John Buchan (187[illegible] and successful literary and public [illegible] educated in Glasgow, where his father wa[illegible] Free Church minister in the Gorbals, but his childhood holidays were spent in the Scottish border country.

After graduating at Glasgow University, Buchan took a scholarship to Oxford where he wrote his first two historical novels while still an undergraduate. With interests in law and journalism, he worked for the British High Commission in South Africa at the end of the Boer War. Returning to London in 1903, he eventually became a director of Thomas Nelson the publishers. Buchan worked for the Ministry of Information during the First War, and also wrote a substantial history of the conflict. He became a Tory M.P. for the Scottish Universities from 1927 to 1935, in which year he was appointed Governor-General of Canada as Lord Tweedsmuir.

Buchan took pride in the craft of storytelling and he is probably best known for his Richard Hannay thrillers, with six titles ranging from *The Thirty-Nine Steps* in 1915, to *The Island of Sheep* in 1936. His other fiction includes *John Burnet of Barns* (1898); *Prester John* (1910); *The Power-House* (1913); *Huntingtower* (1922); *John Macnab* (1925); *The Dancing Floor* (1926); *Witch Wood* (1927); and *Sick Heart River*, published posthumously in 1941.

Buchan's health had never been strong, yet he achieved an enormous literary output in the course of his life, with no fewer than 30 novels and over 60 non-fiction books, including fine biographies of Walter Scott and James Graham, the Marquis of Montrose, whom he greatly admired. His autobiography, *Memory Hold-the-door*, was published in the year of his death from a cerebral stroke.

Waterstones June 2022

JOHN BUCHAN

The Leithen Stories

THE POWER-HOUSE 1913

JOHN MACNAB 1925

THE DANCING FLOOR 1926

SICK HEART RIVER 1941

Introduced by

CHRISTOPHER HARVIE

CANONGATE

Edinburgh · London

This edition first published as a Canongate Classic in 2000
by Canongate Books Ltd,
14 High Street, Edinburgh, EH1 1TE

The Power-House first published in 1913
John Macnab first published in 1925
The Dancing Floor first published in 1926
Sick Heart River first published in 1941

The publishers gratefully acknowledge general
subsidy from the Scottish Arts Council towards
the Canongate Classics series and a specific
grant towards the publication of this title

British Library Cataloguing-in-Publication Data
A catalogue record for this book is available on
request from the British Library

ISBN 978 0 86241 995 0

Typeset by Hewer Text UK Ltd, Edinburgh

Printed and bound by Clays Ltd, Elcograf S.p.A.

www.canongate.tv

Introduction

I

> . . . you are a man of good commonplace intelligence. Pray forgive the lukewarmness of the phrase; it is really a high compliment, for I am an austere critic. But you also possess a quite irrelevant gift of imagination. Not enough to affect your balance, but enough to do what your mere lawyer's talent could never have done. You have achieved a feat which is given to few – you have partially understood me.

The prototype Buchan villain, Andrew Lumley in *The Power House* (1913) got closer to nailing Sir Edward Leithen than anyone else. Leithen, the first and last of Buchan's heroes, and the one closest in character to his author, was also his most enigmatic. It's possible to construct his biography – Buchan's characters, popping up from novel to novel, usually have well-realised backgrounds – but Buchan on Leithen is uncharacteristically sketchy. He tells us he was born in 1879 and a Scots Calvinist, but nothing about his presumably Peeblesshire family, save for a somewhat dim nephew, Charles. He is a Tory MP and a barrister in *The Power-House*, yet in *The Dancing Floor* he seems to have acquired his knighthood as Solicitor-General pre-war. He was only elected in 1910, and couldn't have been in the wartime government, as he was serving at the front; and, unusually, he doesn't go on the bench. He comes awkwardly close to his creator, and seems to operate as an intellectual filing-cabinet for preoccupations and speculations which Buchan wanted to keep at one remove from himself. To compare him with another lone barrister in London, Anthony Trollope's moving portrait of the widowed Sir Thomas Underwood in the otherwise rather silly *Ralph the Heir* (1871), is to see how flat a character he initially is.

II

The Leithen stories, nevertheless, contain the heart of the Buchan matter, political and philosophical, bringing out tantalising glimpses of work which a more troubled man – 'serious unto death', as Carlyle put it – might have turned into a golden lyric. Perhaps this was also apparent to Buchan himself: that what came naturally and fluently to him was something deadly serious to his younger Scots contemporaries. Buchan/Leithen never gave up his day job – or indeed jobs – for the 'determined stupor' of the full-time writer, as did Edwin Muir, Hugh MacDiarmid, Eric Linklater or Lewis Grassic Gibbon – and at a further remove, W.B. Yeats and Ezra Pound. *The Power-House* announces the terrific anarchy to be loosed upon the world, *John Macnab* the recuperative power of the pastoral. *The Dancing Floor* is in its way a fire sermon with the kindling material of tradition, sex and violence. In *Sick Heart River* in particular it's possible to hear echoes of a flyting between MacDiarmid's pitiless mysticism of the material in 'On a Raised Beach' and Buchan's own theism, going on behind his post-imperial project of creating a common Canadian culture.

With the practically-minded Buchan there was always a resistance to 'inoppugnable realities': that sense of being ensnared by circumstances and irreversible political change. But in the 1920s as an MP he may have felt that he had made a false move: he was a political 'lieutenant' who would never be a leader, partly because of his health, partly because he wouldn't commit himself 100 per cent to the party game. He was doomed to see mediocre Tory contemporaries scale heights interdicted to him. One book which doesn't appear here, the implausible *Gap in the Curtain* (1932) has Leithen narrating an uncharacteristically stodgy political tale. 'The Rt. Hon. David Mayot' could have concerned a real, and gripping episode in which Buchan was involved – the formation of Ramsay MacDonald's National Government the previous August – but it reeks of Asquith's day, not Baldwin's.

III

Leithen/Buchan's career is therefore something of a 'bag-end of life', of speculative enterprises worked out better elsewhere. But what remains is considerable. If, as Roderick Watson and Douglas Gifford have argued, a salient feature of the Scottish renaissance was a preoccupation with the socialising functions of myths and archetypes, then few writers were richer in this respect than Buchan, throughout his career concerned with 'the causal and the casual' in politics. This was something he gained from older contemporaries such as Andrew Lang, John Veitch and J.G. Frazer. The political was something from which they recoiled; yet perhaps the most famous line in all Buchan, Lumley's warning to Leithen: 'You think that a wall as solid as the earth separates civilisation from barbarism. I tell you the division is a thread, a sheet of glass . . .' could almost have been plucked directly from the second volume of *The Golden Bough* (1892):

> It is not our business here to consider what bearing the permanent existence of such a solid layer of savagery beneath the surface of society, and unaffected by the superficial changes of religion and culture, has on the future of humanity. The dispassionate observer, whose studies have led him to plumb its depths, can hardly regard it as otherwise than as a standing menace to civilisation. We seem to move on a thin crust which may at any time be rent by the subterranean forces slumbering below.

This in turn related to a metaphor running back via Disraeli, Carlyle and Goethe to the geological debates of the Enlightenment. *The Power-House* shows the super-intellect Lumley – with more than a few resemblances to Buchan's hero Arthur Balfour – brought down by the 'commonplace' Leithen, and an enthusiastic but bungling Labour MP. This was one way of saying that to Buchan the security of 1913 Britain *was* genuine, and not canvas painted to look like stone and stretched over a chasm. This didn't last: by August 1914 the reign of Saturn had been resumed.

IV

The war made Buchan's 'shockers' famous. It also delivered blow after shattering blow through the loss of family and friends: all the more severe because his deskbound jobs deprived him of the exhilaration of survival which his French contemporary Henri Barbusse celebrated in *Under Fire* (1916). But war propaganda was complex enough to be recuperative; it also involved Buchan in probing German nationality via German psychoanalysis. Catherine Carswell wrote that he had mastered all the standard texts 'with attention and respect', which certainly meant Freud and Jung.

Freudian traces in Buchan are pretty limited, although the distinguished Scots psychoanalyst Jock Sutherland argued that his relationship to his mother might repay study. Jung, an exact contemporary and, like Buchan, a son of the Calvinist manse, was likely to be a more agreeable ideologue; but both would lead back to the huge myth-kitty of Victorian anthropology, *The Golden Bough* in particular, because of their interest in custom and habit, totem and taboo.

John Macnab (1925) seems remote from such concerns, the most lighthearted of Buchan's novels, with its origins in Captain Brander Dunbar's challenge to Lord Abinger at Inverlochy in 1897, and its stunning descriptions of the treacherous beauty of the West Highlands. But it becomes equally freighted with significance. Editing *The Northern Muse* (1924), his fine anthology of Scots vernacular poetry, Buchan doubtless remembered that his great predecessor in this business, Allan Ramsay senior, had used the politics of pastoral in his *Gentle Shepherd* exactly two centuries earlier. This was still acted by village companies into Buchan's childhood, reminding the folk of a protest against misgovernment which was both Jacobite and radical.

This comes out in the election meeting, with its contrast between Lord Lamancha's meaningless party oration, and Archie Roylance's love-kindled idealism. It owes something to Disraeli – Buchan snitching one of his best jokes – but also in the background is Arthur Hugh Clough's *The Bothie of Tober Na Vuolich* (1848) in which a group of Oxford men on a highland reading party are faced with old inequalities, love, and the prospect of a new beginning. If it doesn't work quite as well as that masterly *réprise* of Peacock and Scott, *Castle Gay* (1930), put this down to Buchan's problems with the highlands and a landscape which, however beautiful, was empty of people. Border pastoral had a somewhat different meaning for those who had been driven forth by the shepherds, the Cheviot and the stag, and Gerard Craig Sellar, Buchan's host at Ardtornish, was the grandson of Patrick Sellar, the Duke of Sutherland's evicter-in-chief, a name which still inspires strong emotions. On the other hand, the highlanders do get the last word, the sporting gents' destinies being firmly in the scaly, crafty, hands of Fish Benjie.

Craig-Sellar also had a hand in *The Dancing Floor* (1926) which followed quickly after *John Macnab*. Inspired by a huge, silent house on one of the Petali Islands, north-east of Athens, visited while on Craig-Sellar's yacht in 1910, it was a reworking, at novel length, of a much earlier short story 'Basilissa' (1914), published not long after *The Power House*, and also in *Blackwood's*. Vernon Milburne is a young English country gentleman happened on by Leithen after an accident (does Leithen never encounter, by accident, somewhere terribly boring?). He is haunted by an annual dream about a fire in a room, each year advancing towards him. Leithen provides the link to a strange house on a Greek island and an ordeal he must endure, and the mysterious figure of Koré Arabin. Travelling in the Aegean, he discovers the house, residence of Koré's father Shelley Arabin, an English *littérateur* far gone in nameless decadence. Furious against their landlord, the locals perceive Milburne as being the priest-king 'who slew the slayer and shall himself be slain', who must marry the daughter of the hated house, and then be sacrificed with her. All this has more than a whiff of Arthur Machen, even of Dennis Wheatley, about it. It's with a start that one remembers that the Plakos business was right in the time and place of a quite different sort of villain: Eric Ambler's Dimitrios Makropolos.

In the earlier novels Leithen is energetic and self-confident. It is quite otherwise in *Sick Heart River* (1941), written while Buchan, now Lord Tweedsmuir, was Governor-General of Canada and published after his death. It puzzled his staff, who found it sombre and introverted. The dying Leithen is involved in no thriller plot, but the task of finding a French-Canadian financier, Francis Gaillard, who has disappeared in the Canadian North, something complicated by the fact that Lew Frizel, brother of Leithen's guide, seems to have gone crazily off in search of an edenic valley, the Sick Heart River. The quest for the two deranged men also becomes a quest for a nation. The Sick Heart, although tranquil and green, is dead. When Leithen gets Lew out he has to minister to 'the madness of the north' which has afflicted all the *voyageurs*. They might also be suffering from the malaise of Canada – its division by region and racial group – something which became obvious to Buchan on his tours as Governor-General. Leithen finds himself acting as a sort of medicine man. His moment of choice comes in the camp of the Hare Indians, who have, following an epidemic, become totally demoralised. Is Leithen to go back to England – now at war – or to stay and organise, with Gaillard, the hunting of winter food?

> Compared to his companions Leithen suddenly saw himself founded solidly, like an oak. He was drawing life from deep sources. Death, if it came, was no blind trick of fate, but a thing accepted and therefore mastered.

Leithen ends up as more than a sacrificial Frazerian priest-king. He provides, by hunting, a function which antedates the Demeter goddess, and concurs with a leading myth of the Scots renaissance, particularly salient in Neil Gunn and Lewis Grassic Gibbon: the 'golden age' of the hunting horde.

V

Throughout the four books Buchan seems to be preoccupied with what the *literati* of the eighteenth century would have called 'notions' derived from philosophy and anthropology, or had these confirmed by his wartime experience. The first was the fragility of civilisation. A somewhat thetorical apprehension in his pre-war books, this had now become reality. Man's capability of generating evil was far greater because of the eclipse of the constraints Buchan associated with western Christendom, and Lumley's reference to China introduces the 'Asiatic' combination of the wielding of power and its abnegation that Buchan elaborated in his master-villain Dominick Medina in *The Three Hostages* (1924). This 're-barbarisation' would loom over *The Dancing Floor* – Plakos wasn't far from Smyrna, and its appalling massacre in 1922 – and even the japes of *John Macnab*. Young Claybody's private army – a Highland *Freikorps*? – draws on the unemployed set adrift by the post-war slump. Buchan's German friends like Moritz Bonn would make him aware of where this could lead.

Linked to this was something he derived from Freud via Frazer: the role of repressive doctrine. To Buchan this stemmed from over-mechanistic religion which recoiled from the cycle of nature, and bred evil and sexual perversion. If Shelley Arabin was based on Lord Byron, whose private letters had horrified Buchan – if not Henry James – investigating them in 1905, then the impact of Calvinist repression of the sort dramatically evident in *Witch Wood* (1928) couldn't be discounted. The young Buchan who had gone to Brasenose hoping to study under Walter Pater, would also have known all about Gilles de Rais, *quondam* ally of Joan of Arc, pederast and child-murderer, central to J.–K. Huysmans' *Là-Bas* (1891).

Finally, myth and ritual gave to a humanity assailed by 'mass culture' and 'mass politics' a prospect of ecological harmony. Buchan was reared in an intellectual tradition in which the scientific had always been related to the anthropological and the theological: by the Scottish Enlightenment, by Carlyle, by Robertson Smith and Frazer, and a growing Scots' fascination with psychoanalysis. Getting to the heart of the matter seemed necessary in the post-war turmoil, when the structures of liberal capitalism were collapsing. In *The Dancing Floor* Vernon Milburne recognises the rituals of Plakos as ultimately benign, going back not just beyond Christianity but predating the 'noisy, middle-class family party' of the Greek gods: 'You may call her Demeter, or Aphrodite, or Hera, but she is the same, the Virgin and the Mother, the "mistress of wild things", the "priestess of the new birth in spring".'

In *Sick Heart River* this 'natural theology' is assimilated not so much into the Canadian Indians' respect for their natural environment – the Hares are their environment's victims – but into the quandary of the 'true' Canadians, the half-breed Frizels. The pollution and environmental destruction that Gaillard's factory has inflicted on the Clairefontaine, are the cognate penalty of mechanistic 'civilisation'. Making the connection, and consequently the new Canada, is the ideal for which Leithen ultimately sacrifices himself.

Buchan/Leithen was a product of that peculiar involvement of the Scots with empire, whereby patronage, career-development and economic exploitation were also linked up with the drive to understand so typical of a Scots-influenced intelligentsia. Buchan's first publication in 1894 had been *Essays and Apothegms of Francis Lord Bacon:* 'all knowledge was his province'. His mission to know, but also to evangelise, made him what H.G. Wells called in, *The New Machiavelli* (1911) – with Buchan's friend G.M. Trevelyan in mind – a secular monk. Wells didn't mean this in any kindly sense, believing that science and sexual hedonism were delightfully compatible. Leithen's motor was quite obviously sublimation in the Freudian sense, but he was no less of a scientist for ending up a priest-king.

Christopher Harvie

(This introduction benefitted from discussions with my wife Virginia, the Rev. James Greig and Owen Dudley Edwards. Responsibility for any mistakes is mine alone. C.H.)

THE POWER-HOUSE

Contents

TO MAJOR-GENERAL
SIR FRANCIS LLOYD, K.C.P.

My Dear General,

A recent tale of mine has, I am told, found favour in the dug-outs and billets of the British front, as being sufficiently short and sufficiently exciting for men who have little leisure to read. My friends in that uneasy region have asked for more. So I have printed this story, written in the smooth days before the war, in the hope that it may enable an honest man here and there to forget for an hour the too urgent realities. I have put your name on it, because among the many tastes which we share, one is a liking for precipitous yarns.

J.B.

Preface by the Editor

WE WERE AT Glenaicill – six of us – for the duck-shooting, when Leithen told us this story. Since five in the morning we had been out on the skerries, and had been blown home by a wind which threatened to root the house and its wind-blown woods from their precarious lodgment on the hill. A vast nondescript meal, luncheon and dinner in one, had occupied us till the last daylight departed, and we settled ourselves in the smoking-room for a sleepy evening of talk and tobacco.

Conversation, I remember, turned on some of Jim's trophies which grinned at us from the firelit walls, and we began to spin hunting yarns. Then Hoppy Bynge, who was killed next year on the Bramaputra, told us some queer things about his doings in New Guinea, where he tried to climb Carstensz, and lived for six months in mud. Jim said he couldn't abide mud – anything was better than a country where your boots rotted. (He was to get enough of it last winter in the Ypres Salient.) You know how one tale begets another, and soon the whole place hummed with odd recollections, for five of us had been a good deal about the world.

All except Leithen, the man who was afterwards Solicitor-General, and, they say, will get to the Woolsack in time. I don't suppose he had ever been farther from home than Monte Carlo, but he liked hearing about the ends of the earth.

Jim had just finished a fairly steep yarn about his experiences on a Boundary Commission near Lake Chad, and Leithen got up to find a drink.

'Lucky devils,' he said. 'You've had all the fun out of life. I've had my nose to the grindstone ever since I left school.'

I said something about his having all the honour and glory.

'All the same,' he went on, 'I once played the chief part in a rather exciting business without ever once budging from London. And the joke of it was that the man who went out to look for adventure only saw a bit of the game, and I who sat in my chambers saw it all and pulled the strings. "They also serve who only stand and wait," you know.'

Then he told us this story. The version I give is one he afterwards wrote down, when he had looked up his diary for some of the details.

ONE

Beginning of the Wild-Goose Chase

IT ALL STARTED one afternoon early in May when I came out of the House of Commons with Tommy Deloraine. I had got in by an accident at a by-election, when I was supposed to be fighting a forlorn hope, and as I was just beginning to be busy at the Bar I found my hands pretty full. It was before Tommy succeeded, in the days when he sat for the family seat in Yorkshire, and that afternoon he was in a powerful bad temper. Out of doors it was jolly spring weather; there was greenery in Parliament Square and bits of gay colour, and a light wind was blowing up from the river. Inside a dull debate was winding on, and an advertising member had been trying to get up a row with the Speaker. The contrast between the frowsy place and the cheerful world outside would have impressed even the soul of a Government Whip.

Tommy sniffed the spring breeze like a supercilious stag.

'This about finishes me,' he groaned. 'What a juggins I am to be mouldering here! Joggleberry is the celestial limit, what they call in happier lands the pink penultimate. And the frowst on those back benches! Was there ever such a moth-eaten old museum?'

'It is the Mother of Parliaments,' I observed.

'Damned monkey-house,' said Tommy. 'I must get off for a bit or I'll bonnet Joggleberry or get up and propose a national monument to Guy Fawkes or something silly.'

I did not see him for a day or two, and then one morning he rang me up and peremptorily summoned me to dine with him. I went, knowing very well what I should find. Tommy was off next day to shoot lions on the Equator, or something equally unconscientious. He was a bad acquaintance for a placid, sedentary soul like me, for though he could work like a Trojan when the fit took him, he was never at the same job very long. In the same week he would harass an Under-Secretary about horses for the Army, write voluminously to the press about a gun he had invented for potting aeroplanes, give a fancy-dress ball which he forgot to attend, and get into the semi-final of the racquets championship. I waited daily to see him start a new religion.

That night, I recollect, he had an odd assortment of guests. A Cabinet Minister was there, a gentle being for whom Tommy professed public scorn and private affection; a sailor; an Indian cavalry fellow; Chapman, the Labour member, whom Tommy called Chipmunk; myself, and old Milson of the Treasury. Our host was in tremendous form, chaffing everybody, and sending Chipmunk into great rolling gusts of merriment. The two lived adjacent in Yorkshire, and on platforms abused each other like pickpockets.

Tommy enlarged on the misfits of civilised life. He maintained that none of us, except perhaps the sailor and the cavalryman, were at our proper jobs. He would have had Wytham – that was the Minister – a cardinal of the Roman Church, and he said that Milson should have been the Warden of a college full of port and prejudice. Me he was kind enough to allocate to some reconstructed Imperial General Staff, merely because I had a craze for military history. Tommy's perception did not go very deep. He told Chapman he should have been a lumberman in California. 'You'd have made an uncommon good logger, Chipmunk, and you know you're a dashed bad politician.'

When questioned about himself he became reticent, as the newspapers say. 'I doubt if I'm much good at any job,' he confessed, 'except to ginger up my friends. Anyhow I'm getting out of this hole. Paired for the rest of the session with a chap who has lockjaw. I'm off to stretch my legs and get back my sense of proportion.'

Some one asked him where he was going, and was told 'Venezuela, to buy Government bonds and look for birds' nests.'

Nobody took Tommy seriously, so his guests did not trouble to bid him the kind of farewell a prolonged journey would demand. But when the others had gone, and we were sitting in the little back smoking-room on the first floor, he became solemn. Portentously solemn, for he wrinkled up his brows and dropped his jaw in the way he had when he fancied he was in earnest.

'I've taken on a queer job, Leithen,' he said, 'and I want you to hear about it. None of my family know, and I would like to leave some one behind me who could get on to my tracks if things got troublesome.'

I braced myself for some preposterous confidence, for I was experienced in Tommy's vagaries. But I own to being surprised when he asked me if I remembered Pitt-Heron.

I remembered Pitt-Heron very well. He had been at Oxford with me, but he was no great friend of mine, though for about two years Tommy and he had been inseparable. He had had a prodigious reputation for cleverness with everybody but the college authorities, and used to spend his vacations doing mad things in the Alps and the Balkans, and writing about them in the halfpenny press. He was enormously rich – cottonmills and Liverpool ground-rents – and being without a father, did pretty much what his fantastic taste dictated. He was rather a hero for a bit after he came down, for he had made some wild journey in the neighbourhood of Afghanistan, and written an exciting book about it.

Then he married a pretty cousin of Tommy's, who happened to be the only person that ever captured my stony heart, and settled down in London. I did not go to their house, and soon I found that very few of his friends saw much of him either. His travels and magazine articles suddenly stopped, and I put it down to the common course of successful domesticity. Apparently I was wrong.

'Charles Pitt-Heron,' said Tommy, 'is blowing up for a most thundering mess.'

I asked what kind of mess, and Tommy said he didn't know. 'That's the mischief of it. You remember the wild beggar he used to be, always off on the spree to the Mountains of the Moon or somewhere. Well, he has been damping down his fires lately, and trying to behave like a respectable citizen, but God knows what he has been thinking! I go a good deal to Portman Square, and all last year he has been getting queerer.'

Questions as to the nature of the queerness only elicited the fact that Pitt-Heron had taken to science with some enthusiasm.

'He has got a laboratory at the back of the house – used to be the billiard-room – where he works away half the night. And Lord! The crew you meet there! Every kind of heathen – Chinese and Turks, and long-haired chaps from Russia, and fat Germans. I've several times blundered into the push.

They've all got an odd secretive air about them, and Charlie is becoming like them. He won't answer a plain question or look you straight in the face. Ethel sees it too, and she has often talked to me about it.'

I said I saw no harm in such a hobby.

'I do,' said Tommy grimly. 'Anyhow, the fellow has bolted.'

'What on earth—' I began, but was cut short.

'Bolted without a word to a mortal soul. He told Ethel he would be home for luncheon yesterday, and never came. His man knew nothing about him, hadn't packed for him or anything; but he found he had stuffed some things into a kit-bag and gone out by the back through the mews. Ethel was in terrible straits and sent for me, and I ranged all yesterday afternoon like a wolf on the scent. I found he had drawn a biggish sum in gold from the bank, but I couldn't find any trace of where he had gone.

'I was just setting out for Scotland Yard this morning when Tomlin, the valet, rang me up and said he had found a card in the waistcoat of the dress clothes that Charles had worn the night before he left. It had a name on it like Konalevsky, and it struck me that they might know something about the business at the Russian Embassy. Well, I went round there, and the long and short of it was that I found there was a fellow of that name among the clerks. I saw him, and he said he had gone to see Mr Pitt-Heron two days before with a letter from some Embassy chap. Unfortunately the man in question had gone off to New York next day, but Konalevsky told me one thing which helped to clear up matters. It seemed that the letter had been one of those passports that Embassies give to their friends – a higher-powered sort than the ordinary make – and Konalevsky gathered from something he had heard that Charles was aiming at Moscow.'

Tommy paused to let his news sink in.

'Well, that was good enough for me. I'm off tomorrow to run him to ground.'

'But why shouldn't a man go to Moscow if he wants?' I said feebly.

'You don't understand,' said the sage Tommy. 'You don't know old Charles as I know him. He's got into a queer set, and there's no knowing what mischief he's up to. He's perfectly capable of starting a revolution in Armenia or somewhere merely to see how it feels like to be a revolutionary. That's the damned thing about the artistic temperament. Anyhow, he's got to chuck it. I won't have Ethel scared to death by his whims. I am going to hale him back from Moscow, even if I have to pretend he's an escaped lunatic. He's probably like enough one by this time if he has taken no clothes.'

I have forgotten what I said, but it was some plea for caution. I could not see the reason for these heroics. Pitt-Heron did not interest me greatly, and the notion of Tommy as a defender of the hearth amused me. I thought that he was working on very slight evidence, and would probably make a fool of himself.

'It's only another of the man's fads,' I said. 'He never could do things like an ordinary mortal. What possible trouble could there be? Money?'

'Rich as Crœsus,' said Tommy.

'A woman?'

'Blind as a bat to female beauty.'

'The wrong side of the law?'

'Don't think so. He could settle any ordinary scrape with a cheque.'

'Then I give it up. Whatever it is, it looks as if Pitt-Heron would have a companion in misfortune before you are done with the business. I'm all for you taking a holiday, for at present you are a nuisance to your friends and a disgrace to your country's legislature. But for goodness' sake curb your passion for romance. They don't like it in Russia.'

Next morning Tommy turned up to see me in Chambers. The prospect of travel always went to his head like wine. He was in wild spirits, and had forgotten his anger at the defaulting Pitt-Heron in gratitude for his provision of an occupation. He talked of carrying him off to the Caucasus when he had found him, to investigate the habits of the Caucasian stag.

I remember the scene as if it were yesterday. It was a hot May morning, and the sun which came through the dirty window in Fountain Court lit up the dust and squalor of my working chambers. I was pretty busy at the time, and my table was well nourished with briefs. Tommy picked up one and began to read it. It was about a new drainage scheme in West Ham. He tossed it down and looked at me pityingly.

'Poor old beggar!' he said. 'To spend your days on such work when the world is chock-full of amusing things. Life goes roaring by and you only hear the echo in your stuffy rooms. You can hardly see the sun for the cobwebs on these windows of yours. Charles is a fool, but I'm blessed if he isn't wiser than you. Don't you wish you were coming with me?'

The queer thing was that I did. I remember the occasion, as I have said, for it was one of the few on which I have had a pang of dissatisfaction with the calling I had chosen. As Tommy's footsteps grew faint on the stairs I suddenly felt as if I were missing something, as if somehow I were out of it. It is an unpleasant feeling even when you know that the thing you are out of is foolishness.

Tommy went off at 11 from Victoria, and my work was pretty well ruined for the day. I felt oddly restless, and the cause was not merely Tommy's departure. My thoughts kept turning to the Pitt-Herons – chiefly to Ethel, that adorable child unequally yoked to a perverse egoist, but a good deal to the egoist himself. I have never suffered much from whimsies, but I suddenly began to feel a curious interest in the business – an unwilling interest, for I found it in my heart to regret my robust scepticism of the night before. And it was more than interest. I had a sort of presentiment that I was going to be mixed up in the affair more than I wanted. I told myself angrily that the life of an industrious common-law barrister could have little to do with the wanderings of two maniacs in Muscovy. But, try as I might, I could not get rid of the obsession. That night it followed me into my dreams, and I saw myself with a knout coercing Tommy and Pitt-Heron in a Russian fortress which faded away into the Carlton Hotel.

Next afternoon I found my steps wending in the direction of Portman Square. I lived at the time in Down Street, and I told myself I would be none the worse of a walk in the Park before dinner. I had a fancy to see Mrs Pitt-Heron, for, though I had only met her twice since her marriage, there had been a day when we were the closest of friends.

I found her alone, a perplexed and saddened lady with imploring eyes. Those eyes questioned me as to how much I knew. I told her presently that I had seen Tommy and was aware of his errand. I was moved to add that she might count on me if there were anything she wished done on this side of the Channel.

She was very little changed. There was still the old exquisite slimness, the old shy courtesy. But she told me nothing. Charles was full of business and becoming very forgetful. She was sure the Russian journey was all a stupid mistake.

He probably thought he had told her of his departure. He would write; she expected a letter by every post.

But her haggard eyes belied her optimism. I could see that there had been odd happenings of late in the Pitt-Heron household. She either knew or feared something – the latter, I thought, for her air was more of apprehension than of painful enlightenment.

I did not stay long, and, as I walked home, I had an awkward feeling that I had intruded. Also I was increasingly certain that there was trouble brewing, and that Tommy had more warrant for his journey than I had given him credit for. I cast my mind back to gather recollections of Pitt-Heron, but all I could find was an impression of a brilliant, uncomfortable being, who had been too fond of the byways of life for my sober tastes. There was nothing crooked in him in the wrong sense, but there might be a good deal that was perverse. I remember consoling myself with the thought that, though he might shatter his wife's nerves by his vagaries, he would scarcely break her heart.

To be watchful, I decided, was my business. And I could not get rid of the feeling that I might soon have cause for all my vigilance.

TWO

I First Hear of Mr Andrew Lumley

A FORTNIGHT LATER – to be accurate, on the 21st of May – I did a thing I rarely do, and went down to South London on a County Court case. It was an ordinary taxi-cab accident, and, as the solicitors for the company were good clients of mine and the regular County Court junior was ill in bed, I took the case to oblige them. There was the usual dull conflict of evidence. An empty taxi-cab, proceeding slowly on the right side of the road and hooting decorously at the corners, had been run into by a private motor-car which had darted down a side street. The taxi had been swung round and its bonnet considerably damaged, while its driver had suffered a dislocated shoulder. The bad feature in the case was that the motor-car had not halted to investigate the damage, but had proceeded unconscientiously on its way, and the assistance of the London police had been called in to trace it. It turned out to be the property of a Mr Julius Pavia, a retired East India merchant, who lived in a large villa in the neighbourhood of Blackheath, and at the time of the accident it had been occupied by his butler. The company brought an action for damages against its owner.

The butler, Tuke by name, was the only witness for the defence. He was a tall man, with a very long, thin face, and a jaw, the two parts of which seemed scarcely to fit. He was profuse in his apologies on behalf of his master, who was abroad. It seemed that on the morning in question – it was the 8th of May – he had received instructions from Mr Pavia to convey a message to a passenger by the Continental express from Victoria, and had been hot on this errand when he met the taxi. He was not aware that there had been any damage, thought it only a slight grazing of the two cars, and on his master's behalf consented to the judgment of the court.

It was a commonplace business, but Tuke was by no means a commonplace witness. He was very unlike the conventional butler, much liker one of those successful financiers whose portraits you see in the picture papers. His little eyes were quick with intelligence, and there were lines of ruthlessness around his mouth, like those of a man often called to decisive action. His story was simplicity itself, and he answered my questions with an air of serious candour. The train he had to meet was the 11 a.m. from Victoria, the train by which Tommy had travelled. The passenger he had to see was an American gentleman, Mr Wright Davies. His master, Mr Pavia, was in Italy, but would shortly be home again.

The case was over in twenty minutes, but it was something unique in my professional experience. For I took a most intense and unreasoning dislike to that bland butler. I cross-examined with some rudeness, was answered with steady courtesy, and hopelessly snubbed. The upshot was that I lost my temper, to the surprise of the County Court judge. All the way back I was both angry and ashamed of myself. Halfway home I realised that the accident had happened on the very day that Tommy left London. The coincidence merely flickered across my mind, for there could be no earthly connection between the two events.

That afternoon I wasted some time in looking up Pavia in the directory. He was there sure enough as the occupier of a suburban mansion called the White Lodge. He had no city address, so it was clear that he was out of business. My irritation with the man had made me inquisitive about the master. It was a curious name he bore, possibly Italian, possibly Goanese. I wondered how he got on with his highly competent butler. If Tuke had been my servant I would have wrung his neck or bolted before a week was out.

Have you ever noticed that, when you hear a name that strikes you, you seem to be constantly hearing it for a bit? Once I had a case in which one of the parties was called Jubber, a name I had never met before, but I ran across two other Jubbers before the case was over. Anyhow, the day after the Blackheath visit I was briefed in a big Stock Exchange case, which turned on the true ownership of certain bearer bonds. It was a complicated business, which I need not trouble you with, and it involved a number of consultations with my lay clients, a famous firm of brokers. They produced their books, and my chambers were filled with glossy gentlemen talking a strange jargon.

I had to examine my clients closely on their practice in

treating a certain class of bearer security, and they were very frank in expounding their business. I was not surprised to hear that Pitt-Heron was one of the most valued names on their lists. With his wealth he was bound to be a good deal in the city. Now I had no desire to pry into Pitt-Heron's private affairs, especially his financial arrangements, but his name was in my thoughts at the time, and I could not help looking curiously at what was put before me. He seemed to have been buying these bonds on a big scale. I had the indiscretion to ask if Mr Pitt-Heron had long followed this course, and was told that he had begun to purchase some six months before.

'Mr Pitt-Heron,' volunteered the stockbroker, 'is very closely connected in his financial operations with another esteemed client of ours, Mr Julius Pavia. They are both attracted by this class of security.'

At the moment I scarcely noted the name, but after dinner that night I began to speculate about the connection. I had found out the name of one of Charles's mysterious new friends. It was not a very promising discovery. A retired East India merchant did not suggest anything wildly speculative, but I began to wonder if Charles's preoccupation, to which Tommy had been witness, might not be connected with financial worries. I could not believe that the huge Pitt-Heron fortunes had been seriously affected, or that his flight was that of a defaulter, but he might have got entangled in some shady city business which preyed on his sensitive soul. Somehow or other I could not believe that Mr Pavia was a wholly innocent old gentleman; his butler looked too formidable. It was possible that he was blackmailing Pitt-Heron, and that the latter had departed to get out of his clutches.

But on what ground? I had no notion as to the blackmailable thing that might lurk in Charles's past, and the guesses which flitted through my brain were too fantastic to consider seriously. After all, I had only the flimsiest basis for conjecture. Pavia and Pitt-Heron were friends; Tommy had gone off in quest of Pitt-Heron; Pavia's butler had broken the law of the land in order, for some reason or other, to see the departure of the train by which Tommy had travelled. I remember laughing at myself for my suspicions, and reflecting that, if Tommy could see into my head, he would turn a deaf ear in the future to my complaints of his lack of balance. But the thing stuck in my mind, and I called again that week on Mrs Pitt-Heron. She had had no word from her husband, and only a bare line from Tommy, giving his Moscow address. Poor child, it was a wretched business for her. She had to keep a smiling face to the world, invent credible tales to account for her husband's absence, and all the while anxiety and dread were gnawing at her heart. I asked her if she had ever met a Mr Pavia, but the name was unknown to her. She knew nothing of Charles's business dealings, but at my request she interviewed his bankers, and I heard from her next day that his affairs were in perfect order. It was no financial crisis which had precipitated him abroad.

A few days later I stumbled by the merest accident upon what sailors call a 'cross-bearing'. At the time I used to 'devil' a little for the Solicitor-General, and 'note' cases sent to him from the different Government offices. It was thankless work, but it was supposed to be good for an ambitious lawyer. By this prosaic channel I received the first hint of another of Charles's friends.

I had sent me one day the papers dealing with the arrest of a German spy at Plymouth, for at the time there was a sort of epidemic of roving Teutons, who got themselves into compromising situations, and gravely troubled the souls of the Admiralty and the War Office. This case was distinguished from the common ruck by the higher social standing of the accused. Generally the spy is a photographer or bag-man who attempts to win the bibulous confidence of minor officials. But this specimen was no less than a professor of a famous German university, a man of excellent manners, wide culture, and attractive presence, who had dined with Port officers and danced with Admirals' daughters. I have forgotten the evidence, or what was the legal point submitted for the Law Officers' opinion; in any case it matters little, for he was acquitted. What interested me at the time were the testimonials as to character which he carried with him. He had many letters of introduction. One was from Pitt-Heron to his wife's sailor uncle; and when he was arrested one Englishman went so far as to wire that he took upon himself the whole costs of the defence. This gentleman was a Mr Andrew Lumley, stated in the papers sent me to be a rich bachelor, a member of the Athenaeum and Carlton Clubs, and a dweller in the Albany.

Remember that, till a few weeks before, I had known nothing of Pitt-Heron's circle, and here were three bits of information dropping in on me unsolicited, just when my interest had been awakened. I began to get really keen, for every man at the bottom of his heart believes that he is a born detective. I was on the look-out for Charles's infrequent friends, and I argued that if he knew the spy and the spy knew Mr Lumley, the odds were that Pitt-Heron and Lumley were acquaintances. I hunted up the latter in the Red Book. Sure enough he lived in the Albany, belonged to half a dozen clubs, and had a country house in Hampshire.

I tucked the name away in a pigeon-hole of my memory, and for some days asked every one I met if he knew the philanthropist of the Albany. I had no luck till the Saturday, when, lunching at the club, I ran against Jenkinson, the art critic.

I forget if you know that I have always been a bit of a connoisseur in a mild way. I used to dabble in prints and miniatures, but at that time my interest lay chiefly in Old Wedgwood, of which I had collected some good pieces. Old Wedgwood is a thing which few people collect seriously, but the few who do are apt to be monomaniacs. Whenever a big collection comes into the market it fetches high prices, but it generally finds its way into not more than half a dozen hands. Wedgwoodites all know each other, and they are less cut-throat in their methods than most collectors. Of all I have ever met Jenkinson was the keenest, and he would discourse for hours on the 'feel' of good jasper, and the respective merits of blue and sage-green grounds.

That day he was full of excitement. He babbled through luncheon about the Wentworth sale, which he had attended the week before. There had been a pair of magnificent plaques, with a unique Flaxman design, which had roused his enthusiasm. Urns and medallions and what not had gone to this or that connoisseur, and Jenkinson could quote their prices, but the plaques dominated his fancy, and he was furious that the nation had not acquired them. It seemed that he had been to South Kensington and the British Museum, and all sorts of dignitaries, and he thought he might yet persuade the authorities to offer them if the purchaser would resell. They had been bought by Lutrin for a well-known private collector, by name Andrew Lumley.

I pricked up my ears and asked about Mr Lumley.

Jenkinson said he was a rich old buffer who locked up his things in cupboards and never let the public get a look at them.

He suspected that a lot of the best things at recent sales had found their way to him, and that meant that they were put in cold storage for good.

I asked if he knew him.

No, he told me, but he had once or twice been allowed to look at his things for books he had been writing. He had never seen the man, for he always bought through agents, but he had heard of people who knew him. 'It is the old silly game,' he said. 'He will fill half a dozen houses with priceless treasures, and then die, and the whole show will be sold at auction and the best things carried off to America. It's enough to make a patriot swear.'

There was balm in Gilead, however. Mr Lumley apparently might be willing to resell the Wedgwood plaques if he got a fair offer. So Jenkinson had been informed by Lutrin, and that very afternoon he was going to look at them. He asked me to come with him, and, having nothing to do, I accepted.

Jenkinson's car was waiting for us at the club door. It was closed, for the afternoon was wet. I did not hear his directions to the chauffeur, and we had been on the road ten minutes or so before I discovered that we had crossed the river and were traversing South London. I had expected to find the things in Lutrin's shop, but to my delight I was told that Lumley had taken delivery of them at once.

'He keeps very few of his things in the Albany except his books,' I was told. 'But he has a house at Blackheath which is stuffed from cellar to garret.'

'What is the name of it?' I asked with a sudden suspicion.

'The White Lodge,' said Jenkinson.

'But that belongs to a man called Pavia,' I said.

'I can't help that. The things in it belong to old Lumley, all right. I know, for I've been three times there with his permission.'

Jenkinson got little out of me for the rest of the ride. Here was excellent corroborative evidence of what I had allowed myself to suspect. Pavia was a friend of Pitt-Heron; Lumley was a friend of Pitt-Heron; Lumley was obviously a friend of Pavia, and he might be Pavia himself, for the retired East India merchant, as I figured him, would not be above an innocent impersonation. Anyhow, if I could find one or the other, I might learn something about Charles's recent doings. I sincerely hoped that the owner might be at home that afternoon when we inspected his treasures, for so far I had found no one who could procure me an introduction to that mysterious old bachelor of artistic and philo-Teutonic tastes.

We reached the White Lodge about half-past three. It was one of those small, square, late-Georgian mansions which you see all around London – once a country-house among fields, now only a villa in a pretentious garden. I looked to see my super-butler Tuke, but the door was opened by a female servant who inspected Jenkinson's card of admission, and somewhat unwillingly allowed us to enter.

My companion had not exaggerated when he described the place as full of treasures. It was far more like the shop of a Bond Street art-dealer than a civilised dwelling. The hall was crowded with Japanese armour and lacquer cabinets. One room was lined from floor to ceiling with good pictures, mostly seventeenth-century Dutch, and had enough Chippendale chairs to accommodate a public meeting. Jenkinson would fain have prowled round, but we were moved on by the inexorable servant to the little back room where lay the objects of our visit. The plaques had been only half-unpacked, and in a moment Jenkinson was busy on them with a magnifying glass, purring to himself like a contented cat.

The housekeeper stood on guard by the door, Jenkinson was absorbed, and after the first inspection of the treasures I had leisure to look about me. It was an untidy little room, full of fine Chinese porcelain in dusty glass cabinets, and in a corner stood piles of old Persian rugs.

Pavia, I reflected, must be an easy-going soul, entirely oblivious of comfort, if he allowed his friend to turn his dwelling into such a pantechnicon. Less and less did I believe in the existence of the retired East India merchant. The house was Lumley's, who chose to pass under another name during his occasional visits. His motive might be innocent enough, but somehow I did not think so. His butler had looked too infernally intelligent.

With my foot I turned over the lid of one of the packing-cases that had held the Wedgwoods. It was covered with a litter of cotton-wool and shavings, and below it lay a crumpled piece of paper. I looked again, and saw that it was a telegraph form. Clearly somebody, with the telegram in his hand, had opened the cases, and had left it on the top of one, whence it had dropped to the floor and been covered by the lid when it was flung off.

I hope and believe that I am as scrupulous as other people, but then and there came on me the conviction that I must read that telegram. I felt the gimlet eye of the housekeeper on me, so I had recourse to craft. I took out my cigarette case as if to smoke, and clumsily upset its contents amongst the shavings. Then on my knees I began to pick them up, turning over the litter till the telegram was exposed.

It was in French, and I read it quite clearly. It had been sent from Vienna, but the address was in some code. '*Suivez à Bokhare Saronov*' – these were the words. I finished my collection of the cigarettes, and turned the lid over again on the telegram, so that its owner, if he chose to look for it diligently, might find it.

When we sat in the car going home, Jenkinson absorbed in meditation on the plaques, I was coming to something like a decision. A curious feeling of inevitability possessed me. I had collected by accident a few odd, disjointed pieces of information, and here by the most amazing accident of all was the connecting link. I knew I had no evidence to go upon which would have convinced the most credulous common jury. Pavia knew Pitt-Heron; so probably did Lumley . . . Lumley knew Pavia, possibly was identical with him. Somebody in Pavia's house got a telegram in which a trip to Bokhara was indicated. It didn't sound much. Yet I was absolutely convinced, with the queer subconscious certitude of the human brain, that Pitt-Heron was or was about to be in Bokhara, and that Pavia-Lumley knew of his being there and was deeply concerned in his journey.

That night after dinner I rang up Mrs Pitt-Heron.

She had had a letter from Tommy, a very dispirited letter, for he had had no luck. Nobody in Moscow had seen or heard of any wandering Englishman remotely like Charles; and Tommy, after playing the private detective for three weeks, was nearly at the end of his tether and spoke of returning home.

I told her to send him the following wire in her own name: '*Go on to Bokhara. Have information you will meet him there.*'

She promised to send the message next day, and asked no further questions. She was a pearl among women.

THREE

Tells of a Midsummer Night

HITHERTO I HAD been the looker-on; now I was to become a person of the drama. That telegram was the beginning of my active part in this curious affair. They say that everybody turns up in time at the corner of Piccadilly Circus if you wait long enough. I was to find myself like a citizen of Baghdad in the days of the great Caliph, and yet never stir from my routine of flat, chambers, club, flat.

I am wrong: there was one episode out of London, and that perhaps was the true beginning of my story.

Whitsuntide that year came very late, and I was glad of the fortnight's rest, for Parliament and the Law Courts had given me a busy time. I had recently acquired a car and a chauffeur called Stagg, and I looked forward to trying it in a tour in the West Country. But before I left London I went again to Portman Square.

I found Ethel Pitt-Heron in grave distress. You must remember that Tommy and I had always gone on the hypothesis that Charles's departure had been in pursuance of some mad scheme of his own which might get him into trouble. We thought that he had become mixed up with highly undesirable friends, and was probably embarking in some venture which might not be criminal but was certain to be foolish. I had long rejected the idea of blackmail, and convinced myself that Lumley and Pavia were his colleagues. The same general notion, I fancy, had been in his wife's mind. But now she had found something which altered the case.

She had ransacked his papers in the hope of finding a clue to the affair which had taken him abroad, but there was nothing but business letters, notes of investments, and such-like. He seemed to have burned most of his papers in the queer laboratory at the back of the house. But, stuffed into the pocket of a blotter on a bureau in the drawing-room where he scarcely ever wrote, she had found a document. It seemed to be the rough draft of a letter, and it was addressed to her. I give it as it was written; the blank spaces were left blank in the manuscript.

> You must have thought me mad, or worse, to treat you as I have done. But there was a terrible reason, which some day I hope to tell you all about. I want you as soon as you get this to make ready to come out to me at . . . You will travel by . . . and arrive at . . . I enclose a letter which I want you to hand in deepest confidence to Knowles, the solicitor. He will make all arrangements about your journey and about sending me the supplies of money I want. Darling, you must leave as secretly as I did, and tell nobody anything, not even that I am alive – that least of all. I would not frighten you for worlds, but I am on the edge of a horrible danger, which I hope with God's help and yours to escape . . .

That was all obviously the draft of a letter which he intended to post to her from some foreign place. But can you conceive a missive more calculated to shatter a woman's nerves? It filled me, I am bound to say, with heavy disquiet. Pitt-Heron was no coward, and he was not the man to make too much of a risk. Yet it was clear that he had fled that day in May under the pressure of some mortal fear.

The affair in my eyes began to look very bad. Ethel wanted me to go to Scotland Yard, but I dissuaded her. I have the utmost esteem for Scotland Yard, but I shrank from publicity at this stage. There might be something in the case too delicate for the police to handle, and I thought it better to wait.

I reflected a great deal about the Pitt-Heron business the first day or two of my trip, but the air and the swift motion helped me to forget it. We had a fortnight of superb weather, and sailed all day through a glistening green country under the hazy blue heavens of June. Soon I fell into the blissful state of physical and mental ease which such a life induces. Hard toil, such as deer-stalking, keeps the nerves on the alert and the mind active, but swimming all day in a smooth car through a heavenly landscape mesmerises brain and body.

We ran up the Thames valley, explored the Cotswolds, and turned south through Somerset till we reached the fringes of Exmoor. I stayed a day or two at a little inn high up in the moor, and spent the time tramping the endless ridges of hill or scrambling in the arbutus thickets where the moor falls in steeps to the sea. We returned by Dartmoor and the south coast, meeting with our first rain in Dorset, and sweeping into sunlight again on Salisbury Plain. The time came when only two days remained to me. The car had behaved beyond all my hopes, and Stagg, a sombre and silent man, was lyrical in its praise.

I wanted to be in London by the Monday afternoon, and to insure this I made a long day of it on the Sunday. It was the long day which brought our pride to a fall. The car had run so well that I resolved to push on and sleep in a friend's house near Farnham. It was about half-past eight, and we were traversing the somewhat confused and narrow roads in the neighbourhood of Wolmer Forest, when, as we turned a sharp corner, we ran full into the tail of a heavy carrier's cart. Stagg clapped on the brakes, but the collision, though it did no harm to the cart, was sufficient to send the butt-end of something through our glass screen, damage the tyre of the near front wheel, and derange the steering-gear. Neither of us suffered much hurt, but Stagg got a long scratch on his cheek from broken glass, and I had a bruised shoulder.

The carrier was friendly but useless and there was nothing for it but to arrange for horses to take the car to Farnham. This meant a job of some hours, and I found on inquiry at a neighbouring cottage that there was no inn where I could stay within eight miles. Stagg borrowed a bicycle somehow and went off to collect horses, while I morosely reviewed the alternatives before me.

I did not like the prospect of spending the June night beside my derelict car, and the thought of my friend's house near Farnham beckoned me seductively. I might have walked there, but I did not know the road, and I found that my shoulder was paining me, so I resolved to try to find some gentleman's house in the neighbourhood where I could borrow a conveyance. The south of England is now so densely peopled by Londoners that even in a wild district, where there are no inns and few farms, there are certain to be several week-end cottages.

I walked along the white ribbon of road in the scented June dusk. At first it was bounded by high gorse, then came patches of open heath, and then woods. Beyond the woods I found a park railing, and presently an entrance-gate with a lodge. It seemed to be the place I was looking for, and I woke the lodge-keeper, who thus early had retired to bed. I asked the name of the owner, but was told the name of the place instead – it was High Ashes. I asked if the owner was at home, and got a sleepy nod for answer.

The house, as seen in the half-light, was a long white-washed cottage, rising to two storeys in the centre. It was plentifully covered with creepers and roses, and the odour of flowers was mingled with the faintest savour of wood-smoke, pleasant to a hungry traveller in the late hours. I pulled an old-fashioned bell, and the door was opened by a stolid young parlour-maid.

I explained my errand, and offered my card. I was, I said, a Member of Parliament and of the Bar, who had suffered a motor accident. Would it be possible for the master of the house to assist me to get to my destination near Farnham? I was bidden to enter, and wearily seated myself on a settle in the hall.

In a few minutes an ancient housekeeper appeared, a grim dame whom at other times I should have shunned. She bore, however, a hospitable message. There was no conveyance in the place, as the car had gone that day to London for repairs. But if I cared to avail myself of the accommodation of the house for the night it was at my service. Meantime my servant could be looking after the car, and a message would go to him to pick me up in the morning.

I gratefully accepted, for my shoulder was growing trouble-some, and was conducted up a shallow oak staircase to a very pleasant bedroom with a bathroom adjoining. I had a bath, and afterwards found a variety of comforts put at my service from slippers to razors. There was also some Elliman for my wounded shoulder. Clean and refreshed I made my way downstairs and entered a room from which I caught a glow of light.

It was a library, the most attractive I think I have ever seen. The room was long, as libraries should be, and entirely lined with books, save over the fireplace, where hung a fine picture which I took to be a Raeburn. The books were in glass cases, which showed the beautiful shallow mouldings of a more artistic age. A table was laid for dinner in a corner, for the room was immense, and the shaded candlesticks on it, along with the late June dusk, gave such light as there was. At first I thought the place was empty, but as I crossed the floor a figure rose from a deep chair by the hearth.

'Good evening, Mr Leithen,' a voice said. 'It is a kindly mischance which gives a lonely old man the pleasure of your company.'

He switched on an electric lamp, and I saw before me what I had not guessed from the voice, an old man. I was thirty-four at the time, and counted anything over fifty old, but I judged my host to be well on in the sixties. He was about my own size, but a good deal bent in the shoulders, as if from study. His face was cleanshaven and extraordinarily fine, with every feature delicately chiselled. He had a sort of Hapsburg mouth and chin, very long and pointed, but modelled with a grace which made the full lower lip seem entirely right. His hair was silver, brushed so low on the forehead as to give him a slightly foreign air, and he wore tinted glasses, as if for reading.

Altogether it was a very dignified and agreeable figure who greeted me in a voice so full and soft that it belied his obvious age.

Dinner was a light meal, but perfect in its way. There were soles, I remember, an exceedingly well-cooked chicken, fresh strawberries, and a savoury. We drank a '95 Perrier-Jouet and some excellent Madeira. The stolid parlour-maid waited on us, and, as we talked of the weather and the Hampshire roads, I kept trying to guess my host's profession. He was not a lawyer, for he had not the inevitable lines on the cheek. I thought that he might be a retired Oxford don, or one of the higher civil servants, or perhaps some official of the British Museum. His library proclaimed him a scholar, and his voice a gentleman.

Afterwards we settled ourselves in armchairs, and he gave me a good cigar. We talked about many things – books, the right furnishing of a library, a little politics, in deference to my M.P.-ship. My host was apathetic about party questions, but curious about defence matters, and in his way an amateur strategist. I could fancy his indicting letters to *The Times* on national service.

Then we wandered into foreign affairs, where I found his interest acute, and his knowledge immense. Indeed he was so well informed that I began to suspect that my guesses had been wrong, and that he was a retired diplomat. At that time there was some difficulty between France and Italy over customs duties, and he sketched for me with remarkable clearness the weak points in the French tariff administration.

I had been recently engaged in a big South American railway case, and I asked him a question about the property of my clients. He gave me a much better account than I had ever got from the solicitors who briefed me.

The fire had been lit before we finished dinner, and presently it began to burn up and light the figure of my host, who sat in a deep armchair. He had taken off his tinted glasses, and as I rose to get a match I saw his eyes looking abstractedly before him.

Somehow they reminded me of Pitt-Heron. Charles had always a sort of dancing light in his, a restless intelligence which was at once attractive and disquieting. My host had this and more. His eyes were paler than I had ever seen in a human head – pale, bright, and curiously wild. But, whereas Pitt-Heron's had only given the impression of reckless youth, this man's spoke of wisdom and power as well as of endless vitality.

All my theories vanished, for I could not believe that my host had ever followed any profession. If he had, he would have been at the head of it, and the world would have been familiar with his features. I began to wonder if my recollection was not playing me false, and I was in the presence of some great man whom I ought to recognise.

As I dived into the recesses of my memory I heard his voice asking if I were not a lawyer.

I told him, Yes. A barrister with a fair common-law practice and some work in Privy Council appeals.

He asked me why I chose the profession.

'It came handiest,' I said. 'I am a dry creature, who loves facts and logic. I am not a flier, I have no new ideas, I don't want to lead men, and I like work. I am the ordinary educated Englishman, and my sort gravitates to the Bar. We like feeling that, if we are not the builders, at any rate we are the cement of civilisation.'

He repeated the words 'cement of civilisation' in his soft voice.

'In a sense you are right. But civilisation needs more than the law to hold it together. You see, all mankind are not equally willing to accept as divine justice what is called human law.'

'Of course there are further sanctions,' I said. 'Police and armies and the goodwill of civilisation.'

He caught me up quickly. 'The last is your true cement. Did you ever reflect, Mr Leithen, how precarious is the tenure of the civilisation we boast about?'

'I should have thought it fairly substantial,' I said, 'and – the foundations grow daily firmer.'

He laughed. 'That is the lawyer's view, but, believe me, you are wrong. Reflect, and you will find that the foundations are sand. You think that a wall as solid as the earth separates civilisation from barbarism. I tell you the division is a thread, a sheet of glass. A touch here, a push there, and you bring back the reign of Saturn.' It was the kind of paradoxical, undergraduate speculation which grown men indulge in sometimes after dinner. I looked at my host to discover his mood, and at the moment a log flared up again.

His face was perfectly serious. His light wild eyes were intently watching me.

'Take one little instance,' he said. 'We are a commercial world, and have built up a great system of credit. Without our cheques and bills of exchange and currency the whole of our life would stop. But credit only exists because behind it we have a standard of value. My Bank of England notes are worthless paper unless I can get sovereigns for them if I choose. Forgive this elementary disquisition, but the point is important. We have fixed a gold standard, because gold is sufficiently rare, and because it allows itself to be coined into a portable form. I am aware that there are economists who say that the world could be run equally well on a pure credit basis, with no metal currency at the back of it; but, however sound their argument may be in the abstract, the thing is practically impossible. You would have to convert the whole of the world's stupidity to their economic faith before it would work.

'Now, suppose something happened to make our standard of value useless. Suppose the dream of the alchemists came true, and all metals were readily transmutable. We have got very near it in recent years, as you will know if you interest yourself in chemical science. Once gold and silver lost their intrinsic value, the whole edifice of our commerce would collapse. Credit would become meaningless, because it would be untranslatable. We should be back at a bound in the age of barter, for it is hard to see what other standard of value could take the place of the precious metals. All our civilisation, with its industries and commerce, would come toppling down.

Once more, like primitive man, I would plant cabbages for a living, and exchange them for services in kind from the cobbler and the butcher. We should have the simple life with a vengeance, not the self-conscious simplicity of the civilised man, but the compulsory simplicity of the savage.'

I was not greatly impressed by the illustration. 'Of course there are many key-points in civilisation,' I said, 'and the loss of them would bring ruin. But those keys are strongly held.'

'Not so strongly as you think. Consider how delicate the machine is growing. As life grows more complex, the machinery grows more intricate, and therefore more vulnerable. Your so-called sanctions become so infinitely numerous that each in itself is frail. In the Dark Ages you had one great power – the terror of God and His Church. Now you have a multiplicity of small things, all delicate and fragile, and strong only by our tacit agreement not to question them.'

'You forget one thing,' I said, 'the fact that men really are agreed to keep the machine going. That is what I called the "goodwill of civilisation".'

He got up from his chair and walked up and down the floor, a curious dusky figure lit by the rare spurts of flame from the hearth.

'You have put your finger on the one thing that matters. Civilisation is a conspiracy. What value would your police be if every criminal could find a sanctuary across the Channel, or your law courts, if no other tribunal recognised their decisions? Modern life is the silent compact of comfortable folk to keep up pretences. And it will succeed till the day comes when there is another compact to strip them bare.'

I do not think that I have ever listened to a stranger conversation. It was not so much what he said – you will hear the same thing from any group of half-baked young men – as the air with which he said it. The room was almost dark, but the man's personality seemed to take shape and bulk in the gloom. Though I could scarcely see him, I knew that those pale strange eyes were looking at me. I wanted more light, but did not know where to look for a switch. It was all so eerie and odd that I began to wonder if my host were not a little mad. In any case, I was tired of his speculations.

'We won't dispute on the indisputable,' I said. 'But I should have thought that it was the interest of all the best brains of the world to keep up what you call the conspiracy.'

He dropped into his chair again.

'I wonder,' he said slowly. 'Do we really get the best brains working on the side of the compact? Take the business of Government. When all is said, we are ruled by the amateurs and the second-rate. The methods of our departments would bring any private firm to bankruptcy. The methods of Parliament – pardon me – would disgrace any board of directors. Our rulers pretend to buy expert knowledge, but they never pay the price for it that a businessman would pay, and if they get it they have not the courage to use it. Where is the inducement for a man of genius to sell his brains to our insipid governors?

'And yet knowledge is the only power – now as ever. A little mechanical device will wreck your navies. A new chemical combination will upset every rule of war. It is the same with our commerce. One or two minute changes might sink Britain to the level of Ecuador, or give China the key of the world's wealth. And yet we never dream that these things are possible. We think our castles of sand are the ramparts of the universe.'

I have never had the gift of the gab, but I admire it in others. There is a morbid charm in such talk, a kind of exhilaration, of which one is half ashamed. I found myself interested, and more than a little impressed.

'But surely,' I said, 'the first thing a discoverer does is to make his discovery public. He wants the honour and glory, and he wants money for it. It becomes part of the world's knowledge, and everything is readjusted to meet it. That was what happened with electricity. You call our civilisation a machine, but it is something far more flexible. It has the power of adaptation of a living organism.'

'That might be true if the new knowledge really became the world's property. But does it? I read now and then in the papers that some eminent scientist has made a great discovery. He reads a paper before some Academy of Science, and there are leading articles in it, and his photograph adorns the magazines. That kind of man is not the danger. He is a bit of the machine, a party to the compact. It is the men who stand outside it that are to be reckoned with, the artists in discovery who will never use their knowledge till they can use it with full effect. Believe me, the biggest brains are without the ring which we call civilisation.'

Then his voice seemed to hesitate. 'You may hear people say

that submarines have done away with the battleship, and that aircraft have annulled the mastery of the sea. That is what our pessimists say. But do you imagine that the clumsy submarine or the fragile aeroplane is really the last word of science?'

'No doubt they will develop,' I said, 'but by that time the power of the defence will have advanced also.'

He shook his head. 'It is not so. Even now the knowledge which makes possible great engines of destruction is far beyond the capacity of any defence. You see only the productions of second-rate folk who are in a hurry to get wealth and fame. The true knowledge, the deadly knowledge, is still kept secret. But, believe me, my friend, it is there.'

He paused for a second, and I saw the faint outline of the smoke from his cigar against the background of the dark. Then he quoted me one or two cases, slowly, as if in some doubt about the wisdom of his words.

It was these cases that startled me. They were of different kinds – a great calamity, a sudden breach between two nations, a blight on a vital crop, a war, a pestilence. I will not repeat them. I do not think I believed in them then, and now I believe less. But they were horribly impressive, as told in that quiet voice in that sombre room on that dark June night. If he was right, these things had not been the work of Nature or accident, but of a devilish art. The nameless brains that he spoke of, working silently in the background, now and then showed their power by some cataclysmic revelation. I did not believe him, but, as he put the case, showing with strange clearness the steps in the game, I had no words to protest.

At last I found my voice.

'What you describe is super-anarchy, and yet it makes no headway. What is the motive of those diabolical brains?'

He laughed. 'How should I be able to tell you? I am a humble inquirer, and in my researches I come on curious bits of fact. But I cannot pry into motives. I only know of the existence of great extra-social intelligences. Let us say that they distrust the machine. They may be idealists and desire to make a new world, or they may simply be artists, loving for its own sake the pursuit of truth. If I were to hazard a guess, I should say that it took both types to bring about results, for the second find the knowledge and the first the will to use it.'

A recollection came back to me. It was of a hot upland meadow in Tyrol, where among acres of flowers and beside a leaping stream I was breakfasting after a morning spent in climbing the white crags. I had picked up a German on the way, a small man of the Professor class, who did me the honour to share my sandwiches. He conversed fluently but quaintly in English, and he was, I remember, a Nietzschean and a hot rebel against the established order. 'The pity,' he cried, 'is that the reformers do not know, and those who know are too idle to reform. Some day there will come the marriage of knowledge and will, and then the world will march.'

'You draw an awful picture,' I said. 'But if those extra-social brains are so potent, why after all do they effect so little? A dull police-officer, with the machine behind him, can afford to laugh at most experiments in anarchy.'

'True,' he said, 'and civilisation will win until its enemies learn from it the importance of the machine. The compact must endure until there is a counter-compact. Consider the ways of that form of foolishness which today we call nihilism or anarchy. A few illiterate bandits in a Paris slum defy the world, and in a week they are in jail. Half a dozen crazy Russian intellectuals in Geneva conspire to upset the Romanovs, and are hunted down by the police of Europe. All the Governments and their not very intelligent police forces join hands, and hey, presto! there is an end of the conspirators. For civilisation knows how to use such powers as it has, while the immense potentiality of the unlicensed is dissipated in vapour. Civilisation wins because it is a worldwide league; its enemies fail because they are parochial. But supposing . . .' Again he stopped and rose from his chair. He found a switch and flooded the room with light. I glanced up blinking to see my host smiling down on me, a most benevolent and courteous old gentleman. He had resumed his tinted glasses. 'Forgive me,' he said, 'for leaving you in darkness while I bored you with my gloomy prognostications. A recluse is apt to forget what is due to a guest.'

He handed the cigar-box to me, and pointed to a table where whisky and mineral waters had been set out.

'I want to hear the end of your prophecies,' I said. 'You were saying—?'

'I said – supposing anarchy learned from civilisation and became international. Oh, I don't mean the bands of advertising donkeys who call themselves International Unions of Workers and such-like rubbish. I mean if the real brainstuff of the world were internationalised. Suppose that the links in the cordon of civilisation were neutralised by other links in a far more potent chain. The earth is seething with incoherent power and unorganised intelligence. Have you ever reflected on the case of China? There you have millions of quick brains stifled in trumpery crafts. They have no direction, no driving power, so the sum of their efforts is futile, and the world laughs at China. Europe throws her a million or two on loan now and then, and she cynically responds by begging the prayers of Christendom. And yet, I say, supposing—'

'It's a horrible idea,' I said, 'and, thank God, I don't believe it possible. Mere destruction is too barren a creed to inspire a new Napoleon, and you can do with nothing short of one.'

'It would scarcely be destruction,' he replied gently. 'Let us call it iconoclasm, the swallowing of formulas, which has always had its full retinue of idealists. And you do not want a Napoleon. All that is needed is direction, which could be given by men of far lower gifts than a Bonaparte. In a word, you want a Power-House, and then the age of miracles will begin.'

I got up, for the hour was late, and I had had enough of this viewy talk. My host was smiling, and I think that smile was the thing I really disliked about him. It was too – what shall I say – superior and Olympian.

As he led me into the hall he apologised for indulging his whims. 'But you, as a lawyer, should welcome the idea. If there is an atom of truth in my fancies, your task is far bigger than you thought. You are not defending an easy case, but fighting in a contest where the issues are still doubtful. That should encourage your professional pride.'

By all the rules I should have been sleepy, for it was past midnight, and I had had a long day in the open air. But that wretched talk had unsettled me, and I could not get my mind off it. I have reproduced very crudely the substance of my host's conversation, but no words of mine could do justice to his eerie persuasiveness. There was a kind of magnetism in the man, a sense of vast powers and banked-up fires, which would have given weight to the tritest platitudes. I had a horrible feeling that he was trying to convince me, to fascinate me, to prepare the ground for some proposal. Again and again I told myself it was crazy nonsense, the heated dream of a visionary, but again and again I came back to some detail which had a horrid air of reality. If the man was a romancer he had an uncommon gift of realism.

I flung open my bedroom window and let in the soft air of the June night and the scents from leagues of clover and pines and sweet grasses. It momentarily refreshed me, for I could not believe that this homely and gracious world held such dire portents.

But always that phrase of his, the 'Power-House,' kept recurring. You know how twisted your thoughts get during a wakeful night, and long before I fell asleep towards morning I had worked myself up into a very complete dislike of that bland and smiling gentleman, my host. Suddenly it occurred to me that I did not know his name, and that set me off on another train of reflection.

I did not wait to be called, but rose about seven, dressed, and went downstairs. I heard the sound of a car on the gravel of the drive, and to my delight saw that Stagg had arrived. I wanted to get away from the house as soon as possible, and I had no desire to meet its master again in this world.

The grim housekeeper, who answered my summons, received my explanation in silence. Breakfast would be ready in twenty minutes; eight was Mr Lumley's hour for it.

'Mr Andrew Lumley?' I asked with a start.

'Mr Andrew Lumley,' she said.

So that was my host's name. I sat down at a bureau in the hall and did a wildly foolish thing.

I wrote a letter, beginning 'Dear Mr Lumley', thanking him for his kindness and explaining the reason of my early departure. It was imperative, I said, that I should be in London by midday. Then I added: 'I wish I had known who you were last night, for I think you know an old friend of mine, Charles Pitt-Heron.'

Breakfastless I joined Stagg in the car, and soon we were swinging down from the uplands to the shallow vale of the Wey. My thoughts were very little on my new toy or on the midsummer beauties of Surrey. The friend of Pitt-Heron, who knew about his going to Bokhara, was the maniac who dreamed of the 'Power-House'. There were going to be dark scenes in the drama before it was played out.

FOUR

I Follow the Trail of the Super-Butler

MY FIRST THOUGHT, as I journeyed towards London, was that I was horribly alone in this business.

Whatever was to be done I must do it myself, for the truth was I had no evidence which any authority would recognise. Pitt-Heron was the friend of a strange being who collected objects of art, probably passed under an alias in South London, and had absurd visions of the end of civilisation. That, in cold black and white, was all my story came to. If I went to the police they would laugh at me, and they would be right.

Now I am a sober and practical person, but, slender though my evidence was, it brought to my mind the most absolute conviction. I seemed to know Pitt-Heron's story as if I had heard it from his own lips – his first meeting with Lumley and their growing friendship; his initiation into secret and forbidden things; the revolt of the decent man, appalled that his freakishness had led him so far; the realisation that he could not break so easily with his past, and that Lumley held him in his power; and last, the mad flight under the pressure of overwhelming terror.

I could read, too, the purpose of that flight. He knew the Indian frontier as few men know it, and in the wild tangle of the Pamirs he hoped to baffle his enemy. Then from some far refuge he would send for his wife, and spend the rest of his days in exile. It must have been an omnipotent terror to drive such a man, young, brilliant, rich, successful, to the fate of an absconding felon.

But Lumley was on his trail. So I read the telegram I had picked up on the floor of the Blackheath house, and my business was to frustrate the pursuit. Some one must have gone to Bokhara, some creature of Lumley's, perhaps the super-butler I had met in the County Court. The telegram, for I had noted the date, had been received on the 27th day of May. It was now the 15th of June, so if some one had started immediately on its receipt, in all probability he would by now be in Bokhara.

I must find out who had gone, and endeavour to warn Tommy. I calculated that it would have taken him seven or eight days to get from Moscow by the Transcaspian; probably he would find Pitt-Heron gone, but inquiries would set him on the track. I might be able to get in touch with him through the Russian officials. In any case, if Lumley were stalking Pitt-Heron, I, unknown and unsuspected, would be stalking Lumley.

And then in a flash I realised my folly.

The wretched letter I had written that morning had given the whole show away. Lumley knew that I was a friend of Pitt-Heron, and that I knew that he was a friend of Pitt-Heron. If my guess was right, friendship with Lumley was not a thing Charles was likely to confess to, and he would argue that my knowledge of it meant that I was in Charles's confidence. I would therefore know of his disappearance and its cause, and alone in London would connect it with the decorous bachelor of the Albany. My letter was a warning to him that he could not play the game unobserved, and I, too, would be suspect in his eyes.

It was no good crying over spilt milk, and Lumley's suspicions must be accepted. But I confess that the thought gave me the shivers. The man had a curious terror for me, a terror I cannot hope to analyse and reproduce for you. My bald words can give no idea of the magnetic force of his talk, the sense of brooking an unholy craft. I was proposing to match my wits against a master's – one, too, who must have at his command an organisation far beyond my puny efforts. I have said that my first feeling was that of loneliness and isolation; my second was one of hopeless insignificance. It was a boy's mechanical toy arrayed against a Power-House with its shining wheels and monstrous dynamos.

My first business was to get into touch with Tommy.

At that time I had a friend in one of the Embassies, whose acquaintance I had made on a dry-fly stream in Hampshire. I will not tell you his name, for he has since become a great figure in the world's diplomacy, and I am by no means certain that the part he played in this tale was strictly in accordance with official etiquette. I had assisted him on the legal side in some of the international worries that beset all Embassies, and we had reached the point of intimacy which is marked by the use of Christian names and by dining frequently together. Let us call him Monsieur Felix. He was a grave young man, slightly my senior, learned, discreet, and ambitious, but with an engaging boyishness cropping up now and then under the official gold lace. It occurred to me that in him I might find an ally.

I reached London about eleven in the morning, and went straight to Belgrave Square. Felix I found in the little library off the big secretaries' room, a sunburnt sportsman fresh from a Norwegian salmon-river. I asked him if he had half an hour to spare, and was told that the day was at my service.

'You know Tommy Deloraine?' I asked.

He nodded.

'And Charles Pitt-Heron?'

'I have heard of him.'

'Well, here is my trouble. I have reason to believe that Tommy has joined Pitt-Heron in Bokhara. If he has, my mind will be greatly relieved, for, though I can't tell you the story, I can tell you that Pitt-Heron is in very considerable danger. Can you help me?'

Felix reflected. 'That should be simple enough. I can wire in cypher to the Military Governor. The police there are pretty efficient, as you may imagine, and travellers don't come and go without being remarked. I should be able to give you an answer within twenty-four hours. But I must describe Tommy. How does one do that in telegraphese?'

'I want you to tell me another thing,' I said. 'You remember that Pitt-Heron has some reputation as a Central Asian traveller. Tommy, as you know, is as mad as a hatter. Suppose these two fellows at Bokhara, wanting to make a long trek into wild country – how would they go? You've been there, and know the lie of the land.'

Felix got down a big German atlas, and for half an hour we pored over it. From Bokhara, he said, the only routes for madmen ran to the south. East and north you got into Siberia; west lay the Transcaspian desert; but southward you might go through the Hissar range by Pamirski Post to Gilgit and Kashmir, or you might follow up the Oxus and enter the north of Afghanistan, or you might go by Merv into north-eastern Persia. The first he thought the likeliest route, if a man wanted to travel fast.

I asked him to put in his cable a suggestion about watching the Indian roads, and left him with a promise of early enlightenment.

Then I went down to the Temple, fixed some consultations, and spent a quiet evening in my rooms. I had a heavy sense of impending disaster, not unnatural in the circumstances. I really cannot think what it was that held me to the job, for I don't mind admitting that I felt pretty queasy about it. Partly, no doubt, liking for Tommy and Ethel, partly regret for that unfortunate fellow Pitt-Heron, most of all, I think, dislike of Lumley. That bland superman had fairly stirred my prosaic antipathies.

That night I went carefully over every item in the evidence to try and decide on my next step. I had got to find out more about my enemies. Lumley, I was pretty certain, would baffle me, but I thought I might have a better chance with the super-butler. As it turned out, I hit his trail almost at once.

Next day I was in a case at the Old Bailey. It was an important prosecution for fraud, and I appeared, with two leaders, for the bank concerned. The amazing and almost incredible thing about this story of mine is the way clues kept rolling in unsolicited, and I was to get another from this dull prosecution. I suppose that the explanation is that the world is full of clues to everything, and that if a man's mind is sharp-set on any quest, he happens to notice and take advantage of what otherwise he would miss. My leaders were both absent the first day, and I had to examine our witnesses alone.

Towards the close of the afternoon I put a fellow in the box, an oldish, drink-sodden clerk from a Cannon Street bucket-shop. His evidence was valuable for our case, but I was very doubtful how he would stand a cross-examination as to credit. His name was Routh, and he spoke with a strong north-country accent. But what caught my attention was his face. His jaw looked as if it had been made in two pieces which did not fit, and he had little, bright, protuberant eyes. At my first glance I was conscious of a recollection.

He was still in the box when the Court rose, and I informed the solicitors that before going further I wanted a conference with the witness. I mentioned also that I should like to see him alone. A few minutes later he was brought to my chambers, and I put one or two obvious questions on the case, till the managing clerk who accompanied him announced with many excuses that he must hurry away. Then I shut the door, gave Mr Routh a cigar, and proceeded to conduct a private inquiry.

He was a pathetic being, only too ready to talk. I learned the squalid details of his continuous misfortunes. He had been the son of a dissenting minister in Northumberland, and had drifted through half a dozen occupations till he found his present unsavoury billet. Truth was written large on his statement; he had nothing to conceal, for his foible was folly, not crime, and he had not a rag of pride to give him reticence. He boasted that he was a gentleman and well-educated, too, but he had never had a chance. His brother had advised him badly; his brother was too clever for a prosaic world; always through his reminiscences came this echo of fraternal admiration and complaint.

It was about the brother I wanted to know, and Mr Routh was very willing to speak. Indeed, it was hard to disentangle facts from his copious outpourings. The brother had been an engineer and a highly successful one; had dallied with politics, too, and had been a great inventor. He had put Mr Routh on to a South American speculation, where he had made a little money, but speedily lost it again. Oh, he had been a good brother in his way, and had often helped him, but he was a busy man, and his help never went quite far enough. Besides, he did not like to apply to him too often. I gathered that the brother was not a person to take liberties with.

I asked him what he was doing now.

'Ah,' said Mr Routh, 'that is what I wish I could tell you. I will not conceal from you that for the moment I am in considerable financial straits, and this case, though my hands are clean enough, God knows, will not make life easier for me. My brother is a mysterious man, whose business often takes him abroad. I have never known even his address, for I write always to a London office from which my communications are forwarded. I only know that he is in some big electrical business, for I remember that he once let drop the remark that he was in charge of some power station. No, I do not think it is in London; probably somewhere abroad. I heard from him a fortnight ago, and he told me he was just leaving England for a couple of months. It is very annoying, for I want badly to get into touch with him.'

'Do you know, Mr Routh,' I said, 'I believe I have met your brother. Is he like you in any way?'

'We have a strong family resemblance, but he is taller and slimmer. He has been more prosperous, and has lived a healthier life, you see.'

'Do you happen to know,' I asked, 'if he ever uses another name? I don't think that the man I knew was called Routh.'

The clerk flushed. 'I think it highly unlikely that my brother would use an alias. He has done nothing to disgrace a name of which we are proud.'

I told him that my memory had played me false, and we parted on very good terms. He was an innocent soul, one of those people that clever rascals get to do their dirty work for them. But there was no mistaking the resemblance. There, without the brains and force and virility, went my super-butler of Blackheath, who passed under the name of Tuke.

The clerk had given me the name of the office to whose address he had written to his brother. I was not surprised to find that it was that of the firm of stockbrokers for whom I was still acting in the bearer-bonds case where I had heard Pavia's name.

I rang up the partner whom I knew, and told him a very plausible story of having a message for one of Mr Pavia's servants, and asked him if he were in touch with them and could forward letters. He made me hold the line, and then came back and told me that he had forwarded letters for Tuke, the butler, and one Routh who was a groom or foot-man. Tuke had gone abroad to join his master and he did not know his address. But he advised me to write to the White Lodge.

I thanked him and rang off. That was settled, anyhow. Tuke's real name was Routh, and it was Tuke who had gone to Bokhara.

My next step was to ring up Macgillivray at Scotland Yard and get an appointment in half an hour's time. Macgillivray had been at the Bar – I had read in his chambers – and was now one of the heads of the Criminal Investigation Department. I was about to ask him for information which he was in no way bound to give me, but I presumed on our old acquaintance. I asked him first whether he had ever heard of a secret organisation which went under the name of the Power-House. He laughed out loud at my question.

'I should think we have several hundreds of such pet names on our records,' he said. 'Everything from the Lodge of the Baldfaced Ravens to Solomon's Seal No. X. Fancy nomenclature is the relaxation of the tired anarchist, and matters very little. The dangerous fellows have no names, no numbers even, which we can get hold of. But I'll get a man to look up our records. There may be something filed about your Power-House.'

My second question he answered differently. 'Routh! Routh! Why, yes, there was a Routh we had dealings with a dozen years ago when I used to go the North-Eastern circuit. He was a trade-union official who bagged the funds, and they couldn't bring him to justice because of the ridiculous extra-legal status they possess. He knew it, and played their own privileges against them. Oh yes, he was a very complete rogue. I once saw him at a meeting in Sunderland, and I remember his face – sneering eyes, diabolically clever mouth, and with it all as smug as a family butler. He has disappeared from England – at least we haven't heard of him for some years, but I can show you his photograph.'

Macgillivray took from a lettered cabinet a bundle of cards, selected one, and tossed it towards me. It was that of a man of thirty or so, with short side-whiskers and a drooping moustache. The eyes, the ill-fitting jaw, and the brow were those of my friend Mr Tuke, brother and patron of the sorrowful Mr Routh, who had already that afternoon occupied my attention.

Macgillivray promised to make certain inquiries, and I walked home in a state of elation. Now I knew for certain who had gone to Bokhara, and I knew something, too, of the traveller's past. A discredited genius was the very man for Lumley's schemes – one who asked for nothing better than to use his brains outside the ring-fence of convention. Somewhere in the wastes of Turkestan the ex-trade-union official was in search of Pitt-Heron. I did not fancy that Mr Tuke would be very squeamish.

I dined at the club and left early. Going home, I had an impression that I was being shadowed.

You know the feeling that some one is watching you, a sort of sensation which the mind receives without actual evidence. If the watcher is behind, where you can't see him, you have a cold feeling between your shoulders. I daresay it is a legacy from the days when the cave-man had to look pretty sharp to keep from getting his enemy's knife between the ribs.

It was a bright summer evening, and Piccadilly had its usual crowd of motor-cars and buses and foot passengers. I halted twice, once in St James's Street and once at the corner of Stratton Street, and retraced my steps for a bit; and each time I had the impression that some one a hundred yards or so off had done the same. My instinct was to turn round and face him, whoever he was, but I saw that that was foolishness. Obviously in such a crowd I could get no certainty in the matter, so I put it out of my mind.

I spent the rest of the evening in my rooms, reading cases and trying to keep my thoughts off Central Asia. About ten I was rung up on the telephone by Felix. He had had his answer from Bokhara. Pitt-Heron had left with a small caravan on June 2nd by the main road through the Hissar range. Tommy had arrived on June 10th, and on the 12th had set off with two servants on the same trail. Travelling the lighter of the two, he should have overtaken Pitt-Heron by the 15th at latest.

That was yesterday, and my mind was immensely relieved. Tommy in such a situation was a tower of strength, for, whatever his failings in politics, I knew no one I would rather have with me to go tiger-shooting.

Next day the sense of espionage increased. I was in the habit of walking down to the Temple by way of Pall Mall and the Embankment, but, as I did not happen to be in Court that morning, I resolved to make a detour and test my suspicions. There seemed to be nobody in Down Street as I emerged from my flat, but I had not walked five yards before, turning back, I saw a man enter from the Piccadilly end, while another moved across the Hertford Street opening. It may have been only my imagination, but I was convinced that these were my watchers.

I walked up Park Lane, for it seemed to me that by taking the Tube at the Marble Arch Station I could bring matters to the proof. I have a knack of observing small irrelevant details, and I happened to have noticed that a certain carriage in the train which left Marble Arch about 9.30 stopped exactly opposite the exit at the Chancery Lane Station, and by hurrying up the passage one could just catch the lift which served an earlier train, and so reach the street before any of the other travellers.

I performed this manoeuvre with success, caught the early lift, reached the street, and took cover behind a pillar-box, from which I could watch the exit of passengers from the stairs. I judged that my tracker, if he missed me below, would run up the stairs rather than wait on the lift. Sure enough, a breathless gentleman appeared, who scanned the street eagerly, and then turned to the lift to watch the emerging passengers. It was clear that the espionage was no figment of my brain.

I walked slowly to my chambers, and got through the day's work as best I could, for my mind was preoccupied with the unpleasant business in which I found myself entangled. I would have given a year's income to be honestly quit of it, but there seemed to be no way of escape. The maddening thing was that I could do so little. There was no chance of forgetting anxiety in strenuous work. I could only wait with the patience at my command, and hope for the one chance in a thousand which I might seize. I felt miserably that it was no game for me. I had never been brought up to harry wild beasts and risk my neck twice a day at polo like Tommy Deloraine. I was a peaceful sedentary man, a lover of a quiet life, with no appetite for perils and commotions. But I was beginning to realise that I was very obstinate.

At four o'clock I left the Temple and walked to the Embassy. I had resolved to banish the espionage from my mind, for that was the least of my difficulties.

Felix gave me an hour of his valuable time. It was something that Tommy had joined Pitt-Heron, but there were other matters to be arranged in that far country. The time had come, in my opinion, to tell him the whole story.

The telling was a huge relief to my mind. He did not laugh at me as I had half feared, but took the whole thing as gravely as possible. In his profession, I fancy, he had found too many certainties behind suspicions to treat anything as trivial. The next step, he said, was to warn the Russian police of the presence of the man called Sarenov and the super-butler. Happily we had materials for the description of Tuke or Routh, and I could not believe that such a figure would be hard to trace. Felix cabled again in cypher, asking that the two should be watched, more especially if there was reason to believe that they had followed Tommy's route. Once more we got out the big map and discussed the possible ways. It seemed to me a land created by Providence for surprises, for the roads followed the valleys, and to the man who travelled light there must be many short cuts through the hills.

I left the Embassy before six o'clock and, crossing the Square engrossed with my own thoughts, ran full into Lumley.

I hope I played my part well, though I could not repress a

start of surprise. He wore a grey morning-coat and a white top-hat, and looked the image of benevolent respectability.

'Ah, Mr Leithen,' he said, 'we meet again.'

I murmured something about my regrets at my early departure three days ago, and added the feeble joke that I wished he would hurry on his Twilight of Civilisation, for the burden of it was becoming too much for me.

He looked me in the eyes with all the friendliness in the world. 'So you have not forgotten our evening's talk? You owe me something, my friend, for giving you a new interest in your profession.'

'I owe you much,' I said, 'for your hospitality, your advice, and your warnings.'

He was wearing his tinted glasses, and peered quizzically into my face.

'I am going to make a call in Grosvenor Place,' he said, 'and shall beg in return the pleasure of your company. So you know my young friend, Pitt-Heron?'

With an ingenuous countenance I explained that he had been at Oxford with me and that we had common friends.

'A brilliant young man,' said Lumley. 'Like you, he has occasionally cheered an old man's solitude. And he has spoken of me to you?'

'Yes,' I said, lying stoutly. 'He used to tell me about your collections.' (If Lumley knew Charles well he would find me out, for the latter would not have crossed the road for all the treasures of the Louvre.)

'Ah, yes, I have picked up a few things. If ever you should care to see them I should be honoured. You are a connoisseur? Of a sort? You interest me, for I should have thought your taste lay in other directions than the dead things of art. Pitt-Heron is no collector. He loves life better than art, as a young man should. A great traveller, our friend – the Laurence Oliphant or Richard Burton of our day.'

We stopped at a house in Grosvenor Place, and he relinquished my arm. 'Mr Leithen,' he said, 'a word from one who wishes you no ill. You are a friend of Pitt-Heron, but where he goes you cannot follow. Take my advice and keep out of his affairs. You will do no good to him, and you may bring yourself into serious danger. You are a man of sense, a practical man, so I speak to you frankly. But, remember, I do not warn twice.'

He took off his glasses, and his light, wild eyes looked me

straight in the face. All benevolence had gone, and something implacable and deadly burned in them. Before I could say a word in reply he shuffled up the steps of the house and was gone.

FIVE

I Take a Partner

THAT MEETING WITH Lumley scared me badly, but it also clinched my resolution. The most pacific fellow on earth can be gingered into pugnacity. I had now more than my friendship for Tommy and my sympathy with Pitt-Heron to urge me on. A man had tried to bully me, and that roused all the worst stubbornness of my soul. I was determined to see the game through at any cost.

But I must have an ally if my nerves were to hold out, and my mind turned at once to Tommy's friend, Chapman. I thought with comfort of the bluff independence of the Labour member. So that night at the House I hunted him out in the smoking-room.

He had been having a row with the young bloods of my party that afternoon and received me ungraciously.

'I'm about sick of you fellows,' he growled. (I shall not attempt to reproduce Chapman's accent. He spoke rich Yorkshire, with a touch of the drawl of the western dales.) 'They went and spoiled the best speech, though I say it as shouldn't, which this old place has heard for a twelvemonth. I've been workin' for days at it in the Library. I was tellin' them how much more bread cost under Protection, and the Jew Hilderstein started a laugh because I said kilometres for kilogrammes. It was just a slip o' the tongue, for I had it right in my notes, and besides, these furrin words don't matter a curse. Then that young lord as sits for East Claygate gets up and goes out as I was gettin' into my peroration, and he drops his topper and knocks off old Higgins's spectacles, and all the idiots laughed. After that I gave it them hot and strong, and got called to order. And then Wattles, him as used to be as good a Socialist as me, replied for the Government and his blamed Board, and said that the Board thought this and the Board thought that, and was blessed if the Board would stir its stumps. Well I mind the day when I was hanging on to the

Board's coat-tails in Hyde Park to keep it from talking treason.'

It took me a long time to get Chapman settled down and anchored to a drink.

'I want you,' I said, 'to tell me about Routh – you know the fellow I mean – the ex-union-leader.'

At that he fairly blazed up.

'There you are, you Tories,' he shouted, causing a pale Liberal member on the next sofa to make a hurried exit. 'You can't fight fair. You hate the unions, and you rake up any rotten old prejudice to discredit them. You can find out about Routh for yourself, for I'm damned if I help you.'

I saw I could do nothing with Chapman unless I made a clean breast of it, so for the second time that day I told the whole story.

I couldn't have wished for a better audience. He got wildly excited before I was half through with it. No doubt of the correctness of my evidence ever entered his head, for, like most of his party, he hated anarchism worse than capitalism, and the notion of a highly-capitalised, highly-scientific, highly-undemocratic anarchism fairly revolted his soul. Besides, he adored Tommy Deloraine.

Routh, he told me, had been a young engineer of a superior type, with a job in a big shop at Sheffield. He had professed advanced political views, and, although he had strictly no business to be there, had taken a large part in trade union work, and was treasurer of one big branch. Chapman had met him often at conferences and on platforms, and had been impressed by the fertility and ingenuity of his mind and the boldness of his purpose. He was the leader of the left wing of the movement, and had that gift of half-scientific, half-philosophic jargon which is dear at all times to the hearts of the half-baked. A seat in Parliament had been repeatedly offered him, but he had always declined; wisely, Chapman thought, for he judged him the type which is more effective behind the scenes.

But with all his ability he had not been popular. 'He was a cold-blooded, sneering devil,' as Chapman put it, 'a sort of Parnell. He tyrannised over his followers, and he was the rudest brute I ever met.'

Then followed the catastrophe, in which it became apparent that he had speculated with the funds of the union and had lost a large sum. Chapman, however, was suspicious of these losses, and was inclined to suspect that he had the money all the time in a safe place. A year or two earlier the unions, greatly to the disgust of old-fashioned folk, had been given certain extra-legal privileges, and this man Routh had been one of the chief advocates of the unions' claims. Now he had the cool effrontery to turn the tables on them, and use those very privileges to justify his action and escape prosecution.

There was nothing to be done. Some of the fellows, said Chapman, swore to wring his neck, but he did not give them the chance. He had disappeared from England, and was generally believed to be living in some foreign capital.

'What I would give to be even with the swine!' cried my friend, clenching and unclenching his big fist. 'But we're up against no small thing in Josiah Routh. There isn't a crime on earth he'd stick at, and he's as clever as the old Devil, his master.'

'If that's how you feel, I can trust you to back me up,' I said. 'And the first thing I want you to do is to come and stay at my flat. God knows what may happen next, and two men are better than one. I tell you frankly, I'm nervous, and I would like to have you with me.'

Chapman had no objection. I accompanied him to his Bloomsbury lodgings, where he packed a bag, and we returned to the Down Street flat. The sight of his burly figure and sagacious face was relief to me in the mysterious darkness where I now found myself walking.

Thus began my housekeeping with Chapman, one of the queerest episodes in my life. He was the best fellow in the world, but I found that I had misjudged his character. To see him in the House you would have thought him a piece of granite, with his Yorkshire bluntness and hard, downright, north-country sense. He had all that somewhere inside him, but he was also as romantic as a boy. The new situation delighted him. He was quite clear that it was another case of the strife between Capital and Labour – Tommy and I standing for Labour, though he used to refer to Tommy in public as a 'gilded popinjay,' and only a month before had described me in the House as a 'viperous lackey of Capitalism.' It was the best kind of strife in which you had not to meet your adversary with long-winded speeches, but might any moment get a chance to pummel him with your fists. He made me ache with laughter. The spying business used to rouse him to fury. I don't think he was tracked as I was, but he chose to fancy he was, and was guilty of assault and battery on one butcher's boy, two cabbies, and a gentleman who turned out to be a bookmaker's assistant. This side of him got to be an infernal nuisance, and I had many rows with him. Among other things, he chose to suspect my man Waters of treachery – Waters, who was the son of a gardener at home, and hadn't wits enough to put up an umbrella when it rained.

'You're not taking this business rightly,' he maintained one night. 'What's the good of waiting for these devils to down you? Let's go out and down them.' And he announced his intention, from which no words of mine could dissuade him, of keeping watch on Mr Andrew Lumley at the Albany.

His resolution led to a complete disregard of his Parliamentary duties. Deputations of constituents waited for him in vain. Of course he never got a sight of Lumley. All that happened was that he was very nearly given in charge more than once for molesting peaceable citizens in the neighbourhood of Piccadilly and Regent Street.

One night on my way home from the Temple I saw in the bills of the evening papers the announcement of the arrest of a Labour Member. It was Chapman, sure enough. At first I feared that he had got himself into serious trouble, and was much relieved to find him in the flat in a state of blazing anger. It seemed that he had found somebody whom he thought was Lumley, for he only knew him from my descriptions. The man was in a shop in Jermyn Street, with a car waiting outside, and Chapman had – politely, as he swore – asked the chauffeur his master's name. The chauffeur had replied abusively, upon which Chapman had hailed him from the driver's seat and shaken him till his teeth rattled. The owner came out, and Chapman was arrested and taken off to the nearest police-court. He had been compelled to apologise, and had been fined five pounds and costs.

By the mercy of Heaven the chauffeur's master was a money-lender of evil repute, so the affair did Chapman no harm. But I was forced to talk to him seriously. I knew it was no use explaining that for him to spy on the Power-House was like an elephant stalking a gazelle. The only way was to appeal to his incurable romanticism.

'Don't you see,' I told him, 'that you are playing Lumley's game? He will trap you sooner or later into some escapade which will land you in jail, and where will I be then? That is what he and his friends are out for. We have got to meet cunning with cunning, and lie low till we get our chance.'

He allowed himself to be convinced and handed over to me the pistol he had bought, which had been the terror of my life.

'All right,' he said, 'I'll keep quiet. But you promise to let me into the big scrap when it comes off.'

I promised. Chapman's notion of the grand finale was a Homeric combat in which he would get his fill of fisticuffs.

He was an anxiety, but all the same he was an enormous comfort. His imperturbable cheerfulness and his racy talk were the tonics I wanted. He had plenty of wisdom, too. My nerves were getting bad those days, and, whereas I had rarely touched the things before, I now found myself smoking cigarettes from morning till night. I am pretty abstemious, as you know, but I discovered to my horror that I was drinking far too many whiskies-and-sodas. Chapman knocked me off all that, and got me back to a pipe and a modest nightcap. He did more, for he undertook to put me in training. His notion was that we should win in the end by superior muscles. He was a square, thick-set fellow, who had been a good middle-weight boxer. I could box a bit myself, but I improved mightily under his tuition. We got some gloves, and used to hammer each other for half an hour every morning. Then might have been seen the shameful spectacle of a rising barrister with a swollen lip and a black eye arguing in court and proceeding of an evening to his country's legislature, where he was confronted from the opposite benches by the sight of a Leader of the People in the same vulgar condition.

In those days I wanted all the relief I could get, for it was a beastly time. I knew I was in grave danger, so I made my will and went through the other doleful performances consequent on the expectation of a speedy decease. You see I had nothing to grip on, no clear job to tackle, only to wait on the off-chance, with an atmosphere of suspicion thickening around me. The spying went on – there was no mistake about that – but I soon ceased to mind it, though I did my best to give my watchers little satisfaction. There was a hint of bullying about the spying. It is disconcerting at night to have a man bump against you and look you greedily in the face.

I did not go again to Scotland Yard, but one night I ran across Macgillivray in the club.

He had something of profound interest to tell me. I had asked about the phrase, the 'Power-House'. Well, he had come across it, in the letter of a German friend, a private letter, in which the writer gave the results of his inquiries into a curious affair which a year before had excited Europe.

I have forgotten the details, but it had something to do with the Slav States of Austria and an Italian Students' Union, and it threatened at one time to be dangerous. Macgillivray's correspondent said that in some documents which were seized he found constant allusion to a thing called the *Krafthaus*, evidently the headquarters staff of the plot. And this same word *Krafthaus* had appeared elsewhere in a sonnet of a poet-anarchist who shot himself in the slums of Antwerp, in the last ravings of more than one criminal, in the extraordinary testament of Professor M of Jena, who, at the age of thirty-seven, took his life after writing a strange mystical message to his fellow-citizens.

Macgillivray's correspondent concluded by saying that, in his opinion, if this *Krafthaus* could be found, the key would be discovered to the most dangerous secret organisation in the world. He added that he had some reason to believe that the motive power of the concern was English.

'Macgillivray,' I said, 'you have known me for some time, and I fancy you think me a sober and discreet person. Well, I believe I am on the edge of discovering the secret of your *Krafthaus*. I want you to promise me that if in the next week I send you an urgent message you will act on it, however fantastic it seems. I can't tell you more. I ask you to take me on trust, and believe that for anything I do I have tremendous reasons.'

He knit his shaggy grey eyebrows and looked curiously at me. 'Yes, I'll go bail for your sanity. It's a good deal to promise, but if you make an appeal to me, I will see that it is met.'

Next day I had news from Felix. Tuke and the man called Saronov had been identified. If you are making inquiries about anybody it is fairly easy to find those who are seeking for the same person, and the Russian police, in tracking Tommy and Pitt-Heron, had easily come on the two gentlemen who were following the same trail. The two had gone by Samarkand, evidently intending to strike into the hills by a shorter route than the main road from Bokhara. The frontier posts had been warned, and the stalkers had become the stalked.

That was one solid achievement, at any rate. I had saved Pitt-Heron from the worst danger, for first I had sent him Tommy, and now I had put the police on guard against his enemies. I had not the slightest doubt that enemies they were. Charles knew too much, and Tuke was the man appointed to reason with him, to bring him back, if possible, or if not – as Chapman had said – the ex-union leader was not the man to stick at trifles.

It was a broiling June, the London season was at its height, and I had never been so busy in the Courts before. But that crowded and garish world was little more than a dream to me. I went through my daily tasks, dined out, went to the play, had consultations, talked to my fellows, but all the while I had the feeling that I was watching somebody else perform the same functions. I believe I did my work well, and I know I was twice complimented by the Court of Appeal.

But my real interests were far away. Always I saw two men in the hot glens of the Oxus, with the fine dust of the *loess* rising in yellow clouds behind them. One of these men had a drawn and anxious face, and both rode hard. They passed by the closes of apricot and cherry and the green watered gardens, and soon the Oxus ceased to flow wide among rushes and water-lilies and became a turbid hill-stream. By-and-by the roadside changed, and the horses of the travellers trod on mountain turf, crushing the irises and marigolds and thyme. I could feel the free air blowing from the roof of the world, and see far ahead the snowy saddle of the pass which led to India.

Far behind the riders I saw two others, and they chose a different way, now over waterless plateaux, now in rugged *nullahs*. They rode the faster and their route was the shorter. Sooner or later they must catch up the first riders, and I knew, though how I could not tell, that death would attend the meeting.

I, and only I, sitting in London four thousand miles away, could prevent disaster. The dream haunted me at night, and often, walking in the Strand or sitting at a dinner-table, I have found my eyes fixed clearly on the shining upland with the thin white mountains at the back of it, and the four dots, which were men, hurrying fast on their business.

One night I met Lumley. It was at a big political dinner given by the chief of my party in the House of Lords – fifty or sixty guests, and a blaze of stars and decorations. I sat near the bottom of the table, and he was near the top, sitting between a famous General and an ex-Viceroy of India. I asked my right-hand neighbour who he was, but he could not tell me. The same question to my left-hand neighbour brought an answer.

'It's old Lumley. Have you never met him? He doesn't go out much, but he gives a man's dinner now and then, which are the best in London. No. He's not a politician, though he favours our side, and I expect has given a lot to our funds. I can't think why they don't make him a Peer. He's enormously rich and very generous, and the most learned old fellow in Britain. My Chief' – my neighbour was an Under-Secretary – 'knows him, and told me once that if you wanted any out-of-the-way bit of knowledge you could get it by asking Lumley. I expect he pulls the strings more than anybody living. But he scarcely ever goes out, and it's a feather in our host's cap to have got him tonight. You never see his name in the papers, either. He probably pays the Press to keep him out, like some of those millionaire fellows in America.' I watched him through dinner. He was the centre of the talk at his end of the table. I could see the blue ribbon bulging out on Lord Morecambe's breast as he leaned forward to question him. He was wearing some foreign orders, including the Legion of Honour, and I could hear in the pauses of conversation echoes of his soft rich voice. I could see him beaming through his glasses on his neighbours, and now and then he would take them off and look mildly at a speaker. I wondered why nobody realised, as I did, what was in his light wild eyes.

The dinner, I believe, was excellent, and the company was good, but down at my end I could eat little, and I did not want to talk. Here in this pleasant room, with servants moving softly about, and a mellow light on the silver from the shaded candles, I felt the man was buttressed and defended beyond my reach. A kind of despairing hatred gripped me when I looked his way. For I was always conscious of that other picture, the Asian desert, Pitt-Heron's hunted face, and the grim figure of Tuke on his trail. That, and the great secret wheels of what was too inhuman to be called crime, moving throughout the globe under this man's hand.

There was a party afterwards, but I did not stay. No more did Lumley, and for a second I brushed against him in the hall at the foot of the big staircase.

He smiled on me affectionately.

'Have you been dining here? I did not notice you.'

'You had better things to think of,' I said. 'By the way, you gave me good advice some weeks ago. It may interest you to hear that I have taken it.'

'I am so glad,' he said softly. 'You are a very discreet young man.'

But his eyes told me that he knew I lied.

SIX

The Restaurant in Antioch Street

I WAS WORKING late at the Temple next day, and it was nearly seven before I got up to go home. Macgillivray had telephoned to me in the afternoon saying he wanted to see me and suggesting dinner at the club, and I had told him I should come straight there from my Chambers. But just after six he had rung me up again and proposed another meeting-place.

'I've got some very important news for you and want to be quiet. There's a little place where I sometimes dine – Rapaccini's, in Antioch Street. I'll meet you there at half-past seven.'

I agreed, and sent a message to Chapman at the flat, telling him I would be out to dinner. It was a Wednesday night, so the House rose early. He asked me where I was dining and I told him, but I did not mention with whom. His voice sounded very cross, for he hated a lonely meal. It was a hot, still night, and I had had a heavy day in Court, so heavy that my private anxieties had almost slipped from my mind. I walked along the Embankment, and up Regent Street towards Oxford Circus. Antioch Street, as I had learned from the directory, was in the area between Langham Place and Tottenham Court Road. I wondered vaguely why Macgillivray should have chosen such an out-of-the-way spot, but I knew him for a man of many whims.

The street, when I found it, turned out to be a respectable little place – boarding-houses and architects' offices, with a few antiquity shops, and a picture-cleaner's. The restaurant took some finding, for it was one of those discreet establishments, common enough in France, where no edibles are displayed in the British fashion, and muslin half-curtains deck the windows. Only the doormat, lettered with the proprietor's name, remained to guide the hungry.

I gave a waiter my hat and stick and was ushered into a garish dining-room, apparently full of people. A single violinist was discoursing music from beside the grill. The occupants were not quite the kind one expects to find in an eating-house in a side street. The men were all in evening dress with white waistcoats, and the women looked either demi-mondaines or those who follow their taste in clothes. Various eyes looked curiously at me as I entered. I guessed that the restaurant had by one of those odd freaks of Londoners become for a moment the fashion.

The proprietor met me half-way up the room. He might call himself Rapaccini, but he was obviously a German.

'Mr Geelvrai,' he nodded. 'He has engaged a private room. Vill you follow, sir?'

A narrow stairway broke into the wall on the left side of the dining-room. I followed the manager up it and along a short corridor to a door which filled its end. He ushered me into a brightly-lit little room where a table was laid for two.

'Mr Geelvrai comes often here,' said the manager. 'He vill be lat – sometimes. Everything is ready, sir. I hope you vill be pleased.'

It looked inviting enough, but the air smelt stuffy. Then I saw that, though the night was warm, the window was shut and the curtains drawn. I pulled back the curtains, and to my surprise saw that the shutters were closed.

'You must open these,' I said, 'or we'll stifle.'

The manager glanced at the window. 'I vill send a waiter,' he said, and departed. The door seemed to shut with an odd click.

I flung myself down in one of the arm-chairs, for I was feeling pretty tired. The little table beckoned alluringly, for I was also hungry. I remember there was a mass of pink roses on it. A bottle of champagne, with the cork loose, stood in a wine-cooler on the sideboard, and there was an unopened bottle beside it. It seemed to me that Macgillivray, when he dined here, did himself rather well.

The promised waiter did not arrive, and the stuffiness was making me very thirsty. I looked for a bell, but could not see one. My watch told me it was now a quarter to eight, but there was no sign of Macgillivray. I poured myself out a glass of champagne from the opened bottle, and was just about to drink it, when my eye caught something in a corner of the room.

It was one of those little mid-Victorian corner tables – I believe they call them 'what-nots' – which you will find in any boarding-house littered up with photographs and coral and

'Presents from Brighton'. On this one stood a photograph in a shabby frame, and I thought I recognised it.

I crossed the room and picked it up. It showed a man of thirty, with short side-whiskers, an ill-fitting jaw, and a drooping moustache. The duplicate of it was in Macgillivray's cabinet. It was Mr Routh, the ex-union leader.

There was nothing very remarkable about that after all, but it gave me a nasty shock. The room now seemed a sinister place, as well as intolerably close. There was still no sign of the waiter to open the window, so I thought I would wait for Macgillivray downstairs.

But the door would not open. The handle would not turn. It did not seem to be locked, but rather to have shut with some kind of patent spring. I noticed that the whole thing was a powerful piece of oak with a heavy framework, very unlike the usual flimsy restaurant doors.

My first instinct was to make a deuce of a row and attract the attention of the diners below. I own I was beginning to feel badly frightened. Clearly I had got into some sort of trap. Macgillivray's invitation might have been a hoax, for it is not difficult to counterfeit a man's voice on the telephone. With an effort I forced myself into calmness. It was preposterous to think that anything could happen to me in a room not thirty feet from where a score or two of ordinary citizens were dining. I had only to raise my voice to bring inquirers.

Yes, but above all things I did not want a row. It would never do for a rising lawyer and a Member of Parliament to be found shouting for help in an upper chamber of a Bloomsbury restaurant. The worst deductions would be drawn from the open bottle of champagne. Besides, it might be all right after all. The door might have got stuck. Macgillivray at that very moment might be on his way up.

So I sat down and waited. Then I remembered my thirst, and stretched out my hand to the glass of champagne.

But at that instant I looked towards the window, and set down the wine untasted.

It was a very odd window. The lower end was almost flush with the floor, and the hinges of the shutters seemed to be only on one side. As I stared I began to wonder whether it was a window at all.

Next moment my doubts were solved. The window swung open like a door, and in the dark cavity stood a man.

Strangely enough I knew him. His figure was not one that is readily forgotten.

'Good evening, Mr Docken,' I said; 'will you have a glass of champagne?'

A year before, on the South-Eastern Circuit, I had appeared for the defence in a burglary case. Criminal law was not my province, but now and then I took a case to keep my hand in, for it is the best training in the world for the handling of witnesses. This case had been peculiar. A certain Bill Docken was the accused, a gentleman who bore a bad reputation in the eyes of the police. The evidence against him was strong, but it was more or less tainted, being chiefly that of two former accomplices – a proof that there is small truth in the proverbial honour among thieves. It was an ugly business, and my sympathies were with the accused, for though he may very well have been guilty, yet he had been the victim of a shabby trick. Anyhow I put my back into the case, and after a hard struggle got a verdict of 'Not Guilty'. Mr Docken had been kind enough to express his appreciation of my efforts, and to ask in a hoarse whisper how I had 'squared the old bird', meaning the Judge. He did not understand the subtleties of the English law of evidence.

He shambled into the room, a huge hulking figure of a man, with the thickness of chest which under happier circumstances might have made him a terror in the prize-ring. His features wore a heavy scowl which slowly cleared to a flicker of recognition.

'By God, it's the lawyer-chap,' he muttered.

I pointed to the glass of champagne. 'I don't mind if I do,' he said. ' 'Ere's 'ealth!' He swallowed the wine at a gulp and wiped his mouth on his sleeve. ' 'Ave a drop yourself, guv'nor,' he added. 'A glass of bubbly will cheer you up.'

'Well, Mr Docken,' I said, 'I hope I see you fit.' I was getting wonderfully collected now that the suspense was over.

'Pretty fair, sir. Pretty fair. Able to do my day's work like an honest man.'

'And what brings you here?'

'A little job I'm on. Some friends of mine wants you out of the road for a bit and they've sent me to fetch you. It's a bit of luck for you that you've struck a friend. We needn't 'ave no unpleasantness, seein' we're both what you might call men of the world.'

'I appreciate the compliment,' I said. 'But where do you propose to take me?'

'Dunno. It's some lay near the Docks. I've got a motor-car waitin' at the back of the 'ouse.'

'But supposing I don't want to go?'

'My orders admits no excuse,' he said solemnly. 'You're a sensible chap, and can see that in a scrap I could down you easy.'

'Very likely,' I said. 'But, man, you must be mad to talk like that. Downstairs there is a dining-room full of people. I have only to lift my voice to bring the police.'

'You're a kid,' he said scornfully. 'Them geysers downstairs are all in the job. That was a flat-catching rig to get you up here so as you wouldn't suspect nothing. If you was to go down now – which you ain't going to be allowed to do – you wouldn't find a blamed soul in the place. I must say you're a bit softer than I 'oped after the 'andsome way you talked over yon old juggins with the wig at Maidstone.'

Mr Docken took the bottle from the wine-cooler and filled himself another glass.

It sounded horribly convincing. If I was to be kidnapped and smuggled away, Lumley would have scored half a success. Not the whole; for, as I swiftly reflected, I had put Felix on the track of Tuke, and there was every chance that Tommy and Pitt-Heron would be saved. But for myself it looked pretty black. The more my scheme succeeded the more likely the Power-House would be to wreak its vengeance on me once I was spirited from the open-air world into its dark labyrinths. I made a great effort to keep my voice even and calm.

'Mr Docken,' I said, 'I once did you a good turn. But for me you might be doing time now instead of drinking champagne like a gentleman. Your pals played you a pretty low trick and that was why I stuck out for you. I didn't think you were the kind of man to forget a friend.'

'No more I am,' said he. 'The man who says Bill Docken would go back on a pal is a liar.'

'Well, here's your chance to pay your debts. The men who employ you are my deadly enemies and want to do me in. I'm not a match for you. You're a stronger fellow and can drag me off and hand me over to them. But if you do I'm done with. Make no mistake about that. I put it to you as a decent fellow. Are you going to go back on the man who has been a good friend to you?'

He shifted from one foot to another with his eyes on the ceiling. He was obviously in difficulties. Then he tried another glass of champagne.

'I dursn't, guv'nor. I dursn't let you go. Them I work for would cut my throat as soon as look at me. Besides, it ain't no good. If I was to go off and leave you there'd be plenty more in this 'ouse as would do the job. You're up against it, guv'nor. But take a sensible view and come with me. They don't mean you no real 'arm. I'll take my Bible oath on it. Only to keep you quiet for a bit, for you've run across one of their games. They won't do you no 'urt if you speak 'em fair. Be a sport and take it smiling-like.'

'You're afraid of them,' I said.

'Yuss. I'm afraid. Black afraid. So would you be if you knew the gents. I'd rather take on the whole Rat Lane crowd – you know them as I mean – on a Saturday night when they're out for business than go back to my gents and say as 'ow I had shirked the job.'

He shivered. 'Good Lord, they'd freeze the 'eart out of a bull-pup.'

'You're afraid,' I said slowly. 'So you're going to give me up to the men you're afraid of to do as they like with me. I never expected it of you, Bill. I thought you were the kind of lad who would send any gang to the devil before you'd go back on a pal.'

'Don't say that,' he said almost plaintively. 'You don't 'alf know the 'ole I'm in.' His eye seemed to be wandering, and he yawned deeply.

Just then a great noise began below. I heard a voice speaking, a loud peremptory voice. Then my name was shouted: 'Leithen! Leithen! Are you there?'

There could be no mistaking that stout Yorkshire tongue. By some miracle Chapman had followed me and was raising Cain downstairs.

My heart leaped with the sudden revulsion. 'I'm here,' I yelled. 'Upstairs. Come up and let me out!'

Then I turned with a smile of triumph to Bill.

'My friends have come,' I said. 'You're too late for the job. Get back and tell your masters that.'

He was swaying on his feet, and he suddenly lurched towards me. 'You come along. By God, you think you've done me. I'll let you see.'

His voice was growing thick and he stopped short. 'What the 'ell's wrong with me?' he gasped. 'I'm goin' all queer.'

He was like a man far gone in liquor, but three glasses of champagne would never have touched a head like Bill's. I saw what was up with him. He was not drunk, but drugged.

'They've doped the wine,' I cried. 'They put it there for me to drink it and go to sleep.'

There is always something which is the last straw to any man. You may insult and outrage him and he will bear it patiently, but touch the quick in his temper and he will turn. Apparently for Bill drugging was the unforgivable sin. His eye lost for a moment its confusion. He squared his shoulders and roared like a bull.

'Doped, by God!' he cried. 'Who done it?'

'The men who shut me in this room. Burst that door and you will find them.'

He turned a blazing face on the locked door and hurled his huge weight on it. It cracked and bent, but the lock and hinges held. I could see that sleep was overwhelming him and that his limbs were stiffening, but his anger was still strong enough for another effort. Again he drew himself together like a big cat and flung himself on the woodwork. The hinges tore from the jambs and the whole outfit fell forward into the passage in a cloud of splinters and dust and broken plaster.

It was Mr Docken's final effort. He lay on the top of the wreckage he had made, like Samson among the ruins of Gaza, a senseless and slumbering hulk.

I picked up the unopened bottle of champagne. It was the only weapon available and stepped over his body. I was beginning to enjoy myself amazingly.

As I expected, there was a man in the corridor, a little fellow in waiter's clothes with a tweed jacket instead of a dress-coat. If he had a pistol I knew I was done, but I gambled upon the disinclination of the management for the sound of shooting.

He had a knife, but he never had a chance to use it. My champagne bottle descended on his head and he dropped like a log.

There were men coming upstairs – not Chapman, for I still heard his hoarse shouts in the dining-room. If they once got up they could force me back through that hideous room by the door through which Docken had come, and in five minutes I should be in their motor-car.

There was only one thing to do. I jumped from the stair-head right down among them. I think there were three, and my descent toppled them over. We rolled in a wild whirling mass and cascaded into the dining-room, where my head bumped violently on the parquet.

I expected a bit of a grapple, but none came. My wits were pretty woolly, but I managed to scramble to my feet. The heels of my enemies were disappearing up the staircase. Chapman was pawing my ribs to discover if there were any bones broken. There was not another soul in the room except two policemen who were pushing their way in from the street. Chapman was flushed and breathing heavily: his coat had a big split down the seams at the shoulder, but his face was happy as a child's.

I caught his arm and spoke in his ear. 'We've got to get out of this at once. How can we square these policemen? There must be no inquiry and nothing in the papers. Do you hear?'

'That's all right,' said Chapman. 'These bobbies are friends of mine, two good lads from Wensleydale. On my road here I told them to give me a bit of law and follow me, for I thought they might be wanted. They didn't come too soon to spoil sport, for I've been knocking furriners about for ten minutes. You seem to have been putting up a tidy scrap yourself.'

'Let's get home first,' I said, for I was beginning to think of the bigger thing.

I wrote a chit for Macgillivray which I asked one of the constables to take to Scotland Yard. It was to beg that nothing should be done yet in the business of the restaurant, and above all, that nothing should get into the papers. Then I asked the other to see us home. It was a queer request for two able-bodied men to make on a summer evening in the busiest part of London, but I was taking no chances. The Power-House had declared war on me, and I knew it would be war without quarter.

I was in a fever to get out of that place. My momentary lust of battle had gone, and every stone of that building seemed to me a threat. Chapman would have liked to spend a happy hour rummaging through the house, but the gravity of my face persuaded him. The truth is, I was bewildered. I could not understand the reason of this sudden attack. Lumley's spies must long ago have told him enough to connect me with the Bokhara business. My visits to the Embassy alone were proof enough. But now he must have found something new, something which startled him, or else there had been wild doings in Turkestan.

I won't forget that walk home in a hurry. It was a fine July twilight. The streets were full of the usual crowd, shop-girls in thin frocks, promenading clerks, and all the flotsam of a London summer. You would have said it was the safest place on earth. But I was glad we had the policeman with us, who at the end of one beat passed us on to his colleague, and I was glad of Chapman. For I am morally certain I would never have got home alone.

The queer thing is that there was no sign of trouble till we got into Oxford Street. Then I became aware that there were people on these pavements who knew all about me. I first noticed it at the mouth of one of those little dark side-alleys which run up into mews and small dingy courts. I found myself being skilfully edged away from Chapman into the shadow, but I noticed it in time and butted my way back to the pavement. I couldn't make out who the people were who hustled me. They seemed nondescripts of all sorts, but I fancied there were women among them.

This happened twice, and I got wary, but I was nearly caught before we reached Oxford Circus. There was a front of a big shop rebuilding, and the usual wooden barricade with a gate. Just as we passed it there was a special throng on the pavement, and I, being next the wall, got pushed against the gate. Suddenly it gave, and I was pressed inward. I was right inside before I realised my danger, and the gate was closing. There must have been people there, but I could see nothing in the gloom.

It was no time for false pride. I yelled to Chapman, and the next second his burly shoulder was in the gap. The hustlers vanished, and I seemed to hear a polite voice begging my pardon.

After that Chapman and I linked arms and struck across Mayfair. But I did not feel safe till I was in the flat with the door bolted.

We had a long drink, and I stretched myself in an armchair, for I was as tired as if I had come out of a big game of Rugby football.

'I owe you a good deal, old man,' I said. 'I think I'll join the Labour Party. You can tell your fellows to send me their whips. What possessed you to come to look for me?'

The explanation was simple. I had mentioned the restaurant in my telephone message, and the name had awakened a recollection in Chapman's mind. He could not fix it at first, but by-and-by he remembered that the place had cropped up in the Routh case. Routh's London headquarters had been at the restaurant in Antioch Street. As soon as he remembered this he got into a taxi and descended at the corner of the street, where by sheer luck he fell in with his Wensleydale friends.

He said he had marched into the restaurant and found it empty, but for an ill-favoured manager, who denied all knowledge of me. Then, fortunately, he chose to make certain by shouting my name, and heard my answer. After that he knocked the manager down, and was presently assaulted by several men whom he described as 'furrin muck'. They had knives, of which he made very little, for he seems to have swung a table as a battering-ram and left sore limbs behind him.

He was on the top of his form. 'I haven't enjoyed anything so much since I was a lad at school,' he informed me. 'I was beginning to think your Power-House was a wash-out, but Lord! it's been busy enough tonight. This is what I call life!'

My spirits could not keep pace with his. The truth is that I was miserably puzzled – not afraid so much as mystified. I couldn't make out this sudden dead-set at me. Either they knew more than I bargained for, or I knew far too little.

'It's all very well,' I said, 'but I don't see how this is going to end. We can't keep up the pace long. At this rate it will be only a matter of hours till they get me.'

We pretty well barricaded ourselves in the flat, and, at his earnest request, I restored to Chapman his revolver.

Then I got the clue I had been longing for. It was about eleven o'clock, while we were sitting smoking, when the telephone bell rang. It was Felix who spoke.

'I have news for you,' he said. 'The hunters have met the hunted, and one of the hunters is dead. The other is a prisoner in our hands. He has confessed.'

It had been black murder in intent. The frontier police had shadowed the two men into the cup of a glen, where they met Tommy and Pitt-Heron. The four had spoken together for a little, and then Tuke had fired deliberately at Charles and had grazed his ear. Whereupon Tommy had charged him and knocked the pistol from his hand. The assailant had fled, but a long shot from the police on the hillside had toppled him over. Tommy had felled Saronov with his fists, and the man had abjectly surrendered. He had confessed, Felix said, but what the confession was he did not know.

SEVEN

I Find Sanctuary

MY NERVOUSNESS AND indecision dropped from me at the news. I had won the first round, and I would win the last, for it suddenly became clear to me that I had now evidence which would blast Lumley. I believed that it would not be hard to prove his identity with Pavia and his receipt of the telegram from Saronov; Tuke was his creature, and Tuke's murderous mission was his doing. No doubt I knew little and could prove nothing about the big thing, the Power-House, but conspiracy to murder is not the lightest of criminal charges. I was beginning to see my way to checkmating my friend, at least so far as Pitt-Heron was concerned. Provided – and it was a pretty big proviso – that he gave me the chance to use my knowledge.

That, I foresaw, was going to be the difficulty. What I knew now Lumley had known hours before. The reason of the affair at Antioch Street was now only too clear. If he believed that I had damning evidence against him – and there was no doubt he suspected it – then he would do his best to stop my mouth. I must get my statement lodged in the proper quarter at the earliest possible moment.

The next twenty-four hours, I feared, were going to be too sensational for comfort. And yet I cannot say that I was afraid. I was too full of pride to be in a funk. I had lost my awe of Lumley through scoring a point against him. Had I known more I should have been less at my ease. It was this confidence which prevented me doing the obvious safe thing – ringing up Macgillivray, telling him the gist of my story, and getting him to put me under police protection. I thought I was clever enough to see the thing through myself. And it must have been the same over-confidence which prevented Lumley getting at me that night. An organisation like his could easily have got into the flat and done for us both. I suppose the explanation is that he did not yet know how much I knew, and was not ready to take the last steps in silencing me. I sat up till the small hours, marshalling my evidence in a formal statement and making two copies of it. One was destined for Macgillivray and the other for Felix, for I was taking no risks. I went to bed and slept peacefully, and was awakened as usual by Waters. My man slept out, and used to turn up in the morning about seven. It was all so normal and homely that I could have believed my adventures of the night before a dream. In the summer sunlight the ways of darkness seemed very distant. I dressed in excellent spirits and made a hearty breakfast. Then I gave the docile Chapman his instructions. He must take the document to Scotland Yard, ask to see Macgillivray, and put it into his hands. Then he must ring me up at once at Down Street and tell me that he had done this. I had already telephoned to my clerk that I would not be at the Temple that day. It seems a simple thing to travel less than a mile in the most frequented part of London in broad daylight and perform an easy act like carrying a letter; but I knew that Lumley's spies would be active, and would connect Chapman sufficiently with me to think him worth following. In that case there might be an attempt at violence. I thought it my duty to tell him this, but he laughed me to scorn. He proposed to walk, and he begged to be shown the man who would meddle with him. Chapman, after last night, was prepared to take on all comers. He put my letter to Macgillivray in his inner pocket, buttoned his coat, crushed down his felt hat on his head, and defiantly set forth.

I expected a message from him in half an hour, for he was a rapid walker. But the half-hour passed, then the three-quarters, and nothing happened. At eleven I rang up Scotland Yard, but they had no news of him.

Then I became miserably anxious, for it was clear that some disaster had overtaken my messenger. My first impulse was to set out myself to look for him, but a moment's reflection convinced me that that would be playing into the enemy's hands. For an hour I wrestled with my impatience, and then a few minutes after twelve I was rung up by St Thomas's Hospital.

A young doctor spoke, and said that Mr Chapman had asked him to tell me what had happened. He had been run down by a motor-car at the corner of Whitehall, nothing serious – only a bad shake and some scalp wounds. In a day or so he would be able to leave.

Then he added what drove the blood from my heart. 'Mr Chapman personally wished me to tell you,' he said, 'that the letter has gone.' I stammered some reply asking his meaning. 'He said he thinks,' I was told, 'that, while he was being assisted to his feet, his pocket was picked and a letter taken. He said you would know what he meant.'

I knew only too well what he meant. Lumley had got my statement, and realised precisely how much I knew and what was the weight of evidence against him. Before he had only suspected, now he knew. He must know, too, that there would be a copy somewhere which I would try to deliver. It was going to be harder than I had fancied to get my news to the proper ears, and I had to anticipate the extreme of violence on the part of my opponents.

The thought of the peril restored my coolness. I locked the outer door of my flat, and telephoned to the garage where I kept my car, bidding Stagg call for me at two o'clock precisely. Then I lit a pipe and strove to banish the whole business from my thoughts, for fussing would do me no good.

Presently it occurred to me to ring up Felix and give him some notion of the position. But I found that my telephone was now broken and connection was impossible. The spoken as well as the written word was to be denied me. That had happened in the last half-hour, and I didn't believe it was by accident. Also my man Waters, whom I had sent out on an errand after breakfast, had never returned. The state of siege had begun.

It was a blazing hot midsummer day. The water-carts were sprinkling Piccadilly, and looking from my window I could see leisurely and elegant gentlemen taking their morning stroll. A florist's cart full of roses stood below me in the street. The summer smell of town – a mixture of tar, flowers, dust, and patchouli – rose in gusts through the hot air. It was the homely London I knew so well, and I was somehow an exile from it. I was being shepherded into a dismal isolation, which, unless I won help, might mean death. I was cool enough now, but I will not deny that I was miserably anxious. I cursed my false confidence the night before. By now I might have had Macgillivray and his men by my side. As it was, I wondered if I should ever see them.

I changed into a flannel suit, lunched off sandwiches and a whisky-and-soda, and at two o'clock looked for Stagg and my car. He was five minutes late, a thing which had never happened before. But I never welcomed anything so gladly as the sight of that car. I had hardly dared to hope that it would reach me.

My goal was the Embassy in Belgrave Square, but I was convinced that if I approached it directly I should share the fate of Chapman. Worse, for from me they would not merely snatch the letter. What I had once written I could write again, and if they wished to ensure my silence it must be by more drastic methods. I proposed to baffle my pursuers by taking a wide circuit round the western suburbs of London, returning to the Embassy when I thought the coast clear. It was a tremendous relief to go down the stairs and emerge into the hot daylight. I gave Stagg his instructions, and lay back in the closed car with a curious fluttering sense of anticipation. I had begun the last round in a wild game. There was a man at the corner of Down Street who seemed to peer curiously at the car. He was doubtless one of my watchers. We went up Park Lane into the Edgware Road, my instructions to Stagg being to make a circuit by Harrow and Brentford. Now that I was ensconced in my car I felt a trifle safer, and my tense nerves relaxed. I grew drowsy and allowed myself to sink into a half doze. The stolid back of Stagg filled my gaze, as it had filled it a fortnight ago on the western road, and I admired lazily the brick-red of his neck. He had been in the Guards, and a Boer bullet at Modder River had left a long scar at the nape of his neck, which gave to his hair the appearance of being badly cut. He had told me the story on Exmoor.

Suddenly I rubbed my eyes. There was no scar there; the hair of the chauffeur grew regularly down to his coat-collar. The resemblance had been perfect, the voice was Stagg's, but clearly it was not Stagg who now drove my car.

I pulled the blind down over the front window as if to shelter myself from the sun. Looking out, I saw that we were some distance up the Edgware Road, nearing the point where the Marylebone Road joins it. Now or never was my chance, for at the corner there is always a block in the traffic.

The car slowed down in obedience to a policeman's uplifted hand, and very gently I opened the door on the left side. Since the car was new it opened softly, and in two seconds I had stepped out, shut it again, and made a dive between a butcher's cart and a motor-bus for the side-walk. I gave one glance back and saw the unconscious chauffeur still rigid at the wheel.

I dodged unobtrusively through the crowd on the pavement, with my hand on my breast-pocket to see that my paper was still there. There was a little picture-shop near by to which I used to go occasionally, owned by a man who was an adept at cleaning and restoring. I had sent him customers and he was likely to prove a friend. So I dived into his doorway, which made a cool pit of shade after the glaring street, and found him, spectacles on nose, busy examining some dusty prints.

He greeted me cordially and followed me into the back shop.

'Mr Levison,' I said, 'have you a back door?'

He looked at me in some surprise. 'Why, yes; there is the door into the lane which runs from Edgeley Street into Connaught Mews.'

'Will you let me use it? There is a friend outside whom I wish to avoid. Such things happen, you know.'

He smiled comprehendingly. 'Certainly, sir. Come this way.' And he led me through a dark passage hung with dingy Old Masters to a little yard filled with the debris of picture frames. There he unlocked a door in the wall and I found myself in a narrow alley. As I emerged I heard the bell of the shop-door ring. 'If any one inquires, you have not seen me here, remember,' I said, and Mr Levison nodded. He was an artist in his small way and liked the scent of a mystery.

I ran down the lane and by various cross streets made my way into Bayswater. I believed that I had thrown my trackers for the moment off the scent, but I had got to get to the Embassy, and that neighbourhood was sure to be closely watched. I came out on the Bayswater Road pretty far west, and resolved to strike south-east across the Park. My reason was that the neighbourhood of Hyde Park Corner was certain at that time of day to be pretty well crowded, and I felt more security in a throng than in the empty streets of Kensington. Now that I come to think of it, it was a rash thing to do, for since Lumley knew the full extent of my knowledge, he was likely to deal more violently with me than with Chapman, and the seclusion of the Park offered him too good a chance.

I crossed the riding-track, and struck over the open space where the Sunday demonstrations are held. There was nothing there but nurses and perambulators, children at play, and dogs being exercised. Presently I reached Grosvenor Gate, where on the little green chairs well-dressed people were taking the air. I recognised several acquaintances, and stopped for a moment to talk to one of them. Then I emerged in Park Lane, and walked down it to Hamilton Place.

So far I thought I had not been followed, but now once more I had the indefinable but unerring sensation of being watched. I caught a man looking eagerly at me from the other side of the street, and it seemed to me that he made a sign to some one farther off. There was now less than a quarter of a mile between me and Belgrave Square, but I saw that it would be a hard course to cover.

Once in Piccadilly, there could be no doubt about my watchers. Lumley was doing the thing in style this time. Last night it had only been a trial trip, but now the whole energies of the Power-House were on the job. The place was filled with the usual mid-season crowd, and I had to take off my hat several times. Up in the bow-window of the Bachelors' Club a young friend of mine was writing a letter and sipping a long drink with an air of profound boredom. I would have given much for his *ennui*, for my life at the moment was painfully exciting. I was alone in that crowd, isolated and proscribed, and there was no help save in my own wits. If I spoke to a policeman he would think me drunk or mad, and yet I was on the edge of being made the victim of a far subtler crime than fell within the purview of the Metropolitan force.

Now I saw how thin is the protection of civilisation. An accident and a bogus ambulance, false charge and a bogus arrest – there were a dozen ways of spiriting me out of this gay, bustling world. I foresaw that, if I delayed, my nerve would break, so I boldly set off across the road.

I jolly nearly shared the fate of Chapman. A car which seemed about to draw up at a club door suddenly swerved across the street, and I had to dash to an island to escape it. It was no occasion to hesitate, so, dodging a bus and missing a motor-bicycle by a hair's breadth, I rushed across the remaining distance and reached the railings of the Green Park.

Here there were fewer people, and several queer things began to happen. A little group of workmen with their tools were standing by the kerb, and they suddenly moved towards me. A pavement artist, who looked like a cripple, scrambled to his feet and moved in the same direction. There was a policeman at the corner, and I saw a well-dressed man go up to him, say something and nod in my direction, and the policeman too began to move towards me.

I did not await them. I took to my heels and ran for my life down Grosvenor Place.

Long ago at Eton I had won the school mile, and at Oxford I was a second string for the quarter. But never at Eton or at Oxford did I run as I ran then. It was blisteringly hot, but I did not feel it, for my hands were clammy and my heart felt like a cold stone. I do not know how the pursuit got on, for I did not think of it. I did not reflect what kind of spectacle I must afford running like a thief in a London thoroughfare on a June afternoon. I only knew that my enemies were around and behind me, and that in front, a few hundred yards away, lay safety.

But even as I ran I had the sense to think out my movements, and to realise that the front door of the Embassy was impossible. For one thing, it would be watched, and for another, before the solemn footmen opened it, my pursuers would be upon me. My only hope was the back door.

I twisted into the Mews behind the north side of the Square, and as I turned I saw two men run up from the Square as if to cut me off. A whistle was blown, and more men appeared – one entering from the far end of the Mews, one darting from a public-house door, and one sliding down a ladder from a stable-loft. This last was nearest me, and tried to trip me, but I rejoice to say that a left-hander on the chin sent him sprawling on the cobbles. I remembered that the Embassy was the fifth house from the end, and feverishly I tried to count the houses by their backs. It is not so easy as it sounds, for the modern London householder studs his back premises with excrescences which seem to melt into his neighbour's. In the end I had to make a guess at the door, which, to my joy, was unlocked. I rushed in and banged it behind me.

I found myself in a stone passage, with on one side a door opening on a garage. There was a wooden staircase leading to an upper floor, and a glass door in front, which opened into a large disused room full of boxes. Beyond were two doors, one of which was locked. The other abutted on a steep iron stairway, which obviously led to the lower regions of the house.

I ran down the stair – it was no more than a ladder – crossed a small courtyard, traversed a passage, and burst into the kitchen, where I confronted an astonished white-capped chef in the act of lifting a pot from the fire.

His face was red and wrathful, and I thought that he was going to fling the pot at my head. I had disturbed him in some delicate operation, and his artist's pride was outraged.

'Monsieur,' I stammered in French, 'I seek your pardon for my intrusion. There were circumstances which compelled me to enter this house by the back premises. I am an acquaintance of his Excellency, your patron, and an old friend of Monsieur Felix. I beg you of your kindness to direct me to Monsieur Felix's room, or to bid some one take me there.'

My abject apologies mollified him.

'It is a grave offence, monsieur,' he said, 'an unparalleled offence, to enter my kitchen at this hour. I fear you have irremediably spoiled the new casserole dish that I was endeavouring to compose.'

I was ready to go on my knees to the offended artist.

'It grieves me indeed to have interfered with so rare an art, which I have often admired at his Excellency's table. But there is danger behind me, and an urgent mission in front. Monsieur will forgive me? Necessity will sometimes overrule the finest sensibility.'

He bowed to me, and I bowed to him, and my pardon was assured.

Suddenly a door opened, another than that by which I had entered, and a man appeared whom I took to be a footman. He was struggling into his livery coat, but at the sight of me he dropped it. I thought I recognised the face as that of the man who had emerged from the public-house and tried to cut me off.

''Ere, Mister Alphonse,' he cried, ''elp me to collar this man. The police are after 'im.'

'You forget, my friend,' I said, 'that an Embassy is privileged ground which the police can't enter. I desire to be taken before his Excellency.'

'So that's yer game,' he shouted. 'But two can play at that. 'Ere, give me an 'and, moosoo, and we'll 'ave him in the street in a jiffey. There's two 'undred of the best in our pockets if we 'ands 'im over to them as wants 'im.'

The cook looked puzzled and a little frightened.

'Will you allow them to outrage your kitchen – an Embassy kitchen, too – without your consent?' I said.

'What have you done?' he asked in French.

'Only what your patron will approve,' I replied in the same tongue. '*Messieurs les assassins* have a grudge against me.'

He still hesitated, while the young footman advanced on me. He was fingering something in his trousers-pocket which I did not like.

Now was the time when, as they say in America, I should have got busy with my gun; but alas! I had no gun. I feared supports for the enemy, for the footman at the first sight of me had run back the way he had come, and I had heard a low whistle.

What might have happened I do not know, had not the god appeared from the machine in the person of Hewins, the butler.

'Hewins,' I said, 'you know me. I have often dined here, and you know that I am a friend of Monsieur Felix. I am on my way to see him on an urgent matter, and for various reasons I had to enter by Monsieur Alphonse's kitchen. Will you take me at once to Monsieur Felix?'

Hewins bowed, and on his imperturbable face there appeared no sign of surprise. 'This way, sir,' was all he said.

As I followed him I saw the footman plucking nervously at the something in his trousers-pocket. Lumley's agents apparently had not always the courage to follow his instructions to the letter, for I made no doubt that the order had been to take me alive or dead.

I found Felix alone, and flung myself into an armchair.

'My dear chap,' I said, 'take my advice and advise His Excellency to sack the red-haired footman.'

From that moment I date that sense of mastery over a situation which drives out fear. I had been living for weeks under a dark pall, and suddenly the skies had lightened. I had found sanctuary. Whatever happened to me now the worst was past, for I had done my job.

Felix was looking at me curiously, for, jaded, scarlet, dishevelled, I was an odd figure for a London afternoon. 'Things seem to have been marching fast with you,' he said.

'They have, but I think the march is over. I want to ask several favours. First, here is a document which sets out certain facts. I shall ring up Macgillivray at Scotland Yard and ask him to come here at 9.30 this evening. When he comes I want you to give him this and ask him to read it at once. He will know how to act on it.'

Felix nodded. 'And the next?'

'Give me a telegraph form. I want a wire sent at once by

some one who can be trusted.' He handed me a form and I wrote out a telegram to Lumley at the Albany, saying that I proposed to call upon him that evening at eight sharp, and asking him to receive me.

'Next?' said Felix.

'Next and last, I want a room with a door which will lock, a hot bath, and something to eat about seven. I might be permitted to taste Monsieur Alphonse's new casserole dish.'

I rang up Macgillivray, reminded him of his promise, and told him what awaited him at 9.30. Then I had a wash, and afterwards at my leisure gave Felix a sketch of the day's doings. I have never felt more completely at my ease, for whatever happened I was certain that I had spoiled Lumley's game. He would know by now that I had reached the Embassy, and that any further attempts on my life and liberty were futile. My telegram would show him that I was prepared to offer terms, and I would certainly be permitted to reach the Albany unmolested. To the meeting with my adversary I looked forward without qualms, but with the most lively interest. I had my own theories about that distinguished criminal, and I hoped to bring them to the proof.

Just before seven I had a reply to my wire. Mr Lumley said he would be delighted to see me. The telegram was directed to me at the Embassy, though I had put no address on the one I sent. Lumley, of course, knew all my movements. I could picture him sitting in his chair, like some Chief of Staff, receiving every few minutes the reports of his agents. All the same, Napoleon had fought his Waterloo.

EIGHT

The Power-House

I LEFT BELGRAVE Square about a quarter to eight and retraced my steps along the route which for me that afternoon had been so full of tremors. I was still being watched – a little observation told me that – but I would not be interfered with, provided my way lay in a certain direction. So completely without nervousness was I that at the top of Constitution Hill I struck into the Green Park and kept to the grass till I emerged into Piccadilly opposite Devonshire House. A light wind had risen, and the evening had grown pleasantly cool. I met several men I knew going out to dinner on foot, and stopped to exchange greetings. From my clothes they thought I had just returned from a day in the country.

I reached the Albany as the clock was striking eight. Lumley's rooms were on the first floor, and I was evidently expected, for the porter himself conducted me to them and waited by me till the door was opened by a manservant.

You know those rococo, late Georgian, Albany rooms, large, square, clumsily corniced. Lumley's was lined with books, which I saw at a glance were of a different type from those in his working library at his country house. This was the collection of a bibliophile, and in the light of the summer evening the rows of tall volumes in vellum and morocco lined the walls like some rich tapestry.

The valet retired and shut the door, and presently from a little inner chamber came his master. He was dressed for dinner, and wore more than ever the air of the eminent diplomat. Again I had the old feeling of incredulity. It was the Lumley I had met two nights before at dinner, the friend of Viceroys and Cabinet Ministers. It was hard to connect him with Antioch Street or the red-haired footman with a pistol. Or with Tuke? Yes, I decided, Tuke fitted into the frame. Both were brains cut loose from the decencies that make life possible.

'Good evening, Mr Leithen,' he said pleasantly. 'As you have fixed the hour of eight, may I offer you dinner?'

'Thank you,' I replied, 'but I have already dined. I have chosen an awkward time, but my business need not take long.'

'So?' he said. 'I am always glad to see you at any hour.'

'And I prefer to see the master rather than the subordinates who have been infesting my life during the past week.'

We both laughed. 'I am afraid you have had some annoyance, Mr Leithen,' he said. 'But remember, I gave you fair warning.'

'True. And I have come to do the same kindness to you. That part of the game, at any rate, is over.'

'Over?' he queried, raising his eyebrows.

'Yes, over,' I said, and took out my watch. 'Let us be quite frank with each other, Mr Lumley. There is really very little time to waste. As you have doubtless read the paper which you stole from my friend this morning, you know more or less the extent of my information.'

'Let us have frankness by all means. Yes, I have read your paper. A very creditable piece of work, if I may say so. You will rise in your profession, Mr Leithen. But surely you must realise that it carries you a very little way.'

'In a sense you are right. I am not in a position to reveal the full extent of your misdeeds. Of the Power-House and its doings I can only guess. But Pitt-Heron is on his way home, and he will be carefully safeguarded on that journey. Your creature, Saronov, has confessed. We shall know more very soon, and meantime I have clear evidence which implicates you in a conspiracy to murder.'

He did not answer, but I wished I could see behind his tinted spectacles to the look in his eyes. I think he had not been quite prepared for the line I took.

'I need not tell you, as a lawyer, Mr Leithen,' he said at last, 'that what seems good evidence on paper is often feeble enough in Court. You cannot suppose that I will tamely plead guilty to your charges. On the contrary, I will fight them with all the force that brains and money can give. You are an ingenious young man, but you are not the brightest jewel of the English Bar.'

'That also is true. I do not deny that some of my evidence may be weakened at the trial. It is even conceivable that you may be acquitted on some technical doubt. But you have forgotten one thing. From the day you leave the Court you will be a suspected man. The police of all Europe will be on your trial. You have been highly successful in the past, and why? Because you have been above suspicion, an honourable and distinguished gentleman, belonging to the best clubs, counting as your acquaintances the flower of our society. Now you will be a suspect, a man with a past, a centre of strange stories. I put it to you – how far are you likely to succeed under these conditions?'

He laughed.

'You have a talent for character-drawing, my friend. What makes you think I can work only if I live in the limelight of popularity?'

'The talent you mention,' I said. 'As I read your character – and I think I am right – you are an artist in crime. You are not the common cut-throat who acts out of passion or greed. No, I think you are something subtler than that. You love power, hidden power. You flatter your vanity by despising mankind and making them your tools. You scorn the smattering of inaccuracies which passes for human knowledge, and I will not venture to say you are wrong. Therefore, you use your brains to frustrate it. Unhappily the life of millions is built on that smattering, so you are a foe to society. But there would be no flavour in controlling subterranean things if you were yourself a mole working in the dark. To get the full flavour, the irony of it all, you must live in the light. I can imagine you laughing in your soul as you move about our world, praising it with your lips, patting it with your hands, and kicking its props away with your feet. I can see the charm of it. But it is over now.'

'Over?' he asked.

'Over,' I repeated. 'The end has come, the utter, final, and absolute end.'

He made a sudden, odd, nervous movement, pushing his glasses close back upon his eyes.

'What about yourself?' he said hoarsely. 'Do you think you can play against me without suffering desperate penalties?'

He was holding a cord in his hand with a knob on the end of it. He now touched a button in the knob, and there came the faint sound of a bell.

The door was behind me, and he was looking beyond me towards it. I was entirely at his mercy, but I never budged an inch. I do not know how I managed to keep calm, but I did it, and without much effort. I went on speaking, conscious that the door had opened and that some one was behind me.

'It is really quite useless trying to frighten me. I am safe, because I am dealing with an intelligent man, and not with the ordinary half-witted criminal. You do not want my life in silly revenge. If you call in your man and strangle me between you what earthly good would it do you?'

He was looking beyond me, and the passion – a sudden white-hot passion like an epilepsy – was dying out of his face.

'A mistake, James,' he said. 'You can go.'

The door closed softly at my back.

'Yes. A mistake. I have a considerable admiration for you, Mr Lumley, and should be sorry to be disappointed.'

He laughed quite like an ordinary mortal. 'I am glad this affair is to be conducted on a basis of mutual respect. Now that the melodramatic overture is finished let us get to the business.'

'By all means,' I said. 'I promised to deal with you frankly. Well, let me put my last cards on the table. At half-past nine precisely the duplicate of that statement of mine which you annexed this morning will be handed to Scotland Yard. I may add that the authorities there know me, and are proceeding under my advice. When they read that statement they will act on it. You have therefore about one hour and a half, or say one and three-quarters, to make up your mind. You can still secure your freedom, but it must be elsewhere than in England.'

He had risen to his feet, and was pacing up and down the room.

'Will you oblige me by telling me one thing,' he said. 'If you believe me to be, as you say, a dangerous criminal, how do you reconcile it with your conscience to give me a chance of escape? It is your duty to bring me to justice.'

'I will tell you why,' I said. 'I, too, have a weak joint in my armour. Yours is that you can only succeed under the disguise of high respectability. That disguise, in any case, will be stripped from you. Mine is Pitt-Heron. I do not know how far he has entangled himself with you, but I know something of his weakness, and I don't want his career ruined and his wife's heart broken. He has learned his lesson, and will never mention you and your schemes to a mortal soul. Indeed, if I can help it, he will never know that any one shares his secret. The price of the chance of escape I offer you is that Pitt-Heron's past be buried for ever.'

He did not answer. He had his arms folded, walking up and down the room, and suddenly seemed to have aged enormously. I had the impression that I was dealing with a very old man.

'Mr Leithen,' he said at last, 'you are bold. You have a frankness which almost amounts to genius. You are wasted in your stupid profession, but your speculative powers are not equal to your other endowments, so you will probably remain in it, deterred by an illogical scruple from following your true bent. Your true *métier*, believe me, is what shallow people call crime. Speaking "without prejudice", as the idiot solicitors say, it would appear that we have both weak spots in our cases. Mine, you say, is that I can only work by using the conventions of what we agreed to call the Machine. There may be truth in that. Yours is that you have a friend who lacks your iron-clad discretion. You offer a plan which saves both our weaknesses. By the way, what is it?'

I looked at my watch again. 'You have ample time to catch the night express to Paris.'

'And if not?'

'Then I am afraid there may be trouble with the police between ten and eleven o'clock.'

'Which, for all our sakes, would be a pity. Do you know you interest me uncommonly, for you confirm the accuracy of my judgment. I have always had a notion that some day I should run across, to my sorrow, just such a man as you. A man of very great intellectual power I can deal with, for that kind of brain is usually combined with the sort of high-strung imagination on which I can work. The same with your over-imaginative man. Yes, Pitt-Heron was of that type. Ordinary brains do not trouble me, for I puzzle them. Now, you are a man of good commonplace intelligence. Pray forgive the lukewarmness of the phrase; it is really a high compliment, for I am an austere critic. If you were that and no more you would not have succeeded. But you possess also a quite irrelevant gift of imagination. Not enough to upset your balance, but enough to do what your mere lawyer's talent could never have done. You have achieved a feat which is given to few – you have partially understood me. Believe me, I rate you high. You are the kind of foursquare being bedded in the concrete of our civilisation, on whom I have always felt I might some day come to grief . . . No, no, I am not trying to wheedle you. If I thought I could do that I should be sorry, for my discernment would have been at fault.'

'I warn you,' I said, 'that you are wasting precious time.'

He laughed quite cheerfully. 'I believe you are really anxious about my interests,' he said. 'That is a triumph indeed. Do you know, Mr Leithen, it is a mere whimsy of fate that you are not my disciple. If we had met earlier, and under other circumstances, I should have captured you. It is because you have in you a capacity for discipleship that you have succeeded in your opposition.'

'I abominate you and all your works,' I said, 'but I admire your courage.'

He shook his head gently.

'It is the wrong word. I am not courageous. To be brave means that you have conquered fear, but I have never had any fear to conquer. Believe me, Mr Leithen, I am quite impervious to threats. You come to me tonight and hold a pistol to my head. You offer me two alternatives, both of which mean failure. But how do you know that I regard them as failure? I have had what they call a good run for my money. No man since Napoleon has tasted such power. I may be willing to end it. Age creeps on and power may grow burdensome. I have always sat loose from common ambitions and common affections. For all you know I may regard you as a benefactor.'

All this talk looks futile when it is written down, but it was skilful enough, for it was taking every atom of exhilaration out of my victory. It was not idle brag. Every syllable rang true, as I knew in my bones. I felt myself in the presence of something enormously big, as if a small barbarian was desecrating the colossal Zeus of Pheidias with a coal hammer. But I also felt it inhuman and I hated it, and I clung to that hatred.

'You fear nothing and you believe nothing,' I said. 'Man, you should never have been allowed to live.'

He raised a deprecating hand. 'I am a sceptic about most things,' he said, 'but, believe me, I have my own worship. I venerate the intellect of man. I believe in its undreamed-of possibilities, when it grows free like an oak in the forest and is not dwarfed in a flower-pot. From that allegiance I have never wavered. That is the God I have never forsworn.'

I took out my watch.

'Permit me again to remind you that time presses.'

'True,' he said, smiling. 'The continental express will not wait upon my confession. Your plan is certainly conceivable. There may be other and easier ways. I am not certain. I must think. Perhaps it would be wiser if you left me now, Mr Leithen. If I take your advice there will be various things to do. In any case there will be much to do.'

He led me to the door as if he were an ordinary host speeding an ordinary guest. I remember that on my way he pointed out a set of Aldines and called my attention to their beauty. He shook hands quite cordially and remarked on the fineness of the weather. That was the last I saw of this amazing man.

It was with profound relief that I found myself in Piccadilly in the wholesome company of my kind. I had carried myself boldly enough in the last hour, but I would not have gone through it again for a king's ransom. Do you know what it is to deal with a pure intelligence, a brain stripped of every shred of humanity? It is like being in the company of a snake.

I drove to the club and telephoned to Macgillivray, asking him to take no notice of my statement till he heard from me in the morning. Then I went to the hospital to see Chapman.

That Leader of the People was in a furious temper, and he was scarcely to be appeased by my narrative of the day's doings. Your Labour Member is the greatest of all sticklers for legality, and the outrage he had suffered that morning had grievously weakened his trust in public security. The Antioch Street business had seemed to him eminently right; if you once got mixed up in melodrama you had to expect such things. But for a Member of Parliament to be robbed in broad daylight next door to the House of Commons upset the foundations of his faith. There was little the matter with his body, and the doctor promised that he would be allowed up next day, but his soul was a mass of bruises.

It took me a lot of persuasion to get him to keep quiet. He wanted a public exposure of Lumley, a big trial, a general ferreting out of secret agents, the whole winding up with a speech in Parliament by himself on this latest outrage of Capitalism. Gloomily he listened to my injunction to silence. But he saw the reason of it, and promised to hold his tongue out of loyalty to Tommy. I knew that Pitt-Heron's secret was safe with him.

As I crossed Westminster Bridge on my way home, the night express to the Continent rumbled over the river. I wondered if Lumley was on board, or if he had taken one of the other ways of which he had spoken.

NINE

Return of the Wild Geese

I DO NOT think I was surprised at the news I read in *The Times* next morning.

Mr Andrew Lumley had died suddenly in the night of heart failure, and the newspapers woke up to the fact that we had been entertaining a great man unawares. There was an obituary in 'leader' type of nearly two columns. He had been older than I thought – close on seventy – and *The Times* spoke of him as a man who might have done anything he pleased in public life, but had chosen to give to a small coterie of friends what was due to the country. I read of his wit and learning, his amazing connoisseurship, his social gifts, his personal charm. According to the writer, he was the finest type of cultivated amateur, a Beckford with more than a Beckford's wealth and none of his folly. Large private charities were hinted at, and a hope was expressed that some part at least of his collections might come to the nation.

The halfpenny papers said the same thing in their own way. One declared he reminded it of Atticus, another of Mæcenas, another of Lord Houghton. There must have been a great run on biographical dictionaries in the various offices. Chapman's own particular rag said that, although this kind of philanthropist was a dilettante and a back-number, yet Mr Lumley was a good specimen of the class and had been a true friend to the poor. I thought Chapman would have a fit when he read this. After that he took in the *Morning Post*.

It was no business of mine to explode the myth. Indeed I couldn't even if I had wanted to, for no one would have believed me unless I produced proofs, and these proofs were not to be made public. Besides, I had an honest compunction. He had had, as he expressed it, a good run for his money, and I wanted the run to be properly rounded off.

Three days later I went to the funeral. It was a wonderful occasion. Two eminent statesmen were among the pall-bearers.

Royalty was represented, and there were wreaths from learned societies and scores of notable people. It was a queer business to listen to that stately service, which was never read over stranger dust. I was thinking all the time of the vast subterranean machine which he had controlled, and which now was so much old iron. I could dimly imagine what his death meant to the hosts who had worked blindly at his discretion. He was a Napoleon who left no Marshals behind him. From the Power-House came no wreaths or newspaper tributes, but I knew that it had lost its power.

De mortuis, etc. My task was done, and it only remained to get Pitt-Heron home.

Of the three people in London besides myself who knew the story – Macgillivray, Chapman, and Felix – the two last might be trusted to be silent, and Scotland Yard is not in the habit of publishing its information. Tommy, of course, must some time or other be told; it was his right; but I knew that Tommy would never breathe a word of it. I wanted Charles to believe that his secret died with Lumley, for otherwise I don't think he would have ever come back to England.

The thing took some arranging, for we could not tell him directly about Lumley's death without giving away the fact that we knew of the connection between the two. We had to approach it by a roundabout road. I got Felix to arrange to have the news telegraphed to and inserted by special order in a Russian paper which Charles could not avoid seeing.

The device was successful. Calling at Portman Square a few days later, I learned from Ethel Pitt-Heron's glowing face that her troubles were over. That same evening a cable to me from Tommy announced the return of the wanderers.

It was the year of the Chilean Arbitration, in which I held a junior brief for the British Government, and that and the late sitting of Parliament kept me in London after the end of the term. I had had a bad reaction from the excitements of the summer, and in these days I was feeling pretty well hipped and overdone. On a hot August afternoon I met Tommy again.

The sun was shining through my Temple chambers, much as it had done when he started. So far as I remember, the West Ham brief which had aroused his contempt was still adorning my table. I was very hot and cross and fagged, for I had been engaged in the beastly job of comparing half a dozen maps of a despicable little bit of South American frontier.

Suddenly the door opened, and Tommy, lean and sunburnt, stalked in.

'Still at the old grind,' he cried, after we had shaken hands. 'Fellows like you give me a notion of the meaning of Eternity.'

'The same uneventful, sedentary life,' I replied. 'Nothing happens except that my scale of fees grows. I suppose nothing will happen till the conductor comes to take the tickets. I shall soon grow fat.'

'I notice it already, my lad. You want a bit of waking up or you'll get a liver. A little sensation would do you a pot of good.'

'And you?' I asked. 'I congratulate you on your success. I hear you have retrieved Pitt-Heron for his mourning family.'

Tommy's laughing eyes grew solemn.

'I have had the time of my life,' he said. 'It was like a chapter out of the Arabian Nights with a dash of Fenimore Cooper. I feel as if I had lived years since I left England in May. While you have been sitting among your musty papers we have been riding like mosstroopers and seeing men die. Come and dine tonight and hear about our adventures. I can't tell you the full story, for I don't know it, but there is enough to curl your hair.'

Then I achieved my first and last score at the expense of Tommy Deloraine.

'No,' I said, 'you will dine with me instead, and I will tell you the full story. All the papers on the subject are over there in my safe.'

JOHN MACNAB

To
ROSALIND MAITLAND

Contents

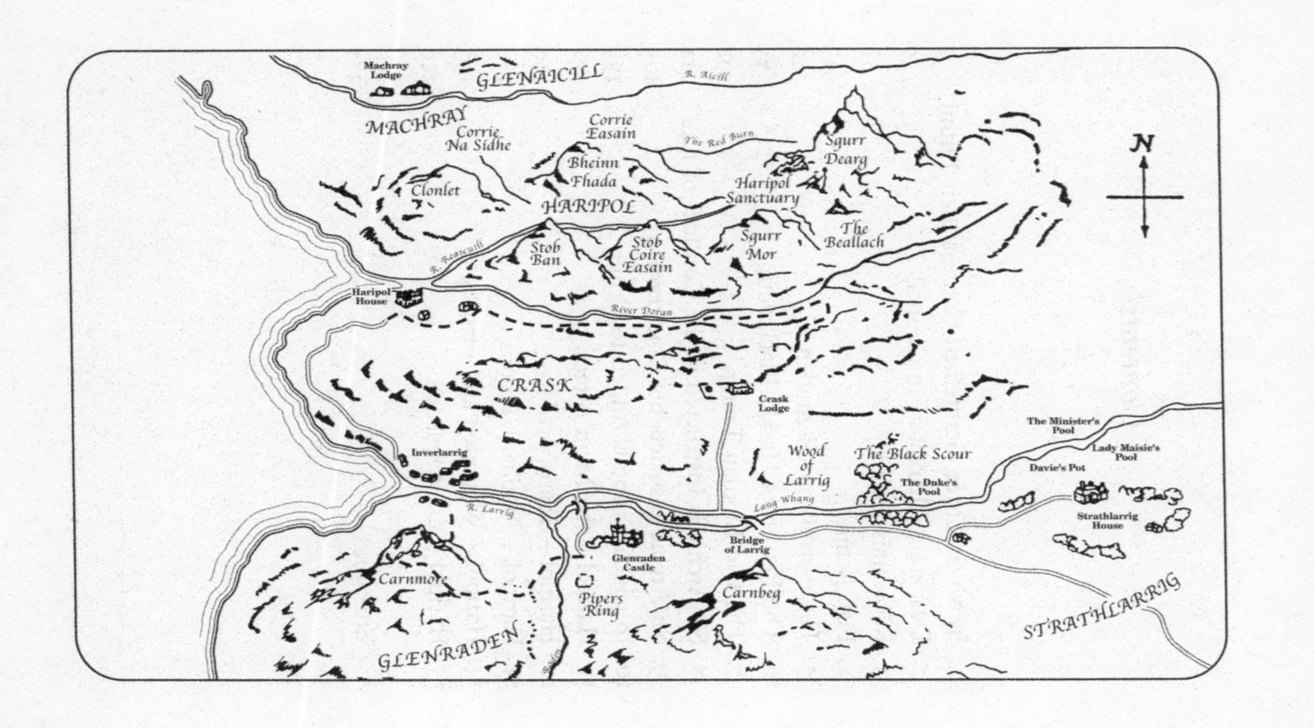

N
Machray Lodge
GLENAICILL
R. Aicill
MACHRAY
Corrie Na Sidhe
Corrie Easain
The Red Burn
Sgurr Dearg
Bheinn Fhada
Clonlet
Haripol Sanctuary
HARIPOL
Stob Ban
Stob Coire Easain
Sgurr Mor
The Beallach
R. Reascuill
Haripol House
River Doran
CRASK
Crask Lodge
Inverlarrig
Wood of Larrig
The Black Scour
The Duke's Pool
The Minister's Pool
Lady Maisie's Pool
Davie's Pot
Strathlarrig House
Lang Whang
R. Larrig
Bridge of Larrig
Glenraden Castle
Carnmore
Pipers Ring
Carnbeg
GLENRADEN
STRATHLARRIG

ONE

In which Three Gentlemen Confess their Ennui

THE GREAT DOCTOR stood on the hearth-rug looking down at his friend who sprawled before him in an easy-chair. It was a hot day in early July, and the windows were closed and the blinds half-down to keep out the glare and the dust. The standing figure had bent shoulders, a massive clean-shaven face, and a keen interrogatory air, and might have passed his sixtieth birthday. He looked like a distinguished lawyer, who would soon leave his practice for the Bench. But it was the man in the chair who was the lawyer, a man who had left forty behind him, but was still on the pleasant side of fifty.

'I tell you for the tenth time that there's nothing the matter with you.'

'And I tell you for the tenth time that I'm miserably ill.'

The doctor shrugged his shoulders. 'Then it's a mind diseased, to which I don't propose to minister. What do you say is wrong?'

'Simply what my housekeeper calls a "no-how" feeling.'

'It's clearly nothing physical. Your heart and lungs are sound. Your digestion's as good as anybody's can be in London in Midsummer. Your nerves – well, I've tried all the stock tests, and they appear to be normal.'

'Oh, my nerves are all right,' said the other wearily.

'Your brain seems good enough, except for this dismal obsession that you are ill. I can find no earthly thing wrong, except that you're stale. I don't say run-down, for that you're not. You're stale in mind. You want a holiday.'

'I don't. I may *need* one, but I don't *want* it. That's precisely the trouble. I used to be a glutton for holidays, and spent my leisure moments during term planning what I was going to do. Now there seems to be nothing in the world I want to do – neither work nor play.'

'Try fishing. You used to be keen.'

'I've killed all the salmon I mean to kill. I never want to look the ugly brutes in the face again.'

'Shooting?'

'Too easy and too dull.'

'A yacht.'

'Stop it, old fellow. Your catalogue of undesired delights only makes it worse. I tell you that there's nothing at this moment which has the slightest charm for me. I'm bored with my work, and I can't think of anything else of any kind for which I would cross the street. I don't even want to go into the country and sleep. It's been coming on for a long time – I daresay it's due somehow to the war – but when I was in office I did not feel it so badly, for I was in a service and not my own master. Now I've nothing to do except to earn an enormous income, which I haven't any need for. Work comes rolling in – I've got retainers for nearly every solvent concern in this land – and all that happens is that I want to strangle my clerk and a few eminent solicitors. I don't care a tinker's curse for success, and what is worse, I'm just as apathetic about the modest pleasures which used to enliven my life.'

'You may be more tired than you think.'

'I'm not tired at all.' The speaker rose from his chair yawning, and walked to the windows to stare into the airless street. He did not look tired, for his movements were vigorous, and, though his face had the slight pallor of his profession, his eye was clear and steady. He turned round suddenly.

'I tell you what I've got. It's what the Middle Ages suffered from – I read a book about it the other day – and its called *taedium vitae*. It's a special kind of ennui. I can diagnose my ailment well enough, and Shakespeare has the words for it. I've come to a pitch where I find "nothing left remarkable beneath the visiting moon."'

'Then why do you come to me, if the trouble is not with your body?'

'Because you're *you*. I should come to you just the same if you were a vet, or a bone-setter, or a Christian Scientist. I want your advice, not as a fashionable consultant, but as an old friend and a wise man. It's a state of affairs that can't go on. What am I to do to get rid of this infernal disillusionment? I can't go through the rest of my life dragging my wing.'

The doctor was smiling.

'If you ask my professional advice,' he said, 'I am bound to tell you that medical science has no suggestion to offer. If you consult me as a friend, I advise you to steal a horse in some part of the world where a horse-thief is usually hanged.'

The other considered. 'Pretty drastic prescription for a man who has been a Law Officer of the Crown.'

'I speak figuratively. You've got to rediscover the comforts of your life by losing them for a little. You have good food and all the rest of it at your command – well, you've got to be in want for a bit to appreciate them. You're secure and respected and rather eminent – well, somehow or other get under the weather. If you could induce the newspapers to accuse you of something shady and have the devil of a job to clear yourself it might do the trick. The fact is, you've grown too competent. You need to be made to struggle for your life again – your life or your reputation. You have to find out the tonic of difficulty, and you can't find it in your profession. Therefore I say "Steal a horse."'

A faint interest appeared in the other's eyes.

'That sounds to me good sense. But, hang it all, it's utterly unpractical. I can't go looking for scrapes. I should feel like play-acting if in cold blood I got myself into difficulties, and I take it that the essence of your prescription is that I must feel desperately in earnest.'

'I'm not prescribing. Heaven forbid that I should advise a friend to look for trouble. I'm merely stating how in the abstract I regard your case.'

The patient rose to go. 'Miserable comforters are ye all,' he groaned. 'Well, it appears you can do nothing for me except to suggest the advisability of crime. I suppose it's no good trying to make you take a fee?'

The doctor shook his head. 'I wasn't altogether chaffing. Honestly, you would be the better of dropping for a month or two into another world – a harder one. A hand on a cattleboat, for instance.'

Sir Edward Leithen sighed deeply as he turned from the doorstep down the long hot street. He did not look behind him, or he would have seen another gentleman approach cautiously round the corner of a side-street, and, when the coast was clear, ring the doctor's bell. He was so completely fatigued with life that he neglected to be cautious at crossings, as was his habit, and was all but slain by a motor-omnibus. Everything seemed weary and over-familiar – the summer smell of town, the din of traffic, the panorama of faces, pretty women shopping, the occasional sight of a friend. Long ago, he reflected with disgust, there had been a time when he had enjoyed it all.

He found sanctuary at last in the shade and coolness of his club. He remembered that he was dining out, and bade the porter telephone that he could not come, giving no reason. He remembered, too, that there was a division in the House that night, an important division advertised by a three-line whip. He declined to go near the place. At any rate, he would have the dim consolation of behaving badly. His clerk was probably at the moment hunting feverishly for him, for he had missed a consultation in the great Argentine bank case which was in the paper next morning. That also could slide. He wanted, nay, he was determined, to make a mess of it.

Then he discovered that he was hungry, and that it was nearly the hour when a man may dine. 'I've only one positive feeling left,' he told himself, 'the satisfaction of my brute needs. Nice position for a gentleman and a Christian!'

There was one other man in the dining-room, sitting at the little table in the window. At first sight he had the look of an undergraduate, a Rugby Blue, perhaps, who had just come down from the University, for he had the broad, slightly stooped shoulders of the football-player. He had a ruddy face, untidy sandy hair, and large reflective grey eyes. It was those eyes which declared his age, for round them were the many fine wrinkles which come only from the passage of time.

'Hullo, John,' said Leithen. 'May I sit at your table?'

The other, whose name was Palliser-Yeates, nodded.

'You may certainly eat in my company, but I've got nothing to say to you, Ned. I'm feeling as dried-up as a dead starfish.'

They ate their meal in silence, and so preoccupied was Sir Edward Leithen with his own affairs that it did not seem to him strange that Mr Palliser-Yeates, who was commonly a person of robust spirits and plentiful conversation, should have the air of a deaf-mute. When they had reached the fish, two other diners took their seats and waved them a greeting. One of them was a youth with lean, high-coloured cheeks, who limped slightly; the other a tallish older man with a long dark face, a small dark moustache, and a neat pointed chin which gave him something of the air of a hidalgo. He looked weary and glum, but his companion seemed to be in the best of tempers, for his laugh rang out in that empty place with a startling boyishness. Mr Palliser-Yeates looked up angrily, with a shiver.

'Noisy brute, Archie Roylance!' he observed. 'I suppose he's above himself since Ascot. His horse won some beastly race, didn't it? It's a good thing to be young and an ass.'

There was that in his tone which roused Leithen from his apathy. He cast a sharp glance at the other's face.

'You're off-colour.'

'No,' said the other brusquely. 'I'm perfectly fit. Only I'm getting old.'

This was food for wonder, inasmuch as Mr Palliser-Yeates had a reputation for a more than youthful energy and, although forty-five years of age, was still accustomed to do startling things on the Chamonix *aiguilles*. He was head of an eminent banking firm and something of an authority on the aberrations of post-war finance.

A gleam of sympathy came into Leithen's eyes.

'How does it take you?' he asked.

'I've lost zest. Everything seems more or less dust and ashes. When you suddenly wake up and find that you've come to regard your respectable colleagues as so many fidgety old women and the job you've given your life to as an infernal squabble about trifles – why, you begin to wonder what's going to happen.'

'I suppose a holiday ought to happen.'

'The last thing I want. That's my complaint. I have no desire to do anything, work or play, and yet I'm not tired – only bored.'

Leithen's sympathy had become interest.

'Have you seen a doctor?'

The other hesitated. 'Yes,' he said at length. 'I saw old Acton Croke this afternoon. He was no earthly use. He advised me to go to Moscow and fix up a trade agreement. He thought that might make me content with my present lot.'

'He told *me* to steal a horse.'

Mr Palliser-Yeates stared in extreme surprise. 'You! Do you feel the same way? Have you been to Croke?'

'Three hours ago. I thought he talked good sense. He said I must get into a rougher life so as to appreciate the blessings of the life that I'm fed up with. Probably he is right, but you can't take that sort of step in cold blood.'

Mr Palliser-Yeates assented. The fact of having found an associate in misfortune seemed to enliven slightly, very slightly, the spirits of both. From the adjoining table came, like an echo from a happier world, the ringing voice and hearty laughter of youth. Leithen jerked his head towards them.

'I would give a good deal for Archie's gusto,' he said. 'My sound right leg, for example. Or, if I couldn't I'd like Charles Lamancha's insatiable ambition. If you want as much as he wants, you don't suffer from tedium.'

Palliser-Yeates looked at the gentleman in question, the tall dark one of the two diners. 'I'm not so sure. Perhaps he has got too much too easily. He has come on uncommon quick, you know, and, if you do that, there's apt to arrive a moment when you flag.'

Lord Lamancha – the title had no connection with Don Quixote and Spain, but was the name of a shieling in a Border glen which had been the home six centuries ago of the ancient house of Merkland – was an object of interest to many of his countrymen. The Marquis of Liddesdale, his father, was a hale old man who might reasonably be expected to live for another ten years and so prevent his son's career being compromised by a premature removal to the House of Lords. He had a safe seat for a London division, was a member of the Cabinet, and had a high reputation for the matter-of-fact oratory which has replaced the pre-war grandiloquence. People trusted him, because, in spite of his hidalgo-ish appearance, he was believed to have that combination of candour and intelligence which England desires in her public men. Also he was popular, for his record in the war and the rumour of a youth spent in adventurous travel touched the imagination of the ordinary citizen. At the moment he was being talked of for a great Imperial post which was soon to become vacant, and there was gossip, in the alternative, of a Ministerial readjustment which would make him the pivot of a controversial Government. It was a remarkable position for a man to have won in his early forties, who had entered public life with every disadvantage of birth.

'I suppose he's happy,' said Leithen. 'But I've always held that there was a chance of Charles kicking over the traces. I doubt if his ambition is an organic part of him and not stuck on with pins. There's a fundamental daftness in all Merklands. I remember him at school.'

The two men finished their meal and retired to the smoking-room, where they drank their coffee abstractedly. Each was thinking about the other, and wondering what light the other's case could shed on his own. The speculation gave each a faint glimmer of comfort.

Presently the voice of Sir Archibald Roylance was heard, and that ebullient young man flung himself down on a sofa beside Leithen, while Lord Lamancha selected a cigar. Sir Archie settled his game leg to his satisfaction, and filled an ancient pipe.

'Heavy weather,' he announced. 'I've been tryin' to cheer up old Charles and it's been like castin' a fly against a thirty-mile gale. I can't make out what's come over him. Here's a deservin' lad like me struggling at the foot of the ladder and not cast down, and there's Charles high up on the top rungs as glum as an owl and declarin' that the whole thing's foolishness. Shockin' spectacle for youth.'

Lamancha, who had found an arm-chair beside Palliser-Yeates, looked at the others and smiled wryly.

'Is that true, Charles?' Leithen asked. 'Are you also feeling hipped? Because John and I have just been confessing to each other that we're more fed up with everything in this gay world than we've ever been before in our useful lives.'

Lamancha nodded. 'I don't know what has come over me. I couldn't face the House to-night, so I telephoned to Archie to come and cheer me. I suppose I'm stale, but it's a new kind of staleness, for I'm perfectly fit in body, and I can't honestly say I feel weary in mind. It's simply that the light has gone out of the landscape. Nothing has any savour.'

The three men had been at school together, they had been contemporaries at the University, and close friends ever since. They had no secrets from each other. Leithen, into whose face and voice had come a remote hint of interest, gave a sketch of his own mood, and the diagnosis of the eminent consultant. Archie Roylance stared blankly from one to the other, as if some new thing had broken in upon his simple philosophy of life.

'You fellows beat me,' he cried. 'Here you are, every one of you a swell of sorts, with everything to make you cheerful, and you're grousin' like a labour battalion! You should be jolly well ashamed of yourselves. It's fairly temptin' Providence. What you want is some hard exercise. Go and sweat ten hours a day on a steep hill, and you'll get rid of these notions.'

'My dear Archie,' said Leithen, 'your prescription is too crude. I used to be fond enough of sport, but I wouldn't stir a foot to catch a sixty-pound salmon or kill a fourteen pointer. I don't want to. I see no fun in it. I'm *blasé.* It's too easy.'

'Well, I'm dashed! You're the worst spoiled chap I ever heard of, and a nice example to democracy.' Archie spoke as if his gods had been blasphemed.

'Democracy, anyhow, is a good example to us. I know now why workmen strike sometimes and can't give any reason. We're on strike – against our privileges.'

Archie was not listening. 'Too easy, you say?' he repeated. 'I call that pretty fair conceit. I've seen you miss birds often enough, old fellow.'

'Nevertheless, it seems to me too easy. Everything has become too easy, both work and play.'

'You can screw up the difficulty, you know. Try shootin' with a twenty bore, or fishin' for salmon with a nine-foot rod and a dry-fly cast.'

'I don't want to kill anything,' said Palliser-Yeates. 'I don't see the fun of it.'

Archie was truly shocked. Then a light of reminiscence came into his eye. 'You remind me of poor old Jim Tarras,' he said thoughtfully.

There were no inquiries about Jim Tarras, so Archie volunteered further news.

'You remember Jim? He had a little place somewhere in Moray, and spent most of his time shootin' in East Africa. Poor chap, he went back there with Smuts in the war and perished of blackwater. Well, when his father died and he came home to settle down, he found it an uncommon dull job. So, to enliven it, he invented a new kind of sport. He knew all there was to be known about *shikar,* and from trampin' about the Highlands he had a pretty accurate knowledge of the countryside. So he used to write to the owner of a deer forest and present his compliments, and beg to inform him that between certain dates he proposed to kill one of his stags. When he had killed it he undertook to deliver it to the owner, for he wasn't a thief.'

'I call that poaching on the grand scale,' observed Palliser-Yeates.

'Wasn't it? Most of the fellows he wrote to accepted his

challenge and told him to come and do his damnedest. Little Avington, I remember, turned on every man and boy about the place for three nights to watch the forest. Jim usually worked at night, you see. One or two curmudgeons talked of the police and prosecutin' him, but public opinion was against them – too dashed unsportin'.'

'Did he always get his stag?' Leithen asked.

'In-var-i-ably, and got it off the ground and delivered it to the owner, for that was the rule of the game. Sometimes he had a precious near squeak, and Avington, who was going off his head at the time, tried to pot him – shot a gillie in the leg too. But Jim always won out. I should think he was the best *shikari* God ever made.'

'Is that true, Archie?' Lamancha's voice had a magisterial tone.

'True – as – true. I know all about it, for Wattie Lithgow, who was Jim's man, is with me now. He and his wife keep house for me at Crask. Jim never took but the one man with him, and that was Wattie, and he made him just about as cunning an old dodger as himself.'

Leithen yawned. 'What sort of a place is Crask?' he inquired.

'Tiny little place. No fishin' except some hill lochs and only rough shootin'. I take it for the birds. Most marvellous nestin' ground in Britain barrin' some of the Outer Islands. I don't know why it should be, but it is. Something to do with the Gulf Stream, maybe. Anyhow, I've got the greenshank breedin' regularly and the red-throated diver, and half a dozen rare duck. It's a marvellous stoppin' place in spring too, for birds goin' north.'

'Are you much there?'

'Generally in April, and always from the middle of August till the middle of October. You see, it's about the only place I know where you can do exactly as you like. The house is stuck away up on a long slope of moor, and you see the road for a mile from the windows, so you've plently of time to take to the hills if anybody comes to worry you. I roost there with old Sime, my butler, and the two Lithgows, and put up a pal now and then who likes the life. It's the jolliest bit of the year for me.'

'Have you any neighbours?'

'Heaps, but they don't trouble me much. Crask's the earthenware pot among the brazen vessels – mighty hard to get to and nothing to see when you get there. So the brazen vessels keep to themselves.'

Lamancha went to a shelf of books above a writing-table and returned with an atlas. 'Who are your brazen vessels?' he asked.

'Well, my brassiest is old Claybody at Haripol – that's four miles off across the hill.'

'Bit of a swine, isn't he?' said Leithen.

'Oh, no. He's rather a good old bird himself. Don't care so much for his family. Then there's Glenraden t'other side of the Larrig' – he indicated a point on the map which Lamancha was studying – 'with a real old Highland grandee living in it – Alastair Raden – commanded the Scots Guards, I believe, in the year One. Family as old as the Flood and very poor, but just manage to hang on. He's the last Raden that will live there, but that doesn't matter so much as he has no son – only a brace of daughters. Then, of course, there's the show place, Strathlarrig – horrible great house as large as a factory, but wonderful fine salmon-fishin'. Some Americans have got it this year – Boston or Philadelphia, I don't remember which – very rich and said to be rather high-brow. There's a son, I believe.'

Lamancha closed the atlas.

'Do you know any of these people, Archie?' he asked.

'Only the Claybodys – very slightly. I stayed with them in Suffolk for a covert shoot two years ago. The Radens have been to call on me, but I was out. The Bandicotts – that's the Americans – are new this year.'

'Is the sport good?'

'The very best. Haripol is about the steepest and most sportin' forest in the Highlands, and Glenraden is nearly as good. There's no forest at Strathlarrig, but, as I've told you, amazin' good salmon fishin'. For a west coast river, I should put the Larrig only second to the Laxford.'

Lamancha consulted the atlas again and appeared to ponder. Then he lifted his head, and his long face, which had a certain heaviness and sullenness in repose, was now lit by a smile which made it handsomer and younger.

'Could you have me at Crask this autumn?' he asked. 'My wife has to go to Aix for a cure and I have no plans after the House rises.'

'I should jolly well think so,' cried Archie. 'There's heaps of room in the old house, and I promise you I'll make you comfortable. Look here, you fellows! Why shouldn't all three of you come? I can get in a couple of extra maids from Inverlarrig.'

'Excellent idea,' said Lamancha. 'But you mustn't bother about the maids. I'll bring my own man, and we'll have a male establishment, except for Mrs Lithgow . . . By the way, I suppose you can count on Mrs Lithgow?'

'How do you mean, "count"?' asked Archie, rather puzzled. Then a difficulty struck him. 'But wouldn't you be bored? I can't show you much in the way of sport, and you're not naturalists like me. It's a quiet life, you know.'

'I shouldn't be bored,' said Lamancha, 'I should take steps to prevent it.'

Leithen and Palliser-Yeates seemed to divine his intention, for they simultaneously exclaimed. – 'It isn't fair to excite Archie, Charles,' the latter said. 'You know that you'll never do it.'

'I intend to have a try. Hang it, John, it's the specific we were talking about – devilish difficult, devilish unpleasant, and calculated to make a man long for a dull life. Of course you two fellows will join me.'

'What on earth are you talkin' about?' said the mystified Archie. 'Join what?'

'We're proposing to quarter ourselves on you, my lad, and take a leaf out of Jim Tarras's book.'

Sir Archie first stared, then he laughed nervously, then he called upon his gods, then he laughed freely and long. 'Do you really mean it? What an almighty rag! . . . But hold on a moment. It will be rather awkward for me to take a hand. You see I've just been adopted as prospective candidate for that part of the country.'

'So much the better. If you're found out – which you won't be – you'll get the poaching vote solid, and a good deal more. Most men at heart are poachers.'

Archie shook a doubting head. 'I don't know about that. They're an awfully respectable lot up there, and all those dashed stalkers and keepers and gillies are a sort of trade-union. The scallywags are a hopeless minority. If I get sent to quod—'

'You won't get sent to quod. At the worst it will be a fine, and you can pay that. What's the extreme penalty for this kind of offence, Ned?'

'I don't know,' Leithen answered. 'I'm not an authority on Scots law. But Archie's perfectly right. We can't go making a public exhibition of ourselves like this. We're too old to be listening to the chimes at midnight.'

'Now, look here.' Lamancha had shaken off his glumness and was as tense and eager as a schoolboy. 'Didn't your doctor advise you to steal a horse? Well, this is a long sight easier than horse-stealing. It's admitted that we three want a tonic. On second thoughts Archie had better stand out – he hasn't our ailment, and a healthy man doesn't need medicine. But we three need it, and this idea is an inspiration. Of course we take risks, but they're sound sporting risks. After all, I've a reputation of a kind, and I put as much into the pool as anyone.'

His hearers regarded him with stony faces, but this in no way checked his ardour.

'It's a perfectly first-class chance. A lonely house where you can see visitors a mile off, and an unsociable dog like Archie for a host. We write the letters and receive the answers at a London address. We arrive at Crask by stealth, and stay there unbeknown to the country-side, for Archie can count on his people and my man in a sepulchre. Also we've got Lithgow, who played the same game with Jim Tarras. We have a job which will want every bit of our nerve and ingenuity with a reasonable spice of danger – for, of course, if we fail we should cut queer figures. The thing is simply ordained by Heaven for our benefit. Of course you'll come.'

'I'll do nothing of the kind,' said Leithen.

'No more will I,' said Palliser-Yeates.

'Then I'll go alone,' said Lamancha cheerfully. 'I'm out for a cure, if you're not. You've a month to make up your mind, and meanwhile a share in the syndicate remains open to you.'

Sir Archie looked as if he wished he had never mentioned the fatal name of Jim Tarras. 'I say, you know, Charles,' he began hesitatingly, but was cut short.

'Are you going back on your invitation?' asked Lamancha sternly. 'Very well, then, I've accepted it, and what's more I'm going to draft a specimen letter that will go to your Highland grandee, and Claybody and the American.'

He rose with a bound and fetched a pencil and a sheet of notepaper from the nearest writing-table. 'Here goes – *Sir, I have the honour to inform you that I propose to kill a stag* – or a salmon as the case may be – *on your ground between midnight on*

—— *and midnight* ——. We can leave the dates open for the present. *The animal, of course, remains your property and will be duly delivered to you. It is a condition that it must be removed wholly outside your bounds. In the event of the undersigned failing to achieve his purpose he will pay as forfeit one hundred pounds, and if successful fifty pounds to any charity you may appoint. I have the honour to be, your obedient humble servant.*'

'What do you say to that?' he asked. 'Formal, a little official, but perfectly civil, and the writer proposes to pay his way like a gentleman. Bound to make a good impression.'

'You've forgotten the signature,' Leithen observed dryly.

'It must be signed with a *nom de guerre*.' He thought for a moment. 'I've got it. At once business-like and mysterious.' At the bottom of the draft he scrawled the name 'John Macnab.'

TWO

Desperate Characters in Council

CRASK – WHICH IS properly Craoisg and is so spelled by the Ordnance Survey – when the traveller approaches it from the Larrig Bridge has the air of a West Highland terrier, *couchant* and *regardant*. You are to picture a long tilt of moorland running east and west, not a smooth lawn of heather, but seamed with gullies and patched with bogs and thickets and crowned at the summit with a low line of rocks above which may be seen peeping the spikes of the distant Haripol hills. About three-quarters of the way up the slope stands the little house, whitewashed, slated, grey stone framing the narrow windows, with that attractive jumble of masonry which belongs to an adapted farm. It is approached by a road which scorns detours and runs straight from the glen highway, and it looks south over broken moorland to the shining links of the Larrig, and beyond them to the tributary vale of the Raden and the dark mountains of its source. Such is the view from the house itself, but from the garden behind there is an ampler vista, since to the left a glimpse may be had of the policies of Strathlarrig and even of a corner of that monstrous mansion, and to the right of the tidal waters of the river and the yellow sands on which in the stillest weather the Atlantic frets. Crask is at once a sanctuary and a watchtower; it commands a wide countryside and yet preserves its secrecy, for, though officially approached by a road like a ruler, there are a dozen sheltered ways of reaching it by the dips and crannies of the hill-side.

So thought a man who about five o'clock on the afternoon of the 24th of August was inconspicuously drawing towards it by way of a peat road which ran from the east through a wood of birches. Sir Edward Leithen's air was not more cheerful than when we met him a month ago, except that there was now a certain vigour in it which came from ill-temper. He had been for a long walk in the rain, and the scent of wet bracken and birches and bog myrtle, the peaty fragrance of the hills salted with the tang of the sea, had failed to comfort, though, not so long ago, it had had the power to intoxicate. Scrambling in the dell of a burn, he had observed both varieties of the filmy fern and what he knew to be a very rare cerast, and, though an ardent botanist, he had observed them unmoved. Soon the rain had passed, the west wind blew aside the cloud-wrack, and the Haripol tops had come out black against a turquoise sky, with Sgurr Dearg, awful and remote, towering above all. Though a keen mountaineer, the spectacle had neither exhilarated nor tantalised him. He was in a bad temper, and he knew that at Crask he should find three other men in the same case, for even the debonair Sir Archie was in the dumps with a toothache.

He told himself that he had come on a fool's errand, and the extra absurdity was that he could not quite see how he had been induced to come. He had consistently refused: so had Palliser-Yeates; Archie as a prospective host had been halting and nervous; there was even a time when Lamancha, the source of all the mischief, had seemed to waver. Nevertheless, some occult force – false shame probably – had shepherded them all here, unwilling, unconvinced, cold-footed, destined to a preposterous adventure for which not one of them had the slightest zest . . . Yet they had taken immense pains to arrange the thing, just as if they were all exulting in the prospect. His own clerk was to attend to the forwarding of their letters including any which might be addressed to 'John Macnab.' The newspapers had contained paragraphs announcing that the Countess of Lamancha had gone to Aix for a month, where she would presently be joined by her husband, who intended to spend a week drinking the waters before proceeding to his grouse-moor of Leriot on the Borders. *The Times*, three days ago, had recorded Sir Edward Leithen and Mr John Palliser-Yeates as among those who had left Euston for Edinburgh, and more than one social paragrapher had mentioned that the ex-Attorney-General would be spending his holiday fishing on the Tay, while the eminent banker was to be the guest of the Chancellor of the Exchequer at an informal vacation conference on the nation's precarious finances. Lamancha had been fetched under cover of night by Archie from a station so remote that no one but a lunatic would think of using it. Palliser-Yeates had tramped for two days across the hills from the south, and Leithen himself, having been instructed to bring a Ford car, had had a miserable drive of a hundred and fifty miles in the rain, during which he had repeatedly lost his way. He had carried out his injunctions as to secrecy by arriving at two in the morning by means of this very peat road. The troops had achieved their silent concentration, and the silly business must now begin. Leithen groaned, and anathematised the memory of Jim Tarras.

As he approached the house he saw, to his amazement, a large closed car making its way down the slope. Putting his glass on it, he watched it reach the glen road and then turn east, passing the gates of Strathlarrig, till he lost it behind a shoulder of hill. Hurrying across the stable-yard, he entered the house by the back-door, disturbing Lithgow the keeper in the midst of a whispered confabulation with Lamancha's man, whose name was Shapp. Passing through the gun-room he found, in the big smoking-room which looked over the valley, Lamancha and Palliser-Yeates with the crouch of conspirators flattening their noses on the windowpanes.

The sight of him diverted the attention of the two from the landscape.

'This is an infernal plant,' Palliser-Yeates exclaimed. 'Archie swore to us that no one ever came here, and the second day a confounded great car arrives. Charles and I had just time to nip in here and lock the door, while Archie parleyed with them. He's been uncommon quick about it. The brutes didn't stay for more than five minutes.'

'Who were they?' Leithen asked.

'Only got a side glance at them. They seemed to be a stout woman and a girl – oh, and a yelping little dog. I expect Archie kicked him, for he was giving tongue from the drawing-room.'

The door opened to admit their host, who bore in one hand a large whisky-and-soda. He dropped wearily into a chair, where he sipped the beverage. An observer might have noted that what could be seen of his wholesome face was much inflamed, and that a bandage round chin and cheeks which ended in a top-knot above his scalp gave him the appearance of Ricquet with the Tuft in the fairytale.

'That's all right,' he said, in the tone of a man who has done a good piece of work. 'I've choked off visitors at Crask for a bit, for the old lady will put it all round the country-side.'

'Put what?' said Leithen, and 'Who is the old lady?' asked

Lamancha, and 'Did you kick the dog?' demanded Palliser-Yeates.

Archie looked drearily at his friends. 'It was Lady Claybody and a daughter – I think the second one – and their horrid little dog. They won't come back in a hurry – nobody will come back – I'm marked down as a pariah. Hang it, I may as well chuck my candidature. I've scuppered my prospects for the sake of you three asses.'

'What has the blessed martyr been and done?' asked Palliser-Yeates.

'I've put a barrage round this place, that's all. I was very civil to the Claybodys, though I felt a pretty fair guy with my head in a sling. I bustled about, talking nonsense and offerin' tea, and then, as luck would have it, I trod on the hound. That's the worst of my game leg. The brute nearly had me over, and it started howlin' – you must have heard it. That dog's a bit weak in the head, for it can't help barkin' just out of pure cussedness – Lady Claybody says it's high-strung because of its fine breedin'. It got something to bark for this time, and the old woman had it in her arms fondlin' it and lookin' very old-fashioned at me. It seems the beast's name is Roguie and she called it her darlin' Wee Roguie, for she's pickin' up a bit of Scots since she came to live in these parts . . . Lucky Mackenzie wasn't at home. He'd have eaten it . . . Well, after that things settled down, and I was just goin' to order tea, when it occurred to the daughter to ask what was wrong with my face. Then I had an inspiration.'

Archie paused and smiled sourly.

'I said I didn't know, but I feared I might be sickenin' for small-pox. I hinted that my face was a horrid sight under the bandage.'

'Good for you, Archie,' said Lamancha. 'What happened then?'

'They bolted – fairly ran for it. They did record time into their car – scarcely stopped to say goodbye. I suppose you realise what I've done, you fellows. The natives here are scared to death of infectious diseases, and if we hadn't our own people we wouldn't have a servant left in the house. The story will be all over the country-side in two days, and my only fear is that it may bring some medical officer of health nosin' round . . . Anyhow, it will choke off visitors.'

'Archie, you're a brick,' was Lamancha's tribute.

'I'm very much afraid I'm a fool, but thank Heaven I'm not the only one. Sime,' he shouted in a voice of thunder, 'what's happened to tea?'

The shout brought the one-armed butler and Shapp with the apparatus of the meal, and an immense heap of letters all addressed to Sir Archibald Roylance.

'Hullo! the mail has arrived,' cried the master of the house. 'Now let's see what's the news of John Macnab?'

He hunted furiously among the correspondence, tearing open envelopes and distributing letters to the others with the rapidity of a conjurer. One little sealed packet he reserved to the last, and drew from it three missives bearing the same superscription.

These he opened, glanced at, and handed to Lamancha. 'Read 'em out, Charles,' he said. 'It's the answers at last.'

Lamancha read slowly the first document, of which this is the text:

GLENRADEN CASTLE,
STRATHLARRIG,
Aug. — 19—.

SIR,

I have received your insolent letter. I do not know what kind of rascal you may be, except that you have the morals of a bandit and the assurance of a halfpenny journalist. But since you seem in your perverted way to be a sportsman, I am not the man to refuse your challenge. My reply is, sir, damn your eyes and have a try. I defy you to kill a stag in my forest between midnight on the 28th of August and midnight of the 30th. I will give instructions to my men to guard my marches, and if you should be roughly handled by them you have only to blame yourself.

Yours faithfully,
ALASTAIR RADEN.

John Macnab, Esq.

'That's a good fellow,' said Archie with conviction. 'Just the sort of letter I'd write myself. He takes things in the proper spirit. But it's a blue look-out for your chances, my lads. What old Raden doesn't know about deer isn't knowledge.'

Lamancha read the second reply:

STRATHLARRIG HOUSE,
STRATHLARRIG,
Aug —, 19—.

MY DEAR SIR,

Your letter was somewhat of a surprise, but as I am not yet familiar with the customs of this country, I forbear to enlarge on this point, and since you have marked it 'Confidential' I am unable to take advice. You state that you intend to kill a salmon in the Strathlarrig water between midnight on September 1 and midnight on September 3, this salmon, if killed, to remain my property. I have consulted such books as might give me guidance, and I am bound to state that in my view the laws of Scotland are hostile to your suggested enterprise. Nevertheless, I do not take my stand on the law, for I presume that your proposition is conceived in a sporting spirit, and that you dare me to stop you. Well, sir, I will see you on that hand. The fishing is not that good at present that I am inclined to quarrel about one salmon. I give you leave to use every method that may occur to you to capture that fish, and I promise to use every method that may occur to me to prevent you. In your letter you undertake to use only 'legitimate means.' I would have pleasure in meeting you in the same spirit, but I reckon that all means are counted legitimate in the capture of poachers.

Cordially,
JUNIUS THEODORE BANDICOTT.

Mr J. Macnab.

'That's the young 'un,' Archie observed. 'The old man was christened "Acheson," and don't take any interest in fishin'. He spends his time in lookin' for Norse remains.'

'He seems a decent sort of fellow,' said Palliser-Yeates, 'but I don't quite like the last sentence. He'll probably try shooting, same as his countrymen once did on the Beauly. Whoever gets this job will have some excitement for his money.'

Lamancha read out the last letter:

227 NORTH MELVILLE STREET,
EDINBURGH,
Aug —, 19—.

SIR,

Re *Haripol Forest*

Our client, the Right Honourable Lord Claybody, has read to us on the telephone your letter of Aug. – and has desired us to reply to it. We are instructed to say that our client is at a loss to understand how to take your communication, whether as a piece of impertinence or as a serious threat. If it is the latter, and you persist in your intention, we are instructed to apply to the Court for a summary interdict to prevent your entering upon his lands. We would also point out that under the Criminal Law of Scotland, any person whatsoever who commits a trespass in the daytime by entering upon any land without leave of the proprietor, in pursuit of, *inter alia*, deer, is liable to a fine of £2, while, if such person have his face blackened, or if five or more persons acting in concert commit the trespass, the penalty is £5 (2 & 3 William IV, c. 68).

We are, sir,
Your obedient servants,
PROSSER, MCKELPIE, AND MACLYMONT.

John Macnab, Esq.

Lamancha laughed. 'Is that good law, Ned?'

Leithen read the letter again. 'I suppose so. Deer being *ferae naturae*, there is no private property in them or common law crime in killing them, and the only remedy is to prevent trespass in pursuit of them or to punish the trespasser.'

'It seems to me that you get off pretty lightly,' said Archie. 'Two quid is not much in the way of a fine, for I don't suppose you want to black your faces or march five deep into Haripol . . . But what a rotten sportsman old Claybody is!'

Palliser-Yeates heaved a sigh of apparent relief. 'I am bound to say the replies are better than I expected. It will be a devil of a business, though, to circumvent that old Highland chief, and that young American sounds formidable. Only, if we're caught out there, we're dealing with sportsmen and can appeal to their higher nature, you know. Claybody is probably the easiest proposition so far as getting a stag is concerned, but if we're nobbled by him we needn't look for mercy. Still, it's only a couple of pounds.'

'You're an ass, John,' said Leithen. 'It's only a couple of pounds for John Macnab. But if these infernal Edinburgh lawyers get on the job, it will be a case of producing the person of John Macnab, and then we're all in the cart. Don't you realise that in this fool's game we simply cannot afford to lose – none of us?'

'That,' said Lamancha, 'is beyond doubt the truth, and it's just there that the fun comes in.'

The reception of the three letters had brightened the atmosphere. Each man had now something to think about, and, till it was time to dress for dinner, each was busy with sheets of the Ordnance maps. The rain had begun again, the curtains were drawn, and round a good fire of peats they read and smoked and dozed. Then they had hot baths, and it was a comparatively cheerful and very hungry party that assembled in the dining-room. Archie proposed champagne, but the offer was unanimously declined. 'We ought to be in training,' Lamancha warned him. 'Keep the Widow for the occasions when we need comforting. They'll come all right.'

Palliser-Yeates was enthusiastic about the food. 'I must say, you do us very well,' he told his host. 'These haddocks are the best things I've ever eaten. How do you manage to get fresh sea-fish here?'

Archie appealed to Sime. 'They come from Inverlarrig, Sir Erchibald,' said the butler. 'There's a wee laddie comes up here sellin' haddies verra near every day.'

'Bless my soul, Sime. I thought no one came up here. You know my orders.'

'This is just a tinker laddie, Sir Erchibald. He sleeps in a cairt down about Larrigmore. He just comes wi' his powny and awa' back, and doesna bide twae minutes. Mistress Lithgow was anxious for haddies, for she said gentlemen got awfu' tired of saumon and trout.'

'All right, Sime. I'll speak to Mrs Lithgow. She'd better tell him we don't want any more. By the way, we ought to see Lithgow after dinner. Tell him to come to the smoking-room.'

When Sime had put the port on the table and withdrawn, Leithen lifted up his voice.

'Look here, before we get too deep into this thing, let's make sure that we know where we are. We're all three turned up here – why, I don't know. But there's still time to go back. We realise now what we're in for. Are you clear in your minds that you want to go on?'

'I am,' said Lamancha doggedly. 'I'm out for a cure. Hang it, I feel a better man already.'

'I suppose your profession makes you take risks,' said Leithen dryly, 'Mine doesn't. What about you, John?'

Palliser-Yeates shifted uneasily in his chair. 'I don't want to go on. I feel no kind of keenness, and my feet are rather cold. And yet – you know – I should feel rather ashamed to turn back.'

Archie uplifted his turbaned head. 'That's how I feel, though I'm not on myself in this piece. We've given hostages, and the credit of John Macnab is at stake. We've dared old Raden and young Bandicott, and we can't decently cry off. Besides, I'm advertised as a smallpox patient, and it would be a pity to make a goat of myself for nothing. Mind you, I stand to lose as much as anybody, if we bungle things.'

Leithen had the air of bowing to the inevitable. 'Very well, that's settled. But I wish to Heaven I saw myself safely out of it. My only inducement to go on is to score off that bounder Claybody. He and his attorney's letter put my hackles up.'

In the smoking-room Lamancha busied himself with preparing three slips of paper and writing on them three names.

'We must hold a council of war,' he said. 'First of all, we have taken measures to keep our presence here secret. My man Shapp is all right. What about your people, Archie?'

'Sime and Carfrae have been warned, and you may count on them. They're the class of lads that ask no questions. So are the Lithgows. We've no neighbours, and they're anyway not the gossiping kind, and I've put them on their Bible oath. I fancy they think the reason is politics. They're a trifle scared of you, Charles, and your reputation, for they're not accustomed to hidin' Cabinet Ministers in the scullery. Lithgow's a fine crusted old Tory.'

'Good. Well, we'd better draw for beats, and get Lithgow in.'

The figure that presently appeared before them was a small man, about fifty years of age, with a great breadth of shoulder and a massive face decorated with a wispish tawny beard. His mouth had the gravity and primness of an elder of the Kirk, but his shrewd blue eyes were not grave. The son of a Tweeddale shepherd who had emigrated years before to a cheviot farm in Sutherland, he was in every line and feature the Lowlander, and his speech had still the broad intonation of the Borders. But all his life had been spent in the Highlands on this and that deer forest, and as a young stalker he had been picked out by Jim Tarras for his superior hill craft. To Archie his chief recommendation was that he was a passionate naturalist, who was as eager to stalk a rare bird with a field-glass as to lead a rifle up to deer. Other traits will appear in the course of this narrative; but it may be noted here that he was a voracious reader and in the long winter nights had amassed a store of varied knowledge, which was patently improving his master's mind. Archie was accustomed to quote him for most of his views on matters other than ornithology and war.

'Do you mind going over to that corner and shuffling these slips? Now, John, you draw first.'

Mr Palliser-Yeates extracted a slip from Lithgow's massive hand.

'Glenraden,' he cried. 'Whew! I'm for it this time.'

Leithen drew next. His slip read Strathlarrig.

'Thank God, I've got old Claybody,' said Lamancha. 'Unless you want him very badly, Ned?'

Leithen shook his head. 'I'm content. It would be a bad start to change the draw.'

'Sit down, Wattie,' said Archie. 'Here's a dram for you. We've summoned you to a consultation. I daresay you've been wonderin' what all this fuss about secrecy has meant. I'm going to tell you. You were with Jim Tarras, and you've often told me about his poachin'. Well, these three gentlemen want to have a try at the same game. They're tired of ordinary sport, and want something more excitin'. It wouldn't do, of course, for them to appear under their real names, so they've invented a *nom de guerre* – that's a bogus name, you know. They call themselves collectively, as you might say, John Macnab. John Macnab writes from London to three proprietors, same as Jim Tarras used to do, and proposes to take a deer or a salmon on their property within certain dates. There's copy of the letter, and here are the replies that arrived tonight. Just you read 'em.'

Lithgow, without moving a muscle of his face, took the documents. He nodded approvingly over the original letter. He smiled broadly at Colonel Raden's epistle, puzzled a little at Mr Bandicott's, and wrinkled his brows over that of the Edinburgh solicitors. Then he stared into the fire, and emitted short grunts which might have equally well been chuckles or groans.

'Well, what do you think of the chances?' asked Archie at length.

'Would the gentlemen be good shots?' asked Lithgow.

'Mr Palliser-Yeates, who has drawn Glenraden, is a very good shot,' Archie replied, 'and he has stalked on nearly every forest in Scotland. Lord Lamancha – Charles, you're pretty good, aren't you?'

'Fair,' was the answer. 'Good on my day.'

'And Sir Edward Leithen is a considerable artist on the river. Now, Wattie, you understand that they want to win – want to get the stags and the salmon – but it's absolute sheer naked necessity that, whether they fail or succeed, they mustn't be caught. John Macnab must remain John Macnab, an unknown blighter from London. You know who Lord Lamancha is, but perhaps you don't know that Sir Edward Leithen is a great lawyer, and Mr Palliser-Yeates is one of the biggest bankers in the country.'

'I ken all about the gentlemen,' said Lithgow gravely. 'I was readin' Mr Yeates's letter in *The Times* about the debt we was owin' America, and I mind fine Sir Edward's speeches in Parliament about the Irish Constitution. I didna altogether agree with him.'

'Good for you, Wattie. You see, then, how desperately important it is that the thing shouldn't get out. Mr Tarras didn't much care if he was caught, but if John Macnab is uncovered there will be a high and holy row. Now you grasp the problem, and you've got to pull up your socks and think it out. I don't want your views to-night, but I should like to have your notion of the chances in a general way. What's the bettin'? Twenty to one against?'

'Mair like a thousand,' said Lithgow grimly. 'It will be verra, verra deeficult. It will want a deal o' thinkin'.' Then he added, 'Mr Tarras was an awfu' grand shot. He would kill a runnin' beast at fower hundred yards – aye, he could make certain of it.'

'Good Lord, I'm not in that class,' Palliser-Yeates exclaimed.

'Aye, and he was more than a grand shot. He could creep up to a sleepin' beast in the dark and pit a knife in its throat. The sauvages in Africa had learned him that. There was plenty o' times when him and me were out that it wasna possible to use the rifle.'

'We can't compete there,' said Lamancha dolefully.

'But I wad not say it was impossible,' Lithgow added more briskly. 'It will want a deal o' thinkin'. It might be done on Haripol – I wadna say but it might be done, but yon auld man at Glenraden will be ill to get the better of. And the Strathlarrig water is an easy water to watch. Ye'll be for only takin' shootable beasts, like Mr Tarras, and ye'll not be wantin' to cleek a fish? It might be not so hard to get a wee staggie, or to sniggle a salmon in one of the deep pots.'

'No, we must play the game by the rules. We're not poachers.'

'Then it will be verra, verra deeficult.'

'You understand,' put in Lamancha, 'that, though we count on your help, you yourself mustn't be suspected. It's as important for you as for us to avoid suspicion, for if they got you it would implicate your master, and that mustn't happen on any account.'

'I ken that. It will be verra, verra deeficult. I said the odds were a thousand to one, but I think ten thousand wad be liker the thing.'

'Well, go and sleep on it, and we'll see you in the morning. An' tell your wife I don't want any boys comin' up to the house with fish. She must send elsewhere and buy 'em. Good-night, Wattie.'

When Lithgow had withdrawn the four men sat silent and meditative in their chairs. One would rise now and then and knock out his pipe, but scarcely a word was spoken. It is to be presumed that the thoughts of each were on the task in hand, but Leithen's must have wandered. 'By the way, Archie,' he said, 'I saw a very pretty girl on the road this afternoon, riding a yellow pony. Who could she be?'

'Lord knows!' said Archie. 'Probably one of the Raden girls. I haven't seen 'em yet.'

When the clock struck eleven Sir Archie arose and ordered his guests to bed.

'I think my toothache is gone,' he said, switching off his turban and revealing a ruffled head and scarlet cheek. Then he muttered: 'A thousand to one! Ten thousand to one! It can't be done, you know. We've got to find some way of shortenin' the odds!'

THREE

Reconnaissance

ROSY-FINGERED DAWN, when, attended by mild airs and a sky of Italian blue, she looked in at Crask next morning, found two members of the household already astir. Mr Palliser-Yeates, coerced by Wattie Lithgow, was starting with bitter self-condemnation to prospect what his guide called 'the yont side o' Glenraden.' A quarter of an hour later Lamancha, armed with a map and a telescope, departed alone for the crest of hill behind which lay the Haripol forest. After that peace fell on the place, and it was not till the hour of ten that Sir Edward Leithen descended for breakfast.

The glory of the morning had against his convictions made him cheerful. The place smelt so good within and without, Mrs Lithgow's scones were so succulent, the bacon so crisp, and Archie, healed of the toothache, was so preposterous and mirthful a figure that Leithen found a faint zest again in the contemplation of the future. When Archie advised him to get busy about the Larrig he did not complain, but accompanied his host to the gun-room, where he studied attentively on a large-scale map the three miles of the stream in the tenancy of Mr Bandicott.

It seemed to him that he had better equip himself for the part by some simple disguise, so, declining Archie's suggestion of a kilt, he returned to his bedroom to refit. Obviously the best line was the tourist, so he donned a stiff white shirt and a stiff dress collar with a tartan bow-tie contributed from Sime's wardrobe. Light brown boots in which he had travelled from London took the place of his nailed shoes, and his thick knickerbocker stockings bulged out above them. Sime's watch-chain, from which depended a football club medal, a vulgar green Homburg hat of Archie's, and a camera slung on his shoulders completed the equipment. His host surveyed him with approval.

'The Blackpool season is beginning,' he observed. 'You're

the born tripper, my lad. Don't forget the picture post cards.' A bicycle was found, and the late Attorney-General zigzagged warily down the steep road to the Larrig bridge.

He entered the highway without seeing a human soul, and according to plan turned down the glen towards Inverlarrig. There at the tiny post-office he bought the regulation picture post cards, and conversed in what he imagined to be the speech of Cockaigne with the aged post-mistress. He was eloquent on the beauties of the weather and the landscape and not reticent as to his personal affairs. He was, he said, a seeker for beauty-spots, and had heard that the best were to be found in the demesne of Strathlarrig. 'It's private grund,' he was told, 'but there's Americans bidin' there and they're kind folk and awfu' free with their siller. If ye ask at the lodge, they'll maybe let ye in to photograph.' The sight of an array of ginger-beer bottles inspired him to further camouflage, so he purchased two which he stuck in his side-pockets.

East of the Bridge of Larrig he came to the chasm in the river above which he knew began the Strathlarrig water. The first part was a canal-like stretch among bogs, which promised ill for fishing, but beyond a spit of rock the Larrig curled in towards the road edge, and ran in noble pools and swift streams under the shadow of great pines. This, Leithen knew from the map, was the Wood of Larrigmore, a remnant of the ancient Caledonian Forest. By the water's edge the covert was dark, but towards the roadside the trees thinned out, and the ground was delicately carpeted with heather and thymy turf. There grazed an aged white pony, and a few yards off, on the shaft of a dilapidated fish-cart, sat a small boy.

Leithen, leaning his bicycle against a tree, prospected the murky pools with the air rather of an angler than a photographer, and in the process found his stiff shirt and collar a vexation. Also the ginger-beer bottles bobbed unpleasantly at his side. So, catching sight of the boy, he beckoned him near. 'Do you like ginger-beer?' he asked, and in reply to a vigorous nod bestowed the pair on him. The child returned like a dog to the shelter of the cart, whence might have been presently heard the sound of gluttonous enjoyment. Leithen, having satisfied himself that no mortal could take a fish in that thicket, continued up-stream till he struck the wall of the Strathlarrig domain and a vast castellated lodge.

The lodge-keeper made no objection when he sought

admittance, and he turned from the gravel drive towards the river, which now flowed through a rough natural park. For a fisherman it was the water of his dreams. The pools were long and shelving, with a strong stream at the head and, below, precisely the right kind of boulders and outjutting banks to shelter fish. There were three of these pools – the 'Duke's,' the 'Black Scour,' and 'Davie's Pot,' were the names Archie had told him – and beyond, almost under the windows of the house, 'Lady Maisie's,' conspicuous for its dwarf birches and the considerable waterfall above it. Here he made believe to take a photograph, though he had no idea how a camera worked, and reflected dismally upon the magnitude of his task. The whole place was as bright and open as the Horse Guards Parade. The house commanded all four pools, which he knew to be the best, and even at midnight, with the owner unsuspecting, poaching would be nearly impossible. What would it be when the owner was warned, and legitimate methods of fishing were part of the contract?

After a glance at the house, which seemed to be deep in noontide slumber, he made his inconspicuous way past the end of a formal garden to a reach where the Larrig flowed wide and shallow over pebbles. Then came a belt of firs, and then a long tract of broken water which was obviously not a place to hold salmon. He realised, from his memory of the map, that he must be near the end of the Strathlarrig beat, for the topmost mile was a series of unfishable linns. But presently he came to a noble pool. It lay in a meadow where the hay had just been cut and was liker a bit of Tweed or Eden than a Highland stream. Its shores were low and on the near side edged with fine gravel, the far bank was a green rise unspoiled by scrub, the current entered it with a proud swirl, washed the high bank, and spread itself out in a beautifully broken tail, so that every yard of it spelled fish. Leithen stared at it with appreciative eyes. The back of a moving monster showed in mid-stream, and automatically he raised his arm in an imaginary cast.

The next second he observed a man walking across the meadow towards him, and remembered his character. Directing his camera hastily at the butt-end of a black-faced sheep on the opposite shore, he appeared to be taking a careful photograph, after which he restored the apparatus to its case and turned to reconnoitre the stranger. This proved to be a middle-aged man in ancient tweed knickerbockers of an outrageous pattern known locally as the 'Strathlarrig tartan.' He was obviously a river-keeper, and was advancing with a resolute and minatory air.

Leithen took off his hat with a flourish.

'Have I the honour, sir, to address the owner of this lovely spot?' he asked in what he hoped was the true accent of a tripper.

The keeper stopped short and regarded him sternly.

'What are ye daein' here?' he demanded.

'Picking up a few pictures, sir. I inquired at your lodge, and was told that I might presume upon your indulgence. Pardon me, if I 'ave presumed too far. If I 'ad known that the proprietor was at 'and I would have sought 'im out and addressed my 'umble request to 'imself.'

'Ye're makin' a mistake. I'm no the laird. The laird's awa' about India. But Mr Bandicott – that's him that's the tenant – has given strict orders that naebody's to gang near the watter. I wonder Mactavish at the lodge hadna mair sense.'

'I fear the blame is mine,' said the agreeable tourist. 'I only asked leave to enter the grounds, but the beauty of the scenery attracted me to the river. Never 'ave I seen a more exquisite spot.' He waved his arm towards the pool.

'It's no that bad. But ye maun awa' out o' this. Ye'd better gang by the back road, for fear they see ye frae the hoose.'

Leithen followed him obediently, after presenting him with a cigarette, which he managed to extract without taking his case from his pocket. It should have been a fag, he reflected, and not one of Archie's special Egyptians. As they walked he conversed volubly.

'What's the name of the river?' he asked. 'Is it the Strathlarrig?'

'No, it's the Larrig, and that bit you like sae weel is the Minister's Pool. There's no a pool like it in Scotland.'

'I believe you. There is not,' was the enthusiastic reply.

'I mean for fish. Ye'll no ken muckle aboot fishin'.'

'I've done a bit of anglin' at 'ome. What do you catch here? Jack and perch?'

'Jack and perch!' cried the keeper scornfully. 'Saumon, man. Saumon up to thirty pounds' wecht.'

'Oh, of course, salmon. That must be a glorious sport. But a friend of mine, who has seen it done, told me it wasn't 'ard. He said that even I could catch a salmon.'

'Mair like a saumon wad catch you. Now, you haud down the back road, and ye'll come out aside the lodge gate. And dinna you come here again. The orders is strict, and if auld Angus was to get a grip o' ye, I wadna say what wad happen. Guid day to ye, and dinna stop till ye're out o' the gates.'

Leithen did as he was bid, circumnavigated the house, struck a farm track, and in time reached the high road. It was a very doleful tourist who trod the wayside heather past the Wood of Larrigmore. Never had he seen a finer stretch of water or one so impregnably defended. No bluff or ingenuity would avail an illicit angler on that open greensward, with every keeper mobilised and on guard. He thought less now of the idiocy of the whole proceeding than of the folly of plunging in the dark upon just that piece of river. There were many streams where Jim Tarras's feat might be achieved, but he had chosen the one stretch in all Scotland where it was starkly impossible.

The recipient of the ginger-beer was still sitting by the shafts of his cart. He seemed to be lunching, for he was carving attentively a hunk of cheese and a loaf-end with a gully-knife. As he looked up from his task Leithen saw a child of perhaps twelve summers, with a singularly alert and impudent eye, a much-freckled face, and a thatch of tow-coloured hair bleached almost white by the sun. His feet were bare, his trousers were those of a grown man, tucked up at the knees and hitched up almost under his armpits, and for a shirt he appeared to have a much-torn jersey. Weather had tanned his whole appearance into the blend of greys and browns which one sees on a hill-side boulder. The boy nodded gravely to Leithen, and continued to munch.

Below the wood lay the half-mile where the Larrig wound sluggishly through a bog before precipitating itself into the chasm above the Bridge of Larrig. Leithen left his bicycle by the roadside and crossed the waste of hags and tussocks to the water's edge. It looked a thankless place for the angler. The clear streams of the Larrig seemed to have taken on the colour of their banks, and to drowse dark and deep and sullen in one gigantic peat-hole. In spite of the rain of yesterday there was little current. The place looked oily, stagnant, and unfishable – a tract through which salmon after mounting the fall would hurry to the bright pools above.

Leithen sat down in a clump of heather and lit his pipe. Something might be done with a worm after a spate, he considered, but any other lure was out of the question. The place had its merits for every purpose but taking salmon. It was a part of the Strathlarrig water outside the park pale, and it was so hopeless that it was not likely to be carefully patrolled. The high road, it was true, ran near, but it was little frequented. If only . . . He suddenly sat up, and gazed intently at a ripple on the dead surface. Surely that was a fish on the move . . . He kept his eyes on the river, until he saw something else which made him rub them, and fall into deep reflection . . .

He was roused by a voice at his shoulder.

'What for will they no let me come up to Crask ony mair?' the voice demanded in a sort of tinker's whine.

Leithen turned and found the boy of the ginger-beer.

'Hullo! You oughtn't to do that, my son. You'll give people heart disease. What was it you asked?'

'What . . . for . . . will . . . they . . . no . . . let . . . me come . . . up to Crask . . . ony mair?'

'I'm sure I don't know. What's Crask?'

'Ye ken it fine. It's the big hoose up the hill. I seen you come doon frae it yoursel' this mornin'.'

Leithen was tempted to deny this allegation and assert his title of tourist, but something in the extreme intelligence of the boy's face suggested that such a course might be dangerous. Instead he said, 'Tell me your name, and what's your business at Crask?'

'My name's Benjamin Bogle, but I get Fish Benjie frae most folks. I've sell't haddies and flukes to Crask these twa months. But this mornin' I was tell't no to come back, and when I speired what way, the auld wife shut the door on me.'

A recollection of Sir Archie's order the night before returned to Leithen's mind, and with it a great sense of insecurity. The argus-eyed child, hot with a grievance, had seen him descend from Crask, and was therefore in a position to give away the whole show. What chance was there for secrecy with this malevolent scout hanging around?

'Where do you live, Benjie?'

'I bide in my cairt. My father's in jyle, and my mither's lyin' badly in Muirtown. I sell fish to a' the gentry.'

'And you want to know why you can't sell them at Crask?'

'Aye, I wad like to ken that. The auld wife used to be a kind body and gie me jeely pieces. What's turned her into a draygon?'

Leithen was accustomed, in the duties of his profession, to quick decisions on tactics, and now he took one which was destined to be momentous.

'Benjie,' he said solemnly, 'there's a lot of things in the world that I don't understand, and it stands to reason that there must be more that you don't. I'm in a position in which I badly want somebody to help me. I like the look of you. You look a trusty fellow and a keen one. Is all your time taken up selling haddies?'

''Deed no. Just twa hours in the mornin', and twa hours at nicht when I gang doun to the cobles at Inverlarrig. I've a heap o' time on my hands.'

'Good. I think I can promise that you may resume your trade at Crask. But first I want you to do a job for me. There's a bicycle lying by the roadside. Bring it up to Crask this evening between six and seven. Have you a watch?'

'No, but I can tell the time braw and fine.'

'Go to the stables and wait for me there. I want to have a talk with you.' Leithen produced half a crown, on which the grubby paw of Fish Benjie instantly closed.

'And look here, Benjie. You haven't seen me here, or anybody like me. Above all, you didn't see me come down from Crask this morning. If anybody asks you questions, you only saw a man on a bicycle on the road to Inverlarrig.'

The boy nodded, and his solemn face flickered for a second with a subtle smile.

'Well, that's a bargain.' Leithen got up from his couch and turned down the river, making for the Bridge of Larrig, where the highway crossed. He looked back once, and saw Fish Benjie wheeling his bicycle into the undergrowth of the wood. He was in two minds as to whether he had done wisely in placing himself in the hands of a small ragamuffin, who for all he knew might be hand-in-glove with the Strathlarrig keepers. But the recollection of Benjie's face reassured him. He did not look like a boy who would be the pet of any constituted authority; he had the air rather of the nomad against whom the orderly world waged war. There had been an impish honesty in his face, and Leithen, who had a weakness for disreputable urchins, felt that he had taken the right course. Besides, the young sleuth-hound had got on his trail, and there had been nothing for it but to make him an ally.

He crossed the bridge, avoided the Crask road, and struck

up hill by a track which followed the ravine of a burn. As he walked his mind went back to a stretch on a Canadian river, a stretch of still unruffled water warmed all day by a July sun. It had been as full as it could hold of salmon, but no artifice of his could stir them. There in the later afternoon had come an aged man from Boston, who fished with a light trout rod and cast a deft line, and placed a curious little dry fly several feet above a fish's snout. Then, by certain strange manoeuvres, he had drawn the fly under water. Leithen had looked on and marvelled, while before sunset that ancient man hooked and landed seven good fish . . . Somehow that bit of shining sunflecked Canadian river reminded him of the unpromising stretch of the Larrig he had just been reconnoitring.

At a turn of the road he came upon his host, tramping homeward in the company of a most unprepossessing hound. I paused for an instant to introduce Mackenzie. He was a mongrel collie of the old Highland stock, known as 'beardies,' and his touzled head, not unlike an extra-shaggy Dandie Dinmont's, was set upon a body of immense length, girth and muscle. His manners were atrocious to all except his master, and local report accused him of every canine vice except worrying sheep. He had been christened 'The Bluidy Mackenzie' after a noted persecutor of the godly, by someone whose knowledge of history was greater than Sir Archie's, for the latter never understood the allusion. The name, however, remained his official one; commonly he was addressed as Mackenzie, but in moments of expansion he was referred to by his master as Old Bloody.

The said master seemed to be in a strange mood. He was dripping wet, having apparently fallen into the river, but his spirits soared, and he kept on smiling in a light-hearted way. He scarcely listened to Leithen, when he told him of his compact with Fish Benjie. 'I daresay it will be all right,' he observed idiotically. 'Is your idea to pass off one of his haddies as a young salmon on the guileless Bandicott?' For an explanation of Sir Archie's conduct the chronicler must retrace his steps.

After Leithen's departure it had seemed good to him to take the air, so, summoning Mackenzie from a dark lair in the yard, he made his way to the river – the beat below the bridge and beyond the high road, which was on Crask ground. There it was a broad brawling water, boulder-strewn and shallow, which an active man could cross dry-shod by natural stepping-stones. Sir Archie sat for a time on the near shore, listening to the sandpipers – birds which were his special favourites – and watching the whinchats on the hill-side and the flashing white breasts of the water-ousels. Mackenzie lay beside him, an uneasy sphinx, tormented by a distant subtle odour of badger.

Presently Sir Archie arose and stepped out on the half-submerged boulder. He was getting very proud of the way he had learned to manage his game leg, and it occurred to him that here was a chance of testing his balance. If he could hop across on the stones to the other side he might regard himself as an able-bodied man. Balancing himself with his stick as a rope-dancer uses his pole, he in due course reached the middle of the current. After that it was more difficult, for the stones were smaller and the stream more rapid, but with an occasional splash and flounder he landed safely, to be saluted with a shower of spray from Mackenzie, who had taken the deep-water route.

'Not so bad that, for a crock,' he told himself, as he lay full length in the sun watching the faint line of the Haripol hills overtopping the ridge of Crask.

Half an hour was spent in idleness till the dawning of hunger warned him to return. The crossing as seen from this side looked more formidable, for the first stones could only be reached by jumping a fairly broad stretch of current. Yet the jump was achieved, and with renewed confidence Sir Archie essayed the more solid boulders. All would have gone well had not he taken his eyes from the stones and observed on the bank beyond a girl's figure. She had been walking by the stream and had stopped to stare at the portent of his performance. Now Sir Archie was aware that his style of jumping was not graceful and he was discomposed by his sudden gallery. Nevertheless, the thing was so easy that he could scarcely have failed had it not been for the faithful Mackenzie. That animal had resolved to follow his master's footsteps, and was jumping steadily behind him. But three boulders from the shore they jumped simultaneously, and there was not standing-room for both. Sir Archie, already nervous, slipped, recovered himself, slipped again, and then, accompanied by Mackenzie, subsided noisily into three feet of water.

He waded ashore to find himself faced by a girl in whose face concern struggled with amusement. He lifted a dripping hand and grinned.

'Silly exhibition, wasn't it? All the fault of Mackenzie! Idiotic brute of a dog, not to remember my game leg!'

'You're horribly wet,' the girl said, 'but it was sporting of you to try that crossing. What about dry clothes?'

'Oh, no trouble about that. I've only to get up to Crask.'

'You're Sir Archibald Roylance, aren't you? I'm Janet Raden. I've been with papa to call on you, but you're never at home.'

Sir Archie, having now got the water out of his eyes and hair, was able to regard his interlocutor. He saw a slight girl with what seemed to him astonishingly bright hair and very blue and candid eyes. She appeared to be anxious about his dry clothes, for she led the way up the bank at a great pace, while he limped behind her. Suddenly she noticed the limp.

'Oh, please forgive me, I forgot about your leg. You had another smash, hadn't you, besides the one in the war – steeplechasing, wasn't it?'

'Yes, but it didn't signify. I'm all right again and get about anywhere, but I'm a bit slower on the wing, you know.'

'You're keen about horses?'

'Love 'em.'

'So do I. Agatha – that's my sister – doesn't care a bit about them. She would like to live all the year at Glenraden, but – I'm ashamed to say it – I would rather have a foggy November in Warwickshire than August in Scotland. I simply dream of hunting.'

The ardent eyes and the young grace of the girl seemed marvellous things to Sir Archie. 'I expect you go uncommon well,' he murmured.

'No, only moderate. I only get scratch mounts. You see I stay with my Aunt Barbara, and she's too old to hunt, and has nothing in her stables but camels. But this year . . .' She broke off as she caught sight of the pools forming round Sir Archie's boots. 'I mustn't keep you here talking. You be off home at once.'

'Don't worry about me. I'm wet for days on end when I'm watchin' birds in the spring. You were sayin' about this year?'

Her answer was a surprising question. 'Do you know anybody called John Macnab?'

Sir Archibald Roylance was a resourceful mountebank and did not hesitate.

'Yes. The distiller, you mean? Dhuniewassel Whisky? I've

seen his advertisements – "They drink Dhuniewassel, In cottage and castle—" That chap?'

'No, no, somebody quite different. Listen, please, if you're not too wet, for I want you to help me. Papa has had the most extraordinary letter from somebody called John Macnab, saying he means to kill a stag in our forest between certain dates, and daring us to prevent him. He is going to hand over the beast to us if he gets it and pay fifty pounds, but if he fails he is to pay a hundred pounds. Did you ever hear of such a thing?'

'Some infernal swindler,' said Archie darkly.

'No. He can't be. You see the fifty pounds arrived this morning.'

'God bless my soul!'

'Yes. In Bank of England notes, posted from London. Papa at first wanted to tell him to go to – well, where Papa tells people he doesn't like to go. But I thought the offer so sporting that I persuaded him to take up the challenge. Indeed, I wrote the reply myself. Mr Macnab said that the money was to go to a charity, so Agatha is having the fifty pounds for her native weaving and dyeing – she's frightfully keen about that. But if we win the other fifty pounds papa says the best charity he can think of is to prevent me breaking my neck on hirelings, and I'm to have it to buy a hunter. So I'm very anxious to find out about Mr John Macnab.'

'Probably some rich Colonial who hasn't learned manners.'

'I don't think so. His manners are very good, to judge by his letter. I think he is a gentleman, but perhaps a little mad. We simply *must* beat him, for I've got to have that fifty pounds. And – and I want you to help me.'

'Oh, well, you know – I mean to say – I'm not much of a fellow . . .'

'You're very clever, and you've done all kinds of things. I feel that if you advised us we should win easily, for I'm sure you had far harder jobs in the war.'

To have a pretty young woman lauding his abilities and appealing with melting eyes for his aid was a new experience in Sir Archie's life. It was so delectable an experience that he almost forgot its awful complications. When he remembered them he flushed and stammered.

'Really, I'd love to, but I wouldn't be any earthly good. I'm an old crock, you see. But you needn't worry – your Glenraden gillies will make short work of this bandit. . . . By Jove, I hope you get your hunter, Miss Raden. You've got to have it somehow. Tell you what, if I've any bright idea I'll let you know.'

'Thank you so much. And may I consult you if I'm in difficulties?'

'Yes, of course. I mean to say, No. Hang it, I don't know, for I don't like interferin' with your father's challenge.'

'That means you will. Now, you mustn't wait another moment. Good-bye. Will you come over to lunch at Glenraden?'

Then she broke off and stared at him. 'I forgot. Haven't you smallpox?'

'What! Smallpox? Oh, I see! Has old Mother Claybody been putting that about?'

'She came to tea yesterday twittering with terror, and warned us all not to go within a mile of Crask.'

Sir Archie laughed somewhat hollowly. 'I had a bad toothache and my head tied up, and I daresay I said something silly, but I never thought she would take it for gospel. You see for yourself that I've nothing the matter with me.'

'You'll have pneumonia the matter with you, unless you hurry home. Good-bye. We'll expect you to lunch the day after to-morrow.' And with a wave of her hand she was gone.

The extraordinary fact was that Sir Archie was not depressed by the new tangle which encumbered him. On the contrary, he was in the best of spirits. He hobbled gaily up the by-road to Crask, listened to Leithen, when he met him, with less than half an ear, and was happy with his own thoughts. I am at a loss to know how to describe the first shattering impact of youth and beauty on a susceptible mind. The old plan was to borrow the language of the world's poetry, the new seems to be to have recourse to the difficult jargon of psychologists and physicians; but neither, I fear, would suit Sir Archie's case. He did not think of nymphs and goddesses or of linnets in spring; still less did he plunge into the depths of a subconscious self which he was not aware of possessing. The unromantic epithet which rose to his lips was 'jolly.' This was for certain the jolliest girl he had ever met – regular young sportswoman and amazingly good-lookin', and he was dashed if she wouldn't get her hunter. For a delirious ten minutes, which carried him to the edge of the Crask lawn, he pictured his resourcefulness placed at her service, her triumphant success, and her bright-eyed gratitude.

Then he suddenly remembered that alliance with Miss Janet Raden was treachery to his three guests. The aid she had asked for could only be given at the expense of John Macnab. He was in the miserable position of having a leg in both camps, of having unhappily received the confidences of both sides, and whatever he did he must make a mess of it. He could not desert his friends, so he must fail the lady; wherefore there could be no luncheon for him, the day after to-morrow, since another five minutes' talk with her would entangle him beyond hope. There was nothing for it but to have a return of smallpox. He groaned aloud.

'A twinge of that beastly toothache,' he explained in reply to his companion's inquiry.

When the party met in the smoking-room that night after dinner two very weary men occupied the deepest arm-chairs. Lamancha was struggling with sleep; Palliser-Yeates was limp with fatigue, far too weary to be sleepy. 'I've had the devil of a day,' said the latter. 'Wattie took me at a racing gallop about thirty miles over bogs and crags. Lord! I'm stiff and footsore. I believe I crawled more than ten miles, and I've no skin left on my knees. But we spied the deuce of a lot of ground, and I see my way to the rudiments of a plan. You start off, Charles, while I collect my thoughts.'

But Lamancha was supine.

'I'm too drunk with sleep to talk,' he said. 'I prospected all the south side of Haripol – all this side of the Reascuill, you know. I got a good spy from Sgurr Mor, and I tried to get up Sgurr Dearg, but stuck on the rocks. That's a fearsome mountain, if you like. Didn't see a blessed soul all day – no rifles out – but I heard a shot from the Machray ground. I got my glasses on to several fine beasts. It struck me that the best chance would be in the corrie between Sgurr Mor and Sgurr Dearg – there's a nice low pass at the head to get a stag through and the place is rather tucked away from the rest of the forest. That's as far as I've got at present. I want to sleep.'

Palliser-Yeates was in a very different mood. With an ordnance map spread out on his knees he expounded the result of his researches, waving his pipe excitedly.

'It's a stiff problem, but there's just the ghost of a hope. Wattie admitted that on the way home. Look here, you fellows

– Glenraden is divided, like Gaul, into three parts. There's the Home beat – all the low ground of the Raden glen and the little hills behind the house. Then there's the Carnbeg beat to the east, which is the best I fancy – very easy going, not very high and with peat roads and tracks where you could shift a beast. Last there's Carnmore, miles from anywhere, with all the highest tops and as steep as Torridon. It would be the devil of a business, if I got a stag there, to move it. Wattie and I went round the whole marches, mostly on our bellies. No, we weren't seen – Wattie took care of that. What a noble *shikari* the old chap is!'

'Well, what's your conclusion?' Leithen asked.

Palliser-Yeates shook his head. 'That's just where I'm stumped. Try to put yourself in old Raden's place. He has only one stalker and two gillies for the whole forest, for he's very short-handed, and as a matter of fact he stalks his beasts himself. He'll consider where John Macnab is likeliest to have his try, and he'll naturally decide on the Carnmore beat, for that's by far the most secluded. You may take it from me that he has only enough men to watch one beat properly. But he'll reflect that John Macnab has got to get his stag away, and he'll wonder how he'll manage it on Carnmore, for there's only one bad track up from Inverlarrig. Therefore he'll conclude that John Macnab may be more likely to try Carnbeg, though it's a bit more public. You see, his decision isn't any easier than mine. On the whole, I'm inclined to think he'll plump for Carnmore, for he must think John Macnab a fairly desperate fellow who will aim first at killing his stag in peace, and will trust to Providence for the rest. So at the moment I favour Carnbeg.'

Leithen wrinkled his brow. 'There are three of us,' he said. 'That gives us a chance of a little finesse. What about letting Charles or me make a demonstration against Carnmore, while you wait at Carnbeg?'

'Good idea! I thought of that too.'

'You'd better assume Colonel Raden to be in very full possession of his wits,' Leithen continued. 'The simple bluff won't do – he'll see through it. He'll think that John Macnab is the same wary kind of old bird as himself. I found out in the war that it didn't do to underrate your opponent's brains. He's pretty certain to expect a feint and not to be taken in. I'm for something a little subtler.'

'Meaning?'

'Meaning that you feint in one place, so that your opponent believes it to be a feint and pays no attention – and then you sail in and get to work in that very place.'

Palliser-Yeates whistled. 'That wants thinking over . . . How about yourself?'

'I've studied the river, and you never in your life saw such a hopeless proposition. All the good pools are as open as the Serpentine. Wattie stated the odds correctly.'

'Nothing doing there?'

'Nothing doing, unless I take steps to shorten the odds. So I've taken in a partner.'

The others stared, and even Lamancha woke up.

'Yes. I interviewed him in the stable before dinner. It's the little ragamuffin who sells fish – Fish Benjie is the name he goes by. Archie, I hope you don't mind, but I told him to resume his morning visits. They're my best chance for consultations.'

'You're taking a pretty big risk, Ned,' said his host. 'D'you mean to say you've let that boy into the whole secret?'

'I've told him everything. It was the only way, for he had begun to suspect. I admit it's a gamble, but I believe I can trust the child. I think I know a sportsman when I see him.'

Archie still shook his head. 'There's something else I may as well tell you. I met one of the Raden girls to-day – the younger – she was on the bank when I fell into the Larrig. She asked me point-blank if I knew anybody called John Macnab?'

Lamancha was wide awake. 'What did you say?' he asked sharply.

'Oh, lied of course. Said I supposed she meant the distiller. Then she told me the whole story – said she had written the letter her father signed. She's mad keen to win the extra fifty quid, for it means a hunter for her this winter down in Warwickshire. Yes, and she asked me to help. I talked a lot of rot about my game leg and that sort of thing, but I sort of promised to go and lunch at Glenraden the day after tomorrow.'

'That's impossible,' said Lamancha.

'I know it is, but there's only one way out of it. I've got to have smallpox again.'

'You've got to go to bed and stay there for a month,' said Palliser-Yeates severely. 'Now, look here, Archie. We simply can't have you getting mixed up with the enemy, especially the enemy women. You're much too susceptible and far too great an ass.'

'Of course not,' said Archie, with a touch of protest in his voice. 'I see that well enough, but it's a black look-out for me. I wish to Heaven you fellows had chosen to take your cure somewhere else. I'm simply wreckin' all my political career. I had a letter from my agent tonight, and I should be touring the constituency instead of playin' the goat here. All I've got to say is that you've a dashed lot more than old Raden against you. You've got that girl, crazy about her hunter, and anyone can see that she's as clever as a monkey.'

But the laird of Crask was not thinking of Miss Janet Raden's wits as he went meditatively to bed. He was wondering why her eyes were so blue, and as he ascended the stairs he thought he had discovered the reason. Her hair was spun-gold, but she had dark eye-lashes.

FOUR

Fish Benjie

ON THE ROADS of the north of Scotland, any time after the last snow-wreaths have melted behind the dykes, you will meet a peculiar kind of tinker. They are not the copper-nosed scarecrows of the lowlands, sullen and cringing, attended by sad infants in ramshackle perambulators. Nor are they in any sense gipsies, for they have not the Romany speech or colouring. They travel the roads with an establishment, usually a covered cart and one or more lean horses, and you may find their encampments any day by any burnside. Of a rainy night you can see their queer little tents, shaped like a segment of sausage, with a fire hissing at the door, and the horses cropping the roadside grass; of a fine morning the women will be washing their duds on the loch shore and their young fighting like ferrets among the shingle. You will meet with them in the back streets of the little towns, and at the back doors of wayside inns, but mostly in sheltered hollows of the moor or green nooks among the birches, for they are artists in choosing camping-grounds. They are children of Esau who combine a dozen crafts – tinkering, fish-hawking, besom-making, and the like – with their natural trades of horse-coping and poaching. At once brazen and obsequious, they beg rather as an art than a necessity; they will whine to a keeper with pockets full of pheasants' eggs, and seek permission to camp from a laird with a melting tale of hardships, while one of his salmon lies hidden in the bracken on their cart floor. The men are an upstanding race, keen-eyed, resourceful, with humour in their cunning; the women, till life bears too hardly on them, are handsome and soft-spoken; and the children are burned and weathered like imps of the desert. Their speech is neither lowland nor highland, but a sing-song Scots of their own, and if they show the Celt in their secret ways there is a hint of Norse blood in the tawny hair and blue eyes so common among them.

Ebenezer Bogle was born into this life, and for fifty-five years travelled the roads from the Reay country to the Mearns and from John o'Groats to the sea-lochs of Appin. Sickness overtook him one October when camped in the Black Isle, and, feeling the hand of death on him, he sent for two people. One was the nearest Free Kirk minister – for Ebenezer was theologically of the old school; the other was a banker from Muirtown. What he said to the minister I do not know; but what the banker said to him may be gathered from the fact that he informed his wife before he died that in the Muirtown bank there lay to his credit a sum of nearly three thousand pounds. Ebenezer had been a sober and careful man, and a genius at horse-coping. He had bought the little rough shelties of the North and the Isles, and sold them at lowland fairs, he had dabbled in black cattle, he had done big trade in sheep-skins when a snowstorm decimated the Sutherland flocks, and he had engaged, perhaps, in less reputable ventures, which might be forbidden by the law of the land, but were not contrary, so he believed, to the Bible. Year by year his bank balance had mounted, for he spent little, and now he had a fortune to bequeath. He made no will; all went to his wife, with the understanding that it would be kept intact for his son; and in this confidence Ebenezer closed his eyes.

The wife did not change her habit of life. The son Benjamin accompanied her as before in the long rounds between May and October, and in the winter abode in the fishing quarter of Muirtown, and intermittently attended school. Presently his mother took a second husband, a Catholic Macdonald from the West, for the road is a lonely occupation for a solitary woman. Her new man was a cheerful being – very little like the provident Ebenezer – much addicted to the bottle and a lover of all things but legitimate trade. But he respected the dead man's wishes and made no attempt to touch the hoard in the Muirtown bank; he was kind, too, to the boy, and taught him many things that are not provided for in the educational system of Scotland. From him Benjie learned how to take a nesting grouse, how to snare a dozen things, from hares to roebuck, how to sniggle salmon in the clear pools, and how to poach a hind when the deer came down in hard weather to the meadows. He learned how to tell the hour by the sun, and to find his way by the stars, and what weather was foretold by the starlings packing at nightfall, or the crows sitting with their beaks to the wind, or a badger coming home after daylight.

The boy knew how to make cunning whistles from ash and rowan with which to imitate a snipe's bleat or the call of an otter, and he knew how at all times and in all weathers to fend for himself and find food and shelter. A tough little nomad he became under this tutelage, knowing no boys' games, with scarcely an acquaintance of his age, but able to deal on equal terms with every fisherman, gillie, and tinker north of the Highland line.

It chanced that in the spring of this year Mrs Bogle had fallen ill for the first time in her life. It was influenza, and, being neglected, was followed by pneumonia, so that when May came she was in no condition to take the road. By ill luck her husband had been involved in a drunken row, when he had assaulted two of his companions with such violence and success that he was sent for six months to prison. In these circumstances there was nothing for it but that Benjie should set out alone with the cart, and it is a proof of the stoutheartedness of the family tradition that his mother never questioned the propriety of this arrangement. He departed with her blessing, and weekly despatched to her a much-blotted scrawl describing his doings. There was something of his father's hard fibre in the child, for he was a keen bargainer and as wary as a fox against cajolery. He met friends of his family who let him camp beside them, and with their young he did battle, when they dared to threaten his dignity. Benjie fought in no orthodox way, but like a weasel, using every weapon of tooth and claw, but in his sobbing furies he was unconquerable, and was soon left in peace. Presently he found that he preferred to camp alone, so with his old cart and horse he made his way up and down the long glens of the West to the Larrig. There, he remembered, the fish trade had been profitable in past years, so he sat himself down by the roadside, to act as middleman between the fishing-cobles of Inverlarrig and the kitchens of the shooting lodges. It would be untrue to say that this was his only means of livelihood, and I fear that the contents of Benjie's pot, as it bubbled of an evening in the Wood of Larrigmore, would not have borne inspection by any keeper who chanced to pass. The weekly scrawls went regularly to his now convalescent mother, and once a parcel arrived for him at the Inverlarrig post-office containing a gigantic new shirt, which he used as a blanket. For the rest, he lived as Robinson Crusoe lived, on the country-side around him, asking no news of the outer world.

On the morning of the 27th of August he might have been seen, a little after seven o'clock, driving his cart up the fine beech avenue which led to Glenraden Castle. It was part of his morning round, but hitherto he had left his cart at the lodge-gate, and carried his fish on foot to the house; wherefore he had some slight argument with the lodge-keeper before he was permitted to enter. He drove circumspectly to the back regions, left his fish at the kitchen door, and then proceeded to the cottage of the stalker, one Macpherson, which stood by itself in a clump of firs. There he waited for some time till Mrs Macpherson came to feed her hens. A string of haddocks changed hands, and Benjie was bidden indoors, where he was given a cup of tea, while old Macpherson smoked his early pipe and asked questions. Half an hour later Benjie left, with every sign of amity, and drove very slowly down the woodland road towards the haugh where the Raden, sweeping from the narrows of the glen, spreads into broad pools and shining shallows. There he left the cart and squatted inconspicuously in the heather in a place which commanded a prospect of the home woods. From his observations he was aware that one of the young ladies regularly took her morning walk in this quarter.

Meantime in the pleasant upstairs dining-room of the Castle breakfast had begun. Colonel Alastair Raden, having read prayers to a row of servants from a chair in the window – there was a family tradition that he once broke off in a petiton to call excitedly his Maker's attention to a capercailzie on the lawn – and having finished his porridge, which he ate standing, with bulletins interjected about the weather, was doing good work on bacon and eggs. Breakfast, he used to declare, should consist of no kickshaws like kidneys and omelettes; only bacon and eggs, and plenty of 'em. The master of the house was a lean old gentleman dressed in an ancient loud-patterned tweed jacket and a very faded kilt. Still erect as a post, he had a barrack-square voice, a high-boned, aquiline face, and a kindly but irritable blue eye. His daughters were devoting what time was left to them from attending to the breakfasts of three terriers to an animated discussion of a letter which lay before them. The morning meal at Glenraden was rarely interrupted by correspondence, for the post did not arrive till the evening, but this missive had been delivered by hand.

'He can't come,' the younger cried. 'He says he's seedy again. It may really be smallpox this time.'

'Who can't come, and who has smallpox?' her father demanded.

'Sir Archibald Roylance. I told you I met him and asked him to lunch here today. We really ought to get to know our nearest neighbour, and he seems a very pleasant young man.'

'I think he is hiding a dark secret,' said the elder Miss Raden. 'Nobody who calls there ever finds him in – except Lady Claybody, and then he told her he had smallpox. Old Mr Bandicott said he went up the long hill to Crask yesterday, and found nobody at home, though he was perfectly certain he saw one figure slinking into the wood and another moving away from a window. I wonder if Sir Archibald is really all right. We don't know anything about him, do we?'

'Of course he's all right – bound to be – dashed gallant, sporting fellow. Sorry he's not coming to luncheon – I want to meet him. He's probably afraid of Nettie, and I don't blame him, for she's a brazen hussy, and he does well to be shy of old Bandicott. I'm scared to death by the old fellow myself.'

'You know you've promised to let him dig in the Piper's Ring, papa.'

'I know I have, and I would have promised to let him dig up my lawn to keep him quiet. Never met a man with such a flow of incomprehensible talk. He had the audacity to tell me that I was no more Celtic than he was, but sprung from some blackguard Norse raiders a thousand years back. Judging by the sketch he gave me of their habits, I'd sooner the Radens were descended from Polish Jews.'

'I thought him a darling,' said his elder daughter, 'and with such a beautiful face.'

'He may be a darling for all I know, but his head is stuffed with maggots. If you admired him so much, why didn't you take him off my hands? I liked the look of the young fellow and wanted to have a word with him. More by token' – the Colonel was hunting about for the marmalade – 'what were you two plotting with him in the corner after dinner?'

'We were talking about John Macnab.'

The Colonel's face became wrathful.

'Then I call it dashed unfilial conduct of you not to have brought me in. There was I, deafened with the old man's chatter – all about a fellow called Harald Blacktooth or Bottlenose or some such name, that he swears is buried in my grounds and means to dig up – when I might have been having a really fruitful conversation. What was young Bandicott's notion of John Macnab?'

'Mr Junius thinks he is a lunatic,' said the elder Miss Raden. She was in every way her sister's opposite, dark of hair and eye where Janet was fair, tall where Janet was little, slow and quiet of voice where Janet was quick and gusty.

'I entirely differ from him. I think John Macnab is perfectly sane, and probably a good fellow, though a dashed insolent one. What's Bandicott doing about his river?'

'Patrolling it day and night between the 1st and 3rd of September. He says he's taking no chances, though he'd bet Wall Street to a nickel that the poor poop hasn't the frozenest outside.'

'Nettie, he said nothing of the kind!' Miss Agatha was indignant. 'He talks beautiful English, with no trace of an accent – all Bostonians do, he told me.'

'Anyhow, he asked what steps we were taking and advised us to get busy. We come before him, you know . . . Heavens, papa, it begins tomorrow night! Oh, and I did so want to consult Sir Archibald. I'm sure he could help.'

Colonel Raden, having made a satisfactory breakfast, was lighting a pipe.

'You need not worry, my dear. I'm an old campaigner and have planned out the thing thoroughly. I've been in frequent consultation with Macpherson, and yesterday we had Alan and James Fraser in, and they entirely agreed.'

He produced from his pocket a sheet of foolscap on which had been roughly drawn a map of the estate.

'Now, listen to me. We must assume this fellow Macnab to be in possession of his senses, and to have more or less reconnoitred the ground – though I don't know how the devil he can have managed it, for the gillies have kept their eyes open, and nobody's been seen near the place. Well, here are the three beats. Unless young Bandicott is right and the man's a lunatic, he won't try the Home beat, for the simple reason that a shot there would be heard by twenty people and he could not move a beast twenty yards without being caught. There remains Carnmore and Carnbeg. Macpherson was clear that he would try Carnmore, as being farthest away from the house. But I, with my old campaigning experience' – here Colonel

Raden looked remarkably cunning – 'pointed out at once that such reasoning was rudimentary. I said "He'll bluff us, and just because he thinks that *we* think he'll try Carnmore, he'll try Carnbeg. Therefore, since we can only afford to watch one beat thoroughly, we'll watch Carnbeg." What do you think of that, my dears?'

'I think you're very clever, papa,' said Agatha. 'I'm sure you're right.'

'And you, Nettie?'

Janet was knitting her brows and looking thoughtful.

'I'm . . . not . . . so . . . sure. You see we must assume that John Macnab is very ingenious. He probably made his fortune in the colonies by every kind of dodge. He's sure to be very clever.'

'Well but, my dear,' said her father, 'it's just that cleverness that I propose to match.'

'But do you think you have quite matched it? You have tried to imagine what John Macnab would be thinking, and he will have done just the same by you. Why shouldn't he have guessed the conclusion you have reached and be deciding to go one better?'

'How do you mean, Nettie?' asked her puzzled parent. He was inclined to be annoyed, but experience had taught him that his younger daughter's wits were not to be lightly disregarded.

Nettie took the estate map from his hand and found a stump of pencil in the pocket of her jumper.

'Please look at this, papa. Here is A and B. B offers a better chance, so Macpherson says John Macnab will take B. You say, acutely, that John Macnab is not a fool, and will try to bluff us by taking A. I say that John Macnab will have anticipated your acumen.'

'Yes, yes,' said her father impatiently. 'And then?'

'And will take B after all.'

The Colonel stood rapt in unpleasant meditation for the space of five seconds.

'God bless my soul!' he cried. 'I see what you mean. Confound it, of course he'll go for Carnmore. Lord, this is a puzzle. I must see Macpherson at once. Are you sure you're right, Nettie?'

'I'm not in the least sure. We've only a choice of uncertainties, and must gamble. But, as far as I see, if we must plump for one we should plump for Carnmore.'

Colonel Raden departed from his study, after summoning Macpherson to that shrine of the higher thought, and Janet Raden, after one or two brief domestic interviews, collected her two terriers and set out for her morning walk. The morning was as fresh and bright as April, the rain in the night had set every burn singing, and the thickets and lawns were still damp where the sun had not penetrated. Her morning walk was wont to be a scamper, a thing of hops, skips, and jumps, rather than a sedate progress; but on this occasion, though two dogs and the whole earth invited to hilarity, she walked slowly and thoughtfully. The mossy broken tops of Carnbeg showed above a wood of young firs, and to the right rose the high blue peaks of the Carnmore ground. On which of these on the morrow would John Macnab begin his depredations? He had two days for his exploit; probably he would make his effort on the second day, and devote the first to confusing the minds of the defence. That meant that the problem would have to be thought out anew each day, for the alert intelligence of John Macnab – she now pictured him as a sort of Sherlock Holmes in knickerbockers – would not stand still. The prospect exhilarated, but it also alarmed her; the desire to win a new hunter was now a fixed resolution; but she wished she had a colleague. Agatha was no use, and her father, while admirable in tactics, was weak in strategy; she longed more than ever for the help of that frail vessel, Sir Archie.

Her road led her by a brawling torrent through the famous Glenraden beechwood to the spongy meadows of the haugh, beyond which could be seen the shining tides of the Raden sweeping to the high-backed bridge across which ran the road to Carnmore. The haugh was all bog-myrtle and heather and bracken, sprinkled with great boulders which the river during the ages had brought down from the hills. Half a mile up it stood the odd tumulus called the Piper's Ring, crowned with an ancient gnarled fir, where reposed, according to the elder Bandicott, the dust of that dark progenitor, Harald Blacktooth. If Mr Bandicott proposed to excavate there he had his work cut out; the place was encumbered with giant stones since a thousand floods had washed its sides since it first received the dead Viking. Great birch woods from both sides of the valley descended to the stream, thereby making the excellence of the Home beat, for the woodland stag is a heavier beast than his brother of the high tops.

Close to the road, in a small hollow where one of the rivulets from the woods cut its way though the haugh, she came on an ancient cart resting on its shafts, an ancient horse grazing on a patch of turf among the peat, and a small boy diligently whittling his way through a pile of heather roots. The urchin sprang to his feet and saluted like a soldier.

'Please, lady,' he explained in a high falsetto whine, 'I've gotten permission from Mr Macpherson to make heather besoms on this muir. He's aye been awfu' kind to me, lady.'

'You're the boy who sells fish? I've seen you on the road.'

'Aye, lady, I'm Fish Benjie. I sell my fish in the mornin's and evenin's, and I've a' the day for other jobs. I've aye wanted to come here, for it's the grandest heather i' the countryside; and Mr Macpherson, he kens I'll do nae harm, and I've promised no to kindle a fire.'

The child with the beggar's voice looked at her with such sage and solemn eyes that Janet, who had a hopeless weakness for small boys, sat down on a sun-warmed hillock and stared at him, while he turned resolutely to business.

'If you're hungry, Benjie,' she said, 'and they won't let you make a fire, you can come up to the Castle and get tea from Mrs Fraser. Tell her I sent you.'

'Thank you, lady, but if *you* please, I was gaun to my tea at Mrs Macpherson's. She's fell fond o'my haddies, and she tell't me to tak a look in when I stoppit work. I'm ettlin' to be here for a guid while.'

'Will you come every day?'

'Aye, every day about eight o'clock, and bide till maybe five in the afternoon when I go down to the cobles at Inverlarrig.'

'Now, look here, Benjie. When you're sitting quietly working here I want you to keep your eyes open, and if you see any strange man, tell Mr Macpherson. By strange man I mean somebody who doesn't belong to the place. We're rather troubled by poachers just now.'

Benjie raised a ruminant eye from his besom.

'Aye, lady. I seen a queer man already this mornin'. He cam up the road and syne started off over the bog. He was sweatin' sore, and there was twa men from Strathlarrig wi' him carryin' picks and shovels . . . Losh, there he is comin' back.'

Following Benjie's pointing finger Janet saw, approaching her from the direction of the Piper's Ring, a solitary figure which laboured heavily among the peat-bogs. Presently it was revealed as an elderly man wearing a broad grey wide-awake and a suit of flannel knickerbockers. His enormous horn spectacles clearly did not help his eyesight, for he had almost fallen over the shafts of the fish-cart before he perceived Janet Raden. He removed his hat, bowed with an antique courtesy, and asked permission to recover his breath.

'I was on my way to see your father,' he said at length. 'This morning I have prospected the barrow of Harald Blacktooth, and it is clear to me that I can make no progress unless I have Colonel Raden's permission to use explosives. Only the very slightest use, I promise you. I have located, I think, the ceremonial entrance, but it is blocked with boulders which it would take a gang of navvies to raise with crowbars. A discreet application of dynamite would do the work in half an hour. I cannot think that Colonel Raden would object to my using it when I encounter such obstacles. I assure you it will not spoil the look of the barrow.'

'I'm sure papa will be delighted. You're certain the noise won't frighten the deer? You know the Piper's Ring is in the forest.'

'Not in the least, my dear young lady. The reports will be very slight, scarcely louder than a rifle-shot. I ought to tell you that I am an old hand at explosives, for in my young days I mined in Colorado, and recently I have employed them in my Alaska researches . . .'

'If we go home now,' said Janet, rising, 'we'll just catch papa before he goes out. You're very warm, Mr Bandicott, and I think you would be the better for a rest and a drink.'

'I certainly should, my dear. I was so eager to begin that I bolted my breakfast, and started off before Junius was ready. He proposes to meet me here.'

Benjie, left alone, wrought diligently at his heather roots, whistling softly to himself, and every now and then raising his head to scan the haugh and the lower glen. Presently a tall young man appeared, who was identified as the younger American, and who was duly directed to follow his father to the Castle. The two returned in a little while, accompanied by Agatha Raden, and, while the elder Mr Bandicott hastened to the Piper's Ring, the young people sauntered to the Raden bridge and appeared to be deep in converse. 'Thae twa's weel agreed,' was Benjie's comment. A little before one o'clock the party adjourned to the Castle, presumably for luncheon, and

Benjie, whose noon-tide meal was always sparing, nibbled a crust of bread and a rind of cheese. In the afternoon Macpherson and one of the gillies strolled past, and the head-stalker proved wonderfully gracious, adjuring him, as Janet had done, to keep his eyes open and report the presence of any stranger. 'There'll be the three folk from Strathlarrig howkin' awa there, but if ye see anybody else, away up to the house and tell the wife. They'll no be here for any good.' Benjie promised fervently. 'I've grand een, Mr Macpherson, sir, and though they was to be crawlin' like a serpent I'd be on them.' The head-stalker observed that he was a 'gleg one,' and went his ways.

Despite his industry Benjie was remarkably observant that day, but he was not looking for poachers. He had suddenly developed an acute interest in the deer. His unaided eyes were as good as the ordinary man's telescope, and he kept a keen watch on the fringes of the great birch woods. The excavation at the Piper's Ring kept away any beasts from the east side of the haugh, but on the west bank of the stream he saw two lots of hinds grazing, with one or two young stags among them, and even on the east bank, close in to the edge of the river, he saw hinds with calves. He concluded that on the fringes of the Raden the feeding must be extra good, and, as a steady west wind was blowing, the deer there would not be alarmed by Mr Bandicott's quest. Just after he had finished his bread and cheese he was rewarded with the spectacle of a hummel, a great fellow of fully twenty stone, who rolled in a peat hole and then stood blowing in the shallow water as unconcerned as if he had been on the top of Carnmore. Later in the afternoon he saw a good ten-pointer in the same place, and a little later an eight-pointer with a damaged horn. He concluded that that particular hag was a favourite mud-bath for stags, and that with the wind in the west it was no way interfered with by the activities at the Piper's Ring.

About four o'clock Benjie backed the old horse into the shafts, and jogged up the beech-avenue to Mrs Macpherson's, where he was stayed with tea and scones. There was a gathering outside the door of Macpherson himself and the two gillies, and a strange excitement seemed to have fallen on that stolid community. Benjie could not avoid – indeed, I am not sure that he tried to avoid – hearing scraps of their talk. 'I've been a' round Carnmore,' said Alan, 'and I seen some fine beasts.

They're mostly in a howe atween the two tops, and a man at the Grey Beallach could keep an eye on all the good ground.' 'Aye, but there's the Carn Moss, and the burnheads – there will be beasts there too,' said James Fraser. 'There will have to be a man there, for him at the Grey Beallach would not ken what was happening.' 'And what about Corrie Gall?' asked Macpherson fiercely. 'Ye canna post men on Carnmore – they will have to keep moving; it is that awful broken ground.' Well, there's you and me and James,' said Alan, 'and there's Himself.' 'And that's the lot of us, and every man wanted,' said Macpherson. 'It's what I was always saying – ye will need every man for Carnmore, and must let Carnbeg alone, or ye can watch Carnbeg and not go near Carnmore. We're far ower few.' 'I wass thinking,' said James Fraser, 'that the youngest leddy might be watching Carnbeg.' 'Aye, James' – this satirically from Macpherson – 'and how would the young leddy be keeping a wild man from killing a stag and getting him away?' ''Deed, I don't ken,' said the puzzled James, 'without she took a gun with her and had a shot at him.'

Benjie drove quietly to Inverlarrig for his supply of fish, and did not return to his head-quarters in the Wood of Larrigmore till nearly seven o'clock. At eight, having cooked and eaten his supper, he made a simple toilet, which consisted in washing the fish-scales and the stains of peat from his hands, holding his head in the river, parting his damp hair with a broken comb, and putting over his shoulders a waterproof cape, which had dropped from some passing conveyance and had been found by him on the road. Thus accoutred, he crossed the river and by devious paths ascended to Crask.

He ensconced himself in the stable, where he was greeted sourly by the Bluidy Mackenzie, who was tied up in one of the stalls. There he occupied himself in whistling strathspeys and stuffing a foul clay pipe with the stump of a cigar which he had picked up in the yard. Benjie smoked not for pleasure, but from a sense of duty, and a few whiffs were all he could manage with comfort. The gloaming had fallen before he heard his name called, and Wattie Lithgow appeared. 'Ye're there, ye monkey? The gentlemen are askin' for ye. Quick and follow me. They're in an awfu' ill key the nicht and maunna be keepit waitin'.'

There certainly seemed trouble in the smoking-room when Benjie was ushered in. Lamancha was standing on the hearth-rug with a letter crumpled in his hand, and Sir Archie, waving a missive, was excitedly confronting him. The other two sat in arm-chairs with an air of protest and dejection.

'I forgot all about the infernal thing till I got Montgomery's letter. The 4th of September! Hang it, my assault on old Claybody is timed to start on the 5th. How on earth can I get to Muirtown and back and deliver a speech, and be ready for the 5th? Besides, it betrays my presence in this part of the world. It simply can't be done . . . and yet I don't know how on earth to get out of it? Apparently the thing was arranged months ago.'

'You're for it all right, my son,' cried Sir Archie, 'and so am I. Here's the beastly announcement. "*A Great Conservative Meeting will be held in the Town Hall, Muirtown, on Thursday, September 4th, to be addressed by the Right Hon. the Earl of Lamancha, M.P., His Majesty's Secretary of State for the Dominions. The chair will be taken at 3 p.m. by His Grace the Duke of Angus, K. G. Among the speakers will be Colonel Wavertree, M.P., the Hon. W.J. Murdoch, Ex-Premier of New Caledonia, and Captain Sir Archibald Roylance, D.S.O., prospective Conservative candidate for Wester Ross.*" Oh, will he? Not by a long chalk! Catch me going to such a fiasco, with Charles hidin' here and the show left to the tender mercies of two rotten bad speakers and a prosy chairman.'

'Did you forget about it too?' Leithen asked.

''Course I did,' said Archie wildly. 'How could I think of anything with you fellows turnin' my house into a den of thieves? I forgot about it just as completely as Charles, only it doesn't matter about me, and it matters the devil of a lot about him. I don't stand an earthly chance of winnin' the seat, if, first of all, I mustn't canvass because of smallpox, and, second, my big meetin', on which all my fellows counted, is wrecked by Charles playin' the fool.'

Lamancha's dark face broke into a smile.

'Don't worry, old chap. I won't let you down. But it looks as if I must let down John Macnab, and just when I was gettin' keen about him . . . Hang it, no! There must be a way. I'm not going to be beaten either by Claybody or this damned Tory rally. Ned, you slacker, what's your advice?'

'Have a try at the double event,' Leithen drawled. 'You'll probably make a mess of both, but it's a sporting proposition.'

Archie's face brightened. 'You don't realise how sportin' a

proposition it is. The Claybodys will be there, and they'll be all over you – brother nobleman, you know, and you goin' to poach their stags next day! Hang it, why shouldn't you turn the affair into camouflage? "Out of my stony griefs Bethel I'll raise," says the hymn . . . We'll have to think the thing out very carefully. – Anyway, Charles, you've got to help me with my speech. I don't mind so much lyin' doggo here if I can put in a bit of good work on the 5th . . . Now, Benjie my lad, for your report.'

Benjie, not without a certain shyness, cleared his throat and began. He narrated how, following his instructions, he had secured Macpherson's permission to cut heather for besoms on the Raden haugh. He had duly taken up his post there, had remained till four o'clock, and had seen such and such people and heard this and that talk. He recounted what he could remember of the speeches of Macpherson and the gillies.

'They've got accustomed to the sight of you, I suppose,' Palliser-Yeates said at length.

'Aye, they're accustomed right enough. Both the young lady and Macpherson was tellin' me to keep a look-out for poachers.' Benjie chuckled.

'Then tomorrow you begin to move up to the high ground by the Carnmore peat-road. Still keep busy at your besoms. You understand what I want you for, Benjie? If I kill a stag I have to get it off Glenraden land, and your old fish-cart won't be suspected.'

'Aye, I see that fine. But I've been thinkin' that there's maybe a better way.'

'Go ahead, and let's have it.'

Benjie began his speech nervously, but he soon warmed to it, and borrowed a cigar-box and the fire-irons to explain his case. The interest of his hearers kindled, until all four men were hanging on his words. When he concluded and had answered sundry questions, Sir Archie drew a deep breath and laughed excitedly.

'I suppose there's nothing in that that isn't quite cricket . . . I thought I knew something about bluff, but this – this absolutely vanquishes the band. Benjie, I'm goin' to have you taught poker. You've the right kind of mind for it.'

FIVE

The Assault on Glenraden

SHORTLY AFTER MIDNIGHT of the 28th day of August three men foregathered at the door of Macpherson's cottage, and after a few words took each a different road into the dark wastes of wood and heather. Macpherson contented himself with a patrol of the low ground in the glen, for his legs were not as nimble as they once had been and his back had a rheumaticky stiffness. Alan departed with great strides for the Carnbeg tops, and James Fraser, the youngest and the leanest, set out for Carnmore, with the speed of an Indian hunter . . . Darkness gave place to the translucence of early dawn: the badger trotted home from his wanderings: the hill-fox barked in the cairns to summon his household: sleepy pipits awoke: the peregrine who lived above the Grey Beallach drifted down into the glens to look for breakfast: hinds and calves moved up from the hazel shaws to the high fresh pastures: the tiny prerustling noises of night disappeared in that hush which precedes the awakening of life: and then came the flood of morning gold from behind the dim eastern mountains, and in an instant the earth had wheeled into a new day. A thin spire of smoke rose from Mrs Macpherson's chimney, and presently the three wardens of the marches arrived for breakfast. They reported that the forest was still unviolated, that no alien foot had yet entered its sacred confines. Herd-boys, the offspring of Alan and James Fraser, had taken up their post at key-points, so that if a human being was seen on the glacis of the fort the fact would at once be reported to the garrison.

'I'm thinkin' he'll no come to-day,' said Macpherson after his third cup of tea. 'It will be the morn. The day he will be tryin' to confuse our minds, and that will no be a difficult job wi' you, Alan, my son.'

'He'll come in the da-ark,' said Alan crossly.

'And how would he be gettin' a beast in the dark? The Laird was sayin' that this man John Macnab was a gra-and sportsman. He will not be shootin' at any little staggie, but takin' a sizeable beast, and it's not a howlet could be tellin' a calf from a stag in these da-ark nights. Na, he will not shoot in the night, but he might be travellin' in the night and gettin' his shot in the early mornin'.'

'What for,' Alan asked, 'should he not be havin' his shot in the gloamin' and gettin' the beast off the ground in the da-ark?'

'Because we will be watchin' all hours of the day. Ye heard what the Laird said, Alan Macdonald, and you, James Fraser. This John Macnab is not to shoot a Glenraden beast at all, at all, but if he shoots one he is not to move it one foot. If it comes to fightin', you are young lads and must break the head of him. But the Laird said for God's sake you was to have no guns, but to fight like honest folk with your fists, and maybe a wee bit stick. The Laird was sayin' the law was on our side, except for shootin' . . . Now, James Fraser, you will take the outer marches the day, and keep an eye on the peat-roads from Inverlarrig, and you, Alan, will watch Carnbeg, and I will be takin' the woods myself. The Laird was sayin' that it would be Carnmore the man Macnab would be tryin', most likely at skreigh of day the morn, and he would be hidin' the beast, if he got one, in some hag, and waitin' till the da-ark to shift him. So the morn we will all be on Carnmore, and I can tell you the Laird has the ground planned out so that a snipe would not be movin' without us seein' him.'

The early morning broadened into day, and the glen slept in the windless heat of late August. Janet Raden, sauntering down from the Castle towards the river about eleven o'clock, thought that she had never seen the place so sabbatically peaceful. To her unquiet soul the calm seemed unnatural, like a thick cloak covering some feverish activity. All the household were abroad since breakfast – her father on a preliminary reconnaissance of Carnmore, Agatha and Mr Junius Bandicott on a circuit of Carnbeg, while the gillies and their youthful allies sat perched with telescopes on eyries surveying every approach to the forest. The plans seemed perfect, but the dread of John Macnab, that dark conspirator, would not be exorcised. It was she who had devised the campaign, based on her reading of the enemy's mind; but had she fathomed it, she asked herself? Might he not even now be preparing some master-stroke which would crumble their crude defences? Horrible stories which she had read of impersonation and the shifts of desperate characters recurred to her mind. Was John Macnab perhaps old Mr Bandicott disguised as an archaeologist? Or was he one of the Strathlarrig workmen?

She walked over the moor to the Piper's Ring and was greeted by a mild detonation and a shower of earth. Old Mr Bandicott, very warm and stripped to his shirt, was desperately busy and most voluble about his task. There was no impersonation here, nor in the two fiery-faced labourers who were burrowing their way towards the resting-place of Harald Blacktooth. Nevertheless, her suspicion was not allayed, she felt herself in the antechamber of plotters, and looked any moment to see on the fringes of the wood or on the white ribbon of road a mysterious furtive figure which she would know for a minion of the enemy.

But the minion did not appear. As Janet stood on the rise before the bridge of Raden with her hat removed to let the faint south-west wind cool her forehead, she looked upon a scene of utter loneliness and peace. The party at the Piper's Ring were hidden, and in all the green amphitheatre nothing stirred but the stream. Even Fish Benjie and his horse had been stricken into carven immobility. He had moved away from the road a few hundred yards into the moor, not far from the waterside, and his little figure, as he whittled at his brooms, appeared from where Janet stood to be as motionless as a boulder, while the old grey pony mused upon three legs as rapt and lifeless as an Elgin marble. The two seemed to have become one with nature, and to be as much part of the sleeping landscape as the clump of birches whose leaves did not even shimmer in that bright silent noontide.

The quiet did something to soothe Janet's restlessness, but after luncheon, which she partook of in solitary state, she found it returning. A kind of *folie de doute* assailed her, not unknown to generals in the bad hours which intervene between the inception and execution of a plan. She had a strong desire to ride up to Crask and have a talk with Sir Archie, and was only restrained by the memory of that young man's last letter, and the hint it contained of grave bodily maladies. She did not know whether to believe in these maladies or not, but clearly she could not thrust her company upon one who had shown a marked distaste for it . . . Yet she had her pony saddled and rode slowly in the direction of Strathlarrig, half hoping to see a limping figure on the highway. But not a soul was in sight on the long blinding stretch or at the bridge where the Crask road started up the hill. Janet turned homeward with a feeling that the world had suddenly become dispeopled. She did not turn her head once, and so failed to notice first one figure and then another, which darted across the high road, and disappeared in the thick coverts of the Crask hill-side.

At the Castle she found Agatha and Junius Bandicott having tea, and presently her father arrived in a state of heat and exhaustion. Stayed with a whisky-and-soda, Colonel Raden became communicative. He had been over the high tops of Carnmore, had visited the Carn Moss, and Corrie Gall, had penetrated the Grey Beallach, had heard the tales of the gillies and of the herd-boys in their eyries, and his report was 'all clear.' The deer were undisturbed, according to James Fraser, since the morning. Moreover, the peat-road from Inverlarrig had relapsed owing to recent rains into primeval bog which no wheeled vehicle and few ponies could traverse. The main fortress seemed not only unassailed but unassailable, and Colonel Raden viewed the morrow with equanimity.

The Carnbeg party had a different story to tell, or rather the main members of it had no story at all. Agatha and Junius Bandicott appeared to have sauntered idly into the pleasant wilderness of juniper and heather which lay between the mossy summits, to have lunched at leisure by the famous Cailleach's Well, and to have sauntered home again. They reported that it had been divine weather, for a hill breeze had tempered the heat, and that they had observed the Claybodys' yacht far out at the entrance of Loch Larrig. Also Junius had seen his first blue hare, which he called a 'jack rabbit.' Of anything suspicious there had been neither sign nor sound.

But at this moment a maid appeared with the announcement that 'Macpherson was wanting to see the Colonel,' and presently the head stalker arrived in what John Bunyan calls a 'pelting heat.' Generally of a pale complexion which never tanned, he was now as red as a peony, and his grey beard made a startling contrast with his flamboyant face. Usually he was an embarrassed figure inside the Castle, having difficulties in disposing of his arms and legs, but now excitement made him bold.

'I've seen him, Cornel,' he panted. 'Seen him crawlin' like an adder and runnin' like a sta-ag!'

'Seen who? Get your breath, Macpherson!'

'Him – the man – Macnab. I beg your pardon for my pechin', sir, but I came down the hill like I was a rollin' stone . . . It was up on the backside of Craig Dhu near the old sheep-fauld. I seen a man hunkerin' among the muckle stones, and I got my glass on him, and he was a sma' man that I've never seen afore. I was wild to get a grip of him, and I started runnin' to drive him to the Cailleach's Well, where Miss Agatha and the gentleman was havin' their lunch. He seen me, and he took the road I ettled, and I thought I had him, for, thinks I, the young gentleman is soople and lang in the leg. But he seen the danger and turned off down the burn, and I couldna come near him. It would have been all right if I could have made the young gentleman hear, but though I was roarin' like a stot he was deafer than a tree. Och, it is the great peety.'

'Agatha, what on earth were you doing?' Janet asked severely.

Junius Bandicott blushed hotly. 'I never heard a sound,' he said. 'There must be something funny about the acoustics of that place.'

Colonel Raden, who knew the power of his stalker's lungs, looked in a mystified way from one to the other.

'Didn't you see Macpherson, Agatha?' he asked. 'He must have been in view coming over the shoulder of Craig Dhu.'

It was Agatha's turn to blush, which she did with vigour, and, to Mr Bandicott's eyes, with remarkable grace.

'Ach, I was in view well enough,' went on the tactless Macpherson, 'and I was routin' like a wild beast. But the twa of them was that busy talking they never lifted their eyes, and the man, as I tell you, slippit off down the burn. It is a gre-at peety, whatever.'

'What did you do then?' the Colonel demanded.

'I followed him till I lost him in that awful rough corrie . . . But I seen him again – aye, I seen him again, away over on the Maam above the big wud. Standin', as impident as ye please, on the sky-line.'

'How long after you lost him in the corrie?' Janet asked.

'Maybe half an hour.'

'Impossible,' she said sharply. 'No living man could cover three miles of that ground in half an hour.'

'I was thinkin' the body was the Deevil.'

'You saw a second man. John Macnab has an accomplice.'

Macpherson scratched his shaggy head. 'I wouldn't say but ye're right, Miss Janet. Now I think of it, it was a bigger man. He didn't bide a moment after I caught sight of him, but I got my glass on him, and he was a bigger man. Aye, a bigger man, and, maybe, a younger man.'

'This is very disturbing,' said Colonel Raden, walking to the window and twisting his moustache. 'What do you make of it, Nettie?'

'I think the affair is proceeding, as generals say about their battles, "according to plan." We didn't know before that John Macnab had a confederate, but of course he was bound to have one. There was nothing against it in the terms of the wager.'

'Of course not, of course not. But what the devil was he doing on Carnbeg? There was no shot, Macpherson?'

'There was no shot, and there will be no shot. There wass no beasts the side they were on, and Alan is up there now with one of James's laddies.'

'It's exactly what we expected,' said Janet. 'It proves that we were right in guessing that John Macnab would take Carnmore. He came here today to frighten us about Carnbeg – make us think that he was going to try there, and get us to mass our forces. Tomorrow he'll be on Carnmore, and then he'll mean business. I hoped this would happen, and I was getting nervous when Agatha and Mr Bandicott came home looking as blank as the Babes in the Wood. But I wish I knew which was really John Macnab – the little one or the tall one.'

'What does that matter?' her parent asked.

'Because I should be happier if he were tall. Little men are far more cunning.'

Junius Bandicott, having recovered his composure, chose to be amused. 'I take that as a personal compliment, Miss Janet. I'm pretty big, and I can't say I want to be thought cunning.'

'Then John Macnab will get his salmon,' said Janet with decision.

Junius laughed. 'You bet he won't. I've gotten the place watched like the Rum Fleet at home. A bird can't hardly cough without its being reported to me. My fellows are on to the game, and John Macnab will have to be a mighty clever citizen to come within a mile of the Strathlarrig water. Nobody is allowed to fish it but myself till the 3rd of September is past. I reckon angling just now is the forbidden fruit in this neighbourhood. I've seen but the one fellow fishing in the last three days – on the bit of slack water five hundred yards below the bridge. It belongs to Crask, I think.'

Janet nodded. 'No good except with a worm after a spate. Crask has no fishing worth the name.'

'I saw him from the automobile early this morning,' Junius continued. 'Strange sight he was, too – dressed in pyjamas and rubbers – flogging away at the most helpless stretch you can imagine – dead calm, not a ripple, He had out about fifty yards of line, and when I passed he made a cast which fell with a flop about his ears. Who do you suppose he was? Somebody from Crask?'

Janet, who was the family's authority on Crask, agreed. 'Probably some English servant who came down before breakfast just to say he had fished for salmon.'

After tea Janet went down into the haugh. She met old Mr Bandicott returning from the Piper's Ring, a very grubby old gentleman, and a little dashed in spirits, for he had as yet seen no sign of Harald Blacktooth's coffin. 'Another day's work,' he announced, 'and then I win or lose. I thought I had struck it this afternoon, but it was the solid granite. If the fellow is there he's probably in a rift of the rock. That has been known to happen. The Vikings found a natural fissure, stuck their dead chief in it, and heaped earth above to make a barrow . . .'

Down near the stream she met Benjie, who appeared to have worked late at his besoms, bumping over the moor to the road. He and his old pony made a more idyllic picture than ever in the mellow light of evening, almost too conventionally artistic to be real, she thought, till Benjie's immobile figure woke to life at the sight of her and he pulled his lint-white forelock. 'A grand nicht, lady,' he crooned, and jogged on into the beeches' shade . . . She sat on the bridge and watched the Raden waters pass from gold to amethyst and from amethyst to purple, and then sauntered back through the sweet-smelling dusk. Visions of John Macnab filled her mind, now a tall bravo with a colonial accent, now a gnarled Caliban of infinite cunning and gnome-like agility. Where in this haunted land was he ensconced – in some hazel covert, or in some clachan but-and-ben, or miles distant in a populous hotel, ready to speed in a swift car to the scene of action? . . . Anyhow, in twenty-four hours she would know if she had defeated this insolent challenger. On the eve of battle she had forgotten all about the stakes and her new hunter; it was the honour of Glenraden that was concerned, that little stone castle against the world.

Night fell, cool and cloudless, and the gillies went on their patrols. Carnmore was their only beat, and they returned one at a time to snatch a few hours' rest. At dawn they went out again – with the Colonel, but without Alan, who was to follow after he had had his ration of sleep. It was arranged that the two girls and Junius Bandicott should spend the day on Carnbeg by way of extra precaution, though if a desperate man made the assault there it was not likely that Junius, who knew nothing of deer and had no hill-craft, would be able to stop him.

Janet woke in low spirits, and her depression increased as the morning advanced. She was full of vague forebodings, and of an irritable unrest to which her steady nerves had hitherto been a stranger. She wished she were a man and could be now on Carnmore, for Carnbeg, she was convinced, was out of danger. Junius, splendid in buckskin breeches and a russet sweater, she regarded with disfavour; he was a striking figure, but out of keeping with the hills, the obvious amateur, and she longed for the halting and guileful Sir Archie. Nor was her temper improved by the conduct of her companions. Agatha and Junius seemed to have an inordinate amount to say to each other, and their conversation was idiotic to the ears of a third party. Their eyes were far more on each other than on the landscape, and their telescopes were never in use. But it mattered little, for Carnbeg slept in a primordial peace. Only pipits broke the silence, only a circling merlin made movement in a spell-bound world. There were some hinds on the west side of Craig Dhu, but no stag showed – as was natural, the girl reflected, for in this weather and thus early in the season the stags would be on the highest tops. John Macnab had chosen rightly if he wanted a shot, but there were three gillies and her father to prevent him getting his beast away.

At luncheon, which was eaten by the Cailleach's Well, Junius took to quoting poetry and Agatha to telling, very charmingly, the fairy tales of the glens. To Janet it all seemed wrong; this was not an occasion for literary philandering, when the credit of Glenraden was at stake. But even she was forced to confess that nothing was astir in the mossy wilderness. She climbed to the top of Craig Dhu and had a long spy, but, except for more hinds and one small knobber, living thing there was none. As the afternoon drew on, she drifted away from the two, who, being engrossed with each other, did not notice her departure.

She wandered through the deep heather of the Maam to where the great woods began that dipped to the Raden glen. It was pleasant walking in the cool shade of the pines on turf which was half thyme and milkwort and eyebright, and presently her spirits rose. Now and then, on some knuckle of blaeberry-covered rock which rose above the trees, she would halt, and, stretched at full length, would spy the nooks of the Home beat. There was no lack of deer there. She picked up one group and then another in the aisles and clearings of the woods, and there were shootable stags among them.

A report like a rifle-shot suddenly startled her. Then she remembered old Mr Bandicott down in the haugh, and, turning her glance in that direction, saw a thin cloud of blue smoke floating away from the Piper's Ring.

Slowly she worked her way down-hill, aiming at the haugh about a mile upstream from the excavators. Once a startled hind and calf sprang up from her feet, and once an old fox slipped out of a pile of rocks and revived thoughts of Warwickshire and her problematical hunter. Soon she was not more than three hundred feet above the stream level, and found a bracken-clad hillock where she could lie and watch the scene. There was a roebuck feeding just below her, a roebuck with fine horns, and it amused her to see the beast come nearer and nearer, since the wind was behind him. He got within five yards of the girl, who lay mute as a stone; then some impulse made him look up and meet her eye, and in a second he had streaked into cover.

Amid that delicious weather and in that home of peace Janet began to recapture her usual mirthfulness. She had been right; Carnmore was the place John Macnab would select, unless his heart had failed him, and on Carnmore he would get a warm reception. There was no need to worry any longer about John Macnab . . . Her thoughts went back to Agatha. Clearly Junius Bandicott was in love with her, and probably she would soon be in love with Junius Bandicott. No one could call it anything but a most suitable match, but Janet was vaguely unhappy about it, for it meant a break in their tiny household and the end of a long and affectionate, if occasionally tempestuous, comradeship. She would be very lonely at Glenraden without

Agatha, and what would Agatha do when transplanted to a foreign shore – Agatha, for whom the world was bounded by her native hills? She began to figure to herself what America was like, and, as her pictures had no basis of knowledge, they soon became fantastic, and merged into dreams. The drowsy afternoon world laid its spell upon the girl, and she fell asleep.

She awoke half an hour later with the sound of a shot in her ear. It set her scrambling to her feet till she remembered the excavators at the Piper's Ring, who were out of sight of the knoll on which she stood, somewhat on her right rear. Reassured, she lazily scanned the sleeping haugh, with the glittering Raden in the middle distance, and beyond the wooded slopes of the other side of the glen. She noticed a small troop of deer splashing through the shallows. Had they been scared by Mr Bandicott's explosion? That was odd, for the report had been faint and they were up-wind from it.

They were badly startled, for they raced through the river and disappeared in a few breathless seconds in the farther woods . . . Suddenly a thought made her heart beat wildly, and she raked the ground with her glass . . .

There was something tawny on a patch of turf in a little hollow near the stream. A moment of anxious spying showed her that it was a dead stag. The report had not been Mr Bandicott's dynamite, but a rifle.

Down the hill-side like a startled hind went Janet. She was choking with excitement, and had no clear idea in her head except a determination that John Macnab should not lay hand on the stricken beast. If he had pierced their defences, and got his shot, he would at any rate not get the carcass off the ground. No thought of the stakes and her hunter occurred to her – only of Glenraden and its inviolate honour.

Almost at once she lost sight of the place where the stag lay. She was now on the low ground of the haugh, in a wilderness of bogs and hollows and overgrown boulders, with half a mile of rough country between her and her goal. Soon she was panting hard: presently she had a stitch in her side; her eyes dimmed with fatigue, and her hat flew off and was left behind. It was abominable ground for speed, for there were heather-roots to trip the foot, and mires to engulf it, and noxious stones over which a runner must go warily or break an ankle. On with bursting heart went Janet, slipping, floundering, more than once taking wild tosses. Her light shoes grew leaden, her thin skirts a vast entangling quilt; her side ached and her legs were fast numbing . . . Then, from a slight rise, she had a glimpse of the Raden water, now very near, and the sight of a moving head. Her speed redoubled, and miraculously her aches ceased – the fire of battle filled her, as it had burned in her progenitors when they descended on their foes through the moonlit passes.

Suddenly she was at the scene of the dark deed. There lay the dead stag, and beside it a tall man with his shirt-sleeves turned up and a knife in his hand. That the miscreant should be calmly proceeding to the gralloch was like a fiery stimulant to Janet's spirit. Gone was every vestige of fatigue, and she descended the last slope like a maenad.

'Stop!' she sobbed. 'Stop, you villain!'

The man started at her voice, and drew himself up. He saw a slim dishevelled girl, hatless, her fair locks fast coming down, who, in the attitude of a tragedy queen, stood with uplifted and accusing hand. She saw a tall man, apparently young, with a very ruddy face, a thatch of sandy hair, and ancient, disreputable clothes.

'You are beaten, John Macnab,' cried the panting voice. 'I forbid you to touch that stag. I . . .'

The man seemed to have grasped the situation, for he shut the knife and slipped it back in his pocket. Also he smiled. Also he held both hands above his head.

'*Kamerad!*' he said. 'I acknowledge defeat, Miss Raden.'

Then he picked up his rifle and his discarded jacket, and turned and ran for it. She heard him splashing through the river, and in three minutes he was swallowed up in the farther woods.

The victorious Janet sank gasping on the turf. She wanted to cry, but changed her mind and began to laugh hysterically. After that she wanted to sing. She and she alone had defeated the marauder, while every man about the place was roosting idly on Carnmore. Now at last she remembered that hunter which would carry her in the winter over the Midland pastures. That was good, but to have beaten John Macnab was better . . . And then just a shade of compunction tempered her triumph. She had greatly liked the look of John Macnab. He was a gentleman – his voice bore witness to the fact, and the way he had behaved. *Kamerad!* He must have fought in the war and had no doubt done well. Also, he was beyond question a sportsman. The stag was just the kind of beast that a sportsman would kill – a switch-horn, going back in condition – and he had picked him out of a herd of better beasts. The shot was a workmanlike one – through the neck . . . And the audacity of him! His wits had beaten them all, for he had chosen the Home beat which everyone had dismissed as inviolable. Truly a foeman worthy of her steel, whom like all good fighters after victory she was disposed to love.

Crouched beside the dead stag, she slowly recovered her breath. What was the next move to be? If she left the beast might not John Macnab return and make off with it? No, he wouldn't. He was a gentleman, and would not go back on his admission of defeat. But she was anxious to drain the last drops of her cup of triumph, to confront the idle garrison of Carnmore on its return with the tangible proof of her victory. The stag should be lying at the Castle door, and she herself waiting beside it to tell her tale. She might borrow Mr Bandicott's men to move it.

Hastily doing up her hair, she climbed out of the hollow to the little ridge which gave a prospect over the haugh. There before her, not a hundred yards distant, was the old cart and the white pony of Fish Benjie, looking as if it had been part of the landscape since the beginning of time.

Benjie had wormed his way far into the moss, for he was more than half a mile from the road. It appeared that he had finished his day's work on the besoms, for his pony was in the shafts, and he himself was busy loading the cart with the fruits of his toil. She called out to him, but got no reply, and it was not till she stood beside him that he looked up from his work.

'Benjie,' she said, 'come at once. I want you to help me. Have you been here long?'

'Since nine this mornin', lady.' Benjie's face was as impassive as a stump of oak.

'Didn't you hear a shot?'

'I heard a gude wheen shots. The auld man up at the Piper's Ring has been blastin' awa.'

'But close to you? Didn't you see a man – not five minutes ago?'

'Aye, I seen a man. I seen him crossin' the water. I thought he was a gentleman from the Castle. He had a gun wi' him.'

'It was a poacher, Benjie,' said Janet dramatically. 'The poacher I wanted you to look out for. He has killed a stag, too, but I drove him away. You must help me to get the beast home. Can you get your cart over that knowe?'

'Fine, lady.'

Without more words Benjie took the reins and started the old pony. The cart floundered a little in a wet patch, tittuped over the tussocks, and descended with many jolts to the neighbourhood of the stag – Janet dancing in front of it like an Israelitish priest before the Ark of the Covenant.

The late afternoon was very hot, for down in the haugh the wind had died away. The stag weighed not less than fifteen stone, and before they finished Janet would have called them tons. Yet the great task of transhipment was accomplished. The pony was taken out of the shafts and the cart tilted, and, after some strenuous minutes, the carcase was heaved and pushed and levered on to its floor. Janet, hanging on to the shafts, with incredible exertions pulled them down, while Benjie – a tiny Atlas – prevented the beast from slipping back by bearing its weight on his shoulders. The backboard was put in its place, the mass of brooms and heather piled on the stag, the pony restored to the shafts, and the cortege was ready for the road. Benjie had his face adorned with a new scratch and a quantity of deer's blood, Janet had nobly torn her jumper and one stocking; but these were trivial casulties for so great an action.

'Drive straight to the Castle and tell them to leave the beast before the door. You understand, Benjie? Before the door – not in the larder. I'm going to strike home through the woods, for I'm an awful sight.'

'Ye look very bonny, lady,' said the gallant Benjie as he took up the reins.

Janet watched the strange outfit lumber from the hollow and nearly upset over a hidden boulder. It had the appearance of a moving peat-stack, with a solitary horn jutting heavenwards like a withered branch. Once again the girl subsided on the heather and laughed till she ached.

* * *

The highway by the Larrrig side slept in the golden afternoon. Not a conveyance had disturbed its peace save the baker's cart from Inverlarrig, which had passed about three o'clock. About half-past five a man crossed it – a man who had descended from the hill and used the stepping-stones where Sir Archibald Roylance had come to grief. He was a tall man with a rifle, hatless, untidy and very warm, and he seemed to desire to be unobserved, for he made certain that the road was clear before he ventured on it. Once across, he found shelter in a clump of broom, whence he could command a long stretch of the highway, almost from Glenraden gates to the Bridge of Larrig.

Mr Palliser-Yeates, having reached sanctuary – for behind him lay the broken hillsides of Crask – mopped his brow and lit a pipe. He did not seem to be greatly distressed at the result of the afternoon. Indeed, he laughed – not wildly like Janet, but quietly and with philosophy. 'A very neat hold-up,' he reflected. 'Gad, she came on like a small destroying angel . . . That's the girl Archie's been talking about . . . a very good girl. She looked as if she'd have taken on an army corps . . . Jolly romantic ending – might have come out of a novel. Only it should have been Archie, and a prospect of wedding bells – what? . . . Anyway, we'd have won out all right but for the girl, and I don't mind being beaten by her . . .'

His meditations were interrupted by the sound of furious wheels on the lone highway, and he cautiously raised his head to see an old horse and an older cart being urged towards him at a canter. The charioteer was a small boy, and above the cart sides projected a stag's horn.

Forgetting all precautions, he stood up, and at the sight of him Benjie, not without difficulty, checked the ardour of his much-belaboured beast, and stopped before him.

'I've gotten it,' he whispered hoarsely. 'The stag's in the cairt. The lassie and me histed him in, and she tell't me to drive to the Castle. But when I was out o' sicht o' her, I took the auld road through the wud and here I am. We've gotten the stag off Glenraden ground and we can hide him up at Crask, and I'll slip doun i' the cairt afore mornin' and leave him ootbye the Castle wi' a letter from John Macnab. Fegs, it was a near thing!'

Benjie's voice rose into a shrill paean, his disreputable face shone with unholy joy. And then something in Palliser-Yeates's eyes cut short his triumph.

'Benjie, you little fool, right about turn at once. I'm much obliged to you, but it can't be done. It isn't the game, you know. I chucked up the sponge when Miss Raden challenged me, and I can't go back on that. Back you go to Glenraden and hand over the stag. Quick, before you're missed . . . And look here – you're a first-class sportsman, and I'm enormously grateful to you. Here is something for your trouble.'

Benjie's face grew very red as he swung his equipage round.

'I see,' he said. 'If ye like to be beat by a lassie, dinna blame me. I'm no wantin' your money.'

The next moment the fish-cart was clattering in the other direction.

To a mystified and anxious girl, pacing the gravel in front of the Castle, entered the fish-cart. The old horse seemed in the last stages of exhaustion, and the boy who drove it was a dejected and sparrow-like figure.

'Where in the world have you been?' Janet demanded.

'I was run awa wi', lady,' Benjie whined. 'The auld powny didna like the smell o' the stag. He bolted in the wud, and I didna get him stoppit till verra near the Larrig Bridge.'

'Poor little Benjie! Now you're going to Mrs Fraser to have the best tea you ever had in your life, and you shall also have ten shillings.'

'Thank you kindly, lady, but I canna stop for tea. I maun awa down to Inverlarrig for my fish.' But his hand closed readily on the note, for he had no compunction in taking money from one who had made him to bear the bitterness of incomprehensible defeat.

SIX

The Return of Harald Blacktooth

MISS JANET RADEN had a taste for the dramatic, which that night was nobly gratified. The space in front of the great door of the Castle became a stage of which the sole furniture was a deceased stag, but on which event succeeded event with a speed which recalled the cinema rather than the legitimate drama.

First, about six o'clock, entered Agatha and Junius Bandicott from their casual wardenship of Carnbeg. The effect upon the young man was surprising. Hitherto he had only half believed in John Macnab, and had regarded the defence of Glenraden as more or less of a joke. It seemed to him inconceivable that, even with the slender staffing of the forest, one man could enter and slay and recover a deer. But when he heard Janet's tale he became visibly excited, and his careful and precise English, the bequest of his New England birth, broke down into college slang.

'The man's a crackerjack,' he murmured reverentially. 'He has us all rocketing around the mountain tops, and then takes advantage of my dad's blasting operations and raids the front yard. He can pull the slick stuff all right, and we at Strathlarrig had better get cold towels round our heads and do some thinking. Our time's getting short, too, for he starts at midnight the day after to-morrow . . . What did you say the fellow was like, Miss Janet? Young, and big, and behaved like a gentleman? It's a tougher proposition than I thought, and I'm going home right now to put old Angus through his paces.'

With a deeply preoccupied face Junius, declining tea, fetched his car from the stableyard and took his leave.

At seven-fifteen Colonel Raden, bestriding a deer pony, emerged from the beech avenue, and waved a cheerful hand to his daughters.

'It's all right, my dears. Not a sign of the blackguard. The men will remain on Carnmore till midnight to be perfectly safe, but I'm inclined to think that the whole thing is a fiasco. He has been frightened away by our precautions. But it's been a jolly day on the high tops, and I have the thirst of all creation.'

Then his eyes fell on the stag. 'God bless my soul,' he cried, 'what is that?'

'That,' said Janet, 'is the stag which John Macnab killed this afternoon.'

The Colonel promptly fell off his pony.

'Where – when?' he stammered.

'On the Home beat,' said Janet calmly. The situation was going to be quite as dramatic as she had hoped. 'I saw it fall, and ran hard and got up to it just when he was starting the gralloch. He was really quite nice about it.'

'What did he do?' her parent demanded.

'He held up his hands and laughed and cried '*Kamerad!*' Then he ran away.'

'The scoundrel showed a proper sense of shame.'

'I don't think he was ashamed. Why should he be, for we accepted his challenge. You know, he's a gentleman, papa, and quite young and good looking.'

Colonel Raden's mind was passing through swift stages from exasperation to unwilling respect. It was an infernal annoyance that John Macnab should have been suffered to intrude on the sacred soil of Glenraden, but the man had played the boldest kind of hand, and he had certainly not tailored his beast. Besides, he had been beaten – beaten by a girl, a daughter of the house. The honour of Glenraden might be considered sacrosanct after all.

A long drink restored the Colonel's equanimity, and the thought of their careful preparations expended in the void moved him to laughter.

''Pon my word, Nettie, I should like to ask the fellow to dinner. I wonder where on earth he is living. He can't be far off, for he is due at Strathlarrig very soon. What did young Bandicott say the day was?'

'Midnight, the day after tomorrow. Mr Junius feels very solemn after today, and has hurried home to put his house in order.'

'Nettie,' said the Colonel gravely, 'I am prepared to make the modest bet that John Macnab gets his salmon. Hang it all, if he could outwit us – and he did it, confound him – he is bound to outwit the Bandicotts. I tell you what, John Macnab is a very remarkable man – a man in a million, and I'm very much inclined to wish him success.'

'So am I,' said Janet; but Agatha announced indignantly that she had never met a case of grosser selfishness. She announced, too, that she was prepared to join in the guarding of Strathlarrig.

'If you and Junius are no more use than you were on Carnbeg today, John Macnab needn't worry,' said Janet sweetly.

Agatha was about to retort when there was a sudden diversion. The elder Bandicott appeared at a pace which was almost a run, breathing hard, and with all the appearance of strong excitement. Fifty yards behind him, could be seen the two Strathlarrig labourers, making the best speed they could under the burden of heavy sacks. Mr Bandicott had no breath left to speak, but he motioned to his audience to give him time and permit his henchmen to arrive. These henchmen he directed to the lawn, where they dropped their sacks on the grass. Then, with an air which was almost sacramental, he turned to Colonel Raden.

'Sir,' he said, 'you are privileged – *we* are privileged – to assist in the greatest triumph of modern archaeology. I have found the coffin of Harald Blacktooth with the dust of Harald Blacktooth inside it.'

'The devil you have!' said the Colonel. 'I suppose I ought to congratulate you, but I'm bound to say I'm rather sorry. I feel as if I had violated the tomb of my ancestors.'

'You need have no fear, sir. The dust has been reverently restored to its casket, and tomorrow the Piper's Ring will show no trace of the work. But within the stone casket there were articles which, in the name of science, I have taken the liberty to bring with me, and which will awaken an interest among the learned not less, I am convinced, than Schliemann's discoveries at Mycenae. I have found, sir, incredible treasures.'

'Treasures!' cried all three of his auditors, for the word has not lost its ancient magic.

Mr Bandicott, with the air of one addressing the Smithsonian Institution, signalled to his henchmen, who thereupon emptied the sacks on the lawn. A curious jumble of objects lay scattered under the evening sun – two massive torques, several bowls and flagons, spear-heads from which the hafts had long since rotted, a sword-blade, and a quantity of brooches, armlets, and rings. A dingy enough collection they made to the eyes of the onlookers as Mr Bandicott arranged them in two heaps.

'These,' he said, pointing to the torques, armlets, and flagons, 'are, so far as I can judge, of solid gold.'

The Colonel called upon his Maker to sanctify his soul. 'Gold! These are great things! They must be prodigiously valuable. Are they mine, or yours, or whose?'

'I am not familiar with the law of Scotland on the matter of treasure trove, but I assume that the State can annex them, paying you a percentage of their value. For myself, I gladly waive all claims. I am a man of science, sir, not a treasure-hunter . . . But the merit of the discovery does not lie in those objects, which can be paralleled from many tombs in Scotland and Norway. No, sir, the tremendous, the epoch-making value is to be found in these.' And he indicated some bracelets and a necklace which looked as if they were made of queerly-marked and very dirty shells.

Mr Bandicott lifted one and fingered it lovingly.

'I have found such objects in graves as far apart as the coast of Labrador and the coast of Rhode Island, and as far inland as the Ohio basin. These shells were the common funerary adjunct of the primitive inhabitants of my country, and they are peculiar to the North American continent. Do you see what follows, sir?'

The Colonel did not, and Mr Bandicott, his voice thrilling with emotion, continued:

'It follows that Harald Blacktooth obtained them from the only place he could obtain them, the other side of the Atlantic. There is historical warrant for believing that he voyaged to Greenland; and now we know that he landed upon the main North American continent. The legends of Eric the Red and Leif the Lucky are verified by archaeology. In you, sir, I salute, most reverently salute, the representative of a family to whom belongs the credit hitherto given to Columbus.'

Colonel Raden plucked feebly at his moustache, and Janet, I regret to say, laughed. But her untimely merriment was checked by Mr Bandicott, who was pronouncing a sort of benediction.

'I rejoice that it has been given to me, an American, to solve this secular riddle. When I think that the dust which an hour ago I touched, and which has lain for centuries under that quiet mound, was once the man who, first of Europeans, trod our soil, my imagination staggers. Colonel Raden, I thank you for having given me the greatest moment of my not uneventful life.'

He took off his hat, and the Colonel rather shame-facedly removed his. The two men stood looking solemnly at each other till practical considerations occurred to the descendant of the Viking.

'What are you going to do with the loot?' he asked.

'With your permission, I will take it to Strathlarrig, where I can examine and catalogue it at my leisure. I propose to announce the find at once to the world. Tomorrow I will return with my men and remove the traces of our excavation.'

Mr Bandicott departed in his car, sitting erect at the wheel in a strangely priest-like attitude, while the two men guarded the treasure behind. He had no eyes for the twilight landscape, or he would have seen in the canal-like stretch of the Larrig belonging to Crask, which lay below the rapids and was universally condemned as hopeless for fish, a solitary angler, who, as the car passed, made a most bungling amateurish cast, but who, when the coast was once more clear, flung a line of surprising delicacy. He could not see the curious way in which that angler placed his fly, laying it with a curl a yard above a moving fish, and then sinking it with a dexterous twist: nor did he see, a quarter of an hour later, the same angler land a fair salmon from water in which in the memory of man no salmon had ever been taken before.

Colonel Raden and his daughters stood watching the departing archaeologist, and as his car vanished among the beeches Janet seized her sister and whirled her into a dance. 'Such a day,' she cried, when the indignant Agatha had escaped and was patting her disordered hair. 'Losses – one stag, which was better dead. Gains – defeat of John Macnab, fifty pounds sterling, a share of unknown value in Harald Blacktooth's treasure, and the annexation of America by the Raden family.'

'You'd better say that America has annexed us,' said the still flustered Agatha. 'They've dug up our barrow, and this afternoon Junius Bandicott asked me to marry him.'

Janet stopped in her tracks. 'What did you say?'

'I said "No" of course. I've only known him a week.' But her tone was such as to make her sister fear the worst.

Mr Bandicott was an archaeologist, but he was also a business man, and he was disposed to use the whole apparatus of civilisation to announce his discovery to the world. With a good deal of trouble he got the two chief Scottish newspapers on the telephone, and dictated to them a summary of his story. He asked them to pass the matter on to the London press, and he gave them ample references to establish his good faith. Also he prepared a sheaf of telegrams and cables – to learned societies in Britain and America, to the great New York daily of which he was the principal owner, to the British Museum, to the Secretary for Scotland, and to friends in the same line of scholarship. Having left instructions that these messages should be despatched from Inverlarrig at dawn, he went to bed in a state of profound jubilation and utter fatigue.

Next morning, while his father was absorbed in the remains of Harald Blacktooth, Junius summoned a council of war. To it there came Angus, the head-keeper, a morose old man near six-foot-four in height, clean-shaven, with eyebrows like a penthouse; Lennox, his second-in-command, whom Leithen had met on his reconnaissance; and two youthful watchers, late of Lovat's Scouts, known as Jimsie and Davie. There were others about the place who could be mobilised if necessary, including the two chauffeurs, an under-footman and a valet; but, as Junius looked at this formidable quartet, and reflected on the narrow limit of the area of danger, he concluded that he had all the man-power he needed.

'Now, listen to me, Angus,' he began. 'This poacher Macnab proposes to start in tomorrow night at twelve o'clock, and according to his challenge he has forty-eight hours to get a fish in – up till midnight on the 3rd of September. I want your advice about the best way of checkmating him. You've attended to my orders, and let nobody near the river during the past week?'

'Aye, sir, and there's nobody socht to gang near it,' said Angus. 'The country-side has been as quiet as a grave.'

'Well, it won't be after tomorrow night. You've probably heard that this Macnab killed a stag on Glenraden yesterday – killed it within half a mile of the house, and would have got away with it but for the younger Miss Raden.'

They had heard of it, for the glen had talked of nothing else all night, but they thought it good manners to express amazement. 'Heard ye ever the like?' said one. 'Macnab maun be a fair deevil,' said another. 'If I had just a grip of him,' sighed the blood-thirsty Angus.

'It's clear we're up against something quite out of the common,' Junius went on, 'and we daren't give him the faintest outside chance. Now, let's consider the river. You say you've seen nobody near it.'

'There hasn't been a line cast in the watter forbye your own, sir,' said Angus.

'I just seen the one man fishin' a' week,' volunteered Jimsie. 'It was on the Crask water below the brig. I jaloused that he was one of the servants from Crask, and maybe no very right in the heid. He had no notion of it at all, at all.'

'Well, that's so far good. Now what about the river outside the park? Our beat runs from the Larrig Bridge – what's it like between the bridge and the lodge? You've never taken me fishing there.'

'Ye wad need to be dementit before you went fishin' there,' said Angus grimly. 'There's the stretch above the brig that they ca' the Lang Whang. There was never man killed a saumon in it, for the fish dinna bide, but rin through to the Wood Pule. There's fish in the Wood Pule, but the trees are that thick that ye canna cast a flee. Though I'll no say,' he added meditatively, 'that ye couldna cleek a fish out of it. I'd better put a watcher at the Wood Pule.'

'You may rule that out, for the bargain says "legitimate means," and from all I know of Macnab he's a sportsman and keeps his word. Well, then, we come to the park, where we've five pools – the Duke's, the Black Scour, Davie's Pot, Lady Maisie's, and the Minister's. We've got to keep our eyes skinned there . . . What about the upper water?'

'There's no a fish in it,' said Lennox. 'They canna get past the linn above the Minister's. There was aye talk o' makin' a salmon ladder, but naething was done, and there's nocht above the Minister's but small broon troot.'

'That makes it a pretty simple proposition,' said Junius. 'We've just the five pools to guard. For the form of the thing we'll keep watchers on all night, but we may take it that the danger lies only in the thirty-four hours of daylight. Now, remember, we're taking no chances. Not a soul is to be allowed to fish on the Strathlarrig water till after midnight on the 3rd of September. Not even I or my father. Macnab's a foxy fellow and I wouldn't put it past him to disguise himself as Mr Bandicott or myself. Do you understand? If you see a man near the river, kick him out. If he has a rod in his hand, lock him up in the garage and send for me . . . No, better still. Nobody's to be allowed inside the gates – except Colonel Raden and his daughters. You'd better tell the lodge-keeper, Angus. If anybody comes to call, they must come back another day. These are my orders, you understand, and I fire anyone who disobeys them. If the 3rd of September passes without accident there's twenty dollars – I mean to say, five pounds – for each of you. That's all I've got to say.'

'Will we watch below the park, sir?' Angus asked.

'Watch every damned foot of the water from the bridge to the linns.'

Thus it came about that when Janet Raden took her afternoon ride past the Wood of Larrigmore she beheld a man patrolling the bog like a policeman on point duty, and when she entered the park for a gallop on the smooth turf she observed a picket at each pool. 'Poor John Macnab!' she sighed. 'He hasn't the ghost of a chance. I'm rather sorry my family discovered America.'

Next day, the 1st of September, the Scottish Press published a short account of Mr Bandicott's discovery, and *The Scotsman* had a leader on it. About noon a spate of telegrams began, and the girl who carried them on a bicycle from Inverlarrig had a weary time of it. The following morning the Press of Britain spread themselves on the subject. *The Times* had a leader and an interview with a high authority at the British Museum; the *Daily Mail* had a portrait of Mr Bandicott and a sketch of his past career, a photograph of what purported to be a Viking's tomb in Norway, and a chatty article on the law of treasure-trove. The *Morning Post* congratulated the discoverer in the name of science, but lamented in the name of patriotism that the honour should have fallen to an alien – views which led to an interminable controversy in its pages with the secretary of the Pilgrims' Club and the president of the American Chamber of Commerce. The evening papers had brightly written articles on Strathlarrig, touching on the sport of deer-stalking, Celtic mysticism, the crofter question, and the law dealing with access to mountains. The previous evening, too, the special correspondents had begun to arrive from all points of the compass, so that the little inn of Inverlarrig had people sleeping in its one bathroom and under its dining-room table. By the morning of the 2nd of September the glen had almost doubled its male population.

The morning, after some rain in the night, broke in the thin fog which promised a day of blazing heat. Sir Edward Leithen, taking the air after breakfast, decided that his attempt should be made in the evening, for he wanted the Larrig waters well warmed by the sun for the type of fishing he proposed to follow. Benjie had faithfully reported to him the precautions which the Bandicotts had adopted, and his meditations were not cheerful. With luck he might get a fish, but only by a miracle could he escape unobserved. His plan depended upon the Lang Whang being neglected by the watchers as not worthy of their vigilance, but according to Benjie's account even the Lang Whang had become a promenade. He had now lost any half-heartedness in the business, and his obstinate soul was as set on victory as ever it had been the case in the Law Courts. For the past four days he had thought of nothing else, – his interest in Palliser-Yeates's attack on Glenraden had been notably fainter than that of the others; every energy he had of mind and body was centred upon killing a fish that night and carrying it off. With some amusement he reflected that he had dissipated the last atom of his ennui, and he almost regretted that apathy had been exchanged for this violent pre-occupation.

Presently he turned his steps to the arbour to the east of the garden, which forms at once a hiding-place and a watch-tower. There he found his host busied about the preparation of his speech, with the assistance of Lamancha, who was also engaged intermittently in the study of the ordnance map of Haripol.

'It's a black look-out for you, Ned,' said Sir Archie. 'I hear the Bandicotts have taped off every yard of their water, and have got a man to every three. Benjie says the place only wants a piper or two to be like the Muirtown Highland Gathering. What are you going to do about it?'

'I'm going to have a try this evening. I can't chuck in my hand, but the thing's a stark impossibility. I hoped old Bandicott would be so excited at unearthing the Viking that he would forget about precautions, but he's as active as a beaver.'

'That's the young 'un. He don't give a damn for Vikings, but he's out to protect his fish. You've struck the American business mind, my lad, and it's an awful thing for us casual Britons. I suppose you won't let me come down and watch you. I'd give a lot to see a scrap between you and that troglodyte Angus.'

At that moment Benjie, wearing the waterproof cape of ceremony, presented himself at the arbour door. He bore a letter which he presented to Sir Archie. The young man read it with a face which was at once perplexed and pleased.

'It's from old Bandicott. He says he has got some antiquarian swell – Professor Babwater I think the name is – coming to stay, and he wants me to dine tonight – says the Radens are coming too . . . This is the devil. What had I better do, Charles?'

'Stay at home. You'll put your foot in it somehow if you go. The girl who held up old John will be there, and she's bound to talk about John Macnab, and you're equally bound to give the show away.'

'But I haven't any sort of excuse. Americans are noted for their politeness, and here have I been shutting the door in the face of the poor old chap when he toiled up the hill. He won't understand it, and people will begin to talk, and that's the quickest way to blow the gaff. Besides, I've got to give up this lie about my ill-health if I'm to appear at Muirtown the day after tomorrow. What do *you* say, Ned?'

'I think you'd better go,' Leithen answered. 'We can't have the neighbourhood thinking you are plague-stricken. You'll be drinking port, while I'm being carted by the gillies into the coal-hole. But for Heaven's sake, Archie, go canny. That Raden girl will turn you inside out, if you give her a chance. And don't you try and be clever, whatever happens. If there's a row and you see me being frog-marched into captivity, don't trouble to create a diversion. Behave as if you had never seen me in your life before . . . You hadn't heard of John Macnab except from Miss Raden, and you're desperately keen to hear more, you understand. Play the guileless innocent and rack your brains to think who he can be. Start any hare you like – that he's D'Annunzio looking for excitement . . . or the Poet Laureate . . . or an escaped lunatic. And keep it up that you are in delicate health. Oh, and talk politics – they're safe enough. Babble about the Rally, and how the great Lamancha's coming up for it all the way from the Borders.'

Archie nodded, with a contented look in his eyes. 'I'm goin' to take your advice. Where did you get this note, Benjie? From Mactavish at the lodge? All right, I'll give you a line to take back with you . . . By the way, Ned, what's your get-up to-night? I'd better know beforehand in case of accidents.'

'I'm going to look the basest kind of poaching tramp. I've selected my costume from the combined wardrobes of this household, and I can tell you it's pretty dingy. Mrs Lithgow is at present engaged in clouting the oldest pair of Wattie's breeks for me . . . My only chance is to be a regular ragamuffin, and the worst I need fear then is a rough handling from the gillies. Bandicott, I take it, is not the sort of fellow to want to prosecute. If I'm caught – which is fairly certain – I'll probably get a drubbing and spend the night in a cellar and be given my breakfast next morning and kicked out. It's a different matter for you, Charles, with the legally minded Claybody.'

'What odds are you offerin'?' Sir Archie asked. 'John backed himself and I took a tenner off him. What about an even fiver?'

'I'll give you three to one in five-pound notes that I win,' said Leithen grimly. 'But that's pride, not conviction.'

'Done with you, my lad,' said Sir Archie, and departed to write an acceptance of the invitation to dinner.

Fish Benjie remained behind, and it was clear that he had something to communicate. He caught Lamancha's eye, who gave him the opening he sought by asking what was the news from Strathlarrig. Benjie had the instinct of the ballad-maker, and would begin his longer discourses with an epic flourish of the 'Late at e'en drinkin' the wine' style.

'It was at fower o'clock this mornin' they started,' he announced, 'and they're still comin'.'

'Coming? Who?' Leithen asked.

'Jornalists. The place is crawlin' wi' them. I seen six on bicycles and five in cawrs and twa in the Inverlarrig dowgcairt. They're a' wantin' to see auld Bandicott, but auld Bandicott will no see them. Mactavish stops them at the lodge, and speirs what they want, and they gie him cairds wi' their names prentit, and he sends them up to the hoose, but he'll no let them enter. Syne the message comes back that the maister will see them the day after the morn, but till then naebody maun put a fit inside the gates.'

'What happened then?' Leithen asked with acute interest.

'It hasna happened – it's still happenin'! I never in my life heard sic a lot o' sweer words. Says ane, "Does the auld dotterel think he can defy the British Press? We'll mak his life no worth leevin'." Says another, "I've come a' the gait frae London and I'll no budge till I've seen the banes o' that Viking!" One or twa went back to Inverlarrig, but the feck o' them just scattered like paitricks. They clamb the wall, and they waded up the water, and they got in by the top o' the linns. In half an hour there was half a dizzen o' them inside the Strathlarrig policies. Man' – here he fixed his glowing eye on Leithen – 'if ye had been on the Lang Whang this mornin' ye could have killed a fish and naebody the wiser.'

'Good Lord! Are they there still?'

'Na. They were huntit oot. Every man aboot the place was huntin' them, and Angus was roarin' like a bull. The young Laird thocht they were Bolshies and cam doun wi' a gun. Syne the auld man appeared and spoke them fair and telled them he was terribly sorry, but he couldna see them for twa days, and if they contentit themselves that lang he would hae them a' to their denner and show them everything. After that they gaed awa, but there's aye mair arrivin' and I'm expectin' mair riots. They're forritsome lads, thae jornalists, and a dour crop to shift. But they're kind folk, and gie'd me a shillin' a-piece for advisin' them.'

'What did you advise?'

'I advised them to gang doun to Glenraden,' said Benjie with a goblin smile. 'I said they should gang and howk in the Piper's Ring and they would maybe find mair treasure. Twa-three o' them got spades and picks and startit off. I'm thinkin' Macpherson will be after them wi' a whup.'

Leithen's brows were puckered in thought. 'It looks as if my bet with Archie wasn't so crazy after all. This invasion is bound to confuse Bandicott's plans. And you say it's still going on? The gillies will be weary men before night.'

'They will that,' Benjie assented. 'And there's no a man o' them can rin worth a docken, except Jimsie. Thae jornalists was far soopler.'

'More power to the Press. Benjie, back you go and keep an eye on Strathlarrig, and stir up the journalists to a sense of their rights. Report here this afternoon at four, for we should be on the move by six, and I've a lot to say to you.'

* * *

In the course of the morning Leithen went for a walk among the scaurs and dingles of Crask Hill. He followed a footpath which took him down the channel of a tiny burn and led to a little mantelpiece of a meadow from which Wattie Lithgow drew a modest supply of bog-hay. His mind was so filled with his coming adventure that he walked with his head bent and at a turn of the path nearly collided with a man.

Murmuring a gruff 'Fine day,' he would have passed on, when he became aware that the stranger had halted. Then, to his consternation, he heard his name uttered, and had perforce to turn. He saw a young man, in knickerbockers and heavy nailed boots, who smiled diffidently as if uncertain whether he would be recognised.

'Sir Edward Leithen, isn't it?' he said. 'I once had the pleasure of meeting you, sir, when you lunched with the Lobby journalists. I was then on the Lobby staff of the *Monitor*. My name is Crossby.'

'Of course, of course. I remember perfectly. Let's sit down, Mr Crossby, unless you're in a hurry. Where are you bound for?'

'Simply stretching my legs. I was climbing rocks at Sligachan when my paper wired me to come on here. The Press seem to have gone mad about this Viking's tomb – think they've got hold of a second Tutankhamen. So I got a fisherman to take me and my bicycle over to the mainland and pedalled the rest of the road. I thought I had a graft with old Bandicott, for I used to write for his paper – *The New York Bulletin*, you know – but it appears there's nothing doing. Odd business, for you don't often find Americans shy of the Press. But I think I've found out the reason, and that makes a good enough story in itself. Perhaps you've heard it?'

'No,' said Leithen, 'but I'd like to, if you don't mind. I'm not a journalist, so I won't give you away. Let's have it.'

He stole a glance at his companion, and saw a pleasant, shrewd, boyish face, with the hard sunburnt skin of one in the prime of physical condition. Like many others of his type, Leithen liked journalists as much as he disliked men of letters – the former had had their corners smoothed by a rough life, and lacked the vanity and spiritual pride of the latter. Also he had acquired from experience a profound belief in the honour of the profession, for at various times in his public career he had put his reputation into their hands and they had not failed him.

It was his maxim that if you tried to bamboozle them they were out for your blood, but that if you trusted them they would see you through.

'Let's hear it, Mr Crossby,' he repeated. 'I'm deeply interested.'

'Well, it's a preposterous tale, but the natives seem to believe it. They say that some fellow, who calls himself John Macnab, has dared the magnates in these parts to prevent his killing a stag or a salmon in their preserves. He has laid down pretty stiff conditions for himself, for he has to get his beast off their ground and hand it back to them. They say he has undertaken to pay £500 to any charity the owner names if he succeeds and £1,000 if he fails – so he must have money to burn, and it appears that he has already paid the £500. He started on Glenraden, and the old Highland chief there had every man and boy for three days watching the forest. Then on the third day, when everybody was on the mountain-tops, in sails John Macnab and kills a stag under the house windows. He reckoned on the American's dynamite charges in his search for the Viking to hide his shot. And he would have got away with it too, if one of the young ladies hadn't appeared on the scene and cried 'Desist!' So what does this bandit do but off with his hat, makes his best bow, and says 'Madame, your servant,' and vanishes, leaving the chief richer by a thousand pounds. It's Bandicott's turn today and tomorrow, and the Strathlarrig household is squatting along the river banks, and the hard-working correspondent is chivvied away till the danger is past. I'm for Macnab myself. It warms my heart to think that there's such a sportsman left alive. It's pure Robin Hood.'

Leithen laughed. 'I back him too. Are you going to publish that story?'

'Yes, why not? I've written most of it and it goes by the afternoon post.' Mr Crossby pulled out a note-book and fluttered the leaves.

'I call it "The Return of Harald Blacktooth." Rather neat, I think. The idea is that when they started to dig up the old fellow his spirit reincarnated itself in John Macnab. I hope to have a second instalment, for something's bound to happen at Strathlarrig today or tomorrow. Are you holidaying here, Sir Edward? Crask's the name of this place, isn't it? They told me that that mad fellow Roylance owned it.'

Leithen nodded. He was bracing himself for another

decision of the same kind as he had taken when he met Fish Benjie. Providence seemed to be forcing him to preserve his incognito only by sharing the secret

'But, of course,' Mr Crossby went on, 'my main business here is the Viking, and I'm keen to find some way to get over Bandicott's reticence. I don't want to wait till the day after to-morrow and then come in with the ruck. I wonder . . . would it be too much to ask you to give me a leg up? I expect you know the Bandicotts?'

'Curiously enough, I don't. I am not sure how far I can help you, Mr Crossby, but I rather think you can help me. Are you by any happy chance a long-distance runner?'

The journalist opened his eyes. 'Well, I used to be. South London Harriers, you know. And I'm in fairly good condition at present after ten days on the Coolin rocks.'

'Well, if I can't give you a story, I think I can put you in the way of an adventure. Will you come up to Crask to luncheon and we'll talk it over?'

SEVEN

The Old Etonian Tramp

SIR ARCHIE GOT himself into the somewhat ancient dress-coat which was the best he had at Crask, and about half-past seven started his Hispana (a car in which his friends would not venture with Archie as driver) down the long hill to the gates of Strathlarrig. He was aware that somewhere in the haugh above the bridge was Leithen, but the only figure visible was that of Jimsie, the Strathlarrig gillie, who was moodily prowling about the upper end. As he passed the Wood of Larrigmore Benjie's old pony was grazing at tether, and the old cart rested on its shafts; the embers of a fire still glowed among the pine-needles, but there was no sign of Benjie. He was admitted after a parley by Mactavish the lodge-keeper, and when he reached the door of the house he observed a large limousine being driven off to the back premises by a very smart chauffeur. Only Haripol was likely to own such a car, and Sir Archie reflected with amusement that the host of John Macnab was about to attend a full conclave of the Enemy.

The huge, ugly drawing-room looked almost beautiful in the yellow light of evening. A fire burned on the hearth after the fashion of Highland houses even in summer, and before it stood Mr Acheson Bandicott, with a small clean-shaven man, who was obviously the distinguished Professor in whose honour the feast was given, and Colonel Raden, a picturesque figure in kilt and velvet doublet, who seemed hard put to it to follow what was clearly a technical colloquy. Agatha and Junius were admiring the sunset in the west window, and Janet was talking to a blond young man who seemed possessed of a singularly penetrating voice.

Sir Archie was unknown to most of the company, and when his name was announced everyone except the Professor turned towards him with a lively curiosity. Old Mr Bandicott was profuse in his welcome, Junius no less cordial, Colonel Raden approving, for indeed it was not in human nature to be cold towards so friendly a being as the Laird of Crask. Sir Archie was apologetic for his social misfeasances, congratulatory about Harald Blacktooth, eager to atone for the past by an exuberant neighbourliness. 'Been havin' a rotten time with the toothache,' he told his host. 'I roost up alone in my little barrack and keep company with birds . . . Bit of a naturalist, you know . . . Yes, sir, quite fit again, but my leg will never be much to boast of.'

Colonel Raden appraised the lean, athletic figure. 'You've been our mystery man, Sir Archibald. I'm almost sorry to meet you, for we lose our chief topic of discussion. You're fond of stalking, they tell me. When are you coming to kill a stag at Glenraden?'

'When will you ask me?' Sir Archie laughed. 'I'm still fairly good on the hill, but just now I'm sittin' indoors all day tuggin' at my hair and tryin' to compose a speech.'

Colonel Raden's face asked for explanations.

'Day after tomorrow in Muirtown. Big Unionist meetin', and I've got to start the ball. It's jolly hard to know what to talk about, for I've a pretty high average of ignorance about everything. But I've decided to have a shot at foreign policy. You see, Charles—' Sir Archie stopped in a fright. He had been within an ace of giving the show away.

'Of course. 'Pon my soul I had forgotten that you were our candidate. It's an uphill fight I'm afraid. The people in these parts, sir, are the most obstinate reactionaries on the face of the globe; but they've been voting Liberal ever since the days of John Knox.'

Mr Bandicott regarded Sir Archie with interest.

'So you're standing for Parliament,' he said. 'Few things impress me more in Great Britain than the way young men take up public life as if it were the natural coping-stone to their education. We have no such tradition, and we feel the absence of it. Junius would as soon think of running for Congress as of keeping a faro-saloon. Now I wonder, Sir Archibald, what induced you to take this step?'

But Sir Archie was gone, for he had seen the beckoning eyes of Janet Raden. That young woman, ever since she had heard that the Laird of Crask was coming to dinner, had looked forward to this occasion as her culminating triumph. He had been her confidant about the desperate John Macnab, and from her he must learn the tale of her victory. Her pleasure was increased by the consciousness that she was looking her best, for she knew that her black gown was a good French model and well set off her delicate colouring. She looked with eyes of friendship on him as he limped across the room, and noted his lean distinction. No other country, she thought, produced this kind of slim, graceful, yet weathered and hard-bitten youth.

'Do you know Mr Claybody?'

Mr Claybody said he was delighted to meet his neighbour again. 'It's years,' he said, 'since we met at Ronham. I spend my life in the train now, and never get more than a few days at a time at Haripol. But I've managed to secure a month this year to entertain my friends. I was looking forward in any case to seeing you at Muirtown on the 4th. I've been helping to organise the show, and I consider it a great score to have got Lamancha. This place had never been properly worked, and with a little efficient organisation we ought to put you in right enough. There's no doubt Scotland is changing, and you'll have the tide to help you.'

Mr Claybody was a very splendid person. He looked rather like a large edition of the great Napoleon, for he had the same full fleshy face, and his head was set on a thickish neck. His blond hair was beautifully sleek and his clothes were of a perfection uncommon in September north of the Forth. Not that Mr Claybody was either fat or dandified; he was only what the ballad calls 'fair of flesh,' and he employed a good tailor and an assiduous valet. His exact age was thirty-two, and he did not look older, once the observer had got over his curiously sophisticated eyes.

But Sir Archie was giving scant attention to Mr Claybody.

'Have you heard?' Janet broke out. 'John Macnab came, saw, and didn't conquer.'

'I've heard nothing else in the last two days.'

'And I was right! He is a gentleman.'

'No? Tell me all about the fellow.' Sir Archie's interest was perhaps less in the subject than in the animation which it woke in Janet's eyes.

But the announcement that dinner was served cut short the tale, though not before Sir Archie had noticed a sudden set of Mr Claybody's jaw and a contraction of his eyebrows. 'Wonder if he means to stick to his lawyer's letter,' he communed with himself. 'In that case it's quod for Charles.'

The dining-room at Strathlarrig was a remnant of the old

house which had been enveloped in the immense sheath of the new. It had eighteenth-century panelling unchanged since the days when Jacobite chiefs in lace and tartan had passed their claret glasses over the water, and the pictures were all of forbidding progenitors. But the ancient narrow windows had been widened, and Sir Archie, from where he sat, had a prospect of half a mile of the river, including Lady Maisie's Pool, bathed in the clear amber of twilight. He was on his host's left hand, opposite the Professor, with Agatha Raden next to him: then came Junius: while Janet was between Johnson Claybody and the guest of the occasion.

Mr Claybody still brooded over John Macnab.

'I call the whole thing infernal impertinence,' he said in his loud, assured voice. 'I confess I have ceased to admire undergraduate "rags." He threatens to visit us, and my father intends to put the matter into the hands of the police.'

'That would be very kind,' said Janet sweetly. 'You see, John Macnab won't have the slightest trouble in beating the police.'

'It's the principle of the thing, Miss Raden. Here is an impudent attack on private property, and if we treat it as a joke it will only encourage other scoundrels. If the man is a gentleman, as you say he is, it makes it more scandalous.'

'Come, come, Mr Claybody, you're taking it too seriously.' Colonel Raden could be emphatic enough on the rights of property, but no Highlander can ever grow excited about trespass. 'The fellow has made a sporting offer and is willing to risk a pretty handsome stake. I rather admire what you call his impudence. I might have done the same thing as a young man, if I had had the wits to think of it.'

Mr Claybody was quick to recognise an unsympathetic audience. 'Oh, I don't mean that we're actually going to make a fuss. We'll give him a warm reception if he comes – that's all. But I don't like the spirit. It's too dangerous in these unsettled times. Once let the masses get into their heads that landed property is a thing to play tricks with, and you take the pin out of the whole system. You must agree with me, Roylance?'

Sir Archie, remembering his part, answered with guile. 'Rather! Rotten game for a gentleman, I think. All the same, the chap seems rather a sportsman, so I'm in favour of letting the law alone and dealing with him ourselves. I expect he won't have much of a look in on Haripol.'

'I can promise you he won't,' said Mr Claybody shortly.

Professor Babwater observed that it would be difficult for a descendant of Harald Blacktooth to be too hard on one who followed in Harald's steps. 'The Celt,' he said, 'has always sought his adventures in a fairy world. The Northman was a realist, and looked to tangible things like land and cattle. Therefore he was a conqueror and a discoverer on the terrestial globe, while the Celt explored the mysteries of the spirit. Those who, like you, sir' – he bowed to Colonel Raden – 'have both strains in their ancestry, should have successes in both worlds.'

'They don't mix well,' said the Colonel sadly. 'There was my grandfather, who believed in Macpherson's *Ossian* and ruined the family fortunes in hunting for Gaelic manuscripts on the continent of Europe. And his father was in India with Clive, and thought about nothing except blackmailing native chiefs till he made the place too hot to hold him. Look at my daughters, too. Agatha is mad about poetry and such-like, and Janet is a bandit. She'd have made a dashed good soldier, though.'

'Thank you, papa,' said the lady. She might have objected to the description had she not seen that Sir Archie accepted it with admiring assent.

'I suppose,' said old Mr Bandicott reflectively, 'that the war was bound to leave a good deal of unsettlement. Junius missed it through being too young – never got out of a training camp – but I have noticed that those who fought in France find it difficult to discover a groove. They are energetic enough, but they won't "stay put", as we say. Perhaps this Macnab is one of the unrooted. In your country, where everybody was soldiering, the case must be far more common.'

Mr Claybody announced that he was sick of hearing the war blamed for the average man's deficiencies. 'Every waster,' he said, 'makes an excuse of being shell-shocked. I'm very clear that the war twisted nothing in a man that wasn't twisted before.'

Sir Archie demurred. 'I don't know. I've seen some pretty bad cases of fellows who used to be as sane as a judge, and came home all shot to bits in their mind.'

'There are exceptions, of course. I'm speaking of the general rule. I turn away unemployables every day – good soldiers, maybe, but unemployable – and I doubt if they were ever anything else.'

Something in his tone annoyed Janet.

'You saw a lot of service, didn't you?' she asked meekly.

'No – worse luck! They made me stick at home and slave fourteen hours a day controlling cotton. It would have been a holiday for me to get into the trenches. But what I say is, a sane man usually remained sane. Look at Sir Archibald. We all know what a hectic time he had, and he hasn't turned a hair.'

'I'd like you to give me that in writing,' Sir Archie grinned. 'I've known people who thought I was rather cracked.'

'Anyhow, it made no difference to your nerves,' said Colonel Raden.

'I hope not. I expect that was because I enjoyed the beastly thing. Perhaps I'm naturally a bit of a bandit – like Miss Janet.'

'Perhaps you're John Macnab,' said that lady.

'Well, you've seen him and can judge.'

'No. I'll be a witness for the defence if you're ever accused. But you mustn't be offended at the idea. I suppose poor John Macnab is now crawling round Strathlarrig trying to find a gap between the gillies to cast a fly.'

'That's about the size of it,' Junius laughed. 'And there's twenty special correspondents in the neighbourhood cursing his name. If they get hold of him, they'll be savager than old Angus.'

Mr Bandicott, after calling his guests' attention to the merits of a hock which he had just acquired – it was a Johannisberg with the blue label – declared that in his belief the war would do good to English life, when the first ferment had died away.

'As a profound admirer of British institutions,' he said, 'I have sometimes thought that they needed a little shaking up and loosening. In America our classes are fluid. The rich man of today began life in a shack, and the next generation may return to it. It is the same with our professions. The man who starts in the law may pass to railway management, and end as the proprietor of a department store. Our belief is that it doesn't matter how often you change your trade before you're fifty. But an Englishman, once he settles in a profession, is fixed in it till the Day of Judgment, and in a few years he gets the mark of it so deep that he'd be a fish out of water in anything else. You can't imagine one of your big barristers doing anything else. No fresh fields and pastures new for them. It would be a crime against Magna Carta to break loose and try company-promoting or cornering the meat trade for a little change.'

Professor Babwater observed that in England they sometimes – in his view to the country's detriment – became politicians.

'That's the narrowest groove of all,' said Mr Bandicott with conviction. 'In this country, once you start in on politics you're fixed in a class and members of a hierarchy, and you've got to go on, however unfitted you may be for the job, because it's sort of high treason to weaken. In America a man tries politics as he tries other things, and if he finds the air of Washington uncongenial he quits, or tries newspapers, or Wall Street, or oil.'

'Or the penitentiary,' said Junius.

'And why not?' asked his father. 'I deplore criminal tendencies in any public man, but the possibility of such a downfall keeps the life human. It is very different in England. The respectability of your politicians is so awful that, when one of them backslides, every man of you combines to hush it up. There would be a revolution if the people got to suspect. Can you imagine a Cabinet Minister in the police court on a common vulgar charge?'

Professor Babwater said he could well imagine it – it was where most of them should be; but Colonel Raden agreed that the decencies had somehow to be preserved, even at the cost of a certain amount of humbug. 'But, excuse me,' he added, 'if I fail to see what good an occasional sentence of six months hard would do to public life.'

'I don't want it to happen,' said his host, who was inspired by his own Johannisberg, 'but I'd like to think it *could* happen. The permanent possibility of it would supple the minds of your legislators. It would do this old country a power of good if now and then a Cabinet Minister took to brawling and went to jail.'

It was a topic which naturally interested Sir Archie, but the theories of Mr Bandicott passed by him unheeded. For his seat at the table gave him a view of the darkening glen, and he was aware that on that stage a stirring drama was being enacted. His host could see nothing, for it was behind him; the Professor would have had to screw his head round; to Sir Archie alone was vouchsafed a clear prospect. Janet saw that he was gazing abstractedly out of the window, but she did not realise that his eyes were strained and every nerve in him excitedly alive . . .

For suddenly into his field of vision had darted a man. He was on the far side of the Larrig, running hard, and behind him, at a distance of some forty yards, followed another. At first he thought it was Leithen, but even in the dusk it was plain that it was a shorter man – younger, too, he looked, and of a notable activity. He was gaining on his pursuers, when the chase went out of sight . . . Then Sir Archie heard a far-away whistling, and would have given much to fling open the window and look out . . .

Five minutes passed and again the runner appeared – this time dripping wet and on the near side. Clearly not Leithen, for he wore a white sweater, which was a garment unknown to the Crask wardrobe. He must have been headed off up-stream, and had doubled back. That way lay danger, and Sir Archie longed to warn him, for his route would bring him close to the peopled appendages of Strathlarrig House . . . Even as he stared he saw what must mean the end, for two figures appeared for one second on the extreme left of his range of vision, and in front of the fugitive. He was running into their arms!

Sir Archie seized his glass of the blue-labelled Johannisberg, swallowed the winé the wrong way, and promptly choked.

When the Hispana crossed the Bridge of Larrig His Majesty's late Attorney-General was modestly concealed in a bush of broom on the Crask side, from which he could watch the sullen stretches of the Lang Whang. He was carefully dressed for the part in a pair of Wattie Lithgow's old trousers much too short for him, a waistcoat and jacket which belonged to Sime the butler and which had been made about the year 1890, and a vulgar flannel shirt borrowed from Shapp. He was innocent of a collar, he had not shaved for two days, and as he had forgotten to have his hair cut before leaving London his locks were of a disreputable length. Last, he had a shocking old hat of Sir Archie's from which the lining had long since gone. His hands were sun-burned and grubby, and he had removed his signet-ring. A light ten-foot greenheart rod lay beside him, already put up, and to the tapered line was fixed a tapered cast ending in a strange little cocked fly. As he waited he was busy oiling fly and line.

His glass showed him an empty haugh, save for the figure of Jimsie at the far end close to the Wood of Larrigmore. The sun-warmed waters of the river drowsed in the long dead stretches, curled at rare intervals by the faintest western breeze. The banks were crisp green turf, scarcely broken by a boulder, but five yards from them the moss began – a wilderness of hags and tussocks. Somewhere in its depths he knew that Benjie lay coiled like an adder, waiting on events.

Leithen's plan, like all great strategy, was simple. Everything depended on having Jimsie out of sight of the Lang Whang for half an hour. Given that, he believed he might kill a salmon. He had marked out a pool where in the evening fish were usually stirring, one of those irrational haunts which no piscatorial psychologist has ever explained. If he could fish fine and far, he might cover it from a spot below a high bank where only the top of his rod would be visible to watchers at a distance. Unfortunately, that spot was on the other side of the stream. With such tackle, landing a salmon would be a critical business, but there was one chance in ten that it might be accomplished; Benjie would be at hand to conceal the fish, and he himself would disappear silently into the Crask thickets. But every step bristled with horrid dangers. Jimsie might be faithful to his post – in which case it was hopeless; he might find the salmon dour, or a fish might break him in the landing, or Jimsie might return to find him brazenly tethered to forbidden game. It was no good thinking about it. On one thing he was decided: if he were caught, he would not try to escape. That would mean retreat in the direction of Crask, and an exploration of the Crask coverts would assuredly reveal what must at all costs be concealed. No. He would go quietly into captivity, and trust to his base appearance to be let off with a drubbing.

As he waited, watching the pools turn from gold to bronze, as the sun sank behind the Glenraden peaks, he suffered the inevitable reaction. The absurdities seemed huge as mountains, the difficulties innumerable as the waves of the sea. There remained less than an hour in which there would be sufficient light to fish – Jimsie was immovable (he had just lit his pipe and was sitting in mediation on a big stone) – every moment the Larrig waters were cooling with the chill of evening. Leithen consulted his watch, and found it half-past eight. He had lost his wrist-watch, and had brought his hunter, attached to a thin gold chain. That was foolish, so he slipped the chain from his button-hole and drew it through the arm-hole of his waistcoat.

Suddenly he rose to his feet, for things were happening at the far side of the haugh. Jimsie stood in an attitude of expectation – he seemed to be hearing something far up-stream. Leithen heard it too, the cry of excited men . . . Jimsie stood on one foot for a moment in doubt; then he turned and doubled towards the Wood of Larrigmore . . . The gallant Crossby had got to business and was playing hare to the hounds inside the park wall. If human nature had not changed, Leithen thought, the whole force would presently join the chase – Angus and Lennox and Jimsie and Dave and doubtless many volunteers. Heaven send fleetness and wind to the South London Harrier, for it was his duty to occupy the interest of every male in Strathlarrig till such time as he subsided with angry expostulation into captivity.

The road was empty, the valley was deserted, when Leithen raced across the bridge and up the south side of the river. It was not two hundred yards to his chosen stand, a spit of gravel below a high bank at the tail of a long pool. Close to the other bank, nearly thirty yards off, was the shelf where fish lay of an evening. He tested the water with his hand, and its temperature was at least 60°. His theory, which he had learned long ago from the aged Bostonian, was that under such conditions some subconscious memory revived in salmon of their early days as parr when they fed on surface insects, and that they could be made to take a dry fly.

He got out his line to the required length with half a dozen casts in the air, and then put his fly three feet above the spot where a salmon was wont to lie. It was a curious type of cast, which he had been practising lately in the early morning, for by an adroit check he made the fly alight in a curl, so that it floated for a second or two with the leader in a straight line away from it. In this way he believed that the most suspicious fish would see nothing to alarm him, nothing but a hapless insect derelict on the water.

Sir Archie had spoken truth in describing Leithen to Wattie Lithgow as an artist. His long, straight, delicate casts were art indeed. Like thistledown the fly dropped, like thistledown it floated over the head of the salmon, but like thistledown it was disregarded. There was indeed a faint stirring of curiosity. From where he stood Leithen could see that slight ruffling of the surface which means an observant fish . . .

Already ten minutes had been spent in this barren art. The crisis craved other measures.

His new policy meant a short line, so with infinite stealth and care Leithen waded up the side of the water, sometimes treading precarious ledges of peat, sometimes waist deep in mud and pond-weed, till he was within twenty feet of the fishing-ground. Here he had not the high bank for a shelter, and would have been sadly conspicuous to Jimsie, had that sentinel remained at his post. He crouched low and cast as before with the same curl just ahead of the chosen spot.

But now his tactics were different. So soon as the fly had floated past where he believed the fish to be, he sank it with a dexterous twist of the rod-point, possible only with a short line. The fly was no longer a winged thing; drawn away under water, it roused in the salmon early memories of succulent nymphs . . . At the first cast there was a slight swirl, which meant that a fish near the surface had turned to follow the lure. The second cast the line straightened and moved swiftly up-stream.

Leithen had killed in his day many hundreds of salmon – once in Norway a notable beast of fifty-five pounds. But no salmon he had ever hooked had stirred in his breast such excitement as this modest fellow of eight pounds. ' " 'Tis not so wide as a church-door," ' he reflected with Mercutio, ' "but 'twill suffice" – if I can only land him.' But a dry-fly cast and a ten-foot rod are a frail wherewithal for killing a fish against time. With his ordinary fifteen-footer and gut of moderate strength he could have brought the little salmon to grass in five minutes, but now there was immense risk of a break, and a break would mean that the whole enterprise had failed. He dared not exert pressure; on the other hand, he could not follow the fish except by making himself conspicuous on the greensward. Worst of all, he had at the best ten minutes for the job.

Thirty yards off an otter slid into the water. Leithen wished he was King of the Otters, as in the Highland tale, to summon the brute to his aid.

The ten minutes had lengthened to fifteen – nine hundred seconds of heart-disease – when, wet to the waist, he got his pocket-gaff into the salmon's side and drew it on to the spit of gravel where he had started fishing. A dozen times he thought he had lost, and once when the fish ran straight up the pool his line was carried out to its last yard of backing. He gave thanks to high Heaven, when, as he landed it, he observed that the fly had all but lost its hold and in another minute would have been free. By such narrow margins are great deeds accomplished.

He snapped the cast from the line and buried it in mud. Then cautiously he raised his head above the bank. The gloaming was gathering fast, and so far as he could see the haugh was still empty. Pushing his rod along the ground, he scrambled on to the turf.

Then he had a grievous shock. Jimsie had reappeared, and he was in full view of him. Moreover, there were two men on bicycles coming up the road, who, with the deplorable instinct of human nature, would be certain to join in any pursuit. He was on turf as short as a lawn, cumbered with a tell-tale rod and a poached salmon. The friendly hags were a dozen yards off, and before he could reach them his damning baggage would be noted.

At this supreme moment he had an inspiration, derived from the memory of the otter. To get out his knife, cut a ragged wedge from the fish, and roll it in his handkerchief was the work of five seconds. To tilt the rod over the bank so that it lay in the deep shadow was the work of three more . . . Jimsie had seen him, for a wild cry came down the stream, a cry which brought the cyclists off their machines and set them staring in his direction. Leithen dropped his gaff after the rod, and began running towards the Larrig bridge – slowly, limpingly, like a frightened man with no resolute purpose of escape. And as he ran he prayed that Benjie from the deeps of the moss had seen what had been done and drawn the proper inference.

It was a bold bluff, for he had decided to make the salmon evidence for, not against him. He hobbled down the bank, looking over his shoulder often as if in terror, and almost ran into the arms of the cyclists, who, warned by Jimsie's yells, were waiting to intercept him.He dodged them, however, and cut across to the road, for he had seen that Jimsie had paused and had noted the salmon lying blatantly on the sward, a silver splash in the twilight. Leithen doubled up the road as if going towards Strathlarrig, and Jimsie, the fleet of foot, did not catch up with him till almost on the edge of the Wood of Larrigmore. The cyclists, who had remounted, arrived at the same moment to find a wretched muddy tramp in the grip of a stalwart but breathless gillie.

'I tell ye I was daein' nae harm,' the tramp whined. 'I was walkin' up the water-side – there's nae law to keep a body frae walkin' up a water-side when there's nae fence – and I seen an auld otter killin' a saumon. The fish is there still to prove I'm no leein'.'

'There is a fush, but you wass thinkin' to steal the fush, and you would have had it in your breeks if I hadna seen you. That is poachin', ma man, and you will come up to Strathlarrig. The master said that anyone goin' near the watter was to be lockit up, and you will be lockit up. You can tell all the lees you like in the mornin'.'

Then a thought struck Jimsie. He wanted the salmon, for the subject of otters in the Larrig had been a matter of dispute between him and Angus, and here was evidence for his own view.

'Would you two gentlemen oblige me by watchin' this man while I rin back and get the fush? Bash him on the head if he offers to rin.'

The cyclists, who were journalists out to enjoy the evening air, willingly agreed, but Leithen showed no wish to escape. He begged a fag in a beggar's whine, and, since he seemed peaceable, the two kept a good distance for fear of infection. He stood making damp streaks in the dusty road, a pitiable specimen of humanity, for his original get-up was not improved by the liquefaction of his clothes and a generous legacy of slimy peat. He seemed to be nervous, which indeed he was, for if Benjie had not seized his chance he was utterly done, and if Jimsie should light upon his rod he was gravely compromised.

But when Jimsie returned in a matter of ten minutes he was empty-handed.

'I never kenned the like,' he proclaimed. 'That otter has come back and gotten the fush. Ach, the maleecious brute!'

The rest of Leithen's progress was not triumphant. He was conducted to the Strathlarrig lodge, where Angus, whose temper and wind had alike been ruined by the pursuit of Crossby, laid savage hands upon him, and frog-marched him to the back premises. The head-keeper scarcely heeded Jimsie's tale. 'Ach, ye poachin' va-aga-bond. It is the jyle ye'll get,' he roared, for Angus was in a mood which could only be relieved by violence of speech and action. Rumbling Gaelic imprecations, he hustled his prisoner into an outhouse, which had once been a larder and was now a supplementary garage, slammed and locked the door, and, as a final warning, kicked it viciously with his foot, as if to signify what awaited the culprit when the time came to sit on his case.

Sir Archie, if not a skeleton at the feast, was no better than a shadow. The fragment of drama which he had witnessed had rudely divorced his mind from the intelligent conversation of Mr Bandicott, he was no longer slightly irritated by Mr Claybody, he forgot even the attractions of Janet. What was going on in that twilit vale? Lady Maisie's Pool had still a shimmer of gold, but the woods were now purple and the waterside turf a dim amethyst, the colour of the darkening sky. All sound had ceased except the rare cry of a bird from the hill, and the hoot of a wandering owl . . . Crossby had beyond doubt been taken, but where was Leithen?

He was recalled to his surroundings by Janet's announcement that Mr Bandicott proposed to take them all in his car to the meeting at Muirtown.

'Oh, I say,' he pleaded, 'I'd much rather you didn't. I haven't a notion how to speak – no experience, you see – only about the third time I've opened my mouth in public. I'll make an awful ass of myself, and I'd much rather my friends didn't see it. If I know you're in the audience, Miss Janet, I won't be able to get a word out.'

Mr Bandicott was sympathetic. 'Take my advice, and do not attempt to write a speech and learn it by heart. Fill yourself with your subject, but do not prepare anything except the first sentence and the last. You'll find the words come easily when you once begin – if you have something you really want to say.'

'That's the trouble – I haven't. I'm goin' to speak about foreign policy, and I'm dashed if I can remember which treaty is which, and what the French are making a fuss about, or why the old Boche can't pay. And I keep on mixing up Poincaré and Mussolini . . . I'm goin' to write it all down, and if I'm stuck I'll fish out the paper and read it. I'm told there are fellows in the Cabinet who do that when they're cornered.'

'Don't stick too close to the paper,' the Colonel advised. 'The Highlander objects to sermons read to him, and he may not like a read speech.'

'Whatever he does I'm sure Sir Archibald will be most enlightening,' Mr Bandicott said politely. 'Also I want to hear

Lord Lamancha. We think rather well of that young man in America. How do you rate him here?'

Mr Claybody, as a habitant of the great world, replied. 'Very high in his own line. He's the old-fashioned type of British statesman, and people trust him. The trouble about him and his kind is that they're a little too far removed from the ordinary man – they've been too cosseted and set on a pedestal all their lives. They don't know how to handle democracy. You can't imagine Lamancha rubbing shoulders with Tom, Dick and Harry.'

'Oh, come!' Sir Archie broke in. 'In the war he started as a captain in a yeomanry regiment, and he commanded a pretty rough Australian push in Palestine. His men fairly swore by him.'

'I daresay,' said the other coldly. 'The war doesn't count for my argument, and Australians are not quite what I mean.'

The butler, who was offering liqueurs, was seen to speak confidentially to Junius, who looked towards his father, made as if to speak, and thought better of it. The elder Mr Bandicott was once more holding the table.

'My archaeological studies,' he said, 'and my son's devotion to sport are apt to circumscribe the interest of my visits to this country. I do not spend more than a couple of days in London, and when I am there the place is empty. Sometimes I regret that I have not attempted to see more of English society in recent years, for there are many figures in it I would like to meet. There are some acquaintances, too, that I should be delighted to revive. Do you know Sir Edward Leithen, Mr Claybody? He was recently, I think, the British Attorney-General.'

Mr Claybody nodded. 'I know him very well. We have just briefed him in a big case.'

'Sir Edward Leithen visited us two years ago as the guest of our Bar Association. His address was one of the most remarkable I have ever listened to. It was on John Marshall – the finest tribute ever paid to that great man, and one which I venture to say no American could have equalled. I had very little talk with him, but what I had impressed me profoundly with the breadth of his outlook and the powers of his mind. Yes, I should like to meet Sir Edward Leithen again.'

The company had risen and were moving towards the drawing-room.

'Now I wonder,' Mr Claybody was saying. 'I heard that Leithen was somewhere in Scotland. I wonder if I could get him up for a few days to Haripol. Then I could bring him over here.'

An awful joy fell upon Sir Archie's soul. He realised anew the unplumbed preposterousness of life.

Ere they reached the drawing-room Junius took Agatha aside.

'Look here, Miss Agatha, I want you to help me. The gillies have been a little too active. They've gathered in some wretched hobo they found looking at the river, and they've annexed a journalist who stuck his nose inside the gates. It's the journalist that's worrying me. From his card he seems to be rather a swell in his way – represents the *Monitor* and writes for my father's New York paper. He gave the gillies a fine race for their money, and now he's sitting cursing in the garage and vowing every kind of revenge. It won't do to antagonise the Press, so we'd better let him out and grovel to him, if he wants apologies . . . The fact is, we're not in a very strong position, fending off the newspapers from Harald Blacktooth because of this ridiculous John Macnab. If you could let the fellow out it would be casting oil upon troubled waters. You could smooth him down far better than me.'

'But what about the other? A hobo, you say! That's a tramp, isn't it?'

'Oh, tell Angus to let him out too. Here are the keys of both garages. I don't want to turn this place into a lock-up. Angus won't be pleased, but we have to keep a sharp watch for John Macnab tomorrow, and it's bad tactics in a campaign to cumber yourself with prisoners.'

The two threaded mysterious passages and came out into a moonlit stable-yard. Junius handed the girl a great electric torch. 'Tell the fellow we eat dirt for our servants' officiousness. Offer him supper, and – I tell you what – ask him to lunch the day after tomorrow. No, that's Muirtown day. Find out his address and we'll write to him and give him first chop at the Viking. Blame it all on the gillies.'

Agatha unlocked the door of the big garage and to her surprise found it brilliantly lit with electric light. Mr Crossby was sitting in the driver's seat of a large motor-car, smoking a pipe and composing a story for his paper. At the sight of Agatha he descended hastily.

'We're so sorry,' said the girl. 'It's all been a stupid mistake. But, you know, you shouldn't have run away. Mr Bandicott had to make rules to keep off poachers, and you ought to have stopped and explained who you were.'

To this charming lady in the grass-green gown Mr Crossby's manner was debonair and reassuring.

'No apology is needed. It wasn't in the least the gillies' blame. I wanted some exercise, and I had my fun with them. One of the young ones has a very pretty turn of speed. But I oughtn't to have done it – I quite see that – with everybody here on edge about this John Macnab. Have I your permission to go?'

'Indeed you have. Mr Bandicott asked me to apologise most humbly. You're quite free unless – unless you'd like to have supper before you go.'

Mr Crossby excused himself, and did not stay upon the order of his going. He knew nothing of the fate of his colleague, and hoped that he might pick up news from Benjie in the neighbourhood of the Wood of Larrigmore.

The other garage stood retired in the lee of a clump of pines – a rude, old-fashioned place, which generally housed the station lorry. Agatha, rather than face the disappointed Angus, decided to complete the task of jail-delivery herself. She had trouble with the lock, and when the door opened she looked into a pit of darkness scarcely lightened by the outer glow of moonshine. She flashed the torch into the interior and saw, seated on a stack of petrol tins, the figure of the tramp.

Leithen, who had been wondering how he was to find a bed in that stony place, beheld the apparition with amazement. He guessed that it was one of the Miss Radens, for he knew that they were dining at Strathlarrig. As he stood sheepishly before her his wits suffered a dislocation which drove out of his head the remembrance of the part he had assumed.

'Mr Bandicott sent me to tell you that you can go away,' the girl said.

'Thank you very much,' said Leithen in his ordinary voice.

Now in the scramble up the river bank and in the rough handling of Angus his garments had become disarranged, and his watch had swung out of his pocket. In adjusting it in the garage he had put it back in its normal place, so that the chain showed on Sime's ancient waistcoat. From it depended one of those squat little gold shields which are the badge of athletic prowess at a famous school. As he stood in the light of her torch Agatha noted this shield, and knew what it signified. Also his tone when he spoke had startled her.

'Oh,' she cried, 'you were at Eton?'

Leithen was for a moment nonplussed. He thought of a dozen lies, and then decided on qualified truth.

'Yes,' he murmured shamefacedly. 'Long ago I was at Eton.'

The girl flushed with embarrassed sympathy.

'What – what brought you to this?' she murmured.

'Folly,' said Leithen, recovering himself. 'Drink and suchlike. I have had a lot of bad luck but I've mostly myself to blame.'

'You're only a tramp now?' Angels might have envied the melting sadness of her voice.

'At present. Sometimes I get a job, but I can't hold it down.' Leithen was warming to his work, and his tones were a subtle study in dilapidated gentility.

'Can't anything be done?' Agatha asked, twining her pretty hands.

'Nothing,' was the dismal answer. 'I'm past helping. Let me go, please, and forget you ever saw me.'

'But can't papa . . . won't you tell me your name or where we can find you?'

'My present name is not my own. Forget about me, my dear young lady. The life isn't so bad . . . I'm as happy as I deserve to be. I want to be off, for I don't like to stumble upon gentlefolks.'

She stood aside to let him pass, noting the ruin of his clothes, his dirty unshaven face, the shameless old hat that he raised to her. Then, melancholy and reflective, she returned to Junius. She could not give away one of her own class, so, when Junius asked her about the tramp, she only shrugged her white shoulders. 'A miserable creature. I hope Angus wasn't too rough with him. He looked as if a puff of wind would blow him to pieces.'

* * *

Ten minutes later Leithen, having unobtrusively climbed the park wall and so escaped the attention of Mactavish at the lodge, was trotting at a remarkable pace for a tramp down the road to the Larrig Bridge. Once on the Crask side, he stopped to reconnoitre. Crossby called softly to him from the covert, and with Crossby was Benjie.

'I've gotten the saumon,' said the latter, 'and your rod and gaff too. Hae ye the bit you howkit out o' the fush?'

Leithen produced his bloody handkerchief.

'Now for supper, Benjie, my lad,' he cried. 'Come along, Crossby, and we'll drink the health of John Macnab.'

The journalist shook his head. 'I'm off to finish my story. The triumphant return of Harald Blacktooth is going to convulse these islands tomorrow.'

EIGHT

Sir Archie is Instructed in the Conduct of Life

EARLY NEXT MORNING, when the great door of Strathlarrig House was opened, and the maids had begun their work, Oliphant, the butler – a stately man who had been trained in a ducal family – crossed the hall to reconnoitre the outer world. There he found an under-housemaid nursing a strange package which she averred she had found on the doorstep. It was some two feet long, swathed in brown paper, and attached to its string was a letter inscribed to Mr Junius Bandicott.

The parcel was clammy and Oliphant handled it gingerly. He cut the cord, disentangled the letter, and revealed an oblong of green rushes bound with string. The wrapping must have been insecure, for something forthwith slipped from the rushes and flopped on the marble floor, revealing to Oliphant's disgusted eyes a small salmon, blue and stiff in death.

At that moment Junius, always an early bird, came whistling downstairs. So completely was he convinced of the inviolability of the Strathlarrig waters that the spectacle caused him no foreboding.

'What are you flinging fish about for, Oliphant?' he asked cheerfully.

The butler presented him with the envelope. He opened it and extracted a dirty half sheet of notepaper, on which was printed in capitals 'With the compliments of John Macnab.'

Amazement, chagrin, amusement followed each other on Junius's open countenance. Then he picked up the fish and marched out-of-doors shouting 'Angus' at the top of a notably powerful voice. The sound brought the scared face of Professor Babwater to his bedroom window.

Angus, who had been up since four, appeared from Lady Maisie's Pool, where he had been contemplating the waters. His vigil had not improved his appearance or his temper, for his eye was red and choleric and his beard was wild as a mountain goat's. He cast one look at the salmon, surmised the truth, and held up imploring hands to Heaven.

'John Macnab!' said Junius sternly. 'What have you got to say to that?'

Angus had nothing audible to say. He was handling the fish with feverish hands and peering at its jaws, and presently under his fingers a segment fell out.

'That fush was cleekit,' observed Lennox, who had come up. 'It was never catched with a flee.'

'Ye're a leear,' Angus roared. 'Just tak a look at the mouth of it. There's the mark of the huke, ye gommeril. The fush was took wi' a rod and line.'

'You may reckon it was,' observed Junius. 'I trust John Macnab to abide by the rules of the game.'

Suddenly light seemed to break in on Angus's soul. He bellowed for Jimsie, who was placidly making his way towards the group at the door, lighting his pipe as he went.

'Look at that, James Mackenzie. Aye, look at it. Feast your een on it. You wass tellin' me there wass otters in the Larrig and I said there wass not. You wass tellin' me there wass an otter had a fush last night at the Lang Whang. There's your otter and be damned to ye!'

Jimsie, slow of comprehension, rubbed his eyes.

'Where wass you findin' the fush? Aye, it's the one I seen last night. That otter must be wrang in the heid.'

'It is not wrang in the heid. It's you that are wrang in the heid, James Mackenzie. The otter is a ver-ra clever man, and its name will be John Macnab.' Slowly enlightenment dawned on Jimsie's mind.

'He wass the tramp,' he ingeminated. 'He wass the tramp.'

'And he's still lockit up,' Angus cried joyfully. 'Wait till I get my hands on him.' He was striding off for the garage when a word from Junius held him back.

'You won't find him there. I gave orders last night to let him go. You know, Angus, you told me he was only a tramp that had been seen walking up the river.'

'We will catch him yet,' cried the vindictive head-keeper. 'Get you on your bicycle, Jimsie, and away after him. He'll be on the Muirtown road . . . There's just the one road he can travel.'

'No, you don't,' said Junius. 'I don't want him here. He has beaten us fairly in a match of wits, and the business is finished.'

'But the thing's no possible,' Jimsie moaned. 'The skeeliest fisher would not take a saumon in the Lang Whang with a flee . . . And I wasna away many meenutes . . . And the tramp was a poor shilpit body – not like a fisher or any kind of gentleman at all, at all . . . And he hadna a rod . . . The thing's no possible.'

'Well, who else could it be?'

'I think it was the Deevil.'

Jimsie, cross-examined, went over the details of his evening's experience.

'The journalist may have been in league with him – or he may not,' Junius reflected. 'Anyway, I'll tackle Mr Crossby. I want to find out what I can about this remarkable sportsman.'

'You will not find out anything at all, at all,' said Angus morosely. 'For I tell ye; sir, Jimsie is right in one thing – Macnab is not a man – he is the Deevil.'

'Then we needn't be ashamed of being beat by him . . . Look here, you men. We've lost, but you've had an uncomfortable time these last twenty-four hours. And I'm going to give you what I promised you if we won out. I reckon the market price of salmon is not more than fifty cents a pound. Macnab has paid about thirty dollars a pound for this fish, so we've a fair margin on the deal.'

Mr Acheson Bandicott received the news with composure, if not with relief. Now he need no longer hold the correspondents at arm's length but could summon them to his presence and enlarge on Harald Blacktooth. His father's equanimity cast whatever balm was needed upon Junius's wounded pride, and presently he saw nothing in the affair but comedy. His thoughts turned to Glenraden. It might be well for him to announce in person that the defences of Strathlarrig had failed.

On his way he called at the post-office where Agatha had told him that Crossby was lodging. He wanted a word with the journalist, who clearly must have been *particeps criminis*, and as he could offer as bribe the first full tale of Harald Blacktooth (to be unfolded before the other correspondents arrived for luncheon) he hoped to acquire a story in return. But, according to the post-mistress, Mr Crossby had gone. He had sat up most of the night writing, and, without waiting for breakfast, had paid his bill, strapped on his ruck-sack and departed on his bicycle.

Junius found the Raden family on the lawn, and with them Archie Roylance.

'Got up early to go over my speech for tomorrow,' the young man explained. 'I'm gettin' the dashed thing by heart – only way to avoid regrettable incidents. I started off down the hill repeatin' my eloquence, and before I knew I was at Glenraden gates, so I thought I'd come in and pass the time of day . . . Jolly interestin' dinner last night, Bandicott. I liked your old Professor . . . Any news of John Macnab?'

'There certainly is. He has us beat to a frazzle. This morning there was a salmon on the doorstep presented with his compliments.'

The effect of this announcement was instant and stupendous. The Colonel called upon his gods. 'Not killed fair? It's a stark impossibility, sir. You had the water guarded like the Bank of England.' Archie expressed like suspicions; Agatha was sad and sympathetic, Janet amused and covertly joyful.

'I reckon it was fair enough fishing,' Junius went on. 'I've been trying to puzzle the thing out, and this is what I made of it. Macnab was in league with one of those pressmen, who started out to trespass inside the park and drew off all the watchers in pursuit, including the man at the Lang Whang. He had them hunting for about half an hour, and in that time Macnab killed his fish . . . He must be a dandy at the game, too, to get a salmon in that dead water . . . Jimsie – that's the man who was supposed to watch the Lang Whang – returned before he could get away with the beast, so what does the fellow do but dig a bit out of the fish and leave it on the bank, while he lures Jimsie to chase him. Jimsie saw the fish and put it down to an otter, and by and by caught the man up the road. There must have been an accomplice in hiding, for when Jimsie went back to pick up the salmon it had disappeared. The fellow, who looked like a hobo, was shut up in a garage, and after dinner we let him go, for we had nothing against him, and now he is rejoicing somewhere at our simplicity . . . It was a mighty clever bit of work, and I'm not ashamed to be beaten by that class of artist. I hoped to get hold of the pressman and find out something, but the pressman seems to have leaked out of the landscape.'

'Was that tramp John Macnab?' Agatha asked in an agitated voice.

'None other. You let him out, Miss Agatha. What was he like? I can't get proper hold of Jimsie's talk.'

'Oh, I should have guessed,' the girl lamented. 'For, of

course, I saw he was a gentleman. He was in horrible old clothes, but he had an Eton shield on his watch-chain. He seemed to be ashamed to remember it. He said he had come down in the world – through drink!'

Archie struggled hard with the emotions evoked by this description of an abstemious personage currently believed to be making an income of forty thousand pounds.

'Then we've both seen him,' Janet cried. 'Describe him, Agatha. Was he youngish and big, and fair-haired, and sunburnt? Had he blue eyes?'

'No-o. He wasn't like that. He was about papa's height, and rather slim, I think. He was very dirty and hadn't shaved, but I should say he was sallow, and his eyes – well, they were certainly not blue.'

'Are you certain? You only saw him in the dark.'

'Yes, quite certain. I had a big torch which lit up his whole figure. Now I come to think of it, he had a striking face – he looked like somebody very clever – a judge perhaps. That should have made me suspicious, but I was so shocked to see such a downfall that I didn't think about it.'

Janet looked wildly around her. 'Then there are two John Macnabs.'

'Angus thinks he is the Devil,' said Junius.

'It looks as if he were a syndicate,' said Archie, who felt that some remark was expected of him.

'Well, I'm not complaining,' said Junius. 'And now we're off the stage, and can watch the play from the boxes. I hope you won't be shocked, sir, but I wouldn't break my heart if John Macnab got the goods from Haripol.'

'By Gad, no!' cried the Colonel. ' 'Pon my soul, if I could get in touch with the fellow I'd offer to help him – though he'd probably be too much of a sportsman to let me. That young Claybody wants taking down a peg or two. He's the most insufferably assured young prig I ever met in my life.'

'He looked the kind of chap who might turn nasty,' Sir Archie observed.

'How do you mean?' Junius asked. 'Get busy with a gun – that sort of thing?'

'Lord, no. The Claybodys are not likely to start shootin'. But they're as rich as Jews, and they're capable of hirin' prize-fighters or puttin' a live wire round the forest. Or I'll tell you what they might do – they might drive every beast on Haripol over the marches and keep 'em out for three days. It would wreck the ground for the season, but they wouldn't mind that – the old man can't get up the hills and the young 'un don't want to.'

'Agatha, my dear,' said her father, 'we ought to return the Claybody's call. Perhaps Mr Junius would drive us over there in his car this afternoon. For, of course, you'll stay to luncheon, Bandicott – and you, too, Roylance.'

Sir Archie stayed to luncheon; he also stayed to tea; and between these meals he went through a surprising experience. For, after the others had started for Haripol, Janet and he drifted aimlessly towards the Raden bridge and then upward through the pinewoods on the road to Carnmore. The strong sun was tempered by the flickering shade of the trees, and, as the road wound itself out of the crannies of the woods to the bare ridges, light wandering winds cooled the cheek, and, mingled with the fragrance of heather and the rooty smell of bogs, came a salty freshness from the sea. The wide landscape was as luminous as April – a bad presage for the weather, since the Haripol peaks, which in September should have been dim in a mulberry haze, stood out sharp like cameos. The two did not talk much, for they were getting beyond the stage where formal conversation is felt to be necessary. Sir Archie limped along at a round pace, which was easily matched by the girl at his side. Both would instinctively halt now and then, and survey the prospect without speaking, and both felt that these pregnant silences were bringing them very near to one another.

At last the track ran out in screes, and from a bald summit they were looking down on the first of the Carnmore corries. Janet seated herself on a mossy ledge of rock and looked back into the Raden glen, which from that altitude had the appearance of an enclosed garden. The meadows of the lower haugh lay green in the sun, the setting of pines by some freak of light was a dark and cloudy blue, and the little castle rose in the midst of the trees with a startling brightness like carven marble. The picture was as exquisite and strange as an illumination in a missal.

'Gad, what a place to live in!' Sir Archie exclaimed.

The girl, who had been gazing at the scene with her chin in her hands, turned on him eyes which were suddenly wistful and rather sad. As contrasted with her sister's, Janet's face had a fine hard finish which gave it a brilliancy like an eager boy's. But now a cloud-wrack had been drawn over the sun.

'We've lived there,' she said, 'since Harald Blacktooth – at least papa says so. But the end is very near now. We are the last of the Radens. And that is as it should be, you know.'

'I'm hanged if I see that,' Sir Archie began, but the girl interrupted.

'Yes, it is as it should be. The old life of the Highlands is going, and people like ourselves must go with it. There's no reason why we should continue to exist. We've long ago lost our justification.'

'D'you mean to say that fellows like Claybody have more right to be here?'

'Yes. I think they have, because they're fighters and we're only survivals. They will disappear, too, unless they learn their lesson . . . You see, for a thousand years we have been going on here, and other people like us, but we only endured because we were alive. We have the usual conventional motto on our coat of arms – *Pro Deo et Rege* – a Heralds' College invention. But our Gaelic motto was very different – it was "Sons of Dogs, come and I will give you flesh." As long as we lived up to that we flourished, but as soon as we settled down and went to sleep and became *rentiers* we were bound to decay . . . My cousins at Glenaicill were just the same. Their motto was "What I have I hold," and while they remembered it they were great people. But when they stopped holding they went out like a candle, and the last of them is now living in St Malo and a Lancashire cotton-spinner owns the place . . . When we had to fight hard for our possessions all the time, and give flesh to the sons of dogs who were our clan, we were strong men and women. There was a Raden with Robert Bruce – he fell with Douglas in the pilgrimage to the Holy Sepulchre – and a Raden died beside the King at Flodden – and Radens were in everything that happened in the old days in Scotland and France. But civilisation killed them – they couldn't adapt themselves to it. Somehow the fire went out of the blood, and they became vegetables. Their only claim was the right of property, which is no right at all.'

'That's what the Bolsheviks say,' said the puzzled Sir Archie.

'Then I'm a Bolshevik. Nobody in the world today has a right to anything which he can't justify. That's not politics, it's the way nature works. Whatever you've got – rank or power or fame or money – you've got to justify it, and keep on justifying it, or go under. No law on earth can buttress up a thing which nature means to decay.'

'D'you know that sounds to me pretty steep doctrine?'

'No, it isn't. It isn't doctrine, and it isn't politics, it's common sense. I don't mean that we want some silly government redistributing everybody's property. I mean that people should realise that whatever they've got they hold under a perpetual challenge, and they are bound to meet that challenge. Then we'll have living creatures instead of mummies.'

Sir Archie stroked his chin thoughtfully. 'I daresay there's a lot in that. But what would Colonel Raden say to it?'

'He would say I was a bandit. And yet he would probably agree with me in the end. Agatha wouldn't, of course. She adores decay – sad old memories and lost causes and all the rest of it. She's a sentimentalist, and she'll marry Junius and go to America, where everybody is sentimental, and be the sweetest thing in the Western hemisphere, and live happy ever after. I'm quite different. I believe I'm kind, but I'm certainly hard-hearted. I suppose it's Harald Blacktooth coming out.'

Janet had got off her perch, and was standing a yard from Sir Archie, her hat in her hand and the light wind ruffling her hair. The young man, who had no skill in analysing his feelings, felt obscurely that she fitted most exquisitely into the picture of rock and wood and water, that she was, in very truth, a part of his clean elemental world of the hill-tops.

'What about yourself?' she asked. 'In the words of Mr Bandicott, are you going to make good?'

She asked the question with such an air of frank comradeship that Sir Archie was in no way embarrassed. Indeed he was immensely delighted.

'I hope so,' he said. 'But I don't know . . . I'm a bit of a slacker. There doesn't seem much worth doing since the war.'

'What nonsense! You find a thousand things worth doing, but they're not enough – and they're not big enough. Do you mean to say you want to hang up your hat at your age and go to sleep? You need to be challenged.'

'I expect I do,' he murmured.

'Well, *I* challenge you. You're fit and you're young, and you did extraordinarily well in the war, and you've hosts of friends, and – and – you're well off, aren't you?'

'Pretty fair. You see, I had a long minority, and – oh yes, I've far more money than I want.'

'There you are. I challenge you. You're bound to justify what you've got. I won't have you idling away your life till you end as the kind of lean brown old gentleman in a bowler hat that one sees at Newmarket. It's a very nice type, but it's not good enough for you, and I won't have it. You must not be a dilettante pottering about with birds and a little sport and a little politics.'

Sir Archie had been preached at occasionally in his life, but never quite in this way. He was preposterously pleased and also a little solemnised.

'I'm quite serious about politics.'

'I wonder,' said Janet, smiling. 'I don't mean scraping into Parliament, but real politics – putting the broken pieces together, you know. Papa and the rest of our class want to treat politics like another kind of property in which they have a vested interest. But it won't do – not in the world we live in today. If you're going to do any good you must feel the challenge and be ready to meet it. And then you must become yourself a challenger. You must be like John Macnab.'

Sir Archie stared.

'I don't mean that I want you to make poaching wagers like John. You can't live in a place and play those tricks with your neighbours. But I want you to follow what Mr Bandicott would call the 'John Macnab proposition.' It's so good for everybody concerned. Papa has never had so much fun out of his forest as in the days he was repelling invasion, and even Mr Junius found a new interest in the Larrig . . . I'm all for property, if you can defend it; but there are too many fatted calves in the world.'

Sir Archie suddenly broke into loud laughter.

'Most people tell me I'm too mad to do much good in anything. But you say I'm not mad enough. Well, I'm all for challengin' the fatted calves, but I don't fancy that's the road that leads to the Cabinet. More like the jail, with a red flag firmly clenched in my manly hand.'

The girl laughed too. 'Papa says that the man who doesn't give a damn for anybody can do anything he likes in the world. Most people give many damns for all kinds of foolish things. Mr Claybody, for example – his smart friends, like Lord Lamancha and the Attorney-General – what is his name? –

Leithen? – and his silly little position, and his father's new peerage. But you're not like that. I believe that all wisdom consists in caring immensely for the few right things and not caring a straw about the rest.'

Had anyone hinted to Sir Archie that a young woman on a Scots mountain could lecture him gravely on his future and still remain a ravishing and adorable thing he would have dismissed the suggestion with incredulity. At the back of his head he had that fear of women as something mysterious and unintelligible which belongs to a motherless and sisterless childhood, and a youth spent almost wholly in the company of men. He had immense compassion for a sex which seemed to him to have a hard patch to hoe in the world, and this pitifulness had always kept him from any conduct which might harm a woman. His numerous fancies had been light and transient like thistledown, and his heart had been wholly unscathed. Fear that he might stumble into marriage had made him as shy as a woodcock – a fear not without grounds, for a friend had once proposed to write a book called *Lives of the Hunted*, with a chapter on Archie. Wherefore, his hour having come, he had cascaded into love with desperate completeness, and with the freshness of a mind unstaled by disillusion . . . All he knew was that a miraculous being had suddenly flooded his world with a new radiance, and was now opening doors and inviting him to dazzling prospects. He felt at once marvellously confident, and supremely humble. Never had mistress a more docile pupil.

They wandered back to the house, and Janet gave him tea in a room full of faded chintzes and Chinese-Chippendale mirrors. Then, when the sun was declining behind the Carnmore peaks, Sir Archie at last took his leave. His head was in a happy confusion, but two ideas rose above the surge – he would seize the earliest chance of asking Janet to marry him, and by all his gods he must not make a fool of himself at Muirtown. She had challenged him, and he had accepted the challenge; he must make it good before he could become in turn a challenger. It may be doubtful if Sir Archie had any very clear notions on the matter, but he was aware that he had received an inspiration, and that somehow or other everything was now to be different . . . First for that confounded speech. He strove to recollect the sentences which had followed each other so trippingly during his morning's walk. But he could not concentrate his mind. Peace treaties and German reparations and the recognition of Russia flitted from him like a rapid film, to be replaced by a 'close-up' of a girl's face. Besides, he wanted to sing, and when song flows to the lips consecutive thought is washed out of the brain.

In this happy and exalted mood, dedicate to great enterprises of love and service, Sir Archie entered the Crask smoking-room, to be brought heavily to earth by the sordid business of John Macnab.

Leithen was there, reading a volume of Sir Walter Scott with an air of divine detachment. Lamancha, very warm and dishevelled, was endeavouring to quench his thirst with a large whisky-and-soda; Palliser-Yeates, also the worse for wear, lay in an attitude of extreme fatigue on a sofa; Crossby, who had sought sanctuary at Crask, was busy with the newspapers which had just arrived, while Wattie Lithgow stood leaning on his crook staring into vacancy, like a clown from some stage Arcadia.

'Where on earth have you been all day, Archie?' Lamancha asked sternly.

'I walked over to Glenraden and stayed to luncheon. They're all hot on your side there – Bandicott too. There's a general feelin' that young Claybody wants takin' down a peg.'

'Much good that will do us. John and Wattie and I have been crawling all day round the Haripol marches. It's pretty clear what they'll do – you think so, Wattie?'

'Alan Macnicol is not altogether a fule. Aye, I ken fine what they'll dae.'

'Clear the beasts off the ground?' Archie suggested.

'No,' said Lamancha. 'Move them into the Sanctuary, and the Sanctuary is in the very heart of the forest – between Sgurr Mor and Sgurr Dearg at the head of the Reascuill. It won't take many men to watch it. And the mischief is that Haripol is the one forest where it can be done quite simply. It's so infernally rough that if the deer were all over it I would back myself to get a shot with a fair chance of removing the beast, but if every stag is inside an inner corral it will be the devil's own business to get within a thousand yards of them – let alone shift the carcass.'

'If the wind keeps in the west,' said Wattie, 'It is a manifest impossibeelity. If it was in the north there would be a verra wee sma' chance. All other airts are hopeless. We maun just possess our souls in patience, and see what the day brings forth . . . I'll awa and mak arrangements for the morn.'

Lamancha nodded after the retreating figure.

'He is determined to go to Muirtown tomorrow. Says you promised that he should be present when you made your first bow in public, and that he has arranged with Shapp to drive him in the Ford . . . But about Haripol. This idea of Wattie's – and I expect it's right – makes the job look pretty desperate. I had worked out a very sound scheme to set my Lord Claybody guessing – similar to John's Glenraden plan but more ingenious; but what's the use of bluff if every beast is snug in an upper corrie with a cordon of Claybody's men round it? Wattie says that Haripol is fairly crawling with gillies.'

Crossby raised his head from his journalistic researches. 'The papers have got my story all right, I see. The first one, I mean – the "Return of Harald Blacktooth." They've featured it well, too, and I expect the evening papers are now going large on it. But it's nothing to what the second will be tomorrow morning. I'm prepared to bet that our Scottish Tutankhamen drops out of the running, and that the Press of this land thinks of nothing for a week except the salmon Sir Edward got last night. It's the silly season, remember!'

Lamancha's jaw dropped. 'Crossby, I don't want to dash your natural satisfaction, but I'm afraid you've put me finally in the cart. If the public wakes up and takes an interest in Haripol, I may as well chuck in my hand.'

'I wasn't such an ass as to mention Haripol,' said the correspondent.

'No, but of course it will get out. Some of your journalistic colleagues will hear of it at Strathlarrig, and, finding that the interest has departed from Harald Blacktooth, will make a bee-line for Haripol. Your success, which I don't grudge you, will be my ruin. In any case the Claybodys will be put on their mettle, for, if they are beaten by John Macnab, they know they'll be a public laughing-stock . . . What sort of fellow is young Claybody, Archie?'

'Bit shaggy about the heels. Great admirer of yours. Ask Ned – he said he knew Ned very well.'

Leithen raised his eyes from *Redgauntlet*. 'Never heard of the fellow in my life.'

'Oh yes, you have. He said he had briefed you in a big case.'

'Well, you can't expect me to know all my clients any more

than John knows the customers of his little bank.' Leithen relapsed into Sir Walter.

'I'm going to have a bath.' Lamancha rose and cautiously relaxed his weary limbs. 'I seem to be in for the most imbecile escapade in history with about one chance in a billion. That's Wattie's estimate, and he knows what a billion is, which I don't.'

'What about dropping it?' Archie suggested; for, though he was sworn to the 'John Macnab proposition,' he was growing very nervous about this particular manifestation. 'Young Claybody is an ugly customer, and we don't want the thing to end in bad blood. Besides, you're cured already – you told me so yesterday.'

'That's true,' said Lamancha, who was engaged in tossing with Palliser-Yeates for the big bath. 'I'm cured. I never felt keener in my life. I'm so keen that there's nothing on earth you could offer me which would keep me away from Haripol . . . You win, John. Gentlemen of the Guard, fire first, and don't be long about it. I can't stretch myself in that drain-pipe that Archie calls his second bathroom.'

Dinner was a cheerful meal, for Mr Crossby had much to say, Lamancha was in high spirits, and Leithen had the benignity of the successful warrior. But the host was silent and abstracted. He managed to banish Haripol from his mind, but he thought of Janet, he thought of Janet's sermon, and in feverish intervals he tried to think of his speech for the morrow. A sense of a vast insecurity had come upon him, of a shining goal which grew brighter the more he reflected upon it, but of some awkward hurdles to get over first.

Afterwards, when the talk was of Haripol, he turned to the newspapers to restore him to the world of stern realities. He did not read that masterpiece of journalism, Crossby's story, but he found a sober comfort in *The Times'* leading articles and in the political notes. He felt himself a worker among *flâneurs*.

'Here's something about you, Charles,' he said. 'This paper says that political circles are looking forward with great interest to your speech at Muirtown. Says it will be the first important utterance since Parliament rose, and that you are expected to deal with Poincaré's speech at Rheims and a letter by a Boche whose name I can't pronounce.'

'Political circles will be disappointed,' said Lamancha, 'for I haven't read them. Montgomery is taking all the boxes and I haven't heard from the office for three weeks. I can't be troubled with newspapers in the Highlands.'

'Then what are you goin' to say tomorrow?' Archie demanded anxiously.

'I'll think of some rot. Don't worry, old fellow. Muirtown is a second-class show compared to Haripol.'

Archie was really shocked. He was envious of a man who could treat thus cavalierly a task which affected him with horrid forebodings, and also scandalised at the levity of his leaders. It seemed to him that Lamancha needed some challenging. Finding no comfort in his company, he repaired to bed, where healthful sleep was slow in visiting him. He repeated his speech to himself, but it would persist in getting tangled up with Janet's sermon and his own subsequent reflections, so that, when at last he dropped off, it was into a world of ridiculous dreams where a dreadful composite figure – Poincarini or Mussolinaré – sat heavily on his chest.

NINE

Sir Archie Instructs his Countrymen

CROSSBY WAS RIGHT in his forecast. The sudden interest in the Scottish Tutankhamen did not survive the revelation of Harald Blacktooth's reincarnation as John Macnab. The twenty correspondents, after lunching heavily with Mr Bandicott, had been shown the relics of the Viking and had heard their significance expounded by their host and Professor Babwater; each had duly despatched his story, but before night-fall each was receiving urgent telegrams from his paper clamouring for news, not of Harald, but of Harald's successor. Crossby's tale of the frustrated attempt on the Glenraden deer had intrigued several million readers – it was the silly season, remember – and his hint of the impending raid on the Strathlarrig salmon had stirred a popular interest vowed to any lawless mystery and any competitive sport. In the doings of John Macnab were blended the splendid uncertainty of a well-matched prize fight and the delicious obscurity of crime. Next morning the news of John's victory at Strathlarrig was received by the several million readers with an enthusiasm denied to the greater matters of public conduct. John Macnab became a slogan for the newsboy, a flaming legend for bills and headlines, a subject of delighted talk at every breakfast-table. Never had there been a more famous eight-pound salmon since fish first swam in the sea.

It was a cold grey morning when Lamancha and Archie left Crask in the Hispana, bound for the station of Bridge of Gair, fifty miles distant by indifferent hill-roads. Lamancha, who had written for clothes, was magnificently respectable below his heavy ulster – a respectability which was not his usual habit but a concession to the urgent demand for camouflage. He was also in a bad temper, for his legs were still abominably stiff, and, though in need of at least ten hours' sleep, he had been allowed precisely six. At long last, too, his speech had begun to weigh upon him. 'Shut up, Archie,' he had told his host. 'I must collect what's left of my wits, or I'll make an exhibition of myself. You say we get the morning's papers at Bridge of Gair? They may give me a point or two. Lord, it's like one of those beastly mornings in Switzerland when they rake you up at two to climb Mount Blanc and you wish you had never been born.'

Sir Archie had no inclination to garrulity, for black fear had settled on his soul. In a few hours' time he would be doing what he had never done before, standing before a gaping audience which was there to be amused and possibly instructed. He had a speech in his pocket, carefully fashioned in consultation with Lamancha, but he was miserably conscious that it had no relation to his native wood-notes. What was Poincaré to him, or he to Poincaré? Why on earth had he not chosen to speak about something which touched his interests – farming, for example, on which he held views, or the future of the Air Force – instead of venturing in the unknown deserts of foreign affairs? Well, he had burned his boats and must make the best of it. The great thing was to be sure that the confounded speech had been transferred from paper to his memory.

But as the miles slipped behind him he realised with horror that his memory was playing him false. He could not get the bits to fit in; what he had reeled off so smoothly twenty-four hours ago now came out in idiotic shreds and patches. He felt himself slipping into a worse funk than he had ever known in all his tempestuous days . . . For a moment he thought of throwing up the sponge. He might engineer a breakdown – it would have to be a bad spill, for the day was yet young – and so deprive Muirtown of the presence of both Lamancha and himself. It was not the thought of the Conservative cause or his own political chances that made him reject this cowardly expedient. Two reasons dissuaded him: one, that though his friends continually prophesied disaster, he had never yet had a smash with his car, and his pride was involved; the other, that such a course would reveal Lamancha's presence in his company too near the suspect neighbourhood and might expose the secret of John Macnab . . . No, he had to go through with it, and, conning such wretched fragments of his oratory as he could dig out of his recollection, Sir Archie drove the Hispana over the bleak moorlands till he was looking down on the wide strath of the Gair, with the railway line scarring the heather and the hotel chimneys smoking beside a cold blue-grey river. He had glanced now and then at his fellow orator, whose professional apathy he profoundly envied, since for the last dozen miles Lamancha had been peacefully asleep.

They breakfasted at the hotel, and presently sought the station platform in the quest for papers. They were informed that papers came with the train for which they were waiting, and when the said train arrived, half an hour late, and Lamancha, according to arrangement, had sought a seat in the front while Archie favoured the rear, the latter secured a London evening paper of the previous day and that morning's *Scotsman.* The compartment in which he found himself was crowded with sleepy and short-tempered people who had made the night journey from the south. So on a pile of three gun-cases in the corridor Archie sat himself and gave his attention to the enlightened Press of his country.

He rubbed his eyes to make certain that he was not dreaming. For there, in conspicuous print on a prominent page of a respected newspaper, was the name of John Macnab. There was other news: of outrages in Mexico and earthquakes in the Pacific, of the disappearance of a solicitor and the arrival in London of a cinema star, but all seemed dwarfed and paled by Crossby's story. There was news of Harald Blacktooth, too, and authentic descriptions of the treasure-trove, but this was in an unconsidered corner. Cheek by jowl with the leading article was what clearly most interested the editor out of all the events on the surface of the globe – the renascence of Harald Blacktooth phoenix-like from his ashes, and the capture of the Strathlarrig salmon.

Archie read the thing confusedly without taking much of it in. Then he turned to the London evening paper. It was a journal which never objected to breaking up its front page for spicy news, and there on the front page was a summary of the Strathlarrig exploit. Moreover, there was a short hastily compiled article on the subject and a number of stimulating notes. John Macnab was becoming a household name, and the gaze of Britain was being centred on his shy personality. The third act in the drama would be played under bright light to a full gallery . . . Archie's eyes caught the end of the first *Scotsman* leader, which contained a reference to the Muirtown meeting, and a speculation as to what the Secretary of State for the Dominions would say. Archie, too, speculated as to what Lamancha was saying at that moment at the other end of the train.

This new complexity did something to quiet his nerves and take his mind off his approaching ordeal. There was no word in the papers of the coming raid on Haripol – Crossby had had that much sense – but, of course, whatever happened at Haripol would be broadcast through the land. The Claybodys, if they defeated John Macnab, would be famous; ridiculous, if they were beaten; and, while the latter fate might be taken with good humour by the Bandicotts, it would be gall and wormwood to a young gentleman with strong notions on the rights and dignities of landed property. It was mathematically certain that Johnson Claybody, as soon as he saw the newspapers, would devote all the powers of a not insignificant mind and the energies of a stubborn temper to the defence of Haripol. That was bad enough, but the correspondents at Strathlarrig were likely to have heard by this time of the third of John Macnab's wagers, and the attempt might have to be made under their argus-eyed espionage. Altogether, things were beginning to look rather dark for John, and incidentally for Sir Archie.

These morose reflections occupied him till the train stopped at Frew, the ticket-station for Muirtown. Here, according to plan, Sir Archie descended, for he could not arrive at the terminus in Lamancha's company. There was a cold gusty wind from the north-west which promised rain, the sky was overcast, and the sea, half a mile distant across the sand-dunes, was grey and sullen. Sir Archie, having two hours to fill before the official luncheon, resolved to reject the ancient station fly and walk . . . Once again the shadow of his speech descended on him. He limped along the shore road, trying to see the words as he had written them down, trying especially to get the initial sentence clear for each paragraph, for he believed that if he remembered these the rest would follow. The thing went rather better now. Parts came in a cascade of glibness, and he remembered Lamancha's injunction not to be too dapper or too rapid. The peroration was all right, and so was the exordium; only one passage near the middle seemed to offer a snag. He devoted the rest of his walk exclusively to this passage, till he was assured that he had it by heart.

He reached Muirtown within an hour, and decided to kill time by visiting some of his friends among the shopkeepers. The gunmaker welcomed him cordially, and announced his intention of coming to hear him that afternoon. But politics had clearly been ousted from that worthy's head by the newspaper which lay on his counter. 'What about this John Macnab, Sir Erchibald,' he asked.

'What about him? I'm hanged if I know what to think.'

'If Mr Tarras wasn't deid in Africa I would ken fine what to think. The man will likely be a gentleman, and he must be a grand fisher. I ken that bit o' the Larrig, and to get a salmon in it wants a fair demon at the job. Crask is no three miles away. D'ye hear nothing at Crask?'

It was the same wherever he went. The fishmonger pointed to a fish on his slabs, and observed that it would be about the size of the one taken at Strathlarrig. The bookseller, who knew his customer's simple tastes in letters, regretted that no contemporary novel of his acquaintance promised such entertainment as the drama now being enacted in Wester Ross. Tired of needless lying, Sir Archie forsook the shops and went for a stroll beside the harbour. But even there John Macnab seemed to pursue him. Wherever he saw a man with a paper he knew what he was reading, the people at the street corners were no doubt discussing the same subject – nay, he was sure he heard the very words spoken as he passed . . . The sight of a blue poster with his name in large letters reminded him of his duties, and he turned his steps towards the Northern Club.

He was greeted by his host, a Baillie of the town (the Provost belonged to the enemy camp), and was presented to the other guests. 'This is our candidate for Wester Ross, my lord,' and Archie was introduced to Lamancha, who smiled urbanely and remarked that he had had the pleasure of meeting Sir Archibald Roylance before. The Duke of Angus would not arrive till the hour of meeting, but Colonel Wavertree was there, a dapper red-faced gentleman who had an interest in breweries, and Mr Murdoch of New Caledonia – immense, grizzled and bearded, who had left the Lews as a child of three for the climes which had given him fortune. Also there was Lord Claybody, who came forward at once to renew his acquaintance.

'Very glad to see you, Sir Archibald. This is your first big meeting, isn't it? Good luck to you. A straight-forward declaration of principles is what we want from our future member, and I've no doubt we'll get it from you. Johnson sent his humblest apologies. He drove me in this morning, but unfortunately a troublesome bit of business took him back at once.'

Sir Archie thought he knew what that business was. He had always rather liked old Claybody, and now that he had leisure to study him the liking was confirmed. There was much of the son's arrogance about the eyes and mouth, but there was humour, too, which was lacking in Johnson, and his voice had a pleasant Midland burr. But he looked horribly competent and wide-awake. One would, thought Sir Archie, if one had made a great fortune oneself, and he concluded that the owner of Haripol was probably a bad man to get up against.

At luncheon they should have talked of the state of the nation and the future of their party; instead they talked of John Macnab. It was to be noted that Lord Claybody did not contribute much to the talk; he pursed his lips when the name was mentioned, and he did not reveal the challenge to Haripol. Patently he shared his son's views on the matter. But the others made no secret of their interest. Colonel Wavertree, who had come in from a neighbouring grouse-moor, was positive that the ruffian's escapades were not over. 'He'll go round the lot of us,' he said, 'and though it costs him fifty pound a time, I daresay he gets his money's worth. I believe he is paid by the agents to put up the price of Highland places, for if he keeps on it will mean money in the pocket of every sporting tenant, besides the devil of a lot of fun.' Mr Murdoch said it reminded him of the doings of one Pink Jones in New Caledonia forty years ago, and told a long and pointless tale of that hero. As for Lamancha, he requested to be given the whole story, and made very good show of merriment. 'A parcel of under-graduates, I suppose,' he said.

But the Baillie, who gave him the information, was a serious man and disapproved. 'It will get the country-side a bad name, my lord. It is a challenge to law and order. There's too many Bolsheviks about as it is, without this John Macnab aidin' and abettin' them.'

'Most likely the fellow is a sound Tory,' said Lamancha; but the Ballie ventured respectfully to differ. 'If your lordship will forgive me, there's some things too serious for jokin',' he concluded sententiously.

It was a dull luncheon, but to Archie the hours passed like fevered seconds. Agoraphobia had seized him once more, and he felt his tongue dry and his stomach hollow with trepidation. Food did not permit itself to be swallowed, so he contented himself with drinking two whisky-and-sodas. Towards the close of the meal that wild form of valour which we call desperation was growing in him. He could do nothing more about his infernal speech, and must fling himself on fortune.

As they left the table the Baillie claimed him. 'Your agent is here, Sir Archibald. He wanted a word with you before the meeting.'

A lean, red-haired man awaited them in the hall.

'Hullo, Mr Brodie. How are you? Glad to see you. Well, what's the drill for this afternoon?'

'It's that I was wantin' to see ye about, sir. The arrangement was that you should speak first, then Lord Lamancha, then Colonel Wavertree, and Mr Murdoch to finish off. But Baillie Dorrit thinks Lord Lamancha should open, him bein' a Cabinet Minister, and that you should follow.'

'Right-o, Brodie! I'm game for anything you like. I've been a slack candidate up to now, and I don't profess to know the job like you.' Sir Archie spoke with a jauntiness which made his heart sink, but the agent was impressed.

'Fine, sir. I can see ye're in grand fettle. Ye'll have a remarkable audience. There's been a demand for tickets far beyond the capacity o' the hall, and I hear of folk comin' from fifty mile round.'

Every word was like a knell to the wretched Archie, but with his spirits in the depths his manner took on a ghastly exhilaration. He lit a cigar with shaking fingers, patted Brodie on the back, linked his arm with the Baillie's, and in the short walk to the hall chattered like a magpie. So fevered was his behaviour that, as they entered the building by a side-door, Lamancha whispered in his ear, 'Steady, old man. For God's sake, keep your head,' and Archie turned on him a face like a lost soul's.

'I'm goin' over the top,' he said.

The Town Hall of Muirtown, having been built originally for the purpose of a drill-hall, was capable of holding inside its bare walls the better part of two thousand people. This afternoon it was packed to the door, presumably with voters, for the attendants had ruthlessly turned away all juvenile politicians. As Sir Archie took his seat on the platform, while a selection from the Muirtown Brass Band rendered 'Annie Laurie,' he seemed to be looking down as from an aeroplane on a strange, unfeatured country. The faces might have been tomb-stones for all the personality they represented. Some of his friends were there, no doubt, but he could no more have recognised them than he could have picked out the starling which haunted the Crask lawn from a flock seen next day on the hill. The place swam in a mist, like a corrie viewed in the morning from the hill-tops, and he knew that the mist came out of his own quaking soul. He had heard of stage-fright, but had never dreamed that it could be such a blackness of darkness.

The Duke of Angus was very old, highly respected, and almost wholly witless. He had never been very clever – Disraeli, it was said, had refused him the Thistle on the ground that he would eat it – and of late years his mind had retired into a happy vacuity. As a chairman he was mercifully brief. He told a Scots story, at which he shook with laughter, but the point of which he unfortunately left out; he repeated very loudly the names of the speakers – Sir Archie started at the sound of his own like a scared fawn; in a tone which was almost a bellow he uttered the words 'Lord Lamancha,' and then he sat down.

Lamancha had the reputation which is always accorded to a man whose name is often in the newspapers. Most of the audience had never seen him in the flesh, and human nature is grateful for satisfied curiosity. Presently he had them docile under the spell of his charming voice. He never attempted oratory in the grand style, but he possessed all the lesser accomplishments. He had nothing new to say, but he said the old things with a pleasant sincerity and that simplicity which is the result only of a long-practised art. It was the kind of speech of which he had made hundreds and would make hundreds more; there was nothing in it to lay hold of, but it produced an impression of being at once weighty and spontaneous, flattering to the audience and a proof of the speaker's easy mastery of his trade. There was a compliment to the Duke, a warm tribute to Sir Archie, a bantering profession of shyness on the part of a Borderer speaking north of the Forth. Then, by an easy transition, he passed to Highland problems – land, emigration, the ex-service men – and thence to the prime economic needs of Britain since 1918, the relation of these needs to world demands, the necessity of meeting them by using the full assets of an Empire which had been a unit in war and should be a unit in peace. There was little to inspire, but little to question; platitudes were so artfully linked together as to give the impression of a rounded and stable creed. Here was one who spoke seriously, responsibly, and yet with optimism; there was character here, said the ordinary man, and yet obviously a mind as well. Even the stern critics on the back benches had no fault to find with a statement from which they could only dissent with respect. None recognised that it was the manner that bewitched them. Lamancha, who on occasion could be profound, was now only improvising. The matter was a mosaic of bits of old speeches and answers to deputations, which he put together cynically with his left hand. But the manner was superb – the perfect production of a fine voice, the cunning emphasis, the sudden halts, the rounded cadences, the calculated hesitations. He sat down after forty minutes amid a tempest of that applause which is the tribute to professional skill and has nothing to do with conviction.

Sir Archie had listened with awe. Knowing now from bitter experience the thorny path of oratory, he was dumbfounded by this spectacle of a perfection of which he had never dreamed. What a fiasco would his halting utterance be in such company! He glanced at the notes in his hand, but could not read them; he strove to remember his opening sentences, and discovered them elusive. Then suddenly he heard his name spoken, and found himself on his feet.

He was scarcely aware of the applause with which he was greeted. All he knew was that every word of his speech had fled from his memory and would never return. The faces below him were a horrid white blur at which he knew he was foolishly grinning . . . In his pocket was an oration carefully written out. If he were to pluck it forth, and try to read it, he knew that he could not make sense of a word, for his eyes had lost the power of sight . . . Profound inertia seized him; he must do something, but there was a dreadful temptation to do nothing, just to go on grinning, like a man in a nightmare who finds himself in the track of an express train.

Nevertheless, such automata are we, he was speaking. He did not know what he was saying, but as a matter of fact he was repeating the words with which the chairman had introduced him. 'Ladies and gentlemen, we are fortunate in the privilege of having heard so stirring and statesmanlike an address as that which His Majesty's Secretary of State for the Dominions has just delivered. Now we are to hear what our gallant and enterprising friend, the prospective candidate for Wester Ross, has to say to us about the problems which confront the nation.'

He repeated this exordium like a parrot. The audience scented a mild joke, and laughed . . . Then in a twittering falsetto he repeated it again – this time in silence. There was a vague sense that something had gone wrong. He was about to repeat it a third time, and then the crash would have come, and he would have retired gibbering from the field.

The situation was saved by Wattie Lithgow. Seated at the back of the hall, Wattie saw that his master was in deadly peril, and took the only way to save him. He had a voice of immense compass, and he used it to the full.

'Speak up, man,' he roared. 'I canna hear a word ye're sayin'.'

There were shouts of 'Order,' and the stewards glared angrily at Wattie, but the trick had been done. Sir Archie's eyes opened, and he saw the audience no longer like turnips in a field, but as living and probably friendly human beings. Above all, he saw Wattie's gnarled face and anxious eyes. Suddenly his brain cleared, and, had he desired it, he could have reeled off the speech in his pocket as glibly as he had repeated it in the solitude of Crask. But he felt that that was no longer possible. The situation required a different kind of speech, and he believed he could make it. He would speak direct to Wattie, as he had often lectured him in the Crask smoking-room.

'Ladies and gentlemen,' he said – and his voice had become full and confident – 'your "gallant and enterprising friend" is not much of a hand at public speaking. I have still my job to learn, and with your help I hope soon to learn it. What I have to say to you this afternoon is the outcome of my first amateurish study of public questions. You may take it that my views are honest and my own. I am not a gramophone.'

In this last sentence he lied, for what he said was for the most part not his own; it was the sermon which Janet Raden had preached him the day before in the clear air of the Carnmore tops. Mixed up with it were fragments of old discourses of his own to Wattie, and reflections which had come to him in the last ten years of a variegated life. The manner was staccato, the style was slangy and inelegant, but it was not a lesson learned and recited, but words spoken direct to those into whose eyes he was looking. He had found touch with his audience, and he held their attention in a vice.

It was a strange, inconsequent speech, but it had a curious appeal in it – the appeal of youth and candour and courage. It was philosophy rather than politics, a ragged but arresting philosophy. He began by confessing that the war had left the world in a muddle, a muddle which affected his own mind. The only cure was to be honest with oneself, and to refuse to accept specious nonsense and conventional jargon. He told the story from Andersen of the Emperor's New Suit. 'Our opponents call us Tories,' he said; 'they can call us anything they jolly well please. I am proud to be called a Tory. I understand that the name was first given by Titus Oates to those who disbelieved in his Popish Plot. What we want today is Toryism – the courage to give the lie to impudent rogues.'

That was a memory of Leithen's table talk. The rest was all from Janet Raden. He preached the doctrine of Challenge; of no privilege without responsibility, of only one right of man – the right to do his duty; of all power and property held on sufferance. These were the thoughts which had been growing in his head since yesterday afternoon. He spoke of the changing face of the land – the Highlands ceasing to be the home of men and becoming the mere raw material of picture postcards, the old gentry elbowed out and retiring with a few trinkets and pictures and the war medals of their dead to suburban lodgings. It all came of not meeting the challenge . . . What was Bolshevism but a challenge, perhaps a much-needed challenge, to make certain of the faith that was in a man? He had no patience with the timorous and whining rich. No law could protect them unless they made themselves worth protecting. As a Tory, he believed that the old buildings were still sound, but they must be swept and garnished, that the ancient weapons were the best, but they must be kept bright and shining and ready for use. So soon as a cause feared inquiry and the light of day that cause was doomed. The ostrich, hiding its head in the sand, left its rump a fatal temptation to the boot of the passer-by.

Sir Archie was not always clear, he was often ungrammatical, and he nobly mixed his metaphors, but he held his audience tight. He did more, when at the close of his speech he put his case in the form of an apologue – the apologue of John Macnab. The mention of the name brought laughter and loud cheering. John Macnab, he said, was abroad in the world today, like a catfish among a shoal of herrings. He had his defects, no doubt, but he was badly wanted, for he was at bottom a sportsman and his challenge had to be met. Even if the game went against them the challenged did not wholly lose, for they were stirred out of apathy into life.

No queerer speech was ever made by a candidate on his first public appearance. It had no kind of success with the Baillie, nor, it may be presumed, with Lord Claybody; indeed, I doubt if any of the distinguished folk on the platform quite approved of it, except Lamancha. But there was no question of its appeal to the audience, and the applause which had followed Lamancha's peroration was as nothing to that amid which Sir Archie resumed his seat.

At the back of the hall a wild-eyed man sitting near Wattie Lithgow had been vociferous in his plaudits. 'He ca's himsel' a Tory. By God, it's the red flag that he'll be wavin' soon.'

'If you say that again,' said Wattie fiercely, 'I'll smash your heid.'

'Keep your hair on,' was the reply. 'I'm for the young ane, whatever he ca's himsel'.'

Archie sat down with his brain in a whirl, for he had tasted the most delicious of joys – the sense of having moved a multitude. He had never felt happier in his life – or, let it be added, more truly amazed. A fiery trail was over, and brilliantly over. He had spoken straightforwardly to his fellow-mortals with ease and acceptance. The faces below him were no longer featureless, but human and friendly and interesting. He did not listen closely to Colonel Wavertree's remarks, which seemed to be mostly about taxation, or to the Ex-Premier of New Caledonia, who was heavily rhetorical and passionately imperial. Modest as he was, he had a pleased consciousness that, though he might have talked a good deal of rot, he had gripped his hearers as not even Lamancha had gripped them. He searched through the hall for faces to recognise. Wattie he saw, savagely content; the Colonel, too, who looked flushed and happy, and Junius, and Agatha. But there was no sign of Janet, and his failure to find her threw a dash of cold water on his triumph.

The next step was to compass an inconspicuous departure. Lamancha would be escorted in state to the four-forty-five train, and he must join it at Frew. While 'God save the King' was being sung, Sir Archie escaped by a side-door, followed by an excited agent. 'Man, ye went down tremendous,' Brodie gasped. 'Ye changed your mind – ye told me ye were goin' to deal wi' foreign policy. Anyway, ye've started fine, and there'll be no gettin' inside the hall the next time ye speak in Muirtown.'

Archie shook him off, picked up a taxi-cab at the station, and drove to Frew. There, after lurking in the waiting-room, he duly entered a third-class carriage in the rear of the south-going train. At six o'clock he emerged on to the platform at Bridge of Gair, and waited till the train had gone before he followed Lamancha to the hotel. He found his friend thinking only of Haripol. 'I had a difficult job to get rid of Claybody, and had to tell a lot of lies. Said I was going to stay with Lanerick and that my man had gone on there with my luggage. We'd better be off, for we've a big day before us tomorrow.'

But, as the Hispana started up the road to the pass, Lamancha smiled affectionately on the driver and patted his shoulder. 'I've often called you an idiot, Archie, but I'm bound to say today you were an inspired idiot. You may win this seat or not – it doesn't matter – but sooner or later you're going to make a howling success in that silly game.'

Beyond the pass the skies darkened for rain, and it was in a deluge that the car, a little after eight o'clock, crossed the Bridge of Larrig. Archie had intended to go round by one of the peat-roads, but the wild weather had driven everyone to shelter, and it seemed safe to take the straight road up the hill. Shapp, who had just arrived in the Ford, took charge of the car, and Archie and Lamancha sprinted through the drizzle to the back-door.

To their surprise it was locked, and when, in reply to their hammering, Mrs Lithgow appeared, it was only after repeated questions through the scullery-window that she was convinced of their identity and permitted them to enter.

'We've been sair fashed wi' folk,' was her laconic comment, as she retired hastily to the kitchen after locking the door behind them.

In the smoking-room they found the lamps lit, the windows shuttered, Crossby busy with the newspapers, Palliser-Yeates playing patience, and Leithen as usual deep in the works of Sir Walter Scott. 'Well,' was the unanimous question, 'how did it go off?'

'Not so bad,' said Archie. 'Charles was in great form. But what on earth has scared Mrs Lithgow?'

Leithen laid down his book. 'We've had the devil of a time. Our base has been attacked. It looks as if we may have a rearguard action to add to our troubles. We're practically besieged. Two hours ago I was all for burning our ciphers and retiring.'

'Besieged? By whom?'

'By the correspondents. Ever since the early afternoon. I fancy their editors have been prodding them with telegrams. Anyhow, they've forgotten all about Harald Blacktooth and are hot on the scent of John Macnab.'

'But what brought them here?'

'Method of elimination, I suppose. Your journalist is a sharp fellow. They argued that John Macnab must have a base near by, and, as it wasn't Strathlarrig or Glenraden, it was most likely here. Also they caught sight of Crossby taking the air, and gave chase. Crossby flung them off – happily they can't have recognised him – but they had him treed in the stable loft for three hours.'

'Did they see you?'

'No. Some got into the hall and some glued their faces to this window, but John was under the table and I was making myself very small at the back of the sofa . . . Mrs Lithgow handled them like Napoleon. Said the Laird was away and wouldn't be back till midnight, but he'd see them at ten o'clock tomorrow. She had to promise that, for they are determined ruffians. They'd probably still be hanging about the place if it hadn't been for this blessed rain.'

'That's not all,' said Palliser-Yeates. 'We had a visit from a lunatic. We didn't see him, for Mrs Lithgow lured him indoors and has him shut up in the wine-cellar.'

'Good God! What kind of lunatic?' Sir Archie exclaimed.

'Don't know. Mrs Lithgow was not communicative. She said something about smallpox. Maybe he's a fellow-sufferer looking for Archie's company. Anyhow, he's in the wine-cellar for Wattie to deal with.'

Sir Archie rose and marched from the room, and did not return till the party were seated at a late supper. His hair was harassed, and his eyes were wild.

'It wasn't the wine-cellar,' he groaned, 'it was the coal-hole. He's upstairs now having a bath and changing into a suit of my clothes. Pretty short in the temper, too, and no wonder. For Heaven's sake, you fellows, stroke him down when he appears. We've got to bank on his being a good chap and tell him everything. It's deuced hard luck. Here am I just makin' a promising start in my public career, and you've gone and locked up the local Medical Officer of Health who came to inquire into a reputed case of smallpox.'

TEN

In which Crime is Added to Crime

BY the mercy of Providence Doctor Kello fulfilled Archie's definition of a 'good chap.' He was a sandy-haired young man from Dundee, who had been in the Air Force, and on his native dialect had grafted the intricate slang of that service. Archie had found him half-choked with coal-dust and wrath, and abject apologies had scarcely mollified him. But a hot bath and his host's insistence that he should spend the night at Crask – Dr Kello knew very well that at the inn he would get no more than a sofa – had worked a miracle, and he appeared at the supper-table prepared to forgive and forget. He was a little awed by the company in which he found himself, and nervously murmured, 'Pleased to meet ye' in response to the various introductions. A good meal and Archie's Veuve Clicquot put him into humour with himself and at ease with his surroundings. He exchanged war reminiscences, and told stories of his professional life – 'Ye wouldn't believe, I tell ye, what queer folk the Highlanders are' – and when later in the evening Archie, speaking as to a brother airman, made a clean breast of the John Macnab affair, he received the confession with obstreperous hilarity. 'It's the best stunt I ever heard tell of,' he roared, slapping his knee. 'Ye may depend on me to back ye up, too. Is it the journalists that's worrying ye? You leave the merchants to me. I'll shut their mouths for them. Ten o'clock tomorrow, is it? Well, I'll be there with a face as long as my arm, and I'll guarantee to send them down the hill like a kirk emptying.'

All night it rained in bucketfuls, and the Friday morning broke with the same pitiless deluge. Lamancha came down to breakfast in a suit of clothes which would have been refused by a self-respecting tramp, but which, as a matter of fact, had been his stalking outfit for a dozen years. The Merklands were not a dressy family. He studied the barograph, where the needle was moving ominously downward, and considered the dissolving skies and the mist which rose like a wall beyond the terrace.

'It's no good,' he told his host. 'You might as well try to stalk Haripol in a snow blizzard. Today must be washed out, and that leaves us only tomorrow. We'll have to roost indoors, and we're terribly at the mercy of that hive of correspondents.'

The hive came at ten, a waterproofed army defying the weather in the cause of duty. But in front of the door they were met by Dr Kello, with a portentous face.

'Good morning, boys,' he said. 'Sir Archibald Roylance asked me to see ye on his behalf. My name's Kello – I'm Medical Officer of Health for this part of the world. I'm very sorry, but ye can't see Sir Archibald this morning. In fact, I want ye to go away and not come near the place at all.'

He was promptly asked for his reason.

'The fact is that a suspected case of smallpox has been reported from Crask. That's why I'm here. I say "suspected," for, in my own opinion, it's nothing of the sort. But I'm bound to take every precaution, and, for your own sakes, I can't let a man-jack of ye a step nearer.'

The news was received in silence, and added to the depression of the dripping weather. A question was asked.

'No, it's not Sir Archibald. He's as disappointed as you are at not being able to welcome ye. He says if ye come back in forty-eight hours – that's the time when I hope to give the place a clean bill of health – he would like to stand ye drinks and have a crack with ye.'

Five minutes later the doctor returned to the smoking-room. 'They're off like good laddies, and I don't think they'll trouble ye for the next two days. Gosh! They're as feared of infectious diseases as a Highlander. I'll give them a wee while to go down the hill, and then I'll start off home on my motor-bike. I'm very much obliged to you gentlemen for your good entertainment . . . Ye may be sure I'll hold my tongue about the confidence ye've honoured me with. Not a cheep from me! But I can tell ye, I'll be keeping my ears open for word of John Macnab. Good luck to ye, gentlemen!'

The departure of Doctor Kello was followed by the appearance of Wattie Lithgow, accompanied by Benjie, whose waterproof cape of ceremony had now its uses.

'I've got bad news from this laddie,' said the former, lugging Benjie forward by the ear. 'He was at Haripol early this morning and a' the folk there was speakin' about it. Macnicol tell't him—'

'No, he didna,' put in Benjie. 'Macnicol's ower prood to speak to me. I heard it frae the men in the bothy and frae ane o' the lassies up at the big hoose.'

'Weel, what a'body kens is maistly true. Ye'll no guess what yon auld Claybody is daein'. Ye ken he's a contractor, forbye ither things, and he's got the contrack for makin' the big dam at Kinlochbuie. There's maybe a thousand navvies workin' there, and he's bringin' ower a squad o' them – Benjie says mair nor a hundred – to guaird the forest.'

'Ass!' exclaimed Palliser-Yeates. 'He'll drive every beast into Caithness.'

'Na, na. Macnicol is not entirely wantin' in sense. The navvies will no be allowed inside the forest. They'll be a guaird outside – what's that they ca' it? – an outer barrage. Macnicol will see that a' the deer are in the Sanctuary, and in this kind o' weather it will no be that deeficult. But it will be verra deeficult for his lordship to get inside the forest, and it will be verra near an impossibeelity to get a beast out.'

Archie looked round the room. 'Dashed unsportin' I call it. I bet it's the young 'un's idea.'

'Look here, Charles,' said Leithen. 'Isn't it about time to consider whether you shouldn't cry off this Haripol affair? It was different at the start. John and I had a fair sporting chance. Our jobs were steep enough, but yours is absolutely perpendicular . . . The Claybodys are not taking any chances, and a hundred able-bodied navvies is a different-sized proposition to a few gillies. The confounded Press has blazoned the thing so wide that if you're caught you'll be a laughing-stock to the whole civilised world. Don't you see that you simply can't afford to lose, any more than the Claybodys? Then, to put the lid on it, our base is under a perpetual threat from those newspaper fellows. I'd rather have all Scotland Yard after me than the Press – you agree, Crossby? I'm inclined to think that John Macnab has done enough *pour chauffer la gloire*. It's insanity to go on.'

Lamancha shook his head. 'It's all very well for you – you won. I tell you frankly that nothing on earth will prevent me having a try at Haripol. All you say is perfectly true, but I don't choose to listen to it. This news of Wattie's only makes me more determined.'

Leithen subsided into his book, observing – 'I suppose that is because you're a great man. You're a sober enough fellow at most times, but you're able now and then to fling your hat over the moon. You can damn the consequences, which I suppose is one of the tests of greatness. John and I can't, but we admire you, and we'll bail you out.'

It was Sir Archie, strangely enough, who now abetted Lamancha's obstinacy. 'I grant you the odds are stiff,' he declared, 'but that only means that we must find some way to shorten them. Nothing's impossible after yesterday. There was I gibbering with terror and not a notion in my head, and yet I got on fairly well, didn't I, Wattie?'

'Ye made a grand speech, sir. There was some said it was the best speech they ever heard in a' their days. There was one man said ye was haverin', but' – fiercely – 'he didna say it twice.'

'We've the whole day to make a plan,' Archie went on. 'Hang it all, there must be some way to diddle the Claybodys. We've got a pretty good notion of the lie of the land, and Wattie's a perfect Red Indian at getting up to deer. We muster four and a half able-bodied men, counting me as half. And there's Benjie. Benjie, you're a demon at strategy. Have you anything to say?'

'Aye,' said Benjie, 'I've a plan. But ye're ower particular here, and maybe ye wadna like it.' This with a dark glance at Palliser-Yeates, who was leaving the room to get more tobacco.

'We'll have it, all the same. Let's sit down to business. Stick the ordnance map on that table, Charles, and you, Ned, shut that book and give us the benefit of your powerful mind.'

Leithen rose, yawning. 'I've left my pipe in the dining-room. Wait a moment till I fetch it.'

Now Dr Kello, on his departure, had left the front-door of the house open, and the steady downpour of rain blanketed all other sounds from outside. So it came to pass that when Archie's quick ear caught the noise of footsteps on the gravel and he bounded into the hall, he was confronted with the spectacle of Colonel Raden and his daughters already across the doorstep. Moreover, as luck would have it, at that moment Leithen from the dining-room and Palliser-Yeates from his bedroom converged on the same point.

'Hullo, Roylance,' the Colonel cried. 'This is a heathenish

hour for a visit, but we had to have some exercise, and my daughters wanted to come up and congratulate you on your performance yesterday. A magnificent speech, sir! Uncommon good sense! What I—'

But the Colonel stopped short in mystification at the behaviour of his daughters, who were staring with wide eyes at two unknown figures who stood shamefacedly behind Sir Archie. This last, having no alternative, was trying to carry off things with a high hand.

'Let me introduce,' he was proclaiming, 'Sir Edward Leithen – Mr Palliser-Yeates – Miss Raden, Miss Janet Raden, Colonel—'

But he was unheeded. Agatha was looking at Leithen and Janet at Palliser-Yeates, and simultaneously the two ejaculated, 'John Macnab!'

Archie saw that it was all up. Shouting for Mrs Lithgow, he helped his visitors to get out of their mackintoshes, and ordered his housekeeper to have these garments dried. Then he ushered them into the smoking-room where were Lamancha and Crossby and Benjie and a good peat-fire. Wattie, at the first sound of voices, had discreetly retired.

'Come along, Colonel, I'll explain. Very glad to see you – have that chair . . . what about dry stockings? . . .'

But his hospitable bustle was unheeded. The Colonel, hopelessly at sea, was bowing to a tall man who in profound embarrassment was clearing books and papers out of chairs.

'Yes, that's Lord Lamancha. You heard him yesterday. Charles, this is Colonel Raden, and Miss Agatha and Miss Janet. That is Mr Crossby, the eminent journalist. That little scallywag is Fish Benjie, whom I believe you know . . . Sit down, please, all of you. We're caught out and are going to confess. Behold the lair of John Macnab.'

Colonel Raden was recovering himself.

'I read in the papers,' he said, 'that John Macnab is the reincarnation of Harald Blacktooth. In that case we are related. With which of these gentleman have I the honour to claim kin?'

The words, the tone, convinced Sir Archie that the danger was past, and his nervousness fled.

'Properly speakin', you've found three new relatives. There they are. Not bad fellows, though they've been givin' me a hectic time. Now *I* retire – shoes off, feet fired, and turned out to grass. Ned, you've a professional gift of exposition. Fire away, and tell the whole story.'

Sir Edward Leithen obeyed, and it may be said that the tale lost nothing in his telling. He described the case of three gentlemen, not wholly useless to their country, who had suddenly fallen into ennui. He told of a cure, now perfected, but of a challenge not yet complete. 'I've been trying to persuade Lord Lamancha to drop the thing,' he said, 'but the Claybodys have put his back up, and I'm not sure that I blame him. It didn't matter about you or Bandicott, for you took it like sportsmen, and we should have felt no disgrace in being beaten by you. But Claybody is different.'

'By Gad, sir, you are right,' the Colonel shouted, rising to his feet and striding about the room. 'He and his damned navvies are an insult to every gentleman in the Highlands. They're enough to make Harald Blacktooth rise from the dead. I should never think anything of Lord Lamancha again – and I've thought a devilish lot of him up to now – if he took this lying down. Do you know, sir' – turning to Lamancha – 'that I served in the Scots Guards with your father – we called them the Scots Fusilier Guards in those days – and I am not going to fail his son.'

Sir Edward Leithen was a philosopher, with an acute sense of the ironies of life, and as he reflected that here was a laird, a Tory, and a strict preserver of game working himself into a passion over the moral rights of the poacher, he suddenly relapsed into helpless mirth. Colonel Raden regarded him sternly and uncomprehendingly, but Janet smiled, for she too had an eye for comedy.

'I'm tremendously grateful to you,' Lamancha said. 'You know more about stalking than all of us put together, and we want your advice.'

'Janet,' commanded her parent, 'you have the best brain in the family. I'll be obliged if you'll apply it to this problem.'

For an hour the anxious conclave surrounded the spread-out ordnance-map. Wattie was summoned, and with a horny finger expounded the probable tactics of Macnicol and the presumable disposition of the navvy guard. At the end of the consultation Lamancha straightened his back.

'The odds are terribly steep. I can see myself dodging the navvies, and with Wattie's help getting up to a stag. But if Macnicol and the gillies are perched round the Sanctuary they are morally certain to spot us, and, if we have to bolt, there's no chance of getting the beast over the march. That's a hole I see no way out of.'

'Janet,' said the Colonel, 'do you?'

Janet was looking abstractedly out of the window. 'I think it is going to clear up,' she observed, disregarding her father's question. 'It will be a fine afternoon, and then, if I am any judge of the weather, it will rain cats and dogs in the evening.'

'We had better scatter after luncheon,' said Lamancha, 'and each of us go for a long stride. We want to be in training for to-morrow.'

After the Colonel had suggested half a dozen schemes, the boldness of which was only matched by their futility, the Radens rose to go. Janet signalled to Benjie, who slipped out after her, and the two spoke in whispers in the hall, while Archie was collecting the mackintoshes from the kitchen.

'I want you to be at Haripol this afternoon. Wait for me a little on this side of the lodge about half-past three.'

Benjie grinned and nodded. 'Aye, lady, I'll be there.' He, too, had a plan for shortening the odds, and he had so great a respect for Janet's sagacity that he thought it probable that she might have reached his own conclusion.

As Janet had foretold, it was a hot afternoon. The land steamed in the sun, but every hill-top was ominously clouded. While the inhabitants of Crask were engaged in taking stealthy but violent exercise among the sinuousities of Sir Archie's estate, Janet Raden mounted her yellow pony and rode thoughtfully towards Haripol by way of Inverlarrig and the high road. There were various short-cuts, suitable for a wild-cat like Benjie, but after the morning's torrential rains she had no fancy for swollen bogs and streams. She found Benjie lurking behind a boulder near the lodge, and in the shelter of a clump of birches engaged him in earnest conversation. Then she rode decorously through the gates and presented herself at the castle door.

Haripol was immense, new, and, since it had been built by a good architect out of good stone, not without its raw dignity. Janet found Lady Claybody in a Tudor hall which had as much connection with a Scots castle as with a Kaffir kraal. There was a wonderful jumble of possessions – tapestries which included priceless sixteenth-century Flemish pieces, and French fakes of last year; Ming treasures and Munich atrocities; armour of which about a third was genuine; furniture indiscriminately Queen Anne, Sheraton, Jacobean, and Tottenham Court Road; and pictures which ranged from a Sir Joshua (an indifferent specimen) to a recent Royal Academy portrait of Lord Claybody. A feature was the number of electric lamps to illumine the hours of darkness, the supports of which varied from Spanish altar-candlesticks to two stuffed polar bears and a turbaned Ethiopian in coloured porcelain.

Lady Claybody was a heavily handsome woman still in her early fifties. The purchase of Haripol had been her doing, for romance lurked in her ample breast, and she dreamed of a new life in which she should be an unquestioned great lady far from the compromising environment where the Claybody millions had been won. Her manner corresponded to her ambition, for it was stately and aloof, her speech was careful English seasoned with a few laboriously acquired Scots words, and in her household her wish was law. A merciful tyrant, she rarely resorted to ultimata, but when she issued a decree it was obeyed.

She was unaffectedly glad to see Janet, for the Radens were the sort of people she desired as friends. Two days before she had been at her most urbane to Agatha and the Colonel, and now she welcomed the younger daughter as an ambassador from that older world which she sought to make her own. A small terrier drowned her greetings with epileptic yelps.

'Silence, Roguie,' she enjoined. 'You must not bark at a fellow-countrywoman. Roguie, you know, is so high-strung that he reacts to any new face. You find me quite alone, my dear. Our daughters do not join us till next week, when we shall have a houseful for the stalking. Now I am having a very quiet, delicious time drinking in the peace of this enchanted glen.'

She said no word of John Macnab, who was doubtless the primary cause of this solitude. Lord Claybody and Johnson, it appeared, were out on the hill. Janet chattered on the kind of topics which she felt suitable – hunting in the Midlands, the coming Muirtown Gathering, the political meeting of yesterday. 'Claybody thought Sir Archie Roylance rather extravagant,' said the lady, 'but he was greatly impressed with Lord Lamancha's speech. Surely it is absurd that his part of the Highlands, which your sister says was so loyal to Prince Charlie, should be a hot-bed of radicalism. Claybody thinks that that can all be changed, but not with a candidate who truckles to socialist nonsense.'

Janet was demure and acquiescent, sighing when her hostess sighed, condemning when she condemned. Presently the hot sun shining through the windows suggested the open air to Lady Claybody, who was dressed for walking.

'Shall we stroll a little before tea?' she asked. 'Wee Roguie has been cooped indoors all morning, and he loves a run, for he comes of a very sporting breed.'

They set forth accordingly, into gardens bathed in sunshine, and thence to the coolness of beech woods. The Reascuill, after leaving its precipitous glen, flows, like the Raden, for a mile or two in haughlands, which are split by the entry of a tributary, the Doran, which in its upper course is the boundary between Haripol and Crask. Between the two streams stands a wooded knoll which is a chief pleasaunce of the estate. It is a tangle of dwarf birches, bracken and blaeberry, with ancient Scots firs on the summit, and from its winding walks there is a prospect of the high peaks of the forest rising black and jagged above the purple ridges.

At its foot they crossed the road which followed the river into the forest, and Janet caught sight of a group of men lounging by the bridge.

'Have you workmen on the place just now?' she asked.

'Only wood-cutters, I think,' said Lady Claybody.

Wee Roguie plunged madly into the undergrowth, and presently could be heard giving tongue, as if in pursuit of a rabbit. 'Dear little fellow!' said his mistress. 'Hear how he loves freedom!'

The ladies walked slowly to the crest of the knoll, where they halted to admire the view. Janet named the different summits, which looked ominously near, and then turned to gaze on the demesne of Haripol lying green and secure in its cincture of wood and water. 'I think you have the most beautiful place in the Highlands,' she told her hostess. 'It beats Glenraden, for you have the sea.'

'It is very lovely,' was the answer. 'I always think of it as a fortress, where we are defended against the troubles of the world. At Ronham one might as well be living in London, but here there are miles of battlements between us and dull everyday things . . . Listen to Roguie! How happy he is! !'

Roguie's yelps sounded now close at hand, and now far off,

as the scent led him. Presently, as the ladies moved back to the house, the sound grew fainter. 'He will probably come out on the main avenue,' his mistress said. 'I like him to feel really free, but he always returns in good time for his little supper.'

They had tea in the tapestried hall, and then Janet took her leave. 'I want to escape the storm,' she explained, 'for it is certain to rain hard again before night.' As it chanced she did not escape it, but after a wayside colloquy with a small boy, arrived at Glenraden as wet as if she had swum the Larrig. She had sent by Benjie a message to Crask, concerning her share in the plans of the morrow

That night after dinner, while the rain beat on the windows, John Macnab was hard at work. The map was spread out on the table, and Lamancha prepared the orders for the coming action. If we would understand his plan, it is necessary to consider the nature of the terrain. The hill behind Crask rises to a line of small cliffs not unlike a South African *kranz*, and through a gap in the line runs a moorland track which descends by the valley of the Doran till it joins the main road from Inverlarrig almost at Haripol gates. The Doran glen – the Crask march is the stream – is a wide hollow of which the north side is the glacis of the great Haripol peaks. These are, in order from west to east, Stob Ban, Stob Coire Easain, Sgurr Mor, and the superb tower of Sgurr Dearg. Seen from the Crask ridge the summits rise in cones of rock from a glacis which at the foot is heather and scrub and farther up steeps of scree and boulders. Between each peak there is a pass leading over to the deep-cut glen of the Reascuill, which glen is contained on the north by the hills of Machray forest.

It was certain that the navvy cordon would be an outer line of defence, outside the wilder ground of the forest. Wattie expounded it with an insight which the facts were to justify. 'The men will be posted along the north side o' the Doran, maybe half-way up the hill – syne round the west side o' Stob Ban and across the Reascuill at the new fir plantin' – syne up the Machray march along the taps o' Clonlet and Bheinn Fhada. They can leave out Sgurr Dearg, for ye'd hae to be a craw to get ower that side o't. By my way o' thinkin', they'll want maybe three hundred to mak a proper ring, and they'll want them thickest on the Machray side where the ground is roughest. North o' the Doran it's that bare that twa – three men could see the whole hill-side, and Macnicol's no the ane to waste his folk.

The easy road intil the Sanctuary is fae Machray up the Reascuill, and the easy way to get a beast out wad be by the way o' the Red Burn. But the navvies will be as thick as starlin's there, so it's no place for you and me, my lord.'

The Haripol Sanctuary lay at the headwater of the Reascuill, between what was called the Pinnacle Ridge of Sgurr Dearg and the cliffs of Sgurr Mor. As luck would have it, a fairly easy path, known generally as the Beallach, led from it to the glen of the Doran. It was clear that Lamancha must enter from the south, and, if he got a stag, remove it by the same road.

'I'll get ye into the Sanctuary, never fear,' said Wattie grimly, 'There's no a navvy ever whelpit wad keep you and me out. But when we're there, God help us, for we'll hae Macnicol to face. And if Providence is mercifu' and we get a beast, we've the navvies to get it through, and that's about the end o't. Ye canna mak yoursel' inconspicuous when ye're pu'in at a muckle stag.'

'True,' said Lamancha, 'and that's just where Mr Palliser-Yeates comes in . . . John, my lad, your job is to be waiting on the Doran side of the Beallach, and if you see Wattie and me with a beast, to draw off the navvies in that quarter. You had better move west towards Haripol, for there's better cover on that side. D'you think you can do it? You used to have a pretty gift of speed, and you've always had an uncommon eye for ground.'

Palliser-Yeates said modestly that he thought he was up to the job, provided Lamancha did not attract the prior notice of the watchers. Once the pack got on his trail, he fancied he could occupy their attention for an hour or two. The difficulty lay in keeping Lamancha in view, and for that purpose it would be necessary to ensconce himself at the very top of the Beallach, where he could have sight of the upper Sanctuary.

To Leithen fell the onerous task of creating a diversion on the other side of the forest. He must start in the small hours and be somewhere on the Machray boundary when Lamancha was beginning operations. There lay the most obvious danger-point, and there the navvies would probably be thickest on the ground. At all costs their attention – and that of any Haripol gillies in the same quarter – must be diverted from what might be happening in the Sanctuary. This was admittedly a hard duty, but Leithen was willing to undertake it. He was not greatly afraid of the navvies, who are a stiff-jointed race, but the Haripol gillies were another matter. 'You simply must not get caught,' Lamancha told him. 'If you're hunted, make a bee-line north to Machray and Glenaicill – the gillies won't be keen to be drawn too far away from Haripol. You won the school mile in your youth, and you're always in training. Hang it all, you ought to be able to keep Claybody's fellows on the run. I never yet knew a gillie quick on his feet.'

'That's a pre-war notion,' said Palliser-Yeates. 'Some of the young fellows are uncommon spry. Ned may win all right, but it won't be by much of a margin.'

The last point for decision was the transport of the stag. The moor-road from Crask was possible for a light car with a high clearance, and it was arranged that Archie should take the Ford by that route and wait in cover on the Crask side of the Doran. It was a long pull from the Beallach to the stream, but there were tributary ravines where the cover was good – always presuming that Palliser-Yeates had decoyed away the navvy guard.

'Here's the lay-out, then,' said Lamancha at last. 'Wattie and I get into the Sanctuary as best we can and try for a stag. If we get him, we bring him through the Beallach; John views us and shows himself, and draws off the navvies, whom we assume to be few at that point. Then we drag the beast down to the Doran and sling it into Archie's car. Meanwhile Ned is on the other side of the forest, doing his damnedest to keep Macnicol busy . . . That's about the best we can do, but I needn't point out to you that every minute we're taking the most almighty chances. We may never get a shot. Macnicol may be in full cry after us long before we reach the Beallach. The navvies may refuse to be diverted by John, or may come back before we get near Archie's car . . . Ned may pipe to heedless ears, or, worse still, he may be nobbled and lugged off to the Haripol dungeons . . . It's no good looking for trouble before it comes, but I can see that there's a big bank of it waiting for us. What really frightens me is Macnicol and the gillies at the Sanctuary itself. This weather is in our favour, but even then I don't see how they can miss hearing our shot, and that of course puts the lid on it.'

A time-table was drawn up after much discussion. Leithen was to start for Machray at 3 a.m., and be in position about 8. Lamancha and Wattie, about the latter hour, would be attempting to enter the Sanctuary by the Beallach.

Palliser-Yeates must be at his post not later than 9, and Archie with the car should reach the Doran by 10. The hour of subsequent happenings depended upon fate; the thing might be over for good or ill by noon, or it might drag on till midnight.

When the last arrangements had been settled Lamancha squared his back against the mantelpiece and looked round on the company.

'Of course we're all blazing idiots – the whole thing is insanity – but we've done the best we can in the way of preparation. The great thing is for each of us to keep his wits about him and use them, for everything may go the opposite way to what we think. There's no "according to Cocker" in this game.'

Archie was wrinkling his brows.

'It's all dashed ingenious, Charles, but do you think you have any real chance?'

'Frankly, I don't,' was the answer. 'The best we can hope for is to fail without being detected. I think there would be a far-away sporting chance if Macnicol could be tied up. That's what sticks in my gizzard. I don't see how it's possible to get a shot in the Sanctuary without Macnicol spotting it.'

Wattie Lithgow had returned, and caught the last words. He was grinning broadly.

'I'm no positeeve but that Macnicol wull be tied up,' he observed. 'Benjie's here, and he's brocht something wi' him.'

He paused for effect.

'It's a dog – a wee, yelpin' dog.'

'Whose dog?'

'Leddy Claybody's. It seems that at Haripol her leddyship wears the breeks – that the grey mear is the better horse there – and it seems that she's fair besottit on that dog. Benjie was sayin' that if it were lost Macnicol and a'body about the place wad be set lookin' for't, and naething wad be thought of at Haripol till it was fund.'

Archie rose in consternation.

'D'you mean to say – How on earth did the beast come here?'

'It cam here wi' Benjie. It's fine and comfortable in a box in the stable . . . I'm no just clear about what happened afore that, but I think Miss Janet Raden and Benjie gae'd ower to Haripol this afternoon and fund the puir wee beast lost in the wuds.'

Archie did not join in the laughter. His mind held no other emotion than a vast and delighted amazement. The lady who two days before had striven to lift his life to a higher plane, who had been the sole inspiration of his successful speech of yesterday, was now discovered conspiring with Fish Benjie to steal a pup.

ELEVEN

Haripol – the Main Attack

SOME MEN BEGIN the day with loose sinews and a sluggish mind, and only acquire impetus as the hours proceed; others show a declining scale from the vigour of the dawn to the laxity of evening. It was fortunate for Lamancha that he belonged to the latter school. At daybreak he was obstinate, energetic, and frequently ill-tempered, as sundry colleagues in France and Palestine had learned to their cost; and it needed an obstinate man to leave Crask between the hours of five and six in the morning on an enterprise so wild and in weather so lamentable. For the rain came down in sheets, and a wind from the north-east put ice into it. He stopped for a moment on the summit of the Crask ridge, to contemplate a wall of driving mist where should have been a vista of the Haripol peaks. 'This wund will draw beasts intil the Sanctuary without any help from Macnicol,' said Wattie morosely. 'It's ower fierce to last. I wager it will be clear long afore night.'

'It's the weather we want,' said Lamancha, cowering from the violence of the blast.

'For the Sanctuary – maybe. Up till then I'm no sae sure. It's that thick we micht maybe walk intil a navvy's airms.'

The gods of the sky were in a capricious mood. All down the Crask hill-side to the edge of the Doran the wet table-cloth of the fog clung to every ridge and hollow. The stream was in roaring spate, and Lamancha and Wattie, already soaked to the skin, forded it knee-high. They had by this time crossed the moor-road from Crask to Haripol, and marked the nook where in the lee of rocks and birches Archie was to be waiting with the Ford car. Beyond lay the long lift of land to the Haripol peaks. It was rough with boulders and heather, and broken with small gullies, and on its tangled face a man might readily lose himself. Wattie disliked the mist solely because it prevented him from locating the watchers, since his experience of life made him disinclined to leave anything to chance; but he had no trouble in finding his way in it. The consequence was that he took Lamancha over the glacis at the pace of a Ghurka, and in half an hour from the Doran's edge had him panting among the screes just under the Beallach which led to the Sanctuary. Somewhere behind them were the vain navvy pickets, happily evaded in the fog.

Then suddenly the weather changed. The wind shifted a point to the east, the mist furled up, the rain ceased, and a world was revealed from which all colour had been washed, a world as bleak and raw as at its first creation. The grey screes sweated grey water, the sodden herbage was bleached like winter, the crags towering above them might have been of coal. A small fine rain still fell, but the visibility was now good enough to show them the ground behind them in the style of a muddy etching.

The consequence of this revelation was that Wattie shuffled into cover. He studied the hill-side behind him long and patiently with his glass. Then he grunted: 'There's four navvies, as I mak out, but no verra well posted. We cam gey near ane o' them on the road up. Na, they canna see us here, and besides they're no lookin' this airt.' Lamancha tried to find them with his telescope, but could see nothing human in the wide sopping wilderness.

Wattie grumbled as he led the way up a kind of *nullah*, usually as dry as Arabia but now spouting a thousand rivulets, right into the throat of the Beallach. 'It's clearin' just when we wanted it thick. The ways o' Providence is mysteerious . . . Na, na, there's nae road there. That's a fox's track, and it's the deer's road we maun gang. Stags will no climb rocks, sensible beasts . . . The wind's gone, but I wish the mist wad come down again.'

At the top of the pass was a pad of flat ground, covered thick with the leaves of cloudberries. On the right rose the Pinnacle Ridge of Sgurr Dearg, in its beginning an easy scramble which gave no hint of the awesome towers which later awaited the traveller; on the left Sgurr Mor ran up in a steep face of screes. 'Keep doun,' Wattie enjoined, and crawled forward to where two boulders made a kind of window for a view to the north.

The two looked down into three little corries which, like the fingers of a hand, united in the palm of a larger corrie, which was the upper glen of the Reascuill. It was a sanctuary perfectly fashioned by nature, for the big corrie was cut off from the lower glen by a line of boiler-plates like the wall of a great dam, down which the stream plunged in cascades. The whole place was loud with water – the distant roar of the main river, the ceaseless dripping of the cliffs, the chatter and babble of a myriad hidden rivulets. But the noise seemed only to deepen the secrecy. It was a world in monochrome, every detail clear as a wet pebble, but nowhere brightness or colour. Even the coats of the deer had taken on the dead grey of the slaty crags.

Never in his life had Lamancha seen so many beasts together. Each corrie was full of them, feeding on the rough pastures or among the boulders, drifting aimlessly across the spouts of screes below the high cliffs, sheltering in the rushy gullies. There were groups of hinds and calves, and knots of stags, and lone beasts on knolls or in mud-baths, and, since all were restless, the numbers in each corrie were constantly changing.

'Ye gods, what a sight!' Lamancha murmured, his head at Wattie's elbow. 'We won't fail for lack of beasts.'

'The trouble is,' said Wattie, 'that there's ower mony.' Then he added obscurely that 'it might be the day o' Pentecost.'

Lamancha was busy with his glass. Just below him, not three hundred yards off, where the ravine which ran from the Beallach opened out into the nearest corrie, there was a group of deer – three hinds, a little stag, and farther on a second stag of which only the head could be seen.

'Wattie,' he whispered excitedly, 'there's a beast down there – a shootable beast. It's just what we're looking for . . . close to the Beallach.'

'Aye, I see it,' was the answer. 'And I see something mair. There's a man ayont the big corrie – d'ye see yon rock shapit like a puddock-stool? . . . Na, the south side o' the waterfall . . . Well, follow on frae there towards Bheinn Fhada – have ye got him?'

'Is that a man?' asked the surprised Lamancha.

'Where's your een, my lord? It's a man wi' grey breeks and a brown jaicket – an' he's smokin' a pipe. Aye, it's Macqueen. I ken by the lang legs o' him.'

'Is he a Haripol gillie?'

'He's the second stalker. He's under notice, for him and young Mr Claybody doesna agree. Macqueen comes frae the Lowlands, and has a verra shairp tongue. They was oot on the hill last week, and Mr Johnson was pechin' sair gaun up the braes, an' no wonder, puir man. He cries on Macqueen to gang slow, and says, apologetic-like, "Ye see, Macqueen, I've been workin' terrible hard the past year, and it's damaged my wund." Macqueen, who canna bide the sight of him, says, "I'm glad to hear it, sir. I was feared it was maybe the drink." Gey impident!'

'Shocking.'

'Weel, he's workin' off his notice . . . I'm pleased to see him yonder, for it means that Macnicol will no be there. Macnicol' – Wattie chuckled like a dropsical corncrake – 'is maist likely beatin' the roddydendrums for the wee dog. Macqueen is set there so as he can watch this Beallach and likewise the top of the Red Burn on the Machray side, which I was tellin' ye was the easiest road. If ye were to kill that stag doun below he could baith see ye and hear ye, and ye'd never be allowed to shift it a yaird . . . Na, na. Seein' Macqueen's where he is, we maun try the wee corrie right under Sgurr Dearg. He canna see into that.'

'But we'll never get there through all those deer.'

'It will not be easy.'

'And if we get a stag we'll never be able to get it over this Beallach.'

'Indeed it will tak a great deal of time. Maybe a' nicht. But I'll no say it's not possible . . . Onyway, it is the best plan. We will have to tak a lang cast roond, and we maunna forget Macqueen. I'd give a five-pun-note for anither blatter o' rain.'

The next hour was one of the severest bodily trials which Lamancha had ever known. Wattie led him up a chimney of Sgurr Mor, the depth of which made it safe from observation, and down another on the north face, also deep, and horribly loose and wet. This brought them to the floor of the first corrie at a point below where the deer had been observed. The next step was to cross the corrie eastwards towards Sgurr Dearg. This was a matter of high delicacy – first because of the number of deer, second because it was all within view of Macqueen's watch-tower.

Lamancha had followed in his time many stalkers, but he had never seen an artist who approached Wattie in skill. The place was littered with hinds and calves and stags, the cover was patchy at the best, and the beasts were restless. Wherever a route seemed plain the large ears and spindle shanks of a hind appeared to block it. Had he been alone Lamáncha would either have sent every beast streaming before him in full sight of Macqueen, or he would have advanced at the rate of one yard an hour. But Wattie managed to move both circumspectly and swiftly. He seemed to know by instinct when a hind could be bluffed and when her suspicions must be laboriously quieted. The two went for the most part on their bellies like serpents, but théir lowliness of movement would have been of no avail had not Wattie, by his sense of the subtle eddies of air, been able to shape a course which prevented their wind from shifting deer behind them. He well knew that any movement of beasts in any quarter would bring Macqueen's vigilant glasses into use.

Their task was not so hard so long as they were in hollows on the corrie floor. The danger came in crossing the low ridge to that farther corrie which was beyond Macqueen's ken, for, as they ascended, the wind was almost bound to carry their scent to the deer through which they had passed. Wattie lay long with his chin in the mire and his eyes scanning the ridge till he made up his mind on his route. Obviously it was the choice of the least among several evils, for he shook his head and frowned.

The ascent of the ridge was a slow business, and toilful. Wattie was clearly following an elaborate plan, for he zigzagged preposterously, and would wait long for no apparent reason in places where Lamancha was held precariously by half a foothold and the pressure of his nails. Anxious glances were cast over his shoulder at the post where Macqueen was presumably on duty. The stalker's ears seemed of an uncanny keenness, for he would listen hard, hear something, and then utterly change his course. To Lamancha it was all inexplicable, for there appeared to be no deer on the ridge, and the place was so much in the lee that not a breath of wind seemed to be abroad to carry their scent. Hard as his condition was, he grew furiously warm and thirsty, and perhaps a little careless, for once or twice he let earth and stones slip under his feet.

Wattie turned on him fiercely. 'Gang as if ye was growin',' he whispered. 'There's beasts on a' sides.'

Sobered thereby, Lamancha mended his ways, and kept his thoughts rigidly on the job before him. He crept docilely in Wattie's prints, wondering why on a little ridge they should go through exertions that must be equivalent to the ascent of the

Matterhorn. At last his guide stopped. 'Put your head between thae rashes,' he enjoined. 'Ye'll see her.'

'See what?' Lamancha gasped.

'That dour deevil o' a hind.'

There she was, a grey elderly beldame, with her wicked puck-like ears, aware and suspicious, not five yards off.

'We canna wait,' Wattie hissed. 'It's ower dangerous. Bide you here like a stone.'

He wriggled away to his right, while Lamancha, hanging on a heather root, watched the twitching ears and wrinkled nozzle . . . Presently from farther up the hill came a sharp bark, which was almost a bleat. The hind flung up her head and gazed intently . . . Five minutes later the sound was repeated, this time from a lower altitude. The beast sniffed, shook herself, and stamped with her foot. Then she laid back her ears, and trotted quietly over the crest.

Wattie was back again by Lamancha's side. 'That puzzled the auld bitch,' was his only comment. 'We can gang faster now, and God kens we've nae time to loss.'

As Lamancha lay panting at last on the top of the ridge he looked down into the highest of the lesser corries, tucked right under the black cliffs of Sgurr Dearg. It was a little corrie, very steep, and threaded by a burn which after the rain was white like a snow-drift. Vast tumbled masses of stone, ancient rock-falls from the mountain, lay thick as the cottages in a hamlet. At first sight the place seemed to be without deer. Lamancha, scanning it with his glass, could detect no living thing among the debris.

Wattie was calling fiercely on his Maker.

'God, it's the auld hero,' he muttered, his eyes glued to his telescope.

At last Lamancha got his glasses adjusted, and saw what his companion saw. Far up the corrie, on a patch of herbage – the last before the desert of the rocks began – stood three stags. Two were ordinary beasts, shootable, for they must have weighed sixteen or seventeen stone, but with inconsiderable heads. The third was no heavier, but he had a head like a blasted pine – going back fast, for the beast was old, but still with thirteen clearly marked points and a most noble spread of horn.

'It's him,' Wattie crooned. 'It's the auld hero. Fine I ken him, for I seen him on Crask last back-end rivin' at the stacks.

There's no a forest hereaways but they've had a try for him, but the deil's in him, for the grandest shots aye miss. What's your will, my lord? Dod, if John Macnab gets yon lad, he can cock his bonnet.'

'I don't know, Wattie. Is it fair to kill the best beast in the forest?'

'Keep your mind easy about that. Yon's no a Haripol beast. He's oftener on Crask than on Haripol. He's a traiveller, and in one season will cover the feck o' the Hielands. I've heard that oreeginally he cam oot o' Kintail. He's terrible auld – some says a hundred year – and if ye dinna kill him he'll perish next winter, belike, in a snaw-wreath, and that's a puir death to dee.'

'It's a terrible pull to the Beallach.'

'It will be that, but there's the nicht afore us. If we don't take that beast – or one o' the three – I doubt we'll no get anither chance.'

'Push on, then, Wattie. It looks like a clear coast.'

'I'm no so sure. There's that deevil o' a hind somewhere afore us.'

Down through the gaps of the Pinnacle Ridge blew fine streams of mist. They were the precursors of a new storm, for long before the two men had wormed their way into the corrie the mountain before them was blotted out with a curtain of rain, and the wind, which seemed for a time to have died away, was sounding a thousand notes in the Pan's-pipes of the crags.

'Good,' said Lamancha. 'This will blanket the shot.'

'Ba-ad too,' growled Wattie, 'for we'll be duntin' against the auld bitch.'

Lamancha believed he had located the stages well enough to go to them in black darkness. You had only to follow the stream to its head, and they were on the left bank a hundred yards or so from the rocks. But when he reached the burn he found that his memory was useless. There was not one stream but dozens, and it was hard to say which was the main channel. It was a loud world again, very different from the first corrie, but, when he would have hastened, Wattie insisted on circumspection. 'There's the hind,' he said, 'and maybe since we're out o' Macqueen's sicht there's nae need to hurry.'

His caution was justified. As they drew themselves up the side of a small cascade the tops of a pair of antlers were seen over the next rise. Lamancha thought they were those of one of the three stags, but Wattie disillusioned him. 'We're no within six hundred yards o' yon beasts,' he said.

A long circuit was necessary, happily in good cover, and the stream was not rejoined till at a point where its channel bore to the south, so that their wind would not be carried to the beasts below the knoll. After that it seemed advisable to Wattie to keep to the water, which was flowing in a deep-cut bed. It was a job for a merman rather than for breeched human beings, for Wattie would permit of no rising to a horizontal or even to a kneeling position. The burn entered at their collars and flowed steadily through their shirts to an exit at their knees. Never had men been so comprehensively and continuously wet. Lamancha's right arm ached with pulling the rifle along the bank – he always insisted on carrying his weapon himself – while his body was submerged in the icy outflow of Sgurr Dearg's springs.

The pressure of Wattie's foot in his face halted him. Blinking through the spray, he saw his leader's head raised stiffly to the alert in the direction of a little knoll. Even in the thick weather he could detect a pair of bat-like ears, and he realised that these ears were twitching. It did not need Wattie's whisper of 'the auld bitch' to reveal the enemy.

The two lay in the current for what seemed to Lamancha at least half an hour. He had enough hill-craft to recognise that their one hope was to stick to the channel, for only thus was there a chance of their presence being unrevealed by the wind. But the channel led them very close to the hind. If the brute chose to turn her foolish head they would be within view.

With desperate slowness, an inch at a time, Wattie moved upwards. He signed to Lamancha to wait while he traversed a pool where only his cap and nose showed above the water. Then came a peat wallow, when his face seemed to be ground into the moss, and his limbs to be splayed like a frog's and to move with frog-like jerks. After that was a little cascade, and, beyond, the shelter of a big boulder which would get him out of the hind's orbit. Lamancha watched this strange progress with one eye; the other was on the twitching ears. Mercifully all went well, and Wattie's stern disappeared round a corner of rock.

He laboured to follow with the same precision. The pool was easy enough except for the trailing of the rifle. The peat was straightforward going, though in his desire to follow his leader's example he dipped his face so deep in the black slime that his nostrils were plugged with it, and some got into his eyes which he dared not try to remove. But the waterfall was a snag. It was no light task to draw himself up against the weight of descending water, and at the top he lay panting for a second, damming up the flow with his body . . . Then he moved on; but the mischief had been done.

For the sound of the release of the pent-up stream had struck a foreign note on the hind's ear. It was an unfamiliar noise among the many familiar ones which at the moment filled the corrie. She turned her head sharply, and saw something in the burn which she did not quite understand. Lamancha, aware of her scrutiny, lay choking, with the water running into his nose; but the alarm had been given. The hind turned her head, and trotted off up-wind.

The next he knew was Wattie at his elbow making wild signals to him to rise and follow. Cramped and staggering, he lumbered after him away from the stream into a moraine of great granite blocks. 'We're no twa hundred yards from the stags,' the guide whispered. 'The auld bitch will move them, but please God we'll get a shot.' As Lamancha ran he marvelled at Wattie's skill, for he himself had not a notion where in the wide world the beasts might be.

They raced to a knoll, and Wattie flung himself flat on the top.

'There,' he cried. 'Steady, man. Tak the nearest. A hundred yards. Nae mair.'

Lamancha saw through the drizzle three stags moving at a gentle trot to the south – up-wind, for in the corrie the eddies were coming oddly. They were not really startled, but the hind had stirred them. The big stag was in the centre of the three, and the proper shot was the last – a reasonable broadside.

Wattie's advice had been due to his loyalty to John Macnab, and not to his own choice, and this Lamancha knew. The desire of the great stag was on him, as it was on the hunter in Homer, and he refused to be content with the second-best. It was not an easy shot in that bad light, and it is probable that he would have missed; but suddenly Wattie gave an unearthly bark, and for a second the three beasts slowed down and turned their heads towards the sound.

In that second Lamancha fired. The great head seemed to bow itself, and then fling upwards, and all three disappeared at a gallop into the mist.

'A damned poor tailoring shot!' Lamancha groaned.

'He's deid for all that, but God kens how far he'll run afore he drops. He's hit in the neck, but a wee thing ower low . . . We can bide here a while and eat our piece. If ye wasna John Macnab I could be wishin' we had brought a dog.'

Lamancha, cold, wet, and disgusted, wolfed his sandwiches, had a stiff dram from his flask, and smoked a pipe before he started again. He cursed his marksmanship, and Wattie forbore to contradict him; doubtless Jim Tarras had accustomed him to a standard of skill from which this was a woeful declension. Nor would he hold out much hope. 'He'll gang into the first corrie and when he finds the wund different there he'll turn back for the Reascuill. If this was our ain forest and the weather wasna that thick, we might get another chance at him there . . . Oh, aye, he might gang for ten mile. The mist is a good thing, for Macqueen will no see what's happenin', but if it was to lift, and he saw a' the stags in the corrie movin', you and me wad have to find a hidy-hole till the dark . . . Are ye ready, my lord?'

They crossed the ridge which separated them from the first corrie, close to the point where it took off from the *massif* of Sgurr Dearg. It was a shorter road than the one they had come by, and they could take it safely, for they were now moving upwind, owing to the curious eddy from the south. Over the ridge it would be a different matter, for there the wind would be easterly as before. But it was a stiff climb and a slow business, for they had to make sure that they were on the track of the stag.

Wattie trailed the blood-marks like an Indian, noticing splashes on stones and rushes which Lamancha would have missed. 'He's sair hit,' he observed at one point. 'See! He tried that steep bit and couldna manage it. There's the mark o' his feet turnin' . . . He's stoppit here . . . Aye, here's his trail, and it'll be the best for you and me. There's nothing like a wounded beast for pickin' the easiest road.'

On the crest the air stirred freely, and, as it seemed to Lamancha, with a new chill. Wattie gave a grunt of satisfaction, and sniffed it like a pointer dog. He moistened his finger and held it up; then he plucked some light grasses and tossed them into the air.

'That's a mercifu' dispensation! Maybe that shot that ye think ye bauchled was the most providential shot ye ever fired

. . . The wund is shiftin'. I looked for it afore night, but no that early in the day. It's wearin' round to the south. D'ye see what that means?'

Lamancha shook his head. Disgust had made his wits dull.

'Yon beast, as I telled ye, was a traiveller. There's nothing to keep him in Haripol forest. But he'll no leave it unless the wund will let him. Now it looks as if Providence was kind to us. The wund's blawin' from the Beallach, and he's bound to gang up-wund.'

The next half-hour was a period of swift drama. Sure enough, the blood-marks turned up the first corrie in the direction from which the two had come in the morning. As the ravine narrowed the stag had evidently taken to the burn, for there were splashes on the rocks and a tinge of red in the pools.

'He's no far off,' Wattie croaked. 'See, man, he's verra near done. He's slippin' sair.'

And then, as they mounted, they came on a little pool where the water was dammed as if by a landslip. There, his body half under the cascade, lay the stag, stone dead, his great horns parting the fall like a pine swept down by a winter spate.

The two regarded him in silence, till Wattie was moved to pronounce his epitaph.

'It's yersel, ye auld hero, and ye've come by a grand end. Ye've had a braw life traivellin' the hills, and ye've been a braw beast, and the fame o' ye gaed through a' the country-side. Ye micht have dwined awa in the cauld winter an dee'd in the wame o' a snaw-drift. Or ye micht have been massacred by ane o' thae Haripol sumphs wi' ten bullets in the big bag. But ye've been killed clean and straucht by John Macnab, and that is a gentleman's death, whatever.'

'That's all very well,' said Lamancha, 'but you know I tailored the shot.'

'Ye're a fule,' cried the rapt Wattie. 'Ye did no siccan thing. It was a verra deeficult shot, and ye put it deid in the only place ye could see. I will not have seen many better shots at all, at all.'

'What about the gralloch?' Lamancha asked.

'No here. If the mist lifted Macqueen micht see us. It's no fifty yards to the top o' the Beallach, and we'll find a place there for the job.'

Wattie produced two ropes and bound the fore-feet and the

hind-feet together. Then he rapidly climbed to the summit, and reported on his return that the mist was thick there, and that there were no tracks except their own of the morning. It was a weary business dragging the carcass up a nearly perpendicular slope. First with difficulty they raised it out of the burn channel, and then drew it along the steep hill-side. They had to go a long way up the hill-side to avoid the rock curtain on the edge of the Beallach, but eventually the top was reached, and the stag was deposited behind some boulders on the left of the flat ground. Here, even if the mist lifted, they would be hid from the sight of Macqueen, and from any sentries there might be on the Crask side.

Wattie flung off his coat and proceeded with gusto to his gory task. The ravens, which had been following them for the past hour, came nearer and croaked encouragement from the ledges of Sgurr Dearg and Sgurr Mor. Wattie was in high spirits, for he whistled softly at his work; but Lamancha, after his first moment of satisfaction, was restless with anxiety. He had still to get his trophy out of the forest, and there seemed many chances of a slip between his lips and that cup. He was impatient for Wattie to finish, for the air seemed to him lightening. An ominous brightness was flushing the mist towards the south, and the rain had declined to the thinnest of drizzles. He told Wattie his fears.

'Aye, it'll be a fine afternoon. I foresaw that, but that's maybe not a bad thing, now that we're out o' Macqueen's sight.'

Wattie completed his job, and hid the horrid signs below a pile of sods and stones. 'Nae *poch-a-bhuie* for me the day,' he grinned. 'I've other things to think o' besides my supper.' He wiped his arms and hands in the wet heather and put on his coat. Then he produced a short pipe, and, as he turned away to light it, a figure suddenly stood beside Lamancha and made his heart jump.

'My hat!' said Palliser-Yeates, 'what a head! That must be about a record for Wester Ross. I never got anything as good myself. You're a lucky devil, Charles.'

'Call me lucky when the beast is safe at Crask. What about your side of the hill?'

'Pretty quiet. I've been here for hours and hours, wondering where on earth you two had got to . . . There's four fellows stuck at intervals along the hill-side, and I shouldn't take them to be very active citizens. But there's a fifth who does sentry-go, and I don't fancy the look of him so much. Looks a keen chap, and spry on his legs. What's the orders for me? The place has been playing hide-and-seek, and half the time I've been sitting coughing in a wet blanket. If it stays thick I suppose my part is off.'

Wattie, stirred again into fierce life, peered into the thinning fog.

'Damn! The mist's liftin'. I'll get the beast ower the first screes afore it's clear, and once I'm in the burn I'll wait for ye. I can manage the first bit fine mysel' – I could manage it a', if there was nae hurry . . . Bide you here till I'm weel startit, for I don't like the news o' that wandering navvy. And you sir' – this to Palliser-Yeates – 'be ready to show yourself down the hill-side as soon as it's clear enough for the folk to see ye. Keep well to the west, and draw them off towards Haripol. There's a man posted near the burn, but he's the farthest east o' them, and for God's sake keep them to the west o' me and the stag. Ye're an auld hand at the job, and should have nae deeficulty in ficklin' a wheen heavy-fitted navvies. Is Sir Erchibald there wi' the cawr?'

'I suppose so. The time he was due the fog was thick. I couldn't pick him up from here with the glass when the weather cleared, but that's as it should be, for the place he selected was absolutely hidden from this side.'

'Well, good luck to us a'.' Wattie tossed off a dram from the socket of Lamancha's flask, and, dragging the stag by the horns, disappeared in two seconds from sight.

'I'll be off, Charles,' said Palliser-Yeates, 'for I'd better get down-hill and down the glen before I start.' He paused to stare at his friend. 'By Gad, you do look a proper blackguard. Do you realise that you've a face like a nigger and a two-foot rent in your bags? It would be good for Johnson Claybody's soul to see you!'

TWELVE

Haripol – Transport

IT MAY BE doubted whether in clear weather Sir Archie could ever have reached his station unobserved by the watchers on the hill. The place was cunningly chosen, for the road, as it approached the Doran, ran in the lee of a long covert of birch and hazel, so that for the better part of a mile no car on it could be seen from beyond the stream, even from the highest ground. But as the car descended from the Crask ridge it would have been apparent to the sentinels, and its non-appearance beyond the covert would have bred suspicion. As it was the clear spell had gone before it topped the hill, for Sir Archie was more than an hour behind the scheduled time.

This was Janet's doing. She had started off betimes on the yellow pony for Crask, intending to take the by-way from the Larrig side, but before she reached the Bridge of Larrig she had scented danger. One of the correspondents, halted by the roadside with a motor bicycle, accosted her with great politeness and begged a word. She was Miss Raden, wasn't she? and therefore she knew all about John Macnab. He had heard gossip in the glen of the coming raid on Haripol, and understood that this was the day. Would Miss Raden advise him from her knowledge of the country-side? Was it possible to find some coign of vantage from which he might see the fun?

Janet stuck to the simple truth. She had heard the same story, she admitted, but Haripol was a gigantic and precipitous forest, and it was preserved with a nicety unparalleled in her experience. To go to Haripol in the hope of finding John Macnab would be like a casual visit to England on the chance of meeting the King. She advised him to go to Haripol in the evening. 'If anything has happened there,' she said, 'you will hear about it from the gillies. They'll either be triumphant or savage, and in either case they'll talk.'

'We've got to get a story, Miss Raden,' the correspondent

observed dismally, 'and in this roomy place it's like looking for a needle in a hayfield. What sort of people are the Claybodys?'

'You won't get anything from them,' Janet laughed. 'Take my advice and wait till the evening.'

When he was out of sight she turned her pony up the hill and arrived at Crask with an anxious face. 'If these people are on the loose all day,' she told Sir Archie, 'they're bound to spoil sport. They may stumble on our car, or they may see more of Mr Palliser-Yeates's doings than we want. Can nothing be done? What about Mr Crossby?'

Crossby was called into consultation and admitted the gravity of the danger. When his help was demanded, he hesitated. 'Of course I know most of them, and they know me, and they're a very decent lot of fellows. But they're professional men, and I don't see myself taking on the job of gulling them. *Esprit de corps*, you know . . . No, they don't suspect me. They probably think I left the place after I got off the Strathlarrig fish scoop, and that I don't know anything about the Haripol business. I daresay they'd be glad enough to see me if I turned up . . . I might link on to them and go with them to Haripol and keep them in a safe place.'

'That's the plan,' said Archie. 'You march them off to Haripol – say you know the ground – which you do a long sight better than they. Some of the gillies will be hunting the home woods for Lady Claybody's pup. Get them mixed up in that show. It will all help to damage Macnicol's temper, and he's the chap we're most afraid of . . . Besides, you might turn up handy in a crisis. Supposin' Ned Leithen – or old John – has a hard run at the finish you might confuse the pursuit . . . That's the game, Crossby my lad, and you're the man to play it.'

It was after eleven o'clock before the Ford car, having slipped over the pass from Crask in driving sleet, came to a stand in the screen of birches with the mist wrapping the world so close that the foaming Doran six yards away was only to be recognised by its voice. All the way there Sir Archie had been full of forebodings.

'We're givin' too much weight away, Miss Janet,' he croaked. 'All we've got on our side is this putrid weather. That's a bit of luck, I admit. Also we've two of the most compromisin' objects on earth, Fish Benjie and that little brute Roguie . . . Claybody has a hundred navvies, and a pack of gillies, and every beast will be in the Sanctuary, which is as good as inside a barb-wire fence . . . The thing's too ridiculous. We've got to sit in this car and watch an eminent British statesman bein' hoofed off the hill, while old John tries to play the decoy-duck, and Ned Leithen, miles off, is hoppin' like a he-goat on the mountains . . . It's pretty well bound to end in disaster. One of them will be nobbled – probably all three – and when young Claybody asks, "Wherefore this outrage?" I don't see what the cowerin' culprit is goin' to answer and say unto him.'

But when the car stopped in the drip of the birches, and Archie had leisure to look at the girl by his side, he began to think less of impending perils. The place was loud with wind and water, and yet curiously silent. The mist had drawn so close that the two seemed to be shut into a fantastic, secret world of their own. Janet was wearing breeches and a long riding-coat covered by a grey oilskin, the buttoned collar of which framed her small face. Her bright hair, dabbled with raindrops, was battened down under an ancient felt hat. She looked, thought Sir Archie, like an adorable boy. Also for the last half-hour she had been silent.

'You have never spoken to me about your speech,' she said at last, looking away from him.

'Yours, you mean,' he said. 'I only repeated what you said that afternoon on Carnmore. But you didn't hear it. I looked for you everywhere in the hall, and I saw your father and your sister and Bandicott, but I couldn't see you.'

'I was there. Did you think I could have missed it? But I was too nervous to sit with the others, so I found a corner at the back below the gallery. I was quite near Wattie Lithgow.'

Archie's heart fluttered. 'That was uncommon kind. I don't see why you should have worried about that – I mean I'm jolly grateful. I was just going to play the ass of all creation when I remembered what you had said – and – well, I made a speech instead of repeating the rigmarole I had written. I owe everything to you, for, you see, you started me out – I can never feel just that kind of funk again . . . Charles thinks I might be some use in politics . . . But I can tell you when I sat down and hunted through the hall and couldn't see you it took all the gilt off the gingerbread.'

'I was gibbering with fright,' said the girl, 'when I thought you were going to stick. If Wattie hadn't shouted out, I think I would have done it myself.'

After that silence fell. The rain poured from the trees on to the cover of the Ford, and from the cover sheets of water cascaded to the drenched heather. Wet blasts scourged the occupants and whipped a high colour into their faces. Janet arose and got out.

'We may as well be properly wet,' she said. 'If they get the stag as far as the Doran, they must find some way across. There's none at present. Hadn't we better build a bridge?'

The stream, in ordinary weather a wide channel of stones where a slender current falls in amber pools, was now a torrent four yards wide. But it was a deceptive torrent with more noise than strength, and save in the pools was only a foot or two deep. There were many places where a stag could have been easily lugged through by an able-bodied man. But the bridge-building proposal was welcomed, since it provided relief for both from an atmosphere which had suddenly become heavily charged. At a point where the channel narrowed between two blaeberry-thatched rocks it was possible to make an inclined bridge from one bank to the other. The materials were there in the shape of sundry larch-poles brought from the lower woods for the repair of a bridge on the Crask road. Archie dragged half a dozen to the edge and pushed them across. Then Janet marched through the water, which ran close to the top of her riding-boots, and prepared the abutment on the farther shore, weighting the poles down with sods broken from an adjacent bank.

'I'm coming over,' she cried. 'If it will bear a stag, it will bear me.'

'No, you're not,' Archie commanded. 'I'll come to you.'

'The last time I saw you cross a stream you fell in,' she reminded him.

Archie tested the contrivance, but it showed an ugly inclination to behave like a see-saw, being insufficiently weighted on Janet's side.

'Wait a moment. We need more turf,' and she disappeared from sight beyond a knoll. When she returned she was excessively muddy as to hands and garments.

'I slipped in that beastly peat-moss,' she explained. 'I never saw such hags, and there's no turf to be got except with a spade . . . No, you don't! Keep off that bridge, please. It isn't nearly safe yet. I'm going to roll down stones.'

Roll down stones she did till she had erected something very much like a cairn at her end, which would have opposed a considerable barrier to the passage of any stag. Then she announced that she must get clean, and went a few yards down-stream to one of the open shallows, where she proceeded to make a toilet. She stood with the current flowing almost to her knees, suffering it to wash the peat from her boots and the skirts of her oilskin and at the same time scrubbing her grimy hands. In the process her hat became loose, dropped into the stream, and was clutched with one hand, while with the other she restrained the efforts of the wind to uncoil her shining curls.

It was while watching the moving waters at their priest-like task that crisis came upon Sir Archie. In a blinding second he realised with the uttermost certainty that he had found his mate. He had known it before, but now came the flash of supreme conviction . . . For swelling bosoms and pouting lips and soft curves and languishing eyes Archie had only the most distant regard. He saluted them respectfully and passed by the other side of the road – they did not belong to his world. But that slender figure splashing in the tawny eddies made a different appeal. Most women in such a posture would have looked tousled and flimsy, creatures ill at ease, with their careful allure beaten out of them by weather. But this girl was an authentic creature of the hills and winds – her young slimness bent tensely against the current, her exquisite head and figure made more fine and delicate by the conflict. It is a sad commentary on the young man's education, but, while his soul was bubbling with poetry, the epithet which kept recurring to his mind was 'clean-run.' . . . More, far more. He saw in that moment of revelation a comrade who would never fail him, with whom he could keep on all the roads of life. It was that which all his days he had been confusedly seeking.

'Janet,' he shouted against the wind, 'will you marry me?'

She made a trumpet of one hand.

'What do you say?' she cried.

'Will you marry me?'

'Yes,' she turned a laughing face, 'of course I will.'

'I'm coming across,' he shouted.

'No. Stay where you are. I'll come to you.'

She climbed the other bank and made for the bridge of larchpoles, and before he could prevent her she had embarked on that crazy structure. Then that happened which might have been foreseen, since the poles on Archie's side of the stream had no fixed foundation. They splayed out, and he was just in time to catch her in his arms as she sprang.

'You darling girl,' he said, and she turned up to him a face smiling no more, but very grave.

Archie, his arms full of dripping maiden, stood in a happy trance.

'Please put me down,' she said. 'See, the mist is clearing. We must get into cover.'

Sure enough the haze was lifting from the hill-side before them and long tongues of black moorland were revealed stretching up to the crags. They found a place among the birches which gave them a safe prospect and fetched luncheon from the car. Hot coffee from a thermos was the staple of the meal, which they consumed like two preoccupied children. Archie looked at his watch and found it after two-o'clock. 'Something must begin to happen soon,' he said, and they took up position side by side on a sloping rock, Janet with her Zeiss glasses and Archie with his telescope.

His head was a delicious merry-go-round of hopes and dreams. It was full of noble thoughts – about Janet, and himself, and life. And the thoughts were mirthful too – a great, mellow, philosophic mirthfulness. John Macnab was no longer an embarrassing hazard, but a glorious adventure. It did not matter what happened – nothing could happen wrong in this spacious and rosy world. If Lamancha succeeded, it was a tremendous joke, if he failed a more tremendous, and, as for Leithen and Palliser-Yeates, comedy had marked them for its own . . . He wondered what he had done to be blessed with such happiness.

Already the mist had gone from the foreground, and the hills were clear to half-way up the rocks of Sgurr Mor and Sgurr Dearg. He had his glass on the Beallach, on the throat of which a stray sun-gleam made a sudden patch of amethyst.

'I see someone,' Janet cried. 'On the edge of the pass. Have you got it? – on the left-hand side of that spout of stones.'

Archie found the place. 'Got him . . . By Jove, it's Wattie . . . And – and – yes, by all the gods, I believe he's pullin' a stag down . . . Wait a second . . . Yes, he's haulin' it into the burn . . . Well done, our side! But where on earth is Charles?'

The two lay with their eyes glued on the patch of hill, now lit everywhere by the emerging sun. They saw the little figure dip into a hollow, appear again and then go out of sight in the upper part of a long narrow scaur which held the headwaters of a stream – they could see the foam of the little falls farther down. Before it disappeared Archie had made out a stag's head against a background of green moss.

'That's that,' he cried. 'Charles must be somewhere behind protectin' the rear. I suppose Wattie knows what he's doin' and is certain he can't be seen by the navvies. Anyhow, he's well hidden at present in the burn, but he'll come into view lower down when the ravine opens out. He's a tough old bird to move a beast at that pace . . . The question now is, where is old John? It's time he was gettin' busy.'

Janet, whose glass made up in width of range what it lacked in power, suddenly cried out: 'I see him. Look! up at the edge of the rocks – three hundred yards west of the Beallach. He's moving down-hill. I think it's Palliser-Yeates – he's the part of John Macnab I know best.'

Archie found the spot. 'It's old John right enough, and he's doin' his best to make himself conspicuous. Those yellow breeks of his are like a flag. We've got a seat in the stalls and the curtain is goin' up. Now for the fun.'

Then followed for the better part of an hour a drama of almost indecent sensation. Wattie and his stag were forgotten in watching the efforts of an eminent banker to play hare to the hounds of four gentlemen accustomed to labour rather with their hands than with their feet. It was the navvy whose post was almost directly opposite Janet and Archie who first caught sight of the figure on the hill-side. He blew a whistle and began to move uphill, evidently with the intention of cutting off the intruder's retreat to the east and driving him towards Haripol. But the quarry showed no wish to go east, for it was towards Haripol that he seemed to be making, by a long slant down the slopes.

'I've got Number Two,' Janet whispered. 'There – above the patch of scrub – close to the three boulders . . . Oh, and there's Number Three. Mr Palliser-Yeates is walking straight towards him. Do you think he sees him?'

'Trust old John. He's the wiliest of God's creatures, and he hasn't lost much pace since he played outside three-quarters for England. Wait till he starts to run.'

But Mr Palliser-Yeates continued at a brisk walk apparently oblivious of his foes, who were whistling like curlews, till he was very near the embraces of Number Three. Then he went through a very creditable piece of acting. Suddenly he seemed to be stricken with terror, looked wildly around to all the points of the compass, noted his pursuer, and, as if in a panic, ran blindly for the gap between Numbers Two and Three. Number Four had appeared by this time, and Number Four was a strategist. He did not join in the pursuit, but moved rapidly down the glen towards Haripol to cut off the fugitive, should he outstrip the hunters.

Palliser-Yeates managed to get through the gap, and now appeared running strongly for the Doran, which at that point of its course – about half a mile down-stream from Janet and Archie – flowed in a deep-cut but not precipitous channel, much choked with birch and rowan. Numbers Two and Three followed, and also Number One, who had by now seen that there was no need of a rearguard. For a little all four disappeared from sight, and Janet and Archie looked anxiously at each other. Cries, excited cries, were coming upstream, but there was no sign of human beings.

'John can't have been such a fool as to get caught,' Archie grumbled. 'He has easily the pace of those heavy-footed chaps. Wish he'd show himself.'

Presently first one, then a second, then a third navvy appeared on the high bank of the Doran, moving aimlessly, like hounds at fault.

'They've lost him,' Archie cried. 'Where d'you suppose the leery old bird has got to? He can't have gone to earth.'

That was not revealed for about twenty minutes. Then a cry from one of the navvies called the attention of the others to something moving high up on the hill-side.

'It's John,' Archie muttered. 'He must have crawled up one of the side-burns. Lord, that's pretty work.'

The navvies began heavily to follow, though they had a thousand feet of lee-way to make up. But it was no part of Palliser-Yeates's plan to discourage them, since he had to draw them clean away from the danger zone. Already this was almost achieved, for Wattie and his stag, even if he had left the ravine, were completely hidden from their view by a shoulder of hill. He pretended to be labouring hard, stumbling often, and now and then throwing himself on the heather in an attitude of utter fatigue, which was visible to the pursuit below.

'It's a dashed shame,' murmured Archie. 'Those poor

fellows haven't a chance with John. I only hope Claybody is payin' them well for this job.'

The hare let the hounds get within a hundred yards of him. Then he appeared to realise their presence and to struggle to increase his pace, but, instead of ascending, he moved horizontally along the slope, slipping and sprawling in what looked like a desperate final effort. Hope revived in the navvies' hearts. Their voices could be heard – 'You bet they're usin' shockin' language,' said Archie – and Number One, who seemed the freshest, put on a creditable spurt. Palliser-Yeates waited till the man was almost upon him, and then suddenly turned downhill. He ran straight for Number Two, dodged him with that famous swerve which long ago on the football field had set forty thousand people shouting, and went down the hill like a rolling stone. Once past the navvy line, he seemed to slide a dozen yards and roll over, and when he got up he limped.

'Oh, he has hurt himself,' Janet cried.

'Not a bit of it,' said Archie. 'It's the old fox's cunning. He's simply playin' with the poor fellows. Oh, it's wicked!'

The navvies followed with difficulty, for they had no gift of speed on a steep hill-face. Palliser-Yeates waited again till they were very near him, and then, like a hen partridge dragging its wing, trotted down the more level ground by the stream side. The pursuit was badly cooked, but it lumbered gallantly along, Number Four now making the running. A quarter of a mile ahead was the beginning of the big Haripol woods which clothed the western skirts of Stob Ban, and stretched to the demesne itself.

Suddenly Palliser-Yeates increased his pace, with no sign of a limp, and, when he passed out of sight of the two on the rock, was going strongly.

Archie shut up his glass. 'That's a workmanlike show, if you like. He'll tangle them up in the woods, and slip out at his leisure and come home. I knew old John was abso-lute-ly safe. If he doesn't run slap into Macnicol—'

He broke off and stared in front of him. A figure like some ancient earth-dweller had appeared on the opposite bank. Hair, face, and beard were grimed with peat, sweat made furrows in the grime, and two fierce eyes glowered under shaggy eyebrows. Bumping against its knees were the antlers of a noble stag.

'Wattie,' the two exclaimed with one voice.

'You old sportsman,' cried Archie. 'Did you pull that great brute all the way yourself? Where is Lord Lamancha?'

The stalker strode into the water dragging the stag behind him, and did not halt till he had it high on the bank and close to the car. Then he turned his eyes on the two, and wrung the moisture from his beard.

'You needn't worry,' Archie told him. 'Mr Palliser-Yeates has all the navvies in the Haripol woods.'

'So I was thinkin''. I got a glisk of him up the burn. Yon's the soople one. But we've no time to loss. Help me to sling the beast into the cawr. This is a fine hidy-hole.'

'Gad, what a stag!'

'It's the auld beast we've seen for the last five years. Ye mind me tellin' ye that he was at our stacks last winter. Come on quick, for I'll no be easy till he's in the Crask larder.'

'But Lord Lamancha?'

'Never heed him. He's somewhere up the hill. It maitters little if he waits till the darkenin' afore he comes hame. The thing is we've got the stag. Are ye ready?'

Archie started the car, which had already been turned in the right direction. Coats and wraps and heather were piled on the freight, and Wattie seated himself on it like an ancient raven.

'Now, tak a spy afore ye start. Is the place clear?'

Archie, from the rock, reported that the hill-side was empty.

'What about the Beallach?'

Archie spied long and carefully. 'I see nothing there, but of course I only see the south end. There's a rock which hides the top.'

'No sign o' his lordship?'

'Not a sign.'

'Never heed. He can look after himsel' braw and weel. Push on wi' the cawr, sir, for it's time we were ower the hill.'

Archie obeyed, and presently they were climbing the long zigzag to the Crask pass. Wattie on the back seat kept an anxious look-out, issuing frequent bulletins, and Janet swept the glen with her glasses. But no sign of life appeared in the wide sunlit place except a buzzard high in the heavens and a weasel slipping into a cairn. Once the watershed had been crossed Wattie's heart lightened.

'Weel done, John Macnab,' he cried. 'Dod, ye're the great lad. Ye've beaten a hundred navvies and Macnicol and a', and ye've gotten the best heid in the country-side . . . Hae ye a match for my pipe, Sir Erchie? Mine's been in ower mony bogholes to kindle.'

It was a clear, rain-washed world on which they looked, and the sky to the south was all an unbroken blue. The air was not sticky and oppressive like yesterday, but pure and balmy and crystalline. When Crask was reached the stag was decanted with expedition, and Archie addressed Janet with a new authority.

'I'm goin' to take you straight home in the Hispana. You're drippin' wet and ought to change at once.'

'Might I change here?' the girl asked. 'I told them to send over dry things, for I was sure it would be a fine afternoon. You see, I think we ought to go to Haripol.'

'Whatever for?'

'To be in at the finish – and also to give Lady Claybody her dog back. Wee Roguie is rather on my conscience.'

'That's a good notion,' Archie assented. So Janet was handed over to Mrs Lithgow, who admitted that a suitcase had indeed arrived from Glenraden. Archie repaired to the upper bathroom, which Lamancha had aforetme likened to a drain-pipe, and, having bathed rapidly, habited himself in a suit of a reasonable newness and took special pains with his toilet. And all the while he whistled and sang, and generally comforted himself like a madman. Janet was under his roof – Janet would soon always be there – the most miraculous of fates was his! Somebody must be told, so when he was ready he went out to seek the Bluidy Mackenzie and made that serious-minded beast the receptacle of his confidences.

He returned to find a neat and smiling young woman conversing with Fish Benjie, whose task had been that of comforter and friend to Roguie. It appeared that the small dog had been having the morning of his life with the Crask rats and rabbits. 'He's no a bad wee dog,' Benjie reported, 'if they'd let him alane. They break his temper keepin' him indoors and feedin' him ower high.'

'Benjie must come too,' Janet announced. 'It would be a shame to keep him back. You understand – Benjie found Roguie in the woods – which is true, and handed him over to me – which is also true. I don't like unnecessary fibbing.'

'Right-o! Let's have the whole bag of tricks. But, I say,

you've got to stage-manage this show. Benjie and I put ourselves in your hands, for I'm hanged if I know what to say to Lady Claybody.'

'It's quite simple. We're just three nice clean people – well, two clean people – who go to Haripol on an errand of mercy. Get out the Hispana, Archie dear, for I feel that something tremendous may be happening there.'

As they started – Benjie and Roguie on the back seat – Bluidy Mackenzie came into view, hungrily eyeing an expedition from which he seemed to be barred.

'D'you mind if we take Mackenzie,' Archie begged. 'We'll go very slow, and he can trollop behind. The poor old fellow has been havin' a lonely time of it, and there's likely to be such a mix-up at Haripol that an extra hound won't signify.'

Janet approved, and they swung down the hill and on to the highway, as respectable an outfit as the heart could wish, except for the waterproof-caped urchin on the back seat. The casual wayfarer would have noted only a very pretty girl and a well-appointed young man driving an expensive car at a most blameless pace. He could not guess what a cargo of dog-thieves and deer-thieves was behind the shining metal and spruce enamel . . . Benjie talked to Wee Roguie in his own tongue, and what Janet and Archie said in whispers to each other is no concern of this chronicle. The sea at Inverlarrig was molten silver running to the translucent blue of the horizon, the shore woods gleamed with a thousand jewels, the abundant waters splashing in every hollow were channels of living light. The world sang in streams and soft winds, the cries of plover and the pipe of shore-birds, and Archie's heart sang above them all.

Close to Haripol gates a tall figure rose from the milestone as the car slowed down.

'Well, John, my aged sportsman, you did your part like a man. We saw it all.'

'How are things going?'

'Famously.'

'The stag?'

'In the Crask larder.'

'And Charles?'

'Lost. Believed to be still lurkin' in the hills. Look here, John, get in beside Benjie. We are goin' to Haripol and restore the pup. You'll be a tower of strength to us, and old Claybody will be tremendously bucked to meet a brother magnate . . . Really, I mean it.'

'I'm scarcely presentable,' said Palliser-Yeates, taking off an old cap and looking at it meditatively.

'Rot! You're as tidy as you'll ever be. Rather dandified for you. In you get, and don't tread on the hound . . . Bloody, you brute, don't you know a pal when you see him?'

THIRTEEN

Haripol – Auxiliary Troops

HALF-WAY DOWN THE avenue, Archie drew up sharply. 'I forgot about Mackenzie. We can't have him here – he'll play the fool somehow. Benjie, out you go. You're one of the few that can manage him. Here's his lead – you tie him up somewhere and watch for us, and we'll pick you up outside the gates when we start home . . . Don't get into trouble on your own account. I advise you to cut round to the bothies, and try to find out what is happenin'.'

On the massive doorstep of Haripol stood Lady Claybody, parasol in one hand and the now useless dog-whip in the other. She made a motion as if to retreat, but thought better of it. Her face was flushed, and her air had abated something of its serenity. The sight of Janet – for she looked at Archie without recognition – seemed to awake her to the duties of hospitality, and she advanced with outstretched hand. Then a yelp from the side of Palliser-Yeates wrung from her an answering cry. In a trice Wee Roguie was in her arms.

'Yes,' Janet explained sweetly, 'it's Roguie quite safe and well. There's a boy who sells fish at Strathlarrig – Benjie they call him – he found him in the woods and brought him to me. I hope you haven't been worried.'

But Lady Claybody was not listening. She had set the dog on his feet and was wagging her forefinger at him, a procedure which seemed to rouse all the latent epilepsy of his nature. 'Oh, you naughty, naughty Roguie! Cruel, cruel doggie! He loved freedom better than his happy home. Master and mistress have been so anxious about Wee Roguie.'

It was an invocation which lasted for two and a half minutes, till the invoker realised the presence of the men. She graciously shook hands with Sir Archie.

'I drove Miss Janet over,' said the young man, explaining the obvious. 'And I took the liberty of bringin' a friend who is stayin' with me – Mr Palliser-Yeates. I thought Lord

Claybody might like to meet him, for I expect he knows all about him.'

The lady beamed on both. 'This is a very great pleasure, Mr Palliser-Yeates, and I'm sure Claybody will be delighted. He ought to be in for tea very soon.' As it chanced. Lady Claybody had an excellent memory and a receptive ear for talk, and she was aware that in her husband's conversation the name of Paliser-Yeates occurred often, and always in dignified connections.

She led the way through the hall to a vast new drawing-room which commanded a wide stretch of lawns and flower-beds as far as the woods which muffled the mouth of the Reascuill glen. When the party were seated and butler and footman had brought the materials for tea, Lady Claybody – Roguie on a cushion by her side – became confidential.

'We've had such a wearing day, my dear,' she turned to Janet. 'First, the ruffian who calls himself John Macnab is probably trying to poach our forest. The rain yesterday kept him off, but we have good reason to believe that he will come today. Poor Johnson has been on the hill since breakfast. Then, there was the anxiety about Roguie. I've had our people searching the woods and shrubberies, for the little darling might have been caught in a trap . . . Macnicol says there are no traps, but you never can tell. And then, on the top of it all, we've been besieged since quite early in the morning by insolent journalists. No. They hadn't the good manners to come to the house – I should have sent them packing – but they have been over the grounds and buttonholing our servants. They want to hear about John Macnab, but we can't tell them anything, for as yet we know nothing ourselves. I gave orders that they should be turned out of the place – no violence, of course, for it doesn't do to offend the Press – but quite firmly, for they were trespassing. Would you believe it, my dear? they wouldn't go. So our people had simply to drive them out, and it has taken nearly all day, and they may be coming back any moment . . . Something should really be done, Mr Palliser-Yeates, to restrain the licence of the modern Press, with its horrid, vulgar sensationalism and its invasion of all the sanctities of private life.'

Palliser-Yeates cordially agreed. The lady had not looked to Archie for assent, and her manner towards him was a trifle cold. Perhaps it was the memory of her visit a fortnight before when he was sickening for smallpox; perhaps it was her husband's emphatic condemnation of his Muirtown speech.

At this point Lord Claybody entered, magnificent in a kilt of fawn-coloured tweed and a ferocious sporran made of the mask of a dog-otter. The garments, which were aggressively new, did not become his short, square figure.

'I don't think you have met my husband, Miss Raden,' said his wife. Then to Lord Claybody: 'You know Sir Archibald Roylance. And this is Mr Palliser-Yeates, who has been so kind as to come over to see us.'

Palliser-Yeates was greeted with enthusiasm. 'Delighted to meet you, sir. I heard you were in the North. Funny that we've had so much to do with each other indirectly and have never met . . . You've been having a long walk? Well, I know what you need. Cold tea for you. We'll leave the ladies to their gossip and have a whisky-and-soda in the library. I've just had a letter from Dickinson on which I'd like your views. Busy folk like you and me can never make a clean cut of their holiday. There's always something clawing us back to the mill.'

The two men were led off to the library, and Janet was left to entertain her hostess. That lady was in an expansive mood, which may have been due to the restoration of Roguie, but also owed something to the visit of Palliser-Yeates. 'My heart is buried here,' she told the girl. 'Every day I love Haripol more – its beauty and poetry and its – its wonderful traditions. My dream is to make it a centre for all the nicest people to come and rest. Everybody comes to the Highlands now, and we have so much to offer them here . . . Claybody, I may as well admit, is apt to be restless when we are alone. He is not enough of a sportsman to be happy shooting and fishing all day and every day. He has a wonderful mind, my dear, and he wants a chance of exercising it. He needs to be stimulated. Look how his eye brightened when he saw Mr Palliser-Yeates . . . And then, there are the girls . . . I'm sure you see what I mean.'

Janet saw, and set herself to cherish the innocent ambition of her hostess. In view of what might befall at any moment, it was most needful to have the Claybodys in a good humour. Then Lady Claybody, one of whose virtues was a love of fresh air, proposed that they should walk in the gardens. Janet would have preferred to remain in the house, had she been able to think of any kind of excuse, for the out-of-doors at the moment was filled with the most explosive material – Benjie, Mackenzie, an assortment of fugitive journalists, and Leithen and Lamancha somewhere in the hinterland. But she assented with a good grace, and, accompanied by Roguie, who after a morning of liberty had cast the part of lap-dog contemptuously behind him, they sauntered into the trim parterres.

The head-gardener at Haripol was a man of the old school. He loved fantastically shaped beds and geometrical patterns, and geraniums and lobelias and calceolarias were still dear to his antiquated soul. On the lawns he had been given his head, but Lady Claybody, who had accepted new fashions in horticulture as in other things, had constructed a pleasaunce of her own, which with crazy-paving and sundials and broad borders was a very fair imitation of an old English garden. She had a lily-pond and a rosery and many pergolas, and what promised in twenty years to be a fine yew-walk. The primitive walled garden, planted in the Scots fashion a long way from the house, was now relegated to fruit and vegetables.

Lady Claybody was an inaccurate enthusiast. She poured into Janet's ear a flow of botanical information and mispronounced Latin names. Each innovation was modelled on what she had seen or heard of in some famous country house. The girl approved, for in that glen the environment of hill and wood was so masterful that the artifices of man were instantly absorbed. The gardens exhausted, they wandered through the rhododendron thickets, which in early summer were towers of flame, crossed the turbid Reascuill by a rustic bridge, and found themselves in a walk which skirted the stream through a pleasant wilderness. Here an expert from Kew had been turned loose, and had made a wonderful wild garden, in which patches of red-hot pokers and godetia and *Hyacinthus candicans* shone against the darker carpet of the heather. Roguie led the way, and where Roguie's yelps beckoned his mistress followed. Soon the two were nearly a mile from the house, approaching the portals of the Reascuill glen.

Sir Edward Leithen left Crask just as the wet dawn was breaking. He had a very long walk before him, but at that he was not dismayed; what perplexed him was how it was going to end. To the first part, a struggle with wind and rain and many moorland miles, he looked forward with enthusiasm. Long, lonely expeditions had always been his habit, for he was the kind of man who could be happy with his own thoughts. Before it became the fashion he had been a pioneer in guideless climbing in the Alps, and the red-letter days in his memory were for the most part solitary days. He was always in hard condition, and his lean figure rarely knew fatigue; weather he minded little, and he had long ago taught himself how to find his road, even in mist, with map and compass.

So it was with sincere enjoyment that his legs covered the rough miles – along the Crask ridge till it curved round at the head of the Doran and led him to the eastern skirts of Sgurr Dearg. He knew from the map that the great eastern precipice of that mountain was towering above him, but he saw only the white wall of fog a dozen yards off. His aim was to make a circuit of the *massif* and bear round to the pass of the Red Burn, which made a road between Haripol and Machray. He would then be nearly due north of the Sanctuary and exactly opposite where Lamancha proposed to make his entrance . . . A fortnight earlier, when he first came to Crask, he had gone for a walk in far pleasanter weather, and had been acutely bored. Now, with no prospect but a wet blanket of mist, and with no chance of observing bird or plant, he was enjoying every moment of it. More, his thoughts were beginning to turn pleasantly towards the other side of his life – his books and hobbies, the intricacies of politics, the legal practice of which he was a master. He reflected almost with exhilaration on a difficult appeal which would come on in the autumn, when he hoped to induce the House of Lords to upset a famous judgement. He had begun to relish his competence again, even to take a modest pride in his fame; what had been dust and ashes in his mouth a few weeks ago had now an agreeable flavour. Palliser-Yeates was of the same way of thinking. Had he not declared last night that he wanted to give orders again and be addressed as 'sir,' instead of being chivvied about the countryside? And Lamancha? Leithen seriously doubted if Lamancha had ever suffered from quite the same malady. The trouble with him was that he had always a large streak of bandit in his composition, and must now and then give it play. That was what made him the bigger man, perhaps. Charles might take an almighty toss some day, but if he did not he would be first at the post, for he rode more gallantly to win.

'I suppose I may regard myself as cured,' Leithen reflected, as he munched a second breakfast of cheese-sandwiches and raisins somewhere under the north-eastern spur of Sgurr Dearg. But he reflected, too, that he had a horribly difficult day ahead of him, for which he felt a strong distaste. He realised the shrewdness of Acton Croke's diagnosis: he was longing once more for the flesh-pots of the conventional.

His orders had been to get somewhere on the Machray side by eight o'clock, and he saw by his watch that he was ahead of his time. Once he had turned the corner of Sgurr Dearg the wind was shut off and the mist wrapped him closer. He had acquired long ago a fast but regular pace on the hills, and, judging from the time and the known distance, he knew that he must now be very near the Machray march. Presently he had topped a ridge which was clearly a watershed, for the plentiful waters now ran west. Then he began to descend, and soon was brought up by a raging torrent which seemed to be flowing north-west. This must be the Red Burn, coming down from the gullies of Sgurr Dearg, and it was his business to cross it and work his way westward along the edge of the great trough of the Reascuill. But he must go warily, for he was very near the pass, by which, according to the map, a road could be found from Corrie Easain in the Machray forest to the Haripol Sanctuary – the road which, according to Wattie Lithgow, gave the easiest access and would most assuredly be well watched.

He crossed the stream, not without difficulty, and climbed another ridge, beyond which the ground fell steeply. These must be the screes on the Reascuill side, he concluded, so he bore to the right and found, as he expected, that here there was a re-entrant corrie, and that he was on the very edge of the great trough. It was for him to keep this edge, but to go circumspectly, for at any moment he might stumble upon some of Claybody's sentries. His business was to occupy their attention, but he did not see what good he could do. The mist was distraction enough, for in it no man could see twenty yards ahead of him. But it might clear, and in that case he would have his work cut out for him. Meanwhile he must avoid a premature collision.

He avoided it only by a hairsbreadth. Suddenly that happened which at the moment was perplexing Wattie Lithgow and Lamancha a mile off. Corridors opened in the air – dark corridors of dizzy space and black rock seamed with torrents. Leithen found himself looking into a cauldron of which only the bottom was still hid, and at the savage splinters of the Pinnacle Ridge. He was looking at something less welcome, for thirty yards off, on the edge of the scarp, was a group of five men.

They had been boiling tea in billies in the lee of a rock and had been stirred to attention by the sudden clearing of the air. They saw him as soon as he saw them, and in a moment were on their feet and spreading out in his direction. He heard a cry, and then a babble of tongues.

Leithen did the only thing possible. He strode towards them with a magisterial air. They were the real navvy, the hardiest race in the land, sleeping in drainpipes, always dirty and wet, forgetting their sodden labours now and then in sordid drink, but tough, formidable, and resourceful.

'What the devil are you fellows doing here?' he shouted angrily.

At first they took him for a gillie.

'What the hell's your business?' one of them replied, but the advance had halted. As he came nearer, they changed their minds, for Leithen had not the air of a gillie.

'My business is to know what you're doing here – on my land?'

Now Machray forest was not let that season, and this Leithen knew. If any arrangement had been come to with Haripol it could only have been made between the stalkers. It was for him to play the part of the owner.

The men looked nonplussed, for the navvy, working under heavy-handed foremen, is susceptible to the voice of authority.

'We were sent up here to keep a look out,' one answered.

'Look out for what? Who sent you?'

'It was Lord Claybody – we took our orders from Mr Macnicol.'

Leithen sat down on a stone and lit his pipe.

'Well, you're trespassing on Machray – my ground. I don't know what on earth Lord Claybody means. I have heard nothing of it.'

'There's a man tryin' to poach, sir. We were telled to wait here and keep a look-out for him.'

Leithen smiled grimly. 'A pretty look-out you can keep in this weather. But that doesn't touch the point that you're in a place where you've no right to be . . . You poor devils must have been having a rotten time roosting up here.'

He took out his flask.

'Here's something to warm you. There's just enough for a tot apiece.'

The flask was passed round amid murmurs of satisfaction, while Leithen smoked his pipe and surveyed the queer party. 'I call it cruelty to animals,' he said, 'to plant you fellows in a place like this. I hope you're well paid for it.'

'We're gettin' a pound a day, and the man that grips the poacher gets a five-pund note. The name o' the poacher is Macnab.'

'Well, I hope one of you will earn the fiver. Now, look here. I can't have you moving a yard north of this. You're on Machray ground as it is, for my march is the edge of the hill. I don't mind you squatting here, and of course it's no business of mine what you do on Haripol, but you don't stir a foot into Machray. With this wind you'll put all the beasts out of the upper corries.'

He rose and strolled away. 'I must be off. See that you mind what I've said. If you move, it must be into Haripol. A poacher! I never heard such rubbish. Better my job than yours, anyway. Still, I hope you get that fiver!'

Leithen departed in an atmosphere of general good will, and as soon as possible put a ridge between himself and the navvies. It had been a narrow escape, but mercifully no harm was done. He must keep well below the skyline on the Machray side, for there would be watchers elsewhere on the Haripol ground and he was not ready as yet to play the decoy-duck. For it had occurred to him that he was still too far east for his purpose. Those navvies were watching the pass from the Red Burn, and had no concern with what might be happening in the Sanctuary. Indeed, they could not see into it because of the spur which Sgurr Dearg flung out toward the Reascuill. He must be farther down the stream before he tried to interest those who might interfere with Lamancha; so he mended his pace, and, keeping well on the Machray side, made for the hill called Bheinn Fhada, which faced Sgurr Mor across the Reascuill.

Then the mist came down again, and in driving sleet Leithen scrambled among the matted boulders and screes of Bheinn Fhada's slopes. Here he knew he was safe enough, for he was inside the Machray march and out of any possible prospect from the Reascuill. But it was a useless labour, and the return of the thick weather began to try his temper. The good humour of the morning had gone, when it was a delight to be abroad in the wilds alone and to pit his strength against storm and distance. He was growing bored with the whole business and at the same time anxious to play the part which had been set him. As it was, wandering on the skirts of Bheinn Fhada, he was as little use to John Macnab as if he had been reading Sir Walter Scott in the Crask smoking-room.

It took him longer than he expected to pass that weariful mountain, and it was noon before he ate the remnants of the food he had brought in the hollow which lies at the head of the second main Machray corrie, Corrie na Sidhe. Here he observed that sight which at the same moment was perturbing Lamancha on the Beallach looking over to Crask. The mist was thinning – not breaking into gloomy corridors, but lightening everywhere with the sun behind it. The wind, too, had shifted; it was blowing in his face from the south. Suddenly the top of Stob Coire Easain in front of him stood clear and bright, and its upper crags, jewelled with falling waters, rose out of a rainbow haze. Far out on the right he saw a patch of silver which he knew for the sea. Nearer, and far below, was an olive-green splash which must be the Haripol woods. And then, as if under a wizard's wand, the glen below him, from a pit of vapour, became an enamelled cup, with the tawny Reascuill looped in its hollows.

It was time for Leithen to be up and doing. He crawled to a point which gave him cover and a view into the glen, and searched the place long and carefully with his glasses. There must be navvy posts close at hand, but from where he lay he could not command the sinuosities of the hill-side below him. He saw the nest of upper corries which composed the Sanctuary, but not the Beallach, which was hidden by the ridge of Sgurr Mor . . . He lay there for half an hour, uncertain what he should do next. If he descended into the glen it meant certain capture, for he would be cut off by some lower post. The only plan seemed to be to show himself on the upper slopes and then try to draw the pursuit off towards Machray, but he did not see how such a course was going to help Lamancha in the Sanctuary. The plan of campaign, he decided, had been a great deal too elaborate, and his part looked like a wash-out.

He made his way along the hill-side towards the Machray peak which bore the name of Clonlet and the wide skirts of which made one side of the glen above Haripol, the opposite sentinel to Stob Ban. He had got well on to the slopes of that mountain when he detected something in the glen below. Men seemed to be moving down the stream – three at least – and to be moving fast. His sense of duty revived, for here seemed a task to his hand . . . He showed himself on an outjutting knoll and waited. The men below had their eyes about them, for he was almost instantly observed. He heard cries, he saw a hand waved, then he heard a whistle blown . . . After that he began to run.

At this point the chronicler must retrace his steps and follow the doings of Mr Johnson Claybody. That young gentleman had taken the threat of John Macnab most seriously to heart: he felt his honour involved, his sense of property outraged, and he saw the pride of the Claybodys lowered if the scoundrel were victorious on Haripol as he had been at Strathlarrig. Above all he feared the Press, which was making a holiday feature of this monstrous insolence. He it was who had devised the plan of defence, a plan which did credit to his wits. Not only had he placed his sentries with care, but he had arranged for peripatetic gillies to patrol between the stations and form an intelligence service for head-quarters. His *poste de commandement* was at Macnicol's cottage just beyond the gorge of the Reascuill and some two miles from the house.

All morning his temper had been worsening. The news of the journalistic invasion of Haripol, brought to him about ten o'clock by a heated garden-boy, had been the first shock. He had sent a message to his father, handing over to him that problem, with the results which we have seen. Also he was lamentably short of the force he had hoped to muster, owing to his mother's insistence on keeping Macnicol and two of the gillies behind to look for her dog. It was not till close on midday that, after a furious journey to the house in a two-seater car, he was able to recover the services of the head-stalker. Macnicol, he felt, should have been on the edge of the Sanctuary at daybreak; instead he had had to send Macqueen, a surly ruffian whom he had dismissed for insolence, but whose hillcraft he knew to be of the first order. Johnson's plan was that towards midday he himself, with a posse, should patrol the upper forest, so that, if John Macnab should be lurking there, he might drive him north or south against the navvy garrison. East, Sgurr Dearg shut the way, and west lay the grounds of Haripol, where escape would be impossible, since every living thing there was on the watch. Johnson's blood was up. If John Macnab had made his venture, he wanted to share directly in the chase and to be in at the death.

It was after midday before the flying column started. It was composed of Macnicol, Cameron the third stalker, two selected gillies, and three of the navvies who were more mobile than their fellows. Macnicol had prophesied that the weather would clear in the afternoon, so, though the mist was thick at the start, they took the road with confidence. Sure enough, it began to lift before they were half a mile up the glen, and Macnicol grunted his satisfaction.

'Macnab cannot escape noways,' he said. 'But I do not think he has come at all, unless he's daft. He would not get in, but, if he is in, he will never get out.'

Johnson's one fear now was that the assault might not have been made. It would be a poor ending to his strategy if the pool were dragged and no fish were found in it. But presently he was reassured, for at the foot of Bheinn Fhada he met one of the patrolling gillies with tremendous news. A man had been seen that morning by the navvies at the Red Burn. He had passed as the Laird of Machray, and had given them whisky. The gillie knew that the Laird of Machray was a child of three dwelling at Bournemouth, and he had demanded a description of the visitor. It was a tallish man, they said, lean and clean-shaven, rather pale, and with his skin very tight over his cheek-bones. He had looked like a gentleman and had behaved as such. Now the only picture of John Macnab known to the gillies was that which had been broadcast in talk by Angus and Jimsie of Strathlarrig, and that agreed most startlingly with the navvies' account. 'A long, lean dog,' Angus had said, 'and whitish in the face.' Wherefore the gillie had hastened with his tidings to head-quarters.

The news increased Johnson's pace. John Macnab was veritably in the forest, and at the thought he grew both nervous and wroth. There was something supernatural, he felt, about the impudence of a man who could march quietly up to a post of navvies and bluff them. Were all his subtle plans to be foiled? Then, half a mile on, appeared Macqueen, just descended from his eyrie.

Macqueen had to report that half an hour before, when the

mist cleared and he could get a view of the corries, he had seen the deer moving. The wind at the same time had shifted to the south, and the beasts in the corrie below Beallach were frightened. He had seen nothing with his telescope – the beasts had been moved some time before, he thought, for they were well down the hill. In his opinion, if John Macnab was in the forest, he was on or beyond the Beallach.

Johnson considered furiously. 'The fellow was at the Red Burn just before nine o'clock. He must have gone through the Sanctuary to be at the Beallach half an hour ago. Is that possible, Macnicol?'

'I don't ken.' Macnicol scratched his head. 'Macqueen says that only the beasts in the corrie below the Beallach were moved, but if he had gone through the Sanctuary they would have been all rinnin' oot. I'm fair puzzled, sir, unless he cam' doun the water and worked up by Sgurr Mor. That Macnab's a fair deevil.'

'We'll get after him,' said Johnson, and then he stopped short. He had a sudden memory of what had happened at Glenraden. Why should not John Macnab have sent a confederate to gull them into the belief that he was busy in the Sanctuary, while he himself killed a stag in the woods around the house? There were plenty of beasts there, and it would be like his infernal insolence to poach one under the very windows of Haripol. It was true that the woodland stags were not easy to stalk, but Macnab had shown himself a mighty artist.

Johnson had a gift of quick decision. He briefly explained to his followers his suspicions. 'The man at the Beallach may not be the man whom the navvies saw at the Red Burn. The Red Burn fellow may have gone down the Machray side, and be now in the woods . . . Cameron, you take Andrew and Peter, and get down the glen in double-quick time. If you see anybody on Clonlet or in the woods, hunt him like hell. I'll skin you if you let him escape. Drive him right down to the gardens, and send word to the men there to be on the look-out. You'll be a dozen against one. Macnicol, you come with me, and you, Macqueen, and you three fellows, and we'll make for the Beallach. We'll cut up through the Sanctuary, for it don't matter a damn about the deer if we only catch that swine. He's probably lying up there till he can slip out in the darkness . . . And, Cameron, tell them to send a car up the Doran road. I may want a lift home.'

* * *

It was Cameron and his posse who spied Leithen on the side of Clonlet. All three were young men; they had the priceless advantage of acquaintance with the ground, while Leithen knew no more than the generalities of the map. As soon as he saw that he was pursued he turned up-hill with the purpose of making for Machray. He had had a long walk, but he felt fresh enough for another dozen miles or so, and he remembered his instructions to go north, if necessary even into Glenaicill.

But in this he had badly miscalculated. For the whistle of Cameron had alarmed a post of navvies in a nook of hill behind Leithen and at a greater altitude, who had missed him earlier for the simple reason that they had been asleep. Roused now to a sudden attention, they fanned out on the slope and cut him off effectively from any retreat towards Corrie na Sidhe. There were only two courses open to him – to climb the steep face of Clonlet or to go west towards the woods. The first would be hard, he did not even know whether the rock was climbable, and if he stuck there he would be an easy prey. He must go west, and trust to find some way to Machray round the far skirts of the mountain.

Cameron did not hurry, for he knew what would happen. So long as the navvies cut off retreat to the east the victim was safe. Leithen did not realise his danger till he found himself above the woods on a broad grassy ledge just under the sheer rocks of Clonlet. It was the place called Crapnagower, which ended not in a hill-side by which the butt of Clonlet could be turned, but in a bold promontory of rock which fell almost sheer to the meadows of Haripol. Long before he got to the edge he had an uncomfortable suspicion of what was coming, but when he peered over the brink and saw cattle at grass far below him, he had an ugly shock. It looked as if he were cornered, and cornered too in a place far from the main scene of action, where his misfortunes could not benefit Lamancha.

He turned and plunged downward through the woods direct for Haripol. There was still plenty of fight in him, and his pursuers would have a run for their money. These pursuers were not far off. Andrew had climbed the hill and had been moving fast parallel to Leithen, but farther down among the trees. Cameron was on the lower road, a grassy aisle among the thickets, and Peter, the swifter, had gone on ahead to watch the farther slopes. It was not long before Leithen was made aware of Andrew, and the sight forced him to his right in a long slant which would certainly have taken him into the arms of Peter.

But at this moment the Fates intervened in the person of Crossby.

That eminent correspondent, having inspired his fellow-journalists with the spirit of all mischief and thereby sadly broken the peace of Haripol, was now lying up from further pursuit in the woods, confident that he had done his best for the cause. Suddenly he became aware of the ex-Attorney-General descending the hill in leaps and bounds, and a gillie not fifty yards behind on his trail . . . Crossby behaved like Sir Philip Sidney and other cavaliers in similar crises. 'Thy need is the greater,' was his motto, and as Leithen passed he whispered hoarsely to him to get into cover. Leithen, whose head was clear enough though his legs were aching, both heard and saw. He clapped down like a woodcock in a patch of bracken, while Crossby, whose garb and height were much the same as his, became the quarry in his stead.

The chase was not of long duration. The correspondent did not know the ground, nor did he know of the waiting Peter. Left to himself he might have outdistanced Andrew, but he was watched from below by wily eyes. He reached the grassy path, turned to his right, and rounded a corner to be embraced firmly and affectionately by the long arms of the gillie. 'That's five pund in our pockets, Andra, ma man,' the latter observed when the second gillie arrived. 'If this is no John Macnab, it's his brither, and anyway we've done what we were telled.' So, strongly held by the two men, the self-sacrificing Crossby departed into captivity.

Of these doings Leithen knew nothing. He did not believe that Crossby could escape, but the hunt had gone out of his ken. Now it is the nature of man that, once he is in flight, he cannot be content till he finds an indisputable place of refuge. This wood was obviously unhealthy, and he made haste to get out of it. But he must go circumspectly, and the first need was for thicker cover, for this upper part was too open for comfort. Below he saw denser scrub, and he started to make his way to it.

The trouble was that presently he came into Cameron's view. The stalker had heard the crash of Crossby's pursuit, and had not hurried himself, knowing the strategic value of Peter's position. He proposed to wait, in case the fugitive doubled back. Suddenly he caught sight of Leithen farther up the hill, and apparently unfollowed. Had the man given the two gillies the slip? . . . Cameron performed a very creditable piece of stalking. He wormed his way up-hill till he was above the bushes where Leithen was now sheltering. The next thing that much-enduring gentleman knew was that a large hand had been outstretched to grip his collar.

Like a stag from covert Leithen leaped forth, upsetting Cameron with his sudden bound. He broke through the tangle of hazel and wild raspberries, and stayed not on the order of his going. His pace downhill had always been remarkable, and Cameron's was no match for it. Soon he had gained twenty yards, then fifty, but he had no comfort in his speed, for somewhere ahead were more gillies and he was being forced straight on Haripol, which was thick with the enemy.

The only plan in his head was to make for the Reascuill, which as he was aware flowed at this part of its course in a deepcut gorge. He had a faint hope that, once there, he might find a place to lie up in till the darkness, for he knew that the Highland gillie is rarely a rock-climber. But the place grew more horrible as he continued. He was among rhododendrons now, and well-tended grass walks. Yes, there was a rustic arbour and what looked like a summer-seat. The beastly place was a garden. In another minute he would be among flower-pots and vineries with twenty gardeners at his heels. But the river was below – he could hear its sound – so, like a stag hard pressed by hounds, he made for the running water. A long slither took him down a steep bank of what had once been foxgloves, and he found his feet on a path.

And there, to his horror, were two women.

By this time his admirable wind was considerably touched, and the sweat was blinding his eyes, so that he did not see clearly. But surely one of the two was known to him.

Janet rose to the occasion like a bird. As he stood blinking before her she laughed merrily:

'Sir Edward,' she cried, 'where in the world have you been? You've taken a very rough road.' Then she turned to Lady Claybody. 'This is Sir Edward Leithen. He is staying with us and went out for an enormous walk this morning. He is always doing it. It was lucky you came this way, Sir Edward, for we can give you a lift home.'

Lady Claybody was delighted, she said, to meet one of whom she had heard so much. He must come back to the house at once and have tea and see her husband, 'I call this a real romance,' she cried. 'First Mr Palliser-Yeates – and then Sir Edward Leithen dropping like a stone from the hill-side.'

Leithen was beginning to recover himself, 'I'm afraid I was trespassing,' he murmured. 'I tried a short cut and got into difficulties. I hope I didn't alarm you coming down that hill like an avalanche. I find it the easiest way.'

The mystified Cameron stood speechless, watching his prey vanishing in the company of his mistress.

FOURTEEN

Haripol – Wounded and Missing

LAMANCHA WATCHED Palliser-Yeates disappear along the hill-side, and then returned to the hollow top of the Beallach, which was completely cut off from view on either side. All that was now left of the mist was a fleeting vapour twining in scarves on the highest peaks, and the cliffs of Sgurr Dearg and Sgurr Mor towered above him in gleaming stairways. The drenched cloudberries sparkled in the sunlight, and the thousand little rivulets, which in the gloom had been hoarse with menace, made now a pleasant music. Lamancha's spirits rose as the world brightened. He proposed to wait for a quarter of an hour till Wattie with the stag was well down the ravine and Palliser-Yeates had secured the earnest attention of the navvies. Then he would join Wattie and help him with the beast, and within a couple of hours he might be wallowing in a bath at Crask, having bidden John Macnab a long farewell.

Meantime he was thirsty, and laid himself on the ground for a long drink at an icy spring, leaving his rifle on a bank of heather.

When he rose with his eyes dim with water he had an unpleasing surprise. A man stood before him, having in his hands his rifle, which he pointed threateningly at the rifle's owner.

''Ands up,' the man shouted. He was a tall fellow in navvy's clothes, with a shock head of black hair, and a week's beard – an uncouth figure with a truculent eye.

'Put that down,' said Lamancha. 'You fool, it's not loaded. Hand it over. Quick!

For answer the man swung it like a cudgel.

''Ands up,' he repeated. ''Ands up, you——, or I'll do you in.'

By this time Lamancha had realised that his opponent was the peripatetic navvy, whom Palliser-Yeates had reported. An ugly customer he looked, and resolute to earn Claybody's promised reward.

'What do you want?' he asked. 'You're behaving like a lunatic.'

'I want you to 'ands up and come along o' me.'

'Who on earth do you take me for?'

'You're the poacher – Macnab. I seen you, and I seen the old fellow and the stag. You're Macnab, I reckon, and you're the—— I'm after. Up with your 'ands and look sharp.'

Mendacity was obviously out of the question, so Lamancha tried conciliation.

'Supposing I am Macnab – let's talk a little sense. You're being paid for this job, and the man who catches me is to have something substantial. Well, whatever Lord Claybody has promised you I'll double it if you let me go.'

The man stared for a second without answering, and then his face crimsoned. But it was not with avarice but with wrath. 'No, you don't,' he cried. 'By——, you don't come over me that way. I'm not the kind as sells his boss. I'm a white man, I am, and I'll—— well let you see it. 'Ands up, you——, and march. I've a—— good mind to smash your 'ead for tryin' to buy me.'

Lamancha looked at the fellow, his shambling figure contorted by hard toil out of its natural balance, his thin face, his hot, honest eyes, and suddenly felt ashamed. 'I beg your pardon,' he grunted. 'I oughtn't to have said that. I had no right to insult you. But of course I refuse to surrender. You've got to catch me.'

He followed his words by a dive to his right, hoping to get between the man and the Sgurr Mor cliffs. But the navvy was too quick for him, and he had to retreat baffled. Lamancha was beginning to realise that the situation was really awkward. This fellow was both active and resolved; even if he gave him the slip he would be pursued down to the Doran, and the destination of the stag would be revealed . . . But he was by no means sure that he could give him the slip. He was already tired and cramped, and he had never been noted for his speed, like Leithen and Palliser-Yeates . . . He thought of another way, for in his time he had been a fair amateur middle-weight.

'You're an Englishman. What about settling the business with our fists? Put the rifle down, and we'll stand up together.'

The man spat sarcastically. 'Ain't it likely?' he sneered. 'Thank you kindly, but I'm takin' no risks this trip. You've got to 'ands up and let me tie 'em so as you're safe and then come along peaceable. If you don't I'll 'it you as 'ard as Gawd'll let me.'

There seemed to be nothing for it but a scrap, and Lamancha, with a wary eye on the clubbed rifle, waited for his chance. He must settle this fellow so that he should be incapable of pursuit – a nice task for a respectable Cabinet Minister getting on in life. There was a pool beside his left foot, which was the source of one of the burns that ran down into the Sanctuary. Getting this between him and his adversary, he darted towards one end, checked, turned, and made to go round the other. The navvy struck at him with the rifle, and narrowly missed his head. Then he dropped the weapon, made a wild clutch, gripped Lamancha by the coat, and with a sound of rending tweed dragged him to his arms. The next moment the two men were locked in a very desperate and unscientific wrestling bout.

It was a game Lamancha had never played in his life before. He was a useful boxer in his way, but of wrestling he was utterly ignorant, and so, happily, was the navvy. So it became a mere contest of brute strength, waged on difficult ground with boulders, wells, and bog-holes adjacent. Lamancha had an athletic, well-trained body, the navvy was powerful but ill-trained; Lamancha was tired with eight or nine hours' scrambling, his opponent had also had a wearing morning; but Lamancha had led a regular and comfortable life, while the navvy had often gone supperless and had drunk many gallons of bad whisky. Consequently the latter, though the heavier and more powerful man, was likely to fail first in a match of endurance.

At the start, indeed, he nearly won straight away by the vigour of his attack. Lamancha cried out with pain as he felt his arm bent almost to breaking-point and a savage knee in his groin. The first three minutes it was anyone's fight; the second three Lamancha began to feel a dawning assurance. The other's breath laboured, and his sudden spasms of furious effort grew shorter and easier to baffle. He strove to get his opponent on to the rougher ground, while that opponent manoeuvred to keep the fight on the patch of grass, for it was obvious to him that his right course was to wear the navvy down. There were no rules in this game, and it would be of little use to throw him; only by reducing him to the last physical fatigue could he have him at his mercy, and be able to make his own terms.

Presently the early fury of the man was exchanged for a sullen defence. Lamancha was getting very distressed himself, for the navvy's great boots had damaged his shins and torn away strips of stocking and skin, while his breath was growing deplorably short. The two staggered around the patch of grass, never changing grips, but locked in a dull clinch into which they seemed to have frozen. Lamancha would fain have broken free and tried other methods, but the navvy's great hands held him like a vice, and it seemed as if their power, in spite of the man's gasping, would never weaken.

In this preposterous stalemate they continued for the better part of ten minutes. Then the navvy, as soldiers say, resumed the initiative. He must have felt his strength ebbing, and in a moment of violent disquiet have decided to hazard everything. Suddenly Lamancha found himself forced away from the chosen ground and dragged into the neighbouring moraine. They shaved the pool, and in a second were stumbling among slabs and screes and concealed boulders. The man's object was plain: if he could make his lighter antagonist slip he might force him down in a place from which it would not be easy to rise.

But it was the navvy who slipped. He lurched backward, tripping over a stone, and the two rolled into a cavity formed by a boulder which had been split by its fall from Sgurr Mor in some bygone storm. It was three or four feet of a fall, and Lamancha fell with him. There was a cry from the navvy, and the grip of his arms slackened.

Lamancha scrambled out and looked back into the hole where the man lay bunched up as if in pain.

'Hurt?' he asked, and the answer came back, garnished with much profanity, that it was his —— leg.

'I'm dashed sorry. Look here, this fight is off. Let me get you out and see what I can do for you.'

The man, sullen but quiescent, allowed himself to be pulled out and laid on a couch of heather. Lamancha had feared for the thigh or the pelvis and was relieved to find that it was a clean break below the knee, caused by the owner's descent, weighted by his antagonist, on an ugly, sharp-edged stone. But, as he looked at the limp figure, haggard with toil and poor living, and realised that he had damaged it in the pitiful capital which was all it possessed, its bodily strength, he suffered from a pang of sharp compunction. He loathed John Macnab and all his works for bringing disaster upon a poor devil who had to earn his bread.

'I'm most awfully sorry,' he stammered. 'I wouldn't have had this happen for a thousand pounds . . .' Then he broke off, for in the face now solemnly staring at him he recognised something familiar. Where had he seen that long crooked nose before and that cock of the eyebrows?

'Stokes,' he cried, 'You're Stokes, aren't you?' He recalled now the man who had once been his orderly, and whom he had last known as a smart troop sergeant.

The navvy tried to rise and failed. 'You've got my name right, guv'nor,' he said, but it was obvious that in his eyes there was no recognition.

'You remember me – Lord Lamancha?' He had it all now – the fellow who had been a son of one of Tommy Deloraine's keepers – a decent fellow and a humorous, and a good soldier. It was like the cussedness of things that he should go breaking the leg of a friend.

'Gawd!' gasped the navvy, peering at the shameful figure of Lamancha, whose nether garments were now well advanced in raggedness and whose peat-begrimed face had taken on an added dirtiness from the heat of the contest. 'I can't 'ardly believe it's you, sir.' Then, with many tropes of speech, he explained what, had he known, would have happened to Lord Claybody, before he interfered with the game of a gentleman as he had served under.

'What brought you to this?' Lamancha asked.

'I've 'ad a lot of bad luck, sir. Nothing seemed to go right with me after the war. I found the missus 'ad done a bunk, and I 'ad two kids on my 'ands, and there weren't no cushy jobs goin' for the likes of me. Gentlemen everywhere was puttin' down their 'osses, and I 'ad to take what I could get. So it come to the navvyin' with me, like lots of other chaps. The Gov'ment don't seem to care what 'appens to us poor Gawd-forgotten devils, sir.'

The navvy stopped to cough, and Lamancha did not like the sound of it.

'How's your health?' he asked.

'Not so bad, barrin' a bit of 'oarseness.'

'That explains a lot. You'll have consumption if you don't look out. If you had been the man you were five years ago you'd have had me on my back in two seconds . . . I needn't tell you, Stokes, that I'm dashed sorry about this, and I'll do all I can to make it up to you. First, we must get that leg right.'

Lamancha began by retrieving the rifle. It was a light, double-barrelled express which fortunately could be taken to pieces. He had some slight surgical knowledge, and was able to set the limb, and then with strips of his handkerchief and the rifle-barrel to put it roughly into a splint. Stokes appeared to have gone without breakfast, so he was given the few sandwiches which remained in Lamancha's pocket and a stiff dram from his flask. Soon the patient was reclining in comparative comfort on the heather, smoking Lamancha's tobacco in an ancient stump of a pipe, while the latter, with heavy brows, considered the situation.

'You ought to get to bed at once, for you've a devil of a bad cough, you know. And you ought to have a doctor to look after that leg properly, for this contraption of mine is a bit rough. The question is, how am I going to get you down? You can't walk, and you're too much of a heavy-weight for me to carry very far. Also I needn't tell you that this hill-side is not too healthy for me at present. I mean to go down it by crawling in the open and keeping to the gullies, but I can't very well do that with you . . . It looks as if there is nothing for it but to wait till dark. Then I'll nip over to Crask and send some men here with a stretcher.'

Mr Stokes declared that he was perfectly happy where he was, and deprecated the trouble he was giving.

'Trouble,' cried Lamancha, 'I caused the trouble, and I'm going to see you through it.'

'But you'll get nabbed, sir, and there ain't no bloomin' good in my 'avin' my leg broke if Claybody's going to nab you along of it. You cut off, sir, and never 'eed me.'

'I don't want to be nabbed, but I can't leave you . . . Wait a minute! If I followed Wattie – that is my stalker – down to the Doran I could send a message to Crask about a stretcher and men to carry it. I might get some food too. And then I'll come back here, and we'll bukk about Palestine till it's time to go . . . It might be the best way . . .'

But, even as he spoke, further plans were put out of the question by the advent of six men who had come quietly through the Beallach from the Sanctuary, and had unostentatiously taken up positions in a circle around the two ex-antagonists. Lamancha had been so engaged in Stoke's affairs that he had ceased to remember that he was in enemy territory.

His military service had taught him the value of the offensive. The new-comers were, he observed, three navvies, two men who were clearly gillies, and a warm and breathless young man in a suit of a dapperness startling on a wild mountain. This young man was advancing towards him with a determined eye when Lamancha arose from his couch and confronted him.

'Hullo!' he cried cheerfully, 'you come just in time. This poor chap here has had a smash – broken his leg – and I was wondering how I was to get him down the hill.'

Johnson Claybody stopped short. He had rarely seen a more disreputable figure than that which had risen from the heather – dissolute in garments, wild of hair, muddy beyond belief in countenance. Yet these dilapidated clothes had once, very long ago, been made by a good tailor, and the fellow was apparently some kind of a gentleman. He was John Macnab beyond doubt, for in his hand was the butt-end of a rifle. Now Johnson was the type of man who is miserable if he feels himself ill-clad or dirty, and discovers in a sense of tidiness a moral superiority. He rejoiced to have found his enemy, and an enemy over whom he felt at a notable advantage. But, unfortunately for him, no Merkland had ever been conscious of the appearance he represented or cared a straw about it. Lamancha in rags would have cheerfully disputed with an emperor in scarlet, and suffered no loss of confidence because of his garb, since he would not have given it a thought. What he was considering at the moment was the future of the damaged Stokes.

'Who's that?' Johnson asked peremptorily, pointing to the navvy.

His colleagues hastened to inform him. 'It's Jim Stokes,' one of the three navvies volunteered. 'What 'ave you been doing to yourself, Jim?' And Macnicol added: 'That's the man that was to keep movin' along this side o' the hill, sir. I picked him, for he looked the sooplest.'

Then the faithful Stokes uplifted his voice. 'I done as I was told, sir, and kep' movin' all right, but I ain't seen nothing, and then I 'ad a nawsty fall among them blasted rocks and 'urt my leg. This gentleman comes along and finds me and 'as a try at patchin' me up. But for 'im, sir, I'd be lyin' jammed between two stones till the crows 'ad a pick at me.'

'You're a good chap, Stokes,' said Lamancha, 'but you're a liar. This man,' he addressed Johnson, 'was carrying out your orders, and challenged me. I wanted to pass, and he wouldn't let me, so we had a rough-and-tumble, and through no fault of his he took a toss into a hole, and, as you see, broke his leg. I've set it and bound it up, but the sooner we get the job properly done the better. Hang it, it's the poor devil's livelihood. So we'd better push along.'

His tone irritated Johnson. This scoundrelly poacher, caught red-handed with a rifle, presumed to give orders to his own men. He turned fiercely on Stokes.

'You know this fellow? What's his name?'

'I can't say as I rightly knows 'im,' was the answer. 'But 'im and me was in the war, and he once gave me a drink outside Jerusalem.'

'Are you John Macnab?' Johnson demanded.

'I'm anything you please,' said Lamancha, 'if you'll only hurry and get this man to bed.'

'Damn your impudence! What business is that of yours? You've been caught poaching and we'll march you down to Haripol and get the truth out of you. If you won't tell me who you are, I'll find means to make you . . . Macnicol, you and Macqueen get on each side of him, and you three fellows follow behind. If he tries to bolt, club him . . . You can leave this man here. He'll take no harm, and we can send back for him later.'

'I'm sorry to interfere,' said Lamancha quietly, 'but Stokes is going down now. You needn't worry about me. I'll come with you, for I've got to see him comfortably settled.'

'You'll come with us!' Johnson shouted. 'Many thanks for your kindness. You'll damn well be made to come. Macnicol, take hold of him.'

'Don't,' said Lamancha. 'Please don't. It will only mean trouble.'

Macnicol was acutely unhappy. He recognised something in Lamancha's tone which was perhaps unfamiliar to his master – that accent which means authority, and which, if disregarded, leads to mischief. He had himself served in Lovat's Scouts, and the voice of this tatterdemalion was unpleasantly like that of certain high-handed officers of his acquaintance. So he hesitated and shuffled his feet.

'Look at the thing reasonably,' Lamancha said. 'You say I'm a poacher called John Something-or-other. I admit that you have found me walking with a rifle on your ground, and naturally you want an explanation. But all that can wait till we get this man down to a doctor. I won't run away, for I want to satisfy myself that he's going to be all right. Won't that content you?'

Johnson, to his disgust, felt that he was being manoeuvred into a false position. He was by no means unkind, and this infernal Macnab was making him appear a brute. Public opinion was clearly against him; Macnicol was obviously unwilling to act, Macqueen he knew detested him, and the three navvies might be supposed to take the side of their colleague. Johnson set a high value on public opinion, and scrupled to outrage it. So he curbed his wrath, and gave orders that Stokes should be taken up. Two men formed a cradle with their arms, and the cortege proceeded down the hill-side.

Lamancha took care to give his captors no uneasiness. He walked beside Macqueen, with whom he exchanged a few comments on the weather, and he thought his own by no means pleasant thoughts. This confounded encounter with Stokes had wrecked everything, and yet he could not be altogether sorry that it had happened. He had a chance now of doing something for an honest fellow – Stokes's gallant lie to Johnson had convinced Lamancha of his superlative honesty. But it looked as if he were in for an ugly time with this young bounder, and he was beginning to dislike Johnson extremely. There were one or two points in his favour. The stag seemed to have departed with Wattie into the *ewigkeit* and happily no eye at the Beallach had seen the signs of the gralloch. All that Johnson could do was to accuse him of poaching, *teste* the rifle; he could not prove the deed. Lamancha was rather vague about the law, but he was doubtful whether mere trespass was a grave offence. Then the Claybodys would not want to make too much fuss about it, with the journalists booming the doings of John Macnab . . . But wouldn't they? They were the kind of people that liked advertisement, and after all they had scored. What a tale for the cheap papers there would be in the capture of John Macnab! And if it got out who he was? . . . It was very clear that that at all costs must be prevented . . . Had Johnson Claybody any decent feelings to which he could appeal? A sportsman? Well, he didn't seem to be of much account in that line, for he had wanted to leave the poor devil on the hill.

It took some time for the party to reach the Doran, which they forded at a point considerably below Archie's former lair. Lamancha gave thanks for one mercy, that Archie and Wattie seemed to have got clean away. There was a car on the road which caused him a moment's uneasiness, till he saw that it was not the Ford but a large car with an all-weather body coming from Haripol. The driver seemed to have his instructions, for he turned round – no light task in that narrow road with its boggy fringes – and awaited their arrival.

Johnson gave rapid orders. 'You march the fellow down the road, and bring the navvy – better take him to your cottage, Macqueen. I'll go home in the car and prepare a reception for Macnab.'

It may be assumed that Johnson spoke in haste, for he had somehow to work off his irritation, and desired to assert his authority.

'Hadn't Stokes better go in the car?' Lamancha suggested in a voice which he strove to make urbane. 'That journey down the hill can't have done his leg any good.'

Johnson replied by telling him to mind his own business, and then was foolish enough to add that he was hanged if he would have any lousy navvy in his car. He was preparing to enter, when something in Lamancha's voice stopped him.

'You can't,' said the latter. 'In common decency you can't.'

'Who'll prevent me? Now, look here, I'm fed up with your insolence. You'll be well advised to hold your tongue till we make up our minds how to deal with you. You're in a devilish nasty position, Mr John Macnab, if you had the wits to see it. Macnicol, and you fellows, I'll fire the lot of you if he escapes on the road. You've my authority to hit him on the head if he gets nasty.'

Johnson's foot was on the step, when a hand on his shoulder swung him round.

'No, you don't.' Lamancha's voice had lost all trace of civility, for he was very angry. 'Stokes goes in the car and one of the gillies with him. Here you, lift the man in.'

Johnson had grown rather white, for he saw that the situation was working up to the ugliest kind of climax. He felt dimly that he was again defying public opinion, but his fury made him bold. He cursed Lamancha with vigour and freedom, but there was a slight catch in his voice, and a hint of anticlimax in his threats, for the truth was that he was a little afraid. Still it was a flat defiance, though it concluded with a sneering demand as to what and who would prevent him doing as he pleased, which sounded a little weak.

'First,' said Lamancha, 'I should have a try at wringing your neck. Then I should wreck any reputation you may have up and down this land. I promise you I should make you very sorry you didn't stay in bed this morning.' Lamancha had succeeded in controlling himself – in especial he had checked the phrase 'infernal little haberdasher' which had risen to his lips – and his voice was civil and quiet again.

Johnson gave a mirthless laugh. 'I'm not afraid of a dirty poacher.'

'If I'm a poacher that's no reason why you should behave like a cad.'

It is a melancholy fact which exponents of democracy must face that, while all men may be on a level in the eyes of the State, they will continue in fact to be preposterously unequal. Lamancha had been captured in circumstances of deep suspicion which he did not attempt to explain; he had been caught on Johnson's land, by Johnson's servants; the wounded man was in Johnson's pay, and might reasonably be held to be at Johnson's orders; the car was without question Johnson's own. Yet this outrageous trespasser was not only truculent and impenitent; he was taking it upon himself to give orders to gillies and navvies, and to dictate the use of an expensive automobile. The truth is, that if you belong to a family which for a good many centuries has been accustomed to command and to take risks, and if you yourself, in the forty-odd years of your life, have rather courted trouble than otherwise, and have put discipline into Arab caravans, Central African natives, and Australian mounted brigades – well, when you talk about wringing necks your words might carry weight. If, too, you have never had occasion to think of your position, because no one has ever questioned it, and you promise to break down somebody else's, your threat may convince others, because you yourself are so wholly convinced of your power in that direction. It was the complete lack of bluster in Lamancha, his sober matter-of-factness, that made Johnson suddenly discover in this potato-bogle of a man something formidable. He hesitated, the gillies hesitated, and Lamancha saw his chance. Angry as he was, he contrived to be conciliatory.

'Don't let us lose our tempers. I've no right to dictate to you, but you must see that we're bound to look after this poor chap first. After that I'm at your disposal to give you any satisfaction you want.'

Johnson had not been practised in commercial negotiations for nothing. He saw that obstinacy would mean trouble, and would gain him little, and he cast about for a way to save his face. He went through a show of talking in whispers to Macnicol – a show which did not deceive his head-stalker. Then he addressed Macqueen. 'We think we'd better get this fellow off our hands. You take him down in the car to your cottage, and put him in your spare bed. Then come round to the house and wait for me.'

'This is my show, if you'll allow me, sir,' said Lamancha politely. He took a couple of notes from a wad he carried in an inner pocket. 'Get hold of the nearest doctor – you can use the post-office telephone – and tell him to come at once, and get everything you need for Stokes. I'll see you again. Don't spare expense, for I'm responsible.'

The car departed, and the walking party continued its way down the Doran glen. Lamancha's anger was evaporating, philosophy had intervened, and he was prepared to make allowances for Johnson. But he recognised that the situation was delicate and the future cloudy, and, since he saw no way out, decided to wait patiently on events, always premising that on no account must he permit his identity to be discovered. That might yet involve violent action of a nature which he could not foresee. His consolation was the thought of the stag, now without doubt in the Crask larder. If only he could get clear of his captors, John Macnab would have won two out of the three events. Yes, and if Leithen and Palliser-Yeates had not blundered into captivity.

He was presently reassured as to the fate of the latter. When the party entered the wooded lower glen of the Doran it was joined by four weary navvies who had been refreshing themselves by holding their heads in the stream. Interrogated by Macnicol, they told a tale of hunting an elusive man for hours on the hillside, of repeatedly being on the point of laying hold of him, of a demoniac agility and a diabolical cunning, and of his final disappearance into the deeps of the wood. Questioned about Stokes, they knew nothing. He had last been seen by them in the early morning when the mist first cleared, but it was his business to keep moving high up the hill near the rocks and he had certainly not joined in the chase when it started.

Johnson's temper was not improved by this news. Twice he had been put to public shame in front of his servants by this arrogant tramp who was John Macnab. He had been insulted and defied, but he knew in his heart that the true bitterness lay in the fact that he had also been frightened. Anger, variegated by fear, is apt to cloud a man's common sense, and Johnson's usual caution was deserting him. He was beginning to see red, and the news that there had been an accomplice was the last straw. Somehow or other he must get even with this bandit and bring him to the last extremity of disgrace. He must get him inside the splendours of Haripol, where, his foot on his native heath, he would recover the confidence which had been so lamentably to seek on the hill . . . He would, of course, hand him over to the police, but his soul longed for some more spectacular *dénouement* . . .

Then he thought of the journalists, who had made such a nuisance of themselves in the morning. They were certain to be still about the place. If they could see his triumphant arrival at Haripol they would write such a story as would blaze his credit to the world and make the frustrated poacher a laughing-stock.

As it chanced, as they entered one of the woodland drives of Haripol, they met the gillie, Andrew, on his way home for a late tea. He was asked if he had seen any of the correspondents, and replied that he and Peter and Cameron had captured one after a hard chase, who at the moment was in Cameron's charge and using strong language about the liberty of the Press. Andrew was privately despatched to bid Cameron bring his captive, with all civility and many apologies, up to the house, with a message that Mr Claybody would be glad to have a talk with him. Then, with three navvies as a vanguard and four as a rear-guard, Lamancha was conducted down the glade between Johnson and Macnicol – the picture of a criminal in the grip of the law.

That picture was seen by a small boy who was lurking among the bracken. To the eyes of Benjie it spelt the uttermost disaster. The stag was safe at Crask, but the major part of John Macnab was in the hands of his enemies. Benjie thought hard for a minute, and then wriggled back into the covert and ran as hard as he could through the wood. To him at this awful crisis there seemed to be but a single hope. Force must be brought against force. The Bluidy Mackenzie, now tied up under a distant tree, must be launched against the foe. The boy was aware that the dog had accepted him as an ally, but that it had developed for Lamancha the passion of its morose and solitary life.

The prisoner's uneasiness grew with every step he took down the sweet-scented twilit glade. He was being taken to the house, and in that house there would be people – women, perhaps – journalists, maybe – and a most embarrassing situation for a Cabinet Minister. The whole enterprise, which had been so packed with comedy and adventure, was about to end in fiasco and disgrace, and it was he, the promoter, who had let the show down. For the first time since he arrived at Crask Lamancha whole-heartedly wished himself out of the thing with a clean sheet. There was something to be said, after all, for a man keeping to his groove . . .

They emerged from the trees, and before them stretched the lawns, with a large and important mansion at the other end. This was worse than his wildest dreams. He stopped short.

'Look here,' he said, 'isn't it time to end this farce? I admit I was trespassing, and was fairly caught out. Isn't that enough?'

'By Gad, it isn't,' said Johnson, into whose bosom a certainty of triumph and revenge had at last entered. 'Into the house you go, and there we'll get the truth out of you.'

'I'll pay any fine in reason, but I'm damned if I'm going near that house.'

For answer, Johnson nodded to Macnicol, and the two closed in on the prisoner. Lamancha, now really desperate, shook off the stalker and was about to break to his left, when Johnson tackled high and held him.

At the same moment the Bluidy Mackenzie took a hand in the game.

That faithful hound, conducted by Benjie, had just arrived on the scene of action. He saw his adored Lamancha, the first man who had really understood him, being assaulted by another whose appearance he did not favour. Like a stone from a sling he leaped from the covert straight at Mr Johnson Claybody's throat.

It all happened in one crowded instant. Lamancha felt the impact of part of Mackenzie's body, saw Johnson stagger and fall, and next observed his captor running wildly for the house with Mackenzie hot on his trail. Then, with that preposterous instinct to help human against animal which is deeper than reason, he started after him.

Never had a rising young commercial magnate shown a better gift of speed, for a mad dog was his private and particular fear, and this beast was clearly raving mad. Macnicol and the navvies were some twenty yards behind, but Lamancha was a close second. Crying hoarsely, Johnson leaped the flower-beds and doubled like a hare in and out of a pergola. Ahead lay his mother's pet new lily-pond, and, remembering dimly that mad dogs did not love water, he plunged into it, and embraced a lead Cupid in the centre.

Mackenzie loved water like a spaniel, and his great body shot after him. But the immersion caused a second's delay and enabled Lamancha to take a flying leap which brought him almost atop of the dog. He clutched his collar and swung him back, making a commotion in the fountain like a tidal wave. Mackenzie recognised his friend and did not turn on him, but he still strained furiously after Johnson, who was now emerging like Proteus on the far side.

Suddenly the windows of the house, which was not thirty yards off, opened, and the stage filled up with figures. First the amazed eyes of Lamancha saw Crossby entering from the right, evidently a prisoner, in the charge of two gillies. Then at one set of windows appeared Sir Edward Leithen with a scared face, while from the other emerged the forms of Sir Archibald Roylance, Mr Palliser-Yeates, and a stout gentleman in a kilt who might be Lord Claybody. To his mind, keyed by wrath and confusion to expectation of tragedy, there could only be one solution. Others besides himself had failed, and the secret of John Macnab was horridly patent to the world.

'Archie,' he panted, 'for God's sake call off your tripe-hound. I can't hold on any longer . . . He'll eat the little man.'

Lord Claybody had unusual penetration. He observed his son and heir dripping and exhausted on the turf, and a figure, which looked like a caricature in the Opposition Press of an eminent Tory statesman, surrendering a savage hound to a small and dirty boy. Also he saw in the background a group of gillies and navvies. There was mystery here which had better be unriddled away from the gaze of the profane crowd. His eye caught Crossby's and Lamancha's.

'I think you'd better all come indoors,' he said.

FIFTEEN

Haripol – the Armistice

THE GREAT DRAWING-room had lost all its garishness with the approach of evening. Facing eastward, it looked out on lawns now dreaming in a green dusk, though beyond them the setting sun, over-topping the house, washed the woods and hills with gold and purple. Lady Claybody sat on a brocaded couch with something of the dignity of the late Queen Victoria, mystified, perturbed, awaiting the explanation which was her due. Her husband stood before her, a man with such an air of being ready for any emergency that even his kilt looked workmanlike. The embarrassed party from Crask clustered in the background; the shameful figures of Lamancha and Johnson stood in front of the window, thereby deepening the shadow. So electric was the occasion that Lady Claybody, finically proud of her house, did not notice that these two were oozing water over the polished parquet and devastating more than one expensive rug.

Lamancha, now that the worst had happened, was resigned and almost cheerful. Since the Claybodys had bagged Leithen and Palliser-Yeates and detected the complicity of Sir Archie, there was no reason why he should be left out. He hoped, rather vaguely, that his captors might not be inclined to make the thing public in view of certain episodes, but he had got to the pitch of caring very little. John Macnab was dead, and only awaited sepulture and oblivion. He looked towards Johnson, expecting him to take up the tale.

But Johnson had no desire to speak. He had been very much shaken and scared by the Bluidy Mackenzie and had not yet recovered his breath. Also a name spoken by his father, as they entered the room, had temporarily unsettled his wits. It was Lord Claybody who broke the uncomfortable silence.

'Who owns that dog?' he asked, looking, not at Lamancha, but at his son.

'The brute's mine,' said Archie penitently. 'He followed the car, and I left him tied up. Can't think how he got loose and started this racket.'

The master of the house turned to Lamancha. 'How did you come here, my lord? You look as if you had been having a rough journey.'

Lamancha laughed. Happily the waning light did not reveal the full extent of his dirt and raggedness. 'I have,' he said, 'I'm your son's prisoner. Fairly caught out. I daresay you think me an idiot, unless Leithen or Palliser-Yeates has explained.'

Lord Claybody looked more mystified than ever.

'I don't understand. A prisoner?'

'He's John Macnab,' put in Johnson, whose breath was returning, and with it sulkiness. He was beginning to see that there was to be no triumph in this business, and a good deal of unpleasant explanation.

'Well, a third of him,' said Lamancha. 'And as you've already annexed the other two-thirds you have the whole of the fellow under your roof.'

Lord Claybody's gasp suddenly revealed to Lamancha that he had been premature in his confession. How his two friends had got into the Haripol drawing-room he did not know, but apparently it was not as prisoners. The mischief was done, however, and there was no going back.

'You mean to say that you three gentlemen are John Macnab? You have been poaching at Glenraden and Strathlarrig? Does Colonel Raden – does Mr Bandicott know who you are?'

Lamancha nodded. 'They found out after we had had our shot at their preserves. They didn't mind – took it very well indeed. We hope you're going to follow suit?'

'But I am amazed. You had only to send me a note and my forest was at your disposal for as long as you wished. Why – why this – this incivility?'

'I assure you, on my honour, that the last thing we dreamed of was incivility . . . Look here, Lord Claybody, I wonder if I can explain. We three – Leithen, Palliser-Yeates, and myself – found ourselves two months ago fairly fed up with life. We weren't sick, and we weren't tired – only bored. By accident we discovered each other's complaint, and we decided to have a try at curing ourselves by attempting something very difficult and rather dangerous. There was a fellow called Tarras used to play this game – he was before your time – and we resolved to take a leaf out of his book. So we quartered ourselves on Archie

– he's not to blame, remember, for he's been protesting bitterly all along – and we sent out our challenge. Glenraden and Strathlarrig accepted it, so that was all right; you didn't in so many words, but you accepted it by your action, for you took elaborate precautions to safeguard your ground . . . Well, that's all. Palliser-Yeates lost at Glenraden owing to Miss Janet. Leithen won at Strathlarrig, and now I've made a regular hat of things at Haripol. But we're cured, all of us. We're simply longing to get back to the life which in July we thought humbug.'

Lord Claybody sat down in a chair and brooded.

'I still don't follow,' he said. 'You are people who matter a great deal to the world, and there's not a man in this country who wouldn't have been proud to give you the chance of the kind of holiday you needed. You're one of the leaders of my party. Personally, I have always considered you the best of them. I'm looking to Sir Edward Leithen to win a big case for me this autumn. Mr Palliser-Yeates has done a lot of business with my firm, and after the talk I've had with him this afternoon I look to doing a good deal more with him in the future. You had only to give me a hint of what you wished and I would have jumped at the chance of obliging you. You wanted the thrill of feeling like poachers. Well, I would have seen that you got it. I would have turned on every man in the place and used all my wits to make your escapade difficult. Wouldn't that have contented you?'

'No, no,' Lamancha cried. 'You are missing the point. Don't you see that your way would have taken all the gloss off the adventure and made it a game? We had to feel that we were taking real risks – that, being what we were, we should look utter fools if we were caught and exposed.'

'Pardon me, but it is you who are missing the point.' Lord Claybody was smiling. 'You could never have been exposed – except perhaps by those confounded journalists,' he added as he caught sight of Crossby.

'We had the best of them on our side,' Lamancha put in. 'Mr Crossby has backed us up nobly.'

'Well, that only made your position more secure. Colonel Raden and Mr Bandicott accepted your challenge, and in any case they were sportsmen, and you knew it. If they had caught one or the other of you they would never have betrayed you. You must see that. And here at Haripol you were on the safest ground of all. I'm not what they call a sportsman – not yet – but I couldn't give you away. Do you think it conceivable that I would do anything to weaken the public prestige of a statesman I believe in, a great lawyer I brief, and a great banker whose assistance is of the utmost value to me. I'm a man who has made a fortune by my own hard work and I mean to keep it; therefore in these bad times I am out to support anything which buttresses the solid structure of society. You three are part of that structure. You might poach every stag on Haripol, and I should still hold my tongue.'

Lamancha, regardless of the condition of his nether garments, sat down heavily on an embroidered stool which Lady Claybody erroneously believed to have belonged to Marie Antoinette, and dropped his head in his hands.

'Lord, I believe you're right,' he groaned. 'We've all been potting at sitting birds. John, do you hear? We've been making godless fools of ourselves. We thought we had got outside civilisation and were really taking chances. But we weren't. We were all the time as safe as your blessed bank. It can't be done – not in this country anyway. We're in the groove and have got to stay there. We've been a pretty lot of idiots not to think of that.'

Then Johnson spoke. He had been immensely cheered by Lord Claybody's words, for they had seemed to raise Haripol again to that dignity from which it had been in imminent risk of falling.

'I don't complain personally, Lord Lamancha, though you've given me a hard day of it. But I agree with my father – you really were gambling on a certainty and it wasn't very fair to us. Besides, you three, who are the supporters of law and order, have offered a pretty good handle to the enemy, with those infernal journalists advertising John Macnab. There may be a large crop of Macnabs springing up, and you'll be responsible. It's a dangerous thing to weaken the sanctities of property.'

He found, to his surprise, a vigorous opponent in his mother. Lady Claybody had passed from mystification to enlightenment, and from enlightenment to appreciation. It delighted her romantic soul that Haripol should have been chosen for the escapade of three eminent men; she saw tradition and legend already glorifying her new dwelling. Moreover, she scented in Johnson's words a theory of life which was not her own, a mercantile creed which conflicted with her notion of Haripol, and of the future of her family.

'You are talking nonsense, Johnson,' she said, 'You are making property a nightmare, for you are always thinking about it. You forget that wealth is made for man, and not man for wealth. It is the personality that matters. It is so vulgar not to keep money and land and that sort of thing in its proper place. Look at those splendid old Jacobites and what they gave up. The one advantage of property is that you can disregard it.'

This astounding epigram passed unnoticed save by Janet, for the lady, smiling benignly on the poaching trinity, went on to a practical application. 'I think the whole John Macnab adventure has been quite delightful. It has brightened us all up, and I'm sure we have nothing to forgive. I think we must have a dinner for everybody concerned to celebrate the end of it. What Claybody says is perfectly true – you must have known you could count on us, just as much as on Colonel Raden and Mr Bandicott. But since you seem not to have realised that, you have had the fun of thinking you were in real danger, and after all it is what one thinks that matters. I am so glad you are all cured of being bored. But I'm not quite happy about those journalists. How can we be certain that they won't make a horrid story of it?'

'My wife is right,' said Lord Claybody emphatically. 'That is the danger.' He looked at Crossby. 'They are certain to want some kind of account.'

'They certainly will,' said the latter. 'And that account must leave out names and – other details. I don't suppose you want the navvy business made public?'

'Perhaps not. That was Johnson's idea, and I don't consider it a particularly happy inspiration.'

'Well, there is nothing for it but that I should give them the story and expurgate it discreetly. John Macnab has been caught and dismissed with a warning – that's all there is to it. I suppose your gillies won't blab? They can't know very much, but they might give away some awkward details.'

'I'll jolly well see that they don't,' said Johnson. 'But who will you make John Macnab out to be?'

'A lunatic – unnamed. I'll hint at some family skeleton into which good breeding forbids me to inquire. The fact that he has failed at Haripol will take the edge off my colleagues' appetites. If he had got his stag they would have been ramping on the trail. The whole thing will go the way of other stunts, and be forgotten in two days. I know the British Press.'

Within half an hour the atmosphere in that drawing-room had changed from suspicion to something not far from friendliness, but the change left two people unaffected. Johnson, doubtless with Lamancha's behaviour on the hill in his memory, was still sullen, and Janet was obviously ill at ease.

Lamancha, who was suffering a good deal from thirst and hunger and longed for a bath, arose from his stool.

'I think,' he said, 'that we three – especially myself – owe you the most abject apologies. I see now that we were taking no risks worth mentioning, and that what we thought was an adventure was only a *faux pas*. It was abominably foolish, and we are all very sorry about it. I think you've taken it uncommonly well.'

Lord Claybody raised a protesting hand. 'Not another word. I vote we break up this conference and give you something to drink. Johnson's tongue is hanging out of his mouth.'

The voice of Janet was suddenly raised, and in it might have been detected a new timidity. 'I want to apologise also. Dear Lady Claybody, I stole your dog . . . I hope you will forgive me. You see we wanted to do something to distract Macnicol, and that seemed the only way.'

A sudden silence fell. Lady Claybody, had there been sufficient light, might have been observed to flush.

'You – stole – Roguie,' she said slowly, while Janet moved closer to Sir Archie. 'You – stole – Wee Roguie. I think you are the ——'

'But we were very kind to him, and he was very happy.'

'*I* wasn't happy. I scarcely slept a wink. What right had you to touch my precious little dog? I think it is the most monstrous thing I ever heard in my life.'

'I'm so very sorry. Please, please forgive me. But you said yourself that the only advantage of property was that you could disregard it.'

Lady Claybody, to her enormous credit, stared, gasped, and then laughed. Then something in the attitude of Janet and Archie stopped her, and she asked suddenly: 'Are you two engaged?'

'Yes,' said Janet, 'since ten minutes past one this afternoon.'

Lady Claybody rose from the couch and took her in her arms.

'You're the wickedest girl in the world and the most delightful. Oh, my dear, I am so pleased. Sir Archibald, you will let an old woman kiss you. You are brigands, both of you, so you should be very very happy. You must all come and dine here tomorrow night – your father and sister too, and we'll ask the Bandicotts. It will be a dinner to announce your engagement, and also to say good-bye to John Macnab. Poor John! I feel as if he were a real person who will always haunt this glen, and now he is disappearing into the mist.'

'No,' said Lamancha, 'he is being shrivelled up by coals of fire. By the way' – and he turned to Lord Claybody – 'I'll send over the stag in the morning. I forgot to tell you I got a stag – an old beast with a famous head, who used to visit Crask. It will look rather well in your hall. It has been in Archie's larder since the early afternoon.'

Then Johnson Claybody was moved to a course which surprised his audience, and may have surprised himself. His sullenness vanished in hearty laughter.

'I think,' he said, 'I have made rather a fool of myself.'

'I think we have all made fools of ourselves,' said Lamancha.

Johnson turned to his late prisoner and held out his hand.

'Lord Lamancha, I have only one thing to say. I don't in the least agree with my mother, and I'm dead against John Macnab. But I'm *your* man from this day on – whatever line you take. You're my leader, for, by all that's holy, you've a most astonishing gift of getting the goods.'

Epilogue

CROSSBY, FROM WHOM I had most of this narrative, was as good as his word, though it went sorely against the grain. He himself wrote a tale, and circulated his version to his brother journalists, which made a good enough yarn, but was a sad anticlimax to the Return of Harald Blacktooth. He told of a gallant but frustrated attempt on the Haripol Sanctuary, the taking of the culprit, and the magnanimous release by young Mr Claybody of a nameless monomaniac – a gentleman, it was hinted, who had not recovered from the effects of the war. The story did not occupy a prominent page in the papers, and presently, as he had prophesied, the world had forgotten John Macnab, and had turned its attention to the cinema star, just arrived in London, whom for several days, to the disgust of that lady's agents, it had strangely neglected.

The dinner at Haripol, Crossby told me, was a hilarious function, at which four men found reason to modify their opinion of the son of the house, and the host fell in love with Janet, and Archie with his hostess. There is talk, I understand, of making it an annual event to keep green the memory of the triune sportsman who once haunted the place. If you go to Haripol, as I did last week, you will see above the hall chimney a noble thirteen-pointer, and a legend beneath proclaiming that the stag was shot on the Sgurr Dearg beat of the forest by the Earl of Lamancha on a certain day of September in a certain year. Lady Claybody, who does not like stag's heads as ornaments, makes an exception of this; indeed, it is one of her household treasures to which she most often calls her guests' attention.

Janet and Archie were married in November in the little kirk of Inverlarrig, and three busy men cancelled urgent engagements to be there. Among the presents there was one not shown to the public or mentioned in the papers, and a duplicate of it went to Junius and Agatha at their wedding in the following spring. It was a noble loving-cup in the form of a quaich, inscribed as the gift of John Macnab. Below four signatures were engraved – Lamancha, Edward Leithen and John Palliser-Yeates, and last, in a hand of surprising boldness, the honoured name of Benjamin Bogle.

THE DANCING FLOOR

'*Quisque suos patimur Manes*'
Virgil, *Aeneid*, vi. 743

To
Henry Newbolt

NOTE

An episode in this tale is taken from a short story of mine entitled 'Basilissa', published in *Blackwood's Magazine* in 1914.

J.B.

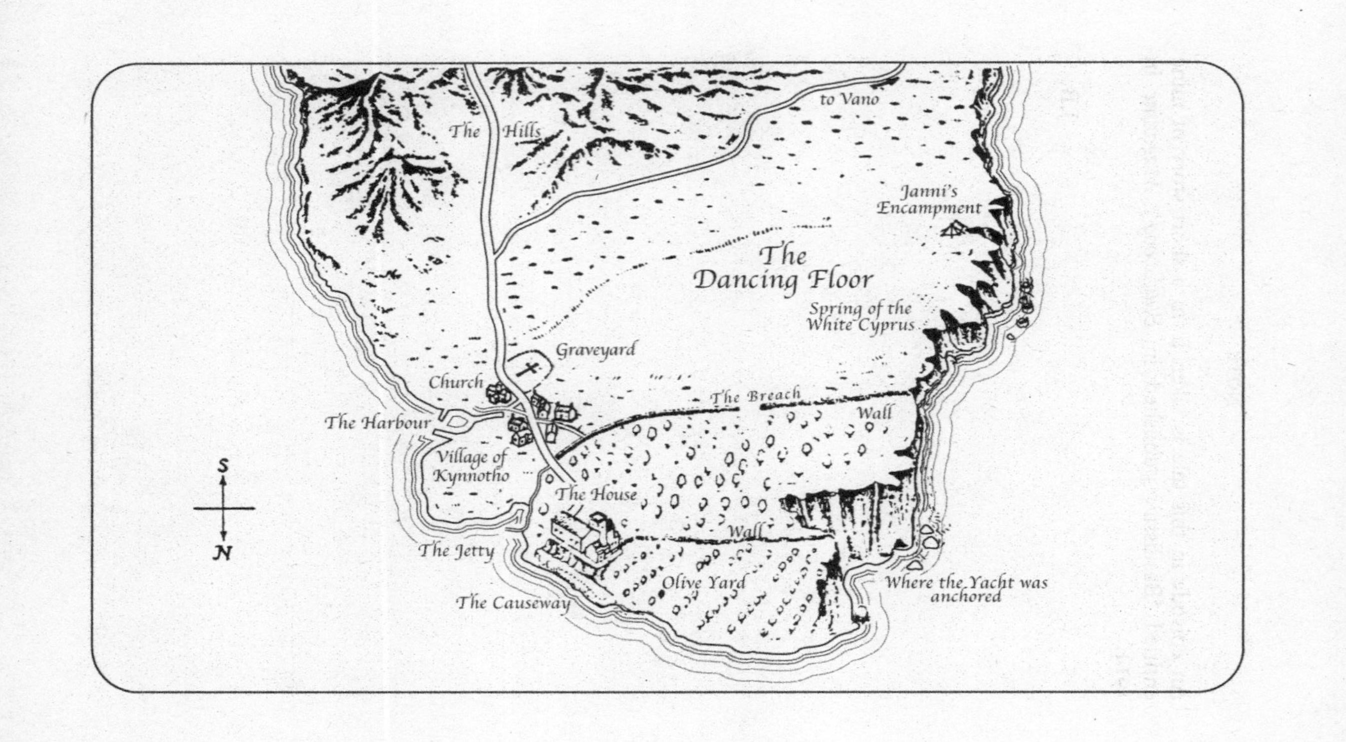
to Vano
The Hills
Janni's Encampment
The Dancing Floor
Spring of the White Cyprus
Graveyard
Church
The Breach
Wall
The Harbour
Village of Kynnotho
The House
Wall
The Jetty
Olive Yard
Where the Yacht was anchored
The Causeway
S
N

Part One

ONE

This story was told me by Leithen, as we were returning rather late in the season from a shooting holiday in North Ontario. There were few passengers, the weather was a succession of snow blizzards and gales, and as we had the smoking-room for the most part to ourselves, we stoked up the fire and fell into a mood of yarns and reminiscences. Leithen, being a lawyer, has a liking for careful detail, and his tale took long in the telling; indeed, snatches of it filled the whole of that rough October passage. The version I have written out is amplified from his narrative, but I think it is accurate, for he took the trouble to revise it.

ROMANCE (HE SAID) is a word I am shy of using. It has been so staled and pawed by fools that the bloom is gone from it, and to most people it stands for a sugary world as flat as an eighteenth-century Arcadia. But, dry stick as I am, I hanker after my own notion of romance. I suppose it is the lawyer in me, but I define it as something in life which happens with an exquisite aptness and a splendid finality, as if Fate had suddenly turned artist – something which catches the breath because it is so wholly right. Also for me it must happen to youth. I do not complain of growing old, but I like to keep my faith that at one stage in our mortal existence nothing is impossible. It is part of my belief that the universe is on the whole friendly to man and that the ordering of the world is in the main benevolent . . . So I go about expecting things, waiting like an old pagan for the descent of the goddess. And once – only once – I caught the authentic shimmer of her wings.

I

My story begins in January 1913, when I took my nephew Charles to dine with the Amysforts for a ball they were giving. Balls are not much in my line, for when I came first to London it was the foolish fashion of young men not to dance, but to lounge superciliously in doorways, while their elders took the floor. I had a good deal of work on hand, and I meant to leave immediately after dinner, but the necessity of launching Charles made me linger through the first few dances. My nephew was a cheerful young gentleman in his second year at Oxford, and it presently appeared that he did not want for friends of his own age. There was a perpetual bandying of nicknames and occult chaff with other fresh-coloured boys.

One in particular caught my attention. He was a tall young man of about Charles's age, who was not dancing but stood beside one of the windows with his head silhouetted against a dark curtain. He was uncommonly handsome after the ordinary English pattern, but our youth is mostly good to behold and that would not have fixed my attention. What struck me was his pose. He was looking at the pretty spectacle with a curious aloofness – with eyes that received much but gave out nothing. I have never seen anyone so completely detached, so clothed with his own atmosphere, and since that is rare at the age of twenty, I asked Charles if he knew him.

'Rather. It's old Milburne. He's up at Magdalen with me. First string for the 'Varsity mile. Believed' – his voice became reverential – 'to be going to knock five seconds off his last year's time. Most awful good chap. Like me to introduce you?'

The young man in response to my nephew's beckoning approached us. 'Hello, Vernon, how's life?' said my nephew. 'Want to introduce you to my uncle – Sir Edward Leithen – big legal swell, you know – good fellow to have behind you if you run up against the laws of England.'

Charles left us to claim a partner, and I exchanged a few commonplaces with his friend, for I too – *consule Planco* – had run the mile. Our short talk was the merest platitudes, but my feeling about his odd distinction was intensified. There was something old-fashioned in his manner – wholly self-possessed yet with no touch of priggishness – a little formal, as if he had schooled himself to be urbanely and delicately on his guard. My guess at the time was that he had foreign blood in him, not from any difference of colouring or feature, but from his silken reserve. We of the North are apt to be angular in our silences; we have not learned the art of gracious reticence.

That boy's face remained clearly fixed in my memory. It is a thing that often happens to me, for without any reason on earth

I will carry about with me pictures of some casual witnesses or clients whom I am bound to recognise if I ever see them again. It is as freakish a gift as that which makes some men remember scraps of doggerel. I saw the face so vividly in my mind that, if I had been an artist, I could have drawn it accurately down to the finest lines of the mouth and the wary courtesy of the eyes. I do not suppose I gave the meeting another conscious thought, for I was desperately busy at the time. But I knew that I had added another portrait to the lumber-room of my absurd memory.

I had meant to go to Scotland that Easter vacation to fish, but a sudden pressure of Crown cases upset all my plans, and I had to limit my holiday to four days. I wanted exercise, so I took it in the most violent form, and went for a walk in the Westmorland hills. The snow lay late that year, and I got the exercise I sought scrambling up icy gullies and breasting north-easters on the long bleak ridges. All went well till the last day, which I spent among the Cartmel fells, intending to catch a train at an obscure station which would enable me to join the night mail for London at Lancaster. You know how those little hills break down in stony shelves to the sea. Well, as luck would have it, I stepped into a hole between two boulders masked with snow, and crawled out with the unpleasing certainty that I had either broken or badly wrenched my ankle. By the time I had hobbled down to the beginning of the stone-walled pastures I knew that it was a twist and not a break, but before I reached a road I knew also that I would never reach the station in time for my train.

It had begun to snow again, the spring dusk was falling, and the place was very lonely. My watch told me that even if I found a farm or inn and hired a trap I should miss my train. The only chance was to get a motor-car to take me to Lancaster. But there was no sign of farm or inn – only interminable dusky snowy fields, and the road was too small and obscure to make a friendly motor-car probable. I limped along in a very bad temper. It was not a matter of desperate urgency that I should be in London next morning, though delay would mean the postponement of a piece of business I wanted to get finished. But the prospect was black for my immediate comfort. The best I could look forward to was a bed in a farm- or a wayside public-house, and a slow and painful journey next day. I was angry with myself for my clumsiness. I had thought my ankles beyond reproach, and it was ridiculous that after three days on rough and dangerous mountains I should come to grief on a paltry hillock.

The dusk thickened, and not a soul did I meet. Presently woods began to creep around the road, and I walked between two patches of blackness in a thin glimmer of twilight which would soon be gone. I was cold and hungry and rather tired, and my ankle gave me a good deal of pain. I tried to think where I was, and could only remember that the station, which had been my immediate objective, was still at least six miles distant. I had out my map and wasted half a dozen matches on it, but it was a map of the hill country and stopped short of my present whereabouts. Very soon I had come to a determination to stop at the first human habitation, were it a labourer's cottage, and throw myself upon the compassion of its inmates. But not a flicker of light could I see to mark the presence of man.

Then something white glimmered faintly on my left, and I saw that it was a wicket gate. This must mean a house near at hand, so I hopefully pushed it open and entered. I found myself in a narrow path running among fir-trees. It was nearly pitch-dark in that place, and I was in fear of losing the road, which was obscured by the fallen snow, and getting lost in a wood. Soon, however, I was clear of the firs and in more open country among what looked like beeches. The wind, too, had swept the path bare, and there was just enough light to make it out as it twined up and down a little glade. I suspected that I was in a demesne of some considerable house and the suspicion became a certainty when my track emerged on a broad gravel drive. After that my way was clear. The drive took me into a park – I knew it was a park because of the frequent swing-gates for cattle – and suddenly it bore to the right and I saw half a dozen irregularly placed lights high up in the air before me. This was the house, and it must be a large one, for some of the lights were far apart.

Five minutes later I found myself ringing the bell in a massive pillared porch, and explaining my case to a very old butler, to whom I gave my card.

'I've had an accident on the hills,' I said, 'and twisted my ankle rather badly. I wonder if I might ask for some assistance – to get to an inn or a station. I'm afraid I don't in the least know where I am.'

'This is Severns Hall, sir,' said the man. 'My master is Mr Vernon Milburne. If you will come in, sir, I will acquaint him with the position.'

'Mr Vernon Milburne?' I cried. 'I believe I have met him. I think he is at Oxford with my nephew.'

'Mr Milburne is a member of the University of Oxford,' said the ancient man. He led me into a vast hall of the worst kind of Victorian Gothic, in which a big bright wood fire crackled. When he saw me clearly the butler proved a very angel of mercy. 'I think, sir, you should first have a little refreshment,' he said, and brought me a whisky-and-soda. Then, while I thawed my frozen bones before the logs, he departed to seek his master.

I was too preoccupied with my own grievances to feel much interest in the fact that I had stumbled upon the dwelling of the boy who had so intrigued me at Lady Amysfort's ball. But as I warmed my hands at the blaze it did occur to me that this was the last kind of house I would have linked him with – this sham-medieval upholstered magnificence. It was Gothic with every merit of Gothic left out, and an air of dull ecclesiasticism hung about it. There was even an organ at one end, ugly and staring, as if it had come out of some *nouveau riche* provincial church. Every bit of woodwork was fretted and tortured into fancy shapes.

I heard a voice at my elbow.

'I think we have met before, Sir Edward,' it said. 'I am so sorry for your misfortune. Let's get the boot off and look at the ankle.'

'It's only a sprain,' I said. 'I really don't want to bother you. If you would be so very kind as to lend me a car to take me to Lancaster, I can manage to travel all right. I ought to be in London tomorrow morning.'

'Nonsense!' He smiled in a pleasant boyish way. 'You are going to stay here tonight, and if you're well enough I'll send you into Lancaster tomorrow. You look simply fagged out. Let's get the boot off and see if we need a doctor.'

He summoned the butler, and the two of them soon had my foot bare, while the boy, who seemed to know something about sprains, ran a light hand over the ankle bone.

'Nothing very bad here,' he said: 'but it must have been jolly painful to walk with. We'll bandage it and you need only limp for a day or two. Beaton, find out if Sir Edward's room is ready. You'd better have a hot bath and then we'll do the bandaging. After that you'll want some food. I'll lend you a dressing-gown and dry clothes.'

The next hour was spent in restoring me to some ease of body. Severns might be an ugly house, but whoever built it had a pretty notion of comfort in bedrooms. I had two rooms, each with a cheerful fire, and when I had had my bath the two Samaritans bandaged my ankle as neatly as a hospital nurse, and helped me into a suit of flannels. Then Vernon disappeared, and when he returned he was dressed for dinner. A table had been laid for me in the sitting-room, and Beaton was waiting to ask me what I would drink.

'Champagne,' said Vernon. 'I prescribe it.'

'But you're making far too much fuss about me,' I protested. 'I can easily dine downstairs with you.'

'I think you ought to dine here. You've put yourself in my hands and I'm your medical adviser.'

He saw me start my meal before he left me.

'Do you mind if I say good night now?' he said. 'You ought to get to bed pretty soon and I have some work I want to do after dinner. Sound sleep and pleasant dreams.'

I dined excellently, and after a single pipe was resolutely put to bed by Beaton the butler. They were benevolent despots in this house who were not to be gainsaid. I was sufficiently weary to be glad to go to sleep, but before I dropped off I wondered just a little at the nature of my reception. There were no other guests, Beaton had told me, and it seemed odd that a boy of nineteen alone in this Gothic mausoleum should show so little desire for human companionship. I should have expected, even if I were not allowed downstairs, to have had him come and talk to me for an hour or so before turning in. What work had he to which he was so faithful? I remembered that Charles had mentioned that he was a bit of a swell at his books, but, as Charles himself had been ploughed for Pass Mods, that might mean very little. Anyhow, there was something morbid about a conscience which at nineteen forced its possessor to work in vacation time after dinner. He had been immensely hospitable, but obviously he had not wanted my company. That aloofness which I had remarked at Lady Amysfort's ball had become a heavy preoccupation. His attitude had been courteously defensive: there had been a screen which robbed his kindness of all geniality. I felt quite distinctly that there was something in or about the house, something connected with himself, from which I was being resolutely excluded.

I slept well, and was awakened by Beaton bringing my early tea. He had undrawn the curtains and opened one of the windows, and a great flood of sunlight and spring airs was pouring through. The storm had passed and April was in her most generous mood. My ankle felt lumpish and stiff, but when Beaton examined it he pronounced that it was mending nicely. 'But you can't press on it today, sir,' he added. 'Mr Vernon won't let you move today . . . Breakfast will be laid in the sitting-room, and Mr Vernon's compliments and he proposes to join you at nine o'clock. I will return and bandage the ankle and assist you to rise as soon as Prayers are over.'

Presently, as I lay watching a ridge of distant hills seen through the window and trying to decide what it could be, the sound of singing rose from some room below me. It must be Prayers. The old-fashioned hymn tune reminded me of my childhood and I wondered how many young men of today kept up the fashion of family worship when alone in a country house. And then I suddenly remembered all about the Milburnes, for they had been my mother's friends.

Humphrey Milburne had been a rich Lancashire cotton-spinner, whose father or grandfather – I forget which – had been one of the pioneers of the industry. I don't think he had ever concerned himself greatly with business, for his *métier* had always been that of the devout layman who is more occupied with church affairs than any bishop. He had been a leader of the Evangelical party, a vigorous opponent of ritualist practices, and a noted organizer of religious revivals. Vague memories of him came back to me from my childhood, for my own family had been of the same persuasion. I had a recollection of a tall bearded man who on a visit to us had insisted on seeing the children, and had set me on his knee, and had asked me, a shivering self-conscious mite, embarrassing questions about my soul. I remembered his wife, Lady Augusta, more clearly. She was a thin little woman who never seemed to be separated from a large squashy Bible stuffed with leaflets and secured by many elastic bands. She had had a knack of dropping everything as she moved, and I had acted as page to retrieve her belongings. She had been very kind to me, for to her grief she had then no children . . . I remembered that a son had at last been born – 'a child of many prayers', my mother had called him. And then came a vague recollection of a tragedy. Lady Augusta had died when the boy was an infant and her husband had followed within the year. After that the Milburnes passed out of my life, except that their nurse had come to us when I was at Eton, and had had much to say of young Master Vernon.

My vague remembrance seemed to explain my host. The child of ageing parents and an orphan from his early years – that would account for his lack of youthful spontaneity. I liked the notion of him I was acquiring; there was something quaint and loyal in his keeping up the family ritual – an evangelical athlete with the looks of Apollo. I had fancied something foreign in his air, but that of course was nonsense. He came of the most prosaic British stock, cotton-spinning Milburnes, and for his mother a Douglas-Ernott, whose family was the quintessence of Whig solidity.

I found Vernon waiting for me in the sunny sitting-room, dressed in rough grey homespun and with an air of being ready for a long day in the open. There was a change in him since the night before. His eyes were a little heavy, as if he had slept badly, but the shutters were lifted from them. His manner was no longer constrained, and the slight awkwardness I had felt in his presence was gone. He was now a cheerful communicative undergraduate.

'Beaton says you had a good night, sir, but you mustn't use that foot of yours. You can't think of London today, you know. I've nothing to do except look after you, so you'd better think of me as Charles with a nephew's privileges. It's going to be a clinking fine day, so what do you say to running up in the car to the moors above Shap and listening to the curlews? In the spring they're the jolliest things alive.'

He was a schoolboy now, looking forward to an outing, and we might have been breakfasting in Oxford rooms before going out with the Bicester. I fell into his holiday mood, and forgot to tell him that I had long ago met his parents. He lent me an ulster and helped me downstairs, where he packed me into the front of a big Daimler and got in beside me. In the clear spring sunshine, with the park a chessboard of green grass and melting snow, and the rooks cawing in the beech tops, Severns looked almost venerable, for its lines were good and the stone was weathering well. He nodded towards the long façades. 'Ugly old thing, when you think of Levens or Sizergh, but it was my grandfather's taste and I mean to respect it. If we get a fine sunset you'll see it light up like an enchanted castle. It's something to be able to see the hills from every window, and to get a glimpse of the sea from the top floor. Goodish sport, too, for we've several miles of salmon and sea trout, and we get uncommon high birds in the upper coverts.'

We sped up by winding hill-roads to the moors, and there were the curlews crying over the snow-patched bent with that note which is at once eerie and wistful and joyful. There were grouse, too, busy about their nesting, and an occasional stone-chat, and dippers flashing their white waistcoats in every beck. It was like being on the roof of the world, with the high Lake hills a little foreshortened, like ships coming over the horizon at sea. Lunch we had with us and ate on a dry bank of heather, and we had tea in a whitewashed moorland farm. I have never taken to anyone so fast as I took to that boy. He was in the highest spirits, as if he had finished some difficult task, and in the rebound he became extraordinarily companionable. I think he took to me also, for he showed a shy but intense interest in my doings, the eagerness with which an undergraduate prospects the channels of the world's life which he is soon to navigate. I had been prepared to find a touch of innocent priggishness, but there was nothing of the kind. He seemed to have no dogmas of his own, only inquiries.

'I suppose a lawyer's training fits a man to examine all kinds of problems – not only legal ones,' he asked casually at luncheon. 'I mean he understands the value of any sort of evidence, for the principles of logical proof are always the same?'

'I suppose so,' I replied, 'though it's only legal conundrums that come my way. I was once asked my opinion on a scientific proof – in the higher mathematics – but I didn't make much of it – couldn't quite catch on to the data or understand the language.'

'Yes, that might be a difficulty,' he admitted. 'But a thing like a ghost story for instance – you'd be all right at that, I suppose?'

The boy had clearly something in his head, and I wondered if the raw magnificence of Serverns harboured any spooks. Could that be the reason of his diffidence on the previous evening?

When we got home we sat smoking by the library fire, and

while I skimmed *The Times* Vernon dozed. He must have been short of his sleep and was now making up for it in the way of a healthy young man. As I watched his even breathing I decided that here there could be no abnormality of body or mind. It was like watching a tired spaniel on the rug, too tired even to hunt in his dreams.

As I lifted my eyes from the paper I saw that he was awake and was looking at me intently, as if he were hesitating about asking me some question.

'I've been asleep,' he apologized. 'I can drop off anywhere after a day on the hills.'

'You were rather sleepless as a child, weren't you?' I asked.

His eyes opened. 'I wonder how you know that?'

'From your old nurse. I ought to have told you that in my boyhood I knew your parents a little. They stayed with us more than once. And Mrs Ganthony came to my mother from you. I was at Eton at the time, and I remember how she used to entertain us with stories about Severns. You must have been an infant when she left.'

'I was four. What sort of things did she tell you?'

'About your bad nights and your pluck. I fancy it was by way of censure of our declamatory habits. Why, after all these years I remember some of her phrases. How did the thing go? "What fidgeted me was the way his lordship 'eld his tongue. For usual he'd shout as lusty as a whelp, but on these mornings I'd find him with his eyes like moons and his skin white and shiny, and never a cheep the whole blessed night, with me lying next door, and a light sleeper at all times, Mrs Wace, ma'am." Was Mrs Wace a sort of Mrs Harris?'

He laughed merrily. 'To think that you should have heard that! No, she was our housekeeper, and Ganthony, who babbled like Sairey Gamp, made a litany of her name. That's the most extraordinary thing I ever heard.'

'You've outgrown that childish ailment anyhow,' I said.

'Yes, I have outgrown it.' My practice with witnesses made me detect just a shade of hesitation.

At dinner he returned to the subject which seemed to interest him, the exact nature of the legal training. I told him that I was an advocate, not a judge, and so had no need to cultivate a judicial mind.

'But you can't do without it,' he protested. 'You have to advise your client and pronounce on his case before you argue it. The bulk of your work must be the weighing of evidence. I should have thought that that talent could be applied to any subject in the world if the facts were sufficiently explained. In the long run the most abstruse business will boil down to a fairly simple deduction from certain data. Your profession enables you to select the relevant data.'

'That may be true in theory but I wouldn't myself rate legal talent so high. A lawyer is apt to lack imagination, you know.' Then I stopped, for I had suddenly the impression that Vernon wanted advice, help of some kind – that behind all his ease he was profoundly anxious, and that a plea, almost a cry, was trembling on his lips. I detest confidences and labour to avoid them, but I could no more refuse this boy than stop my ears against a sick child. So I added, 'Of course lawyers make good confidants. They're mostly decent fellows, and they're accustomed to keeping their mouths shut.'

He nodded, as if I had settled some private scruple, and we fell to talking about spring salmon in the Tay.

'Take the port into the library,' he told Beaton. 'Sir Edward doesn't want coffee. Oh, and see that the fire is good. We shan't need you again tonight. I'll put Sir Edward to bed.'

There was an odd air of purpose about him, as he gave me his arm to the library and settled me with a cigar in a long chair. Then he disappeared for a minute or two and returned with a shabby little clasped leather book. He locked the door and put the key on the mantelpiece, and when he caught me smiling he smiled too, a little nervously.

'Please don't think me an ass,' he said. 'I'm going to ask a tremendous favour. I want you to listen to me while I tell you a story, something I have never told to anyone in my life before . . . I don't think you'll laugh at me, and I've a notion you may be able to help me. It's a confounded liberty, I know, but may I go on?'

'Most certainly,' I said. 'I can't imagine myself laughing at anything you had to tell me; and if there's anything in me that can help you it's yours for the asking.'

He drew a long breath. 'You spoke of my bad nights as a child and I said I had outgrown them. Well, it isn't true.'

2

When Vernon was a very little boy he was the sleepiest and healthiest of mortals, but every spring he had a spell of bad dreams. He slept at that time in the big new night-nursery at the top of the west wing, which his parents had built not long before their death. It had three windows looking out to the moorish flats which run up to the fells, and from one window, by craning your neck, you could catch a glimpse of the sea. It was all hung, too, with a Chinese paper whereon pink and green parrots squatted in wonderful blue trees, and there seemed generally to be a wood fire burning. He described the place in detail, not as it is today, but as he remembered it.

Vernon's recollection of his childish nightmares was hazy. They varied, I gathered, but narrowed down in the end to one type. He used to find himself in a room different from the nursery and bigger, but with the same smell of wood smoke. People came and went, such as his nurse, the butler, Simon the head keeper, Uncle Appleby his guardian, Cousin Jennifer, the old woman who sold oranges in Axby, and a host of others. Nobody hindered them from going away, and they seemed to be pleading with him to come too. There was danger in the place; something was going to happen in the big room, and if by that time he was not gone there would be mischief . . . But it was quite clear to him that he could not go. He must stop there, with the wood smoke in his nostrils, and await the advent of the something. But he was never quite sure of the nature of the compulsion. He had a notion that if he made a rush for the door at Uncle Appleby's heels he would be allowed to escape, but that somehow he would be behaving badly. Anyhow, the place put him into a sweat of fright, and Mrs Ganthony looked darkly at him in the morning.

Those troubled springs continued – odd interludes in a life of nearly unbroken health. Mrs Ganthony left because she could not control her tongue and increased the boy's terrors, and Vernon was nine – he thought – before the dream began to take a really definite shape. The stage was emptying. There was nobody in the room now but himself, and he saw its details a little more clearly. It was not any apartment in Severns. Rather it seemed like one of the big old panelled chambers which he remembered from visits to the Midland country houses of his mother's family, when he had arrived after dark and had been put to sleep in a great bed in a place lit with dancing firelight. In the morning it had looked only an ordinary big room, but at that hour of the evening it had seemed an enchanted cave. The dream-room was not unlike these, for there was the scent of a wood fire and there were dancing shadows, but he could not see clearly the walls or the ceiling, and there was no bed. In one corner was a door which led to the outer world, and through this he knew that he might on no account pass. Another door faced him, and he knew that he had only to turn the handle for it to open.

But he did not want to, for he understood quite clearly what was beyond. There was a second room just like the first one; he knew nothing about it except that opposite the entrance another door led out of it. Beyond was a third chamber, and so on interminably. There seemed to the boy to be no end to this fantastic suite. He thought of it as a great snake of masonry, winding up hill and down dale away to the fells or the sea . . . Yes, but there *was* an end. Somewhere far away in one of the rooms was a terror waiting on him, or, as he feared, coming towards him. Even now it might be flitting from room to room, every minute bringing its soft tread nearer to the chamber of the wood fire.

About this time of his life the dream was an unmitigated horror. Once it came while he was ill with a childish fever, and it sent his temperature up to a point which brought Dr Moreton galloping from Axby. In his waking hours he did not, as a rule, remember it clearly; but during the fever, asleep and awake, that sinuous building, one room thick, with each room opening from the other, was never away from his thoughts. It amazed him to think that outside were the cheerful moors where he hunted for plovers' eggs, and that only a thin wall of stone kept him from pleasant homely things. The thought used to comfort him when he was awake, but in the dream it never came near him. Asleep, the whole world seemed one suite of rooms, and he, a forlorn little prisoner, doomed grimly to wait on the slow coming through the many doors of a fear which transcended word and thought.

He became a silent, self-absorbed boy, and, though the fact of his nightmares was patent to the little household, the details remained locked up in his head. Not even to Uncle Appleby would he tell them, when that gentleman, hurriedly kind, came to visit his convalescent ward. His illness made Vernon grow, and he shot up into a lanky, leggy boy. But the hills soon tautened his sinews, and all the time at his preparatory school he was a healthy and active child. He told me that he tried to exorcise the dream through his religion – to 'lay his burden on the Lord', as the old evangelical phrase has it; but he signally failed, though he got some comfort from the attempt. It was borne in on him, he said, that this was a burden which the Lord had laid quite definitely on him and meant him to bear like a man.

He was fifteen and at Eton when he made the great discovery. The dream had become almost a custom now. It came in April at Severns about Easter-tide – a night's discomfort (it was now scarcely more) in the rush and glory of the holidays. There was a moment of the old wild heart-fluttering; but a boy's fancy is more quickly dulled than a child's, and the endless corridors were now more of a prison than a witch's antechamber. By this time, with the help of his diary, he had fixed the date of the dream; it came regularly on the night of the first Monday of April. Now the year I speak of he had made a long expedition into the hills, and had stridden homeward at a steady four miles an hour among the gleams and shadows of an April twilight. He was alone at Severns, so he had had his supper in the big library, where afterwards he sat watching the leaping flames on the open stone hearth. He was very weary, and sleep fell upon him in his chair. He found himself in the wood-smoke chamber, and before him the door leading to the unknown . . . But it was no indefinite fear that now lay beyond. He knew clearly – though how he knew he could not tell – that each year the something came a room nearer, and was even now but twelve rooms off. In twelve years his own door would open, and then—

He woke in the small hours, chilled and mazed, but with a curious new assurance in his heart. Hitherto the nightmare had left him in gross terror, unable to endure the prospect of its recurrence, till the kindly forgetfulness of youth relieved him. But now, though his nerves were fluttering, he perceived that there was a limit to the mystery. Some day it must declare itself and fight on equal terms.

The discovery opened a new stage in his life. As he thought over the matter in the next few days he had the sense of being forewarned and prepared for some great test of courage. The notion exhilarated as much as it frightened him. Late at night, or on soft dripping days, or at any moment of lessened vitality, he would bitterly wish that he had been born an ordinary mortal. But on a keen morning of frost, when he rubbed himself warm after a cold tub, or at high noon of summer, the adventure of the dream almost pleased him. Unconsciously he must have braced himself to a harder discipline. His fitness, moral and physical, became his chief interest for reasons that would have been unintelligible to his friends or his masters.

He passed through school – as I knew from Charles – an aloof and rather splendid figure, a magnificent athlete with a brain as well as a body, a good fellow in everyone's opinion, but a grave one. He could have had no real intimates, for he never shared the secret of the spring dream. At this period, for some reason which he could not tell, he would have burned his hand off sooner than breathe a hint of it. Pure terror absolves from all conventions and demands a confidant, so terror, I think, must have largely departed from the nightmare as he grew older. Fear, indeed, remained, and awe and disquiet, but these are human emotions, whereas terror is of hell.

Had he told anyone, he would no doubt have become self-conscious and felt acutely his difference from other people, so it was a sound instinct which kept him silent. As it was, he seems to have been an ordinary schoolboy, much liked, and, except at odd moments, unaware of any brooding destiny. As he grew older, and his ambition awoke, the moments when he remembered the dream were apt to be disagreeable, for a boy's ambitions are strictly conventional and his soul revolts at the abnormal. By the time he was ready for the university he wanted above all things to run the mile a second faster than anyone else, and he had hopes of academic distinction, for he was an excellent classic. For most of the year he lived with these hopes and was happy: then came April, and for a short season he was groping in dark places. Just before and after each dream he was in a mood of exasperation; but when it actually came he was plunged in a different atmosphere, and felt the quiver of fear and the quick thrill of expectation.

During his first year at Oxford he had made an attempt to avoid it. He and three others were on a walking tour in Brittany in gusty spring weather, and came late one evening to an inn by an estuary where sea-gulls clattered about the windows. Youth-like they made a great and foolish feast, and sat all night round a bowl of punch, while school songs and 'John Peel' contended with the dirling of the gale. At daylight they took the road again, without having closed an eye, and Vernon told himself that he was rid of his incubus. He wondered at the time why he was not more cheerful, for to his surprise he had a sense of loss, of regret, almost of disappointment.

'That was last year,' he said, and he opened the little locked diary and showed me the entry. 'Last night I went to bed not knowing what to think, but far more nervous than I had been since I was a baby. I hope I didn't show it, but I wasn't much in the mood for guests when you turned up.'

'What happened?' I asked eagerly. 'Did the dream come back?'

He nodded and passed me the diary so that I could read that morning's entry. The dream had not failed him. Once more he had been in the chamber with the wood fire: once again he had peered at the door and wondered with tremulous heart what lay beyond. For the something had come nearer by two rooms, and was now only seven doors away. I read the bare account in his neat, precise handwriting, and it gave me a strong impression of being permitted to peep through a curtain at a stage mysteriously set. I noticed that he had added some lines from Keats's 'Indian Maid's Song':

> I would deceive her,
> And so leave her.
> But ah! she is so constant and so kind.

There was a mark of exclamation against the 'she', as if he found some irony in it.

3

He seemed to be waiting for me to speak, waiting shyly and tensely like a child expecting the judgement of an elder. But I found it hard to know what to say.

'That is a very wonderful story!' I ventured at last. 'I am honoured that you should have chosen me to tell it to. Perhaps it will be a relief to you to know that someone else understands what you are going through . . . I don't suppose you want sympathy, but I would like to congratulate you on your fortitude.'

'I don't need sympathy – or congratulation. But I want help – the help of your brain and your experience . . . You see, in seven years some tremendous experience is coming to me, and I want – I'd like – to know what it is.'

'I wonder if a good doctor wouldn't be the best person to consult.'

'No, no,' he cried almost angrily. 'I tell you there's nothing pathological about it – not now that I'm a man. I don't want it exorcised as if it were an evil spell. I think – now – that I'd break my heart if it all vanished into moonshine . . . I believe in it as I believe in God, and I'm ready to face whatever is coming. But I want to be forewarned and forearmed, if possible, for it's going to be a big thing. If I only knew something about what was coming – even the smallest something!'

Those were the days before psychoanalysis had become fashionable, but even then we had psychologists, and in my bewilderment I tried that tack.

'Might not it all spring from some fright – some strange experience at any rate – which you had as a baby? Such things often make an abiding impression.'

He smiled. 'You're still thinking it is pathological. Fright would account for recurring nightmares, but surely not for a thing so rational as this – a fixed day every year, the same room, the time limit. It would not explain the thing moving on a room last year when I had no dream.'

'I suppose not,' I admitted. 'Have you looked up your family history? I have heard stories of inherited obsessions and premonitions – what they call a "weird" in Scotland.'

'I thought of that, but there's nothing – nothing. There are no Milburne records much beyond my grandfather, and by all accounts they were the most prosaic kind of business men. My mother's family – well, there's plenty of records there and I've waded through most of the muniment-room at Appleby. But there's no hint of anything mysterious in the Douglas-Ernotts. They were a time-serving lot, who knew how the cat was going to jump, but they kept out of crime and shunned anything imaginative like the plague. I shouldn't think one of them had ever an ambition which couldn't be put in terms of office or money, or a regret except that he had missed a chance of getting at the public purse. True-blue Whigs, all of them.'

'Then I'm hanged if I know what to say. But, now you've told me, I want you to remember that you can always count on me. I may not be able to help, but I'm there whenever you want me. Perhaps – you never know – the thing will reveal itself more clearly in the next seven years and come within the scope of my help. I've taken a tremendous liking to you, my dear chap, and we're going to be friends.'

He held out his hand.

'That's kind of you . . . Shall I tell you what I think myself? I was taught to believe that everything in our lives is foreordained by God. No caprice of our own can alter the eternal plan. Now, why shouldn't some inkling of this plan be given us now and then – not knowledge, but just an inkling that we may be ready? My dream may be a heavenly warning, a divine foreshadowing – a privilege, not a cross. It is a reminder that I must be waiting with girt loins and a lit lamp when the call comes. That's the way I look on it, and it makes me happy.'

I said nothing, for I did not share his Calvinism, but I felt that suddenly that library had become rather a solemn place. I had listened to the vow of the young Hannibal at the altar.

TWO

I

I HAVE A PREPOSTEROUS weakness for youth, and I fancy there is something in me which makes it accept me as a coeval. It may be my profession. If you are a busy lawyer without any outside ambitions you spend your days using one bit of your mind, and the rest remains comparatively young and unstaled. I had no wife and few near relations, and while I was daily growing narrower in my outlook on the present and the future I cherished a wealth of sentiment about the past. I welcomed anything which helped me to recapture the freshness of boyhood, and Vernon was like a spring wind in my arid life. Presently we forgot that I was nearly twice his age, and slipped into the manner of contemporaries. He was far more at his ease with me than with the men of his own year. I came to think that I was the only person in the world who *knew* him, for though he had an infinity of acquaintances and a good many people who ranked as friends I suppose I was his only comrade. For I alone knew the story of his dreams.

My flat in Down Street became his headquarters in London, and I never knew when he would stick his head into my Temple chambers and insist on our dining or lunching together. In the following winter I went to Oxford occasionally, nominally to visit Charles; but my nephew led a much occupied life, and it generally ended by my spending my time with Vernon. I kept a horse with the Bicester that season and we hunted occasionally together, and we had sometimes a walk which filled the short winter day, and dined thereafter and talked far into the night. I was anxious to learn how his contemporaries regarded him, and I soon found that he had a prodigious reputation, which was by no means explained by his athletic record. He at once impressed and puzzled his little world. I think it was the sense of brooding power about him which attracted people and also kept them at a respectful distance. His ridiculous good looks and his gentle courtesy seemed to mark him out for universal popularity, but there was too much austerity for a really popular man. He had odd ascetic traits. He never touched wine now, he detested loose talk, and he was a little intolerant of youthful follies. Not that there was anything of the prig in him – only that his character seemed curiously formed and mature. For all his urbanity he had a plain, almost rugged, sagacity in ordinary affairs, a tough core like steel harness under a silk coat. That, I suppose, was the Calvinism in his blood. Had he been a less brilliant figure, he would probably have been set down as 'pi'.

Charles never professed to understand him, and contented himself with prophesying that 'old Vernon would be the devil of a swell some day'. On inquiry I found that none of his friends forecast any special career for him; it would have seemed to them almost disrespectful to condescend upon such details. It was not what Vernon would do that fired their sluggish imaginations, but what they dimly conceived that he already was.

There was the same fastidiousness about all his ways. I have never known a better brain more narrowly limited in its range. He was a first-class 'pure' scholar and had got a Craven and been *proxime* for the Hertford. But he was quite incapable of spreading himself, and his prospects looked bad for 'Greats' since he seemed unable to acquire the smattering of loose philosophy demanded by that school. He was strictly circumscribed in his general reading; I set it down at first to insensitiveness, but came soon to think it fastidiousness. If he could not have exactitude and perfection in his knowledge, he preferred to remain ignorant. I saw in him the makings of a lawyer. Law was just the subject for a finical, exact and scrupulous mind like his. Charles had once in his haste said that he was not a man of the world, and Charles had been right. He was a man of his own world, not the ordinary one. So with his intellectual interests. He would make his own culture, quite regardless of other people. I fancy that he felt that his overmastering private problem made it necessary to husband the energies of his mind.

During that year I think he was quite happy and at peace about the dream. He had now stopped hoping or fearing: the thing had simply become part of him, like his vigorous young body, his slow kindliness, his patient courage. He rarely wanted to talk of it, but it was so much in my thoughts that

I conducted certain researches of my own. I began by trying the psychological line, and plagued those of my acquaintances who had any knowledge of that dismal science. I cannot say I got much assistance. You see I had to state a hypothetical case, and was always met by a demand to produce the patient for cross-examination – a reasonable enough request, which of course I could not comply with. One man, who was full of the new Vienna doctrine, talked about 'complexes' and 'repressions' and suggested that the dream came from a child having been shut up by accident in a dark room. 'If you can dig the memory of it out of his subconsciousness, you will lay that ghost,' he said. I tried one evening to awake Vernon's earliest recollections, but nothing emerged. The dream itself was the furthest-back point in his recollection. In any case I didn't see how such an explanation would account for the steady development of the thing and its periodicity. I thought I might do better with family history, and I gave up a good deal of my leisure to the Douglas-Ernotts. There was nothing to be made of the Ernotts – gross utilitarian Whigs every one of them. The Douglas strain had more mystery in it, but the records of his branch of the great Scottish house were scanty, and sadly impersonal. Douglases many had endured imprisonment and gone to the scaffold, but history showed them as mere sounding names, linked to forays and battles and strange soubriquets, but as vague as the heroes of Homer. As for the Milburnes, I got an ancient aunt who had known Vernon's father to give me her recollections, and a friend on the Northern Circuit collected for me the Lancashire records. The first of them had been a small farmer somewhere on the Ribble: the second had become a mill-owner; and the third in the early nineteenth century had made a great fortune, had been a friend of William Wilberforce and later of Richard Cobden, and had sat in the first Reform parliament. As I looked at the portrait of that whiskered reformer, bland and venerable in his stiff linen and broadcloth, or at the early Millais of his son, the bearded Evangelical, I wondered what in them had gone to the making of Vernon. It was like seeking for the ancestry of a falcon among barnyard fowls.

2

In the spring of 1914 I badly needed a holiday, and Lamancha asked me to go cruising in his yacht. He gave me permission to bring Vernon, whom he knew slightly, for I wanted to be near him on the first Monday of April. We were to join the yacht at Constantinople, and cruise through the Northern Aegean to Athens, and then by way of the Corinth canal to Corfu, where we would catch the steamer for Brindisi and so home. Vernon was at first a little disinclined, for he had a notion that he ought to be at Severns, but when he allowed himself to be persuaded he grew very keen about the trip, for he had been little out of England.

He and I travelled by the Orient Express to Constantinople, and after three days there and one day at Brousa shaped our course westward. We landed one morning on the Gallipoli peninsula, and found birds' eggs on Achi Baba where in a year's time there was to be nothing but barbed wire and trenches. We spent a day at Lemnos, which at that time few people had visited except the British Navy, and then turned south. On the first Monday of April we had half a gale, an uncomfortable thing in those shallow seas. It blew itself out in the afternoon, and after tea we anchored for the night under the lee of a big island. There was a little bay carved out of the side of a hill; the slopes were covered with heath and some kind of scrub, and the young green of crops showed in the clearings. Among the thyme of the nearest headland a flock of goats was browsing, shepherded by a little girl in a saffron skirt, who sang shrilly in snatches. After the yeasty Aegean the scene was an idyll of pastoral peace. Vernon had all day shown signs of restlessness, and he now proposed a walk; so, leaving the others playing bridge, we two were put ashore in the dinghy.

We walked southward towards the other horn of the bay, past little closes of fruit blossom, and thickets of wildwood, and stony patches of downland bright with anemones and asphodel. It was a strange, haunted world, bathed in a twilight of gold and amethyst, filled with a thousand aromatic scents, and very silent except for the wash of the waves and a far-off bleating of goats. Neither of us wanted to talk, being content to drink in the magic of the evening. Vernon walked like a man in a dream, stopping now and then to lift his head and stare up the long scrubby ravines to the sharp line of the crest.

Suddenly a cuckoo's note broke into the stillness and echoed along the hillside. When it died away it seemed to be answered by a human voice, sweet and high and infinitely remote, a voice as fugitive as a scent or a colour.

Vernon stopped short.

'Listen to that,' he cried. 'It is the Spring Song. This has probably been going on here since the beginning of time. They say that nothing changes in these islands – only they call Demeter the Virgin Mary and Dionysos St Dionysius.'

He sat down on a boulder and lit his pipe. 'Let's burn tobacco to the gods,' he said. 'It's too enchanted to hurry through . . . I suppose it's the way I've been educated, but I could swear I've known it all before. This is the season of the Spring Festival, and you may be sure it's the same here today as it was a thousand years before Homer. The winter is over and the Underworld has to be appeased, and then the Goddess will come up from the shades.'

I had never heard Vernon talk like this before, and I listened with some curiosity. I am no classical scholar, but at that moment I too felt the spell of a very ancient and simple world.

'This was the beginning of the year for the Greeks, remember,' he went on – 'for the Greeks as we know them, and for the old Mediterranean peoples before them whose ritual they absorbed. The bones of that ritual never altered . . . You have to begin with purification – to feed the ghosts of the dead in the pot-holes with fireless and wineless sacrifices and so placate them, and to purify your own souls and bodies and the earth by which you live. You have your purgation herbs like buckthorn and agnus castus, and you have your *pharmakos*, your scapegoat, who carries away all impurities. And then, when that is done, you are ready for the coming of the Maiden. It is like Easter after Good Friday – the festival after the fast and penitence. It is always the woman that simple folk worship – the Mother who is also the Maid. Long ago they called her Pandora or Persephone, and now they call her the Blessed Virgin, but the notion is the same – the sinless birth of the divine. You may be sure it is she whom the peasants in this island worship, as their fathers did three thousand years ago – not God the Father.

'The Greeks had only the one goddess,' he went on, 'though she had many names. Later they invented the Olympians – that noisy, middle-class family party – and the priests made a great work with their male gods, Apollo and the like. But the woman came first, and the woman remained. You may call her

Demeter, or Aphrodite, or Hera, but she is the same, the Virgin and the Mother, the "mistress of wild things", the priestess of the new birth in spring. Semele is more than Dionysos, and even to sophisticated Athens the Mailed Virgin of the Acropolis was more than all the pantheon . . . Don't imagine it was only a pretty fancy. The thing had all the beauty of nature, and all the terror too.' He flung back his head and quoted some sonorous Greek.

'What's that?' I asked.

'Euripides,' he replied. 'It has been well translated,' and he quoted:

> For her breath is on all that hath life, and she floats in the air
> Bee-like, death-like, a wonder.

'I can see it all,' he cried. 'The sacred basket, the honey and oil and wine, the torches crimsoning the meadows, the hushed quiet people waiting on the revelation. They are never more than a day or two from starvation all the winter, and the coming of the Maiden is a matter for them of life and death. They wait for her as devout souls today wait for the Easter Resurrection. I can hear the ritual chant and the thin clear music of the flutes . . . Yes, but they were seeing things which are now hid from us – Dionysos with his thyrsus, and goat-feet in the thickets, and the shadows of dancing nymphs! If you starve for three months and put your soul into waiting for the voice from heaven you are in the mood for marvels. Terror and horror, perhaps, but unspeakable beauty, too, and a wild hope. That was the Greek religion, not the Olympians and their burnt offerings. And it is the kind of religion that never dies.'

I thought this pretty good for the scion of an evangelical family, and I said so.

He laughed. 'It isn't my own creed, you know. I dislike all kinds of priestcraft. But, though I'm a stout Protestant, I'm inclined to think sometimes that it is a pity that we have departed from the practice of all other religions and left out the Mother of God . . . Let's go on – I want to see what is on the other side of the cape.'

Beyond the little headland we came suddenly on a very different scene. Here was the harbour of the island. Beside a rude quay some fisherboats lay at anchor with their brown sails furled. Along the waterfront ran a paved terrace, a little dilapidated and with bushes growing in the cracks of the stones. Above rose a great building, showing to seaward as a blank white wall pierced with a few narrow windows. At first sight I took it for a monastery, but a second glance convinced me that its purpose had never been religious. It looked as if it had once been fortified, and the causeway between it and the sea may have mounted guns. Most of it was clearly very old, but the architecture was a jumble, showing here the enriched Gothic of Venice and there the straight lines and round arches of the East. It had once, I conjectured, been the hold of some Venetian sea-king, then the palace of a Turkish conqueror, and was now, perhaps, the manor-house of this pleasant domain. The owners, whoever they might be, were absent, for not a chimney smoked.

We passed the quay and wandered along the great terrace, which was as solidly masoned as a Roman road. For a little the house hung sheer above us, its walls level with the rock, with in three places flights of steps from the causeway ending in small postern doors. Obviously the main entrance was on the other side. There were no huts to be seen, and no sign of life except a little group of fishermen below on the shore, who were sitting round a fire over which a pot was boiling. As we continued along the terrace beyond the house we came to orchards and olive yards, no doubt part of the demesne, and had a glimpse of a rugged coast running out into the sunset.

The place impressed even my sluggish fancy. This great silent castle in the wilds, hung between sky and earth, and all rosy in the last fires of the sun, seemed insubstantial as a dream. I should not have been surprised if it had vanished like a mirage and left us staring at a bare hillside. Only the solid blocks of the causeway bound us to reality. Here, beyond doubt, men had lived and fought far back in the ages. The impression left on my mind was of a place inhabited for aeons, sunk for the moment in sleep, but liable to awake suddenly to a fierce life. As for Vernon he seemed positively rapt.

'There's your castle in Spain,' he cried. 'Odd thing! but I seem to have seen all this before. I knew before we turned the corner that there were olive trees there, and that the rocks tumbled just in that way into the cove. Listen!'

The sound of voices drifted up from the beach, and there was a snatch of a song.

'That's Antiphilos of Byzantium – you remember in the

Anthology – the fisher-boys singing round the broth-pot. Lord what a haunted spot! I'd like to spend the night here.'

I can give no reason for it, but I suddenly felt a strange uneasiness, which made me turn back and stride at a good pace along the terrace. We seemed to have blundered outside the ordinary natural world. I had a feverish desire to get away from the shadow of that pile of masonry, to get beyond the headland and in sight of the yacht. The place was wonderful, secret, beautiful, yet somehow menacing. Vernon clearly felt nothing of all this, for he grumbled at my haste. 'Hang it, we're not walking for a wager,' he complained. 'There's loads of time before dinner . . . I want to stay on here a bit. I never saw such a place.'

At the beginning of the paved terrace close to the quay we came suddenly upon two men, probably from the fishermen's party we had seen on the shore. They were well-set-up fellows, with handsome clear-cut faces, for the true Greek strain is still found in the islands. We came on them by surprise as we turned the corner of a rock and they may have thought from our direction that we were coming from the house. Anyhow they seemed to get the fright of their lives. Both leaped aside and looked at us with startled angry eyes. Then they flung up their right hands; and for a moment I thought they were going to attack us.

But they contented themselves with spitting on their breasts and each holding out a clenched fist with the little finger and the thumb extended. I had seen this before – the ancient protection against the evil eye. But what impressed me was the expression in their faces. It was at Vernon that they stared, and when their stare moved from him it took in the pile of the house above. They seemed to connect us in some way with the house, and in their eyes there was an almost animal fear and hate . . . I looked after them when they had passed, and observed that they were hurrying with bent heads up the path which may have led to their village.

Vernon laughed. 'Queer chaps! They looked as scared as if they had seen Pan.'

'I don't like this place,' I told him when we were approaching the dinghy. 'Some of your infernal gods and goddesses have got loose in it. I feel as if I want to run.'

'Hullo!' he cried. 'You're getting as impressionable as a minor poet . . . Hark! There it is again! Do you hear? The Spring Song?'

But the thin notes which drifted down from the upland no longer seemed to me innocent. There was something horrible about that music.

Next morning, when we were steaming south in calm weather with the island already dim behind us, I found Vernon smoking peacefully on deck and looking at sea-birds through a glass. He nodded gaily as I sat down beside him.

'I had the dream all right – one room nearer. But the room in which I wait has changed. It must be due to being out here, for hitherto I've always spent April in England. I suppose I furnished it unconsciously with things I had seen at home – there was a big lacquer cabinet for one thing, and something like pictures or tapestry on the walls – and there were great silver fire-dogs. But now it's quite bare. The same room of course – I couldn't mistake it – but scarcely any furniture in it except a dark lump in a corner . . . Only the fire-dogs are the same . . . Looks as if the decks were being cleared for action.'

I had expected to find him a little heavy about the eyes, but he appeared as fresh as if he had just come from a morning swim, and his voice had a boyish carelessness.

'Do you know,' he said. 'I've lost every scrap of funk or nervousness about the dream? It's a privilege, not an incubus. Six years to wait! I wish I knew how I was going to put them in. It will be a dull business waiting.'

3

Fate contrived that to Vernon, as to several million others, the next four years should scarcely deserve the name of dull. By the middle of August I was being cursed by a Guards sergeant in Chelsea barracks yard, and Vernon was training with his Yeomanry somewhere in Yorkshire.

My path was plain compared to that of many honest men. I was a bachelor without ties, and though I was beyond the statutory limit for service I was always pretty hard trained, and it was easy enough to get over the age difficulty. I had sufficient standing in my profession to enable me to take risks. But I am bound to say I never thought of that side. I wanted, like everybody else, to do something for England, and I wanted to do something violent. For me to stay at home and serve in some legal job would have been a thousand times harder than to go into the trenches. Like everybody else, too, I thought the war would be short, and my chief anxiety was lest I should miss the chance of fighting. I was to learn patience and perspective during four beastly years.

I went to France in October '14, and Vernon dined with me before I started. He had got a curious notion into his head. He thought that the war would last for full six years, and his reason was that he was convinced that his dream had to do with it. The opening of the last door would be on the battlefield – of that he was convinced. The consequence was that he was in no hurry. My nephew Charles, who was in the same Yeomanry, spent his days pleading to be sent abroad and trying to exchange into any unit he thought would get away first. On the few occasions I met him he raved like a lunatic about the imbecility of a Government that kept him kicking his heels in England. But Vernon, the night he dined with me, was as placid as Buddha. 'I'm learning my job,' he said, 'and I've a mighty lot to learn. I ought to be a fair soldier in six years' time – just when the crisis is due.' But he was very anxious about me, and wanted to get into the Guards to be beside me. Only his fatalism kept him from agitating for a change, for he felt that as he had begun in the Yeomanry, Providence most likely meant him to continue there. He fussed a good deal about how we were to correspond, for I seemed to have taken the place of his family. But on the whole I was happy about him, his purpose was so clear and his mind so perfectly balanced. I had stopped thinking seriously about the dream, for it seemed only a whimsy in the middle of so many urgent realities.

I needn't tell you the kind of time I had in France. It was a long dismal grind, but I had the inestimable advantage of good health, and I was never a day off duty because of sickness. I suppose I enjoyed it in a sense: anyhow I got tremendously keen about my new profession, and rose in it far quicker than I deserved. I was lucky, too. As you know, I stopped something in every big scrap – at Festubert, Loos, Ginchy, Third Ypres, Cambrai and Bapaume – so that I might have covered my sleeve with woundstripes if I had been so minded. But none of the damage was serious and I can hardly find the marks of it today. I think my worst trial was that for more than three years I never had a sight of Vernon.

He went out in the summer of '15 to the Dardanelles and was in the Yeomanry fight at Suvla, where a bit of shrapnel made rather a mess of his left shoulder. After that he was employed on various staff jobs, and during '16 was engaged in some kind of secret service in the Aegean and the Levant. I heard from him regularly, but of course he never spoke of his work. He told me he had learned modern Greek and could speak it like a native, and I fancy he had a hand in Venizelos's revolution. Then he went back to his regiment, and was in the 'Broken Spurs' division when the Yeomanry were dismounted. He was wounded again in Palestine in '17, just before the taking of Jerusalem, and after that was second in command of a battalion.

When I was on leave in February '18 Charles dined with me at the Club – a much older and wiser Charles, with an empty sleeve pinned to his tunic, who was now employed in home training.

'It's a bloody and disgusting war,' said my nephew, 'and if any fellow says he likes it, you can tell him from me that he's a liar. There's only one man I ever met who honestly didn't mind it, and that was old Vernon, and everybody knows that he's cracked.'

He expatiated on the exact nature of Vernon's lunacy.

'Cracked – as – cracked, and a very useful kind of insanity, too. I often wished I had half his complaint. He simply didn't give a hang for the old war. Wasn't interested in it, if you see what I mean. Oh, brave as you-be-damned, of course, but plenty of other chaps were brave. His was the most cold-blooded, unearthly kind of courage. I've seen the same thing in men who were sick of life and wanted to be killed and knew they were going to be killed, but Vernon wasn't that sort. He had no notion of being killed – always planning out the future and talking of what he was going to do after the war. As you know, he got badly mauled at Suvla, and he nearly croaked with malaria in Crete, and he had his head chipped at Neby Samwil, so he didn't bear what you might call a charmed life. But some little bird had whispered in his ear that he wasn't going to be killed, and he believed that bird. You never saw a fellow in your life so much at his ease in a nasty place.

'It wasn't that he was a fire-eater,' Charles went on. 'He never went out to look for trouble. It was simply that it made no difference to him where he was or what he was doing – he was the same composed old fish, smiling away, and keeping quiet and attending to business, as if he thought the whole thing rather foolishness.'

'You describe a pretty high class of soldier,' I said. 'I can't understand why he hasn't gone quicker up the ladder.'

'I can,' said Charles emphatically. 'He was a first-class battalion officer but he wasn't a first-class soldier. The trouble with him, as I say, is that he wasn't interested in the war. He had no initiative, you understand – always seemed to be thinking about something else. It's like Rugby football. A man may be a fine player according to the rules, but unless his heart is in the business and he can think out new tactics for himself he won't be a great player. Vernon wasn't out to do anything more than the immediate situation required. You might say he wasn't deadset enough on winning the war.'

I detected in Charles a new shrewdness. 'How did the others get on with him?' I asked.

'The men believed in him and would have followed him into hell, and of course we all respected him. But I can't say he was exactly popular. Too dashed inhuman for that. He ought to fall in love with a chorus-girl and go a regular mucker. Oh, of course, I like him tremendously and know what a rare good fellow he is! But the ordinary simple-minded, deserving lad jibs at Sir Galahad crossed with the low-church parson and the 'Varsity don.'

The Broken Spurs came to France in the early summer of '18, but I had no chance of meeting them. My life was rather feverish during the last weeks of the campaign, for I was chief staff-officer to my division, and we were never much out of the line. Then, as you know, I nearly came by my end in September, when the Boche made quite a good effort in the way of a gas attack. It was a new gas, which we didn't understand, and I faded away like the grin of the Cheshire cat, and was pretty ill for a time in a base hospital. Luckily it didn't do me any permanent harm, but my complexion will be greenery-yallery till the day of my death.

I awoke to consciousness in a tidy little bed to learn that the war was all but over and the Boche hustling to make peace. It took me some days to get my head clear and take notice, and then, one morning, I observed the man in the bed next to me. His head was a mass of bandages, but there was something about the features that showed which struck me as familiar. As luck would have it, it turned out to be Vernon. He had been badly hit, when commanding his battalion at the crossing of the Scheldt, and for a day or two had been in grave danger. He was recovering all right, but for a time neither of us was permitted to talk, and we used to lie and smile at each other and think of all the stories we would presently tell.

It was just after we got the news of the Armistice that we were allowed to say how d'ye do. We were as weak as kittens, but I, at any rate, felt extraordinarily happy. We had both come through the war without serious damage and a new world lay before us. To have Vernon beside me put the coping-stone on my contentment, and I could see that he felt the same. I remember the thrill I had when we could stretch out our arms and shake hands.

Slowly we began to build up each other's records for the four years. I soon knew, what I had guessed before, the reason of that inhuman composure which Charles had described. Vernon had had a complete assurance that his day of fate was not due yet awhile, and therefore the war had taken a second place in his thoughts. Most men who fought bore the marks of it in harder lines about the mouth and chin and older eyes. But Vernon had kept his youth intact. His face had always had a certain maturity beyond his years, and his eyes had been curiously watchful. These traits were perhaps slightly intensified, but otherwise I noticed no difference.

'You remember what I told you when we last met in October '14?' he said. 'I was wrong and I'm rather sorry. I thought the war would last for six years and that the last stage of my dream would be in the field. That would have been such a simple and right solution. As it is, I must wait.'

I asked if the dream had come regularly in the past four years.

'Quite regularly,' was the answer. 'The room hasn't changed either, except that the dark shadow in the corner has moved, so I think it must be a human figure. The place is quite bare and empty now, except for the silver fire-dogs . . . I think there is a little window in the wall, rather high up.'

'You have only two years more to wait,' I said, 'less – a year and a half.' It was then November '18.

'I know . . . But I am impatient again. I thought the climax would come in the war, so I stopped speculating about it . . . I thought I would be called on as a soldier to do something very difficult, and I was quite ready . . . But that has all gone, and I am back in the fog. I must think it all out again from the beginning.'

THREE

THE IMMEDIATE CONSEQUENCE of peace was to keep Vernon and myself apart. You see, we neither of us got better very quickly. When his wounds were healed a kind of neuritis remained; he was tortured with headaches, didn't sleep well, and couldn't recover his lost weight. He was very patient and cheerful about it, and did obediently what he was told, for his one object seemed to be to get fit again. We returned to England together, but presently the doctors packed him off abroad with instructions to bask in the sun and idle at a Riviera villa which had been dedicated to such cases. So I spent a lonely Christmas in London.

Heaven knows I had nothing to complain of compared with most fellows, but I count the six months after the Armistice the most beastly in my life. I had never been seriously ill before, all the four years of war I had been brimming over with energy, and it was a new experience for me to feel slack and under-engined. The gas had left a sort of poison in my blood which made every movement an effort. I was always sleepy, and yet couldn't sleep, and to my horror I found myself getting jumpy and neurotic. The creak of a cart in the street worried me so that I wanted to cry; London noise was a nightmare, and when I tried the country I had a like horror of its silence. The thing was purely physical, for I found I could think quite clearly and sanely. I seemed to be two persons, one self-possessed enough watching the antics of the other with disgust and yet powerless to stop them.

Acton Croke was reassuring. 'You're a sick man, and you've got to behave as such,' he told me. 'No attempt to get back into harness. Behave as if you were recovering from a severe operation – regular life, no overstrain physical or mental, simply lie fallow and let nature do its work. You have a superb constitution which, given a chance, will pick up its balance. But don't forget that you're passing through a crisis. If you play the fool you may have indifferent health for the rest of your days.'

I was determined that at all events that mustn't happen, so I was as docile as a good child. As I say, I had mighty little to complain of, when you consider the number of good men who, far seedier than I, came back to struggle for their daily bread. I had made a bit of money, so I had a solid hump to live off. Also, I had a chance, if I wished, of becoming one of the law officers of the Crown. I was still a Member of Parliament, and at the December election, though I had never gone near the place, my old constituency had returned me with a majority of more than ten thousand. A pretty gilded position for a demobbed soldier! But for the present I had to put all that aside and think only of getting well.

There has been a good deal of nonsense talked about the horror of war memories and the passionate desire to bury them. The vocal people were apt to be damaged sensitives, who were scarcely typical of the average man. There were horrors enough, God knows, but in most people's recollections these were overlaid by the fierce interest and excitement, even by the comedy of it. At any rate that was the case with most of my friends, and it was certainly the case with me. I found a positive pleasure in recalling the incidents of the past four years. The war had made me younger. You see – apart from regular officers – I had met few of my own years and standing. I had consorted chiefly with youth, and had recovered the standpoint of twenty years ago. That was what made my feeble body so offensive. I could not regard myself as a man in middle age, but as a sick undergraduate whose malady was likely to keep him out of the Boat or the Eleven.

You would have laughed if you could have seen the way I spent my time. I was so angry with my ill health that I liked to keep on reminding myself of the days when I had been at the top of my form. I remember I made out a complete record of my mountaineering exploits, working them out with diagrams from maps and old diaries, and telling myself furiously that what I had once done I could do again . . . I got out my old Oxford texts and used to construe bits of the classics, trying to recapture the mood when those things meant a lot to me . . . I read again all the books which used to be favourites but which I hadn't opened for a score of years. I turned up the cram books for the Bar exams, and the notes I had taken in my early days in chambers and the reports of my first cases. It wasn't sentiment, but a deliberate attempt to put back the clock, and, by recalling the feelings of twenty-five, to convince myself that I had once been a strong man . . . I even made risky experiments. I went up to Oxford in vacation and managed to get put up in my old diggings in the High. That would have been intolerable if they had recalled war tragedies, but they didn't. The men who had shared them with me were all alive – one a Colonial bishop, one a stockbroker, another high up in the Indian Civil Service. It did me good to see the big shabby sitting-room where, in my day, a barrel of beer had adorned one corner. In March, too, I spent three nights at a moorland inn on the Borders which had once been the head-quarters of a famous reading-party. That was not quite so successful, for the weather and the food were vile, and I was driven to reflect on the difference of outlook between twenty and forty-three.

Still my childishness did me good, and I began slowly to gain ground. The spring helped me, which was early that year, you remember, so that the blossom had begun on the fruit trees in the first days of April. I found that it was the time just before the war that it comforted me most to recall, for then I had been healthy enough and a creature more near my present state than the undergraduate of twenty. I think, too, it was because those years were associated with Vernon. He was never much out of my mind, and the reports from him were cheering. The headaches had gone, he had recovered his power of sleep, and was slowly putting on weight. He had taken to sailing a small boat again, had bought a racing cutter, and had come in third in one of the events at the Cannes Regatta.

I had this last news in a letter which reached me while I was staying at Minster Carteron, and it turned my mind back to the yachting trip I had made with Vernon in 1914 in the Aegean. It revived the picture I had almost forgotten – the green island flushed with spring, the twilight haunted with wild music, the great white house hanging like a cliff over the sea. I had felt the place sinister – I remembered the two men with scared faces and their charm against the evil eye – and even after five years a faint aura of distaste lingered about the memory. That was sufficient to awake my interest, and one afternoon I rummaged in the library. Plakos had been the island's name, and I searched for it in gazetteers.

It was the day of the famous April snowstorm which wrought such havoc among English orchards. The windows of the great room were blurred with falling snow, and the fires on the two hearths were hissing and spluttering while I pursued my researches. Folliot, I remember, was dozing beside one of them in an arm-chair. You know old Folliot, with his mild cattish ways and his neat little Louis Napoleon beard. He wants to be the Horace Walpole of our time, and publishes every few years a book of reminiscences, from which it would appear that he has been the confidant of every great man in Europe for the last half-century. He has not much of a mind, but he has a good memory, and after all there is a faint interest about anybody who has dined out in good company for fifty years.

I woke the old fellow when I dropped by misadventure a big atlas on the floor, and he asked testily what I was after.

'I'm trying to find a beastly Greek islet,' I said. 'You haven't by any chance in your travels visited a place called Plakos?'

The name roused him. 'No,' he said, 'but of course I have often heard of it. It belonged to Shelley Arabin.'

'Now, who on earth was Shelley Arabin?'

'You young men!' old Folliot sighed. 'Your memories are so short and your ignorance so vast. Shelley Arabin died last year, and had half a column in *The Times*, but he will have a chapter in my memoirs. He was one of the most remarkable men of his day. Shelley Arabin – to think you never heard of him! Why, I knew his father.'

I drew up an arm-chair to the hearth opposite him. 'It's a foul afternoon,' I said, 'and there's nothing to do. I want to hear about Shelley Arabin. I take it from his name that he was a Levantine.'

Folliot was flattered by my interest. He had begun to bore people, for the war had created a mood unfavourable to his antique gossip. He still stayed a good deal in country houses, but spent most of his time in the libraries and got rather snubbed when he started on his reminiscences.

'Bless you, no! A most ancient English house – the Arabins of Irtling in Essex. Gone out for good now, I fear. As a boy I remember old Tom Arabin – a shaggy old bandit, who came to London once in five years and insulted everybody and then went back again. He used to dine with my family, and I remember watching him arrive, for I had a boyish romance about the man who had been a friend of Byron. Yes, he was with Byron when he died at Missolonghi, and he was an intimate of all the poets of that time – Byron, Shelley – he called his son after Shelley – Keats too, I think – there's a mention of him in the *Letters* I'm almost sure – and he lived with Landor in Italy till they quarrelled. A most picturesque figure, but too *farouche* for comfort. With him a word was a blow, you understand. He married – now, now, who did he marry? – one of the Manorwaters, I fancy. Anyhow, he led her the devil of a life. He bought or stole or acquired somehow the island of Plakos, and used it as a base from which to descend periodically upon the civilized world. Not a pleasant old gentleman, but amazingly decorative. You may have seen his translation of Pindar. I have heard Jebb say that it was a marvellous piece of scholarship, but that his English style was the exact opposite of everything that Pindar stood for. Dear me! How short the world's memory is!'

'I want to hear about his son,' I said.

'You shall – you shall! Poor Shelley, I fear he had not the kind of upbringing which is commonly recommended for youth. Tom disliked his son, and left him to the care of the family priest – they were Catholics of course. All his boyhood he spent in that island among the peasants and the kind of raffish company that his father invited to the house. What kind of company? Well, I should say all the varieties of humbug that Europe produces – soldiers of fortune and bad poets and the gentry who have made their native countries too hot for them. Plakos was the refuge of every brand of outlaw, social and political. Ultimately the boy was packed off to Cambridge, where he arrived speaking English a generation out of date and with the tastes of a Turkish pasha, but with the most beautiful manners. Tom, when he wasn't in a passion, had the graciousness of a king, and Shelley was a young prince in air and feature. He was terribly good-looking in a way no man has a right to be, and that prejudiced him in the eyes of his young contemporaries. Also there were other things against him.'

'How long did Cambridge put up with him?' I asked.

'One year. There was a scandal – rather a bad one, I fancy – and he left under the blackest kind of cloud. Tom would not have him at home, but he gave him a good allowance, and the boy set up in London. Not in the best society, you understand, but he had a huge success in the half-world. Women raved about him, and even when his reputation was at its worst, he would be seen at a few good houses . . . I suppose a lawyer does not concern himself with poetry, but I can assure you that Shelley Arabin made quite a name for himself in the late eighties. I believe bibliophiles still collect his first editions. There was his epic on the Fall of Jerusalem – a very remarkable performance as a travesty of history. And there were his love sonnets, beautiful languid things quite phosphorescent with decay. He carried Swinburne and Baudelaire a stage further. Well, that mood has gone from the world and Shelley Arabin's reputation with it, but at one time sober critics felt obliged to praise him even when they detested him. He was a red-hot revolutionary, too, and used to write pamphlets blackguarding British policy . . . I saw quite a lot of him in those days, and I confess that I found him fascinating. Partly it was his beauty and his air, partly that he was like nobody I had ever met. He could talk wonderfully in his bitter, high-coloured way. But I never liked him. Oh no, I never liked him. There was always a subtle cruelty about him. Old Tom had been a blackguard, but he had had a heart – Shelley behind all his brilliance was ice and stone. I think most people came to feel this, and he had certainly outstayed his welcome before he left London.'

'What made him leave?'

'His father's death. Tom went out suddenly from old age just before the war between Greece and Turkey. Shelley left England with a great gasconade of Greek patriotism – he was going to be a second Byron and smite the infidel. By all accounts he did very little. I doubt if he had old Tom's swashbuckling courage: indeed I have heard ugly stories of the white feather . . . Anyhow England knew him no more. He married a girl he met in Rome – Scotch – a Miss Hamilton, I think, but I never knew of what Hamiltons. He treated her shamefully after the Arabin tradition. She did not live long, and there were no children. I believe, and now Shelley is dead and the Arabins are extinct. Not a pleasant family, you will say, and small loss to the world. But there was a certain quality, too, which under happier circumstances might have made them great. And assuredly they had looks. There was something almost unholy about Shelley's beauty in his early days. It made men instinctively dislike him. If I had had a son I should have liked him to be snub-nosed and bullet-headed, for ugliness in the male is a security for virtue and a passport to popularity.'

This was probably a sentence from one of Folliot's silly books of reminiscences. My curiosity about Plakos was not exhausted and I asked what kind of life had been lived there. 'The house is a tremendous affair,' I said, 'with room for a regiment.'

'I know,' said Folliot, 'and it was often full. I had always a great curiosity to go there, though I dare say I should have found the atmosphere too tropical for my taste. Shelley never invited me, but if I had arrived he could scarcely have turned me away. I entertained the notion at one time, but I kept putting it off till my taste for that kind of adventure declined . . . No, I have never been nearer Plakos than Athens, where I once spent a fortnight when Fanshawe was our Minister there. I asked about Shelley, of course, and Fanshawe gave me an ugly report. Plakos, you must know, is a remote and not over-civilized island where the writ of the Greek Government scarcely runs, so it was very much a patriarchal despotism. I gathered that Shelley was not a popular landlord. There had been many complaints, and one or two really horrid stories of his treatment of the peasantry. It seemed that he saw a good deal of company, and had made his house a resort for the rascality of Europe. The rascality – not merely the folly, as in his father's time. The place fairly stank in Fanshawe's nostrils. "The swine still calls himself an Englishman," he told me, "still keeps his English domicile, so we get the blame of his beastliness. And all the while, too, he is sluicing out venom about England. He is clever enough to keep just inside the tinpot Greek law. I'd give a thousand pounds to see him clapped in gaol." '

I had heard all I wanted to know, and picked up a book, while Folliot busied himself with the newspaper. A little later he interrupted me.

'I have just remembered something else. You knew Wintergreen, the archaeologist? He was at the British School in Athens, and then excavated Hittite remains in Asia Minor. Poor fellow, he died of dysentery as an intelligence officer in Mesopotamia. Well, Wintergreen once spoke to me of Plakos. I suppose he had been there, for he had been everywhere. We were talking, I remember, one night in the club about Gilles de Rais – the French Bluebeard, you know, the friend of Joan of Arc – and I asked if anything approaching that kind of miscreant still existed on the globe. Somebody said that the type was fairly common in the East, and mentioned some Indian potentate. Wintergreen broke in. "You don't need to go to the East," he said. "You can find it in Europe," and he started to speak of Shelley Arabin. I don't recollect what exactly he said, but it was pretty bad, and of course strictly libellous. By his account Shelley had become a connoisseur and high-priest of the uttermost evil, and the cup of his iniquities was nearly full. It seemed that Wintergreen had been in the island excavating some ancient remains and living among the peasants, and had heard tales that sickened him. He thought that some day soon the great house would go flaming to heaven, set alight by an outraged people.

'Well, it hasn't happened.' Folliot returned to his *Times*. 'Shelley has died in his bed, which is perhaps more than he deserved. Not agreeable people, I fear. It is a good thing that he left no posterity.'

That evening I thought a good deal about Plakos. I was glad to have discovered the reason for the aversion which I had felt on our visit, and was inclined to believe that I must be a more sensitive person than my friends would admit. After that the subject passed from my mind.

By the end of April I was so much recovered that I went back to my practice at the Bar, and was almost snowed under by the briefs which descended on my shoulders as soon as there was a rumour of my return. It would have been a difficult job to select, and I dare say I should have slipped into overwork, had I not been made a Law Officer. That, so to speak, canalised my duties, and since my task was largely novel and, at the moment, of extraordinary interest, the change completed my convalescence. In May I was my normal self, and when Vernon returned to England in June he found me eating, sleeping and working as in the old days – a fitter man, indeed, than in 1914, for the war seemed to have drawn off the grosser humours of middle life.

Vernon, too, was fit again. If a young man starts with a fine constitution and a strong character and applies all the powers of his mind to the task of getting well, he is almost certain to succeed. He came back to London a lean, sunburnt creature, with an extraordinarily *rarefied* look about him. He had lost nothing of his youth, indeed he scarcely looked his twenty-five years; but he had been fined down and tautened and tested, so that his face had a new spirituality in it as if there was a light shining behind. I have noticed the same thing in other cases of head wounds. You remember how Jim Barraclough, who used to be a heavy red-haired fellow, came out of hospital looking like a saint in an Italian primitive.

Vernon was changed in other ways. You see, he belonged to a generation which was nearly cleaned out by the war, and he had scarcely a friend of his own year left except my nephew Charles. That should not have meant so much to him as to other people, for he had never depended greatly on friends, but I think the thought of all the boys who had been at school and college with him lying under the sod gave him a feeling of desperate loneliness, and flung him back more than ever on himself. I could see that even I meant less to him than before, though I still meant a good deal.

I was partly to blame for that, perhaps. The war had altered everybody's sense of values, and unconsciously I had come to take his dream less seriously. I had got into a mood of accepting things as they came and living with short horizons, and the long perspective which dominated his thoughts seemed to me a little out of the picture. I was conscious of this change in myself, and strove not to show it, but he must have felt it, and the blinds came down ever so little between us. For it was clear that the dream meant more than ever to him. He was in the last lap now, had rounded the turn and was coming up the straight, and every nerve and sinew were on the stretch. I couldn't quite live up to this ardour, though I tried hard, and with that lightning instinct of his he was aware of it, and was sparing of his confidences. The thing made me miserable, for it increased his loneliness, and I longed for the next year to be over and the apocalyptic to be driven out of his life. The mere fact that I took for granted that nothing would happen showed that I had lost my serious interest in his dream. Vernon had to outgrow a childish fancy, as one outgrows a liability to chicken-pox – that was all.

He had become harder too, as a consequence of loneliness. You remember that curious summer of 1919 when everybody was feverishly trying to forget the war. They were crazy days, when nobody was quite himself. Politicians talked and writers wrote clotted nonsense, statesmen chased their tails, the working-man wanted to double his wages and halve his working hours at a time when the world was bankrupt, youth tried to make up for the four years of natural pleasure of which it had been cheated, and there was a general loosening of screws and a rise in temperature. It was what I had looked for, and I sympathised with a good deal of it, but, Lord bless me! Vernon was like an Israelitish prophet at a feast of Baal. I recalled what Charles had said about him in the war, and I wondered if Charles had not been right. Vernon seemed destitute of common humour.

I took him to dine at the Thursday Club, which had just been started. There he behaved well enough, for he found people who could talk his own language. But I noticed how complete was his apathy when politics were the subject of conversation. He was as uninterested in the setting to rights of the world as a hermit in a cell. He was oddly uncompanionable, too. Burminster's rollicking chaff got nothing out of him but a Mona Lisa smile. 'What has happened to the boy?' that worthy asked me afterwards. 'Shellshock or what? Has he left a bit of his mind out in France? He's the most buttoned-up thing I ever struck.'

He was worse with the ordinary young man. I gave a dinner or two for him, and, as we had one club in common, we occasionally found ourselves together in smoking-room gatherings. I had an immense pity for youth struggling to adjust its poise, and often I could have found it in my heart to be annoyed with Vernon's uncanny balance, which was not far from egotism. These poor lads were splashing about in life, trying to find their feet, and for their innocent efforts he had only a calm contempt. He sat like a skeleton at the feast, when they chattered about their sporting and amorous ventures and discussed with abysmal ignorance how money was to be made in a highly expensive world. I have a vivid recollection of his courteous insulting aloofness.

'What rot to say that the war has done any good,' he remarked to me once as we walked back to the flat. 'It has killed off the men, and left only the half-wits.'

Charles, now endeavouring without much success to earn a living in the City, was vehement on the subject, and he had a characteristic explanation. 'Vernon has become a wonderful old fossil,' he said. 'Not gone to seed, like some of the rest, but a fossil – dried up – mummified. It isn't healthy, and I'm pretty certain about the cause. He's got something on his mind, and I shouldn't be surprised if he was preparing to come an everlasting cropper. I think it's a girl.'

It certainly was not a girl. I often wished it had been, for to a fellow as lonely as Vernon the best cure, as I saw it, would have been to fall in love. People had taken furiously to dancing, and that summer, though there were no big balls, every dinner party seemed to end in a dance, and every restaurant was full of ragtime music and ugly transatlantic shuffling. For youth it was a good way of working off restlessness, and foolish middle age followed the guiding of youth. I had no fault to find with the fashion. The poor girls, starved for four years of their rights, came from dull war-work and shadowed schoolrooms determined to win back something. One could forgive a good deal of shrillness and bad form in such a case. My one regret was that they made such guys of themselves. Well-born young women seemed to have taken for their models the cretinous little oddities of the film world.

One night Vernon and I had been dining at the house of a cousin of mine and had stayed long enough to see the beginning of the dance that followed. As I looked on, I had a sharp impression of the change which five years had brought. This was not, like a pre-war ball, part of the ceremonial of an assured and orderly world. These people were dancing as savages danced – to get rid of or to engender excitement. Apollo had been ousted by Dionysos. The nigger in the band who came forward now and then and sang some gibberish was the true master of ceremonies. I said as much to Vernon, and he nodded. He was watching with a curious intensity the faces that passed us.

'Everybody is leaner,' I said, 'and lighter on their feet. That's why they want to dance. But the women have lost their looks.'

'The women!' he murmured. 'Look at that, I beseech you!'

It was a tall girl, who was dancing with a handsome young Jew, and dancing as I thought, with a notable grace. She was very slim and clearly very young, and I dare say would have been pretty, if she had let herself alone. I caught a glimpse of fine eyes, and her head was set on her neck like a flower on its stalk. But some imp had inspired her to desecrate the gifts of the Almighty. Her hair was bobbed, she had too much paint and powder on her face, she had some kind of barbaric jewels in her ears which put her head out of drawing, and she wore a preposterous white dress. Don't ask me to describe it, for I am not an expert in millinery: but it seemed to me wrong by every canon of decency and art. It had been made, no doubt, with the intention of being provocative, and its audacious lines certainly revealed a great deal of its wearer's body. But the impression was rather of an outrage perpetrated on something beautiful, a foolish ill-bred joke. There was an absurd innocence about the raddled and half-clad girl – like a child who for an escapade has slipped down to the drawing-room in her nightgown.

Vernon did not feel as I felt. His eyes followed her for a little, and then he turned to me with a face like stone.

'So much for our righteous war,' he said grimly. 'It's to produce *that* that so many good fellows died.'

FOUR

EARLY IN NOVEMBER I went down to Wirlesdon for the first big covert shoot. I am not a great performer with the gun, and you will not find me often in the first flight in the hunting-field, but, busy as I was, I made time now for an occasional day's shooting or hunting, for I had fallen in love with the English country, and it is sport that takes you close to the heart of it. Is there anything in the world like the corner of a great pasture hemmed in with smoky-brown woods in an autumn twilight: or the jogging home after a good run when the moist air is quickening to frost and the wet ruts are lemon-coloured in the sunset; or a morning in November when, on some upland, the wind tosses the driven partridges like leaves over tall hedges, through the gaps of which the steel-blue horizons shine? It is the English winter that intoxicates me more even than the English May, for the noble bones of the land are bare, and you get the essential savour of earth and wood and water.

It was a mild evening as we walked back from the last stand to the house, and, though so late in the year, there was still a show in the garden borders. I like the rather languid scent of autumn flowers when it is chastened by a touch of wood smoke from the gardeners' bonfires; it wakes so many memories and sets me thinking. This time my thoughts were chiefly of Vernon, whom I had not seen for several months. We were certainly drawing apart, and I didn't see how it could be avoided. I was back in the ordinary world again, with a mighty zest for it, and he was vowed and consecrated to his extraordinary obsession. I could not take it seriously myself, but about one thing I was grave enough – its effect on Vernon. Nothing would happen when next April came – of that I was convinced, but if nothing happened what would Vernon do? The linch-pin would be out of his life. At twenty-six with a war behind him a man should have found his groove in life, but at twenty-six Vernon would be derelict, like one who has trained himself laboriously for an occupation which is gone. I put aside the notion that anything could happen, for in my new mood I was incredulous of miracles. But my scepticism did not dispel my anxiety.

The hall at Wirlesdon is a big comfortable stone-flagged Georgian place, and before one of the fireplaces, with two great Coromandel screens for a shelter, there was the usual encampment for tea. It was a jolly sight – the autumn dusk in the tall windows, the blazing logs and the group of fresh-coloured young faces. I had gone straight to the covert-side that morning, so I had still to greet my hostess, and I was not clear who were staying in the house. Mollie Nantley, busied in making tea, muttered some indistinct introductions, and I bowed to several unfamiliar young women in riding-habits who were consuming poached eggs. I remembered that this was the Saturday country for the Mivern, and presently one of the red backs turned towards me, and I saw that it was Vernon.

The Mivern cut-away became him uncommonly well, and his splashed breeches and muddy boots corrected the over-precision which was apt to be the fault of his appearance. Once he would have made a bee-line towards me, but now he contented himself with a smile and a wave of his hand. We were certainly drifting apart . . . He was talking to one of the Nantley girls, a pretty shy creature, just out of the schoolroom, and Tom Nantley, her father, made a third in the conversation. As I drank my tea I looked round the little gathering. There were Bill Harcus and Heneage Wotton and young Cheviot who had been of the shooting party. Lady Altrincham was there with her wonderful pearls – she is one of those people whose skin nourishes pearls and she is believed to take them to bed with her. Young Mrs Lamington. who had been walking with the guns, was kicking the burning logs with her mannish shoes and discussing politics with the son of the house, Hugo Brune, who was in Parliament. There were several girls, all with clear skins and shorn curls and slim straight figures. I found myself for the first time approving the new fashion in clothes. These children looked alert and vital like pleasant boys and I have always preferred Artemis to Aphrodite.

But there was one girl who caught and held my eyes. She had been hunting, and her flat-brimmed hat was set deep on her small head and rather tilted back, for her bobbed hair gave it no support. Her figure in a well-cut coat and habit was graceful and workmanlike, and there was a rakish elegance about her pose, as she stood with one foot on the stone curb of the hearth, holding a tea-cup as a Wise Virgin may have carried a lamp. But there was little of the Wise Virgin about her face. Any colour the weather might have whipped into it had disappeared under a recent powdering, and my impression was of very red lips against a dead white background. She had been talking over her left shoulder to her hostess, and now her eyes were roaming about the place, with a kind of arrogant nonchalance. They met mine, and I saw that they were curiously sullen and masterful. Then they passed from me, for a middle-aged lawyer did not interest them, dwelt for a moment on Cheviot and Wotton, who were having an argument about woodcock, and finally rested on Vernon. She had the air of being bored with her company.

Vernon, talking idly to Tom Nantley, suddenly found himself addressed.

'Your mare wants practice in jumping stone walls,' she said. 'You'll cut her knees to ribbons. Better try her in caps next time.'

You can cut into a conversation gracefully, and you can cut in rudely. This girl did it rudely. I could see Vernon's face harden as he replied that this bit of the Mivern country was strange to him.

'It's the only decent going in the shire. I'm sick of the rotten pastures in the vale country. What on earth does one hunt for except for pace?'

'Some of us hunt to follow hounds,' was Vernon's curt rejoinder.

She laughed – a rather ugly hard little laugh. 'Follow your grandmother! If hounds are all you care about you may as well go beagling! Give me a cigarette, will you?'

'Sorry, I haven't any,' he replied.

Several men proffered cases. 'You'll find heaps, Corrie dear,' Mollie Nantley said, 'in the box behind you.' The girl reached behind her for the box and offered it to Vernon. When he declined she demanded a match, and Vernon, with an ill grace, lit her cigarette. It was plain that he detested her manners.

So most certainly did I. The little incident I had witnessed was oddly ill-bred and brazen. And yet 'brazen' was not quite the word, for it implies self-consciousness. This masterful girl had no shadow of doubt as to her behaviour. She seemed to claim the right to domineer, like a barbaric princess accustomed to an obsequious court. Yes, 'barbaric' was the right epithet. Mollie had called her 'Corrie' and the name fitted her. No doubt she had been baptised Cora or Corisande, names which for me recalled the spangles and sawdust of a circus.

She had decided that Vernon was the most interesting of the lot of us, and she promptly annexed him, moving to his side and swinging on an arm of a tapestry chair. But Vernon was a hard fellow to drive against his will. His air was a frigid courtesy, and presently he went up to his hostess. 'We must be off, Lady Nantley,' he said, 'for it's getting dark and we are eight miles from home.' He collected two of the men and three of the hunting girls, like a chaperone at a ball, shook hands with Mollie and Tom, nodded to me, and marched to the door.

The girl, who was apparently my fellow-guest, followed him with her eyes, and her scarlet lips seemed to twitch in a flicker of amusement. If she had been rude, so had been Vernon, and, had she known it, it was something of a triumph to have cracked his adamantine good manners. When the party had gone, she strolled to the front of the hearth, stretched her arms above her head, and yawned.

'Lord, how stiff I am!' she proclaimed. 'Heigho for a bath! I hope you've the right kind of bath salts, Mollie, or I'll be on crutches tomorrow. Come and talk to me, Dolly!' She picked up her crop, made a noose with the lash around the waist of one of the daughters of the house and drew her with her. The child, to my surprise, went smilingly.

I, too, had a bath, and read papers till it was time to dress. I felt happier about Vernon, for the sight of his unmistakable ill-temper seemed to bring him into the common human category. I had never seen him show dislike so markedly to any human being as to that atrocious girl, and I considered that it would be a good thing if his Olympian calm could be ruffled more often in the same way. I wondered casually who she could be, and why the Nantleys should have her to stay. Probably she was some daughter of profiteers who had bought her way into an unfamiliar world, though that would not explain her presence at Wirlesdon. But an ill-bred young woman did not interest me enough for my thoughts to dwell long on her, and my only prayer was that I might not be placed next her at dinner.

It was a very young party which I found assembled in Mollie's sitting-room, and a hasty glance convinced me that I would be sent in with Mrs Lamington. Old Folliot was there, and presently he sidled up to me to tell me a new piece of gossip. Having been out all day in strong air I was ravenous, and impatient for the announcement of dinner.

'Now, who are we waiting for?' Tom Nantley fussed around. 'Oh, Corrie, of course. Corrie is always late. Confound that girl, she has probably gone to sleep in her bath. Pam, you go and dig her out . . . Hullo, here she comes at last!'

In her hunting-kit she had looked handsome in an outlandish way, but as she swept down – without any apology – on our hungry mob there was no question of her beauty. For one thing she walked superbly. Few women can walk, and the trouble about the new fashion in clothes is that it emphasizes ugly movement. She wore a gown of a shade of green which would have ruined most people's looks, but she managed to carry it off, and something more. For a young girl she was far too heavily made up, but that too she forced one to accept. I suddenly had a new view of her, and realized that there was quality here, a masterfulness which might charm, an arrogance which perhaps was not *blasé* but virginal.

I realised, too, that I had seen her before. This was the girl whom Vernon and I had watched at my cousin's dance in July. I wondered if he had understood this in their encounter at the tea-table.

I had barely recovered from this surprise, when I had another. Folliot's hand was on my arm and he was purring in my ear:

'We talked once of Shelley Arabin, and I told you he left no children. My memory betrayed me, for that young lady is his daughter. She has the true Arabin eyes and all their unfathomable conceit. She is what in my day we would have called "shocking bad form". Rather common, I think.'

From which I knew that she must have dealt hardly with old Folliot.

At dinner I sat between Mollie and Mrs Lamington, and since my hostess had the garrulous Cheviot on her right hand, I devoted myself to my other neighbour. That charming lady, who gives to political intrigue what time she can spare from horse-flesh, had so much to tell me that I had no need to exert myself. She was eloquent on the immense importance of certain pending Imperial appointments, especially on the need of selecting men with the right kind of wives, the inference being that George Lamington's obvious deficiencies might be atoned for by the merits of his lady. I must have assented to everything that she said, for she told Mollie afterwards that the war had improved me enormously and had broadened my mind. But as a matter of fact I was thinking of Miss Arabin.

She sat nearly opposite to me, and I could watch her without staring. Her manner seemed to alternate between an almost hoydenish vivacity and complete abstraction. At one moment she would have her young neighbours laughing and protesting volubly, and then she would be apparently deaf to what they said, so that they either talked across her or turned to their other partners . . . In these latter moods her eyes seemed almost sightless, so wholly were they lacking in focus or expression. Sometimes they rested on the table flowers, sometimes on the wall before her, sometimes on Mrs Lamington and myself – but they were always unseeing. Instead of their former sullenness, they seemed to have a brooding innocence . . . I noticed, too, the quality of her voice when she spoke. It was singularly arresting – clear, high and vital. She talked the usual staccato slang, but though she rarely finished a sentence grammatically, the cadence and intonation were always rounded off to a satisfying close. Only her laugh was ugly, as if it were a forced thing. Every other sound that came from her had a musical completeness.

She had the foreign trick of smoking before the close of dinner, and, as if to preserve her beautiful fingers from contamination, before lighting a cigarette she would draw on her right hand a silk glove of the same colour as her gown. The Nantleys seemed to be accustomed to this habit, but it at last withdrew Mrs Lamington from her Imperial propaganda.

'What an extraordinary young woman!' she whispered to me. 'Who is she? Is she a little mad, or only foreign?'

I paraphrased old Folliot in my reply: 'Pure English, but lives abroad.'

The green glove somehow recalled that April evening at Plakos. This outlandish creature was interesting, for God knew what strange things were in her upbringing and her ancestry. Folliot was an old fool; she might be odious, but she was assuredly not 'common'. As it chanced the end of dinner found her in one of her fits of absent-mindedness, and she trailed out of the room with the other women like a sleepwalker. The two youngsters who had been her companions at table stared after her till the door closed.

Later in the drawing-room I returned to my first impression. The girl was detestable. I would have liked a sleepy evening of bridge, but the young harpy turned the sober halls of Wirlesdon into a cabaret. She behaved like a man-eating shark, and swept every male, except Tom Nantley, Folliot and myself, into her retinue. They danced in the library, because of its polished empty floor, and when I looked in I saw that the kind of dances were not what I should have chosen for youth, and was glad that Pam and Dolly had been sent to bed. I heard a clear voice declaring that it was 'devilish slow' and I knew to whom the voice belonged. At the door I passed old Folliot on his way to his room, and he shook his head and murmured 'Common.' This time I almost agreed with him.

In the drawing-room I found my hostess skimming the weekly press and drew up a chair beside her. Mollie Nantley and I count cousinship, though the relation is slightly more remote, and she has long been my very good friend. She laid down her paper and prepared to talk.

'I was so glad to see Colonel Milburne again. He looks so well too. But, Ned dear, you ought to get him to go about more, for he's really a little old-maidish. He was scared to death by Corrie Arabin.'

'Well, isn't she rather – shall we say disconcerting? More by token, who is she?'

'Poor little Corrie! She's the only child of a rather horrible man who died last year – Shelley Arabin. Did you never hear of him? He married a sort of cousin of mine and treated her shamefully. Corrie had the most miserable upbringing – somewhere in Greece, you know, and in Rome and Paris, and at the worst kind of girls' school where they teach the children to be snobs and powder their noses and go to confession. The school wouldn't have mattered, for the Arabins are Romans, and Corrie couldn't be a snob if she tried, but her home life would have ruined St Theresa. She was in London last summer with the Ertzbergers, and I was rather unhappy about her living among cosmopolitan Jew *rastaquouères*, so I am trying to do what I can for her this winter. Fortunately she has taken madly to hunting and she goes most beautifully. She has never had a chance, poor child. You must be kind to her, Ned.'

I said that I was not in the habit of being brutal to young women, but that she was not likely to want my kindness. 'She seems to be a success in her way. These boys follow her like sheep.'

'Oh, she has had one kind of success, but not the best kind. She casts an extraordinary spell over young men, and does not care a straw for one of them. I might be nervous about Hugo, but I'm not in the least, for she is utterly sexless – more like a wild boy. It is no good trying to improve her manners, for she is quite unconscious of them. I don't think there is an atom of harm in her, and she has delightful things about her – she is charming to Pam and Dolly, and they adore her, and she is simply the most honest creature ever born. She must get it from her mother, for Shelley was an infamous liar.'

Mollie's comely face, with her glorious golden-red hair slightly greying at the temples, had a look of compassionate motherliness. With all her vagueness, she is one of the shrewdest women of my acquaintance, and I have a deep respect for her judgement. If she let her adored Pam and Dolly make friends of Miss Arabin, Miss Arabin must be something more than the cabaret girl of my first impression.

'But I'm not happy about her,' Mollie went on. 'I can't see her future. She ought to marry, and the odds are terribly against her marrying the right man. Boys flock after her, but the really nice men – like Colonel Milburne – fly from her like the plague. They don't understand that her bad form is not our bad form, but simply foreignness . . . And she's so terribly strong-minded. I know that she hates everything connected with her early life, and yet she insists on going back to that Greek place. Her father left her quite well off, I believe – Tom says so and he has looked into her affairs – and she ought to settle down here and acclimatise herself. All her superficial oddities would soon drop off, for she is so clever she could make herself whatever she wanted. It is what she wants, too, for she loves England and English ways. But there is a touch of "daftness" about her, a kind of freakishness which I can never understand. I suppose it is the Arabin blood.'

Mollie sighed.

'I try to be tolerant about youth,' she added, 'but I

sometimes long to box its ears. Besides, there is the difficulty about the others. I am quite sure of Corrie up to a point, but I can't be responsible for the young men. George Cheviot shows every inclination to make a fool of himself about her, and what am I to say to his mother? Really, having Corrie in the house is like domesticating a destroying angel.'

'You're the kindest of women,' I said, 'but I think you've taken on a job too hard for you. You can't mix oil and wine. You'll never fit Miss Arabin into your world. She belongs to a different one.'

'I wonder what it is?'

A few hours ago I should have said it was the world of cabarets and Riviera hotels and Ertzbergers. After what you have told me I'm not so sure. But anyhow it's not our world.'

As I went to bed I heard the jigging of dance music from the library, and even in so large a house as Wirlesdon its echoes seemed to pursue me as I dropped into sleep. The result was that I had remarkable dreams, in which Miss Arabin, dressed in the spangles of a circus performer and riding a piebald horse, insisted on my piloting her with the Mivern, while the Master and Vernon looked on in stony disapproval.

The next morning was frosty and clear, and I came down to breakfast to find my hostess alone in the dining-room.

'Corrie behaved disgracefully last night,' I was informed. 'She started some silly rag with George Cheviot and made hay of Mr Harcus's bedroom. Tom had to get up and read the Riot Act in the small hours. I have been to her room and found her asleep, but as soon as she wakes I am going to talk to her very seriously. It is more than bad manners, it is an offence against hospitality.'

I went to church with Tom and his daughters, and when we returned we found Miss Arabin breakfasting before the hall fire on grapes and coffee, with the usual young men in attendance. If she had been given a lecture by her hostess, there was no sign of it in her face. She looked amazingly brilliant – all in brown, with a jumper of brown arabesque and long amber ear-rings. A russet silk glove clothed the hand in which she held her cigarette.

Vernon came over to luncheon and sat next to Mollie, while at the other end of the table I was placed between Miss Arabin and Lady Altrincham. The girl scarcely threw a word to me, being occupied in discussing quite intelligently with Hugo

Brune the international position of Turkey. I could not avoid overhearing some of their talk, and I realised that when she chose she could behave like a civilised being. It might be that Mollie's morning discourse had borne fruit. Her voice was delightful to listen to, with its full clear tones and delicate modulations. And then, after her habit, her attention wandered, and Hugo's platitudes fell on unheeding ears. She was staring at a picture of a Jacobean Nantley on the wall, and presently her eyes moved up the table and rested on Vernon.

She spoke to me at last.

'Who is the man next to Mollie – the man who came to tea last night? You know him, don't you?'

I told her his name.

'A soldier?' she asked.

'Has been. Does nothing at present. He has a place in Westmorland.'

'You are friends?'

'The closest.' There was something about the girl's brusqueness which made me want to answer in monosyllables. Then she suddenly took my breath away.

'He is unhappy,' she said. 'He looks as if he had lost his way.'

She turned to Hugo, and, with an urbanity which I had thought impossible, apologised for her inattention and took up the conversation at the point at which she had dropped it.

Her words made me keep my eyes on Vernon. Unhappy! There was little sign of it in his lean smiling face, with the tanned cheeks and steady eyes. Mollie was clearly delighted with him; perhaps her maternal heart had marked him down for Dolly. Lost his way? On the contrary he seemed at complete ease with the world. Was this strange girl a sorceress to discover what was hidden deep in only two men's minds? I had a sense that Vernon and Miss Arabin, with nothing on earth in common, had yet a certain affinity. Each had a strain of romance in them – romance and the unpredictable.

Vernon had motored over to Wirlesdon and proposed to walk back, so I accompanied him for part of the road. I was glad of a chance for a talk, for I was miserably conscious that we were slipping away from each other. I didn't see how I could help it, for I was immersed in practical affairs, while he would persist in living for a dream. Before the war I had been half under the spell of that dream, but four years' campaigning had given me a distaste for the fantastic and set my feet very solidly on the rock of facts. Our two circles of comprehension, which used to intersect, had now become self-contained.

I asked him what he was doing with himself, and he said hunting and shooting and dabbling in books. He was writing something – I think about primitive Greek religion, in consequence of some notions he had picked up during his service in the Aegean.

'Seriously, old fellow,' I said, 'isn't it time you settled down to business? You are twenty-five, you have first-class brains, and you are quite fit now. I can't have you turning into a *flâneur*.'

'There is no fear of that,' he replied rather coldly. 'I am eager for work, but I haven't found it yet. My training isn't finished. I must wait till after next April.'

'But what is going to happen after that?'

'I don't know. I must see what happens *then*.'

'Vernon,' I cried, 'we are old friends and I am going to speak bluntly. You really must face up to facts. What is going to happen next April? What *can* happen? Put it at its highest. You may pass through some strange mental experience. I can't conceive what it may be, but suppose the last door does open and you see something strange and beautiful or even terrible – I don't know what. It will all happen inside your mind. It will round off the recurring experiences you have had from childhood, but it can't do anything more.'

'It will do much more,' he said. 'It will be the crisis of my life . . . Why have you become so sceptical, Ned? You used to think as I do about it.'

'It will only be a crisis if you make it so, and it's too risky. Supposing on the other hand that nothing happens. You will have keyed your whole being up to an expectation which fails. You will be derelict, cut clean from your moorings. It's too risky, I tell you.'

He shook his head. 'We have fallen out of understanding each other. Your second alternative is impossible. I know it in my bones. Something will happen – must happen – and then I shall know what I have to do with my life. It will be the pistol-shot for the start.'

'But, my dear old man, think of the hazard. You are staking everything on a wild chance. Heaven knows, I'm not unsympathetic. I believe in you – I believe in a way in the reality of the dream. But life is a prosaic thing, and if you are to have marvels in it you should take them in your stride. I want to see you with some sort of policy for the future, and letting the last stage of your dream drop in naturally into a strategic plan. You can't at twenty-five sit waiting on a revelation. You must shape your own course, and take the revelation when it comes. If you don't, you'll find yourself derelict. Damn it, you're far too good to be a waif.'

He smiled a little sadly. 'We're pretty far apart now, I'm afraid. Can't you see that the thing is too big a part of me to be treated as a side-show? It's what I've been sent into the world for. I'm waiting for my marching orders.'

'Then you're waiting for a miracle,' I said testily.

'True. I am waiting for a miracle,' he replied. 'We needn't argue about it, Ned, for miracles are outside argument. In less than six months I will know. Till then I am content to live by faith.'

After leaving him, I walked back to the house in an uncomfortable frame of mind. I realised that the affection between us was as deep as ever, but I had a guilty sense of having left him in the lurch. He was alone now, whereas once I had been with him, and I hated to think of his loneliness.

As I crossed the bridge between the lakes I met Miss Arabin sauntering bareheaded in the autumn sunlight. I would have passed on, with a curt greeting, for I was in no mood to talk trivialities to a girl I disliked, but to my surprise she stopped and turned with me up the long grassy aisle which led to the gardens.

'I came out to meet you,' she said. 'I want to talk to you.'

My response cannot have been encouraging, but she took no notice of that.

'You're a lawyer, aren't you?' she went on. 'Mollie says you are very clever. You look clever.'

I dare say I grinned. I was being comprehensively patronised.

'Well, I want you to help me. I have some tiresome legal complications to disentangle, and my solicitor is a sheep. I mean to sack him.'

I explained the etiquette of my profession.

'Oh, then you can tell him what to do. You'll understand his silly talk, which I don't. You make him obey you.'

'My dear young lady,' I said, 'I cannot undertake private business. You see I'm in the employ of the Government.'

'Don't be afraid, I can pay you all right.' The words were too naïve to be insulting.

I said nothing, and she darted before me and looked me in the face.

'You mean that you won't help me?' she asked.

'I mean that I'm not allowed,' I replied.

Without another word she swung round and disappeared up a side glade. As she vanished among the beech-trees, a figure as russet as the drift of leaves, I thought I had never seen anything more quick and slender, and I fervently hoped that I should never see her again.

FIVE

IN THAT HOPE I was mistaken. A fortnight later the Treasury Solicitor sent me the papers in one of those intricate international cases which were the debris of the war. It was a claim by a resident abroad, who had not lost his British nationality, for compensation for some oppressive act of one of the transient Greek Governments. I left the thing to my 'devil', and just skimmed his note before the necessary conference with the plaintiff's solicitors. To my surprise I saw that it had to do with the island of Plakos and the name of Arabin.

Mr Mower, of the reputable firm of Mower & Lidderdale, was not unlike a sheep in appearance – a Leicester ewe for choice. He had a large pale high-boned face, rimless spectacles, a crop of nice fleecy white-hair, and the bedside manner of the good family solicitor. My hasty study of the papers showed me that the oppressive acts were not denied, but that the title of the plaintiff was questioned.

'This is a matter of domestic law,' I said – 'the *lex loci rei sitæ*. If the title to the land is disputed, it is a case for the Greek courts.'

'We have reason to believe that the defence is not seriously put forward, for the title is beyond dispute, and we are at a loss to understand the attitude of the Greek Government. The documents are all in our possession, and we took Mr Blakeney's advice on them. His opinion is among the papers left with you – and you will see that he has no doubt on the matter.'

Mr Blakeney certainly had not, as I saw from his opinion, nor had my 'devil'. The latter characterised the defence as 'monstrous'. It seemed to be based on an arbitrary act of the old Greek National Assembly of 1830. My note said that the title was complete in every respect, and that the attempt to question it seemed to be a species of insanity. A name caught my attention.

'What is Koré?' I asked.

'It is Miss Arabin's Christian name. Greek, I presume,' said Mr Mower, very much in the tone in which Mr Pecksniff observed, 'Pagan, I regret to say.'

I read the note again, and Blakeney's opinion. Blakeney was an authority from whom I was not disposed to differ, and the facts seemed too patent for argument. As I turned over the papers I saw the name of another solicitor on them.

'You have not always acted for the Arabin family?' I asked.

'Only within the last few months. Derwents were the family solicitors, but Miss Arabin was dissatisfied with them and withdrew her business. Curiously enough, they advised that the claim of the Greek Government was good, and should not be opposed.'

'What!' I exclaimed. Derwents are one of the best firms in England, and the senior partner, Sebastian Derwent, was my oldest client. He was not only a sound lawyer, but a good scholar and a good fellow. What on earth had induced him to give such paradoxical advice?

I told Mr Mower that the matter seemed plain enough, but that for my own satisfaction I proposed to give further consideration to the papers. I took them home with me that evening, and the more I studied them the less I could understand Derwent's action. The thing seemed a bluff so impudent as to be beyond argument. The abstract of title was explicit enough, and Blakeney, who had had the original documents, was emphatic on the point. But the firm of Derwents was not in the habit of acting without good cause . . . I found myself becoming interested in the affair. Plakos was still a disquieting memory, and the outrageous girl at Wirlesdon was of a piece with its strangeness.

A day or two later I was dining at the Athenaeum before going down to the House, and I saw Sebastian Derwent eating a solitary meal at an adjacent table. I moved over beside him, and after some casual conversation I ventured to sound him on the subject. With another man it might have been a delicate task, but we were old and confidential friends.

I told him I had had the Plakos case before me. 'You used to act for the Arabins?' I said.

He nodded, and a slight embarrassment entered his manner. 'My father and grandfather too before me. The firm had a difficult time with old Tom Arabin. He had a habit of coming down to the office with a horsewhip, and on one occasion my grandfather was compelled to wrest it from him, break it over his knee and pitch it into the fire.'

'I can imagine easier clients. But I am puzzled about that preposterous Greek claim. I can't think how it came to be raised, for it is sheer bluff.'

He reddened a little and crumbled his bread.

'I advised Miss Arabin not to dispute it,' he said.

'I know, and I can't imagine why. You advised her to sit down under a piece of infamous extortion.'

'I advised her to settle it.'

'But how can you settle a dispute when all the rights are on one side? Do you maintain that there was any law or equity in the Greek case?'

He hesitated for a second. 'No,' he said, 'the claim was bad in law. But its acceptance would have had certain advantages for Miss Arabin.'

I suppose I looked dumbfounded. 'It's a long story,' he said, 'and I'm not sure that I have the right to tell it to you.'

'Let us leave it at that, then. Of course it's no business of mine.' I did not want to embarrass an old friend.

But he seemed disinclined to leave it. 'You think I have acted unprofessionally?' he ventured.

'God forbid! I know you too well, and I don't want to poke my nose into private affairs.'

'I can tell you this much. Miss Arabin is in a position of extreme difficulty. She is alone in the world without a near relation. She is very young and not quite the person to manage a troublesome estate.'

'But surely that is no reason why she should surrender her patrimony to a bogus demand?'

'It would not have been exactly surrender. I advised her not to submit but to settle. Full compensation would have been paid if she had given up Plakos.'

'Oh, come now,' I cried. 'Who ever heard of voluntary compensation being paid by a little stony-broke Government in Eastern Europe?'

'It would have been arranged,' he said. 'Miss Arabin had friends – a friend – who had great influence. The compensation was privately settled and it was on a generous scale. Miss Arabin has fortunately other sources of income than Plakos: indeed I do not think she draws any serious revenue from the island. She would have received a sum of money in payment, the interest on which would have added substantially to her income.'

'But I still don't see the motive. If the lady is not worried about money, why should her friends be so anxious to increase her income?'

Mr Derwent shook his head. 'Money is not the motive. The fact is that Plakos is a troublesome property. The Arabin family have never been popular, and the inhabitants are turbulent and barely civilised. The thing is weighing on her mind. It is not the sort of possession for a young girl.'

'I see. In order to rid Miss Arabin of a *damnosa hæreditas* you entered into a friendly conspiracy. I gather that she saw through it.'

He nodded. 'She is very quick-witted, and was furious at the questioning of her title. That was my mistake. I underrated her intelligence. I should have had the thing more ingeniously framed. I can assure you that my last interview with her was very painful. I was forced to admit the thinness of the Greek claim, and after that I had a taste of Tom Arabin's temper. She is an extraordinary child, but there is wonderful quality in her, wonderful courage. I confess I am thankful as a lawyer to be rid of her affairs, but as a friend of the family I cannot help being anxious . . . She is so terribly alone in the world.'

'That is a queer story,' I said. 'Of course you behaved as I should have expected, but I fancy that paternal kindliness is thrown away on that young woman. I met her a few weeks ago in a country house, and she struck me as peculiarly able to look after herself. One last question. Who is the friend who is so all-powerful at Athens?'

'That I fear I am not at liberty to tell you,' was the answer.

This tale whetted my curiosity. From old Folliot I had learned something of the record of the Arabins, and I had my own impression of Plakos as clear as a cameo. Now I had further details in my picture. Koré Arabin (odd name! I remembered from my distant schooldays that Koré was Greek for a 'maiden' – it had nothing to do with Corisande of the circus) was the mistress of that sinister island and that brooding house of a people who detested her race. There was danger in the place, danger so great that some friend unknown was prepared to pay a large price to get her out of it, and had involved in the plot the most decorous solicitor in England. Who was this friend? I wanted to meet him and to hear more of

Plakos, for I realised that he and not Derwent was the authority.

Speculation as to his identity occupied a good deal of my leisure, till suddenly I remembered what Lady Nantley had told me. Miss Arabin had been living in London with the Ertzbergers before she came to Wirlesdon. The friend could only be Theodore Ertzberger. He had endless Greek connections, was one of the chief supporters of Venizelos, and it was through his house that the new Greek loan was to be issued. I had met him, of course, and my recollection was of a small bright-eyed man with a peaked grey beard and the self-contained manner of the high financier. I had liked him and found nothing of the *rastaquouère* in him to which Mollie objected. His wife was another matter. She was a large flamboyant Belgian Jewess, a determined social climber and a great patron of art and music, who ran a salon and whose portraits were to be found in every exhibition of the young school of painters. It was borne in on me that my curiosity would not be satisfied till I had had a talk with Ertzberger.

Lady Amysfort arranged the meeting at a Sunday luncheon when Madame Ertzberger was mercifully stricken with influenza.

Except for the hostess, it was a man's party, and afterwards she manoeuvred that Ertzberger and I should be left alone in a corner of the big drawing-room.

I did not waste time beating about the bush, for I judged from his face that this man would appreciate plain dealing. There was something simple and fine about his small regular features and the steady regard of his dark eyes.

'I am glad to have this chance of a talk with you,' I said. 'I have lately been consulted about Plakos and Miss Arabin's claim against the Greek Government. Also a few weeks ago I had the pleasure of meeting Miss Arabin. The whole business interests me strongly – not as a lawyer but as a human being. You see, just before the war I happened to visit Plakos and I can't quite get the place out of my head. You are a friend of hers, and I should like to know something more about the island. I gather that it's not the most comfortable kind of estate.'

He looked me straight in the face. 'I think you know Mr Sebastian Derwent,' he said.

'I do. And he gave me a hint of Miss Arabin's difficulties and the solution proposed. His conduct may not have been strictly professional, but it was extraordinarily kind. But let me make it quite clear that he never mentioned your name, or gave me any sort of clue to it. I guessed that you were the friend, because I knew that Miss Arabin had been staying in your house.'

'You guessed rightly. It is not a thing that I naturally want made public, but I am not in the least ashamed of the part I played. I welcome the opportunity of discussing it with you. It is a curious thing, but Miss Arabin has already spoken of you to me.'

'She asked me to advise her, and I'm afraid was rather annoyed when I told her that I couldn't take private practice.'

'But she has not given up the notion. She never gives up any notion. She has somehow acquired a strong belief in your wisdom.'

'I am obliged to her, but I am not in a position to help.'

He laid his hand on my arm. 'Do not refuse her,' he said earnestly. 'Believe me, no woman ever stood in more desperate need of friends.'

His seriousness impressed me. 'She has a loyal one in you, at any rate. And she seems to be popular and to have a retinue of young men.'

He looked at me sharply. 'You think she is a light-headed girl, devoted to pleasure – rather second-rate pleasure – a little ill-bred perhaps. But you are wrong, Sir Edward. Here in England she is a butterfly – dancing till all hours, a madcap in town and in the hunting-field, a bewitcher of foolish boys. Oh, bad form I grant you – the worst of bad form. But that is because she comes here for an anodyne. She is feverishly gay because she is trying to forget – trying not to remember that there is tragedy waiting behind her.'

'Where?' I asked.

'In the island of Plakos.'

Tragedy – that was the word he used. It had an incongruous sound to me, sitting in a warm London drawing-room after an excellent luncheon, with the sound of chatter and light laughter coming from the group around my hostess. But he had meant it – his grave voice and burdened face showed it – and the four walls seemed to fade into another picture – a twilight by a spring sea, and under a shadowy house two men with uplifted hands and hate and fear in their eyes.

'If you will do me the honour to listen,' Ertzberger was

speaking, 'I should like to tell you more about Miss Arabin's case.'

'Have you known her long?' I asked. A sudden disinclination had come over me to go further in this affair. I felt dimly that if I became the recipient of confidences I might find myself involved in some distasteful course of action.

'Since she was a child, I had dealings with her father – business dealings – he was no friend of mine – but there was a time when I often visited Plakos. I can claim that I have known Miss Arabin for nearly fifteen years.'

'Her father was a bit of a blackguard?'

'None of the words we use glibly to describe evil are quite adequate to Shelley Arabin. The man was rotten to the very core. His father – I remember him too – was unscrupulous and violent, but he had a heart. And he had a kind of burning courage. Shelley was as hard and cold as a stone, and he was also a coward. But he had genius – a genius for wickedness. He was beyond all comparison the worst man I have ever known.'

'What did he do?' I asked. 'I should have thought the opportunities for wrong-doing in a remote island were limited.'

'He was a student of evil. He had excellent brains and much learning and he devoted it all to researches in devilry. He had his friends – people of his own tastes who acknowledged him as their master. Some of the gatherings at Plakos would have made Nero vomit. Men and women both . . . The place stank of corruption. I have only heard the orgies hinted at – heathenish remnants from the backstairs of the Middle Ages. And on the fringes of that hell the poor child grew up.'

'Unsmirched?'

'Unsmirched! I will stake my soul on that. A Muse, a Grace, a nymph among satyrs. Her innocence kept her from understanding. And then as she grew older and began to have an inkling of horrors she was in flaming revolt . . . I managed to get her sent away, first to school, then to my wife's charge. Otherwise I think there would have been a tragedy.'

'But surely with her father's death the danger is gone.'

He shook his head. 'Plakos is a strange place, for the tides of civilisation and progress seem to have left it high and dry. It is a relic of old days, full of wild beliefs and pagan habits. That was why Shelley could work his will with it. He did not confine his evil-doing to his friends and the four walls of his house. He laid a spell of terror on the island. There are horrid tales – I won't trouble you with them – about his dealings with the peasants, for he revelled in corrupting youth. And terror grew soon into hate, till in his last days the man's nerve broke. He lived his last months in gibbering fear. There is something to be said after all for medieval methods. Shelley was the kind of scoundrel whom an outraged people should have treated with boiling oil.'

'Does the hatred pursue his daughter?' I asked.

'Most certainly. It took years for Plakos to recognise Shelley's enormities, and now the realisation has become cumulative, growing with every month. I have had inquiries made – it is easy for me since I have agents everywhere in the Aegean – and I can tell you the thing has become a mania. The war brought the island pretty near starvation, for the fishing was crippled and a succession of bad seasons spoiled the wretched crops. Also there was a deadly epidemic of influenza. Well, the unsettlement of men's minds, which is found all over the world today, has become in Plakos sheer madness. Remember, the people are primitive, and have savagery in their blood and odd faiths in their hearts. I do not know much about these things, but scholars have told me that in the islands the old gods are not altogether dead. The people have suffered and they blame their sufferings on the Arabins, till they have made a monstrous legend of it. Shelley is in hell and beyond their reach, but Shelley's daughter is there. She is the witch who has wronged them, and they are the kind of folk who are capable of witch-burning.'

'Good God!' I cried. 'Then the girl ought never to be allowed to return.'

'So I thought, and hence my little conspiracy which failed. I may tell you in confidence that it was I who prompted the action of the Greek Government and was prepared to find the compensation. But I was met by a stone wall. She insists on holding on to the place. Worse, she insists on going back. She went there last spring, and the spring is a perilous time, for the people have had the winter to brood over their hatred. I do not know whether she is fully conscious of the risk, for sometimes I think she is still only a child. But last year she was in very real danger, and she must have felt it. Behind all her bravado I could see that she was afraid.'

It was an odd tale to hear in a commonplace drawing-room,

and it was odder to hear it from such a narrator. There was nothing romantic about Ertzberger. I dare say he had the imaginative quickness of his race, but the dominant impression was of solid good sense. He looked at the thing from a business man's point of view, and the cold facts made him shudder.

'What on earth is her reason?' I asked. 'Has she any affection for Plakos?'

'She hates it. But there is some stubborn point of honour which forbids her to let it go. She has her grandfather's fierce obstinacy. Fate has dared her to defend her own, and she has accepted the challenge . . . It is not merely the sense of property. I think she feels that she has a duty – that she cannot run away from the consequences of her father's devilry. Her presence there at the mercy of the people is a kind of atonement.'

'Has she any friends in the island?'

'An old steward is the only man in the house. She may have her well-wishers outside, but they cannot be many, for she has not lived continuously there for years. Last spring I tried to have her guarded, but she saw through my plan and forbade it. All I could do was to have the place watched on my own account. This winter my information is that things are worse. There is famine in the hills, and the hillmen are looking with jealous eyes towards the house by the sea. The stories grow wilder, too.'

'What kind?'

'Oh, witchcraft. That the Arabins are sorcerers and that she herself is a witch. Every misfortune in the island is laid to her account. God knows what may happen this spring, if she persists in going back! My hope was that she might find some lover who would make her forget the obsession, but on the contrary the obsession has made her blind to lovers. Perhaps you have noticed it . . . She seems to flirt outrageously, but she keeps every man at a distance . . . Now, do you understand Miss Arabin a little better?'

I was beginning to. A picture was growing up in my mind of something infinitely pathetic, and terribly alone. A child terrified by a nightmare life which she did not understand – carried off to a new environment from which she extracted what was more feverish and vulgar, for she had no canons, yet keeping through it all a pitiful innocence – returning to a half-comprehension which revolted her soul – resolute to face the consequences of the past with an illogical gallantry. I did not know when I had heard a tale that so moved me.

'You will not refuse her if she asks your help?' Ertzberger pleaded.

'But what can I do?' I said. 'I'm a lawyer and she doesn't want legal advice, even if I were free to give it her.'

'She has got the notion that you can help her. Don't ask me why or how. Call it a girl's fancy and make the best of it. I cannot influence her. Derwent couldn't, but you may, because for some reason or other she believes that you are wise . . . I think . . . I think that she thinks that you can tell her what precisely she has to fear in Plakos. There is a mass of papers, you know.'

'What to fear!' I exclaimed. 'Surely you have just made that plain. A famished and half-civilised peasantry with a long record of ill treatment. Isn't that enough?'

'There may be something more,' Ertzberger said slowly. 'She has an idea that there is something more . . . and she is terrified of that something. If you can get rid of her terrors you will be doing a humane act, Sir Edward. The trouble, as I have told you, is that she will take so few into her confidence.'

'Look here, Mr Ertzberger,' I said. 'I will be quite frank with you. Miss Arabin did not attract me – indeed I have not often been more repelled by a young woman. But what you have said puts a new complexion on her behaviour. Tell her I am willing to do my best for her, to advise her, to help her in any way I can. But if she wouldn't listen to you, you may be certain she won't listen to me.'

'That's very good of you,' he said, rising. 'She proposes to go to Plakos in March. Pray God we can put some sanity into her in the next three months.'

SIX

TWO DAYS LATER I had to go north by an early train from Euston, and opposite my platform a special was waiting, to take a hunting party down to somewhere in the Shires. Around the doors of the carriages stood a number of expensive-looking young people, among whom I recognised Miss Arabin. She wore a long fur coat and sniffed at a bunch of violets, while in her high clear voice she exchanged badinage with two young men. As she stood with one foot on the carriage step, her small head tilted backward, her red lips parted in laughter, it was hard to connect her with the stricken lady of Ertzberger's story. Just as the special was leaving I saw Vernon hurry up, also in hunting-kit. He cast one glance at Miss Arabin, and found a seat in another carriage. I hoped the Pytchley would have a fast day, for I did not see these two fraternising during waits at covert-side.

Curiously enough I saw the girl again the same week, also in a railway train. I was returning from Liverpool, and our trains halted beside each other at Rugby. She was alone in her carriage, the winter dusk was falling but the lights were not yet lit, and I saw her only faintly, silhouetted against the farther window. She was not asleep, but her head was sunk as if in a dream. In the few seconds during which I watched I had a strong impression of loneliness, almost of dejection. She was alone with her thoughts, and they were heavy.

That evening on my return to my flat I found a big parcel of papers. Characteristically there was no covering letter or identification of any sort, but a glance showed me what they were. My time after dinner that night was at my own disposal, and I devoted it to reading them. I believe I would have put aside work of whatever urgency for that purpose, for Plakos had begun to dominate my thoughts.

The papers were a curious jumble – no legal documents, but a mass of family archives and notes on the island. I observed that there was nothing concerned with Shelley. Most of the things had to do with old Tom Arabin – correspondence, original and copied, which had passed between him and his friends or enemies. There were letters from Byron and Shelley and Trelawny, one from no less a person than Sir Walter Scott, many from John Cam Hobhouse, official dispatches from the British Foreign Office, a formal note or two from Castlereagh, and several long and interesting epistles from Canning, who seemed to have had some friendship for the old fellow. There was a quantity, too, of correspondence with Continental statesmen, and I observed several famous names. All this I put on one side, for it did not concern my purpose.

Then there was old Tom Arabin's diary, which I skimmed. It was a very human and explosive document, but there was little about Plakos in it. Tom was more interested in the high politics of Europe than in the little domain he had acquired. Next I turned up a manuscript history of the island in French, written apparently about 1860 by a Greek of the name of Karapanos. This was a dull work, being merely a summary of the island's record under Venetian and Turkish rule, and the doings of its people in the War of Liberation. Then came a bundle of early nineteenth-century maps and charts, and some notes on olive culture. There was a batch, too, of verses in Greek and English, probably Tom's work and not very good. There was a pedigree of the Arabin family in the old Irtling days, and a great deal more junk which had not even an antiquarian interest. I shoved away the papers with a sense of failure. There was nothing here to throw light on Plakos; if such material existed it must have been in Shelley's papers, of which his daughter had doubtless made a bonfire.

Then I noticed something among the notes on olive culture, and drew out a thick old-fashioned envelope heavily sealed with green wax, which bore the Arabin device of a Turk's head. I opened it and extracted a sheet of yellowish parchment, covered closely with Greek characters. I was taught Greek at school, though I have forgotten most of it, but I never professed to be able to read even the printed Greek of the fifteenth and sixteenth centuries. This document seemed to be of that date, and its insane ligatures and contractions completely defeated me. But there might be something in these hieroglyphics, so I bundled up the rest of the papers and locked the envelope in a dispatch box.

Next day I paid a visit to a Chancery barrister of my acquaintance whose hobby was medieval Greek and who had written a monograph on Aldus Manutius. He examined the thing with delight, pronounced the calligraphy fifteenth century and promised to write out the contents for me in decent Greek script.

It was not till early in the New Year that I got the manuscript back from him. The task, he said, had been very difficult, and though he was pretty certain that he had got the transliteration correct, he did not profess to be able to construe it. 'I'm a typographer,' he wrote, 'not a scholar. The thing, too, is obviously corrupt, and I should call it the work of an uneducated man who copied what he did not understand. But it is very curious. It seems to be an account of a place called Kynaetho. Better show it to—' and he mentioned several names.

I did not happen to know any of the people he cited, and it occurred to me that I might consult Vernon. He was, I knew, a fine scholar, and he had kept up his interest in Greek literature. So I sent the original and the modern version to him, saying that the document had come into my hands professionally and I should like to know if he could make anything of it.

Next day I had Vernon on the telephone and he seemed to be excited. 'Where on earth did you pick up that thing?' he asked. 'I suppose it isn't a fake?'

'Genuine enough,' I replied, 'but I can't tell you its story yet. Can you make sense of it?'

'I wouldn't say exactly "sense", but I can translate it after a fashion. I worked at it last night till the small hours. If I knew the *provenance* of the manuscript, I might be able to understand it better. Come and dine tonight, and we'll talk about it.'

Vernon had taken a flat in Cleveland Row, and it was a proof of our gradual estrangement that till that evening I had never been inside its doors. Indeed we had not met since that Sunday at Wirlesdon.

'I saw you at Euston one morning before Christmas,' I said. 'Miss Arabin was going to hunt in the same train.'

'Miss Arabin?' he puzzled. 'I don't think I know—'

'The queer girl who was at Wirlesdon.'

'Is that her name? I didn't know it. She rides well, but her manners are atrocious. Lord, how I dislike these *déracinés*!

Let's get dinner over, for I've a lot to say to you about your jigsaw puzzle. It's extremely interesting, you know.'

Later in the evening he put before me several sheets of foolscap on which he had written the translation in his small beautiful hand.

'The thing is headed *Ta Exotika*,' he said. 'That puzzled me at first, till I remembered the phrase in Basil of Cæsarea. It was the word used by the early Christians to describe the old divinities. Whoever wrote this – I don't mean the fifteenth-century scribe, but the original author – was no doubt a Christian, and he is describing a belief and a rite which existed in his time at a place called Kynaetho.'

'Where is that?'

'I'm hanged if I know. It's a fairly common place name in Greece. There's one in Arcadia.'

I read his translation and could not make much of it. It reminded me of a schoolboy's version of a bit of Herodotus. 'In Kynaetho,' said the writer. 'there is a custom at the Spring Festival of welcoming the Queen (*Despoina* was the word) with the rites of the tympanon and the kestos, such as they use in the Mysteries. There is a certain sacred place, a well beside a white cypress, from which all save the purified are excluded. In Kynaetho the Queen is known as Fairborn (Kalligenia). In winter the Queen is asleep but she wakes in Spring, wherefore the Spring month is called by her name . . . .' After this came a fuller description of the rites and a lot of talk about 'mantic birds'.

'There's nothing much in the first part,' said Vernon. 'It's the ordinary ceremony of the rebirth of Demeter. But notice that she is called "Lady of the Wild Things". There was a mighty unpleasant side to Demeter as well as an idyllic one, and it didn't do to take liberties with the Queen of the Shades. But read on.'

The writer went on to say that in time of great distress at Kynaetho there was a different ceremony. It then became necessary to invite not only the Mistress but the Master. For this purpose a virgin and a youth must be chosen and set apart in a hallowed place, and fed upon sacred food. The choosing was done by the victor in a race, who was given the name of King. Then on the appointed day, after the purification, when the dithyramb had been sung, Bromios would be born from Semele in the fire, and with him would come the

Mistress. After that the place would be loved by the Gods and corn and oil and wine would be multiplied.

That was the gist of the story. The manuscript must have been imperfect, for there were gaps and some obvious nonsense, and there were fragments of verse quoted which I took to be part of the dithyramb. One ran like this:

> Io, Kouros most great. I give thee hail.
> Come, O Dithyrambos, Bromios come, and bring with thee
> Holy hours of thy most holy Spring . . .
> Then will be flung over earth immortal a garland of flowers.
> Voices of song will rise among the pipes,
> The Dancing Floor will be loud with the calling of crowned Semele.

I laid the paper down. Vernon was watching me with bright eyes.

'Do you see what it is? Some of those lines I recognise. They come from the Hymn of the Kouretes, which was discovered the other day in Crete, and from the Pæan to Dionysos found at Delphi, and there is a fragment of Pindar in them too. We know Koré, the Maiden, and we know the Kouros, who might be any male god – Dionysos or Zeus or Apollo – but this is the only case I ever heard of where both Koré and Kouros are found in the same ceremony. Kynaetho, wherever it was, must have fairly gone on the bust . . . It's amazingly interesting and that's why I want to know the story of the manuscript. I tell you it's a find of the first importance to scholarship. Look at the other things too – the sacred race and the winner called the King, just like the Basileus at the Olympic games.

'And there's more,' he went on. 'Look at the passage about the hallowing of the maiden and the youth. How does it go?' He picked up the paper and read: ' "Then the Consecrator shall set aside a youth and a virgin, who shall remain consecrate in a sanctity which for all others shall be a place unapproachable. For seven days they shall be fed with pure food, eggs and cheese and barley-cakes and dried figs and water from the well by the white cypress." Do you see what that means? It was a human sacrifice. The fellow who wrote this skates lightly over the facts – I don't believe he was a Christian after all, or he wouldn't have taken it so calmly. The boy and the girl had to die before the Gods could be re-born.

You see, it was a last resource – not an annual rite, but one reserved for a desperate need. All the words are ritual words – *horkos*, the sanctuary, and *abatos*, the *tabu* place, and *hosioter*, the consecrator. If we knew exactly what *hosiotheis* meant we should know a good deal about Greek religion. There were ugly patches in it. People try to gloss over the human sacrifice side, and of course civilised Greeks like the Athenians soon got rid of it; but I haven't a doubt the thing went on all through classical times in Thessaly and Epirus and Arcadia and some of the islands. Indeed in the islands it survived till almost the other day. There was a case not so long ago in Santorini.'

He pressed me to tell him the origin of the paper, but I felt reluctant to mention Miss Arabin. He was so deeply prejudiced against the girl, that it seemed unfair to reveal to him even the most trivial of her private affairs. I put him off by saying it was the property of a client, and that I would find out its history and tell him later.

'I have made a copy of the Greek text,' he said. 'May I keep it?'

I told him, certainly. And that was all that happened during the evening. Formerly we would have sat up talking and smoking till all hours, but now I felt that the curtain was too heavy between us to allow of ordinary conversation. We would get at once into difficult topics. Besides I did not want to talk. The fact was that I was acquiring an obsession of my own – a tragic defiant girl moving between mirthless gaiety and menaced solitude. She might be innocent of the witchcraft in which Plakos believed, but she had cast some outlandish spell over me.

Before the end of the week Miss Arabin rang me up.

'You're Sir Edward Leithen? I sent you some papers. Have you looked at them?'

I told her I had.

'Then you had better come and talk to me. Come on Saturday and I'll give you luncheon. Half-past one.'

There was no word of thanks for my trouble, but I obeyed the summons as if it had been a royal command. She had taken a flat in a block off Berkeley Square, and I wondered what sort of environment she had made for herself. I think I expected a slovenly place full of cushions and French novels and hot-house flowers. Instead I found a large room wholly without frippery – a big bare writing-table, leather arm-chairs like a man's smoking-room, and on the walls one or two hunting prints and some water-colour sketches of English landscape. There were few books, and those I looked at were county history. It was a mild frosty day and the windows were wide open. The only decorations were some dogwood branches and hedgerow berries – the spoil which townsfolk bring back in winter from country week-ends.

She was in tweeds, for she was off to Wirlesdon that afternoon, and – perhaps in my honour – she had forborne to powder her face. Once again I was struck by the free vigour of her movements, and the quick vitality of her eyes. The cabaret atmosphere was clearly no part of the real woman; rather, as I now saw her, she seemed to carry with her a breath of the fields and hills.

At luncheon we talked stiltedly of the Nantleys and hunting. but no sooner was coffee served than she came to business.

'Theodore has told you about me? You see the kind of fence I'm up against. What I want to know is just exactly how high and thick it is, and that no one can tell me. I liked your looks the first time I saw you, and everyone says you are clever. Now, understand one thing about me. I'm not going to show the white feather. Whatever it is, I'm going to stick it out. Have you that clear in your head?'

As I looked at the firm little chin I believed her.

'Well, can you enlighten me about the fence? You've heard all that Theodore has to say, and you know the cheerful sort of family I belong to. Did you find anything in the papers?'

'You've read them yourself?' I asked.

'I tried to, but I'm not clever, you see. I thought my grandfather's journal great nonsense. I had never heard of most of the names. But you're good at these things. Did you make nothing of them?'

'Nothing.' I ran over the items in the bundle, not mentioning the Greek manuscript, which seemed to me to have nothing to do with the subject. 'But there must be other papers.'

She flushed slightly. 'There were many others, but I burned them. Perhaps you can guess why.'

'Miss Arabin,' I said, 'I want to help you, but I don't think we need bother about the papers. Let's go back to the beginning. I suppose it's no use my urging you to get out of Plakos, settle in England and wipe all the past out of your memory?'

'Not the slightest.'

'I wonder why. After all it's only common sense.'

'Common cowardice,' she retorted, with a toss of her head. 'I have known Theodore all my life and I have forbidden him to raise that question. I have known you about a month and I forbid *you*.'

There was something so flat-footed and final about her that I laughed. She stared at me haughtily for a moment, and then laughed also.

'Go on with what you were saying,' she said. 'I stay at Plakos, and you must make your book for that. Now then.'

'Your family was unpopular – I understand, justly unpopular. All sorts of wild beliefs grew up about them among the peasants and they have been transferred to you. The people are half savages, and half starved, and their mood is dangerous. They are coming to see in you the cause of their misfortunes. You go there alone and unprotected and you have no friends in the island. The danger is that, after a winter of brooding, they may try in some horrible way to wreak their vengeance on you. That is what I learned from Mr Ertzberger.'

The summary, as I made it, sounded unpleasant enough, but the girl did not seem to feel it so. She nodded briskly. 'That, at any rate, is what Theodore says. He thinks they may make me a sacrifice. Stuff and nonsense, *I* say.'

The word 'sacrifice' disquieted me. It reminded me of the Greek which Vernon had translated.

'Some risk there must be,' I went on, 'but what I cannot tell is the exact amount of it. Even among a savage people unpopularity need not involve tragedy. You were in Plakos last spring. Tell me what happened.'

She fitted a cigarette into a long amber holder, and blew a cloud of smoke which she watched till it disappeared.

'Nothing much. I was left entirely to myself. There was only one servant in the house, old Mitri the steward, and I had also my maid. The whole establishment was sent to Coventry. We had to get our food from the mainland, for we could buy nothing, except now and then a little milk through Mitri's married daughter. It wasn't pleasant, I can tell you. But the worst was when I went for a walk. If I met a man he would make the sign of the evil eye and spit. If I spoke to a child its mother would snatch it up and race indoors with it. The girls and women all wore blue beads as a charm against me and carried garlic. I could smell it wherever I went. Sometimes I wanted to cry and sometimes I wanted to swear, but you can do nothing with a silent boycott. I could have shaken the fools.'

'What had they against you? Did you ever find out?'

'Oh, Mitri used to tell us gossip that he had heard through his daughter, but Mitri isn't too popular himself, and he is old and can go about very little. It seemed they called me Basilissa. That means Queen and sounds friendly enough, but I think the word they really used was *diabolissa*, which means a she-devil. The better disposed ones thought I was a Nereid – that's what they call fairies – but some said I was a *strigla* – that's a horrible kind of harpy, and some thought I was a *vrykolakas*, which is a vampire. They used to light little fires in the graveyards to keep me away. Oh, I got very sick of my reputation. It was a hideous bore not to be able to go anywhere without seeing scared people dodging up by-ways, and making the sign of the cross and screaming for their children – simply damnable.'

'It must have been damnable. I should have thought it rather terrifying too.'

'Don't imagine that they frightened me. I was really more sorry than angry. They were only foolish people scared half out of their minds, and, after all, my family has done a good deal to scare them. It is folly – nothing but folly, and the only way to beat folly is to live it down. I don't blame the poor devils, but I'm going to bring them to a better mind. I refuse to run away because of a pack of fairy tales.'

'There were no hostile acts?' I asked.

She seemed to reflect. 'No,' she answered. 'One morning we found a splash of blood on the house door, which sent old Mitri to his prayers. But that was only a silly joke.'

'Mr Ertzberger hinted that there might be trouble this year from the people in the hills?'

Her face hardened.

'I wish to Heaven I knew that for certain. It would be the best news I ever got. Those hillmen are not my people, and if they interfere I will have them whipped off the place. I will not have any protection against my own peasantry – Theodore is always pressing me, but I won't have it – it would spoil everything – it wouldn't be the game. But if those filthy mountaineers come within a mile of Plakos I will hire a regiment to shoot them down. Pray God they come. We of the coast have always hated the mountains, and I believe I could rally my people.'

'But I thought you owned the whole island?'

'No one owns the hills. My grandfather obtained the seigneury of Plakos, but he never claimed more than the good land by the sea. The hills have always been a no-man's-land full of bandits. We paid them dues – I still pay them – and we did not quarrel, but there was no coming and going between us. They are a different race from our pure Greek stock – mongrels of Slav and Turk, I believe.'

The spirit of the girl comforted me. If Ertzberger's news was true, it might save the situation, and bring the problem out of the realm of groping mystery to a straightforward defence of property . . . But after all the hills were distant, and the scared tenants were at the house door. We must face the nearer peril.

'Is there no one in the village,' I said, 'whom you can have it out with? No big farmer? What about the priests?'

She shook her head. 'No one. The priests do not love my family, for they call themselves Christians, while we are Catholics.'

Twenty years spent in examining witnesses has given me an acute instinct about candour. There was that in the girl's eyes and voice as she spoke which told me that she was keeping something back, something which made her uneasy.

'Tell me everything,' I said. 'Has no priest talked to you?'

'Yes, there was one. I will tell you. He is an old man, and very timid. He came to me at night, after swearing Mitri to tell no one. He urged me to go away for ever.'

Her eyes were troubled now, and had that abstracted look which I had noted before.

'What was his reason?'

'Oh, care for his precious church. He was alarmed about what had happened at Easter.'

She stopped suddenly.

'Have you ever been in Greece at Easter – during the Great Week? No? Then you cannot imagine how queer it is. The people have been starved all Lent, living only on cuttle-fish soup and bread and water. Everyone is pale and thin and ill-tempered. It is like a nightmare.'

Then in rapid staccato sentences she sketched the ritual. She described the night of Good Friday, when the bier with the figure of the crucified Christ on it stands below the chancel step, and the priests chant their solemn hymn, and the women kiss the dead face, and the body is borne out to burial. With torches and candles flickering in the night wind, it is carried through the village streets, while dirges are sung, and the tense crowd breaks now and then into a moan or a sigh. Next day there is no work done, but the people wander about miserably, waiting on something which may be either death or deliverance. That night the church is again crowded, and at midnight the curtains which screen the chancel are opened, and the bier is revealed – empty, but for a shroud. 'Christ is risen,' the priest cries, as a second curtain is drawn back, and in the sanctuary in an ineffable radiance stands the figure of the risen Lord. The people go mad with joy, they light their tapers at the priest's candle, and like a procession of Bacchanals stream out, shouting 'He is risen indeed'. Then to the accompaniment of the firing of guns and the waving of torches the famished peasants, maddened by the miracle they have witnessed, feast till morning on wine and lamb's flesh in the joy of their redemption.

She drew the picture for me so that I saw it as if with my own eyes, and my imagination quickened under the spell of her emotion. For here was no longer the cool matter-of-fact young woman of the world, with no more than tolerance for the folly of superstition. It was someone who could enter into that very mood, and feel its quivering nerves and alternate despair and exultation.

'What had the priest to complain of?' I asked.

'He said that the people were becoming careless of the Easter holiness. He said that last year the attendance at the rite was poor. He feared that they were beginning to think of something else.'

'Something else!' Two of the most commonplace words in the language. She spoke them in an even voice in an ordinary London dining-room, with outside the wholesome bustle of London and the tonic freshness of an English winter day. She was about to go off to a conventional English week-end party at a prosaic country house. But the words affected me strangely, for they seemed to suggest a peril far more deadly than any turbulence of wild men from the hills – a peril, too, of which she was aware.

For she was conscious of it – that was now perfectly clear to me – acutely conscious. She had magnificent self-command, but fear showed out from behind it, like light through the crack of a shutter. Her courage was assuredly not the valour of ignorance. She was terrified, and still resolute to go on.

It was not my business to add to that terror. Suddenly I had come to feel an immense pity and reverence for this girl. Ertzberger was right. Her hardness, her lack of delicacy and repose, her loud frivolity, were only on the surface – a protective sheathing for a tormented soul. Out of a miserable childhood and a ramshackle education she had made for herself a code of honour as fine and as hard as steel. It was wildly foolish, of course, but so perhaps to our dull eyes the innocent and the heroic must always be.

Perhaps she guessed my thoughts. For when she spoke again it was gently, almost hesitatingly.

'I scarcely hoped that you could tell me anything about Plakos. But I rather hoped you would say I am right in what I am doing. Theodore has been so discouraging . . . I rather hoped from your face that you would take a different view. You wouldn't advise me to run away from my job—?'

'God forbid that I should advise you at all,' I said. 'I see your argument, and, if you will let me say so, I profoundly respect it. But I think you are trying yourself – and your friends also – too high. You must agree to some protection.'

'Only if the hill folk give trouble. Don't you see, protection would ruin everything if I accepted it against my own people? I must trust myself to them – and – and stick it out myself. It is a sort of atonement.'

Then she got up briskly and held out her hand. 'Thank you very much, Sir Edward. It has done me good to talk to you. I must be off now or I'll miss my train. I'll give your love to Mollie and Tom.'

'We shall meet again. When do you leave England?'

'Not till March. Of course we'll meet again. Let me know if you have any bright idea . . . Elise, Elise! Where's that fool woman?'

Her maid appeared.

'Get a taxi at once,' she ordered. 'We haven't any time to waste, for I promised to pick up Lord Cheviot at his flat.'

I asked one question as I left. 'Have you ever heard of a place called Kynaetho?'

'Rather. It's the big village in Plakos close to the house.'

SEVEN

I ONCE READ in some book about Cleopatra that that astonishing lady owed her charm to the fact that she was the last of an ancient and disreputable race. The writer cited other cases – Mary of Scots, I think, was one. It seemed, he said, that the quality of high-coloured ancestors flowered in the ultimate child of the race into something like witchcraft. Whether they were good or evil, they laid a spell on men's hearts. Their position, fragile and forlorn, without the wardenship of male kinsfolk, set them on a romantic pinnacle. They were more feminine and capricious than other women, but they seemed, like Viola, to be all the brothers as well as all the daughters of their father's house, for their soft grace covered steel and fire. They were the true sorceresses of history, said my author, and sober men, not knowing why, followed blindly in their service.

Perhaps Koré Arabin was of this sisterhood. At any rate one sober man was beginning to admit her compelling power. I could not get the girl from my thoughts. For one thing I had awakened to a comprehension of her beauty. Her face was rarely out of my mind, with its arrogant innocence, its sudden brilliancies and its as sudden languors. Her movements delighted me, her darting grace, the insolent assurance of her carriage, and then, without warning, the relapse into the child or the hoyden. Even her bad manners soon ceased to annoy me, for in my eyes they had lost all vulgarity. They were the harshnesses of a creature staving off tragedy. Indeed it was her very extravagances that allured, for they made me see her as a solitary little figure set in a patch of light on a great stage among shadows, defying of her own choice the terrors of the unknown.

What made my capture complete was the way she treated me. She seemed to have chosen me as her friend, and to find comfort and security in being with me. To others she might be rude and petulant, but never to me. Whenever she saw me she would make straight for me, like a docile child waiting for orders. She would dance or sit out with me till her retinue of youth was goaded to fury. She seemed to guess at the points in her behaviour which I did not like and to strive to amend them. We had become the closest friends, and friendship with Koré Arabin was a dangerous pastime.

The result was that I was in a fair way of making a fool of myself. No . . . I don't think I was in love with her. I had never been in love in my life, so I was not an expert on the subject, but I fancied that love took people in a different way. But I was within measurable distance of asking her to be my wife. My feeling was a mixture of affection and pity and anxiety. She had appealed to me, and I had become her champion. I wanted to protect her, but how was a middle-aged lawyer to protect a determined girl from far-away perils which he did not comprehend? The desperate expedient of marriage occurred to me, but I did not believe she would accept me, and, if she did, would not the mating of age and youth be an outrage and a folly? Nevertheless I was in a mood to venture even on that.

I must have presented a strange spectacle to my friends. There were other men of forty in London at the time who behaved as if they were twenty-five – one buxom Cabinet Minister was to be seen at every dance – but none, I am certain, cut an odder figure than I. The dancing Cabinet Minister sought the ball-room for exercise, because he preferred dancing to golf. I had no such excuse, for I danced comparatively little; my object was patently the society of one particular lady. In Koré's train I found myself in strange haunts. I followed her into the Bohemian *coulisses* to which Shelley Arabin's daughter had an entrée – queer studio parties in Chelsea where the women were shorn and the men left shaggy: the feverish literary and artistic salons of the emancipated and rather derelict middle-class: dances given at extravagant restaurants by the English and foreign new-rich, where I did not know or wish to know one single soul. Also we appeared together at houses which I had frequented all my life, and there my friends saw me. Of course they talked. I fancy that for about two months I was the prime subject of London gossip. I didn't care a hang, for I was in a queer obstinate excitable mood. We hunted together, too, and there is no such nursery of scandal as the hunting-field. With a great deal of work on hand I found this new life a considerable strain, and I was perfectly conscious that I was playing the fool. But, though I don't think I was in love with her, I simply could not let the girl out of my sight.

Now and then my conscience awoke and I realised with a shock that the time was slipping past, and that the real problem was still unsolved. I knew that I could not shake Koré in her resolution, and I suppose I hoped blindly that something would occur to prevent her acting on it. That something could only be a love affair. I was perfectly certain that she was not in love with me, but she might accept me, and at the back of my head I had the intention of putting it to the test. Ertzberger had divined what was going on and seemed to approve. 'A boy is no use to her,' he said more than once. 'Besides she wouldn't look at one. She must marry a grown man.' He implied that I filled the bill, and the man's assumption gave me an absurd pleasure. If anyone had told me that I would one day go out of my way to cultivate a little Jew financier, I would have given him the lie, yet the truth is that, when I was not with Koré, I hungered for Ertzberger's company. He alone understood what was in my mind, and shared my anxieties. 'She must not go back,' he kept declaring; 'at all costs she must be kept away from Plakos – at any rate during this spring. I get disquieting reports. There is mischief brewing in the hills, and the people of the coast have had a bitter winter of famine. There has been a lot of sickness too, and in the village at the house gates the mortality among the children has been heavy.'

'You mean Kynaetho?' I asked.

'Kynaetho.' He looked at me curiously. 'You seem to have been getting up the subject . . . Well, I don't like it. If she goes there in April there may be a disaster. Upon my soul, we should be justified in having her kidnapped and shut up in some safe place till the summer. So far as I can learn, the danger is only in the spring. Once let the people see the crops springing and the caiques bringing in fish, and they will forget their grievances.'

Early in March I was dining with the Nantleys, and after dinner Mollie took me aside for a talk. As I have told you, she is one of my oldest friends, for when I was a grubby little private schoolboy and she was a girl of thirteen we used to scamper about together. I had had her son Hugo in my chambers, before he went into Parliament, and Wirlesdon has always been a sort of home to me. Mollie was entitled to say anything she liked, but when she spoke it was rather timidly.

'I hear a good deal of talk about you,' she said, 'and I can't help noticing too. Do you think it is quite fair, Ned?'

'Fair to whom?' I asked.

'To Koré Arabin. You're different from the boys who run after her. You're a distinguished man with a great reputation. Is it fair to her to turn her head?'

'Is that very likely? What if she has turned mine?'

'Do you really mean that?' she cried. 'I never thought of it in that way. Do you honestly want to marry her?'

'I don't know . . . I don't know what I want except that I must stand by her. She's in an appallingly difficult position, and badly needs a friend.'

'Yes. But there's only one way in which a man can protect a young woman. Do you mean to marry her?'

'She wouldn't accept me.'

'But you mean to ask her?'

'It may come to that,' I said.

'But, Ned dear, can't you see it wouldn't do? Koré is not the right sort of wife for you. She's–she's too— Well, you've a career before you. Is she the woman to share it with you?'

'It's not many months since at Wirlesdon you implored my charity for Miss Arabin.'

'Oh, I don't want to say a word against her, and if you were really desperately in love I would say nothing and wish you luck. But I don't believe you are. I believe it's what you say – charity, and that's a most rotten foundation to build on.'

Mollie in such affairs is an incurable romantic.

'I promise never to ask her to marry me unless I am in love,' I said.

'Well, that means you are not quite in love yet. Hadn't you better draw back before it is too late? I can't bear to see you making a bad blunder, and Koré, dear child, would be a bad blunder for you. She's adorably pretty, and she has wonderful qualities, but she is a little savage, and very young, and quite unformed. Really, really it wouldn't do.'

'I admit the difficulties, my dear Mollie. But never mind me, and think of Miss Arabin. You said yourself that she was English at heart and would be very happy settled in England.'

'But not with you.'

'She wouldn't accept me, and I may never propose. But if I did, and she accepted me, why not with me?'

'Because you're you – because you're too good for a rash experiment.'

'I'm not good enough for her, for I'm too old, as you've just told me. But anyhow your argument thinks principally of me, not of Miss Arabin. It is she who matters.'

Mollie rose with a gesture of impatience. 'You are hopeless, Ned. I'm sick of you hard, unsusceptible, ambitious people. You never fall in love in your youth, but wait till after forty and then make idiots of yourselves.'

I had a different kind of remonstrance from Vernon. We saw little of each other in these days beyond a chance word in the street or a casual wave of the hand in the club smoking-room. When I thought of him it was with a sense of shame that I had let him slip so hopelessly out of my life. Time had been when he was my closest friend, and when his problem was also my problem. Now the whole story of his dream seemed a childish fancy.

One night in March I found him waiting for me in my rooms.

'I came round to say good-bye,' he said. 'I shall probably leave London very soon.'

It shows how completely I had forgotten his affairs that I did not remember that his particular crisis was drawing near, that, as he believed, the last door in his dream-world would soon be opened.

Then, before I could ask about his plans, he suddenly broke out:

'Look here, I hope there's no truth in what people tell me.'

His tone had the roughness of one very little at his ease, and it annoyed me. I asked coldly what he meant.

'You know what I mean – that you're in love with Miss What's-her-name – the girl I met at Wirlesdon.'

'I don't know that you've any right to ask the question, and I'm certainly not going to answer it.'

'That means that you are in love,' he cried. 'Good God, man, don't tell me that you want to marry that – that tawdry girl!'

I must have reddened, for he saw that he had gone too far.

'I don't mean that – I apologise. I have no reason to say anything against her.'

Then his tone changed.

'Ned, old man, we have been friends for a long time and you must forgive me if I take liberties. We have never had any secrets from each other. My own affairs give me a good deal to think about just now, but I can't go away with an easy mind till I know the truth about you. For God's sake, old fellow, don't do anything rash. Promise me you won't propose to her till I come back in April.'

His change of manner had softened me, and as I saw the trouble in his honest eyes I felt a return of the old affection.

'Why are you anxious on my account?'

'Because,' he said solemnly, 'I know that if you married that girl our friendship would be over. I feel it in my bones. She would always come between us.'

'I can't make any promises of that kind. But one thing I can promise – that no woman will ever break our friendship.'

'You don't understand. Some women wouldn't, but that girl—! Well, I can say no more. Good-bye, Ned. I'll hunt you up when I come back.'

He left me with a feeling of mingled regret and irritation. I hated to go against Vernon's wishes, but his manner when he had spoken of Koré, the look in his eyes, the inflection of his voice, conveyed an utter distaste which made me angry. I pictured him at Severns nursing his unreasoning dislike of the poor child. Vernon, as my nephew Charles had said, was a prig, and his narrow world had room only for blameless and vapid virginity. The promise he had asked of me was an outrage.

Yet I kept a promise which I had never made. For suddenly Cinderella disappeared from the ball. After a country-house dance I drove her back to town in my car, and left her at the door of her flat. During the long drive she had talked more seriously than I had ever known her to talk before, had spoken of herself and her affairs with a kind of valiant simplicity. The only sophisticated thing about her was her complexion. All day afterwards my conviction was growing that she was the woman for me, that I could make her not only secure but happy. We were by way of dining with the Lamanchas, and I think if we had met that night I should have asked her to marry me . . . But we did not meet, for by the evening she was gone.

I looked for her in vain in the Lamanchas' drawing-room and my hostess guessed what I sought. 'I'm so sorry about

Koré Arabin,' she whispered to me. 'She was coming tonight, but she telephoned this afternoon that she was unexpectedly called out of town.' I did not enjoy my dinner, and as soon as I could decently leave I hurried off to her flat. It was shut up, and from the porter on the ground floor I learned that she and her maid had left with a quantity of luggage to catch the night boat to France. He was positive that she had gone abroad, for he had seen the foreign labels, and Miss Arabin had told him she would not be back for months. The keys of the flat had been sent to her solicitors.

With a very uneasy mind I drove to the Ertzbergers' house in Belgrave Square. Ertzberger had just come in from a City dinner, and his wife seemed to be giving some kind of musical party, for the hall was full of coats and hats and extra footmen, and the jigging of fiddles drifted down the staircase. He took me to his study at the back of the house, and when he heard my news his face grew as solemn as my own. There was nothing to be done that night, for the Continental mail had long since gone, so I went back to my chambers with a pretty anxious mind. I felt that I had let something rare and precious slip out of my hand, but far more that this preciousness was in instant danger. Honestly I don't think that I was much concerned about myself. I wanted Koré Arabin saved – for me – for everyone – for the world. If I was in love with her it was with an affection more impersonal than usually goes by that name. It was as if an adored child had gone missing.

Regardless of our many engagements, Ertzberger and I appeared on the doorstep of Messrs Mower & Lidderdale, the solicitors, at the hour when according to the information given me by telephone the senior partner usually arrived. Mr Mower confirmed our fears. Miss Arabin had returned to Plakos; she had been preparing for some weeks for the journey; he had not advised it – indeed he had not been asked his advice nor would he have dared to volunteer it. 'A very strong-minded young lady,' he repeated – 'I might almost say strong-headed.' She had sold the lease of her flat, and had left no instructions about her return. Yes, she was well supplied with money. Miss Arabin was her own mistress absolutely, for her father had created no trust. He had nothing more to tell us, and Ertzberger departed for the City and I for the Temple.

In the afternoon I was rung up by Ertzberger in my room in

the House of Commons. He had been making inquiries, he said – he had his own ways of doing that sort of thing – and he had discovered that Koré had recently sold large parcels of stocks. She had been selling out steadily throughout the winter, and now had practically no investments left. The proceeds had been deposited on current account in her bank. There his information stopped, but he was profoundly disquieted. 'That child has all her fortune in cash under her hand,' he said, 'and God knows what she means to do with it. Any moment she may beggar herself, and no one can prevent her.'

That night I understood that my infatuation was over, if indeed it had ever existed. I wanted the girl safe, and I did not care who saved her, but I wanted it so much that at the moment nothing in heaven or earth seemed to matter in comparison.

It was now near the end of March, the Courts had just risen and Parliament was about to adjourn for the Easter vacation. I had a good deal of important work on hand, but I was entitled to a holiday, and I thought I could arrange for at any rate a fortnight's absence from town. But whether I could arrange it or not I meant to go, for I could no more settle to my tasks than a boy can settle to Tacitus on the day he is playing for his school. When Ertzberger according to our arrangement turned up at my chambers that night after dinner, he found me busy with an atlas and a Continental Bradshaw.

'I am going to Plakos,' I said.

'That is good. You are still a young man, and you have been a soldier. It is very good. But if you had not gone, I had decided to go myself.'

'This is Wednesday. Miss Arabin left last night. She will get there – when?'

He made some calculations. 'Not before Tuesday. You might overtake her, but I do not think that is necessary. Easter is the danger point and the Greek Easter is still a fortnight off. Besides you must stop a day in Athens.'

'I shall want help. Can you get me half-a-dozen handy fellows I can trust?'

'I had thought of that. Indeed I telegraphed about it this afternoon. I can find you the men – and money, of course, if you want it. I will find you a lieutenant, too, and make all arrangements about transport. That at least I can do. You realise, Sir Edward, that there is a certain danger in this enterprise?'

'I realise that Miss Arabin in a week's time will be in deadly danger . . . I must have a day or two to wind up my work here. I think I can leave on Saturday morning.'

As a matter of fact I left London on the Friday night.

Part Two

EIGHT

I CAME TO Plakos in a blind sea-fog. After a day and a night of storm the wind died utterly, and we made the isle on a compass course, feeling our way in by constant soundings. A thick salt dew hung on every stay and hawser, the deck and bulwarks swam with moisture, and our coats were in an instant drenched as if we had been out in a hurricane. Sea and land alike were invisible. The air was thick and oppressive to the breath, and every muscle in the body felt weak and flaccid. Also there was a strange quiet – only the ripple caused by our slow movement and the creak of sodden cordage. I might have been a shade looking on an island of the dead.

I had reached Athens in record time, but there I found a weariful delay. In spite of Ertzberger's influence the wheels were clogged. I was met at the Piraeus by his agent, one Constantine Maris, whose instructions were to hold himself at my disposal. I took to Maris at once – a young fellow of thirty, who had been in the Greek regular army and had been the right-hand man of Zimbrakis when at Salonika his troops declared for Venizelos. He had been all through the war till it ended in Bulgaria's submission, had been twice wounded and once in prison, and had been chosen by Ertzberger to represent him in Athens because of his truculent honesty and tireless energy. Both in character and appearance he was more like a Frenchman than a Greek – a Norman, for choice, for he had reddish-brown hair and a high- bridged northern nose. He had the additional merit of being well educated, having put in two years at the Sorbonne: and he talked excellent French. His family were of Athens, but his mother, I think, was from one of the islands. He had the looks and manners of a soldier.

But Maris had found the task set him almost impossible. Ertzberger had bidden him get together a batch of reliable fellows who would obey orders and ask no questions, but as we rumbled Athens-ward from the Piraeus in the little train he confessed that such men were not to be found. In the war it was otherwise, but the best had all gone back to the country villages. He had collected a dozen but he was not enthusiastic about them, except a certain Janni, who had been a corporal in his old battalion. When he paraded them for my inspection I was inclined to agree with him. They were an odd mixture – every kind of clothes from the dirty blue jeans of the stoker to the black coat and pointed yellow shoes of the clerk – ages from nineteen to sixty – physique from prize-fighter to sneak-thief. All had served in the war, however, and the best of them, Janni, had an empty left sleeve. After much consultation we dismissed two and were left with ten who at any rate looked honest. Whether they would be efficient was another matter. Maris proposed to arm them with revolvers, but not till we got to Plakos, in case they started shooting up the town. They were told that they were wanted as guards for an estate which was threatened by brigands, but I doubt if they believed it. The younger ones seemed to think that our object was piracy.

Transport was another problem. I had hoped to be able to hire a small steam yacht, but such a thing was not to be had, and the best we could do was to induce a dissolute-looking little Leghorn freighter, named the *Santa Lucia*, to go out of its way and touch at Plakos. Maris told the captain a yarn about men being needed there for making a new sea-wall. The boat was bound for the Dodecanese, and would pick us up on her return a fortnight later.

Before we rounded Cape Sunium we got into foul weather, a heavy north-easter and violent scurries of rain. Our ruffians were all sea-sick and lay about like logs, getting well cursed by the Italian sailors, while Maris and I in the one frowzy little cabin tried to make a plan of campaign. I found out at once that Maris was well informed about the situation in Plakos, partly from Ertzberger and partly from his own knowledge. He knew about Shelley Arabin's career, which seemed to be the common talk of the Aegean. Of Koré he had heard nothing save from Ertzberger, but he had much to tell me of Plakos and its people. They had a name for backwardness and turbulence, and the Government seemed to leave them very much to themselves. There were gendarmes, of course, in the island, but he fancied they didn't function. But the place had sent good soldiers to Venizelos, and its people were true Hellenes. After an interval when he expatiated on that Hellenic empire of the islands which was the dream of good Venizelists, he returned to their superstition. 'That is the curse of my countrymen,' he cried. 'They are priest-ridden.' He was himself, he told me, a free-thinker and despised all mumbo-jumbo.

I told him that the trouble was not with the priests, but he did not seem to understand, and I did not attempt to explain.

Our task as he saw it was straightforward enough – to protect the House during the Easter season when fear of the girl as a witch and the memory of Shelley's misdeeds might induce some act of violence. There was also the trouble with the hill folk, and this seemed to him the greater danger. The dwellers in the stony mountains which filled the centre and south of the island had always been out of hand, and, since the winter had been cruel and the war had unsettled the whole earth, he thought it likely that they might have a try at looting the House, which they no doubt held to be full of treasure, since the Arabins had a name for wealth. I could see that he didn't quite believe in danger from the coast folk, however beastly their superstitions might be. He had the Greek respect for a mountaineer and contempt for the ordinary peasant.

We studied the map – a very good one prepared for the British Navy – and on Maris's advice I decided to begin by dividing our forces. My first business was to get into the House and discover how things were going. But with danger threatening from the hills it would be unwise for all of us to concentrate in a place from which egress might be difficult. Now the House stood at the north-west corner of the island, and the hill country began about ten miles to the south-east. He proposed to send five of our men, under Corporal Janni, to a little port called Vano on the west coast some miles south of the House. They would take supplies with them – we were well provided with these – and reconnoitre towards the hills, giving out that they were a Government survey party. The rest of us would land at the House, and, after satisfying ourselves about the position, would get in touch with Janni by the overland route. Our first business was strictly reconnaissance: Janni could not hope to prevent mischief from the hills if it were really on its way, but he could satisfy himself as to its extent and character, and then join us in the defence of the House, which was our main task. Maris was confident about this. He did not see how a dozen armed men in a strong place could fail to hold off a mob of undisciplined peasants.

For an extra payment the captain of the *Santa Lucia* was induced to carry Janni and his men to Vano. Weapons were served out to all, and I gave Janni a map which he professed to be able to read. Then in the shrouding fog Maris and I and our five got into the ship's one boat and were rowed ashore. We had our supplies both of food and ammunition in half-a-dozen wooden cases, and the wretched cockle was pretty low in the water. I knew from my former visit that the landing-place was just below the House, and the fog seemed to me a godsend, for it would enable us to get indoors unobserved. My only doubt was the kind of reception we might get from Koré.

As it turned out, the mist was our undoing. We were landed at a stone jetty in a dead white blanket which made it difficult to see a yard ahead. Our baggage was put on shore, the boat started back, and in a moment both sound and sight of it were swallowed up. It was an eerie business, and I felt the craziness of our errand as I stood blinking on the wet cobbles. There was no human being about, but the dim shapes of several caiques and some kind of lugger seemed to show below us as we started along the jetty. Our five ruffians had recovered from their sea-sickness, and, feeling solid ground beneath them, were inclined to be jolly. One of them started a song, which I promptly checked. Maris ordered them to wait behind with the boxes, and to keep dead quiet, while he and I prospected inland.

My recollection of that visit in 1914 was hazy, for I had only seen the landing-place from the causeway above it, and at the time I had been too preoccupied to observe accurately. But I was pretty certain that at the shore end of the jetty there were some rough stone steps which led to the causeway. I groped for them in the mist but could not find them. Instead I came on a broad track which bore the mark of wheels and which led away to the left. I waited for the steep to begin, but found no sign of it. The land was dead flat for a long way, and then I came on a rough boundary wall.

It was an orchard with blossoming trees – that much I could see through the brume – and at the end was a cottage. My first thought was to retrace my steps and try a cast to the right, for I still believed that we had found the proper landing-place, and had somehow missed the causeway. But, as I hesitated, there came one of those sudden clearings in the air which happen in the densest fogs, and I had a prospect of some hundreds of yards around me. We were on the edge of a village, the cottage we had reached was at the extreme seaward end a little detached from the rest; beyond lay what seemed to be a shallow valley with no sign of the House and its embattled hill.

It would have been well for us if there and then we had turned and gone back to the jetty, even at the risk of relinquishing our supplies and having to scramble for miles along a difficult shore. For, of course, we had come in that infernal fog to the wrong place. The skipper had landed us at Kynaetho instead of below the House, and though I knew from the map that Kynaetho was at the House's gates, yet it was on the east side, distant at least two miles by coast from the spot which Vernon and I had visited.

It was Maris who decided me. The cottage seemed a solitary place where discreet inquiries might be made without rousing attention. He had little stomach for wandering around Plakos in fog, and we had our five men and the baggage to think of. I followed him into the rough courtyard, paved with cobbles, and strewn with refuse. The low walls were washed with red ochre and above the lintel a great black pentacle was painted. Also over the door was hung a bunch of garlic.

There was a woman standing in the entry watching us. Maris took off his hat with a flourish, and poured out a torrent of soft-sounding dialect. She replied in a harsher accent, speaking with the back of her throat. She seemed to be inviting us to enter, but her face was curiously without expression, though her eyebrows worked nervously. She was a middle-aged woman, terribly disfigured by smallpox; her features were regular, and she had large, prominent, vacant black eyes. She was not in the least repulsive, but somehow she was not reassuring.

As we entered the cottage she called out to someone at the back. A second later I heard footsteps as of a child running.

Maris, as I learned afterwards, told her the story we had agreed on – that we were a Government survey party sent from Athens to make a map of the island. Then he felt his way to more delicate subjects. This was Kynaetho, he understood? There was a large house near which belonged to some foreigners? English, weren't they? Where, exactly, did it lie from the village, for, if he might venture to explain what madam no doubt knew, one must have a starting-point for a survey, and the Government had chosen that house?

The woman's eyebrows twitched, and she crossed herself. She flung a hand over her left shoulder. 'The place is there,' she said. 'I know nothing of it. I do not speak of it.'

All the time she was looking at us with her staring empty eyes, and I realised that she was in an extreme fright. There was certainly nothing in our appearance to discompose her, and I had the uneasy feeling which one has in the presence of a human being who is suffering from an emotion that one cannot fathom. Maris whispered to me that he did not like the look of things. 'She has not offered us food,' he said.

Her ear must have caught some sound from out-of-doors, for her face suddenly showed relief. She walked to a window and cried to someone outside. Then she turned to us. 'There are men now to speak with you.' She had found her tongue, for as she hustled us out she kept muttering, with sidelong glances at us, what seemed to be an invocation to Saint Nicolas. Also she gripped Maris violently by the shoulder and spat words into his ear. He told me afterwards that she was advising him not to be a fool and to go home.

The little courtyard had filled with people, most of them men, but with two or three old crones in the forefront. Their aspect was not threatening, but rather puzzled and timid. The men took off their hats in response to Maris's bow, and politely waited for him to speak. I noticed that they were a well-made, upstanding lot, but with the same flat expressionlessness as the woman of the cottage, and I guessed that that was a mask to hide fear.

Maris told them the same story of our errand. He said – I repeat what he told me later – that our men and baggage were still down by the beach, and that he wanted to be directed to the inn. There was dead silence. The little crowd stared at us as if their lives depended on it, but not a syllable came in reply.

This made Maris angry. 'Are you dumb mules,' he asked, 'not to answer a simple question? I have heard that you of the islands boasted of your hospitality. Is this the way to treat strangers?'

Still no answer. His taunts were as futile as his exposition. But, since I had nothing to do but to look on, I saw something which made me uneasy. The crowd was drawing together, and each was covertly touching the other's sleeve. There was a purpose in this mob, a purpose of action, and I don't like that kind of purpose when it is accompanied by fear.

'Since you will not speak,' Maris cried, 'I will go to your priest. Where is his dwelling? Or do you treat your church as you treat your visitors?'

This time he got a reply. A dozen voices spoke, and a dozen hands pointed towards the village.

'It seems you are not dumb after all? We will seek a lodging from the priest, who doubtless has some regard for his country's Government. We have baggage with us – boxes of instruments and food – and they are now at the jetty. I want two able-bodied fellows to help carry them, and I will pay them well. Who offers?'

But no one offered. Once again they were like gaping cattle. And then an old beldam in the foreground, who had been crossing herself vigorously, cried out a monosyllable and it was taken up in a shout.

Maris turned to me with an angry smile. 'They are advising us to go home. I can mention an island, my friend, in which there is going to be trouble. Let us go back to the shore. Perhaps the sight of our belongings will change their mind.'

They did not obstruct us, but opened a lane for us to pass – opened it with feverish haste, as if they were afraid of coming too near us. The fog had now thinned to a light haze, through which I already felt the glow of the sun. As we moved shorewards they trailed after us, keeping always a respectful distance, and halted fifty yards from the jetty.

Our five fellows were sitting smoking on the boxes, and since we could get no help from the villagers there was nothing for it but to carry the baggage ourselves. My first notion was to go straight to the House, of which by this time I could judge the whereabouts, and it would have been well for us perhaps if I had acted on that impulse. But, until I had prepared the way, I was shy of facing Koré Arabin with a defence force which would make her furious, and I had a notion too that if I marched in broad daylight to the House gates there might be trouble with these scared and sullen natives. So I decided to go first to the inn, where we could leave our stuff, and then to interview the priest. After all, I knew from Koré that the priest was alarmed about the local situation, and from him I might get some counsel. It seemed to me a case for wary walking.

I could have laughed at that progress villagewards, if I hadn't been so anxious. The mob in front of us had doubled in size, and retreated mechanically before us till we were in the village street. The sun was now bright in the sky, and I had a view of the straggling houses, grouped thickly in the centre where there seemed to be a kind of *place*, and thinning out into farms and enclosures on the slopes of the green hills. It was a wide, shallow vale bounded on the south by low ridges; but on the west rose a higher tree-clad hill, and there were glimpses of white masonry which I took to be the House. Once we were in the village the crowd was enlarged by women and children. They kept a good distance, retiring a pace for every step we took, and when we entered the untidy square they huddled against the house doors as if they were forming guard. They were perfectly silent, even the children. It was an eerie business, I can assure you, promenading before that speechless, staring gallery. They were not an ill-looking race, as I have said, for the men were mostly well-built and upstanding, and though the old wives looked like the Witch of Endor the young ones were often comely. But you could see that they were bitter poor, for their cheeks were thin and their eyes hollow. And beyond doubt they were in the throes of some nervous terror. I felt as if at any moment something might snap and the air be filled with a wild screaming.

The inn was easy enough to find. A big plane tree grew before it, and in the yard behind the low whitewashed walls grew a second, beside a stone fountain which had not been erected within these last five hundred years. The place was only a wineshop, with no guest-rooms for travellers, but there were ample outbuildings where our men could encamp. But there was no sign of any landlord. Maris and I pushed indoors and found no trace of life in the big drinking-room with its sanded floor, or in the purlieus beyond. The inn folk must have gone to swell the crowd in the street. But we found a reasonably clean barn at the back of the yard, and there Maris bade our fellows make their quarters, get ready their breakfast and await our return. Then the two of us set out to find the priest.

The villagers had not pressed nearer. When we emerged into the street they were standing as we had left them, patiently staring. Maris cried out, asking to be shown the priest's house, and at that the spell seemed to be broken, for there was a shout in reply. A visit to the priest seemed to be in the popular view the right course for us to take. We were directed to a house a hundred yards on, next door to a squat church, and to my surprise we were not followed. Once they had seen us enter, the crowd remained to watch the inn door.

The priest had evidently been apprised of our coming. His dwelling was only a bigger cottage, but in the furnishing of it there were a few signs of a class above the peasantry – a shelf of books, one or two gaudy religious pictures, a Swiss cuckoo clock, and, incongruously enough, two of the cheap copies of Tanagra statuettes which they sell in the Athens shops. I dare say he imagined that they were figures of saints. He was an old man, nearer eighty than seventy to my eye, and much bent in the shoulders. An unkempt beard fell over his chest, and his white hair was long and brushed back from his forehead like a recent fashion among young men in England. The skin was waxen white, and the lines on his face were like the grey shadows in a snowdrift. His eyes were mild, benevolent and fanatical. He looked stupid but kind and, like everybody else in that mad place, horribly frightened.

With him Maris went straight to the point.

'We are a Government survey party, Pappa,' he said. 'But that story is for the peasants. To you we open our hearts. This gentleman is a colonel in the army of Britain, and likewise a member of the British Government. He is also a friend of the lady in the House of Plakos. What gadfly has bitten the people of this island? Come! We know much already but we would hear your tale.'

The priest – his venerable name was Hieronymos – was ready enough to tell. With a wealth of gesticulation remarkable in one so ancient, but always with a lowered voice, he repeated crudely what we already knew. The people of Plakos had suffered much and long, and were now resolved to make an end of their incubus. The girl was a witch and they had determined that she must die. They were only waiting till the convenient season. All this he said in the most matter-of-fact tone, as if it were a natural sequence of cause and effect.

'But you would not consent to such barbarity?' Maris asked.

'My consent is not asked,' he replied. 'Beyond doubt the woman is evil and comes of an evil stock. But the Scriptures teach mercy, and, though doubtless death is deserved, I would not counsel it. For if she is evil she is also witless. Why else did she return here, when she knew that the whole island desired her death? Did I not go to her secretly, as Nicodemus went to our Lord, and besought her never to return? And she has given immense sums of money to her enemies. Me she gave gold for the Church and that I have secure, but she has given it to others who have bought guns. The men from the hills, who are most bitter against her, carry rifles bought with her money.'

Now I knew why the foolish child had realised her investments.

The priest was gaining confidence.

'The death of a witch may be a righteous deed,' he said, 'but the hearts of this people are not righteous. They are dabbling in a blacker magic than hers, for they are following the Outland Things. And that is heresy and blasphemy, which in the eyes of Holy Church are sins not less mortal than witchcraft.'

Real anger, the jealous anger of a priest for his own prerogatives, blazed in his old eyes. He used for 'outland things' the word *exotika*, the very word which had puzzled Vernon in the manuscript I gave him, till he found help from Basil of Caesarea. The word caught my ear and I made Maris translate for me. He had clearly no compassion for poor Koré, but he was up in arms for his Church. Maris tried to probe the trouble, but he got the vaguest answers. The man seemed eager to unburden his soul and yet terrified to speak, and his eyes were always turning to the window and the closed street door.

Last Eastertide there had been a lamentable neglect of sacred rites. This year the carelessness was complete. Holy Week had begun, but the minds of the people were not on its solemnities. 'They fast indeed,' he said, 'but they do not pray.' They had gone a-whoring after other gods, and what those other gods were it did not become a Christian man to consider. They meditated a sacrifice, but they had forgotten the sacrifice on which their salvation hung. 'There is a madness which surges up at times in these islands. It happened so in my grandfather's day in Santorini, and there is no quelling it till some black deed has been done and the people come to their right minds in a bitter repentance.' He, their priest, had become less regarded than a cur dog. Men stopped talking in the streets when he drew near, and would not meet his eyes. If he spoke, they moved off. They were conscious of a guilty purpose, and yet resolved on it, and he was powerless to check them. 'They will come back, doubtless, and bemoan their folly, but in the meantime they are breaking the hearts of the saints and loading their miserable souls with sin.'

Then he broke off and his face took an expression of shrewdness.

'You have brought men with you. How many?'

Maris told him ten stout fellows all armed.

'What foolishness!' he cried. 'The Government should have sent a regiment – a regiment with cannons. The madmen in Plakos are fifty times your number, and they have the hill folk at their back, and that is a thousand more.'

'Nevertheless,' said Maris, 'we may be sufficient to garrison the House, and protect the lady. I have heard that it is a strong place.'

He looked at us queerly. 'No garrison is sufficient against fire. They will burn the House and all that is in it . . . Listen to me, sirs. I do not think as you think. I have no care for the woman nor for any of her accursed race, but I have much care for the souls of this wayward people, and would save them from mortal sin. There are no two ways about it – the woman must burn or she must depart. Can you carry her off?'

Maris translated to me rapidly. 'Things look ugly,' he said, 'and I rather think this old one talks sense. But to carry off the lady we must have a ship, and God knows where we shall find one. At Vano perhaps? Maybe we did wrong to separate our forces. It strikes me that the sooner we get into touch with friend Janni the better. It is indicated that one of us must presently make his way into the House, and that one had better be you. Let us interrogate the old one about the topography of this damned village.'

'You must enter the House,' said the priest, in reply to Maris's question, 'but it will be a task, I promise you, for Digenes the Cyprian. The place is guarded at all hours, and no one enters or leaves it without the knowledge of the warders. But it might be achieved by bold men under cover of dark. The moon is nearing its full, and when it has set in the small hours there might be a chance.'

I got out the map of the island, and tried to get him to give me my bearings. But he was hopeless with a map, and instead on the white hearth-stone he drew a plan of his own. The main road to the House from Kynaetho ran west from the village square, up a lane lined with crofts and past a big olive grove, till it reached the wood of chestnuts which was the beginning of the demesne. All the ground on this side rose steeply, and there were dwellings almost to the gates, so that it would be hard to escape detection. To the left the slopes curved in a shallow vale, bounded on the east by the main road to the hills and to Vano, and to south and west by a rim of upland beyond which lay the rugged coastline and the sea. This vale was broad and flat, and tilted up gently towards the west, and it bore the curious name of the Dancing Floor. In the old days, said the priest, the *panegyria* were held in it, the island festivals before poverty and madness came to Plakos. The Dancing Floor bordered on the demesne, and he thought that a way of entry might be found there.

I made Maris ask about the shore road, but the priest was emphatic against it. There was no way into the House on that side except by the staircases from the jetty, which Vernon and I had seen in 1914, and there it was certain the watchers would be most vigilant. Besides the staircases were disused, and he believed that the postern doors had been walled up. The cliffs could not be climbed, and if the coast was followed towards the south the difficulties increased. From my recollection of the place, I thought he exaggerated, but I was not prepared to bank on a dim memory.

'There is no time to lose,' he said, with an earnestness which convinced me that, though our motives might be different, our purposes were alike. 'In two days it will be Good Friday, and the night after comes the solemn hour when our Lord breaks the bonds of death. I grievously fear that that is the hour which my foolish folk have fixed for this sacrilege. If great sin is to be averted, the woman must be gone by then and the House given to the flames. The flames, I say, for whatever happens, there will be no peace in Plakos till it is in ashes. But let it be burned honestly and religiously, and not made an altar to the outland devils whom Holy Church has long ago cast into the darkness.'

The problem seemed to me to be clarifying itself. I was inclined to think that the priest was too badly scared to take a balanced view of things, and also too wrapped up in his religious anxieties. I agreed that we must somehow induce Koré to come away, and that for this purpose we must get all our ten men together and beg, borrow or steal some kind of boat. It was also plain that the sooner I got inside the House the better, for Koré would need some persuading. I was not able to view the black magic of the villagers quite seriously. It was obviously a real peril, but it was so wholly outside the range of my mental conception that I took it as a straightforward risk, like that from a wild animal or a thunderstorm.

Maris and I had a short talk in French and settled our plans. He would go back to the inn and see our fellows fixed up for the night. Then he would make his way on foot towards Vano and get into touch with Janni. We fixed a point on his map, on the edge of the cliffs about two miles south of the House, where he was to bring Janni and his posse, and where next morning I was to take out the others to join him. There seemed no risk in leaving the five men in the inn for the night. The villagers would scarcely interfere with strangers who purported to be a Government survey party and had no desire to move. Nor was it likely that any obstacle would be set in the way of Maris's own journey. After all he was moving towards Vano and away from the prohibited area.

My own case was more intricate. If I went back to the inn, it would be harder to make my way from it to the Dancing Floor, for I should have the village street to go through. We put this to the priest, and he proved unexpectedly helpful. Why should I not stay on in his house till the evening? The church was adjacent, and behind the church lay the graveyard, by which a road could be found to the Dancing Floor. He would give me food, if I cared to share his humble meal. The old fellow might be a bigot, but he was honest and friendly and patently on our side. I beamed on him and thanked him in dumb show, while Maris made ready to start.

'Get into the House somehow and fix up a plan with the lady,' he said. 'That is the first job. You are quite clear about the rendezvous on the cliffs? You had better get back to the inn somehow, and tomorrow morning bring the men to join me there. The village will think we've started on our surveying – and a long way off the danger-point. You will have to open the boxes and make each man carry his own supplies. You have your gun?'

I patted my pocket. 'Yes, but there isn't going to be any shooting. We haven't a dog's chance at that game, with Miss Arabin arming the natives with Mauser rifles.'

NINE

MANY TIMES THAT day I wished that my education had included modern Greek. Through the hot afternoon and evening I remained in the little room, bored and anxious and mystified, while the priest sat opposite me, a storehouse of vital knowledge which I could not unlock. I raked up my recollection of classical Greek and tried him with a sentence or two, but he only shook his head. Most of the time he read in a little book, a breviary no doubt, and his lips muttered. An old woman came in and made ready a meal. We lunched off onion soup and black bread and a very odd-tasting cheese, and I was given a glass of some wine which smacked of turpentine. I smoked one of the two cigarettes left in my case, and afterwards fell asleep. When I woke the old man was sitting just as I had left him, but he had laid down his book and seemed to be praying. There was no reserve now in the old face; I saw the age of it, and the innocence, and also the blind fear. He seemed to be pleading fiercely with his God, and his mouth worked like a child's in a passion of disquiet.

Of course I might have strolled out-of-doors, and gone back to the inn, where I could have seen our five men and retrieved my pipe and pouch. It struck me that we were behaving like fools; we had come to visit the House, and we ought to lose no time in getting there. My nap had put our previous talk out of my head, and I found myself on my feet in a sudden impulse. Then I remembered how Maris had enjoined the utmost caution, and I remembered, too, the look of those queer people in the street. The House was *tabu*, and if I was seen going towards it I should be stopped, and I might even precipitate some wild mischief without Maris to help me. There in the priest's homely kitchen, with a belt of golden light on the floor and the hum of flies in the window, I had an acute sense of being among shadows which might suddenly turn into monstrous forms of life. The whole island seemed to me like a snake still numb from the winter cold but thawing fast into a malignant activity. And meantime Koré was all alone in that ill-omened House with the circle of hate closing around her, and I, who had come there to protect her, was still outside the cordon. I cursed the infernal fog which had brought us so fatally out of our course: and I resolved that no power on earth would hinder me, when the dark came, from piercing the barrier.

The presbytery opened into a narrow lane with outbuildings in front of it, but from the window I could see a corner of the main street. The sun poured into the lane, and I watched the little green lizards on the wall beyond. There was scarcely a sign of life in the segment I saw of the main street; indeed there was a silence strange in a village, so that every tiny natural noise – the chirping of grasshoppers, the slow flight of a dove – came with a startling clearness. Once a woman with a shawl over her head hurried past the opening. There should have been children playing at the corner, but there were no children nor any sound of them. Never a cart rumbled by, nor mule nor horse crossed my line of vision. The village seemed to be keeping an eerie fast.

One man indeed I saw – a big fellow with a white blouse and long boots of untanned leather. He stood staring down the alley, and I noticed that he carried a rifle. I beckoned to the priest and we watched him together out of a corner of the window. The old man shook his head violently and muttered something which ended in 'bounos'. Then he added between his teeth a word which sounded like 'Callicantzari'. I had heard that word from Maris as a term of abuse – he had said, I remember, that it meant men who become beasts, like the ancient Centaurs. I guessed that this fellow must be one of the mountain-men, who were now in league with their old enemies of the coast. If they were among the besiegers. Koré could no longer refuse our help. 'I will hire a regiment to shoot them down,' she had furiously told me. But what good was *our* help likely to be?

The sight of that fellow put an edge to my discomfort, and before the shadows had begun to fall I was roaming about the little room like a cat in a cage. The priest left me, and presently I heard the ringing of a bell. In the quiet, now deepened by the hush of twilight, the homely sound seemed a mockery – like the striking of the bells of a naval battery I once heard on the

Yser. Then, in the midst of mud and death, it had incongruously suggested tea on the cool deck of a liner; now this tintinnabulation with its call to a meek worship had the same grotesque note of parody. Clearly there were no worshippers. I went to the back of the cottage, and from the window of the bare little bedroom had a view of the church in that amethyst gloaming. It was a baroque edifice, probably five centuries old, but renovated during the last fifty years, and in part painted a violent red. Beside it was a tiny bell-tower, obviously far more ancient. I could see a faint light in the window, and beyond that a dark clump of ilex above which the evening star was rising.

When the priest returned it was almost dark. He lit a lamp and carefully locked the door and shuttered the window. His barren service seemed to weigh heavily on him, for he moved wearily and did not raise his long-lidded eyes. It was borne in on me that at any price I must find some means of communicating with him, for my hour of action was approaching.

I tried him in French, but he never lifted his head.

Then it occurred to me that even a priest of the Greek church must know a little Latin. I used the English pronunciation, and though he did not understand me, he seemed to realise what tongue I was talking, for he replied in a slow broad Latin. I could not follow it, but at any rate we had found a common speech. I tore a page from my notebook and was about to write, when he snatched it and the pencil from my hand. There was something he badly wanted to say to me. He hesitated a good deal, and then in laborious capitals he wrote: '*Si populus aliquid periculi tibi minatur, invenies refugium in ecclesia.*' Then he scored out '*refugium*' and wrote in '*sanctuarium*'.

'*Quid periculi?*' I wrote.

He looked at me helplessly, and spread out his hands. Danger, he seemed to suggest, lay in every quarter of the compass.

We used up five pages in a conversation in the doggiest kind of style. My Latin was chiefly of the legal type, and I often used a word that puzzled him, while he also set me guessing with phrases which I suppose were ecclesiastical. But the result was that he repeated the instructions he had given me through Maris. If I was to enter the House, the only way was by the Dancing Floor – it took me some time to identify '*locus saltatorum*' – and to climb the great wall which separated it from the demesne. But it would be guarded, probably by the '*incolæ montium*', and I must go warily, and not attempt it till the moon was down. Also I must be back before the first light of dawn.

I showed him my pistol, but he shook his head violently and went through a pantomime, the meaning of which was clear enough. I was not to shoot, because, though the guards were armed, there would be no shooting. But all the same I was in some deadly danger. He scribbled in abusive Latin that the people I had to fear were '*pagani, nefasti, mysteriorum abominabilium cultores*'. If I were seen and pursued my only hope was to reach the church. Not his house – that was no use – but the church. Twice he printed in emphatic capitals: '*Pete sanctuarium ecclesiæ.*'

Then he took me into his little bedroom, and showed me the lie of the land. The moon was now up, the fog of the morning had gone out of the air, and the outline of the church and the bell-tower and the ilex grove beyond might have been cut in amber and jet. Through the trees there appeared a faint reddish glow as if fires were burning. I asked what this might be, and after a good deal of biting the stump of my pencil he wrote that there lay the graveyard, and the lights were burning '*ut vrykolakes absint*'. He seemed to doubt whether I could follow his meaning, but I did, for I knew about this from Koré – how the peasants kept lamps at the grave-heads to ward off vampires.

He was clear that I must traverse the valley of the Dancing Floor while the moon was up, for otherwise I should miss my way. He looked at me appraisingly and wrote 'You are a soldier', implying, as I took it, that there was cover for a man accustomed to use cover. Then he drew a plan on which he marked my road. If I skirted the graveyard I should find myself on a hillside which sloped towards the Dancing Floor. I must keep to this ridge, which was the northern containing wall of the place, till I reached the boundaries of the House. On no account must I go down into the valley, and when I asked why, he said that it was '*nefasta*'. That could not mean merely that it was well-guarded, but that it was held in dread by the people of Kynaetho, a dread which their priest shared.

I left the house just after eleven o'clock. Our long silent sederunt had made the two of us good friends, for he wept at parting and insisted on blessing me and kissing me on the forehead. I was on his side, on the side of his Church, a crusader going into peril in a strife with heathenish evil.

It was a marvellous night for scent and colour, but as silent as the deeps of the sea. I got with all speed into the shade of the ilexes, and climbed up a rocky slope so that I looked down on the village graveyard beyond the trees. Dozens of little lights twinkled in it like fireflies, those undying lamps which were lit to preserve the inmates from outrage by the terrible demons that enter into the bodies of the dead. Suddenly I remembered with horror that it was Koré against whom these precautions were taken – Koré, now because of her crazy gallantry alone in a doomed House, dreaming perhaps that she was winning back the hearts of her people, and knowing little of the dark forces massing against her out of the ancientry of time. There was that in this mania of superstition which both infuriated and awed me; it was a thing against which a man could find no weapon. And I had the ironic recollection of how little more than a week earlier, in a case before the Judicial Committee of the Privy Council, I had been defending the legalisation of certain African rites, on the ground that what to one man was superstition might to another be an honest faith. I had struck a belief which had the compelling power of a fanatical religion, though it was born of the blackness of night.

The hillside was a mass of scrub and boulder, giving excellent cover, and, since the ridge shut me off from the village, I could move with reasonable speed and safety. My spirits were rising with the exercise, and the depression which had overwhelmed me in the priest's house was lifting. Then suddenly I topped a rise and found myself looking down on the Dancing Floor.

It was not a valley so much as an upland meadow, for there was no stream in it nor had there ever been one, and, though tilted up gently towards the west, most of it was as flat as a cricket-field. There it lay in the moonlight, yellow as corn in its cincture of broken ridges, a place plainly hallowed and set apart. All my life I have cherished certain pictures of landscape, of which I have caught glimpses in my travels, as broken hints of a beauty of which I hoped some day to find the archetype. One is a mountain stream running in broad shallows and coming down through a flat stretch of heather from a confusion of blue mountains. Another is a green meadow, cut off like a garden from neighbouring wildernesses, secret and yet offering a wide horizon, a place at once a sanctuary and a watchtower. This type I have found in the Scottish Borders, in the Cotswolds, once in New Hampshire, and plentifully in the Piedmont country of Virginia. But in the Dancing Floor I had stumbled upon its archetype. The moonlight made the farther hills look low and near, and doubtless lessened the size of the level ground, but the constriction only served to increase its preciousness.

I sat down and stared at the scene, and in that moment I underwent a great lightening of spirit. For this meadow was a happy place, the home of gentle and kindly and honourable things. Mildness and peace brooded over it. The priest had said that it was '*nefasta*', but he could only have meant that it was sacred. Sacred indeed it must be, what the Greeks of old called a *temenos*, for the dullest could not be blind to the divinity that dwelt here. I had a moment of wonder why the Arabins, lords of the island, had not included a spot so gracious in their demesne, until I saw that that could not be. The Dancing Floor must be open to the winds and the starry influences and the spirits of earth; no human master could own or enclose it.

You will call me fantastic, but, dull dog as I am, I felt a sort of poet's rapture as I looked at those shining spaces, and at the sky above, flooded with the amber moon except on the horizon's edge where a pale blue took the place of gold and faint stars were pricking. The place was quivering with magic drawn out of all the ages since the world was made, but it was good magic. I had felt the oppression of Kynaetho, the furtive frightened people, the fiasco of Eastertide, the necromantic lamps beside the graves. These all smacked evilly of panic and death. But now I was looking on the Valley of the Shadow of Life. It was the shadow only, for it was mute and still and elusive. But the presage of life was in it, the clean life of fruits and flocks, and children and happy winged things, and that spring purity of the earth which is the purity of God.

The moon was declining, but it would be at least two hours before I could safely approach the House. The cover was good. I was protected by the ridge from the side of the village, and no human being was likely to be abroad on the Dancing Floor. I decided that I must get within sight of my destination before the light failed and spy out the land. It was rough going among the ribs of rock and stone-falls and dense thickets of thorn and arbutus, but sometimes I would come on a patch of turf drenched with dew and scented with thyme. All the myrrh of Arabia was in the place, for every foot of sward I trod on and every patch of scrub I brushed through was aromatic, and in the open places there was the clean savour of night and the sea. Also at my left hand and below lay the Dancing Floor, lambent under the moon like the cool tides of a river.

By and by I came to the end of the ridge, and had a view of the crest where the House stood. There was a blur of ebony which must be the wood that surrounded it, and bounding it a ribbon of silver-grey. I puzzled at this, till I realised that it was the wall of which the priest had spoken – a huge thing, it seemed, of an even height, curving from the dip where the village lay and running to what seemed to be the seaward scarp of the island. I was now in the danger zone, and it behoved me to go warily, so I found a shelter where the cover of the ridge ended and studied the details of the scene. The wall could not be less than fifteen feet in height, and it appeared to be regularly masoned and as smooth as the side of a house. In that landscape it was a startling intrusion of something crude and human, a defiance of nature. Shelley Arabin had built it for the sake of his sinister privacy, but why had he built it so high? And then I guessed the reason. He wanted to shut out the Dancing Floor from his life. That blessed place would have been a mute protest against his infamies.

There was a black patch in the even sheen of the wall. I wormed my way a little nearer and saw that for perhaps a dozen yards the wall had been broken down. I could see the ragged edges and the inky darkness of the shrubberies beyond. This had been done recently, perhaps within the last month. And then I saw something more. There were men – guards – stationed at the gap. I made out their figures, and they seemed to have the baggy white shirts of the mountaineer I had seen in the village. Also they were armed. One stood in the gap, and the two others patrolled the sides, and I could see that they carried rifles at the trail. It seemed absurd that three men were needed for that tiny entrance, and I concluded that they wanted each other's company. There must be something in the task which put a heavy strain on their courage. I noticed, too, that they kept their faces resolutely averted from the Dancing Floor. When one moved he walked with his head screwed round facing the House. The shining meadow might be *nefasta*, as the priest had said, or it might be too sacred at this solemn hour of night for the profane gaze.

When I had watched them for a little it seemed to me that, though the moon had not set, these fellows were too preoccupied to be dangerous, and that I might safely continue my reconnaissance. There was not much cover, but the declining moon made an olive shadow at the upper end of the Dancing Floor, and I proceeded to crawl across it like a gillie after deer. I went very cautiously, stopping every now and then to prospect, but I found the wall now beyond my range and I had to chance the immobility of the sentries. My breeches were sopping with dew before I reached the point which I judged to be out of sight of the gap. The wall, as I had observed, curved at the sea end, and once there – unless there were further guards – I should be at liberty to test my climbing powers. The thing looked a most formidable barrier, but I was in hopes that it might be turned where it abutted on the cliffs.

Before I realised it I was looking down on the sea.

The coast bent inward in a little bight, and a hundred feet below me the water lapped on a white beach. It was such a revelation of loveliness as comes to a man only once or twice in his lifetime. I fancy that the short commons on which I had subsisted all day and the sense of dwelling among portents had keyed me up to a special receptiveness. Behind me was the Dancing Floor, and in front a flood of translucent colour, the shimmer of gold, the rarest tints of sapphire and amethyst, fading into the pale infinity of the sky. I had come again into a world which spoke. From below came the sound of dreamily moving water, of sleepy pigeons in the rocks. Recollections of poetry fleeted through my mind:

> Where Helicon breaks down
> In cliff to the sea . . .
> Where the moon-silver'd inlets
> Send far their light voice –

Yes, but something was wanting. There should have been white flocks on the sward, something to link up nature with the homely uses of man, in order to produce the idyllic. This place was not idyllic, it was magical and unearthly. Above me was a walled mystery, within which evil had once been followed and a greater evil might soon be done, and there were men with quaking hearts bent upon ancient devilries.

I followed the edge of the scarp as it rose to the highest point where the wall ended. There I had a sharp disappointment. The wall ran sheer to the edge of the cliff, and a steep buttress descended to the face of the limestone crag. The stone was as smooth as a water-worn pebble. I have been a rock-climber since I was an undergraduate, and have faced in my time some awkward problems, but this was starkly impossible. Even with a companion and a rope I do not believe it could have been done, and to attempt it alone meant the certainty of a broken neck.

I prospected eastward along the wall and found no better hope there. The thing was simply not to be climbed except by a lizard. If I had had Maris with me I might have stood on his shoulders and made a jump for the coping; as it was it might have been a hundred feet high instead of fifteen for all the good it was to me. There were no branches about to make a ladder, or loose stones to make a cairn – nothing but the short downland turf.

The sight of this insuperable obstacle effectively put a stop to my brief exhilaration of spirit. I felt small and feeble and futile. It was imperative that I should get into the House without further delay and see Koré, and yet the House was as impracticable as the moon, now swiftly setting. The rapid darkening of the world pointed out the only road. I must dodge the sentries and get through the breach in the wall. It was a wild notion, but my growing ill-temper made me heedless of risks. The men had no pistols, only rifles, and were probably not too ready in the use of them. After all I had played this game before with success. In the first winter of the war, when I was a subaltern, I used to be rather good at wriggling across no-man's-land and eaves-dropping beside the German trenches.

I didn't give my resolution time to weaken, but in the shadow of the wall made the best pace I could towards the gap. It was now really dark, with only a faint glow from the stars, and I moved in what seemed to my eyes impenetrable shade after the brightness of the moon. I was wearing rubber-soled boots and cloth gaiters, my garments were subfusc in colour, and I have always been pretty light on my feet. I halted many times to get my bearings, and presently I heard the sound of a man's tread. So far as I could judge before, two of the sentries had their patrol well away from the wall, and I might escape their notice if I hugged the stones. But one had had his stand right in the breach, and with him I would have difficulty. My hope was to dart through into the shelter of the thick shrubbery. Even if they fired on me they would be likely to miss, and I believed that they would not follow me into the demesne.

I edged my way nearer, a foot at a time, till I guessed by the sound that I was inside the beat of the patrols. I had no white about me, for my shirt and collar were drab, and I kept my face to the wall. Suddenly my hands felt the ragged edge of the gap and I almost stumbled over a fallen stone. Here it was very dark and I had the shadow of the trees inside to help me. I held my breath and listened, but I could not hear any noise from within the breach. Had the sentry there deserted his post?

I waited for a minute or so, trying to reckon up the chances. The tread of the man on my right was clear, and presently I could make out also the movement of the man on my left. Where was the third? Suddenly I heard to the right the sound of human speech. The third must be there. There was a sparkle of fire, too. The third sentry had gone to get a light for his cigarette.

Now was my opportunity, and I darted into the darkness of the gap. I was brought up sharp and almost stunned by a blow on the forehead. There was a gate in the gap, a stout thing of wattles with a pole across. I strained at it with my hands, but it would not move.

There was nothing for it but to bolt. The sentries had been alarmed – probably horribly alarmed – by the noise, and were drawing together. The only safety lay in violent action, for they had a means of getting light and would find me if I tried to lurk in the shadows. I raised my arms in the orthodox ghostly fashion, howled like a banshee, and broke for the open.

I was past them before they could stop me and plunging down the slope towards the Dancing Floor. I think that for the first moments they were too scared to shoot, for they must have believed that I had come out of the forbidden House, and when they recovered their nerve I was beyond their range. The upper slope was steep, and I went down it as Pate-in-Peril in *Redgauntlet* went down Errickstane-brae. I rolled over and over, found my feet, lost them again, and did not come to rest till I was in the flats of the meadow. I looked back and saw a light twinkling at the gap. The guards there must have been amazed to find the gate intact and were now doubtless at their prayers.

I did not think that, even if they believed me flesh and blood, they would dare to follow me to the Dancing Floor. So I made my way down it at a reasonable pace, feeling rather tired, rather empty and very thirsty. On the road up I had decided that there was no stream in it, but almost at once I came to a spring. It was a yard across, bubbling up strongly, and sending forth a tiny rill which presently disappeared in some fissure of the limestone. The water was deliciously cold and I drank pints of it. Then it occurred to me that I must put my best foot forwards, for there was that trembling in the eastern sky which is the presage of dawn. My intention was to join my fellows in the inn courtyard, and meet Maris there in the morning. After all the inhabitants of Kynaetho had nothing as yet against me. All they knew of me was that I was a surveyor from the Government at Athens, whose presence no doubt was unwelcome but who could hardly be treated as an enemy.

I reached the eastern bounds of the Dancing Floor, and scrambled up on the ridge above the ilexes of the graveyard. The lamps were still twinkling like glow-worms among the graves. From there it was easy to get into the lane where stood the priest's house, and in a few minutes I was in the main village street. The chilly dawn was very near and I thought lovingly of the good food in our boxes. My first desire was a meal which should be both supper and breakfast.

The door of the courtyard stood open, and I pushed through it to the barn beyond. The place was empty – not a sign of men or baggage. For a moment I thought they might have been given quarters in the inn, till I remembered that the inn had no guest-room. I tried the other outbuildings – a stable, a very dirty byre, a place which looked like a granary. One and all were empty.

It was no use waking the landlord, for he probably would not answer, and in any case I did not understand his tongue. There was nothing for it but to go back to the priest. My temper was thoroughly embittered, and I strode out of the courtyard as if I were at home in my own village.

But my entrance had been observed, and the street was full of people. I doubt if Kynaetho slept much these days, and now it seemed that from every door men and women were emerging. There was something uncanny in that violent vigilance in the cold grey light of dawn. And the crowd was no longer inert. In a second I saw that it was actively hostile, that it wanted to do me a mischief, or at any rate to lay hands on me. It closed in on me from every side, and yet made no sound.

It was now that I had my first real taste of fear. Before I had been troubled and mystified, but now I was downright afraid. Automatically I broke into a run, for I remembered the priest's advice about the church.

My action took them by surprise. Shouts arose, meaningless shouts to me, and I broke through the immediate circle with ease. Two fellows who moved to intercept me I handed off in the best Rugby football style. The street was empty before me and I sprinted up it at a pace which I doubt if I ever equalled in my old running days.

But I had one determined pursuer. I caught a glimpse of him out of a corner of my eye, one of the young men from the hills, a fellow with a dark hawk-like face and a powerful raking stride. In my then form he would have beaten me easily if the course had been longer, but it was too short to let him develop his speed. Yet he was not a yard behind me when I shot through the open door of the church.

I flung myself gasping on the floor behind one of the squat pillars. As I recovered my breath I wondered why no shot had been fired. A man with a gun could have brought me down with the utmost ease, for I had been running straight in the open. My second thought was that the priest had been right. The peasant had stopped in his tracks at the church door. I had found safety for the moment – a sanctuary or, it might be, a prison.

TEN

THE MORNING LIGHT was filtering through the windows, and since the glass was a dirty yellow, the place seemed still to be full of moonshine. As my eyes grew accustomed to it, I made out the features of the interior. A heavy curtain separated the sanctuary from the chancel; the floor was of rough stone, worn with the feet and knees of generations of worshippers: there were none of the statues and images which one is accustomed to in a Roman church, not even a crucifix, though there may have been one above the hidden altar. From a pillar hung an assortment of votive offerings, crutches, oar-blades, rudders of ships, old-fashioned horn spectacles. The walls were studded with little ikons of saints, each one with its guttering lamp before it. The place smelt dank and unused and mouldy, like a kirk in winter-time in some Highland glen. Behind me the open door showed an oval of pure pale light.

I was in a mood of profound despondency which was very near despair. The men had gone and with them our stores of food and ammunition. God knew where Maris was or how I should find him again. The village was actively hostile, and I was shut up in the church as in a penitentiary. I was no nearer Koré than when we landed – farther away indeed, for I had taken the wrong turning, and she was shut off from me by mountainous barriers. I could have laughed bitterly when I thought of the futility of the help which I had been so confident of giving her. And her danger was far more deadly than I had dreamed. She was the mark of a wild hate which had borrowed some wilder madness out of the deeps of the past. She had spoken of a 'sacrifice'. That was the naked truth of it; any moment tragedy might be done, some hideous rite consummated, and youth and gallantry laid on a dark altar.

The thought drove me half crazy. I fancy the lack of food and sleep had made me rather light-headed, for I sat in a stupor which was as much anger as pity – anger at those blinded islanders, at my own feebleness, at Koré's obstinacy. This was succeeded by an extreme restlessness. I could not stay still, but roamed about examining the ill-favoured ikons. There was a little recess on the right of the chancel which was evidently the treasury, for I found a big chest full of dusty vestments and church plate. Sacrilege must have been an unknown crime in Kynaetho, for the thing was unlocked.

Then I noticed a strange object below the chancel step. It seemed to be a bier with a shrouded figure laid on it. The sight gave me a shock, for I thought it a dead body. Reluctantly I approached it and drew back the shroud, expecting to see the corpse of a peasant.

To my amazement it was a figure of Christ – a wooden image, rudely carved but with a strange similitude of life. It reminded me of a John the Baptist by Donatello which I once saw in Venice. The emaciated body was naked but for the loin cloth, the eyes were closed, the cheeks sunken. It was garishly painted, and the stigmata were done in a crude scarlet. But there was power in it, and dignity and a terrible pitifulness. I remembered Koré's story. This was the figure which on the night of Good Friday, after the women had kissed and wailed over it, was borne in procession among the village lanes and then restored to its sepulchre. This was the figure which at the Easter Resurrection stood in a blaze of candles before the altar, the Crucified and Risen Lord.

That sight worked a miracle with me. I suddenly felt that I was not alone, but had august allies. The Faith was behind me, that faith which was deep in the heart of Kynaetho though for the moment it was overlaid. The shabby church, the mazed and ignorant priest took on suddenly a tremendous significance . . . They were the visible sign and warrant of that creed which we all hold dumbly, even those who call themselves unbelievers – the belief in the ultimate omnipotence of purity and meekness.

I reverently laid the shroud again over the figure, and must have stood in a muse before it, till I found that the priest had joined me. He knelt beside the bier, and said his prayers, and never have I heard such an agony of supplication in a man's voice. I drew back a little, and waited. When he had finished he came to me and his eyes asked a question.

I shook my head and got out my notebook.

He asked me if I had breakfasted, and when I wrote the most

emphatic negative which my Latin could compass, he hobbled off and returned with some food under his cassock. It was only cheese and black bread, but I ate it wolfishly and felt better for it. I looked on the old man now with a sincere liking, for he was my host and my ally, and I think he had changed his attitude towards me. Those minutes beside the bier had established a bond between us.

In the recess I have mentioned there was a door which I had not hitherto noticed. This opened into a kind of sacristy, where the priest kept his odds and ends. There was a well in the floor of it, covered by an immense oaken lid, a well of cold water of which I had a long drink. The old man drew several buckets, and set about cleaning the chancel, and I was glad to lend a hand. I spent the better part of the morning like a housemaid on my knees scrubbing the floor and the chancel step, while he was occupied inside the sanctuary. The physical exertion was an anodyne to my thoughts, which in any case were without purpose. I could do nothing till the night came again.

On one of my journeys to the sacristy to fetch water I saw a face at the little window, which opened on the yard of the priest's house. To my immense relief it was Maris, very dirty and dishevelled, but grinning cheerfully. That window was a tight fit, but he managed to wriggle half through and a strong pull from me did the rest. He drank like a thirsty dog out of my bucket, and then observed that a church had its drawbacks as a resort, since one couldn't smoke.

'I have much to tell you, my friend,' he said, 'but first I must interview his Holiness. By God, but he has the mischievous flock.'

I do not know what he said to the priest, but he got answers which seemed to give him a melancholy satisfaction. The old man spoke without ever looking up, and his voice was flat with despair. Often he shook his head, and sometimes he held up his hand as if to avert a blasphemy. Maris turned to me with a shrug of the shoulders. 'This madness is beyond him, as it is beyond me. It is a general breaking down of wits. What can you and I, soldiers though we be, do against insanity? Presently I must sleep, and you too, my friend, to judge by your heavy eyes. But first I make my report.'

'I suppose we are safe here?' I said.

'Safe enough, but impotent. We can take our sleep

confidently, but it is hard to see that we can do much else. We are in quarantine, if you understand. But to report—'

He had gone to the inn the night before, and found our five men supping and playing cards like Christians. They seemed to understand what was required of them – to wait for me and then join Janni and the others at the rendezvous on the western cliffs. So far as he could judge they had had no communication of any kind with the people of the village. Then he had set out with an easy mind on the road to Vano. No one had hindered him; the few villagers he met had stared but had not attempted even to accost him. So over the moonlit downs he went, expecting to find Janni and the other five in bivouac in the open country towards the skirts of the hills.

He found Janni alone – on the roadside some miles east of Vano, squatted imperturbably by a fire, in possession of five revolvers and ample stores, but without a single follower. From the one-armed corporal he heard a strange tale. The party had made Vano before midday in the *Santa Lucia*, had landed, and marched inland from the little port, without apparently attracting much attention. He himself had explained to the harbour-master that they had been sent to do survey work, and the wineshop, where they stopped for a drink, heard the same story. They had then tramped up the road from Vano to the hills, stopping at the little farms to pass the time of day and pick up news. They heard nothing till nightfall, when they encamped beside a village among the foothills. There Janni talked to sundry villagers and heard queer stories of Kynaetho. There was a witch there who by her spells had blighted the crops and sent strange diseases among the people, and the cup of her abominations was now full. St Dionysius had appeared to many in a dream summoning them to Kynaetho in the Great Week, and the best of the young men had already gone thither.

That was all that Janni heard, for being the man in authority he spoke only with the elders, and they were wary in their talk. But the others, gossiping with the women, heard a fuller version which scared them to the bone. Your Greek townsman is not a whit less superstitious than the peasant, and he lacks the peasant's stolidity, and is prone to more speedy excitement. Janni did not know exactly what the women had told his men, except that Kynaetho was the abode of vampires and harpies for whom a surprising judgement was preparing, and that no stranger could enter the place without dire misfortune. There might be throat-cutting, it was hinted, on the part of the young men now engaged in a holy war, and there would for certain be disaster at the hand of the *striglas* and *vrykolakes* in the House, for to them a stranger would be easy prey.

Whatever it was, it brought the men back to Janni gibbering with terror and determined to return forthwith to Vano. The island was accursed and the abode of devils innumerable, and there was nothing for honest men to do but to flee. They would go back to Vano and wait on a boat, the *Santa Lucia* or some other. To do the rascals justice, Janni thought that they might have faced the throat-cutting, but the horrors of the unseen and the occult were more than they could stomach. Janni, who was a rigid disciplinarian, had fortunately possessed himself of their pistols when they encamped for the night, and he was now in two minds whether he should attempt to detain them by force. But the sight of their scared eyes and twitching lips decided him that he could do nothing in their present mood, and he resolved to let them go back to Vano till he had seen Maris and received instructions. They had already had wages in advance, and could fend for themselves till he made a plan. So he doled out to each man a share of the supplies and watched them scurry off in the direction of the coast, while he smoked his pipe and considered the situation. There about two in the morning Maris found him.

The defection of these five men suggested to Maris that the same kind of trouble might be expected with the batch in Kynaetho. So he and Janni humped the stores and started off across the downs to the rendezvous on the cliffs which he had settled with me. That occupied a couple of hours, and there Janni was left with orders not to stir till he was summoned. The place was a hollow on the very edge of the sea, far removed from a road or a dwelling – a lucky choice, for it had been made at haphazard from the map without any local knowledge. Then Maris set off at his best pace for Kynaetho, skirting the Dancing Floor on the south, and striking the road to Vano a mile or so from the village.

There he met the rest of our posse, and a more dilapidated set of mountebanks he declared he had never seen. So far as he could gather from their babble, they had been visited in the small hours by a deputation of villagers, who had peremptorily ordered them to depart. The deputation backed its plea not by threats but by a plain statement of facts. Kynaetho was labouring under a curse which was about to be removed. No doubt the villagers expounded the nature of the curse with details which started goose-flesh on their hearers. What was about to be done was Kynaetho's own affair, and no stranger could meddle with it and live. They may have enforced their argument with a sight of their rifles, but probably they did not need any mundane arguments to barb the terror which their tale inspired. For they succeeded in so putting a fear of unknown horrors into these five Athens guttersnipes that they decamped without a protest. They did not even stay to collect some provender, but fled for their lives along the Vano road.

When Maris met them they were padding along in abject panic. One man still carried unconsciously a tin from which he had been feeding, another clutched a crumpled pack of cards. They had their pistols, but they had no thought of using them. Pantingly they told their story, irking to be gone, and when Maris seemed to be about to detain them they splayed away from him like frightened sheep. Like Janni, he decided that it was no good to try to stop them – indeed he was pretty clear by now that even if they stayed they would be useless for the job we had in hand. He cursed their female relatives for several generations and speeded the hindmost on his way with a kick.

His next business was to find me, and he concluded that I would probably be still in the neighbourhood of the House. So, as the moon was down, he retraced his steps by the south side of the Dancing Floor and reached the edge where the wall abutted on the cliffs probably an hour after I had been there. He shared my view about the impracticality of an entrance to the demesne at that point. As it was now almost daylight he did not dare to follow the wall, but returned to Janni on the cliffs, who gave him breakfast. He was getting anxious about my doings, for he argued that if I returned to the inn to look for the men there would probably be trouble. It seemed to him important that the village should still believe him to have gone off, so he was determined not to show himself. But he must get in touch with me, and for that purpose he decided first to draw the priest's house. He had a difficult journey in the broad daylight by way of the graveyard. It would have been impossible, he said, if the village had been living its normal life, for he had to pass through a maze of little fields and barns. But all farm work seemed to have been relinquished, and not a soul was to be seen at the lower end of the Dancing Floor. Everybody, except the guards round the House, seemed to be huddling in the village street. In the end he got into the priest's house, found it empty and followed on to the church.

I told him briefly my doings of the night. I could see that he was completely in the dark as to what was happening, except that Kynaetho, under the goad of some crazy superstition, intended very resolute mischief to the House and its chatelaine. You see he had not talked to Koré – had indeed never seen her, nor had he read the disquieting manuscript which Vernon had translated for me. I did not see how I could enlighten him, for on that side he was no scholar, and was too rooted in his brand of minor rationalism to take my tale seriously. It was sufficient that we were both agreed that the House must be entered, and Koré willy-nilly removed.

'But we have no ship,' he cried. 'The lady would be no safer in the open than in the House, for they mean most certainly that she shall die. I think it may come to putting our backs to the wall, and the odds are unpleasant. We cannot telegraph for help, for the office is in the village and it has been destroyed. I have ascertained that there is no wire at Vano, or elsewhere in the island.'

Things looked pretty ugly, as I was bound to admit. But there was one clear and urgent duty, to get into the House and find Koré. Before we lay down to snatch a little sleep, we made a rough plan. Maris would try the coast to the north and see if an entrance could be effected by a postern above the jetty where Vernon and I had first landed. He thought that he had better undertake this job, for it meant skirting the village, and he believed he might pass in the darkness as one of the men from the hills. He could talk the language, you see, and, if accosted, could put up some kind of camouflage. I was to make for Janni, and then the two of us would try along the shore under the cliffs in the hope that some gully might give us access to the demesne north of the point where the wall ended. We were to rendezvous about breakfast time at Janni's camp, and from the results of the night frame a further programme.

I slept without a break till after eight o'clock in the evening, when the priest woke us and gave us another ration of the eternal bread and cheese. I felt frowsy and dingy and would have given much for a bath. The priest reported that the day in the village had passed without incident, except that there had been a great gathering in the central square and some kind of debate. He had not been present, but the thing seemed to have deepened his uneasiness. 'There is no time to lose,' he told Maris, 'for tomorrow is Good Friday, and tomorrow I fear that unhallowed deeds may be done.' Maris discussed his route with him very carefully, and several more pages of my note-book were used up in plans. It was going to be a ticklish business to reach the jetty – principally, I gathered, because of the guards who watched all the sides of the demesne which were not bounded by the cliffs or the great wall. But the priest seemed to think it possible, and Maris's Gascon soul had illimitable confidence.

My road was plain – up the ridge on the south side of the Dancing Floor till it ended at the sea, a matter of not more than four miles. I skirted as before the little graveyard with its flickering lamps, and then made a cautious traverse of a number of small fields each with its straw-covered barn. Presently I was out on the downs, with the yellow levels of the Dancing Floor below me on the right. I was in a different mood from the previous night, for I was now miserably conscious of the shortness of our time and the bigness of our task. Anxiety was putting me into a fever of impatience and self-contempt. Here was I, a man who was reckoned pretty competent by the world, who had had a creditable record in the war, who was considered an expert at getting other people out of difficulties – and yet I was so far utterly foiled by a batch of barbarian peasants. I simply dared not allow my mind to dwell on Koré and her perils, for that way lay madness. I had to try to think of the thing objectively as a problem to be solved, but flashes of acute fear for the girl kept breaking through to set my heart beating.

I found Janni cooking supper by his little fire in a nook of the downs, and the homely sight for the moment comforted me. The one-armed corporal was, I dare say, by nature and upbringing as superstitious as any other Greek peasant, but his military training had canalised his imagination, and he would take no notice of a legend till he was ordered to by his superior officer. He reminded me of the policeman Javert in *Les Misérables*: his whole soul was in the ritual of his profession, and it must have been a black day for Janni when the war stopped. Maris, whom he worshipped blindly, had bidden him take instructions from me, and he was ready to follow me into the sea. Mercifully his service at Salonika had taught him a few English words and a certain amount of bad French, so we could more or less communicate.

He had supplies with him, so I had a second supper – biscuits and sardines and coffee, which after two days of starvation tasted like nectar and ambrosia. Also he had a quantity of caporal cigarettes with which I filled my pockets. Our first business was to get down to the beach, and fortunately he had already discovered a route a few hundred yards to the south, where a gully with a stone shoot led to the water's edge. Presently we stood on the pebbly shore looking out to the luminous west over a sea as calm as a millpond. I would have liked to bathe, but decided that I must first get the immediate business over.

That shore was rough going, for it was à succession of limestone reefs encumbered with great boulders which had come down from the rocks during past winters. The strip of beach was very narrow and the overhang of the cliffs protected us from observation from above, even had any peasant been daring enough to patrol the Dancing Floor by night. We kept close to the water where the way was easiest, but even there our progress was slow. It took us the better part of an hour to get abreast of the point where the wall ended. There the cliffs were at least two hundred feet high and smooth as the side of a cut loaf. Crowning them we could see the dark woodlands of the demesne.

My object was to find a route up them, and never in all my mountaineering experience had I seen a more hopeless proposition. The limestone seemed to have no fissures, and the faces had weathered smooth. In the Dolomites you can often climb a perpendicular cliff by the countless little cracks in the hard stone, but here there were no cracks, only a surface glassy like marble. At one point I took off my boots and managed to ascend about twenty yards, when I was brought up sharp by an overhang, could find no way to traverse, and had my work cut out getting down again. Janni was no cragsman, and in any case his one arm made him useless.

Our outlook ahead was barred by a little cape, and I was in hopes that on the other side of that the ground might become easier. We had a bad time turning it, for the beach stopped and the rock fell sheer to the water. Happily the water at the point was shallow, and, partly wading and partly scrambling, we managed to make the passage. In the moonlight everything was clear as day, and once round we had a prospect of a narrow bay, backed by the same high perpendicular cliffs and bounded to the north by a still higher bluff which ended to seaward in a sheer precipice.

I sat down on a boulder with a sinking heart to consider the prospect. It was more hopeless than the part we had already prospected. There was no gully or chimney in the whole glimmering semi-circle, nothing but a rim of unscalable stone crowned with a sharp-cut fringe of trees. Beyond the bluff lay the oliveyards which I had seen six years before when I landed from the yacht, but I was pretty certain that we would never get round the bluff. For the margin of shore had now disappeared, and the cliffs dropped sheer into deep water.

Suddenly Janni by my side grunted and pointed to the middle of the little bay. There, riding at anchor, was a boat.

At first it was not easy to distinguish it from a rock, for there was no riding light shown. But, as I stared at it, I saw that it was indeed a boat – a yawl-rigged craft of, I judged, about twenty tons. It lay there motionless in the moonlight, a beautiful thing which had no part in that setting of stone and sea – a foreign thing, an intruder. I watched it for five minutes and nothing moved aboard.

The sight filled me with both hope and mystification. Here was the 'ship' which Maris had postulated. But who owned it and what was it doing in this outlandish spot, where there was no landing? It could not belong to Kynaetho, or it would have been lying at the jetty below the House or in the usual harbour. Indeed it could not belong to Plakos at all, for, though I knew little about boats, I could see that the cut of this one spoke of Western Europe. Was anyone on board? It behoved me forthwith to find that out.

I spoke to Janni, and he whistled shrilly. But there was no answer from the sleeping bay. He tried again several times without result. If we were to make inquiries, it could only be by swimming out. Janni of course was no swimmer, and besides the responsibility was on me. I can't say I liked the prospect, but in three minutes I had stripped and was striking out in the moon-silvered water.

The fresh cold aromatic sea gave me new vigour of body and mind. I realised that I must proceed warily. Supposing there was someone on board, someone hostile, I would be completely at his mercy. So I swam very softly up to the stern and tried to read the name on it. There was a name, but that side was in shadow and I could not make it out. I swam to the bows and there again saw a name of which I could make nothing, except that the characters did not seem to me to be Greek.

I trod water and took stock of the situation. It was the kind of craft of which you will see hundreds at Harwich and Southampton and Plymouth – a pleasure boat, obviously meant for cruising, but with something of the delicate lines of a racer. I was beginning to feel chilly, and felt that I must do something more than prospect from the water. I must get on board and chance the boat being empty or the owner asleep.

There was a fender amidships hanging over the port side. I clutched this, got a grip of the gunwale, and was just about to pull myself up, when a face suddenly appeared above me, a scared, hairy face, surmounted by a sort of blue nightcap. Its owner objected to my appearance, for he swung a boathook and brought it down heavily on the knuckles of my left hand. That is to say, such was his intention, but he missed his aim and only grazed my little finger.

I dropped off and dived, for I was afraid that he might start shooting. When I came up a dozen yards off and shook the water out of my eyes, I saw him staring at me as if I was a merman, with the boathook still in his hand.

'What the devil do you mean by that?' I shouted, when I had ascertained that he had no pistol. 'What boat is it? Who are you?'

My voice seemed to work some change in the situation, for he dropped the boathook, and replied in what sounded like Greek. I caught one word 'Ingleez' several times repeated.

'I'm English.' I cried. 'English . . . philos . . . philhellene – damn it, what's the Greek for a friend?'

'Friend,' he repeated, 'Ingleez,' and I swam nearer.

He was a tough-looking fellow, dressed in a blue jersey and what appeared to be old flannel bags, and he looked honest, though puzzled. I was now just under him, and smiling for all I was worth. I put a hand on the fender again, and repeated the word 'English'. I also said that my intentions were of the best, and I only wanted to come aboard and have a chat. If he was well disposed towards England, I thought he might recognise the sound of the language.

Evidently he did, for he made no protest when I got both hands on the gunwale again. He allowed me to get my knee up on it, so I took my chance and swung myself over. He retreated a step and lifted the boathook, but he did not attempt to hit me as I arose like Proteus out of the sea and stood dripping on his deck.

I held out my hand, and with a moment's hesitation he took it. 'English . . . friend,' I said, grinning amicably at him, and to my relief he grinned back.

I was aboard a small yacht, which was occidental in every line of her, the clean decks, the general tidy workmanlike air. A man is not at his most confident standing stark naked at midnight in a strange boat, confronting somebody of whose speech he comprehends not one word. But I felt that I had stumbled upon a priceless asset if I could only use it, and I was determined not to let the chance slip. He poured out a flow of Greek, at which I could only shake my head and murmur 'English'. Then I tried the language of signs, and went through a vigorous pantomime to explain that, though I could not speak his tongue, I had a friend on shore who could. The yacht had a dinghy. Would he row me ashore and meet my friend?

It took me the devil of a time to make this clear to him, and I had to lead him to where the dinghy lay astern, point to it, point to the shore, point to my dumb mouth and generally behave like a maniac. But he got it at last. He seemed to consider, then he dived below and returned with a thing like an iron mace which he brandished round his head as if to give me to understand that if I misbehaved he could brain me. I smiled and nodded and put my hand on my heart, and he smiled back.

Then his whole manner changed. He brought me a coat and an ancient felt hat and made signs that I should put them on. He dived below again and brought up a bowl of hot cocoa which did me good, for my teeth were beginning to chatter. Finally he motioned me to get into the dinghy and set his mace beside him, took the sculls and pulled in the direction I indicated.

Janni was sitting smoking on a stone, the image of innocent peace. I cried out to him before we reached shore, and told him that this was the skipper and that he must talk to him. The two began their conversation before we landed, and presently it seemed that Janni had convinced my host that we were respectable. As soon as we landed I started to put on my clothes, but first I took the pistol from my coat pocket and presented the butt-end to my new friend. He saw my intention, bowed ceremoniously, and handed it back to me. He also pitched the mace back into the dinghy, as if he regarded it as no longer necessary.

He and Janni talked volubly and with many gesticulations, and the latter now and then broke off to translate for my benefit. I noticed that as time went on the seaman's face, though it remained friendly, grew also obstinate.

'He says he awaits his master here,' said Janni, 'but who his master is and where he is gone he will not tell. He says also that this island is full of devils and bad men and that on no account will he stay on it.'

I put suggestions to Janni, which he translated, but we could get nothing out of the fellow, except the repeated opinion – with which I agreed – that the island was full of devils and that the only place for an honest man was the water. About his master he remained stubbornly silent. I wanted him to take me in his boat round the farther bluff so that we could land on the oliveyard slopes and possibly get in touch with Maris, but he peremptorily refused. He would not leave the bay, which was the only safe place. Elsewhere were the men and women of Plakos, who were devils.

After about an hour's fruitless talk I gave it up. But one thing I settled. I told him through Janni that there were others besides ourselves and himself who were in danger from the devils of the island. There was a lady – an English lady – who was even now in dire peril. If we could bring her to the spot would he be on the watch and take her on board?

He considered this for a little and then agreed. He would not leave the island without his master, but he would receive the lady if necessary, and if the devils followed he would resist them. He was obviously a fighting man, and I concluded he would be as good as his word. Asked if in case of pursuit he would put to sea, he said, 'No, not till his master returned.' That was the best I could make of him, but of that precious master he refused to speak a syllable. His own name he said was George – known at home as Black George, to distinguish him from a cousin, George of the Harelip.

We parted in obscure friendliness. I presented him with my empty cigarette-case and he kissed me on both cheeks. As I handed him back the garments which he had lent me to cover my nakedness, I noticed a curious thing. The coat was an aquascutum so old that the maker's tab had long since gone from it. But inside the disreputable felt hat I saw the name of a well-known shop in Jermyn Street.

ELEVEN

JANNI AND I returned to the camp before dawn. For some unknown reason a heavy weariness overcame me on the way back, and I could scarcely drag my limbs over the last half-mile of shore and up the stone-shoot to the edge of the downs. I dropped on the ground beside the ashes of the fire, and slept like a drugged man.

When I woke it was high forenoon. The sun was beating full on the little hollow, and Janni was cooking breakfast. My lethargy had gone and I woke to a violent anxious energy. Where was Maris? He ought to have rejoined us, according to plan, before sunrise. But Janni had seen no sign of him. Had he got into the House? Well, in that case he would find means to send us a message, and to send it soon, for this was Good Friday, the day which the priest feared. I was in a fever of impatience, for I had found a boat, a means of escape of which Maris did not know. If he was in the House, I must get that knowledge to him, and he in turn must get in touch as soon as possible with me. Our forces were divided, with no link of communication.

I did my best to possess my soul in that hot scented forenoon, but it was a hard job, for the sense of shortening time had got on my nerves. The place was cooled by light winds from the sea, and for Janni, who lay on his back and consumed cigarettes, it was doubtless a pleasant habitation. Rivers of narcissus and iris and anemone flooded over the crest and spilled into the hollow. The ground was warm under the short herbage, and from it came the rich clean savour of earth quickening after its winter sleep under the spell of the sun. The pigeons were cooing in the cliffs below me and the air was full of the soft tideless swaying of the sea. But for all the comfort it gave me I might have been stretched on frozen bricks in a dungeon. I was constantly getting up and crawling to a high point which gave me a view of the rim of the downs up to the wall, and eastwards towards the Vano road. But there was no sign of Maris in the wide landscape.

About one o'clock the thing became unbearable. If Maris was in the House I must find touch with him: if he had failed, I must make the attempt myself. It was a crazy thing to contemplate in broad daylight, but my anxiety would not let me stay still. I bade Janni wait for me, and set off towards the Vano road, with the intention of trying Maris's route of the previous night and making a circuit by the east side of the village towards the jetty.

I had the sense to keep on the south side of the ridge out of sight of the Dancing Floor and the high ground beyond it. There was not a soul to be seen in all that grassy place; the winding highway showed no figure as far as the eye could reach; even the closes and barns clustered about the foot of the Dancing Floor seemed untenanted of man or beast. I gave the village a wide berth, and after crossing some patches of cultivation and scrambling through several ragged thickets found myself due east of Kynaetho and some three hundred feet above it.

There I had the prospect of the church rising above a line of hovels, a bit of the main street, the rear of the inn, and the houses which straggled seaward towards the jetty. The place had undergone another transformation, for it seemed to be deserted. Not one solitary figure appeared in the blinding white street. Everyone must be indoors engaged in some solemn preparation against the coming night. That gave me a hope that the northern approaches to the House might be unguarded. So great was my anxiety that I set off at a run, and presently had reached the high ground which overlooked the road from the village to the harbour. Here I had to go circumspectly, for once I descended to the road I would be in view of anyone on the jetty, and probably, too, of the northernmost houses in the village.

I scanned the foreground long and carefully with my glass, and decided that no one was about, so I slipped down from the heights, crossed the road a hundred yards above the harbour, and dived into the scrub which bordered the beach on the farther side. Here I was completely sheltered, and made good going till I rounded a little point and came into a scene which was familiar. It was the place where six years before Vernon and I had landed from Lamancha's yacht. There were the closes of fruit blossom, the thickets, the long scrubby ravine where we had listened to the Spring Song. I had a sudden sense of things being predestined, of the ironical fore-ordination of life.

I knew what to expect. Round the horn of the little bay where I stood lay the House with its jetty and the causeway and the steep stairs to the postern gates. My success thus far had made me confident and I covered the next half-mile as if I were walking on my own estate. But I had the wit to move cautiously before I passed the containing ridge, and crept up to the skyline.

It was well that I did so, for this was what I saw. On the jetty there were guards, and there were posts along the causeway. More, some change had been wrought in the seaward wall of the House. The huge place rose, blank and white, in its cincture of greenery, but at the points where the steps ended in postern doors there seemed to be a great accumulation of brushwood which was not the work of nature. My glass told me what it was. The entrance was piled high with faggots. The place had been transformed into a pyre.

But it was not that sight which sent my heart to my boots – I had been prepared for that or any other devilry: it was the utter impossibility of effecting an entrance. The fabric rose stark and silent like a prison, and round it stood the wardens.

I didn't wait long, for the spectacle made me mad. I turned and retraced my steps, as fast as I could drag my legs, for every ounce of vigour had gone out of me. It was a dull listless automation that recrossed the harbour road, made the long circuit east of the village, and regained the downs beyond the Dancing Floor. When I staggered into camp, where the placid Janni was playing dice, it was close on five o'clock.

I made myself a cup of tea and tried to piece the situation together. Maris could not have entered the House – the thing was flatly impossible, and what had happened to him I could only guess. Where he had failed I certainly could not succeed, for the cliffs, the wall and the guards shut it off impenetrably from the world. Inside was Koré alone – I wondered if the old servant whom she had called Mitri was with her, or the French maid she had had in London – and that night would see the beginning of the end. The remembrance of the faggots piled about the door sent a horrid chill to my heart. The situation had marched clean outside human power to control it. I thought with scorn of my self-confidence. I had grievously muddled every detail, and was of as little value as if I had remained in my Temple chambers. Pity and fear for the girl made me clench my hands and gnaw my lips. I could not stay still. I decided once more to prospect the line of the cliffs.

One-armed Janni was no use, so I left him behind. I slid down the stone-shoot and in the first cool of evening scrambled along that arduous shore. When I had passed the abutment of the wall I scanned with my glass every crack in the cliffs, but in daylight they looked even more hopeless than under the moon. At one place a shallow gully permitted me to reach a shelf, but there I stuck fast, for the rock above could only have been climbed by a hanging rope. The most desperate man – and by that time I was pretty desperate – could not find a way where the Almighty had decided that there should be none. I think that if there had been the faintest chance I would have taken it, in spite of the risks; I would have ventured on a course which at Chamonix or Cortina would have been pronounced suicidal; but here there was not even the rudiments of a course – nothing but that maddening glassy wall.

By and by I reached the cape beyond which lay the hidden bay and Black George with his boat. It occurred to me that I had not prospected very carefully the cliffs in this bay, and in any case I wanted to look again at the boat, that single frail link we had with the outer world. But first I stripped and had a bathe, which did something to cool the fret of my nerves. Then I waded round the point to the place where Janni and I had talked with the seaman.

Black George had gone. There was not a trace of him or the boat in the shining inlet into which the westering sun was pouring its yellow light. What on earth had happened? Had his mysterious master returned? Or had he been driven off by the islanders? Or had he simply grown bored and sailed away? The last solution I dismissed: Black George, I was convinced, was no quitter.

The loss of him was the last straw to my hopelessness. I was faced with a situation with which no ingenuity or fortitude could grapple – only some inhuman skill in acrobatics or some Berserker physical powers which I did not possess. I turned my glass listlessly on the cliffs which lined the bay. There was nothing to be done there. They were as sheer as those I had already prospected, and, although more rugged and broken, it was by means of great noses of smooth rock on which only a fly could move.

I was sitting on the very boulder which Janni had occupied the night before, and I saw on the shingle one or two of his cigarette stumps. And then I saw something else.

It was a cigarette end, but not one of Janni's caporals. Moreover it had been dropped there during the past day. Janni's stumps, having been exposed to the night dews, were crumpled and withered; this was intact, the butt end of an Egyptian cigarette of a good English brand. Black George must have been here in the course of the day. But I remembered that Black George had smoked a peculiarly evil type of Greek tobacco. Perhaps he had been pilfering his master's cigarettes? Or perhaps his master had come back?

I remembered that he had refused to utter one word about that master of his. Who could he be? Was he an Englishman? He might well be, judging from Black George's reverence for the word 'English'. If so, what was he doing in Plakos, and how had he reached this spot, unless he had the wings of a bird? If he had come along the downs and the shore Janni would have seen him . . . Anyhow, he was gone now, and our one bridge with a sane world was broken.

I made my way back to Janni with a feeling that I had come to the edge of things and would presently be required to go over the brink. I was now quite alone – as much alone as Koré – and fate might soon link these lonelinesses. I had had this feeling once or twice in the war – that I was faced with something so insane that insanity was the only course for me, but I had no notion what form the insanity would take, for I still saw nothing before me but helplessness. I was determined somehow to break the barrier, regardless of the issue. Every scrap of manhood in me revolted against my futility. In that moment I became primitive man again. Even if the woman were not my woman she was of my own totem, and whatever her fate she should not meet it alone.

Janni had food ready for me, but I could not eat it. I took out my pistol, cleaned and reloaded it, and told Janni to look to his. I am not much of a pistol shot, but Janni, as I knew from Maris, was an expert. There would be something astir when the moon rose, and I had an intuition that the scene would be the Dancing Floor. The seaward end of the House might be the vital point in the last stage of the drama, but I was convinced that the Dancing Floor would see the first act. It was the holy ground, and I had gathered from the priest that some dark ritual would take the place of the Good Friday solemnity.

There was only one spot where Janni and I might safely lie hidden, and at the same time look down on the Dancing Floor, and that was in the shadow of the wall between the guarded breach and the cliffs. There were large trees there and the progress of the moon would not light it up, whereas everywhere else would be clear as noonday. Moreover it was the strategic point, for whatever mischief was intended against the House would pass through the breach and therefore under our eyes. But it was necessary to get there before the moon was fully risen, for otherwise to men coming from the village we should be silhouetted against the cliff edge. I cut Janni's supper short and we started out, using every crinkle of the ground as cover, much as stalkers do when they are fetching a circuit and know that the deer are alarmed and watchful.

We had not much more than a mile to go, and by the route we chose we managed, as it happened, to keep wholly out of sight of the Dancing Floor. Janni – no mountaineer – grumbled at my pace, for I had acquired an extraordinary lightness of limb so that I felt as if I could have flown. I was puzzled to explain this, after my listlessness of the day, but I think it was due partly to tense nerves and partly to the magic of the evening. The air was cool and exhilarating, and when the moon rose with a sudden glory above the House it was as tonic as if one had plunged into water . . . Soon we were on the edge of the inky belt of shadow and moving eastward to get nearer the breach. But now I noticed something I had forgotten. The wall curved outward, and beyond that bulge – a couple of hundred yards from the breach – the light flooded to the very edge of the stone. We came to a halt at the apex of the curve, flat on our faces, and I turned to reconnoitre the Dancing Floor.

I wish to Heaven that I had the gift of words. It is too much to ask a man whose life has been spent in drawing pleadings and in writing dull legal opinions to describe a scene which needs the tongue or pen of a poet. For the Dancing Floor was transfigured. Its lonely beauty had been decked and adorned, as an altar is draped for high festival. On both slopes people clustered, men, women and children, all so silent that I thought I could hear them breathe. I thought, too, that they mostly wore white – at any rate the moonlight gave me the impression of an immense white multitude, all Kynaetho and doubtless half the hills. The valley was marked out like a race-course. There seemed to be posts at regular intervals in a broad oval, and at each post was a red flicker which meant torches. The desert had become populous, and the solitary places blossomed with roses of fire.

The people were clustered towards the upper end, making an amphitheatre of which the arena was the Dancing Floor, and the entrance to the stage the breach in the wall of the House. I saw that this entrance was guarded, not as before by three sentries, but by a double line of men who kept an avenue open between them. Beyond the spectators and round the arena was the circle of posts, and between them lay the Dancing Floor, golden in the moon, and flanked at its circumference by the angry crimson of the torches. I noticed another thing. Not quite in the centre but well within the arena was a solitary figure waiting. He was in white – gleaming white, and, so far as I could judge, he was standing beside the spring from which I had drunk the night before.

I have set out the details of what I saw, but they are only the beggarly elements, for I cannot hope to reproduce the strangeness which caught at the heart and laid a spell on the mind. The place was no more the Valley of the Shadow of Life, but Life itself – a surge of daemonic energy out of the deeps of the past. It was wild and yet ordered, savage and yet sacramental, the home of an ancient knowledge which shattered for me the modern world and left me gasping like a cave-man before his mysteries. The magic smote on my brain, though I struggled against it. The passionless moonlight and the passionate torches – that, I think, was the final miracle – a marrying of the eternal cycle of nature with the fantasies of man.

The effect on Janni was overwhelming. He lay and gibbered prayers with eyes as terrified as a deer's, and I realised that I need not look for help in that quarter. But I scarcely thought of him, for my trouble was with myself. Most people would call me a solid fellow, with a hard head and a close-texture mind, but if they had seen me then they would have changed their view. I was struggling with something which I had never known before, a mixture of fear, abasement and a crazy desire to worship. Yes – to worship. There was that in the scene which wakened some ancient instinct, so that I felt it in me to join the votaries.

It took me a little time to pull myself together. I looked up at the dome of the sky, where on the horizon pale stars were showing. The whole world seemed hard and gem-like and unrelenting. There was no help there. Nature approved this ritual. And then a picture flashed into my mind which enabled me to recover my wits. It was the carven Christ lying in its shroud in the bier in the deserted church. I am not a religious man in the ordinary sense – only a half-believer in the creed in which I was born. But in that moment I realised that there was that in me which was stronger than the pagan, an instinct which had come down to me from believing generations. I understood then what were my gods. I think I prayed. I know that I clung to the memory of that rude image as a Christian martyr may have clung to his crucifix. It stood for all the broken lights which were in me as against this ancient charmed darkness.

I was steadier now and with returning sanity came the power of practical thought. Something, someone, was to be brought from the House. Was there to be a trial in that arena? Or a sacrifice? No – I was clear that tonight was only the preparation, and that the great day was the morrow. There was no sound from the gathering. I could not see the faces, but I knew that everyone, down to the smallest child, was awed and rapt and expectant. No crowd, hushing its breath in the decisive moments of a great match, was ever more rigidly on the stretch. The very air quivered with expectation.

Then a movement began. Figures entered the arena at the end farthest from me – men, young men, naked I thought at first, till my glass showed me that each wore a sort of loin-cloth or it may have been short drawers . . . They aligned themselves, like runners at the start of a race, and still there was no sound. The figure who had been standing by the well was now beside them and seemed to be speaking softly. Each held himself tense, with clenched hands, and his eyes on the ground. Then came some kind of signal and they sprang forward.

It was a race – such a race as few men can have witnessed. The slim youths kept outside the torches, and circled the arena of the Dancing Floor. Over the moonlit sward they flew, glimmering like ghosts – once round, a second time round. And all the while the crowd kept utter silence.

I ran the mile myself at school and college, and know something about pace. I could see that it was going to be a close finish. One man I noted, I think the very fellow who had hunted me into the church – he ran superbly and won a lead at the start. But the second time round I fancied another, a taller and leaner man who had kept well back in the first round, and was slowly creeping ahead. I liked his style, which was oddly like the kind of thing we cultivate at home, and he ran with judgement too. Soon he was abreast of the first man, and then he sprinted and took the lead. I was wondering where the finish would be, when he snatched a torch from one of the posts, ran strongly up the centre of the Dancing Floor and plunged the flame in the spring.

Still there was no sound from the crowd. The winner stood with his head bent, a noble figure of youth who might have stepped from a Parthenon frieze. The others had gone: he stood close beside the well with the white-clad figure who had acted as master of ceremonies – only now the victor in the race seemed to be the true master, on whom all eyes waited.

The sight was so strange and beautiful that I watched it half in a trance. I seemed to have seen it all before, and to know the stages that would follow . . . Yes, I was right. There was a movement from the crowd and a man was brought forward. I knew the man, though he wore nothing but pants and a torn shirt. One could not mistake the trim figure of Maris, or his alert bird-like head.

He stood confronting the beautiful young barbarian beside the spring, looking very much as if he would like to make a fight of it. And then the latter seemed to speak to him, and to lay a hand on his head. Maris submitted, and the next I saw was that the runner had drawn a jar of water from the well and was pouring it over him. He held it high in his arms and the water wavered and glittered in the moonshine; I could see Maris spluttering and wringing out his wet shirt-sleeves.

With that recollection flooded in on me. This was the ceremonial of which Vernon had read to me from Koré's manuscript. A virgin and a youth were chosen and set apart in a hallowed place, and the chooser was he who was victor in a race and was called the King. The victims were hallowed with water from the well by the white cypress. I was looking at the well, though the cypress had long since disappeared. I was looking at the King, and at one of those dedicated to the sacrifice. The other was the girl in the House . . . Vernon had said that if we know what the word *hosiotheis* meant we should know a good deal about Greek religion. That awful knowledge was now mine.

It was as I expected. The consecrator and the consecrated were moving, still in the same hushed silence, towards the *horkos* – the sanctuary. The torches had been extinguished as soon as the victor plunged his in the spring, and the pure light of the moon seemed to have waxed to an unearthly brightness. The two men walked up the slope of the Dancing Floor to the line of guards which led to the breach in the wall. I could not hold my glass because of the trembling of my hands, but I could see the figures plainly – the tall runner, his figure poised like some young Apollo of the great age of art, his face dark with the sun but the skin of his body curiously white. Some youth of the hills, doubtless – his crisp hair seemed in the moonlight to be flaxen. Beside him went the shorter Maris, flushed and truculent. He must have been captured by the guards in his attempt on the House, and as a stranger and also a Greek had been put forward as the male victim.

I was roused by the behaviour of Janni. He had realised that his beloved *capitaine* was a prisoner, towards whom some evil was doubtless intended, and this understanding had driven out his fear and revived his military instincts. He was cursing fiercely and had got out his pistol.

'Sir,' he whispered to me, 'I can crawl within shot, for the shadow is lengthening, and put a bullet into yon bandit. Then in the confusion my *capitaine* will escape and join us and break for the cliffs. These people are sheep and may not follow.'

For a second it appeared to me the only thing to do. This evil Adonis was about to enter the House and on the morrow Koré and Maris would find death at his hands, for he was the sacrificer. I seemed to see in his arrogant beauty the cruelty of an elder world. His death would at any rate shatter the ritual.

And then I hesitated and gripped Janni firmly by his one arm. For, as the two men passed out of my sight towards the breach in the wall, I had caught a glimpse of Maris's face. He was speaking to his companion, and his expression was not of despair and terror, but confident, almost cheerful. For an instant the life of the young runner hung on a thread, for I do not think that Janni would have missed. Then I decided against the shot, for I felt that it was a counsel of despair. There was something which I did not comprehend, for Maris's face had given me a glimmer of hope.

I signed to Janni and we started crawling back towards the cliffs. In that hour the one thing that kept me sane was the image of the dead Christ below the chancel step. It was my only link with the reasonable and kindly world I had lost.

TWELVE

I HAD ONLY one impulse at that moment – an overwhelming desire to get back to the church and look again at the figure on the bier. It seemed to me the sole anchor in the confusion of uncharted tides, the solitary hope in a desert of perplexities. I had seen ancient magic revive and carry captive the hearts of a people. I had myself felt its compelling power. A girl whom I loved and a man who was my companion were imprisoned and at the mercy of a maddened populace. Maris was, like Ulysses, an old campaigner and a fellow of many wiles, but what could Maris do in the face of multitudes? An unhallowed epiphany was looked for, but first must come the sacrifice. There was no help in the arm of flesh, and the shallow sophistication of the modern world fell from me like a useless cloak. I was back in my childhood's faith, and wanted to be at my childhood's prayers.

As for Janni he had a single idea in his head, to follow his captain into the House and strike a blow for him, and as he padded along the seaward cliffs he doubtless thought we were bent on attacking the place from another side. We took pretty much the road I had taken in the morning, skirting the Dancing Floor on its southern edge. One strange thing I saw. The Dancing Floor was still thronged, though a space was kept clear in the centre round the well. Clearly it was no longer *tabu*, but a place of holiday. Moreover, the people seemed to intend to remain there, for they had lit fires and were squatting round them, while some had already stretched themselves to sleep. Kynaetho had moved in a body to the scene of the sacrament.

When we reached the fringe of the village I saw that I had guessed correctly. There was not a sign of life in the streets. We walked boldly into the central square, and it might have been a graveyard. Moreover, in the graveyard itself the lamps by the graves had not been lit. Vampires were apparently no longer to be feared, and that struck me as an ill omen. Keats's lines came into my head about the 'little town by river or sea shore' which is 'emptied of its folk this pious morn'. Pious morn!

And then above us, from the squat campanile, a bell began to toll – raggedly, feebly, like the plaint of a child. Yet to me it was also a challenge.

The church was bright with moonshine. The curtains still shrouded the sanctuary, and there were no candles lit, nothing but the flickering lamps before the ikons. Below the chancel step lay the dark mass which contained the shrouded Christ. Janni, like myself, seemed to find comfort in being here. He knelt at a respectful distance from the bier and began to mutter prayers. I went forward and lifted the shroud. The moon coming through one of the windows gave the carved wood a ghastly semblance of real flesh, and I could not bear to look on it. I followed Janni's example and breathed incoherent prayers. I was bred a Calvinist, but in that moment I was not worshipping any graven image. My prayer was to be delivered from the idolatry of the heathen.

Suddenly the priest was beside me. In one hand he held a lighted candle, and the other carried a censer. He seemed in no way surprised to see us, but there was that about him which made me catch my breath. The man had suddenly become enlarged and ennobled. All the weakness had gone out of the old face, all the languor and bewilderment out of the eyes, the shoulders had straightened, his beard was no longer like a goat's, but like a prophet's. He was as one possessed, a fanatic, a martyr.

He had forgotten that I knew no Greek, for he spoke rapidly words which sounded like a command. But Janni understood, and went forward obediently to the bier. Then I saw what he meant us to do. We were to take the place of the absent hierophants and carry the image of the dead Christ through the bounds of the village. The bier was light enough even for one-armed Janni to manage his share. The shroud was removed, he took the fore-end, and I the back, and behind the priest we marched out into the night.

The streets were deathly still, the cool night air was unruffled by wind, so that the candle burned steadily; the golden dome of the sky was almost as bright as day. Along the white beaten road we went, and then into the rough cobbles of the main street. I noticed that though the houses were empty every house door was wide open. We passed the inn and came into the road to the harbour and to the cottage among fruit trees where I had first made inquiries. Then we turned up the hill where lay the main entrance to the House, past little silent untenanted crofts and oliveyards which were all gleaming grey and silver. The old man moved slowly, swinging his censer, and intoning what I took to be a dirge in a voice no longer tremulous, but masterful and strong, and behind him Janni and I stumbled along bearing the symbol of man's salvation.

I had never been present at a Greek Good Friday celebration, but Koré had described it to me – the following crowds tortured with suspense, the awed kneeling women, the torches, the tears, the universal lamentation. Then the people sorrowed, not without hope, for their dead Saviour. But the ordinary ceremonial can never have been so marvellous as was our broken ritual that night. We were celebrating, but there were no votaries. The torches had gone to redden the Dancing Floor, sorrow had been exchanged for a guilty ecstasy, the worshippers were seeking another Saviour. Our rite was more than a commemoration, it was a defiance, and I felt like a man who carries a challenge to the enemy.

The moon had set and darkness had begun before we returned to the church. Both Janni and I were very weary before we laid down our burden in the vault below the nave, a place hewn out of the dry limestone rock. By the last flickering light of the candle I saw the priest standing at the head of the bier, his hands raised in supplication, his eyes bright and rapt and unseeing. He was repeating a litany in which a phrase constantly recurred. I could guess its meaning. It must have been 'He will yet arise'.

'I slept till broad daylight in the priest's house on the priest's bed,' while Janni snored on a pile of sheepskins. Since Kynaetho was deserted, there was no reason now for secrecy, for the whole place, and not the church only, had become a sanctuary. The aged woman who kept house for the priest gave us a breakfast of milk and bread, but we saw no sign of him, and I did not wish to return to the church and disturb his devotions. I wondered if I should ever see him again; it was a toss-up if I should ever see anybody again after this day of destiny. We had been partners in strange events and I could not leave him without some farewell, so I took the book of his which seemed to be most in use, put two English five-pound notes inside, and did my best in laboriously printed Latin to explain that this was a gift for the Church and to thank him and wish him well.

I did another thing, for I wrote out a short account of the position, saying that futher information might be obtained from Erizberger and Vernon Milburne. Anything might happen today, and I wanted to leave some record for my friends. I addressed the document under cover to the priest, and – again in Latin – begged him, should anything happen to me, to see that it reached the British Minister in Athens. That was about all I could do in the way of preparation, and I had a moment of grim amusement in thinking how strangely I, who since the war had seemed to be so secure and cosseted, had moved back to the razor-edge of life.

I have said that there was no need for secrecy, so we walked straight through the village towards the harbour. Janni had made a preliminary survey beyond the graveyard in the early morning, and had reported that the people of Kynaetho were still encamped around the Dancing Floor. The trouble would not begin till we approached the House, for it was certain that on that day of all days the guards would be vigilant. We were both of us wholly desperate. We simply had to get in, and to get in before the evening: for that purpose anything, even wholesale homicide, was legitimate. But at the same time it would do not good to get caught, even if we succeeded in killing several of our captors.

I think I had a faint unreasonable hope that we should find the situation at the causeway more promising than it had appeared on the day before. But when – after a walk where we had seen no trace of man or beast – we came to the crest of the little cape beyond which lay the jetty and the House, I had a sad disillusionment. The place was thick with sentries. I saw the line of them along the causeway and at the head of the jetty; moreover there seemed to be men working to the left of the House where there was a cluster of outbuildings descending to the shallow vale up which ran the road from the sea. My glass showed me what they were doing. They were piling more straw and brushwood, so that from the outbuildings, which were probably of wood and would burn like tinder, the flames might have easy access to the windows of the House. The altar was being duly prepared for the victim.

Long and carefully I prospected the ground. There was

cover enough to take us down to within a few yards of the jetty. If I tried to cross it I should be within view of the people on the causeway, and even if I got across unobserved there was the more or less open beach between the causeway and the sea. It was true that directly under the wall I should be out of sight of the causeway guards, but then again, though I could get shelter behind some of the boulders, I could not move far without being noticed by whoever chose to patrol the jetty. Nevertheless that was the only road for me, for my object was to get to the far end of the causeway, where before the cliffs began there were oliveyards and orchards, through which some route must be possible to the House.

I considered the left side of the picture, where the valley led upwards past the outbuildings. That way I could see no hope, for if I succeeded in passing the faggot-stackers I would only reach the confines of the main entrance to the demesne from Kynaetho, which was certain to be the best warded of all.

I had also to consider what to do with Janni. He would be a useful ally if it came to a scrap, but a scrap would be futile against such numbers, and in stalking or climbing his lack of an arm would be a serious handicap. Besides, if our business was to escape observation, one man would be better than two . . . But it was possible that he might create a diversion. Supposing he tried the road on the left up the valley and made himself conspicuous, he might draw off attention while I crossed the jetty and got under the lee of the causeway wall. That meant of course that one of us would be put out of action, but unless we tried something of the kind we should both fail.

I put the thing to him, as we lay among the scrubby arbutus, and though he clearly did not like the proposal, since his notion was to manhandle somebody on Maris's behalf, he was too good a soldier not to see the sense of it. He pointed out various difficulties, and then shook his head like a dog and said that he agreed. For his own sake I forbade any shooting. If he were merely hunted and captured, it was unlikely that any harm would befall him. He could explain that he was one of the survey party who had lost the others, and at the worst he would be shut up temporarily in some barn. He might even find the means to make himself useful later in the day.

So it was settled that I should try to worm my way as near to the jetty as the cover would allow. He was to watch my movements and when he saw my hand raised three times he was to march boldly towards the jetty. I would not be able to see what was happening, so when he was pursued and started up the little valley he was to shout as if in alarm. That would be the signal to me that the sentry had left the jetty and that I might try to cross it.

I started out at once on my first stage. As I have said, the cover was good – boulders overgrown with heath and vines, and patches of arbutus and a very prickly thorn. I tried to behave as if I were on a Scotch hill stalking alone, with deer where the sentries stood. It was not a very difficult passage, for my enemies had no eyes for the ground on my side, their business being to prevent egress from the House. After about half an hour's careful crawling, I found myself within six yards of the jetty looking through the tangle to the rough masonry of it, with a sideways view of the point where it joined the causeway. I could see none of the guards, but I heard distinctly the sound of their speech. I had marked the spot where I now lay before I started, and knew that it was within sight of Janni. So I straightened myself and thrice raised my arms above the scrub.

For a minute or two nothing happened. Janni must have started but had not yet attracted attention. I raised my body as far as I dared, but I could only see the shoreward end of the jetty – neither the jetty itself nor any part of the causeway. I waited for a cry, but there was no sound. Was Janni being suffered to make his way up the little valley unopposed?

Then suddenly a moving object flashed into my narrow orbit of vision. It must be one of the watchers from the causeway, and he was in a furious hurry – I could hear the scruff of his heelless boots on the dry stones as he turned a corner . . . He must be in pursuit of Janni . . . There would no doubt be others too at the job. Their silence might be a ritual business. *Favete linguis*, perhaps? If Janni shouted I never heard him.

I resolved to take the chance, and bolted out of cover to the jetty. In two bounds I was beyond it and among the gravel and weed of the farther beach. But in that short progress I saw enough of the landscape to know that I was undiscovered, that there was nobody on the causeway within sight, or at the mouth of the little glen. Janni had certainly been followed, and by this time was no doubt in the hands of the Philistines out of my ken.

I ran close under the lee of the sea-wall, and at first I had a wild hope of getting beyond the causeway into the region of the olive groves before the sentries returned. But some remnant of prudence made me halt and consider before I attempted the last open strip of beach. There I had a view of the bit of the causeway towards the jetty, and suddenly figures appeared on it, running figures, like men returning to duty after a hasty interlude. If I had moved another foot I should have been within view.

There was nothing for it but to wait where I was. I crouched in a little nook between a fallen boulder and the wall, with the weedy rim of the causeway six feet above me. Unless a man stood on the very edge and peered down I was safe from observation. But that was the sum of my blessings. I heard soft feet above me as the men returned to their posts, and I dared not move a yard. It was now about two in the afternoon; I had brought no food with me, though I found a couple of dusty figs in my pocket; the sun blazed on the white wall and the gravel of the shore till the place was like a bakehouse; I was hot and thirsty, and I might have been in the middle of the Sahara for all the chance of a drink. But the discomfort of my body was trivial compared with the disquiet of my mind.

For I found myself in a perfect fever of vexation and fear. The time was slipping past and the crisis was nigh, and yet, though this was now my fourth day on the island, I was not an inch farther forward than the hour I landed. My worst fears – nay, what had seemed to me mere crazy imaginings – had been realised. I was tortured by the thought of Koré – her innocent audacities, her great-hearted courage, her loneliness, her wild graces. 'Beauteous vain endeavour' – that was the phrase of some poet that haunted me and made me want to howl like a wolf. I realised now the meaning of a sacrifice and the horror of it. The remembrance of the slim victor in the race, beautiful and pitiless, made me half-crazy. Movement in that place was nearly impossible, but it was utterly impossible that I should stay still. I began in short stages to worm my way along the foot of the wall.

I do not suppose that the heat of that April afternoon was anything much to complain of, but my fever of mind must have affected my body, for I felt that I had never been so scorched and baked in my life. There was not a scrap of shade, the rocks almost blistered the hand, the dust got into my throat and nose and made me furiously thirsty, and my head ached as if I had a sunstroke . . . The trouble was with the jetty and the watchers on it, for I was always in view of them. Had they detected a movement below the wall, a single glance would have revealed me. So I had to make my stages very short, and keep a wary outlook behind . . . There seemed to be much astir on the jetty. Not only the guards, but other figures appeared on it, and I saw that they were carrying up something from a boat at anchor. That I think was what saved me. Had the sentries had nothing to do but to stare about them I must have been discovered, but the portage business kept them distracted.

The minutes seemed hours to my distraught mind, but I did indeed take an inconceivable time crawling along that grilling beach, with the cool sea water lapping not a dozen yards off to give point to my discomfort. When I reached the place where the causeway ceased, and long ribs of rock took the place of the boulders of the shore, I found by my watch that it was nearly six o'clock. The discovery put quicksilver into my weary limbs. Looking back I saw that I was out of sight of the jetty, and that a few yards would put me out of sight of the causeway. I wriggled into the cover of a bush of broom, lay on my back for a minute or two to rest, and then made for the shade of the oliveyards.

The place was weedy and neglected – I don't know anything about olive culture, but I could see that much. There was a wilderness of a white umbelliferous plant and masses of a thing like a spineless thistle. I pushed uphill among the trees, keeping well in the shade, with the west front of the House glimmering through the upper leaves at a much higher elevation. Above me I saw a deeper shadow which I took to be cypresses, and beyond them I guessed must lie the demesne. I hoped for a gate, and in any case expected no more than a hedge and a palisade.

Instead I found a wall. There was a door to be sure, but it was no use to me, for it was massive and locked. I might have known that Shelley Arabin would leave no part of his cursed refuge unbarricaded. I sat and blinked up at this new obstacle, and could have cried with exasperation. It seemed to run direct from the House to the edge of the cliffs which began about a quarter of a mile to my right, and was an exact replica of the wall above the Dancing Floor.

I decided that it was no good trying it at the House end, for there I should certainly be in view of some of the guards. The masonry was comparatively new and very solid, and since none of the olive trees grew within four yards of it, it was impossible to use them as a ladder. Already I felt the approach of night, for the sun was well down in the west and a great tide of sunset was flooding the sky. I do not think I have ever before felt so hopeless or so obstinate. I was determined to pass that wall by its abutment on the cliffs or break my neck in the effort.

My memory of the next hour is not very clear. All I know is that in the failing daylight I came to the cliffs' edge and found an abutment similar to the one at the Dancing Floor. Similar, but not the same. For here some storm had torn the masonry and it seemed to me that it might be passed. The rock fell steep and smooth to the sea, but that part which was the handiwork of man was ragged. I took off my boots and flung them over the wall by way of a gage of battle, and then I started to make the traverse.

It was a slow and abominable business, but I do not think it would have been very difficult had the light been good, for the stone was hard enough and the cracks were many. But in that dim gloaming with a purple void beneath me, with a heart which would not beat steadily and a head which throbbed with pain, I found it very near the limit of my powers. I had to descend before I could traverse, and the worst part was the ascent on the far side. I knew that, when I at last got a grip of a wind-twisted shrub and tried to draw myself over the brink, it needed every ounce of strength left in me. I managed it and lay gasping beside the roots of a great pine – inside the demesne at last.

When I got my breath I found that I had a view into the narrow cove where Janni and I had seen the boat. Black George had returned, and returned brazenly, for he was showing a riding light. A lantern swung from the mast, and, more, there was a glow from the cabin skylight. I wondered what was going on in the little craft, and I think the sight gave me a grain of comfort, till I realised that I was hopelessly cut off from Black George. What was the good of a link with the outer world, when unscalable walls and cliffs intervened – when at any moment murder might be the end of everything?

Murder – that was the word which filled my head as I pushed inland. I had never thought of it in that way, but of course I was out to prevent murder. To prevent it? More likely to share in it . . . I had no plan of any kind, only a desire to be with Koré, so that she should not be alone. It was her loneliness that I could not bear . . . And anyhow I had a pistol and I would not miss the runner. 'The priest who slew the slayer and shall himself be slain' – the tag came unbidden to my lips. I think I must have been rather light-headed.

The last fires of the sunset did not penetrate far into the pine wood, the moon had not yet risen, and as I ran I took many tosses, for the place was very dark. There were paths, but I neglected them, making straight for where I believed the House to lie. I was not exact in my course, for I bore too much to the right in the direction of the breach in the wall at the Dancing Floor. Soon I was among shrubberies in which rides had been cut, but there were still many tall trees to make darkness. I thought I saw to the right, beyond where the wall lay, a reddish glow. That would be the torches on the Dancing Floor where the people waited for the epiphany.

Suddenly on my left front a great blaze shot up to heaven. I knew it was the signal that the hour had come. The outbuildings had been fired, and the House would soon be in flames. The blaze wavered and waned, and then waxed to a mighty conflagration as the fire reached something specially inflammable. In a minute that wood was bright as with an obscene daylight. The tree trunks stood out black against a molten gold, which at times crimsoned and purpled in a devilish ecstasy of destruction.

I knew now where the House lay. I clutched my pistol, and ran down a broad path, with a horrid fear that I was too late after all. I ran blindly, and had just time to step aside to let two figures pass.

They were two of the guards – hillmen by their dress – and even in my absorption I wondered what had happened to them. For they were like men demented, with white faces and open mouths. One of them stumbled and fell, and seemed to stay on his knees for a second praying, till his companion lugged him forward. I might have faced them with impunity, for their eyes were sightless. Never have I seen men suffering from an extremer terror.

The road twisted too much for my haste, so I cut across country. The surge and crackle of the flames filled the air, but it seemed as if I heard another sound, the sound of running feet, of bodies, many bodies, brushing through the thicket. I was close on the House now, and close on the road which led to it from the broken wall and the Dancing Floor. As I jumped a patch of scrub and the gloom lightened in the more open avenue, I bumped into another man and saw that it was Maris.

He was waiting, pistol in hand, beside the road, and in a trice had his gun at my head. Then he recognised me and lowered it. His face was as crazy as the hillmen's who had passed me, and he still wore nothing but breeches and a ragged shirt, but his wild eyes seemed to hold also a dancing humour.

'Blessed Jesu!' he whispered, 'you have come in time. The fools are about to receive their Gods. You have your pistol? But I do not think there will be shooting.'

He choked suddenly as if he had been struck dumb, and I too choked. For I looked with him up the avenue towards the burning House.

Part Three

THIRTEEN

THIS PART OF the story (said Leithen) I can only give at second-hand. I have pieced it together as well as I could from what Vernon told me, but on many matters he was naturally not communicative, and at these I have had to guess for myself . . .

Vernon left England the day after the talk with me which I have already recorded, sending his boat as deck cargo to Patras, while he followed by way of Venice. He had a notion that the great hour which was coming had best be met at sea, where he would be far from the distractions and littlenesses of life. He took one man with him from Wyvenhoe, a lean gipsy lad called Martell, but the boy fell sick at Corfu and he was obliged to send him home. In his stead he found an Epirote with a string of names, who was strongly recommended to him by one of his colleagues in the old Aegean Secret Service. From Patras they made good sailing up the Gulf of Corinth, and, passing through the Canal, came in the last days of March to the Piraeus. In that place of polyglot speech, whistling engines and the odour of gas-works, they delayed only for water and supplies, and presently had rounded Sunium, and were beating up the Euripus with the Attic hills rising sharp and clear in the spring sunlight.

He had no plans. It was a joy to him to be alone with the racing seas and the dancing winds, to scud past the little headlands, pink and white with blossom, or to lie of a night in some hidden bay beneath the thymy crags. He had discarded the clothes of civilisation. In a blue jersey and old corduroy trousers, bareheaded and barefooted, he steered his craft and waited on the passing of the hours. His mood, he has told me, was one of complete happiness, unshadowed by nervousness or doubt. The long preparation was almost at an end. Like an acolyte before a temple gate, he believed himself to be on the threshold of a new life. He had that sense of unseen hands which comes to all men once or twice in their lives, and both hope and fear were swallowed up in a calm expectancy.

Trouble began under the snows of Pelion as they turned the north end of Euboea. On the morning of the first Monday in April the light winds died away, and foul weather came out of the north-west. By midday it was half a gale, and in those yeasty shallow seas, with an iron coast to port and starboard, their position was dangerous. The nearest harbour was twenty miles distant, and neither of the crew had ever been there before. With the evening the gale increased, and it was decided to get out of that maze of rocky islands to the safer deeps of the Aegean.

It was a hard night for the two of them, and there was no chance of sleep. More by luck than skill they escaped the butt of Skiathos, and the first light found them far to the south-east among the long tides of the North Aegean. They ran close-reefed before the gale, and all morning with decks awash nosed and plunged in seas which might have been the wintry Atlantic. It was not till the afternoon that the gale seemed to blow itself out and two soaked and chilly mortals could relax their vigil. Soon bacon was frizzling on the cuddy-stove, and hot coffee and dry clothes restored them to moderate comfort.

The sky cleared, and in bright sunlight, with the dregs of the gale behind him, Vernon steered for the nearest land, an island of which he did not trouble to read the name, but which the chart showed to possess good anchorage. Late in the evening, when the light was growing dim, they came into a little bay carved from the side of a hill. They also came into fog. The wind had dropped utterly, and the land which they saw was only an outline in the haze. When they cast anchor the fog was rolling like a tide over the sea, and muffling their yards. They spent a busy hour or two, repairing the damage of the storm, and then the two of them made such a meal as befits those who have faced danger together. Afterwards Vernon, as his custom was, sat alone in the stern, smoking and thinking his thoughts. He wrote up his diary with a ship's lantern beside him, while the mist hung about him low and soft as an awning.

He had leisure now for the thought which had all day been at the back of his mind. The night – the great night – had passed and there had been no dream. The adventure for which all his life he had been preparing himself had vanished into the

Aegean tides. The hour when the revelation should have come had been spent in battling with the storm, when a man lives in the minute at grips with too urgent realities.

His first mood was one of dismal relaxedness. He felt as useless as an unstrung bow. I, the only man to whom he had ever confided his secret, had been right, and the long vigil had ended in fiasco. He tried to tell himself that it was a relief, that an old folly was over, but he knew that deep down in his heart there was bitter disappointment. The fates had prepared the stage, and rung up the curtain and lo! there was no play. He had been fooled, and somehow the zest and savour of life had gone from him. After all, no man can be strung high and then find his preparations idle without suffering a cruel recoil.

And then anger came to stiffen him – anger at himself. What a God-forsaken ass he had been, frittering away his best years in following a phantom! . . . In his revulsion he loathed the dream which he had cherished so long. He began to explain it away with the common sense which on my lips he had accounted blasphemy . . . The regular seasonal occurrence was his own doing – he had expected it and it had come – a mere case of subjective compulsion . . . The fact that each year the revelation had moved one room nearer was also the result of his willing it to be so, for subconsciously he must have desired to hasten the consummation . . . He went through every detail, obstinately providing some rationalistic explanation for each. I do not think he can have satisfied himself, but he was in the mood to deface his idols, and one feeling surged above all others – that he was done with fancies now and for ever. He has told me that the thing he longed for chiefly at that moment was to have me beside him that he might make formal recantation.

By and by he argued himself into some philosophy. He had dallied certain years, but he was still young and the world was before him. He had kept his body and mind in hard training, and that at any rate was not wasted, though the primal purpose had gone. He was a normal man now among normal men, and it was his business to prove himself. He thought in his Calvinistic way that the bogus vision might have been sent to him for a purpose – the thing might be hallucination, but the *askesis* which it had entailed was solid gain . . . He fetched from his locker the little book in which he had chronicled his inner life, and wrote in it 'Finis'. Then he locked it and flung the key overboard. The volume would be kept at Severns to remind him of his folly, but it would never be opened by him.

By this time he was his own master again. He would sail for England next morning and get hold of me and make a plan for his life.

He was now conscious for the first time of his strange environment. The boat was in a half-moon of bay in an island of which he had omitted to notice the name but whose latitude and longitude he roughly knew. The night was close around him like a shell, for the fog had grown thicker, though the moon behind it gave it an opaque sheen. It was an odd place in which to be facing a crisis . . .

His thoughts ran fast ahead to the career which he must shape from the ruins of his dream. He was too late for the Bar. Business might be the best course – he had big interests in the north of England which would secure him a footing, and he believed that he had the kind of mind for administration . . . Or politics? There were many chances for a young man in the confused post-bellum world . . .

He was absorbed in his meditations and did not hear the sound of ears or the grating of a boat alongside. Suddenly he found a face looking at him in the ring of lamplight – an old bearded face curiously wrinkled. The eyes, which were shrewd and troubled, scanned him for a second or two, and then a voice spoke:

Will the Signor come with me?' it said in French.

Vernon, amazed at this apparition which had come out of the mist, could only stare.

'Will the Signor come with me?' the voice spoke again. 'We have grievous need of a man.'

Vernon unconsciously spoke not in French but in Greek. 'Who the devil are you, and where do you come from?'

'I come from the House. I saw you enter the bay before the fog fell. Had there been no fog, they would not have let me come to you.'

'Who are "they"?' Vernon asked.

But the old man shook his head. 'Come with me and I will tell you. It is a long story.'

'But what do you want me to do? Confound it. I'm not going off with a man I never saw before who can't tell me what he wants.'

The old man shrugged his shoulders despairingly. 'I have no

words,' he said. 'But Mademoiselle Elise is waiting at the jetty. Come to her at any rate and she will reason with you.'

Vernon – as you will admit, if I have made his character at all clear to you – had no instinct for melodrama. He had nothing in him of the knight-errant looking for adventure, and this interruption out of the fog and the sea rather bored him than otherwise. But he was too young to be able to refuse such an appeal. He went below and fetched his revolver and an electric torch which he stuffed into a trouser pocket. He cried to the Epirote to expect him when he saw him, for he was going ashore.

'All right,' he said. 'I'll come and see what the trouble is.'

He dropped over the yacht's side into the cockleshell of a boat, and the old man took up the sculls. The yacht must have anchored nearer land than he had thought, for in five minutes they had touched a shelving rock. Somebody stood there with a lantern which made a dull glow in the fog.

Vernon made out a middle-aged woman with the air and dress of a lady's maid. She held the lantern close to him for a moment, and then turned wearily to the other. 'Fool, Mitri!' she cried. 'You have brought a peasant.'

'Nay,' said the old man, 'he is no peasant. He is a Signor, I tell you.'

The woman again passed the light of her lantern over Vernon's face and figure. 'His dress is a peasant's, but such clothes may be a nobleman's whim. I have heard it of the English.'

'I am English,' said Vernon in French.

She turned on him with a quick movement of relief.

'You are English . . . and a gentleman? But I know nothing of you . . . . only that you have come out of the sea. Up in the House we women are alone, and my mistress has death to face, or worse than death. We have no claim on you, and if you give us your service it means danger – oh, what danger! See, the boat is there. You can return in it and go away, and forget that you have been near this accursed place. But, O Monsieur, if you hope for Heaven and have pity on a defenceless angel, you will not leave us.'

Vernon's blood was slow to stir, and, as I have said, he had no instinct for melodrama. This gesticulating French maid was like something out of an indifferent play.

'Who is your mistress?' he asked. 'Did she send you for me?'

The woman flung up her hands.

'I will speak the truth. My mistress does not know you are here. Only Mitri and I saw you. She will not ask help, for she is foolishly confident. She is proud and fearless, and will not believe the evidence of her eyes. She must be saved in spite of herself. I fear for her and also for myself, for the whole House is doomed.'

'But, Mademoiselle, you cannot expect me to intrude uninvited on your mistress. What is her name? What do you want me to do?'

She clutched his arm and spoke low and rapidly in his ear.

'She is the last of her line, you must know – a girl with a wild estate and a father dead these many months. She is good and gracious, as I can bear witness, but she is young and cannot govern the wolves who are the men of these parts. They have a long hatred of her house, and now they have it rumoured that she is a witch who blights the crops and slays the children . . . Once, twice, they have cursed our threshold and made the blood mark on the door. We are prisoners now, you figure. They name her Basilissa, meaning the Queen of Hell, and there is no babe but will faint with fright if it casts eyes on her, and she as mild and innocent as Mother Mary . . . The word has gone round to burn the witch out, for the winter has been cruel and they blame their sorrows on her. The hour is near, and unless salvation comes she will go to God in the fire.'

There was something in the hoarse excited voice which forbade Vernon to dismiss lightly this extraordinary tale. The woman was patently terrified and sincere. It might be a trap, but he had his pistol, and from an old man and a woman he had nothing to fear. On the other hand there might be some desperate need which he could not disregard. It seemed to him that he was bound to inquire further.

'I am willing to go to your mistress,' he said, and the woman, murmuring 'God's mercy', led the way up a steep causeway to some rocky steps cut in a tamarisk thicket.

She stopped half-way to whisper an injunction to go quietly. 'They cannot see us in this blessed fog,' she whispered, 'but they may hear us.' Then to Vernon: 'They watch us like wild beasts, Monsieur; their sentries do not permit us to leave the House, but this night the kind God has fooled them. But they cannot be far off, and they have quick ears.'

The three crept up the rock staircase made slippery by the

heavy mist. Presently a great wall of masonry rose above them, and what seemed the aperture of a door. 'Once,' the woman whispered, 'there were three such posterns, but two were walled up by my lady's father – walled up within, with the doors left standing. This our enemies do not know and they watch all three, but this the least, for it looks unused. Behold their work!'

Vernon saw that tall bundles of brushwood had been laid around the door, and that these had with difficulty been pushed back when it was opened.

'But what . . .?' he began.

'It means that they would burn us,' she hissed. 'Now, Monsieur, do you believe my tale, and, believing, does your courage fail you?'

To Vernon, shy, placid, a devotee of all the conventions, it was beginning to seem a monstrous thing to enter this strange house at the bidding of two servants, primed with a crazy tale, to meet an owner who had given no sign of desiring his presence. A woman, too – apparently a young woman. The thing was hideously embarrassing, the more so as he suddenly realised that he was barefooted, and clad in his old jersey and corduroys. I think he would have drawn back except for the sight of the faggots – that and the woman's challenge to his courage. He had been 'dared' like a schoolboy, and after twenty-four hours fighting with storms and the shattering of the purpose of a lifetime he was in that half-truculent, half-reckless mood which is prone to accept a challenge. There was business afoot, it appeared, ugly business.

'Go on. I will see your mistress,' he said.

With a key the old man unlocked the door. The lock must have been recently oiled, for it moved easily. The three now climbed a staircase which seemed to follow the wall of a round tower. Presently they came into a stone hall with ancient hangings like the banners in the church. From the open frame of the lantern a second was kindled, and the two lights showed a huge desolate place with crumbling mosaics on the floor and plaster dropping from the walls and cornices. There was no furniture of any kind and the place smelt damp and chilly like a vault.

'These are unused chambers,' the woman said, and her voice was no longer hushed but high-pitched with excitement. 'We live only on the landward side.'

Another heavy door was unlocked, and they entered a corridor where the air blew warmer, and there was a hint of that indescribable scent which comes from human habitation. The woman stopped and consulted in whispers with the old man. Now that she had got Vernon inside, her nervousness seemed to have increased. She turned to him at last:

'I must prepare my mistress. If Monsieur will be so good he will wait here till I fetch him.'

She opened a door and almost pushed Vernon within. He found himself in black darkness, while the flicker of the lantern vanished round a bend in the corridor.

FOURTEEN

FROM HIS POCKET Vernon drew his electric torch and flashed it round the room in which he found himself. It was the extreme opposite of the empty stone hall, for it was heavily decorated and crowded with furniture. Clearly no one had used it lately, for dust lay on everything and the shutters of the windows had not been unbarred for months. It had the air, indeed, of a lumber-room, into which furniture had been casually shot. The pieces were for the most part fine and costly. There were several Spanish cabinets, a wonderful red-lacquer couch, quantities of Oriental rugs which looked good, and a litter of Chinese vases and antique silver lamps.

But it was not the junk which filled it that caught Vernon's eye. It was the walls which had been painted and frescoed in one continuous picture. At first he thought it was a Procession of the Hours or the Seasons, but when he brought his torch to bear on it he saw that it was something very different. The background was a mountain glade, and on the lawns and beside the pools of a stream figures were engaged in wild dances. Pan and his satyrs were there, and a bevy of nymphs, and strange figures half animal, half human. The thing was done with immense skill – the slanted eyes of the fauns, the leer in a contorted satyr face, the mingled lust and terror of the nymphs, the horrid obscenity of the movements. It was a carnival of bestiality that stared from the four walls. The man who conceived it had worshipped darker gods even than Priapus.

There were other things which Vernon noted in the jumble of the room. A head of Aphrodite, for instance – Pandemia, not Urania. A broken statuette of a boy which made him sick. A group of little figures which were a miracle in the imaginative degradation of the human form. Not the worst relics from the lupanars of Pompeii compared with these in sheer subtlety of filth. And all this in a shuttered room stifling with mould and disuse.

There was a door at the farther end which he found unlocked. The room beyond was like a mortuary – the walls painted black and undecorated save for one small picture. There was a crack in the shutters here, and perhaps a broken window, for a breath of the clean sea air met him. There was no furniture except an oblong piece of yellow marble which seemed from the rams' heads and cornucopias to be an old altar. He turned his torch on the solitary picture. It represented the stock scene of Salome with the head of John the Baptist, a subject which bad artists have made play with for the last five hundred years. But this was none of the customary daubs, but the work of a master – a perverted, perhaps a crazy, genius. The woman's gloating face, the passion of the hands caressing the pale flesh, the stare of the dead eyes, were wonderful and awful. If the first room had been the shrine of inhuman lust, this had been the chapel of inhuman cruelty.

He opened another door and found himself in a little closet, lined to the ceiling with books. He knew what he would find on the shelves. The volumes were finely bound, chiefly in vellum, and among them were a certain number of reputable classics. But most belonged to the backstairs of literature – the obscenities of Greek and of silver Latin, the diseased sidewalks of the Middle Ages, the aberrations of the moderns. It was not common pornography: the collection had been made by someone who was a scholar in vice.

Vernon went back to the first room, nauseated and angry. He must get out of this damned place, which was, or had been, the habitation of devils. What kind of owner could such a house possess? The woman had said that it was a young girl, as virtuous as the Virgin. But, great God! how could virtue dwell in such an environment.

He had opened the door to begin his retreat when a lantern appeared in the corridor. It was the woman, and with a finger on her lips she motioned him back into the room.

'My mistress is asleep,' she said, 'and it would not be well to wake her. Monsieur will stay here tonight and speak with her in the morning?'

'I will do nothing of the kind,' said Vernon. 'I am going back to my boat.'

The woman caught his involuntary glance at the wall paintings and clutched his arm. 'But that is not her doing,' she cried. That was the work of her father, who was beyond belief wicked. It is his sins that the child is about to expiate. The people have condemned her, but you surely would not join in their unjust judgement.'

'I tell you I will have nothing to do with the place. Will you kindly show me the way back?'

Her face hardened. 'I cannot. Mitri has the key.'

'Well, where the devil is Mitri?'

'I will not tell . . . O Monsieur, I beseech you, do not forsake us. There has been evil in this House enough to sink it to hell, but my mistress is innocent. I ask only that you speak with her. After that, if you so decide, you can go away.'

The woman was plainly honest and in earnest, and Vernon was a just man. He suddenly felt that he was behaving badly. There could be no harm in sleeping a night in the house, and in the morning interviewing its owner. If it was a case of real necessity he could take her and her maid off in his boat . . . After all there might be serious trouble afoot. The sight of those hideous rooms had given him a sharp realisation of the ugly things in life.

He was taken to a clean, bare little attic at the top of the house which had once no doubt been a servant's quarters. Having been up all the previous night, his head had scarcely touched the rough pillow before he was asleep. He slept for ten hours, till he was awakened by Mitri, who brought him hot water and soap and a venerable razor with which he made some attempt at a toilet. He noticed that the fog was still thick, and from the garret window he looked into an opaque blanket.

He had wakened with a different attitude towards the adventure in which he found himself. The sense of a wasted youth and defrauded hopes had left him; he felt more tightly strung, more vigorous, younger; he also felt a certain curiosity about this Greek girl who in an abominable house was defying the lightnings.

Mitri conducted him to the first floor, where he was taken charge of by the Frenchwoman.

'Do not be afraid of her,' she whispered. 'Deal with her as a man with a woman and make her do your bidding. She is stiff-necked towards me, but she may listen to a young man, especially if he be English.'

She ushered Vernon into a room which was very different from the hideous chambers he had explored the night before. It was poorly and sparsely furnished, the chairs were chiefly wicker, the walls had recently been distempered by an amateur hand, the floor was of bare scrubbed boards. But a bright fire burned on the hearth, there was a big bunch of narcissus on a table set for breakfast, and flowering branches had been stuck in the tall vases beside the chimney. Through the open window came a drift of fog which intensified the comfort of the fire.

It was a woman's room for on a table lay some knitting and a piece of embroidery, and a small ivory housewife's case bearing the initials 'K.A.'. There were one or two books also, and Vernon looked at them curiously. One was a book of poems which had been published in London a month before. This Greek girl must know English; perhaps she had recently been in England . . . He took up another volume, and to his amazement it was a reprint of Peter Beckford's *Thoughts on Hunting*. He could not have been more surprised if he had found a copy of the *Eton Chronicle*. What on earth was the mistress of a lonely Aegean island doing with Peter Beckford?

The fire crackled cheerfully, the raw morning air flowed through the window, and Vernon cast longing eyes on the simple preparations for breakfast. He was ferociously hungry, and he wished he were now in the boat, where the Epirote would be frying bacon . . .

There was another door besides that by which he had entered, and curiously enough it was in the same position as the door in the room of his dream. He angrily dismissed the memory of that preposterous hallucination, but he kept his eye on the door. By it no doubt the mistress of the house would enter, and he wished she would make haste. He was beginning to be very curious about this girl . . . Probably she would be indignant and send him about his business, but she could scarcely refuse to give him breakfast first. In any case there was the yacht . . . There was a mirror above the mantelpiece in which he caught a glimpse of himself. The glimpse was not reassuring. His face was as dark as an Indian's, his hair wanted cutting, and his blue jersey was bleached and discoloured with salt water. He looked like a deckhand on a cargo boat. But perhaps a girl who read Beckford would not be pedantic about appearances. He put his trust in Peter—

The door had opened. A voice, sharp-pitched and startled, was speaking, and to his surprise it spoke in English.

'Who the devil are you?' it said.

He saw a slim girl, who stood in the entrance poised like a runner, every line of her figure an expression of amazement. He had seen her before, but his memory was wretched for women's faces. But the odd thing was that, after the first second, there was recognition in her face.

'Colonel Milburne!' said the voice. 'What in the name of goodness are you doing here?'

She knew him, and he knew her, but where – when – had they met? He must have stared blankly, for the girl laughed.

'You have forgotten,' she said. 'But I have seen you out with the Mivern, and we met at luncheon at Wirlesdon in the winter.'

He remembered now, and what he remembered chiefly were the last words he had spoken to me on the subject of this girl. The adventure was becoming farcical.

'I beg your pardon,' he stammered. 'You are Miss Arabin. I didn't know—'

'I am Miss Arabin. But why the honour of an early morning call from Colonel Milburne?'

'I came here last night in a yacht.' Vernon was making a lame business of his explanation, for the startled angry eyes of his hostess scattered his wits. 'I anchored below in the fog, and an old man came out in a boat and asked me to come ashore. There was a woman on the beach – your maid – and she implored my help – told a story I didn't quite follow—'

'The fog!' the girl repeated. 'That of course explains why you were allowed to anchor. In clear weather you would have been driven away.'

She spoke in so assured a tone that Vernon was piqued.

'The seas are free,' he said. 'Who would have interfered with me? Your servants?'

She laughed again, mirthlessly. 'My people. Not my servants. Continue. You came ashore and listened to Elise's chatter. After that?'

'She said you were asleep and must not be wakened, but that I should speak to you in the morning. She put me up for the night.'

'Where?' she asked sharply.

'In a little room on the top floor.'

'I see. "Where you sleeps you breakfasts." Well, we'd better have some food.'

She rang a little silver handbell, and the maid, who must have been waiting close at hand, appeared with coffee and boiled eggs. She cast an anxious glance at Vernon as if to inquire how he had fared at her mistress's hands.

'Sit down,' said the girl when Elise had gone, 'I can't give you much to eat, for these days we are on short rations. I'm sorry but there's no sugar. I can recommend the honey. It's the only good thing in Plakos.'

'Is this Plakos? I came here once before – in 1914 – in a steam yacht. I suppose I am in the big white house which looks down upon the jetty. I could see nothing last night in the fog. I remember a long causeway and steps cut in the rock. That must have been the road I came.'

She nodded. 'What kind of sailor are you to be so ignorant of your whereabouts? Oh, I see, the storm! What's the size of your boat?'

When he told her, she exclaimed. 'You must have had the devil of a time, for it was a first-class gale. And now on your arrival in port you are plunged into melodrama. You don't look as if you had much taste for melodrama, Colonel Milburne.'

'I haven't. But is it really melodrama? Your maid told me a rather alarming tale.'

Her eyes had the hard agate gleam which he remembered from Wirlesdon. Then he had detested her, but now, as he looked at her, he saw that which made him alter his judgement. The small face was very pale, and there were dark lines under the eyes. This girl was undergoing some heavy strain, and her casual manner was in the nature of a shield.

'Is it true?' he asked.

'So-so. In parts, no doubt. I am having trouble with my tenants, which I am told is a thing that happens even in England. But that is my own concern, and I don't ask for help. After breakfast I would suggest that you go back to your yacht.'

'I think you had better come with me. You and your maid. I take it that the old man Mitri can fend for himself.'

'How kind of you!' she cried in a falsetto, mimicking voice. 'How extraordinarily kind! But you see I haven't asked your help, and I don't propose to accept it . . . You're sure you won't have any more coffee! I wonder if you could give me a cigarette? I've been out of them for three days.'

She lay back in a wicker chair, rocking herself and lazily blowing smoke clouds. Vernon stood with his back to the fire and filled a pipe.

'I don't see how I can go away,' he said, 'unless I can convince myself that you're in no danger. You're English, and a woman, and I'm bound to help you whether you want it or not.' He spoke with assurance now, perhaps with a certain priggishness. The tone may have offended the girl, for when she spoke it was with a touch of the insolence which he remembered at Wirlesdon.

'I'm curious to know what Elise told you last night.'

'Simply that you were imprisoned here by the people of Plakos – that they thought you a witch and might very likely treat you in the savage way that people used to treat witches.'

She nodded. 'That's about the size of it. But what if I refuse to let anyone interfere in a fight between me and my own people? Supposing this is something which I must stick out for the sake of my own credit? What then, Colonel Milburne? You have been a soldier. You wouldn't advise me to run away.'

'That depends,' said Vernon. 'There are fights where there can be no victory – where the right course is to run away. Your maid told me something else. She said that the evil reputation you had among the peasants was not your own doing – that of course I guessed – but a legacy from your family, who for very good reasons were unpopular. Does that make no difference?'

'How?'

'Why, there's surely no obligation in honour to make yourself a vicarious sacrifice for other people's misdeeds!'

'I – don't – think I agree. One must pay for one's race as well as for oneself.'

'Oh, nonsense! Not the kind of thing your family seem to have amused themselves with.'

'What do you mean?'

'I was put into a room last night –' Vernon spoke hesitatingly – 'and I saw some books and paintings. They were horrible. I understood – well, that the peasants might have a good deal of reason – something to say for themselves, you know. Why should you suffer for that swinishness?'

The morning sun had broken through the fog and was

shining full on the girl's face. She sprang to her feet, and Vernon saw that she had blushed deeply.

'You entered those rooms!' she cried. 'That fool Elise! I will have her beaten. Oh, I am shamed . . . Get off with you! You are only making me wretched. Get off while there's time.'

The sight of her crimson face and neck moved Vernon to a deep compassion.

'I refuse to leave without you, Miss Arabin,' he said. 'I do not know much, but I know enough to see that you are in deadly danger. I can no more leave you here than I could leave a drowning child in the sea. Quick! Get your maid and pack some things and we'll be gone.'

She stood before him, an abashed obstinate child.

'I won't go . . . I hate you . . . You have seen – oh, leave me, if you have any pity.'

'You come with me.'

'I won't!' Her lips were a thin line, and the shut jaws made a square of the resolute little face.

'Then I shall carry you off. I'm very sorry, Miss Arabin, but I'm going to save you in spite of yourself.'

Vernon had his hand stretched out to the silver handbell to summon Elise, when he found himself looking at a small pistol. He caught her wrist, expecting it to go off, but nothing happened. It dropped into his hand and he saw that it was unloaded.

He rang the bell.

'All the more reason why you should come with me if you are so badly armed.'

The girl stood stiff and silent, her eyes and cheeks burning, as Elise entered.

'Pack for your mistress,' he told the maid. 'Bring as little baggage as possible, for there isn't much room.' The woman hurried off gladly to do his bidding.

'Please don't make a scene,' he said. 'You will have to come in the end and some day you will forgive me.'

'I will not come,' she said, 'but I will show you something.'

Life seemed to have been restored to her tense body, as she hurried him out of the room along a corridor, and up a flight of stairs to a window which looked seaward.

The last wreath of fog had disappeared, and the half-moon of bay lay blue and sparkling. Down at the jetty were men and boats, but out on the water there was no sign of the anchored yacht.

'What does that mean?' Vernon cried.

'It means that your boat has gone. When the air cleared the people saw it, and have driven your man away . . . It means that you, like me, are a prisoner!'

FIFTEEN

AS VERNON LOOKED at the flushed girl, whose voice as she spoke had at least as much consternation in it as triumph, he experienced a sudden dislocation of mind. Something fell from him – the elderliness, the preoccupation, the stiff dogma of his recent years. He recaptured the spirit which had open arms for novelty. He felt an eagerness to be up and doing – what, he was not clear – but something difficult and high-handed. The vanishing of his dream had left the chambers of his mind swept and garnished, and youth does not tolerate empty rooms.

Also, though I do not think that he had yet begun to fall in love with Koré, he understood the quality of one whom aforetimes he had disliked both as individual and type. This pale girl, dressed like a young woman in the Scotch shooting lodge, was facing terror with a stiff lip. There was nothing raffish or second-rate about her now. She might make light of her danger in her words, but her eyes betrayed her.

It was about this danger that he was still undecided. You see, he had not, like me, seen the people of the island, felt the strain of their expectancy, or looked on the secret spaces of the Dancing Floor. He had come out of the storm to hear a tale told in the fog and darkness by an excited woman. That was all – that and the hideous rooms at which he had had a passing glance. The atmosphere of the place, which I had found so unnerving, had not yet begun to affect him.

'My fellow will come back,' he said, after scanning the empty seas. 'He has his faults, but he is plucky and faithful.'

'You do not understand,' the girl said. 'He would be one against a thousand. He may be as brave as a lion, but they won't let him anchor, and if they did they would never let you and me join him. I have told you we are prisoners – close prisoners.'

'You must tell me a great deal more. You see, you can't

refuse my help now, for we are in the same boat. Do you mind if we go back to where we breakfasted, for I left my pipe there.'

She turned without a word and led him back to her sitting-room, passing a woebegone Elise who, with her arms full of clothes, was told that her services were now needless. The windows of the room looked on a garden which had been suffered to run wild but which still showed a wealth of spring blossom. Beyond was a shallow terrace and then the darkness of trees. A man's head seemed to move behind a cypress hedge. The girl nodded towards it. 'One of my gaolers,' she said.

She stood looking out of the window with her eyes averted from Vernon and seemed to be forcing herself to speak.

'You have guessed right about my family,' she said. 'And about this house. I am cleaning it slowly – I must do it myself. Elise and I, for I do not want strangers to know . . . This room was as bad as the other two till I white-washed the walls. The old furniture I am storing till I have time to destroy it. I think I will burn it, for it has hideous associations for me. I would have had the whole house in order this spring if my foolish people had not lost their heads.'

A 'tawdry girl', that was how Vernon had spoken of her to me. He withdrew the word now. 'Tawdry' was the last adjective he would use about this strange child, fighting alone to get rid of a burden of ancient evil. He had thought her a modish, artificial being, a moth hatched out of the latest freak of fashion. Now she seemed to him a thousand years removed from the feverish world which he had thought her natural setting. Her appeal was her extreme candour and simplicity, her utter, savage, unconsidering courage.

'Let us take the family for granted,' Vernon said gently. 'I can't expect you to talk about that. I assume that there was that in your predecessor's doings which gave these islanders a legitimate grievance. What I want to know is what they are up to now. Tell me very carefully everything that has happened since you came here a week ago.'

She had little to tell him. She had been allowed to enter the House by the ordinary road from the village, and after that the gates had been barred. When she had attempted to go for a walk she had been turned back by men with rifles – she did not tell Vernon how the rifles had been procured. The hillmen had joined with the people of the coast – you could always tell a hillman by his dress – though the two used to be hereditary enemies. That made her angry and also uneasy; so did the curious methodical ways of the siege. They were not attempting to enter the House – she doubted if any one of them would dare to cross the threshold – they were only there to prevent her leaving it. She herself, not the looting of the House, must be their object. Mitri was permitted to go to the village, but he did not go often, for he came back terrified and could not or would not explain his terrors. No communication had been held with the watchers, and no message had come from them. She had tried repeatedly to find out their intentions, but the sentinels would not speak, and she could make nothing of Mitri. No, she was not allowed into the demesne. There were sentries there right up to the house wall – sentries night and day.

Vernon asked her about supplies. She had brought a store with her which was not yet exhausted, but the people sent up food every morning. Mitri found it laid on the threshold of the main door. Curious food – barley cakes and honey and cheese and eggs and dried figs. She couldn't imagine where they got it from, for the people had been starving in the winter. Milk, too – plenty of milk, which was another unexpected thing.

Water – that was the oddest business of all. The House had a fine well in the stableyard on the east side. This had been sealed up and its use forbidden to Mitri. But morning and night buckets of fresh water were brought to the door – whence, she did not know. 'It rather restricts our bathing arrangements,' she said.

She told the story lightly, with a ready laugh, as if she were once more mistress of herself. Mistress of her voice she certainly was, but she could not command her eyes. It was these that counteracted the debonair tones and kept tragedy in the atmosphere.

Vernon, as I have said, had not the reason which I had for feeling the gravity of the business. But he was a scholar, and there were details in Koré's account which startled him.

'Tell me about the food again. Cheese and honey and barley cakes, dried figs and eggs – nothing more?'

'Nothing more. And not a great deal of that. Not more than enough to feed one person for twenty-four hours. We have to supplement it from the stores we brought.'

'I see . . . It is meant for you personally – not for your

household. And the water? You don't know what spring it comes from?'

She shook her head. 'There are many springs in Plakos. But why does our commissariat interest you?'

'Because it reminds me of something I have read somewhere. Cheese and honey and barley cakes – that is ritual food. Sacramental, if you like. And the water. Probably brought from some sacred well. I don't much like it. Tell me about the people here, Miss Arabin. Are they very backward and superstitious?'

'I suppose you might call them that. They are a fine race to look at, and claim to be pure Greek – at least the coast folk. The hillmen are said to be mongrels, but they are handsome mongrels and fought bravely in the war. But I don't know them well for I left when I was a child, and since my father died I have only seen the people of Kynaetho.'

'Kynaetho?' Vernon cried out sharply, for the word was like a bell to ring up the curtain of memory.

'Yes, Kynaetho. That is the village at the gate.'

Now he had the clue. Kynaetho was the place mentioned in the manuscript fragment which he had translated for me. It was at Kynaetho that the strange rite was performed of the Koré and the Kouros. The details were engraven on his memory, for they had profoundly impressed him and he had turned them over repeatedly in his mind. He had thought he had discovered the record of a new ritual form; rather it appeared that he had stumbled upon the living rite itself.

'I begin – to understand,' he said slowly. 'I want you to let me speak to Mitri. Alone, if you please. I have done this work before in the war, and I can get more out of that kind of fellow if I am alone with him. Then I shall prospect the land.'

He found Mitri in his lair in the ancient kitchen. With the old man there was no trouble, for when he found that his interlocutor spoke Greek fluently he overflowed in confidences.

'They will burn this House,' he said finally. 'They have piled faggots on the north and east sides where the wind blows. And the time will be Easter eve.'

'And your mistress?'

Mitri shrugged his shoulders. 'There is no hope for her, I tell you. She had a chance of flight and missed it, though I pled with her. She will burn with the House unless—'

He looked at Vernon timidly, as if he feared to reveal something.

'Unless—?' said Vernon.

'There is a rumour in Kynaetho of something else. In that accursed village they have preserved tales of the old days, and they say that on the night of Good Friday there will be *panegyria* on the Dancing Floor. There will be a race with torches, and he who wins will be called King. To him it will fall to slay my mistress in order that the Ancient Ones may appear and bless the people.'

'I see,' said Vernon. 'Do you believe in that rubbish?'

Mitri crossed himself and called the Panagia to witness that he was a Christian and after God and the Saints loved his mistress.

'That is well. I trust you, Mitri; and I will show you how you can save her. You are allowed to leave the House?'

'Every second day only. I went yesterday, and cannot go again till tomorrow. I have a daughter married in the village, whom I am permitted to visit.'

'Very well. We are still two days from Good Friday. Go down to the village tomorrow and find out all about the plans for Good Friday evening. Lie as much as you like. Say you hate your mistress and will desert her whenever you are bidden. Pretend you're on the other side. Get their confidence . . . A madness has afflicted this island and you are the only sane Christian left in it. If these ruffians hurt your mistress, the Government – both in Athens and in London – will send soldiers and hang many. After that there will be no more Kynaetho. We have got to prevent the people making fools of themselves. Your mistress is English and I am English, and that is why I stay here. You do exactly as I tell you and we'll win through.'

It was essential to encourage Mitri, for the old man was patently torn between superstitious fear and fidelity to Koré and only a robust scepticism and a lively hope would enable him to keep his tail up and do his part. Vernon accordingly protested a confidence which he was very far from feeling. It was arranged that Mitri should go to Kynaetho next morning after breakfast and spend the day there.

After that, guided by the old man, Vernon made a circuit of the House. From the top windows he was able to follow the lie of the land – the postern gates to the shore, the nest of stables and outbuildings on the east with access to the shallow glen running up from the jetty, the main entrance and the drive from Kynaetho, the wooded demesne ending at the cliffs, and the orchards and oliveyards between the cliffs and the causeway. The patrols came right up to the House wall, and on various sides Vernon had a glimpse of them. But he failed to get what he specially sought, a prospect of any part of the adjoining coastline beyond the little bay. He believed that his yacht was somewhere hidden there, out of sight of the peasants. He was convinced that the Epirote would obey orders and wait for him, and would not go one yard farther away than was strictly necessary. But he was at a loss to know how to find him, if he were penned up in this shuttered mausoleum.

He returned to find Koré sewing by the window of the breakfast room. He entered quietly and had a momentary glimpse of her before she was conscious of his presence. She was looking straight before her with vacant eyes, her face in profile against the window, a figure of infinite appeal. Vernon had a moment of acute compunction. What he had once thought and spoken of this poor child seemed to him now to have been senseless brutality. He had called her tawdry and vulgar and shrill, he had thought her the ugly product of the ugly after-the-war world. But there she sat like a muse of meditation, as fine and delicate as a sword-blade. And she had a sword's steel, too, for had she not faced unknown peril for a scruple?

'What does Mitri say?' she asked in a voice which had a forced briskness in it.

'I shall know more tomorrow night, but I have learned something. You are safe for the better part of three days – till some time on Good Friday evening. That is one thing. The other is that your scheme of wearing down the hostility of your people has failed. Your islanders have gone stark mad. The business is far too solemn for me to speak smooth things. They have resurrected an old pagan rite of sacrifice. *Sacrifice*, do you understand? This House will be burned, and if they have their will you will die.'

I was beginning to guess as much. I don't want to die, for it means defeat. But I don't think I am afraid to die. You see – life is rather difficult – and not very satisfactory. But tell me more.'

Vernon gave her a sketch of the ritual of Kynaetho. 'It was

your mentioning the name that brought it back to me. I have always been interested in Greek religion, and by an amazing chance I came on this only a month or so ago. Leithen – the lawyer – you know him, I think – gave me a bit of medieval Greek manuscript to translate, and part of it had this rite.'

'Leithen,' she cried. 'Sir Edward? Then he found it among the papers I lent him. Why didn't he tell me about it?'

'I can't imagine.'

'Perhaps he thought I wouldn't have believed it. I wouldn't a month ago. Perhaps he thought he could prevent me coming here. I think he did his best. I had to go off without saying goodbye to him, and he was my greatest friend.'

'He happens to be also my closest friend. If you had known about this – this crazy ritual, would you have come?'

She smiled. 'I don't know. I'm very obstinate, and I can't bear to be bullied. These people are trying to bully me . . . But of course I didn't know how bad it was . . . And I didn't know that I was going to land you in this mess. That is what weighs on my mind.'

'But you didn't invite me here. You told me to clear out.'

'My servants invited you and therefore I am responsible . . . Oh, Colonel Milburne, you must understand what I feel. I haven't had an easy life, for I seem to have been always fighting, but I didn't mind it as long as it was my own fight. I felt I had to stick it out, for it was the penalty I paid for being an Arabin. But whatever paying was to be done I wanted to do it myself . . . Otherwise, don't you see, it makes the guilt of my family so much heavier . . . And now I have let you in for it, and that is hell – simply hell!'

Vernon had suddenly an emotion which he had never known before – the exhilaration with which he had for years anticipated the culmination of his dream, but different in kind, nobler, less self-regarding. He felt keyed up to any enterprise, and singularly confident. There was tenderness in his mood, too, which was a thing he had rarely felt – tenderness towards this gallant child.

'Listen to me, Miss Arabin. I have two things to say to you. One is that I glory in being here. I wouldn't be elsewhere for the world. It is a delight and a privilege. The other is that we are going to win out.'

'But how?'

'I don't know yet. We will find a way. I am as certain of it as that I am standing here. God doesn't mean a thing like this to be a blind *cul-de-sac.*'

'You believe in God? I wish I did. I think I only believe in the Devil.'

'Then you believe in God. If evil is a living thing, good must be living as well – more indeed, or the world would smash . . . Look here, we've two days to put in together. There is nothing we can do for the present, so we must find some way to keep our nerves quiet. Let's pretend we're in an ordinary English country house and kept indoors by rain.'

So the two of them made plans to pass the time, while the clear spring sunlight outside turned Vernon's pretence into foolishness. They played piquet, and sometimes he read to her – chiefly Peter Beckford. The florid eighteenth-century prose, the tags of Augustan poetry, the high stilts, the gusto, carried their thoughts to the orderly world of home. I have no wish to speculate about the secrets of a friend, but I fancy that the slow hours spent together brought understanding. Koré must have told him things which she had kept back from me, for the near prospect of death breaks down many barriers. I think, too, that he may have told her the story of his boyish dream – he must have, for it bore directly on the case. With his sense of predestination he would draw from it a special confidence, and she would be made to share it. He had undergone a long preparation for something which had ended in mist, but the preparation might point to success in a great reality . . .

Late the following afternoon old Mitri returned. Vernon saw him first alone, and got from him the details of the next evening's ceremonial. There was to be a race among the young men on the Dancing Floor as soon as the moon rose, and the victor would be called the King. Some of the news which Mitri had gathered was unexpected, some incomprehensible, but in the main it agreed with his own version. The victor would choose a victim – a male victim, clearly, for the female victim was already chosen. The two would enter the House, and on the next night – the eve of this grim Easter – the sacrifice would be accomplished. Beyond that Mitri could say nothing except that the people looked for a mighty miracle; but the manuscript had told what the miracle would be.

'Who will be the runners?' Vernon asked.

'The fleetest among the young men, both of the village and the hills.'

It was characteristic of Vernon's fatalism that he had not troubled to make even the rudiments of a plan till he had heard Mitri's tidings. Now the thing began to unfold itself. The next step at any rate was clearly ordained.

'Will everybody be known to each other?' he said.

'Faith, no. Kynaetho till now has had few dealings with the hill folk, and the villagers in the hills are generally at strife with each other. Tomorrow night there will be many strangers, and no questions will be asked, for all will be allies in this devilry.'

'Do I speak like a Greek?'

'You speak like a Greek, but like one from another island.'

'And I look like an islander?'

Mitri grinned. 'There are few as well-looking. But if your face were darkened, you would pass. There is a place, a little remote place in the hills, Akte by name, where the folk are said to have white skins like you, Signor.'

'Well, attend, Mitri. I am a man from Akte who has been at the wars, and has just returned. That will account for my foreign speech.'

'The Signor jests. He has a stout heart that can jest—'

'I'm not jesting. I'm going to compete in the race tomorrow night. What is more, I'm going to win. I've been a bit of a runner in my time, and I'm in hard training.'

A faint spark appeared in the old man's eye.

'The Signor will no doubt win if he runs. And if he ever reaches the Dancing Floor he will not be troubled with questions. But how will he reach the Dancing Floor?'

'I intend to get out of the House early tomorrow morning. There are several things I want to do before the race. Have you any rags with which I can imitate the dress of a hillman?'

Mitri considered. Shirt and breeches he had, but no boots. A cap might be improvised, but boots?

'Remember I have only just returned to Akte, and have brought the fashion of the war with me. So I can make shift with home-made puttees. Anything else?'

'The men around the House will not let you pass.'

'They'll have to. I'm one of themselves, and you've got to coach me in local customs. You have twelve hours before you in which to turn me into a respectable citizen of Akte. If any awkward questions are asked I propose to be truculent. A soldier is going to stand no nonsense from civilians, you know.'

Mitri considered again. 'It will be best to go by the main road to Kynaetho.'

'No, I'm going by the causeway. I want to see what lies beyond it to the west.'

'The cliffs are there and there is no road.'

'I will find one.'

Mitri shook his head. He had apparently little belief in the scheme, but an hour later, after Vernon had given Koré a sketch of his intentions, he arrived with an armful of strange garments. Élise at her mistress's request had collected oddments of fabrics, and brought part of the contents of the linen-cupboard.

'We are about,' Vernon told a mystified Koré, 'to prepare for private theatricals. Puttees are my most urgent need, and that thin shirt of yours will be the very thing.'

Since Koré still looked puzzled he added: 'We're cast for parts in a rather sensational drama. I'm beginning to think that the only way to prevent it being a tragedy is to turn it into a costume-play.'

SIXTEEN

VERY EARLY NEXT morning, before the blue darkness had paled into dawn, Vernon swung his legs out of an upper window of the House, crawled along the broad parapet and began to descend by a waterpipe in an angle between the main building and the eastern wing. This brought him to the roof of one of the out-buildings, from which it was possible for an active man to reach the road which ran upward from the jetty. He had been carefully prepared by Mitri for his part. The loose white shirt and the short mountain tunic were in order. Mitri's breeches had proved too scanty, but Elise had widened them, and the vacant space about his middle was filled with a dirty red cummerbund, made of one of Mitri's sashes, in which were stuck a long knife and his pistol. A pair of Mitri's home-made shoes of soft untanned hide were supplemented by home-made puttees. He had no hat; he had stained his face, hands and arms beyond their natural brown with juice from Mitri's store of pickled walnuts; and – under the critical eye of Koré – had rubbed dirt under his eyes and into his finger-nails till he looked the image of a handsome, swaggering, half-washed soldier. More important, he had been coached by Mitri in the speech of the hills, the gossip which might have penetrated to the remote Akte, and the mannerisms of the hillmen, which were unpleasingly familiar to the dwellers by the sea.

All this care would have been useless had Vernon not been in the mood to carry off any enterprise. He felt the reckless audacity of a boy, an exhilaration which was almost intoxication, and the source of which he did not pause to consider. Above all he felt complete confidence. Somehow, somewhere, he would break the malign spell and set Koré beyond the reach of her enemies.

He reached ground fifty yards south of the jetty and turned at once in the direction of the sea. At the beginning of the causeway he met a man.

'Whither away, brother?' came the question, accompanied by the lift of a rifle.

Vernon gave the hillman's greeting. He loomed up tall and formidable in the half-darkness.

'I go beyond the causeway to the oliveyards,' he said carelessly, as if he condescended in answering.

'By whose orders?'

'We of Akte do not take orders. I go at the request of the Elders.'

'You are of Akte?' said the man curiously. He was very willing to talk, being bored with his long night-watch. 'There are none of Akte among us, so far as I have seen. The men of Akte live in the moon, says the proverb. But . . .' this after peering at Vernon's garb – 'these clothes were never made in the hills.'

'I am new back from the war, and have not seen Akte these three years. But I cannot linger, friend.'

'Nay, bide a little. It is not yet day. Let us talk of Akte. My father once went there for cattle . . . Or let us speak of the war. My uncle was in the old war and my young nephew was . . . If you will not bide, give me tobacco.'

Vernon gave him a cigarette. 'These are what we smoked in Smyrna,' he said. 'They are noble stuff.'

Half-way along the causeway a second guard proved more truculent. He questioned the orders of the Elders, till Vernon played the man from Akte and the old soldier, and threatened to fling him into the sea. The last sentry was fortunately asleep. Vernon scrambled over the fence of the oliveyards, and as the sun rose above the horizon was striding with long steps through the weedy undergrowth.

His object was not like mine when I travelled that road, to get inside the demesne; he wanted to keep out of it, and to explore the bit of coast under it, since it seemed from the map to be the likeliest place to find his boat. The Epirote, he was convinced, would obey his instructions faithfully, and when driven away from his old anchorage would not go a yard more than was necessary. So, after being stopped as I had been by the wall which ran to the cliffs, he stuck to the shore. He picked his way under the skirts of the great headland till the rock sank sheer into deep water. There was nothing for it now but to swim, so he made a bundle of his shirt and jacket and bound them with the cummerbund on his shoulders, took his pistol in his teeth and slipped into the cold green sea. Mitri's breeches were a nuisance, but he was a strong swimmer, and in five minutes was at the point of the headland.

He found a ledge of rock which enabled him to pull up his shoulders and reconnoitre the hidden bay. There to his joy was the yacht, snugly anchored half-way across. There was no sign of life on board, for doubtless the Epirote was below cooking his breakfast. Vernon had no desire to make himself conspicuous by shouting, for the demesne and the watchers were too near, so he dropped back into the water and struck out for the boat. Ten minutes later he was standing dripping on the deck, and the Epirote was welcoming him with maledictions on Plakos.

He stripped off his wet clothes, and put on his old aquascutum till they should be dried. Then he breakfasted heartily, while Black George gave an account of his stewardship. When Vernon did not return he had not concerned himself greatly, for the affairs of his master were no business of his. But in the morning, when the fog began to lift, men had put off from shore in a boat and had demanded the reason of his presence. The interview had been stormy, for he had declined to explain, holding that if his master chose to land secretly by night, and rude fellows appeared with the daylight, it would be wise to tell the latter nothing. His interviewers had been more communicative. They had been very excited and had tried to alarm him with foolish tales of witches. But it was clear that they had meant mischief, for all were armed, and when at the point of several rifle barrels they had ordered him to depart, it seemed to him the part of a wise man to obey. He had feigned fear and deep stupidity, and had upped sail and done their bidding. Then, looking for a refuge, he had seen the great curtain of cliff and had found this little bay. Here he hoped he was secure, for there was no passage along the shore, and the people of Plakos did not seem during these days to be sailing the seas. He could be observed, of course, from the cliff tops, but these were shrouded in wood and looked unfrequented.

'Did I not well, Signor?' he asked anxiously.

'You did well. Have you seen no one?'

'No islander. Last night two men came about midnight. One was a crippled Greek and the other man, I judge, English.'

Vernon woke to the liveliest interest, but Black George told a halting tale. 'He swam out and wakened me, and at first, fearing trouble, I would have brained him. Since he could not speak my tongue, I rowed ashore with him and saw the Greek . . . He was an Englishman, beyond doubt, and a Signor, so I gave him food.'

'What did he want with you?'

'Simply that I should stay here. He had a story of some lady to whom the devils of this island meant mischief, and he begged me to wait in case the lady should seek to escape.'

No cross-examination of Vernon's could make Black George amplify the tale. He had not understood clearly, he said, for the English Signor could not speak his tongue and the Greek who interpreted was obviously a fool. But he had promised to remain, which was indeed his duty to his master. No. He had spoken no single word of his master. He had not said he was an Englishman. He had said nothing.

Vernon puzzled over the matter but could make nothing of it. He did not credit the story of an Englishman in Plakos who knew of Koré's plight, and came to the conclusion that Black George had misunderstood his visitor's talk. He had the day before him, and his first act was to row ashore to the other point of the bay – the place from which Janni and I had first espied the yacht. There he sat for a little and smoked, and it was one of his cigarette ends that I found the same afternoon. A scramble round the headland showed him the strip of beach below the Dancing Floor, but it occurred to him that there was no need to go pioneering along the coast – that he had a yacht and could be landed wherever he pleased. So he returned to Black George, and the two hoisted sail and made for open sea.

The day was spent running with the light north-west wind behind them well to the south of Plakos, and then tacking back till about sunset they stood off the north-east shore. It was a day of brilliant sun, tempered by cool airs, with the hills of the island rising sharp and blue into the pale spring sky. Vernon found to his delight that he had no trepidation about the work of the coming night. He had brought with him the copy he had made of his translation of Koré's manuscript, and studied it as a man studies a map, without any sense of its strangeness. The madmen of Plakos were about to revive an ancient ritual, where the victor in a race would be entrusted with certain barbarous duties. He proposed to be the victor, and so to defeat the folly. The House would be burnt, and in the confusion he would escape with Koré to the yacht, and leave the unhallowed isle for ever. The girl's honour would be satisfied, for she would have stuck it out to the last. Once he had convinced himself that she would be safe, he let his mind lie fallow. He dreamed and smoked on the hot deck in the bright weather, as much at his ease as if the evening were to bring no more than supper and sleep.

In the early twilight the yacht's dinghy put him ashore on a lonely bit of coast east of the village. Black George was ordered to return to his former anchorage and wait there; if on the following night he saw a lantern raised three times on the cliff above, he was to come round to the oliveyards at the far end of the causeway. At this stage Vernon's plan was for a simple escape in the confusion of the fire. He hoped that the postern gate of the jetty would be practicable; if not he would find some way of reaching the oliveyards from the demesne. The whole affair was viewed by him as a straightforward enterprise – provided he could win the confounded race.

But with his landing on Plakos in the spring gloaming his mood began to change. I have failed in my portrayal of Vernon if I have made you think of him as unimaginative and insensitive. He had unexpected blind patches in his vision and odd callosities in his skin, but for all that he was highly strung and had an immense capacity for emotion, though he chose mostly to sit on the safety valve. Above all he was a scholar. All his life he had been creating imaginative pictures of things, or living among the creations of other men. He had not walked a mile in that twilight till he felt the solemnity of it oppressing his mind.

I think it was chiefly the sight of the multitude moving towards the Dancing Floor, all silent, so that the only sound was the tread of feet. He had been in doubt before as to where exactly the place was, but the road was blazed for him like the roads to Epsom on Derby Day. Men, women, children, babes-in-arms, they were streaming past the closes at the foot of the glade, past the graveyard, up the aisle of the Dancing Floor. It was his first sight of it – not as I had seen it solitary under the moon, but surging with a stream of hushed humanity. It had another kind of magic, but one as potent as that which had laid its spell on me. I had seen the temple in its loneliness, he saw it thronged with worshippers.

No one greeted him or even noticed him; he would probably

have passed unregarded if he had been wearing his ordinary clothes. The heavy preoccupation of the people made them utterly incurious. He saw men dressed as he was, and he noted that the multitude moved to left and right as if by instinct, leaving the central arena vacant. Dusk had fallen, and on the crown of the ridge on his right he saw dimly what he knew to be the trees of the demesne. He saw, too, that a cluster seemed to be forming at the lower end of the arena, apart from the others, and he guessed that these were the competitors in the race. He made his way towards them, and found that he had guessed rightly. It was a knot of young men, who were now stripping their clothes, till they stood naked except for the sashes twisted around their middle. Most were barefoot, but one or two had raw-hide brogues. Vernon followed their example, till he stood up in his short linen drawers. He retained Mitri's shoes, for he feared the flints of the hillside. There were others in the group, older men whom he took to be the Elders of whom Mitri had spoken, and there was one man who seemed to be in special authority and who wore a loose white cassock.

It was now nearly dark, and suddenly, like the marks delimiting a course, torches broke into flame. These points of angry light in the crowded silence seemed to complete the spell. Vernon's assurance had fled and left behind it an unwilling awe and an acute nervousness. All his learning, all his laborious scholarship quickened from mere mental furniture into heat and light. His imagination as well as his nerves were on fire. I can only guess at the thoughts which must have crowded his mind. He saw the ritual, which so far had been for him an antiquarian remnant, leap into a living passion. He saw what he had regarded coolly as a barbaric survival, a matter for brutish peasants, become suddenly a vital concern of his own. Above all, he felt the formidableness of the peril to Koré. She had dared far more than she knew, far more than he had guessed; she was facing the heavy menace of a thousand ages, the devils not of a few thousand peasants but of a whole forgotten world . . . And in that moment he has told me that another thing became clear to him – she had become for him something altogether rare and precious.

The old man in the white ephod was speaking. It was a tale which had obviously been told before to the same audience, for he reminded them of former instructions. Vernon forced himself to concentrate on it an attention which was half paralysed by that mood of novel emotion which had come upon him. Some of it he failed to grasp, but the main points were clear – the race twice round the arena outside the ring of torches, the duty of the victor to take the last torch and plunge it in the sacred spring. The man spoke as if reciting a lesson, and Vernon heard it like a lesson once known and forgotten. Reminiscences of what he had found in classical by-ways hammered on his mind, and with recollection came a greater awe. It was only the thought of Koré that enabled him to keep his wits. Without that, he told me, he would have sunk into the lethargy of the worshippers, obedient, absorbed in expectancy.

Then came the start, and the race which Janni and I watched from our hiding-place in the shadows under the wall. He got off the mark clumsily, and at first his limbs seemed heavy as lead. But the movement revived him and woke his old racing instinct. Though he had not run for years, he was in hard training, and towards the close of the first round his skill had come back to him and he was in the third place, going well within his powers. In the second round he felt that the thing was in his hands. He lay close to the first man, passed him before the final straight, and then forged ahead so that in the last hundred yards he was gaining ground with every stride. He seized the torch at the winning-post and raced to where in the centre of the upper glade a white figure stood alone. With the tossing of the flame into the well he straightened his body and looked round, a man restored to his old vigour and ready for swift action.

His account of the next stage was confused, for his mind was on Koré and he was going through a violent transformation of outlook. The old man was no longer repeating a rehearsed lesson, but speaking violently like one in a moment of crisis. He addressed Vernon as 'You of the hills', and told him that God had placed the fate of Kynaetho in his hands – which God he did not particularise. But from his excited stammering something emerged that chilled Vernon's blood . . . He was to wait in the House till moonrise of the next night. The signal was to be the firing of the place. With the first flames he was to perform the deed to which he had been called. 'Choose which way you please,' said the old man, 'provided that they die.' Then he would leave the House by the main door and join the young men without. 'They will be gathered there till they come who will come.' The door would be closed behind him till it was opened by the fire . . . 'They who will come are Immortals.'

The man's voice was high-pitched with passion, and his figure, solitary in the bright moonshine in that ring of silent folk, had something in it of the awful and the sacramental. But Vernon's thoughts were not on it, but on the news which meant the downfall of his plans. His mind worked now normally and sanely; he was again a man of the modern world. The young men – of course they would be there – the Kouretes to greet the Kouros. He might have known it, if he had only thought. But how was Koré to escape from those frenzied guardians? He had imagined that with the fire the vigilance of the watch would be relaxed and that it would be easy to join Black George and the boat. But with the fire there was to be a thronging of the hierophants towards the House, and what was inside would be kept inside till the place was a heap of ashes.

The man was speaking again. He had made some signal, for three figures had approached the well. 'The woman is within,' he said, 'and it is for you to choose the man. Your choice is free among the people of Plakos, but we have one here, a young man, a Greek, but a stranger. He would doubtless be acceptable.'

The half-clad Maris cut an odd figure as, in the grip of two stalwart peasants, he was led forward for inspection. His face was white and set, and his eyes were furious. 'No willing victim this,' thought Vernon, 'but so much the better, for he and I are in the same boat and I must make him an ally.' From the way he carried himself he saw that Maris had been drilled, and he considered that a soldier might be useful. 'I choose this man,' he said.

A jar was given him, and he filled it from the spring and emptied it on Maris's head and shoulders. His own clothes were also brought, but he contented himself with Mitri's sash, of which he made a girdle and into which he stuck his own pistol and Mitri's knife. 'I have no need of the rest,' he said, for he was beginning to enter into the spirit of the part. Then he knelt while the old man laid a hand on his head and pronounced some consecration. 'Come,' he said to Maris, and the two moved up the slope of the Dancing Floor towards the breach in the wall.

He had almost forgotten his anxiety in the wonder of the scene. He seemed to be set on a stage in a great golden amphitheatre, and Maris and the guards who accompanied him were no more than stage properties. All human life had for the moment gone, and he was faced with primordial elements – the scented shell of earth, the immense arch of the sky and the riding moon, and, as he climbed the slope, an infinity of shining waters. The magic weighed on him, a new magic, for the ruthlessness of man was submerged in the deeper ruthlessness of nature . . . And then, as he passed the fringe of the spectators and caught a glimpse of pallid strained faces, he got his bearings again. It was man he had to cope with, crazy, fallible, tormented man. He felt the pity and innocence of it behind the guilt, and in an instant he regained confidence . . . Maris was stumbling along, walking painfully like one unaccustomed to going on bare feet, casting fierce startled glances about him. As they approached the breach in the wall Vernon managed to whisper to him to cheer up, for no ill would befall him. 'I am your friend,' he said; 'together we will make an end of this folly,' and the man's face lightened.

It was this look on Maris's face which I saw from my hiding-place and which made me forbid Janni's pistol shot.

SEVENTEEN

THE GREAT DOORS clanged behind them, and Vernon, who had been given the key by the guards, turned it in the lock. In spite of the reassuring words he had spoken to Maris he thought that his companion might attack him, so he steered wide of him and in the inky darkness fell over a basket of logs. The mishap wrung from him a very English expletive. Then he shouted on Mitri to bring a light.

He heard Maris's excited voice. 'Who are you? Who in God's name are you? Are you English?'

'Of course I am English. Confound it. I believe I have cracked my shin. Mitri, you idiot, where are you?'

The old man appeared from a corridor with a lantern shaking in his hand. He had no words, but stared at the two as if he were looking on men risen from the dead.

Where's your mistress? In her sitting-room? For God's sake get me some clothes – my old ones, and bring something for this gentleman to put on. Any old thing will do. Get us some food too, for we're starving. Quick, man. Leave the lantern here.'

By the slender light, set on a table in the great stone hall, the two men regarded each other.

You want to know who I am,' said Vernon. 'I'm an Englishman who came here three nights ago in a yacht. I happened to have met Miss Arabin before. I found out what the people of Plakos were up to, and it seemed to me that the best thing I could do was to win the race tonight. I needn't tell you about that, for you saw it . . . Now for yourself. I gather that you also are unpopular in this island?'

Maris gave a short sketch of his career, and Vernon convinced himself by a few questions that he spoke the truth, for the Greek had served alongside the British at Salonika.

'I came here to protect the lady,' Maris concluded.

'Who sent you?'

'Mr Ertzberger. I had a companion, an English colonel who is also in your Parliament, and a great milord. Leithen is his name.'

'God bless my soul! Leithen! Oh, impossible! Quick! Tell me more. Where is he now?'

'That I do not know. Yesterday evening we separated, each seeking to find some way of entering this House. I blundered badly, and was taken by the guards on the seaward front. My friend must also have failed, or he would be here, but I do not think he has been taken.'

The knowledge that I was somewhere in the island gave Vernon, as he told me, a sudden acute sense of comfort. I must have been the visitor to the yacht. He cross-examined Maris, who knew nothing of the boat's existence, and Maris agreed that the stranger who had gone aboard must have been myself. 'The Greek who was with him,' he said, 'was doubtless my corporal, Janni, the one man in my batch of fools who kept his head.'

Mitri returned with Vernon's clothes, and an ancient dressing-gown for Maris. He also brought a bowl of milk and some cakes and cheese. Questions trembled on his lips, but Vernon waved him off. 'Go and tell your mistress that we will come to her in a quarter of an hour. And have a bed made ready for this gentleman.'

As Vernon dressed he had a look at his companion, now grotesquely robed in a gown too large for him, and dirty and scratched from his adventures. It was the mercy of Providence that had given him such a colleague, for he liked the man's bold hard-bitten face and honest eyes. Here was a practical fellow, and he wanted something exceedingly prosaic and practical to counteract the awe which still hovered about his mind. He fought to keep at a distance the memory of the silence and the torches and the shining spaces of the Dancing Floor. This man did not look susceptible.

'I need not tell you that we are in the devil of a tight place, Captain Maris. Do you realise precisely the meaning of the performance we have just witnessed?'

Maris nodded. 'Since yesterday. It has been most pointedly explained to me. I am one victim for the sacrifice, and the lady of this house is the other, and you are the priest.'

'We have the better part of twenty-four hours' grace. After that?'

'After that this House will be burned. You may go forth, if you have the nerve to play the part. The lady and I – no. We are supposed to die when the fire begins, but if we do not die by your hand we will die in the flames.'

'There is no way of escape?'

'None,' said Maris cheerfully. 'But with your help I think we will do some mischief first. God's curse on the swine!'

'And the lady?'

Maris shrugged his shoulders.

'Till this evening,' said Vernon, 'I thought I had a plan. I was pretty certain I could win the race, and I proposed to reason with the male victim who came back with me, or club him on the head. I thought that when the fire began there would be confusion and that the people would keep outside the wall. My boat is lying below the cliffs and I hoped to carry the lady there. But now I know that that is impossible. There will be a concourse of the young men outside the door at the moment of the burning, and the House will be watched more closely than ever. Do you know what the people expect?'

Maris spat contemptuously. 'I heard some talk of the coming of Gods. The devil take all priests and their lying tales.'

'They await the coming of Gods. You are not a classical scholar Captain Maris, so you cannot realise, perhaps, just what that means. We are dealing with stark madness. These peasants are keyed up to a tremendous expectation. A belief has come to life, a belief far older than Christianity. They expect salvation from the coming of two Gods, a youth and a maiden. If their hope is disappointed, they will be worse madmen than before. Tomorrow night nothing will go out from this place, unless it be Gods.'

'That is true. The lady and I will without doubt die at the threshold, and you also, my friend. What arms have we?'

'I have this revolver with six cartridges. The lady has a toy pistol, but, I think, no ammunition. The men without are armed with rifles.'

'Ugly odds. It is infamous that honest folk and soldiers should perish at the hands of the half-witted.'

'What about Leithen? He is outside and has come here expressly to save the lady.'

Maris shook his head. 'He can do nothing. They have set up a cordon, a barrage, which he cannot penetrate. There is no hope in the island, for every man and woman is under the Devil's spell. Also the telegraph has been cut these three days.'

'Do you see any chance?'

Maris cogitated. 'We have twenty-four hours. Some way of escape might be found by an active man at the risk of a bullet or two. We might reach your boat.'

'But the lady?'

'Why, no. Things look dark for the poor lady. We came here to protect her, and it seems as if we can do no more than die with her . . . I would like to speak with that old man about clothes. A soldier does not feel at his bravest when he is barefoot and unclad save for pants and a ragged shirt. I refuse to go to Paradise in this dressing-gown.'

Maris's cheerful fortitude was balm to Vernon's mind, for it seemed to strip the aura of mystery from the situation, and leave it a straight gamble of life and death. If Koré was to be saved it must be through Maris, for he himself was cast for another part.

'Come and let me present you to the lady,' he said. 'We must have some plan to sleep on.'

Koré was in her sitting-room, and as she rose to meet them he saw that her face was very white.

'I heard nothing,' she said hoarsely, 'though Mitri says that there are thousands in the glade beyond the wall. But I saw a red glow from the upper windows.'

'That was the torches which lined the stadium. I have been running a race, Miss Arabin, and have been lucky enough to win. Therefore we have still twenty-four hours of peace. May I present Captain Maris of the Greek Army? He asked me to apologise for his clothes.'

The Greek bowed gallantly and kissed her hand.

'Captain Maris came here to protect you. He came with a friend of ours, Sir Edward Leithen.'

'Sir Edward Leithen?' the girl cried. 'He is here?'

'He is in the island, but he is unable to join us in the House. Captain Maris tried, and was unfortunately captured. He was handed over to me as the victor of the race, and that is why he is here. But Sir Edward must be still scouting around the outposts, and it is pretty certain that he won't find a way in. I'm afraid we must leave him out of account . . . Now I want you to listen to me very carefully, for I've a good deal to say to you. I'm going to be perfectly candid, for you're brave enough to hear the worst.'

Vernon constructed three cigarettes out of his pipe tobacco and tissue paper from the illustrations in Peter Beckford. Koré did not light hers, but sat waiting with her hands on her knees.

'They think you a witch, because of the habits of your family. That you have long known. In the past they have burned witches in these islands, and Plakos remembers it. But it remembers another thing – the ancient ritual I told you of, and that memory which has been sleeping for centuries has come to violent life. Perhaps it would not have mastered them if the mind of the people had not been full of witch-burning. That, you see, gave them one victim already chosen, and in Captain Maris, who is of their own race and also a stranger, they have found the other.'

'I see all that,' the girl said slowly. 'Of course I did not know when I left London – I couldn't have guessed – I thought it was a simple business which only needed a bold front, and I was too vain to take advice . . . Oh, forgive me. My vanity has brought two innocent people into my miserable troubles . . .'

'I told you yesterday that we were going to win. You must trust me, Miss Arabin. And, for Heaven's sake, don't imagine that I blame you. I think you are the bravest thing God ever made. I wouldn't be elsewhere for worlds.'

Her eyes searched his face closely, and then turned to Maris, who instantly adopted an air of bold insouciance.

'You are good men . . . But what can you do? They will watch us like rats till the fire begins, and then – if we are not dead – they will kill us . . . They will let no one go from this House – except their Gods.'

These were the very words Vernon had used to Maris, and since they so wholly expressed his own belief, he had to repudiate them with a vehement confidence.

'No,' he said, 'you forget that there are two things on our side. One is that, as the winner of the race, I am one of the people of Plakos. I can safely go out at the last moment and join their young men. I speak their tongue and I understand this ritual better than they do themselves. Surely I can find some way of driving them farther from the House so that in the confusion Maris can get you and your maid off unobserved. Mitri, too—'

'Mitri,' she broke in, 'has permission from our enemies to go when he pleases. But he refuses to leave us.'

'Well, Mitri also. The second thing is that I have found my

boat and got in touch with my man. He is lying in the bay below the cliffs, and I have arranged that on a certain signal he will meet you under the oliveyards. There is a gate in the wall there of which Mitri no doubt has the key. Once aboard, you are as safe as in London.'

'And you?'

'Oh, I will take my chance. I am a hillman from Akte and can keep up the part till I find some way of getting off.'

'Impossible!' she cried. 'When they find that their Gods have failed them they will certainly kill you. Perhaps it is because I was born here, but though I have only heard of this ritual from you, I feel somehow as if I had always known it. And I know that if the one sacrifice fails, there will be another.'

She rang the little silver bell for Mitri. 'Show this gentleman his room,' she looked towards Maris. 'You have already had food? Good night, Captain Maris. You must have had a wearing day, and I order you to bed.'

When they were alone she turned to Vernon. 'Your plan will not work. I can make a picture of what will happen tomorrow night – I seem to see every detail clear, as if I had been through it all before – and your plan is hopeless. You cannot draw them away from the House. They will be watching like demented wolves . . . And if you did and we escaped, what on earth would become of you?'

'I should be one of them – a sharer in their disappointment – probably forgotten.'

'Not you. You are their high-priest, and an angry people always turns on their priest.'

'There might be a bit of a row, but I dare say I could hold my own.'

'Against thousands – mad thousands? You would be torn in pieces even though they still believed you were a hillman from Akte.'

'I'll take the risk. It is no good making difficulties, Miss Arabin. I admit that the case is pretty desperate, but my plan has at any rate a chance.'

'The case is utterly desperate, and that is why your plan is no good. Desperate cases need more desperate remedies.'

'Well, what do you suggest?'

She smiled. 'You are very tired and so am I. We have a day and a night left us and we can talk in the morning . . . I told you when you first came here that I refused to run away. Well, I – don't – think – I have changed my mind . . .'

The difficulty of telling this part of the story (said Leithen) is that it must be largely guess-work. The main facts I know, but the affair had become so strange and intimate that neither Koré nor Vernon would speak of it, while Maris was only vaguely aware of what was happening. It must have been some time on the Friday morning that the two met again. I can picture Vernon racking his brains to supplement his fragile plan, turning sleeplessly in his bed, hunting out Maris in the early morn to go wearily over the slender chances. Koré, I imagine, slept dreamlessly. She had reached her decision, and to her strong and simple soul to be resolved was to be at peace. Vernon was a fine fellow – I have known few finer – but there were lumpish elements in him, while the girl was all pure spirit.

But I can reconstruct the meeting of the two in the bare little sitting-room – without Maris – for that much Vernon has told me. I can see Vernon's anxious face, and the girl's eyes bright with that innocent arrogance which once in my haste I had thought ill-breeding.

'I am not going to run away from my people,' she said. 'I am going to meet them.'

Vernon asked her meaning and she replied:

'I said yesterday that no one would be permitted to leave the House, unless in the eyes of the watchers they were Gods. Well, the Gods will not fail them . . . Listen to me. I have tried to purify this place, but there can be only one purification and that is by fire. It had to come, and it seems to me right that it should come from the hands of those who have suffered. After that I go out as a free woman – and to a free woman nothing is impossible.'

I think that for a little he may not have understood her. His mind, you see, had been busy among small particulars, and the simplicity of her plan would not at once be comprehended. Then there came for him that moment of liberation, when the world clarifies and what have been barrier mountains become only details in a wide prospect. The extreme of boldness is seen to be the true discretion, and with that mood comes a sharp uplift of spirit.

'You are right,' he cried. 'We will give them their Gods.'

'Gods?' She stopped him. 'But I must go alone. You have no part in this trial. But if I win all this household will be safe.

Most of these people have never seen me, and Kynaetho knows me only as a girl in old country clothes from whom they kept their eyes averted. I can dress for a different part, and they will see someone who will be as new to them as if the Panagia had come down from Heaven. But you—'

'They will not be content with one divinity,' he broke in. 'They await a double epiphany, remember – the Koré and the Kouros. That is the point of the occasion. We must be faithful to the letter of the rite. After all they know less of me than of you. They saw me win a race, a figure very much like the others in the moonlight . . . To those who may recognise me I am an unknown hillman of Akte. Why should not the Kouros have revealed himself the day before, and be also the Basileus?'

She looked at him curiously as if seeing him for the first time as a bodily presence. I can fancy that for the first time she may have recognised his beauty and strength.

'But you are not like me,' she urged. 'You have not an old burden to get rid of. I am shaking off the incubus of my youth, and going free, like the Gods. What you call the epiphany is not only for Plakos but for myself, and nothing matters, not even death. I can play the part, but can you? To me it is going to be the beginning of life, but to you it can only be an adventure. Chivalry is not enough.'

'To me also it is the beginning of life,' he answered. Then he returned to the tale of his boyhood's dream. 'When it vanished in the storm a few nights ago I hated it, for I felt that it had stolen years from my life. But now I know that nothing is wasted. The door of the last of the dream-rooms has opened and you have come in. And we are going to begin life – together.'

A strange pair of lovers, between whom no word of love had yet been spoken! By very different roads both had reached a complete assurance, and with it came exhilaration and ease of mind. Maris during the long spring day might roam about restlessly, and Mitri and Elise fall to their several prayers, but Vernon and Koré had no doubts. While I, outside the wall, was at the mercy of old magics, a mere piece of driftwood tossed upon undreamed-of tides, the two in the House had almost forgotten Plakos. It had become to them no more than a background for their own overmastering private concerns. The only problem was for their own hearts; for Koré to shake off for good the burden of her past and vindicate her fiery purity, that virginity of the spirit which could not be smirched by man or matter; for Vernon to open the door at which he had waited all his life and redeem the long preparation of his youth. They had followed each their own paths of destiny, and now these paths had met and must run together. That was the kind of thing that could not be questioned, could not even be thought about; it had to be accepted, like the rising sun. I do not think that they appreciated their danger, as I did, for they had not been, like me, down in the shadows. They were happy in their half-knowledge, and in that blessed preoccupation which casts out fear.

But some time in the afternoon he drew for the girl a picture of the ancient rite, and he must have been inspired, for, as she once recounted it to me, he seems to have made his book learning like the tale of an eye-witness.

'Why do you tell me this?' she asked.

'Because if we are to play our part we must understand that there is beauty as well as terror in this worship.'

'You speak as if you were a believer.'

He laughed. 'There is truth in every religion that the heart of man ever conceived. It is because of that that we shall win.'

But I think his confidence was less complete than hers. I judge from what Maris told me that, though Vernon was what the Scotch call 'fey' during those last hours, he retained something of his old careful prevision. As the twilight fell he took Maris aside and gave him his pistol. 'Mitri has orders as soon as he gets out of the House to take a lantern to the cliffs and make the signal for my boat. He has a key and will open the door in the oliveyard wall. Miss Arabin and I are staking everything on a mighty gamble. If it succeeds, I think that the people will be in a stupor and we shall have an opportunity to join you. But if it fails – well, they will tear us to pieces. You must be close to us and await events. If the worst happens, one of these bullets is for the lady. 'Swear to me on your honour as a soldier.'

EIGHTEEN

I TAKE UP the tale now (said Leithen) at the point where I fell in with Maris in the avenue which led to the gap in the wall. As I have told you, I had stumbled through the undergrowth with the blazing House making the place an inferno of blood-red aisles and purple thickets. Above the roar of the flames I heard the noise of panic-driven feet, of men plunging in haste – two indeed I had met, who seemed to be in the extremity of fear. For myself I was pretty nearly at the end of my tether. I was doddering with fatigue, and desperate with anxiety, and the only notion in my head was to use the dregs of my strength to do something violent. I was utterly in the dark, too. I did not know but that Koré might be already beyond my help, for that crimson grove seemed to reek of death.

And then I blundered into Maris, saw something in his face which gave me a surge of hope, and with his hand on my arm turned my eyes up the avenue.

The back part of the House and the outbuildings were by this time one roaring gust of flame, but the front was still untouched, and the fan of fire behind it gave it the concave darkness of a shell – a purple dark which might at any moment burst into light. The glow beyond the façade was reflected farther down the avenue, which was as bright as day, but the House end was shadowed, and the two figures which I saw seemed to be emerging from a belt of blackness between two zones of raw gold. I therefore saw them first as two dim white forms, which, as they moved, caught tints of flame . . .

Put it down to fatigue, if you like, or to natural stupidity, but I did not recognise them. Besides, you see, I knew nothing of Vernon's presence there. My breath stopped and I felt my heart leap to my throat. What I saw seemed not of the earth – immortals, whether from Heaven or Hell, coming out of the shadows and the fire in white garments, beings that no elements could destroy. In that moment the most panicky of the guards now fleeing from the demesne was no more abject believer than I.

And then another fugitive barged into me, and Maris caught him by the arm and cuffed his ears. I saw that it was Janni, but the sight meant nothing to me. The corporal seemed to be whimpering with terror, and Maris talked fiercely to him, but I did not listen. He quieted him, and then he took us both by an arm and hurried us with him towards the gap. It was what I wanted to do. I dared not look again on that burning pageant.

The next I knew I was beyond the wall on the edge of the Dancing Floor. I do not know how I got there, for my legs seemed to have no power in them, and I fancy that Maris dragged us both. The scared guards must have preceded us, for behind was emptiness, save for the presences in the avenue. The thick trees partly blanketed the fire, but the light from the burning roof fell beyond them and lit up redly the scarp on which we stood. A rival light, too, was coming into being. The rising moon had already flooded the far hills, and its calm radiance was sweeping over the hollow packed with the waiting multitude.

At first I saw only the near fringes of the people – upturned faces in the uncanny light of the fire. But as I looked, the unfeatured darkness beyond changed also into faces – faces spectral in the soft moonshine. I seemed to be standing between two worlds, one crimson with terror and the other golden with a stranger spell, but both far removed from the kindly works of men.

Maris had pulled us aside out of the line of the breach in the wall, where the avenue made a path for the glow of the fire. We were in full view of the people, but they had no eyes for us, for their gaze was concentrated on the breach. The fugitive guards had by this time been absorbed, and their panic had not communicated itself to the great multitude. For a second I forgot my own fears in the amazing sight before me . . . The crowded Dancing Floor was silent; in face of that deep stillness the crackle and roar of the fire seemed no more than the beating of waves on a far-away coast. Though the moon made the hills yellow as corn, it left the upturned faces pale. I was looking down on a sea of white faces – featureless to me, masks of strained expectation. I felt the influence from them beat upon me like a wind. The fierce concentration of mingled hope and fear – wild hope, wilder fear – surged up to me, and clutched at my nerves and fired my brain. For a second I was as exalted as the craziest of them. Fragments of the dithyramb which Vernon had translated came unbidden to my lips – 'Io, Kouros most great . . . Come, O come, and bring with thee – holy hours of thy most holy Spring.'

The spell of the waiting people made me turn, as they had turned, to the gap in the wall. Through it, to the point where the glow of the conflagration mingled with the yellow moonlight, came the two figures.

I think I would have dropped on my knees, but that Maris fetched me a clout on the back, and his exultant voice cried in my ear. 'Bravo,' he cried. 'By the Mother of God, they win! That is a great little lady!'

There was something in the familiarity, the friendly roughness of the voice which broke the spell. I suddenly looked with seeing eyes, and I saw Koré.

She was dressed in white, the very gown which had roused Vernon's ire at my cousin's dance the summer before. A preposterous garment I had thought it, the vagary of an indecent fashion. But now – ah now! It seemed the fitting robe for youth and innocence – divine youth, heavenly innocence – clothing but scarcely veiling the young Grace who walked like Persephone among the spring meadows. *Vera incessu patuit Dea*. It was not Koré I was looking at, but *the* Koré, the immortal maiden, who brings to the earth its annual redemption.

I was a sane man once more, and filled with another kind of exaltation. I have never felt so sharp a sense of joy. God had not failed us. I knew that Koré was now not only safe but triumphant.

And then I recognised Vernon.

I did not trouble to think by what mad chance he had come there. It seemed wholly right that he should be there. He was dressed like the runner of the day before, but at the moment I did not connect the two. What I was looking at was an incarnation of something that mankind has always worshipped – youth rejoicing to run its race, that youth which is the security of this world's continuance and the earnest of Paradise.

I recognised my friends and yet I did not recognise them, for they were transfigured. In a flash of insight I understood that it was not the Koré and the Vernon that I had known, but new creations. They were not acting a part, but living it. They, too, were believers; they had found their own epiphany, for they had found themselves and each other. Each other! How I knew it I do not know, but I realised that it was two lovers that stood on the brink of the Dancing Floor. And I felt a great glow of peace and happiness.

With that I could face the multitude once more. And then I saw the supreme miracle.

People talk about the psychology of a crowd, how it is different in kind from the moods of the men who compose it. I dare say that is true, but if you have each individual strained to the extreme of tension with a single hope, the mood of the whole is the same as that of the parts, only multiplied a thousandfold. And if the nerve of a crowd goes there is a vast cracking, just as the rending of a tree-trunk is greater than the breaking of a twig.

For a second – not more – the two figures stood on the edge of the Dancing Floor in the sight of the upturned eyes. I do not think that Koré and Vernon saw anything – they had their own inward vision. I do not know what the people saw in the presences that moved out of the darkness above them.

But this I saw. Over the multitude passed a tremor like a wind in a field of wheat. Instead of a shout of triumph there was a low murmur as of a thousand sighs. And then there came a surge, men and women stumbling in terror. First the fringes opened and thinned, and in another second, as it seemed to me, the whole mass was in precipitate movement. And then it became panic – naked veritable panic. The silence was broken by hoarse cries of fear. I saw men running like hares on the slopes of the Dancing Floor. I saw women dragging their children as if fleeing from a pestilence . . . In a twinkling I was looking down on an empty glade with the Spring of the White Cypress black and solitary in the moonlight.

I did not doubt what had happened. The people of Plakos had gone after strange gods, but it was only for a short season that they could shake themselves free from the bonds of a creed which they had held for a thousand years. The resurgence of ancient faiths had obsessed but had not destroyed the religion into which they had been born. Their spells had been too successful. They had raised the Devil and now fled from him in the blindest terror. They had sought the outlands, had felt their biting winds, had had a glimpse of their awful denizens, and they longed with the passion of children for their old homely shelters. The priest of Kynaetho would presently have his fill of stricken penitents.

Maris was laughing. I dare say it was only a relief from nervous strain, but it seemed to me an impiety. I turned on him angrily. 'There's a boat somewhere. See that everybody is aboard – the whole household. And bring it round to the harbour where we first landed.'

'Not to the oliveyards?' he asked.

'No, you fool. To the harbour. Plakos is now as safe for us as the streets of Athens.'

Koré and Vernon stood hand in hand like people in a dream. I think they were already dimly aware of what had happened, and were slowly coming back to the ordinary world. The virtue was going out of them, and with the ebbing of their exaltation came an immense fatigue. I never saw human faces so pale.

Vernon was the first to recover. He put his arm round Koré's waist, for without it she would have fallen, but he himself was none too steady on his feet. He recognised me.

'Ned,' he said, in a stammering voice, like a sleepwalker's. 'I heard you were here. It was good of you, old man . . . What do you think . . . now . . . the boat . . .'

'Come along,' I cried, and I took an arm of each. 'The sooner you are on board the better. You want to sleep for a week.' I started them off along the edge of the Dancing Floor.

'Not that way,' he gasped. 'Too risky . . .'

'There is no danger anywhere in this blessed island. Come along. You want food and clothes. It's getting on for midnight and you're both only half-dressed.'

They were like two children pulled out of bed and too drowsy to walk, and I had my work cut out getting them along the ridge. The Dancing Floor was empty, and when we entered the road which led from Kynaetho to the main gate of the House there was also solitude. Indeed, we had to pass through a segment of the village itself, and the place was silent as the grave. I knew where the people were – in and around the church, grovelling in the dust for their sins.

Our going was so slow that by the time we looked down on the harbour the boat was already there. I stopped for a moment and glanced back, for far behind me I heard voices. There was a glow as from torches to the south where the church stood, and a murmur which presently swelled into an excited clamour. Suddenly a bell began to ring, and it seemed as if the noise became antiphonal, voices speaking and others replying. At that distance I could make out nothing, but I knew what the voices said. It was 'Christ is risen – He is risen indeed.'

The moon had set before we put to sea. My last recollection of Plakos is looking back and seeing the House flaming like a pharos on its headland. Then, as we beat outward with the wind, the fire became a mere point of brightness seen at a great distance in the vault of night.

I had no wish or power to sleep. Koré and Vernon, wrapped each in a heap of cloaks, lay in the bows. It was the quietest place, but there was no need of precautions, for they slept like the drugged. Elise, whose nerves had broken down, was in Vernon's berth. Black George had the helm and old Mitri and Janni snored beside him.

I sat amidships and smoked. When the moon went down a host of stars came out, pale and very remote as they always seem in a spring sky. The wind was light and the water slid smoothly past; I knew roughly our bearings, but I had a sense of being in another world and on seas never before sailed by man. The last week had been for me a time of acute anxiety and violent bodily exertion, but a sponge seemed to have passed over the memory of it. Something altogether different filled my mind. I had with my own eyes seen Fate take a hand in the game and move the pieces on the board. The two sleepers in the bows had trusted their destiny and had not been betrayed.

I thought with contrition of my cynicism about Vernon's dream. No doubt it had been a will-o'-the-wisp, but it had been true in purpose, for it had made him wait, alert and aware, on something which had been prepared for him, and if that something was far different from his forecast the long expectation had made him ready to seize it. How otherwise could he, with his decorous ancestry and his prudent soul, have become an adventurer? . . . And Koré? She had stood grimly to the duty which she conceived Fate to have laid upon her, and Fate, after piling the odds against her, had relented. Perhaps that is the meaning of courage. It wrestles with circumstance, like Jacob with the angel, till it compels its antagonist to bless it.

I remembered a phrase which Vernon had once used about

'the mailed virgin'. It fitted this girl, and I began to realise the meaning of virginity. True purity, I thought, whether in woman or man, was something far more than the narrow sex thing which was the common notion of it. It meant keeping oneself, as the Bible says, altogether unspotted from the world, free from all tyranny and stain, whether of flesh or spirit, defying the universe to touch even the outworks of the sanctuary which is one's soul. It must be defiant, not the inert fragile crystal, but the supple shining sword. Virginity meant nothing unless it was mailed, and I wondered whether we were not coming to a better understanding of it. The modern girl, with all her harshness, had the gallantry of a free woman. She was a crude Artemis, but her feet were on the hills. Was the blushing sheltered maid of our grandmother's day no more than an untempted Aphrodite?

These were queer reflections, I know, for a man like me, but they gave me contentment, as if I had somehow made my peace with life. For a long time I listened to the ripple of the water and watched the sky lighten to dim grey and the east flush with sunrise. It had become very cold and I was getting sleepy, so I hunted about for a mattress to make myself a bed. But a thought made me pause. How would these two, who had come together out of the night, shake down on the conventional roads of marriage? To the end of time the desire of a woman should be to her husband. Would Koré's eyes, accustomed to look so masterfully at life, ever turn to Vernon in the surrender of wifely affection? As I looked at the two in the bows I wondered.

Then something happened which reassured me. The girl stirred uneasily as if in a bad dream, turned to where Vernon lay and flung out her hand. Both were sound asleep, but in some secret way the impulse must have been communicated to Vernon, for he moved on his side, and brought an arm, which had been lying loosely on the rug which covered him, athwart Koré's in a gesture of protection.

After that both seemed to be at peace, while the yawl ran towards the mainland hills, now green as a fern in the spring dawn.

SICK HEART RIVER

Part One

'Thus said Alfred:
If thou hast a woe, tell it not to the weakling,
Tell it to thy saddlebow, and ride singing forth.'

Proverbs of Alfred

I

LEITHEN had been too busy all day to concern himself with the thoughts which hung heavily at the back of his mind. In the morning he had visited his bankers to look into his money affairs. These were satisfactory enough: for years he had been earning a large income and spending little of it; his investments were mostly in trustee stocks; he found that he possessed, at a safe computation, a considerable fortune, while his Cotswold estate would find a ready sale. Next came his solicitors, for he was too wise a man to make the mistake of many barristers and tinker with his own will. He gave instructions for bringing the old one up to date. There were a few legacies by way of mementoes to old friends, a considerable gift to his college, donations to certain charities, and the residue to his nephew Charles, his only near relation.

He forced himself to lunch at one of his clubs, in a corner where no one came near him, though Archie Roylance waved a greeting across the dining-room. Then he spent a couple of hours with his clerk in his Temple chambers, looking through the last of his briefs. There were not a great many, since, for some months, he had been steadily refusing work. The batch of cases for opinion he could soon clear off, and one big case in the Lords he must argue next week, for it involved a point of law in which he had always taken a special interest. The briefs for the following term would be returned. The clerk, who had been with him for thirty years, was getting on in life and would be glad to retire on an ample pension. Still, it was a painful parting.

'It's a big loss to the Bar, Sir Edward, sir,' old Mellon said, 'and it's pretty well the end of things for me. You have been a kind master to me, sir, and I'm proud to have served you. I hope you are going to have many happy years yet.'

But there had been a look of pain in the old man's eyes

which told Leithen that he had guessed what he dared not hint at.

He had tea at the House of Commons with the Chief Whip, a youngish man named Ritson, who in the War had been a subaltern in his own battalion. Ritson listened to him with a wrinkled brow and troubled eyes.

'Have you told your local people?' he asked.

'I'll write to them tomorrow. I thought I ought to tell you first. There's no fear of losing the seat. My majority has never been less than six thousand, and there's an excellent candidate ready in young Walmer.'

'We shall miss you terribly, you know. There's no one to take your place.'

Leithen smiled. 'I haven't been pulling my weight lately.'

'Perhaps not. But I'm thinking of what's coming. If there's an election, we're going to win all right, and we'll want you badly in the new Government. It needn't be a law office. You can have your pick of half a dozen jobs. Only yesterday the Chief was speaking to me about you.' And he repeated a conversation he had had with the man who would be the next Prime Minister.

'You're all very kind. But I don't think I want anything. I've done enough, as Napoleon said, "*pour chauffer la gloire.*" '

'Is it your health?' Ritson asked.

'Well, I need a rest. I've been pretty busy all my days and I'm tired.'

The Chief Whip hesitated.

'Things are pretty insecure in the world just now. There may be a crisis any day. Don't you think you ought—'

Leithen smiled.

'I've thought of that. But if I stayed on I could do nothing to help. That isn't a pleasant conclusion to come to, but it's the truth.'

Ritson stood at the door of his room and watched his departing guest going down the corridor to the Central Lobby. He turned to a junior colleague who had joined him—

'I wonder what the devil's the matter! There's been a change in him in the last few months. But he doesn't look a sick man. He was always a bad colour, of course, but Lamancha says he is the hardest fellow he ever knew on the hill.'

The other shook a wise head, 'You never can tell. He had a roughish time in the War and the damage often takes years to come out. I think he's right to slack off, for he must have a gruelling life at the Bar. My father tried to get him the other day as leader in a big case, and he wasn't to be had for love or money. Simply snowed under with work!'

Leithen walked from the House towards his rooms in Down Street. He was still keeping his thoughts shut down, but in spite of himself the familiar streets awakened memories. How often he had tramped them in the far-off days when he was a pupil in chambers and the world was an oyster waiting to be opened. It was a different London then, quieter, cosier, dirtier perhaps, but sweeter smelling. On a summer evening such as this the scents would have been a compound of wood paving, horse-dung, flowers, and fresh paint, not the deadly monotony of petrol. The old land-marks, too, were disappearing. In St James's Street only Mr Lock's modest shop-window and the eighteenth-century facade of Boodle's recalled the London of his youth. He remembered posting up this street with a high heart after he had won his first important case in court . . . and the Saturday afternoon's strolls in it when he had changed his black regimentals for tweeds or flannels . . . and the snowy winter day when a tiny coffin on a gun carriage marked the end of Victoria's reign . . . and the shiny August morning in 1914 when he had been on his way to enlist with a mind half-anxious and half-exulting. He had travelled a good deal in his time, but most of his life had been spent in this square mile of west London. He did not regret the changes; he only noted them. His inner world was crumbling so fast that he had lost any craving for permanence in the externals of life.

In Piccadilly he felt his knees trembling and called a taxi. In Down Street he took the lift to his rooms, though for thirty years he had made a ritual of climbing the stairs.

The flat was full of powdery sunlight. He sank into a chair at the window to get his breath, and regarded the comfortable, shabby sitting-room. Now that he seemed to be looking at it with new eyes he noted details which familiarity had long obscured. The pictures were school and college groups, one or two mountain photographs, and, over the mantelpiece, Raeburn's portrait of his grandfather. He was very little of a connoisseur, though at Borrowby he had three Vandykes which suited its Jacobean solemnity. There were books everywhere; they overflowed into the dining-room and his bedroom and the little hall. He reflected that what with these, and the law library in his chambers and his considerable collection at Borrowby, he must have at least twenty thousand volumes. He had been happy here, happy and busy, and for a moment – for a moment only – he felt a bitter pang of regret.

But he was still keeping his thoughts at a distance, for the time had not come to face them. Memories took the vacant place. He remembered how often he had left these rooms with a holiday zest, and how he had always returned to them with delight, for this, and not Borrowby, was his true home. How many snug winter nights had he known here, cheerful with books and firelight; and autumn twilights when he was beginning to get into the stride of his work after the long vacation; and spring mornings when the horns of elfland were blowing even in Down Street. He lay back in his chair, shut his eyes, and let his memory wander. There was no harm in that, for the grim self-communion he had still to face would have no room for memories. He almost dozed.

The entry of his man, Cruddock, aroused him.

'Lord Clanroyden called you up, sir. He is in town for the night and suggests that you might dine with him. He said the Turf Club at eight. I was to let him know, sir.'

'Tell him to come here instead. You can produce some kind of a dinner?' Leithen rather welcomed the prospect. Sandy Clanroyden would absorb his attention for an hour or two and postpone for a little the settlement with himself which his soul dreaded.

He had a bath and changed. He had been feeling listless and depressed, but not ill, and the cold shower gave him a momentary sense of vigour and almost an appetite for food. He caught a glimpse of himself naked in the long mirror, and was shocked anew by his leanness. He had given up weighing himself, but it looked as if he had lost pounds in the past month.

Sandy arrived on the stroke of eight. Leithen, as he greeted him, reflected that he was the only one of his closer friends whom he could have borne to meet. Archie Roylance's high spirits would have been intolerable, and Lamancha's air of mastery over life, and Dick Hannay's serene contentment.

He did not miss the sharp glance of his guest when he entered the room. Could some rumours have got abroad? It was clear that Sandy was setting himself to play a part, for his manner had not its usual ease. He was not talking at random, but picking his topics.

A proof was that he did not ask Leithen about his holiday plans, which, near the close of the law term, would have been a natural subject. He seemed to feel that his host's affairs might be delicate ground, and that it was his business to distract his mind from some unhappy preoccupation. So he talked about himself and his recent doings. He had just been to Cambridge to talk to the Explorers' Club, and had come back with strong views about modern youth.

'I'm not happy about the young entry. Oh! I don't mean all of it. There's plenty of lads that remind me of my own old lot. But some of the best seem to have become a bit too much introverted – isn't that the filthy word? What's to be done about the Owlish Young, Ned?'

'I don't see much of youth nowadays,' said Leithen. 'I seem to live among fogies. I'm one myself.'

'Rot! You are far and away the youngest of us.'

Again Leithen caught a swift glance at his face, as if Sandy would have liked to ask him something, but forbore.

'Those boys make me anxious. It's right that they should be serious with the world slipping into chaos, but they need not be owlish. They are so darned solemn about their new little creeds in religion and politics, forgetting that they are as old as the hills. There isn't a ha'porth of humour in the bunch, which means, of course, that there isn't any perspective. If it comes to a show-down I'm afraid they will be pretty feeble folk. People with half their brains and a little sense of humour will make rings round them.'

Leithen must have shown his unconcern about the future of the world by his expression, for Sandy searched for other topics. Spring at Laverlaw had been diviner than ever. Had Leithen heard the curlews this year? No? Didn't he usually make a pilgrimage somewhere to hear them? For northerners they, and not the cuckoo, were the heralds of spring . . . His wife was at Laverlaw, but was coming to London next day. Yes, she was well, but—

Again Leithen saw in the other's face a look of interrogation. He wanted to ask him something, tell him something, but did not feel the moment propitious.

'Her uncle has just turned up here. Apparently there's a bit of family trouble to be settled. You know him, don't you? Blenkiron – John Scantlebury Blenkiron?'

Leithen nodded. 'A little. I was his counsel in the

Continental Nickel case some years ago. He's an old friend of yours and Hannay's, isn't he?'

'About the best Dick and I have in the world. Would you like to see him again? I rather think he would like to see you.'

Leithen yawned and said his plans for the immediate future were uncertain.

Just before ten Sandy took his leave, warned by his host's obvious fatigue. He left the impression that he had come to dinner to say something which he had thought had better be left unsaid, and Leithen, when he looked at his face in his dressing-table mirror, knew the reason. It was the face of a very sick man.

That night he had meant, before going to sleep, to have it out with himself. But he found that a weary body had made his brain incapable of coherent thought, so he tumbled into bed.

2

THE reckoning came six hours later, when his bedroom was brightening with the fore-glow of a June dawn. He awoke, as he usually did nowadays, sweating and short of breath. He got up and laved his face with cold water. When he lay down again he knew that the moment had arrived.

Recent events had been confused in a cloud of misery, and he had to disengage the details . . . There was no one moment to which he could point when his health had begun to fail. Two years before he had had a very hard summer at the Bar, complicated by the chairmanship of a Royal Commission, and a trip to Norway for the August sea trout had been disastrous. He had returned still a little fatigued. He no longer got up in the morning with a certain uplift of spirit, work seemed duller and more laborious, food less appetising, sleep more imperative but less refreshing.

During that winter he had had a bout of influenza for the first time in his life. After it he had dragged his wing for a month or two, but had seemed to pick up in the spring when he had had a trip to Provence with the Clanroydens. But the hot summer had given him a set-back, and when he went shooting with Lamancha in the autumn he found to his dismay that he had become short of breath and that the hills were too steep for him. Also he was clearly losing weight. So on his return to London he sought out Acton Croke and had himself examined. The great doctor had been ominously grave. Our fathers, he said, had talked unscientifically about the 'grand climacteric,' which came in the early sixties, but there was such a thing as a climacteric which might come any time in middle life, when the physical powers adjusted themselves to the approach of age. That crisis Leithen was now enduring, and he must go very carefully and remember that the dose of gas he got in the War had probably not exhausted its effect. Croke put him on a diet, prescribed a certain routine of rest and exercise, and made him drastically cut down his engagements. He insisted also on seeing him once a fortnight.

A winter followed for Leithen of steadily declining health. His breath troubled him and a painful sinking in the chest. He rose languidly, struggled through the day, and went to bed exhausted. Every moment he was conscious of his body and its increasing frailty. Croke sent him to a nursing home during the Christmas vacation, and for a few weeks he seemed to be better. But the coming of spring, instead of giving him new vigour, drained his strength. He began to suffer from night sweats which left him very feeble in the morning. His meals became a farce. He drove himself to take exercise, but now a walk round the Park exhausted one who only a few years back could walk down any Highland gillie. Croke's face looked graver with each visit.

Then the day before yesterday had come the crisis. He went by appointment to Croke – and demanded a final verdict. The great doctor gave it: gravely, anxiously, tenderly, as to an old friend, but without equivocation. He was dying, slowly dying.

Leithen's mind refused to bite on the details of his own case with its usual professional precision. He was not interested in these details. He simply accepted the judgment of the expert. He was suffering from advanced tuberculosis, a retarded consequence of his gas poisoning. Croke, knowing his patient's habit of mind, had given him a full diagnosis, but Leithen had scarcely listened to his exposition of the chronic fibrous affection and broncho-pulmonary lesions. The fact was enough for him.

'How long have I to live?' he asked, and was told a year, perhaps a little longer.

'Shall I go off suddenly, or what?' The answer was that there would be a progressive loss of strength until the heart failed.

'You can give me no hope?'

Croke shook his head.

'I dare not. The lesions *might* heal, the fibrous patch *might* disappear, but it would be a miracle according to present knowledge. I must add, of course, that our present knowledge may not be final truth.'

'But I must take it as such, I agree. Miracles don't happen.'

Leithen left Harley Street almost cheerfully. There was a grim satisfaction in knowing the worst. He was so utterly weary that after coffee and a sandwich in his rooms he went straight to bed.

Soon he must think things out, but not at once. He must first make some necessary arrangements about his affairs which would keep him from brooding. That should be the task of the morrow. It all reminded him of his habit as a company commander in the trenches when an attack was imminent: he had busied himself with getting every detail exact, so that his mind had no time for foreboding . . .

As he lay watching his window brighten with the morning he wondered why he was taking things so calmly. It was not courage – he did not consider himself a brave man, though he had never greatly feared death. At the best he had achieved in life a thin stoicism, a shallow fortitude. Insensibility, perhaps, was the best word. He remembered Dr Johnson's reply to Boswell's 'That, sir, was great fortitude of mind.' – 'No, sir, stark insensibility.'

At any rate he would not sink to self-pity. He had been brought up in a Calvinistic household and the atmosphere still clung to him, though in the ordinary way he was not a religious man. For example, he had always had an acute sense of sin, which had made him something of a Puritan in his way of life. He had believed firmly in God, a Being of ineffable purity and power, and consequently had had no undue reverence for man. He had always felt his own insignificance and imperfections and was not inclined to cavil at fate. On the contrary, he considered that fortune had been ludicrously kind to him. He had had fifty-eight years of health and wealth. He had survived the War, when the best of his contemporaries had fallen in swathes. He had been amazingly successful in his profession and had enjoyed every moment of his work. Honours had fallen to him out of all proportion to his merits. He had had a thousand pleasures – books, travel, the best of sport, the best of friends.

His friends – that had been his chief blessing. As he thought of their warm companionship he could not check a sudden wave of regret. *That* would be hard to leave. He had sworn Acton Croke to secrecy, and he meant to keep his condition hidden even from his closest intimates – from Hannay and Clanroyden and Lamancha and Palliser-Yeates and Archie Roylance. He could not endure to think of their anxious eyes. He would see less of them than before, of course, but he would continue to meet them on the old terms. Yes – but how? He was giving up Parliament and the Bar – London, too. What story was he to tell? A craving for rest and leisure? Well, he must indulge that craving at a distance, or otherwise his friends would discover the reason.

But where? . . . Borrowby? Impossible, for it was associated too closely with his years of vigour. He had rejoiced in reshaping that ancient shell into a house for a green old age; he remembered with what care he had planned his library and his garden; Borrowby would be intolerable as a brief refuge for a dying man . . . Scotland? – somewhere in the Lowland hills or on the sounding beaches of the west coast? But he had been too happy there. All the romance of childhood and forward-looking youth was bound up with those places and it would be agony to revisit them.

His memory sprawled over places he had seen in his much-travelled life. There was a certain Greek island where he had once lived dangerously; there were valleys on the Italian side of the Alps, and a *saeter* in the Jotunheim to which his fancy had often returned. But in his survey he found that the charm had gone from them; they were for the living, not the dying. Only one spot had still some appeal. In his early youth, when money had not been plentiful, he had had an autumn shooting trip in northern Quebec because it was cheap. He had come down on foot over the height of land, with a single Montagnais guide back-packing their kit, and one golden October afternoon he had stumbled on a place which he had never forgotten. It was a green saddle of land, a meadow of wild hay among the pines. South from it a stream ran to the St Lawrence; from an adjacent well another trickle flowed north on the Arctic watershed. It had seemed a haven of pastoral peace in a shaggy land, and he recalled how loth he had been to leave it. He had often thought about it, often determined to go back and look for it. Now, as he pictured it in its green security, it seemed the kind of sanctuary in which to die. He remembered its name.

The spring was called Clairefontaine, and it gave its name both to the south-flowing stream and to a little farm below in the valley.

Supposing he found the proper shelter, how was he to spend his closing months? As an invalid, slowly growing feebler, always expectant of death? That was starkly impossible. He wanted peace to make his soul, but not lethargy either of mind or body. The body! – that was the rub. It was failing him, that body which had once been a mettled horse quickly responding to bridle or spur. Now he must be aware every hour of its ignoble frailty . . . He stretched out his arms, flexing the muscles as he used to do when he was well, and was conscious that there was no pith in them.

His thoughts clung to this physical shell of his. He had been proud of it, not like an athlete who guards a treasure, but like a master proud of an adequate servant. It had added much to the pleasures of life . . . But he realised that in his career it had mattered very little to him, for his work had been done with his mind. Labouring men had their physical strength as their only asset, and when the body failed them their work was done. They knew from harsh experience the limits of their strength, what exhaustion meant, and strife against pain and disablement. They had to endure all their days what he had endured to a small degree in the trenches . . . Had he not missed something, and, missing it, had failed somehow in one of the duties of man?

This queer thought kept returning to him with the force of a revelation. His mood was the opposite of self-pity, a feeling that his life had been too cosseted and fur-lined. Only now that his body was failing did he realise how little he had used it . . . Among the oddly assorted beliefs which made up his religious equipment, one was conditional immortality. The soul was only immortal if there was such a thing as a soul, and a further existence had to be earned in this one. He had used most of the talents God had given him, but not all. He had never, except in the War, staked his body in the struggle, and yet that was the stake of most of humanity. Was it still possible to meet that test of manhood with a failing body? . . . If only the War were still going on!

His mind, which had been dragging apathetically along, suddenly awoke into vigour. By God! there was one thing that would not happen. He would not sit down and twiddle his thumbs and await death. His ship, since it was doomed, should go down in action with every flag flying. Lately he had been re-reading *Vanity Fair* and he remembered the famous passage where Thackeray moralises on the trappings of the conventional death-bed, the soft-footed nurses, the hushed voices of the household, the alcove on the staircase in which to rest the coffin. The picture affected him with a physical nausea. That, by God! should never be his fate. He would die standing, as Vespasian said an emperor should . . .

The day had broadened into full sunlight. The white paint and the flowered wallpaper of his bedroom glowed with the morning freshness, and from the street outside came pleasant morning sounds like the jingle of milk-cans and the whistling of errand boys. His mind seemed to have been stabbed awake out of a flat stoicism into a dim but masterful purpose.

He got up and dressed, and his cold bath gave him a ghost of an appetite for breakfast.

3

HIS intention was to go down to his chambers later in the morning and get to work on the batch of cases for opinion. As always after a meal, he felt languid and weak, but his mind was no longer comatose. Already it was beginning to move steadily, though hopelessly, towards some kind of plan. As he sat huddled in a chair at the open window Cruddock announced that a Mr Blenkiron was on the telephone and would like an appointment.

This was the American that Sandy Clanroyden had spoken of. Leithen remembered him clearly as his client in a big case. He remembered, too, much that he had heard about him from Sandy and Dick Hannay. One special thing, too – Blenkiron had been a sick man in the War and yet had put up a remarkable show. He had liked him, and, though he felt himself now cut off from human companionship, he could hardly refuse an interview, for Sandy's sake. The man had probably some lawsuit in hand, and if so it would not take long to refuse.

'If convenient, sir, the gentleman could come along now,' said Cruddock.

Leithen nodded and took up the newspaper.

Blenkiron had aged. Eight years ago Leithen recalled him as a big man with a heavy shaven face, a clear skin, and calm ruminant grey eyes. A healthy creature in hard condition, he could have given a good account of himself with his hands as well as his head. Now he was leaner and more grizzled, and there were pouches under his eyes. Leithen remembered Sandy's doings in South America; Blenkiron had been in that show, and he had heard about his being a sort of industrial dictator in Olifa, or whatever the place was called.

The grey eyes were regarding him contemplatively but keenly. He wondered what they made of his shrunken body.

'It's mighty fine to see you again, Sir Edward. And all the boys, too. I've been stuck so tight in my job down south that I've gotten out of touch with my friends. I'm giving myself a holiday to look them up and to see my little niece. I think you know Babs.'

'I know her well. A very great woman. I had forgotten she was your niece. How does the old gang strike you?'

'Lasting well, sir. A bit older and maybe a bit wiser and settling down into good citizens. They tell me that Sir Archibald Roylance is making quite a name for himself in your Parliament, and that Lord Clanroyden cuts a deal of ice with your Government. Dick Hannay, I judge, is getting hayseed into his hair. How about yourself?'

'Fair,' Leithen said. 'I'm going out of business now. I've worked hard enough to be entitled to climb out of the rut.'

'That's fine!' Blenkiron's face showed a quickened interest. 'I haven't forgotten what you did for me when I was up against the Delacroix bunch. There's no man on the globe I'd sooner have with me in a nasty place than you. You've a mighty quick brain and a mighty sound judgment and you're not afraid to take a chance.'

'You're very kind,' said Leithen a little wearily. 'Well, that's all done with now. I am going out of harness.'

'A man like you can't ever get out of harness. If you lay down one job you take up another.'

Blenkiron's eyes, appraising now rather than meditative, scanned the other's face. He leaned forward in his chair and sank his voice.

'I came round this morning to say something to you, Sir Edward – something very special. Babs has a sister, Felicity – I guess you don't know her, but she's something of a person on our side of the water. Two years younger than Babs, and married to a man you've maybe heard of, Francis Galliard, one of old Simon Ravelston's partners. Young Galliard's gotten a great name in the city of New York, and Felicity and he looked like being a happy pair. But just lately things haven't been going too well with Felicity.'

In common politeness Leithen forced a show of attention, but Blenkiron had noted his dull eyes.

'I won't trouble you with the story now,' he went on, 'for it's long and a bit ravelled, but the gist of it is that Francis Galliard has disappeared over the horizon. Just leaked out of the landscape without a word to Felicity or anybody else. No! There is no suggestion of kidnapping or any dirty work – the trouble is in Francis's own mind. He is a Canuck – a Frenchman from Quebec – and I expect his mind works different from yours and mine. Now, he has got to be found and brought back – first of all to Felicity, and second, to his business, and third, to the United States. He's too valuable a man to lose, and in our present state of precarious balance we just can't afford it.'

Blenkiron stopped as if he expected some kind of reply. Leithen said nothing, but his thoughts had jumped suddenly to the upland meadow of Clairefontaine of which he had been thinking that morning. Odd that that remote memory should have been suddenly dug out of the lumber-room of the past!

'We want help in the job,' Blenkiron continued, 'and it's not going to be easy to find it. We want a man who can piece together the bits that make up the jigsaw puzzle, though we haven't got much in the way of evidence. We want a man who can read himself into Francis's mind and understand the thoughts he might have been thinking, and, most of all, we want a man who can put his conclusions into action. Finding Francis may mean a good deal of bodily wear and tear and taking some risks.'

'I see,' Leithen spoke at last. 'You want a combination of detective, psychologist and sportsman.'

'Yep.' Blenkiron beamed. 'You've hit it. And there's just the one man I know that fills the bill. I've had a talk with Lord Clanroyden and he agrees. If you had been going on at the Bar we would have offered you the biggest fee that any brief ever carried, for there's money to burn in this business – though I don't reckon the fee would have weighed much with you. But you tell me you are shaking loose. Well, here's a job for your leisure and, if I judge you right, it's the sort of job you won't turn down without a thought or two.'

Leithen raised his sick eyes to the eager face before him, a face whose abounding vitality sharpened the sense of his own weakness.

'You've come a little late,' he said slowly. 'I'm going to tell you something which Lord Clanroyden and the others don't know, and will never know – which nobody knows except myself and my doctor – and I want you to promise to keep it secret . . . I'm a dying man. I've only about a year to live.'

He was not certain what he expected, but he was certain it would be something which would wind up this business for good. He had longed to have one confidant, only one, and Blenkiron was safe enough. The sound of his voice speaking these grim words somehow chilled him, and he awaited dismally the conventional sympathy. After that Blenkiron would depart and he would see him no more.

But Blenkiron did not behave conventionally. He flushed deeply and sprang to his feet, upsetting his chair.

'My God!' he cried. 'If I ain't the blightedest, God-darned blundering fool! I might have guessed by your looks you were a sick man, and now I've hurt you in the raw with my cursed egotistical worries . . . I'm off, Sir Edward. Forget you ever saw me. God forgive me, for I won't soon forgive myself.'

'Don't go,' said Leithen. 'Sit down and talk to me. You may be the very man I want.'

4

HIS hostess noticed his slow appraising look round the table, which took each of the guests in turn.

'You were here last in '29,' she said. 'Do you think we have changed?'

Leithen turned his eyes to the tall woman at his left hand. Mrs Simon Ravelston had a beautiful figure, ill-chosen clothes, and the weather-beaten face of an English master of foxhounds. She was magnificently in place on horseback, or sailing a boat, or running with her beagles, but no indoor setting could fit her. Sprung from ancient New England stock, she showed her breeding in a wonderful detachment from the hubbub of life. At her own table she would drift into moods of reverie and stare into vacancy, oblivious of the conversation, and then when she woke up would turn such kind eyes upon her puzzled interlocutor that all offences were forgiven. When her husband had been Ambassador at the Court of St James's she had been widely popular, a magnet for the most sophisticated young men; but of this she had been wholly unconscious. She was deeply interested in life and very little interested in herself.

Leithen answered, 'Yes, I think you all look a little more fine-drawn and harder trained. The men, that is. The women could never change.'

Mrs Ravelston laughed. 'I hope that you're right. Before the depression we were getting rather gross. The old Uncle Sam that we took as our national figure was lean like a Red Indian, but in late years our ordinary type had become round-faced, and puffy, and pallid, like a Latin John Bull. Now we are recovering Uncle Sam, though we have shaved him and polished him up.' Her eyes ran round the table and stopped at a youngish man with strong rugged features and shaggy eyebrows who was listening with a smile to the talk of a very pretty girl.

'George Lethaby, for example. Thank goodness he is a career diplomat and can show himself about the world. I should like people to take him as a typical American.' She lowered her voice, for she was speaking now of her left-hand neighbour, 'Or Bronson, here. You know him, don't you? Bronson Jane.'

Leithen glanced beyond his hostess to where a man just passing into middle life was peering at an illegible menu card. This was the bright particular star of the younger America, and he regarded him with more than curiosity, for he counted upon him for help. On paper Bronson Jane was almost too good to be true. He had been a noted sportsman and was still a fine polo player; his name was a household word in Europe for his work in international finance; he was the Admirable Crichton of his day and it was rumoured that in the same week he had been offered the Secretaryship of State, the Presidency of an ancient University, and the control of a great industrial corporation. He had chosen the third, but seemed to have a foot also in every other world. He had a plain sagacious face, a friendly mouth, and deep-set eyes, luminous and masterful.

Leithen glanced round the table again. The dining-room of the Ravelston house was a homely place; it had no tapestries or panelling, and its pictures were family portraits of small artistic merit. In each corner there were marble busts of departed Ravelstons. It was like the rest of the house, and, like their country homes in the Catskills and on the Blue Ridge, a dwelling which bore the mark of successive generations who had all been acutely conscious of the past. Leithen felt that he might have been in a poor man's dwelling, but for the magnificence of the table flowers and silver and the gold soup plates which had once belonged to a King of France. He let his gaze rest on each of the men.

'Yes,' he told his hostess, 'you are getting the kind of face I like.'

'But not the right colour perhaps,' she laughed. 'Is that worry or too much iced water, I wonder?' She broke off suddenly, remembering her neighbour's grey visage.

'Tell me who the people are,' he said to cover her embarrassment. 'I have met Mr Jane and Mr Lethaby and Mr Ravelston.'

'I want you to know my Simon better,' she said. 'I know why you have come here – Mr Blenkiron told me. Nobody knows about it except in the family. The story is that Mr Galliard has gone to Peru to look into some pitchblende propositions. Simon is terribly distressed and he feels so helpless. You see, we only came back to America from England four months ago, and we have kind of lost touch.'

Simon Ravelston was a big man with a head like Jove, and a noble silvered beard. He was president of one of the chief private banking houses in the world, which under his great-grandfather had financed the first railways beyond the Appalachians, under his grandfather had salved the wreckage of the Civil War, and under his father had steadied America's wild gallop to wealth. He had a dozen partners, most of whom understood the technique of finance far better than himself, but on all major questions he spoke the last word, for he had the great general's gift of reducing complexities to a simple syllogism. In an over-worked world he seemed always to have ample leisure, for he insisted on making time to think. When others of his calling were spending twelve hectic hours daily in their offices, Simon would calmly go fishing. No man ever saw him rattled or hustled, and this Olympian detachment gave him a prestige in two continents against which he himself used to protest vigorously.

'They think I'm wise only because I don't talk when I've

nothing to say,' he used to tell his friends. 'Any fool these days can get a reputation if he keeps his mouth shut.'

He was happy because his mind was filled with happy interests; he had no itching ambitions, he did his jobs as they came along with a sincere delight in doing them well, and a no less sincere delight in seeing the end of them. He was the extreme opposite of the man whose nerves demand a constant busyness because, like a bicyclist, he will fall down if he stays still.

Leithen's gaze passed to a young man who had Simon's shape of head but was built on a smaller and more elegant scale. His hostess followed his eyes.

'That's our boy, Eric, and that's his wife Delia, across the table. Pretty, isn't she? She has the southern complexion, the real thing, which isn't indigestion from too much hot bread at breakfast. What's he doing? He's on the Johns Hopkins staff and is making a big name for himself in lung surgery. Ever since a little boy he's been set on doctoring and nothing would change him. He had a pretty good training – Harvard – two years at Oxford – a year in Paris – a long spell in a Montreal hospital. That's a new thing about our boys, Sir Edward. They're not so set nowadays on big business. They want to do things and make things, and they consider that there are better tools than dollars. George Lethaby is an example. He's a poor man and always will be, for a diplomat can't be a money-maker. But he's a happier man than Harold Downes, though he doesn't look it.'

Mr Lethaby's rugged face happened at the moment to be twisted into an expression of pain out of sympathy with some tale of the woman to whom he was talking, while his *vis-à-vis*, Mr Downes, was laughing merrily at a remark of his neighbour.

'Harold has a hard life,' said Mrs Ravelston. 'He's head of the Fremont Banking Corporation and a St Sebastian for everyone to shoot arrows at. Any more to be catalogued? Why, yes, there are the two biggest exhibits of all.'

She directed Leithen's eyes to two men separated by a handsome old woman whose hair was dressed in the fashion of forty years ago.

'You see the man on the far side of Ella Purchass, the plump little man with the eagle beak who looks like he's enjoying his food. What would you set him down as?'

'Banker? Newspaper proprietor?'

'Wrong. That's Walter Derwent. You've heard of him? His father left him all kinds of wealth, but Walter wasted no time in getting out of oil into icebergs. He has flown and mushed and tramped over most of the Arctic, and there are heaps of mountains and wild beasts named after him. And you'd never think he'd moved further than Long Island. Now place the man on this side of Ella.'

Leithen saw a typical English hunting man – lean brown face with the skin stretched tight over the cheek bones, pale, deep-set eyes, a small clipped moustache, shoulders a little stooped from being much on horse-back.

'Virginian squire,' he hazarded. 'Warrenton at a guess.'

'Wrong,' she laughed. 'He wouldn't be happy at Warrenton, and I'm certain he wouldn't be happy on a horse. His line is deep learning. He's about our foremost pundit – professor at Yale – dug up cities in Asia Minor – edited Greek books. Writes very nice little stories, too. That's Clifford Savory.'

Leithen looked with interest at the pleasant vital face. He knew all about Clifford Savory. There were few men alive who were his equals in classical scholarship, and he had published one or two novels, delicate historical reconstructions, which were masterpieces in their way.

His gaze circled round the table again, noting the friendliness of the men's eyes, the atmosphere of breeding and simplicity and stability. He turned to his hostess—

'You've got together a wonderful party for me,' he said. 'I feel what I always feel when I come here – that you are the friendliest people on earth. But I believe, too, that you are harder to get to know than our awkward, difficult, tongue-tied folk at home. To get to know really well, I mean – inside your plate-armour of general benevolence.'

Mrs Ravelston laughed. 'There may be something in that. It's a new idea to me.'

'I think you are sure of yourselves, too. There is no one at this table who hasn't steady nerves and a vast deal of common sense. You call it poise, don't you?'

'Maybe, but this is a picked party, remember.'

'Because of its poise?'

'No. Because every man here is a friend of Francis Galliard.'

'Friend? Do you mean acquaintance or intimate?'

The lady pursed her lips.

'I'm not sure. I think you are right and that we are not an easy people to be intimate with unless we have been brought up with the same background. Francis, too, is scarcely cut out for intimacy. Did you ever meet him?'

'No. I heard his name for the first time a few weeks ago. Which of you knows him best? Mr Ravelston?'

'Certainly not Simon, though he's his business partner. Francis has a good many sides, and most people know only one of them. Bronson could tell you most about his work. He likes my Eric, but hasn't seen much of him in recent years. I know he used to go duck-shooting in Minnesota with George Lethaby, and he's a trustee of Walter Derwent's Polar Institute. I fancy Clifford Savory is nearer to him than most people. And yet . . . I don't know. Maybe nobody has got to know the real Francis. He has that frank, forthcoming manner which conceals a man, and he's mighty busy too, too busy for intimacies. I used to see him once or twice a week, but I couldn't tell you anything about him that everybody doesn't know. It won't be easy, Sir Edward, to get a proper notion of him from second-hand evidence. Felicity's your best chance. You haven't met Felicity yet?'

'I'm leaving her to the last. What's she like? I know her sister well.'

'She's a whole lot different from Babs. I can tell you she's quite a person.'

Leithen felt that if his hostess had belonged to a different social grade she would have called her a 'lovely woman.' Her meaning was clear. Mrs Galliard was someone who mattered.

He was beginning to feel very weary, and, knowing that he must ration his strength, he made his excuses and did not join the women after dinner. But he spent a few minutes in the library, to which the men retired for coffee and cigars. He had one word with Clifford Savory.

'I heard you five years ago at the Bar Association,' Savory said. 'You spoke on John Marshall. I hope you're going to give me an evening on this visit.'

Bronson Jane accompanied him to the door.

'You're taking it easy, I understand, Sir Edward, and going slow with dinners. What about the Florian tomorrow at half past five? In these hot days that's a good time for a talk.'

5

THE library of the Florian Club looked out on the East River, where the bustle of traffic was now dying down and the turbid waters catching the mellow light of the summer evening. It might have been a room in an old English country house with its Chippendale chairs and bookcases, and the eighteenth-century mezzo-tints on the walls. The two men sat by the open window, and the wafts of cool evening air gave Leithen for the first time that day a little physical comfort.

'You want me to tell you about Francis Galliard?'

Bronson Jane's wholesome face showed no signs of fatigue, though he had been having a gruelling day.

'I'll tell you all I can, but I warn you that it's not much. I suppose I'm as close to him as most people, but I can't say I knew him well. No one does – except perhaps his wife. But I can give you the general lay-out. First of all, he is a French-Canadian. Do you know anything about French Canada?'

'I once knew a little – a long time ago.'

'Well, they are a remarkable race there. They ought to have made a rather bigger show in the world than they have. Here's a fine European stock planted out in a new country and toughened by two centuries of hardship and war. They keep their close family life and their religion intact and don't give a cent for what we call progress. Yet all the time they have a pretty serious fight with nature, so there is nothing soft in them. You would say that boys would come out of those farms of theirs with a real kick in them, for they have always been a race of pioneers. But so far Laurier is their only great man. You'd have thought that now and then they would have produced somebody big in the business line, like the Scots. You have young Highlanders, haven't you, coming out of the same primitive world, who become business magnates? We have had some of them in this country.'

'Yes. That is not uncommon in Scotland.'

'Well, Francis is the only specimen I've struck from French Canada. He came out of a farm in the Laurentians, somewhere back of the Glaubsteins' new pulp town at Chateau-Gaillard. I believe the Gaillards go right back to the Crusades. They came to Canada with Champlain, and were the seigneurs of Chateau-Gaillard, a tract of country as big as Rhode Island. By and by they came down in the world until now they only possess a little bit of a farm at the end of nowhere.'

'What took him out of the farm? The French don't part easily from the land.'

'God knows. Ambition? Poverty? He never told me. I don't just know how he was raised, for he never speaks of his early days. The village school, I suppose, and then some kind of college, for his first notion was to be a priest. He had a pretty good education of an old-fashioned kind. Then something stirred in him and he set off south like the fairy-tale Younger Son, with his pack on his back and his lunch in his pocket. He must have been about nineteen then.'

Leithen's interest quickened. 'Go on,' he said, as Bronson paused. 'How did he make good?'

'I'm darned if I know. There's a fine story there, but I can't get it out of him. He joined a French paper in Boston, and went on to another in Louisiana, and finished up in Chicago on a financial journal. I fancy that several times he must have pretty nearly starved. Then somehow he got into the bond business and discovered that he had a genius for one kind of finance. He was with Connolly in Detroit for a time, and after that with the Pontiac Trust here, and then Ravelstons started out to discover new blood and got hold of him. At thirty-five he was a junior partner, and since then he has never looked back. Today he's forty-three, and there aren't five men in the United States whose repute stands higher. Not bad for a farm boy, I'll say.'

'Does he keep in touch with his people?'

'Not he. That door is closed and bolted. He has never been back to Canada. He's a naturalised American citizen. He won't speak French unless he's forced to, and then it's nothing to boast of. He writes his name "Galliard," not Gaillard. He has let himself become absorbed in our atmosphere.'

'Really absorbed?'

'Well – that's just the point. He has adopted the externals of our life, but I don't know how much he's changed inside. When he married Felicity Dasent five years ago I thought we had got him for keeps. You don't know Mrs Galliard?'

Leithen shook his head. He had been asked this question now a dozen times since he landed.

'No? Well, I won't waste time trying to describe her, for you'll soon be able to judge for yourself; but I should call her a possessive personality, and she certainly annexed Francis. Oh, yes, he was desperately in love and only too willing to do what she told him. He's a good-looking fellow, but he hadn't bothered much about his appearance, so she groomed him up and made him the best-dressed man in New York. They've got a fine apartment in Park Avenue and her dinners have become social events. The Dasents are a horsey family and I doubt if Francis had ever mounted a horse until his marriage, but presently she had him out regularly with the Westbrook. He bought a country place in New Jersey and is going to start in to breed 'chasers. Altogether she gives him a pretty full life.'

'Children?'

'No, not yet. A pity, for a child would have anchored Francis. I expect he has family in his blood like all his race.'

'He never appeared to be restless, did he?' Leithen asked.

'Not that I noticed. He seemed perfectly content. He used to work too hard and wear himself out, and every now and then have to go off for a rest. That's the tom-fool habit we all have here. You see, he hadn't any special tastes outside his business to make him keen about leisure. Felicity changed all that. She isn't anything of the social climber, or ambitious for herself, but she's mighty ambitious for her man. She brought him into all kinds of new circles, and he shines in them, too, for he has excellent brains – every kind of brains. All the gifts which made him a power in business she developed for other purposes. He was always a marvel in a business deal, for he could read other men's minds, and he would have made a swell diplomatist. Well, she turned that gift to social uses, with the result that every type mixes well at their parties. You'll hear as good talk at their table as you'll get anywhere on the civilised globe. He can do everything that a Frenchman can do, or an Englishman or an American. She has made him ten times more useful to Ravelstons than before, for she has made him a kind of national figure. The Administration has taken to consulting him, and he's one of the people that foreigners coming over here have got to see. I fancy she has politics at the back of her mind – last winter, I know, they were a good deal in Washington.'

Bronson lit a fresh cigar.

'All set fair, you'd say, for the big success of our day. And then suddenly one fine morning he slips out of the world like the man in Browning's poem, and God knows what's become of him.'

'You know him reasonably well? Is he happy?'

Bronson laughed. 'That's a question I couldn't answer about my own brother. I doubt if I could answer it about myself. He is gay – that is the French blood, maybe. I doubt if he has ever had time to consider whether he is happy or not, he lives such a bustling life. There can't be much of the introvert in Francis.'

A man had entered the room and was engaged in turning over the magazines on one of the tables.

'Here's Savory,' Bronson whispered. 'Let's have him join us. He's a rather particular friend of Francis.' He raised his voice, 'Hullo, Clifford! Come and have a drink. Sir Edward wants to see you.'

Clifford Savory, looking more like a country squire than ever in his well-cut grey flannels, deposited his long figure in an armchair and sipped the whisky-and-soda which the club servant brought him.

'We were talking about Galliard,' Bronson said. 'Sir Edward has heard a lot about him and is keen to meet him. It's just too bad that he should be out of town at present. It seems that Francis has got a reputation across the water. What was it you wanted to ask, Sir Edward? How much of his quality comes from his French blood?'

Savory joined his finger-tips and regarded them meditatively.

'That's hard to say. I don't know enough of the French in Canada, for they're different from the French in Europe. But I grant you that Galliard's power is exotic – not the ordinary gifts that God has given us Americans. He can argue a case brilliantly with the most close-textured reasoning; but there are others who can do that. His real strength lies in his *flair*, which can't be put down in black and white. He has an extra sense which makes him conscious of things which are still in the atmosphere – a sort of instinct of what people are going to think quite a bit ahead, not only in America, but in England and Europe. His mind is equipped with no end of sensitive antennae. When he trusts that instinct he is never wrong, but now and then, of course, he is over-ridden by prosaic folk. If people had listened to him in '29 we should be better off now.'

'That's probably due to his race,' said Leithen. 'Whenever you get a borderland where Latin and Northman meet, you get this uncanny sensitiveness.'

'Yes,' said Savory, 'and yet in other things his race doesn't show up at all. Attachment to family and birthplace, for instance. Francis has forgotten all about his antecedents. He cares as little about his origin as Melchizedek. He is as rootless as the last-arrived Polish immigrant. He has pulled up his roots in Canada, and I do not think he is getting them down here – too restless for that.'

'Restless?' Leithen queried.

'Well, I mean mobile – always on the move. He is restless in another way, too. I doubt if he is satisfied by what he does, or particularly happy. A man can scarcely be if he lives in a perpetual flux.'

6

A figure was taking shape at the back of Leithen's mind, a figure without material mould, but an outline of character. He was beginning to realise something of the man he had come to seek. The following afternoon, when he stood in the hall of the Galliards' apartment in Park Avenue, he had the chance of filling in the physical details, for he was looking at a portrait of the man.

It was one of the young Van Rouyn's most celebrated achievements, painted two years earlier. It showed a man in riding breeches and a buff leather coat sitting on a low wall above a flower garden. His hair was a little ruffled by the wind, and one hand was repelling the advances of a terrier. Altogether an attractive detail of what should have been a 'conversation piece.' Leithen looked at the picture with the liveliest interest. Galliard was very different from the conception he had formed of him. He had thought of him as a Latin type, slim and very dark, and it appeared that he was more of a Norman, with well-developed shoulders like a football player. It was a pleasant face, the brown eyes were alight with life, and the mouth was both sensitive and firm. Perhaps the jaw was a little too fine drawn, and the air of bonhomie too elaborate to be quite natural. Still, it was a face a man would instinctively trust, the face of a good comrade, and there could be no question about its supreme competence. In every line there was energy and quick decision.

Leithen gazed at it for some time, trying to find what he had expected.

'Do you think it a good likeness?' he asked the woman at his side.

'It's Francis at his best and happiest,' she answered.

Felicity Galliard was a fair edition of her sister Barbara. She was not quite so tall or quite so slim, and with all her grace she conveyed an impression, not only of physical health, but of physical power. There was a charming athleticism about her; she had none of Barbara's airy fragility. Her eyes were like her sister's, a cool grey with sudden lights in them which changed their colour. She was like a bird, always poised to fly, no easy swoop or flutter, but, if need be, a long stern flight against weather and wind.

She led Leithen into the drawing-room. Her house was very different from the Ravelstons', where a variety of oddments represented the tastes of many generations. It was a 'period' piece, the walls panelled in a light, almost colourless wood, the scanty furniture carefully chosen, an Aubusson carpet, and hangings and chintzes of grey and old rose and silver. A Nattier over the fireplace made a centre for the exquisite harmony. It was a room without tradition or even individuality, as if its possessors had deliberately sought out something which should be non-committal, an environment which should neither reflect nor influence them.

'You never met Francis?' she asked as she made tea. 'We have been twice to Europe since we married, but only once in England, and then only for a few days. They were business trips, and he didn't have a moment to himself.'

Her manner was beautifully composed, with no hint of tragedy, but in her eyes Leithen read an anxiety so profound that it was beyond outward manifestation. This woman was living day and night with fear. The sight of her, and of the picture in the hall, moved him strangely. He felt that between the Galliards and the friendly eupeptic people he had been meeting there was a difference, not of degree, but of kind. There was a quality here, undependable, uncertain, dangerous perhaps, but rare and unmistakable. There had been no domestic jar – of that he was convinced. But something had happened to one of them to shatter a happy partnership. If he could discover that something he would have a clue for his quest.

'I have never met your husband,' he said, 'but I've heard a great deal about him, and I think I'm beginning to understand him. That picture in the hall helps, and you help. I know your sister and your uncle, and now that I'm an idle man I've promised to do what I can. If I'm to be of any use, Mrs Galliard, I'm afraid I must ask you some questions. I know you'll answer them frankly. Tell me first what happened when he went away.'

'It was the fourth day of May, a perfect spring day. I went down to Westchester to see an old friend. I said good-bye to Francis after breakfast, and he went to the office. I came back about five o'clock and found a note from him on my writing-table. Here it is.'

She produced from an escritoire a half-sheet of paper. Leithen read –

'*Dearest, I am sick – very sick in mind. I am going away. When I am cured I will come back to you. All my love.*'

'He packed a bag himself – the butler knew nothing about it. He took money with him – at least there was a large sum drawn from his account. No, he didn't wind up things at the office. He left some big questions undecided, and his partners have had no end of trouble. He didn't say a word to any of them, or to anybody else that I know of. He left no clue as to where he was going. Oh, of course, we could have put on detectives and found out something, but we dare not do that. Every newspaper in the land would have started a hue and cry, and there would have been a storm of gossip. As it is, nobody knows about him except his partners, and one or two friends, and Uncle Blenkiron, and Babs and you. You see he may come back any day quite well again, and I would never forgive myself if I had been neurotic and let him down.'

Leithen thought that neurotic was the last word he would have chosen to describe this wise and resolute woman.

'What was he like just before he left? Was there any change in his manner? Had he anything to worry him?'

'Nothing to worry him in business. Things were going rather specially well. And, anyhow, Francis never let himself be worried by affairs. He prided himself on taking things lightly – he was always what the old folk used to call debonair. But – yes, there were little changes in him, I think. All winter he had been almost too good and gentle and yielding. He did everything I asked him without questioning, and that was not always his way . . . Oh! and he did one funny thing. We used to go down to Florida for a fortnight after Christmas – we had a regular foursome for golf, and he liked to bask in the sun. This year he didn't seem to care about it, and I didn't press him, for

I'm rather bored with golf, so we stayed at home. There was a good deal of snow at Combermere – that's our New Jersey home – and Francis got himself somewhere a pair of snow-shoes and used to go for long walks alone. When he came back he would sit by the hour in the library, not dozing, but thinking. I thought it was a good way of resting and never disturbed him.'

'You never asked what he was thinking about?'

'No. He thought a good deal, you see. He always made leisure to think. My only worry was about his absurd modesty. He was sure of himself, but not nearly so sure as I was, and recently when people praised him and I repeated the praise he used to be almost cross. He wrote a memorandum for the Treasury about some tax scheme, and Mr Beverley said that it was a work of genius. When I told him that, I remember he lay back in his chair and said quite bitterly, 'Quel chien de génie!' He never used a French phrase except when he was tired or upset. I remember the look on his face – it was as if I had really pained him. But I could find nothing to be seriously anxious about. He was perfectly fit and well.'

'Did he see much of anybody in particular in the last weeks?'

'I don't think so. We always went about together, you know. He liked to talk to Mr Jane and Mr Savory, and they often dined with us. I think young Eric Ravelston came once or twice to the house – Walter Derwent, too, I think. But he saw far more of me than of anybody else.'

Her face suddenly stiffened with pain.

'Oh, Sir Edward, you don't think that he's dead – that he went away to die?'

'I don't. I haven't any fear of that. Any conclusion of mine would be worthless at the present stage, but my impression is that Mr Galliard's trouble has nothing to do with his health. You and he have made a wonderful life together. Are you certain that he quite fitted into it?'

She opened her eyes.

'He was a huge success in it.'

'I know. But did the success give him pleasure?'

'I'm sure it did. At least for most of the time.'

'Yes, but remember that it was a strange world to him. He hadn't been brought up in it. He may have been homesick for something different.'

'But he loved me!' she cried.

'He loved you. And therefore he will come back to you. But it may be to a different world.'

7

NEW scenes, new faces, the interests of a new problem had given Leithen a few days of deceptive vitality. Then the reaction came, and for a long summer's day he sat on the veranda of his hotel bedroom in body a limp wreck, but with a very active mind. He tried to piece together what he had heard of Galliard, but could reach no conclusion. A highly strung, sensitive being, with Heaven knew what strains in his ancestry, had been absorbed into a new world in which he had been brilliantly successful. And then something had snapped, or some atavistic impulse had emerged from the deeps, something strong enough to break the tie of a happy marriage. The thing was sheer mystery. He had abandoned his old world and had never shown the slightest hankering after it. What had caused this sudden satiety with success?

Bronson Jane and Savory thought that the trouble was physical, a delicate machine over-wrought and over-loaded. The difficulty was that his health had always been perfect, and there was no medical adviser who could report on the condition of his nerves. His friends thought that he was probably lying hidden in some quiet sunny place, nursing himself back to vigour, with the secretiveness of a man to whom a physical breakdown was so unfamiliar that it seemed a portent, almost a crime.

But Savory had been enlightening. Scholarly, critical, fastidious, he had spoken of Galliard, the ordinary successful financier with no special cultural background, with an accent almost of worship.

'This country of ours,' he told Leithen, 'is up against the biggest problem in her history. It is not a single question like slavery or state rights, or the control of monopolies, or any of the straightforward things that have made a crisis before. It is a conglomeration of problems, most of which we cannot define. We have no geographical frontier left, but we've an eternal frontier in our minds. Our old American society is really in dissolution. All of us have got to find a new way of life. You're lucky in England, for you've been at the job for a long time and you make your revolutions so slowly and so quietly that you don't notice them – or anybody else. Here we have to make ours against time, while we keep shouting about them at the top of our voices. Everybody and everything here has to have a new deal, and the different deals have to be fitted together like a jig-saw puzzle, or there will be an infernal confusion. We're a great people, but we're only by fits and starts a nation. You're fortunate in your British Empire. You may have too few folk, and these few scattered over big spaces, but they're all organically connected, like the separate apples on a tree. Our huge population is more like a collection of pebbles in a box. It's only the containing walls of the box that keep them together.'

So much for Savory's diagnosis.

'Francis is just the kind of fellow we need,' he went on. 'He sees what's coming. He's the most intellectually honest creature God ever made. He has a mind which not only cuts like a scalpel, but is rich and resourceful – both critical and creative. He hasn't any prejudices to speak of. He's a fascinating human being and rouses no antagonisms. It looks like he has dragged his anchor at present. But if we could get him properly moored again he's going to be a power for good in this country. We've got to get him back, Sir Edward – the old Francis.'

The old Francis? Leithen had queried.

'Well, with the old genius. But with an extra anchor down. I've never been quite happy about the strength of his moorings.'

8

WALTER Derwent at first had nothing to tell him. Francis Galliard had not been interested in travel in far places. He was treasurer of his Polar Institute, but that was out of personal friendship. Francis had not much keenness in field sports either, though his wife had made him take up fox-hunting. He never went fishing, and in recent years he had not shot much, though he sometimes went after duck to Minnesota and the Virginia shore. He was not much of a bird-shot, but he was deadly with the rifle on the one occasion when Derwent had been with him after deer . . .

Derwent screwed up his pleasant rosy face till, with his eagle beak, he looked like a benevolent vulture. And then suddenly he let drop a piece of information which made Leithen sit up.

'But he did ask me – I remember – if I could recommend him a really first-class guide, a fellow that understood woodcraft and knew the Northern woods. Maybe he was asking on behalf of someone else, for he couldn't have much use himself for a guide.'

'When was that?' Leithen asked sharply.

'Some time after Christmas. Early February, I reckon. Yes, it was just after our Adventurers' Club dinner.'

'Did you recommend one?'

'Yes. A fellow called Lew Frizel, a 'breed, but of a very special kind. His mother was a Cree Indian and his father one of the old-time Hudson's Bay factors. I've had Lew with me on half a dozen trips. I discovered him on a trap-line in northern Manitoba.'

'Where is he now?'

'That's what I can't tell you. He seems to have gone over the horizon. I wanted him for a trip up the Liard this fall, but I can get no answer from any of his addresses. He has a brother Johnny who is about as good, but he's not available, for he has a job with the Canadian Government in one of its parks – Waskesieu, up Prince Albert way.'

Leithen paid a visit to the Canadian Consulate, and after a talk with the Consul, who was an old friend, the telegraph was set in motion. Johnny Frizel, sure enough, had a job as a game warden at Waskesieu.

Another inquiry produced a slender clue. Leithen spent a morning at the Ravelston office and had a long talk with Galliard's private secretary, an intelligent young Yale man. From the office diary he investigated the subjects which had engaged Galliard's attention during his last weeks in New York. They were mostly the routine things on which the firm was then engaged, varied by a few special matters on which he was doing Government work. But one point caught Leithen's eye. Galliard had called for the papers about the Glaubstein pulp mill at Chateau-Gaillard and had even taken them home with him.

'Was there anything urgent about them?' he asked.

The secretary said no. The matter was dead as far as Ravelstons were concerned. They had had a lot to do with financing the original proposition, but long ago they had had their profit and were quit of it.

9

LEITHEN'S last talk was with young Eric Ravelston. During the days in New York he had felt at times his weakness acutely, but he had not been conscious of any actual loss of strength. He wanted to be assured that he had still a modest reservoir to draw upon. The specialist examined him carefully and then looked at him with the same solemn eyes as Acton Croke.

'You know your condition, of course?' he asked.

'I do. A few weeks ago I was told that I had about a year to live. Do you agree?'

'It's not possible to fix a time schedule. You may have a year – or a little less – or a little more. If you went to a sanatorium and lived very carefully you might have longer.'

'I don't propose to lead a careful life. I've only a certain time and a certain amount of dwindling strength. I'm going to use them up on a hard job.'

'Well, in that case you may fluff out very soon, or you may go on for a year or more, for the mind has something to say in these questions.'

'There's no hope of recovery?'

'I'm afraid there's none – that is to say, in the light of our present knowledge. But, of course, we're not infallible.'

'Not even if I turn myself into a complete invalid?'

'Not even then.'

'Good. That's all I wanted to know. Now I've one other question. I'm going to look for Francis Galliard. You know him, but you never treated him, did you?'

Eric Ravelston shook his head.

'He didn't want any treatment. He was as healthy as a hound.'

Something in the young man's tone struck Leithen.

'You mean in body. Had you any doubt about other things – his mind, for instance?'

The other did not at first reply.

'I have no right to say this,' he spoke at last. 'And, anyhow, it isn't my proper subject. But for some time I have been anxious about Francis. Little things, you know. Only a doctor would notice them. I thought that there was something pathological about his marvellous vitality. Once I had Garford, the neurologist, staying with me and the Galliards came to dinner. Garford could not keep his eyes off Francis. After they had gone he told me that he would bet a thousand dollars that he crumpled up within a year . . . So if there's a time limit for you, Sir Edward, there's maybe a time limit also for Francis.'

10

LEITHEN disembarked on a hot morning from the Quebec steamer which served the north shore of the St Lawrence. Chateau-Gaillard was like any other pulp-town – a new pier with mighty derricks, the tall white cylinders of the pulp mill, a big brick office, and a cluster of clapboard shacks which badly needed painting. The place at the moment had a stagnant air, for the old cutting limits had been exhausted and the supply of pulp-wood from the new area was still being organised. A stream came in beyond the pier, and the background was steep scrub-clad hills cleft by a wedge-like valley beyond which there rose distant blue lines of mountain.

For the first mile or two the road up the valley was a hard, metalled highway. Leithen had not often felt feebler in body or more active in mind. Thoreau had been a favourite author of his youth, and he had picked up a copy in New York and had read it on the boat. Two passages stuck in his memory. One was from *Walden* –

'If you stand right fronting and face to face to a fact, you will see the sun glimmer on both its surfaces, as if it were a cimiter, and feel its sweet edge dividing you through the heart and marrow, and so you will happily conclude your mortal career. Be it life or death we crave only reality. If we are really dying, let us hear the rattle in our throat and feel the cold in the extremities; if we are alive, let us go about our business.'

The other was only a sentence –

'The cost of a thing is the amount of what I will call life which is required to be exchanged for it.'

How valuable was that thing for which he was bartering all that remained to him of life? At first Blenkiron's story had been no more than a peg on which to hang a private determination, an excuse, partly to himself and partly to the world, for a defiant finish to his career. The task fulfilled the conditions he wanted – activity for the mind and a final activity for the body. Francis Galliard was a disembodied ghost, a mere premise in an argument.

But now – Felicity had taken shape as a human being. There was an extraordinary appeal in her mute gallantry, her silent, self-contained fortitude. Barbara Clanroyden could not under any circumstances be pathetic; her airy grace was immune from the attacks of fate; she might bend, but she would never break. But her sister offered an exposed front to fortune. She was too hungry for life, too avid of experience, too venturesome, and more, she had set herself the task of moulding her husband to her ambitions. No woman, least of all his wife, would attempt to mould Sandy Clanroyden . . . And the gods had given her tough material – not a docile piece of American manhood, but something exotic and unpredictable, something for which she had acquired a desperate affection, but of which she had only a dim understanding.

As for Francis, that shadow too was taking form. Leithen now had a picture of him in his mind, but it was not that of the portrait in the hall of the Park Avenue apartment. Oddly enough, it was of an older man, with a rough yellow beard. His eyes were different too, wilder, less assured, less benevolent. He told himself that he had reconstructed the physical appearance to match his conception of the character. For he had arrived at a provisional assessment of the man . . . The chains of race and tradition are ill to undo, and Galliard, in his brilliant advance to success, had loosened, not broken them. Something had happened to tighten them again. The pull of an older world had jerked him out of his niche. But how? And whither?

II

THE valley above the township was an ugly sight. The hillsides had been lumbered out and only scrub was left, and the shutes where the logs had been brought down were already tawny with young brushwood. In the bottom was a dam, which had stretched well up the slopes, for the lower scrub was bleached and muddied with water. But the sluices had been opened and the dam had shrunk to a few hundred yards in width, leaving the near hillsides a hideous waste of slime, the colour of a slag-heap. The place was like the environs of a town in the English Black Country.

Suddenly he was haunted by a recollection, a shadow at the back of his mind. The outline of the hills was familiar. Looking back, he realised that he had seen before the bluff which cut the view of the St Lawrence into a wedge of blue water. He had forgotten the details of that journey thirty years ago when he had tramped down from the mountains; but it must have been in this neighbourhood. There was a navvy on some job by the roadside, and he stopped the car and spoke to him.

The man shook his head. 'I'm a newcomer here. There's a guy up there – a Frenchie – maybe he'd tell you.'

Johnny Frizel went up the track in the bush to where a countryman was cutting stakes. He came back and reported.

'He says that before the dam was made there was a fine little river down there. The Clairefontaine was the name of it.'

Leithen's memory woke into vivid life. This valley had been his road down country long ago. He remembered its loveliness when Chateau-Gaillard had been innocent of pulp mills and no more than a hamlet of painted houses and a white church. There had been a strip of green meadow-land by the waterside grazed by old-fashioned French cattle, and the stream had swept through it in deep pools and glittering shallows, while above it pine and birch had climbed in virgin magnificence to the crests. Now all the loveliness had been butchered to enable some shoddy newspaper to debauch the public soul. He had only seen the place once long ago at the close of a blue autumn day, but the desecration beat on his mind like a blow. What had become of the little Clairefontaine farm at the river head, and that delicate place on the height of land which had of late been haunting him? . . . He felt a curious nervousness and it brought on a fit of coughing.

At the end of the dam the road climbed the left side of the valley through patches of spruce and a burnt-out area of blackened stumps. A ridge separated it from the stream, and when it turned again to the water's edge the character of the valley had changed. The Clairefontaine rumbled in a deep gorge, and as the aged Ford wheezed its way up the dusty roads Chateau-Gaillard and its ugliness were shut off and Leithen found himself in a sanctuary of the hills. He could not link up the place with his memory of thirty years ago when he had descended it on foot in the gold and scarlet of autumn. Then it had been a pathway to the outer world; now it was the entry into a secret and strange land. There was no colour in the scene, except the hard blue of the sky. The hot noon had closed down like a lid on an oppressive dull green waste which offered no welcome.

His mind was full of Francis Galliard. Once this had been the seigneur of his family, running back from the tide-water some scores of miles into the wilderness. He felt the man here more vividly than ever before, but he could not affiliate him with the landscape, except that he also was a mystery . . .

Why had his wife and his friends in New York been so oddly supine in looking for him? They had waited and left it for a stranger to take on the job. Fear of publicity, of course, in that over-public world. But was that the only reason? Was there not also fear of Galliard? He was not of their world, and they admired and loved him, but uncomprehendingly. Even Felicity. What did they fear? That they might wreck a subtle mechanism by a too heavy hand? They were all sensitive people and highly intelligent, and they would have not walked so delicately without a cause. Only now, when he was entering the cradle of Galliard's race, did he realise how intricate was the task to which he had set himself. And one to be performed against time. He remembered the young Ravelston's words. There was a time limit for Francis Galliard, as there was one for Edward Leithen.

The valley mounted by steps, each one marked by the thunder of a cataract in the gorge. Presently they rose above the woods, and came out on a stretch of open upland where the stream flowed among patches of crops and meadows of hay. Now his memory was clearer, for he remembered this place in exact detail. There was the farm of Clairefontaine, with its shingled, penthouse roof, its white-painted front, its tall weather-beaten barn, its jumble of decrepit outhouses. There was the little church of the parish, the usual white box, with a tin-coated spire now shining like silver in the sun, and beside it a hump-backed presbytery. And there was something beyond of which the memory was even sharper. For the valley seemed to come to an end, the wooded ranges closed in on it, but there was a crack through which the stream must flow from some distant upland. He knew what lay beyond that nick which was like the back-sight of a rifle.

'We won't stop here,' he told Johnny, who handled the Ford like an artist. 'Go on as far as the road will take us.'

It did not take them far. They bumped among stumps and roots over what was now a mere cart track, but at the beginning of the cleft the track died away into a woodland trail. They got out, and Leithen led the way up the Clairefontaine. There was something tonic in the air which gave him a temporary vigour, and he was surprised that he could climb the steep path without too great discomfort. When they rested on a mossy rock by the stream he found that he ate his sandwiches with some appetite. But after that it was heavy going, for there was the inevitable waterfall to surmount, and, weary and panting, he came out into the ultimate meadow of the Clairefontaine, which was fixed so clearly in his recollection.

It was a cup in the hills, floored not with wild hay, but with short, crisp pasture like an English down. From its sides descended the rivulets which made the Clairefontaine, and in the heart of it was a pool fringed with flags, so clear that through its six-foot depth the little stir in the sand could be seen where the water bubbled up from below. The place was so green and gracious that all sense of the wilds was lost, and it seemed like a garden in a long-settled land, a garden made centuries ago by the very good and the very wise.

But it was a watch-tower as well as a sanctuary. Looking south, the hills opened to show *Le Fleuve*, the great river of Canada, like a pool of colourless light. North were higher mountains, which seemed to draw together with a purpose, huddling to shepherd the streams towards a new goal. They were sending the waters, not to the familiar St Lawrence, but to untrodden Arctic wastes. That was the magic of the place. It was a frontier between the desert and the sown. To Leithen it was something more. He felt again the spell which had captured him here in his distant youth. It was the borderline between the prosaic world, where things went by rule and rote and were all fitted to the human scale, and the world as God first made it out of chaos, which had no care for humanity.

He stretched himself full length on the turf, his eyes feasting on the mystery of the northern hills. Almost he had a sense of physical well-being, for his breath was less troublesome. Then Johnny Frizel came into the picture, placidly smoking an old black pipe. He fitted in well, and Leithen began to reflect on his companion, who had docilely, at the order of his superiors, flown over half Canada to join him.

Johnny was a small man, about five feet six, with broad shoulders and sturdy, bandy legs. He wore an old pair of khaki breeches and a lumberman's laced boots, but the rest of his garb was conventional, for he had put on his best clothes, not knowing what his duties might be. He had a round bullet head covered with black hair cut very short, and his ears stuck out like the handles of a pitcher. His Indian mother showed in his even brown colouring, and his father in his mild, meditative blue eyes. So far Leithen had scarcely realised him, except to admire his speech, which was a wonderful blend of the dialect of the outlands, the slang of America, and literary idioms, for Johnny was a great reader – all spoken in the voice of a Scots shepherd, and with a broad Scots accent. When the War broke out Johnny had been in the Labrador and his brother Lew on the lower Mackenzie, and both, as soon as they got the news, had made a bee-line for France and the front. They had been notable snipers in the Canadian Corps, as the notches on the butts of their service rifles witnessed.

'You have been lent to me, Johnny,' Leithen said. 'Seconded for special service, as we used to say in the army. I had better tell you our job.' Briefly he sketched the story of Francis Galliard.

'This is the place where he was brought up,' he said. 'My notion is that he's in Canada now. I think he is with your brother – at any rate, I know that he was making inquiries about him in the early spring. You haven't heard from your brother lately?'

'Not since Christmas. Lew never troubles to put me wise about his doings. He may be anywhere on God's earth.'

'We want to find out if we can, from old Gaillard at the farm and the priest, if the young Galliard has been here. Or your brother. If my guess is right they won't be very willing to speak, but with luck they may give themselves away. If the young Galliard has been here it gives us a bit of a clue. They are a hospitable lot, so I propose that we quarter ourselves on them for the night to have the chance of a talk. You can put up at the farm, and I dare say I can get a shake-down at the presbytery.'

Johnny nodded approval. His blue eyes dwelt searchingly on Leithen's thin face, from which the flush of bodily exercise had gone, leaving a grey pallor.

They retraced their steps when the sun had sunk behind the hills and the evening glow was beginning, soft as the bloom on a peach. The Ford was turned, and rumbled down the valley until it was parked in the presbytery yard. The priest, Father Paradis, came out to greet them, a tall, lean old man much bent in the shoulders, who, like all Quebec clergy, wore the cassock. He had been gardening, and his lumberjack's boots were coated with soil.

To Leithen's relief Father Paradis spoke the French of France, for, though Canadian born, he had been trained in a seminary at Beauvais.

'But of a surety,' he cried. 'You shall sleep here, monsieur, and share my supper. I have a guest room, though it is as small as the Prophet's Chamber of the Scriptures.'

He would have Johnny stay also.

'No doubt Augustin can lodge Monsieur Frizel, but I fear he will have rough quarters.'

Leithen's kit was left at the presbytery and he and Johnny walked to the farm to pay their respects to the squire of Clairefontaine. He had ascertained that this Augustin Gaillard, to whom the farm had descended, was an uncle of Francis. The priest had given him a rapid sketch of the family history. The mother had died in bearing Francis; the father a year after Francis had left for the States. There had been an elder brother, Paul, who two years ago had disappeared into the north, leaving his uncle from Chateau-Gaillard in his place. There were also two sisters who were Grey Nuns serving somewhere in the west – the priest did not know where.

Augustin Gaillard was a man of perhaps sixty years, with a wisp of grey beard and a moist, wandering eye. Everything about him bespoke the drunkard. His loud-patterned shirt had a ragged collar and sleeves, his waistcoat was discoloured with the dribbling of food, his trousers had holes at the knees, and his bare feet were shod with *bottes-sauvages*. There was nothing in his features to suggest the good breeding which Leithen had noted in the picture of Francis. The house, which was more spacious than the ordinary farm, was in a condition of extreme dirt and disorder. Somewhere in the background Leithen had a glimpse of an ancient crone, who was doubtless the housekeeper.

But Augustin had the fine manners of his race. He placed his dwelling and all that was in it at their disposal. He pressed Leithen to remove himself from the presbytery.

'The good father,' he said, 'has but a poor table. He will give you nothing to drink but cold water.'

Leaving Johnny deep in converse in the *habitant* patois, Leithen went back in the dusk to the presbytery. He was feeling acutely the frailty of his body, as he was apt to do at nightfall. Had he chosen a different course he would be going back to delicate invalid food, to a soft chair and a cool bed; now he must make shift with coarse fare and the hard pallet of the guest room. He wondered for a moment if he had not been every kind of fool.

But no sick-nurse could have been more attentive than Father Paradis. He had killed and cooked a chicken with his own hands. For supper there was soup and the fowl, and coffee made by one who had learned the art in France.

The little room was lit by a paraffin lamp, the smell of which brought back to Leithen faraway days in a Scots shooting box. The old man saw his guest's weakness, and after the meal he put a pillow in his chair and made him rest his legs on a stool.

'I see you are not in good health, monsieur.' he said. 'Do you travel to restore yourself? The air of these hills is well reputed.'

'Partly. And partly in hope of finding a friend. I am an Englishman, as you see, and am a stranger in Canada, though I have visited it once before. On that occasion I came to hunt, but my hunting days are over.'

Father Paradis screwed up his old eyes.

'At home you were perhaps a professor?'

'I have been a lawyer – and also a Member of our Parliament. But my working days are past, and I would make my soul.'

'You are wise. You are then in retreat? You are not, I think, of the Faith?'

Leithen smiled. 'I have my faith to find, and perhaps I have little time in which to find it.'

'There is little time for any of us,' said the old man. He looked at Leithen with eyes long experienced in life, and shook his head sadly.

'I spoke of a friend,' said Leithen. 'Have you had many visitors this summer?'

'Few come here nowadays. A pedlar or two, and a drover in the fall for the farm cattle. There is no logging, for our woods are bare. People used to come up from Chateau-Gaillard on holiday, but Chateau-Gaillard is for the moment stagnant. Except for you and Monsieur Frizel it is weeks since I have seen a stranger.'

'Had you no visitor from New York – perhaps in May? A man of the name of Francis Galliard?'

Leithen, from long practice in cross-examination, was accustomed to read faces. He saw the priest's eyes suddenly go blank, as if a shutter had been drawn over them, and his mouth tighten.

'No man of that name has visited us,' he said.

'Perhaps he did not give that name. The man I mean is still young,' and he described the figure as he had seen it in the New York portrait. 'He is a kinsman, I think, of the folk at the farm.'

Father Paradis shook his head.

'No, there has been no Francis Galliard here.'

But there was that in the old man's eyes which informed Leithen that he was not telling all he knew, and also that no cross-examination would elicit more. His face had the stony secrecy of the confessional.

'Well, I must look elsewhere,' Leithen said cheerfully. 'Tell me of the people at the farm. I understand they are one of the oldest families in Canada.'

Father Paradis's face lightened.

'Most ancient, but now, alas! pitifully decayed. The father was a good man, and a true son of the Church, but his farm failed, for he had little worldly wisdom. As for Augustin, he is, as you see, a drunkard. The son Paul was a gallant young man, but he was not happy on this soil. He was a wanderer, as his race was in the old days.'

'Wasn't there a second son?'

'Yes, but he left us long ago. He forsook his home and his faith. Let us not speak of him, for he is forgotten.'

'Tell me about Paul.'

'You must know, monsieur, that once the Gaillards were a stirring race. They fought with Frontenac against the Iroquois, and very fiercely against the English. Then, when peace came, they exercised their hardihood in distant ventures. Many of the house travelled far into the west and the north, and few of them returned. There was one, Aristide, who searched for the lost British sailor Frankolin – how do you call him? – and won fame. And only the other day there was Paul's uncle – also an Aristide – who found a new road to the Arctic shores and discovered a great river. Its name should be the Gaillard, but they tell me that the maps have the Indian word, the Ghost.'

Leithen, who had a passion for studying maps, remembered the river which flowed from north of the Thelon in the least-known corner of Canada.

'Is that where Paul went?' he asked.

'That is what we think. He was restless ever after his father died. He would go off for months to guide parties of hunters – even down to the Labrador, and in his dreams he had always his uncle Aristide; he was assured he was still alive and that if he went to the Ghost River he would find him. So one day he summons the other uncle, the worthless one, and bids him take over the farm of Clairefontaine.'

'You have heard nothing of him since?'

'Not a word has come. Why should it? He has no care for Clairefontaine . . . Now, monsieur, it is imperative that you go to bed, for you are very weary. I will conduct you to the Prophet's Chamber.'

Leithen was in the habit of falling asleep at once – it was now his one bodily comfort – but this night he lay long awake. He thought that he had read himself into the soul of Francis Galliard, a summary and provisional reading, but enough to give him a starting point. He was convinced beyond doubt that he had come to Clairefontaine in the spring. He could not mistake the slight hesitation in the speech of Father Paradis, the tremor of the eyelids, the twitch of the mouth before it set – he had seen these things too often in the courts to be wrong. The priest had not lied, but he had equivocated, and had he been pressed would have taken refuge in obstinate silence. Francis had been here and had enjoined secrecy on the priest and no doubt on old Augustin. He was on a private errand and wanted to shut out the world.

He could picture the sequence of events. The man, out of tune with his environment, had fallen into the clutches of the past. He had come to Chateau-Gaillard and seen the ravaged valley – ravaged by himself and his associates – and thereby a bitter penitence had been awakened. His purpose now was to make his peace with the past – with his family, his birthplace, and his religion. No doubt he had confessed himself to the priest. Perhaps he had gone, as Leithen had gone, to the secret meadow at the river head, and, looking to the north, had had boyish memories and ambitions awakened. It was his business – so Leithen read his thoughts – to make restitution, to appease his offended household gods. He must shake off the bonds of an alien civilisation, and, like his uncle and his brother and a hundred Gaillards of old, worship at the altars of the northern wilds.

Leithen fell asleep with so clear a picture in his mind that he might have been reading in black and white Francis's confession.

12

'WE go back to Quebec,' he told Johnny next morning. 'But first I want to go up the stream again.'

The mountain meadow haunted his imagination. There, the

afternoon before, he had had the first hour of bodily comfort he had known for months. The place, too, inspired him. It seemed to stiffen his purpose and to quicken his fancy.

Once again he lay on the warm turf beside the spring looking beyond the near forested hills to the blue dimness of the far mountains. It was that halcyon moment of the late Canadian summer when there are no flies, and even the midday is cool and scented, and the first hints of bright colour are stealing into the woods.

'I didn't get a great deal out of the old man,' said Johnny. 'He kept me up till three in the morning listenin' to his stuff. He was soused when he began, and well pickled before he left off, but he was never lit up – the liquor isn't brewed that could light up that old carcase. I guess he's got a grouse against the whole world. But I found out one thing. Brother Lew has been here this year.'

Leithen sat up. 'How do you know?'

'Why, he asked me if I was any relation to another man of my name – a fellow with half a thumb on his left hand and a scar above his right eyebrow. That's Lew to the life, for he got a bit chawed up at Vimy. When I asked more about the chap he felt he had said too much and shut up like a clam. But that means that Lew has been here all right, and that Augustin saw him, for to my certain knowledge Lew was never before east of Quebec, and yon old perisher has never stirred out of this valley. So I guess that Lew and your pal were here, for Lew wouldn't have come on his own.'

Leithen reflected for a moment.

'Was Lew ever at the Ghost River?' he asked. 'I mean the river half-way between Coronation Gulf and the top of Hudson's Bay.'

'Never heard of it. Nope. I'm pretty sure brother Lew was never within a thousand miles of it. It ain't his bailiewick.'

'Well, I fancy he's there now . . . You and I are setting out for the Ghost River.'

13

LEITHEN spent two weary days in Montreal, mostly at the telephone, a business which in London he had always left to Cruddock or his clerk. He knew that the Northland was one vast whispering gallery, and that it was easier to track a man there than in the settled countries, so he hoped to get news by setting the machine of the R.C.M.P. to work. There was telephoning and telegraphing far and wide, but no result. No such travellers as Galliard and Lew Frizel had as yet been reported north of the railways. One thing he did ascertain. The two men had not flown to the Ghost River. That was the evidence of the Air Force and the private aeroplane companies. Leithen decided that this was what he had expected. If Galliard was on a mission of penitence he would travel as his uncle Aristide and his brother Paul had travelled – by canoe and trail. If he had started early in May he should just about have reached the Arctic shores.

The next task was to get a machine for himself. He hired an aeroplane from Air-Canada, a Baird-Sverisk of a recent pattern, and was lucky enough to get one of the best of the northern flyers, Job Teviot, for his pilot, and one Murchison as his mechanic. The contract was for a month, but with provision for an indefinite extension. All this meant bringing in his bankers, and cabling home, and the influence of Ravelstons had to be sought to complete the business. The barometer at Montreal stood above 100°, and there were times before he and Johnny took off when he thought that his next move would be to a hospital.

He felt stronger when they reached Winnipeg, and next day, flying over the network of the Manitoba lakes, he found that he drew breath more easily. He had flown little before, and the air at first made him feel very sleepy. This passed, and, since there was no demand for activity, his mind turned in on itself. He felt like some disembodied creature, for already he seemed to have shed all ordinary interests. Aforetime on his travels and his holidays he had been acutely interested in what he saw and heard, and part of his success at the Bar had been due to the wide range of knowledge thus acquired. But now he had no thoughts except for the job on hand. He had meant deliberately to concentrate on it, in order to shut out fruitless meditations on his own case; but he found that this concentration had come about automatically. He simply was not concerned about other things. In New York he had listened to well-informed talk about politics and business and books, and it had woke no response in his mind. Here in Canada he did not care a jot about the present or future of a great British Dominion. The Canadian papers he glanced at were full of the perilous situation in Europe – any week there might be war.

The news meant nothing to him, though a little while ago it would have sent him home by the next boat. The world had narrowed itself to Francis Galliard and the frail human creature that was following him.

By and by it was the latter that crowded in on his thoughts. Since he had nothing to do except watch a slowly moving landscape and the cloud shadows on lake and forest, he began to reflect on the atom, Edward Leithen, now hurrying above the world. The memory of Felicity kept returning – the sudden anguish in her eyes, her cry 'I love him! I love him!' and he realised how lonely his life had been. No woman had ever felt like that about him; he had never felt like that about any woman. Was it loss or gain? Gain, he told himself, for he implicated no one in his calamity. But had he not led a starved life? A misfit like Galliard had succeeded in gaining something which he, with all his social adaptability, had missed. He found himself in a mood almost of regret. He had made a niche for himself in the world, but it had been a chilly niche. With a start he awoke to the fact that he was very near the edge of self-pity, a thing forbidden.

In a blue windless twilight they descended for the night at a new mining centre on the Dog-Rib River. Johnny pitched a tent and cooked supper, while the pilot and the mechanic found quarters with other pilots who ran the daily air service to the south. There was a plague of black flies and mosquitoes, but Leithen was too tired to be troubled by them, and he had eight hours of heavy, unrefreshing sleep.

When he stood outside the tent next morning, looking over a shining lake and a turbulent river, he had a moment of sharp regret. How often he had stood like this on a lake shore – in Scotland, in Norway, in Canada long ago – and watched the world heave itself out of night into dawn! Like this – but how unlike! Then he had been exhilarated with the prospect of a day's sport, tingling from his cold plunge, ravenous as a hawk for breakfast, the blood brisk in his veins and every muscle in trim. Now he could face only a finger of bacon and a half-cup of tea, and he was weary before the day had begun.

'There's plenty here knows Lew,' Johnny reported. 'They haven't come this way. If they're at the Ghost River, my guess is that they've gone by the Planchette and The Old Man Falls.'

They crossed Great Slave Lake and all morning flew over those plains miscalled the Barrens, which, seen from above, are a delicate lace-work of lakes and streams criss-crossed by ridges of bald rock and banks of gravel, and with now and then in a hollow a patch of forest. They made camp early at the bend of a river, which Johnny called the Little Fish, for Murchison had some work to do on the engine. While Leithen rested by the fire Job went fishing and brought back three brace of Arctic char. He announced that there was another camp round the next bend – a white man in a canoe with two Crees – a sight in that lonely place as unexpected as the great auk. Somewhat refreshed by his supper, Leithen in the long-lighted evening walked upstream to see his neighbour.

He found a middle-aged American cleaning a brace of ptarmigan which he had shot, and doing it most expertly. He was a tall man, in breeches, puttees, and a faded yellow shirt, and Leithen took him for an ordinary trapper or prospector until he heard him speak.

'I saw you land,' the stranger said. 'I was coming round presently to pass the time of day. Apart from my own outfit you are the first man I've seen for a month.'

He prepared a bed of hot ashes, and with the help of rifle rods set the birds to roast. Then he straightened himself, filled a pipe, and had a look at Leithen.

'I'm an American,' he said. 'New York.'

Leithen nodded. He had already detected the unmistakable metropolitan pitch of the voice.

'You're English? Haven't I seen you before? I used to be a good deal in London . . . Hold on a minute. I've got it. I've heard you speak in the British Parliament. That would be in—' And he mentioned a year.

'Very likely,' said Leithen. 'I was in Parliament then. I was Attorney-General.'

'You don't say. Well, we're birds of the same flock. I'm a corporation lawyer. My name's Taverner. Yours – wait a minute – is Leven.'

'Leithen,' the other corrected.

'Odd we should meet here in about the wildest spot in North America. It's easy enough to come by air, like you, but Matthew and Mark and I have taken two blessed months canoeing and portaging from railhead, and it will take us about the same time to get back.'

'Can corporation lawyers with you take four months' holiday?'

Mr Taverner's serious face relaxed in a smile.

'Not usually. But I had to quit or smash. No, I wasn't sick. I was just tired of the dam' racket. I had to get away from the noise. The United States is getting to be a mighty noisy country.'

The cry of a loon broke the stillness, otherwise there was no sound but the gurgle of the river and the grunting of one of the Indians as he cleaned a gun.

'You get silence here,' said Leithen.

'I don't mean physical noise so much. The bustle in New York doesn't worry me more than a little. I mean noise in our minds. You can't get peace to think nowadays.' He broke off. 'You here for the same cause?'

'Partly,' said Leithen. 'But principally to meet a friend.'

'I hope you'll hit him off. It's a biggish country for an assignation. But you don't need an excuse for cutting loose and coming here. I pretend I come to fish and hunt, but I only fish and shoot for the pot. I'm no sort of sportsman. I'm just a poor devil that's been born in the wrong century. There's quite a lot of folk like me. You'd be surprised how many of us slip off here now and then to get a little quiet. I don't mean the hearty, husky sort of fellow who goes into the woods in a fancy mackinaw and spends his time there drinking whisky and playing poker. I mean quiet citizens like myself, who've simply got to breathe fresh air and get the din out of their ears. Canada is becoming to some of us like a medieval monastery to which we can retreat when things get past bearing.'

Taverner, having been without white society for so long, seemed to enjoy unburdening himself.

'I'm saying nothing against my country. I know it's the greatest on earth. But my God! I hate the mood it has fallen into. It seems to me there isn't one section of society that hasn't got some kind of jitters – big business, little business, politicians, the newspaper men, even the college professors. We can't talk except too loud. We're bitten by the exhibitionist bug. We're all boosters and high-powered salesmen and propagandists, and yet we don't know what we want to propagand, for we haven't got any kind of common creed. All we ask is that a thing should be colourful and confident and noisy. Our national industry is really the movies. We're one big movie show. And just as in the movies we worship languishing Wops and little blonde girls out of the gutter, so we pick the same bogus deities in other walks of life. You remember Emerson speaks about some nations as having guano in their destiny. Well, I sometimes think that we have got celluloid in ours.'

There was that in Leithen's face which made Taverner pause and laugh.

'Forgive my rigmarole,' he said. 'It's a relief to get one's peeves off the chest, and I reckon I'm safe with you. You see, I come of New England stock, and I don't fit in too well with these times.'

'Do you know a man called Galliard?' Leithen asked. 'Francis Galliard – a partner in Ravelstons?'

'A little. He's a friend of Bronson Jane, and Bronson's my cousin. Funny you should mention him, for if I had to choose a fellow that fitted in perfectly to the modern machine, I should pick Galliard. He enjoys all that riles me. He's French, and that maybe explains it. I've too much of the Puritan in my blood. You came through New York, I suppose. Did you see Galliard? How is he? I've always had a liking for him.'

'No. He was out of town.'

Leithen got up to go. The long after-glow in the west was fading, and the heavens were taking on the shadowy violet which is all the northern summer darkness.

'When do you plan to end your trip?' Taverner asked as he shook hands.

'I don't know. I've no plans. I've been ill, as you see, and it will depend on my health.'

'This will set you up, never fear. I was a sick man three years ago and I came back from Great Bear Lake champing like a prize-fighter. But take my advice and don't put off your return too late. It don't do to be trapped up here in winter. The North can be a darn cruel place.'

14

LATE next afternoon they reached the Ghost River delta, striking in upon it at an angle from the south-west. The clear skies had gone, and the 'ceiling' was not more than a thousand feet. Low hills rimmed the eastern side, but they were cloaked in a light fog, and the delta seemed to have no limits, but to be an immeasurable abscess of decay. Leithen had never imagined such an abomination of desolation. It was utterly silent, and the only colours were sickly greens and drabs. At first sight he thought he was looking down on a bit of provincial Surrey, broad tarmac roads lined with asphalt footpaths, and behind the trim hedges smooth suburban lawns. It took a little time to realise that the highways were channels of thick mud, and the lawns bottomless quagmires. He was now well inside the Circle, and had expected from the Arctic something cold, hard, and bleak, but also clean and tonic. Instead he found a horrid lushness – an infinity of mire and coarse vegetation, and a superfluity of obscene insect life. The place was one huge muskeg. It was like the no-man's-land between the trenches in the War – a colossal no-man's-land created in some campaign of demons, pitted and pocked with shell-holes from some infernal artillery.

They skirted the delta and came down at its western horn on the edge of the sea. Here there was no mist, and he could look far into the North over still waters eerily lit by the thin evening sunlight. It was like no ocean he had ever seen, for it seemed to be without form or reason. The tide licked the shore without purpose. It was simply water filling a void, a treacherous, deathly waste, pale like a snake's belly, a thing beyond humanity and beyond time. Delta and sea looked as if here the Demiurge had let His creative vigour slacken and ebb into nothingness. He had wearied of the world which He had made and left this end of it to ancient Chaos.

Next morning the scene had changed, and to his surprise he felt a lightening of both mind and body. Sky and sea were colourless, mere bowls of light. There seemed to be no tides, only a gentle ripple on the grey sand. Very far out there were blue gleams which he took to be ice. The sun was warm, but the body of the air was cold, and it had in it a tonic quality which seemed to make his breathing easier. He remembered hearing that there were no germs in the Arctic, that the place was one great sanatorium, but that did not concern one whose trouble was organic decay. Still, he was grateful for a momentary comfort, and he found that he wanted to stretch his legs. He walked to the highest point of land at the end of a little promontory.

It was a place like a Hebridean cape. The peaty soil was matted with berries, though a foot or two beneath was eternal ice. The breeding season was over and the migration not begun, so there was no bird life on the shore; the wild fowl were all in the swamps of the delta. The dead-level of land and sea made the arc of sky seem immense, the 'intense inane' of Shelley's poem. The slight recovery of bodily vigour quickened his imagination. This was a world not built on the human scale, a world made without thought of mankind, a world colourless and formless, but also timeless; a kind of eternity. It would be a good place to die in, he thought, for already the clinging ties of life were loosened and death would mean little since life had ceased.

To his surprise he saw a small schooner anchored at the edge of a sandbank, a startling thing in that empty place. Johnny had joined him, and they went down to inspect it. An Eskimo family was on board, merry, upstanding people from far-distant Gordans Land. The skipper was one Andersen, the son of a Danish whaling captain and an Eskimo mother, and he spoke good English. He had been to Herschell Island to lay in stores, and was now on his way home after a difficult passage through the ice of the Western Arctic. The schooner was as clean as a new pin, and the instruments as well kept as on a man-o'-war. It had come in for fresh water, and Job was able to get from it a few tins of gasolene, for it was a long hop to the next fuelling stage. The visit to the Andersens altered Leithen's mood. Here was a snug life being lived in what had seemed a place of death. It switched his interest back to his task.

Presently he found what he had come to seek. On the way to the tent they came on an Eskimo cemetery. Once there had been a settlement here which years ago had been abandoned. There were half a dozen Eskimo graves, with skulls and bones showing through chinks in the piles of stone, and in one there was a complete skeleton stretched as if on a pyre. There was something more. At a little distance in a sheltered hollow were two crosses of driftwood. One was bent and weathered, with the inscription, done with a hot iron, almost obliterated, but it was possible to read . . . TID. GAIL . . . D. There was a date too blurred to decipher. The other cross was new and it had not suffered the storms of more than a couple of winters. On it one could read clearly PAUL LOUIS GAILLARD and a date eighteen months back.

To Leithen there was an intolerable pathos about the two crosses. They told so much, and yet they told nothing. How had Aristide died? Had Paul found him alive? How had Paul died? Who had put up the memorials? There was a grim drama here at which he could not even guess. But the one question that mattered to him was, had Francis seen these crosses?

Johnny, who had been peering at the later monument, answered that question.

'Brother Lew has been here,' he said.

He pointed to a little St Andrew's cross freshly carved with a knife just below Paul's name. Its ends were funnily splayed out.

'That's Lew's mark,' he said. 'You might say it's a family mark. Long ago, when Dad was working for the Bay, there was a breed of Indians along the Liard, some sort of Slaveys, that had got into their heads that they were kind of Scots, and every St Andrew's Day they would bring Dad a present of a big St Andrew's Cross, very nicely carved, which he stuck above the door like a horse-shoe. So we all got into the way of using that cross as our trade mark, especially Lew, who's mighty particular. I've seen him carve it on a slab to stick above a dog's grave, and when he writes a letter he puts it in somewhere. So whenever you see it you can reckon Lew's ahead of you.'

'They can't be long gone,' said Leithen.

'I've been figuring that out, and I guess they might have gone a week ago – maybe ten days. Lew's pretty handy with a canoe. What puzzles me is where they've gone and how. There's no place hereaways to get supplies, and it's a good month's journey to the nearest post. Maybe they shot caribou and smoked 'em. I tell you what, if your pal's got money to burn, what about him hiring a plane to meet 'em here and pick 'em up? If that's their game it won't be easy to hit their trail. There's only one thing I'm pretty sure of, and that is they didn't go home. If we fossick about we'll maybe find out more.'

Johnny's forecast was right, for that afternoon they heard a shot a mile off, and, going out to inquire, found an Eskimo hunter. At the sight of them the man fled, and Johnny had some trouble rounding him up. When halted he stood like a sullen child, a true son of the Elder Ice, for he had a tattooed face and a bone stuck through his upper lip. Probably he had never seen a white man before. He had been hunting caribou before they migrated south from the shore, and had a pile of skins and high-smelling meat to show for his labours. He stubbornly refused to accompany them back to the tent, so

Leithen left him with Johnny, who could make some shape at the speech of the central Arctic.

When Johnny came back Andersen and the schooner had sailed, and Ghost River had returned to its ancient solitude.

'Lew's been here right enough,' he said. 'He and his boss and a couple of Indians came in two canoes eleven days back – at least I reckoned eleven days as well as I could from yon Eskimo's talk. Two days later a plane arrived for them. The Eskimo has never seen a horse or an automobile, but he knows all about aeroplanes. They handed over the canoes and what was left of the stores to the Indians and shaped a course pretty well due west. They've gotten the start of us by a week or maybe more.'

That night after supper Johnny spoke for the first time at some length.

'I've been trying to figure this out,' he said, 'and here's what I make of it. Mr Galliard comes here and sees the graves of his brother and uncle. So far so good. From what you tell me that's not going to content him. He wants to do something of his own on the same line by way of squarin' his conscience. What's he likely to do? Now, let's see just where brother Lew comes in. I must put you wise about Lew.'

Johnny removed his pipe from his mouth.

'He's a wee bit mad,' he said solemnly. 'He's a great man; the cutest hunter and trapper and guide between Alaska and Mexico, and the finest shot on this continent. But he's also mad – batty – loony – anything you like that's out of the usual. It's a special kind of madness, for in most things you won't find a sounder guy. Him and me was buck privates in the War until they made a sharpshooter of him, and you wouldn't hit a better-behaved soldier than old Lew. I was a good deal in trouble, but Lew never was. He has just the one crazy spot in him, and it reminds me of them Gaillards you talk about. It's a kind of craziness you're apt to find in us Northerners. There's a bit of country he wants to explore, and the thought of it comes between him and his sleep and his grub. Say, did you ever hear of the Sick Heart River?'

Leithen shook his head.

'You would if you'd been raised in the North. It's a fancy place that old-timers dream about. Where is it? Well, that's not easy to say. You've heard maybe of the South Nahanni that comes in the north bank of the Liard about a hundred miles west of Fort Simpson? Dad had a post up the Liard and I was born there, and when I was a kid there was a great talk about the South Nahanni. There's a mighty big waterfall on it, so you can't make it a canoe trip. Some said the valley was full of gold, and some said that it was as hot as hell owing to warm springs, and everybody acknowledged that there was more game there to the square mile than in the whole of America. It had a bad name, too, for at least a dozen folk went in and never came out. Some said that was because of bad Indians, but that was punk, for there ain't no Indians in the valley. Our Indians said it was the home of devils, which sounds more reasonable.'

Johnny stopped to relight his pipe, and for a few minutes smoked meditatively.

'Do you get to the Sick Heart by the South Nahanni?' Leithen asked.

'No, you don't. Lew's been all over the South Nahanni, and barring the biggest grizzlies on earth and no end of sheep and goat and elk and caribou, he found nothing. Except the Sick Heart. He saw it from the top of a mountain, and it sort of laid a charm on him. He said that first of all you had snow mountains bigger than any he had ever seen, and then icefields like prairies, and then forests of tall trees, the same as you get on the coast. And then in the valley bottom, grass meadows and an elegant river. A Hare Indian that was with him gave him the name – the Sick Heart, called after an old-time chief that got homesick for the place and pined away. Lew had a try at getting into it and found it no good – there was precipices thousands of feet that end. But he come away with the Sick Heart firm in his mind, and he ain't going to forget it.'

'Which watershed is it on?' Leithen asked.

'That's what no man knows. Not on the South Nahanni's. And you can't get into it from the Yukon side, by the Pelly or the Peel or the Ross or Macmillan – Lew tried 'em all. So it looks as if it didn't flow that way. The last time I heard him talk about it he was kind of thinking that the best route was up from the Mackenzie, the way the Hare Indians go for their mountain hunting. There's a river there called the Big Hare. He thought that might be the road.'

'Do you think he's gone there now?'

'I don't think, but I suspicion. See here, mister. Lew's a strong character and mighty set on what he wants. He's also a bit mad, and mad folks have persuasive ways with them. He finds this Galliard man keen to get into the wilds, and the natural thing is that he persuades him to go to his particular wilds, which he hasn't had out of his mind for ten years.'

'I think you're probably right,' said Leithen. 'We will make a cast by way of the Sick Heart. What's the jumping-off ground?'

'Fort Bannerman on the Mackenzie,' said Johnny. 'Right, we'll start tomorrow morning. We can send back the planes from there and collect an outfit. We'll want canoes and a couple of Hares as guides.'

And then he fell silent and stared into the fire. Now and then he took a covert glance at Leithen. At last he spoke a little shyly.

'You're a sick man, I reckon. I can't help noticin' it, though you don't make much fuss about it. If Lew's on the Sick Heart and we follow him there it'll be a rough passage, and likely we'll have to go into camp for the winter. I'm wondering can you stand it? There ain't no medical comforts in the Mackenzie mountains.'

Leithen smiled. 'It doesn't matter whether I stand it or not. You're right. I'm a sick man. Indeed, I'm a dying man. The doctors in England did not give me more than a year to live, and that was weeks ago. But I want to find Galliard and send him home, and after that it doesn't matter what happens to me.'

'Is Galliard your best pal?'

'I scarcely know him. But I have taken on the job to please a friend, and I must make a success of it. I want to die on my feet, if you see what I mean.'

Johnny nodded.

'I get you. I'm mighty sorry, but I get you . . . Once I had a retriever bitch, the best hunting dog I ever knew, and her and me had some great times on the hills. She could track a beast all day, and minded a blizzard no more than a spring shower. Well, she got something mortally wrong with her innards, and was dying all right. One morning I missed her from her bed beside the stove, and an Indian told me he'd seen her dragging herself up through the woods in the snow. I followed her trail and found her dead just above the tree line, the place she'd been happiest in when she was well. She wanted to die on her feet. I reckon that's the best way for men and hounds.'

15

FOR three days Leithen was in abject misery. They had no receiver in their plane and therefore no means of getting weather reports, and when they took off the next morning the only change was an increased chill in the air. By midday they had run into fog, and, since in that area Job was uncertain of his compass, they went north again to the Arctic coast, and followed it to the Coppermine. Here it began to blow from the north, and in a series of rainstorms they passed the Dismal Lakes and came to the shore of the Great Bear Lake. Job had intended to pass the night at the Mines, but there was no going further that evening in the mist and drizzle.

Next day they struggled to the Mines with just enough gasolene. Leithen looked so ill that the kindly manager would have put him to bed, but he insisted on restarting in the afternoon. They had a difficult take-off from the yeasty lake – Job insisted on their getting into their life-jackets, for he said that the betting was that in three minutes they would be in the water. The lake was safely crossed, but Job failed to hit off the outlet of the Great Bear River, and with the low 'ceiling' he feared to try a compass course to the Mackenzie because of the Franklin mountains. It was midnight before they struck the outlet and they had another wretched bivouac in the rain.

After that things went better. The weather returned to bright sun, clear skies, and a gentle wind from the north-east. Presently they were above the Mackenzie and far in the west they saw the jumble of dark ridges which were the foothills of the Mackenzie mountains. In the afternoon the hills came closer to the river, and on the left bank appeared a cluster of little white shacks with the red flag of the Hudson's Bay flying from a post.

'Fort Bannerman,' said Johnny, as they circled down. 'That's the Big Hare, and somewhere at the back of it is the Sick Heart. Mighty rough country.'

The inhabitants of the fort were grouped at the mud bank where they went ashore – the Hudson's Bay postmaster, two Oblate Brothers, a fur trader, a trapper in for supplies, and several Indians. The trapper waved a hand to Johnny—

'Hullo, boy!' he said. 'How goes it? Lew's been here. He lit out for the mountains ten days ago.'

Part Two

There is a river, the streams whereof shall make glad the city of God.

Psalm xlvi

I

IT took three days to get the proper equipment together. Johnny was leaving little to chance.

'If we find Lew and his pal we may have to keep 'em company for months. It won't be easy to get to the Sick Heart, but it'll be a darn sight harder to get out. We've got to face the chance of a winter in the mountains. Lucky for us the Hares have a huntin' camp fifty miles up-river. We can dump some of our stuff there and call it our base.'

The first question was that of transport. Water was the easiest until the river became a mountain torrent. The common Indian craft was of moose hides tanned like vellum and stretched on poplar ribs; but Johnny managed to hire from a free-trader a solid oak thirty-foot boat with an outboard motor; and, as subsidiaries, a couple of canoes brought years ago from the south, whose seams had been sewn up with strips of tamarack root and caulked with resin. Two Indians were engaged, little men compared with the big Plains folk, but stalwart for the small-boned Hares. They had the slanting Mongol eyes of the Mackenzie River tribes, and had picked up some English at the Catholic mission school. Something at the back of Leithen's brain christened them Big Klaus and Little Klaus, but Johnny, who spoke their tongue, had other names for them.

Then the Hudson's Bay store laid open its resources, and Johnny was no niggardly outfitter. Leithen gave him a free hand, for they had brought nothing with them. There were clothes to be bought for the winter – parkas and fur-lined jerkins, and leather breeches, and lined boots; gloves and flapped caps, blankets and duffel bags. There were dog packs, each meant to carry twenty-five pounds. There was a light tent – only one, for the Hares would fend for themselves at the up-river camp, and Lew and Galliard were no doubt already well provided. There were a couple of shot-guns and a couple of rifles and ammunition, and there was a folding tin stove. Last came the provender: bacon and beans and flour, salt and sugar, tea and coffee, and a fancy assortment of tinned stuffs.

'Looks like we was goin' to start a store,' said Johnny, 'but we may need every ounce of it and a deal more. If it's a winter-long job we'll sure have to get busy with our guns. Don't look so scared, mister. We've not got to back-pack that junk. The boat'll carry it easy to the Hares' camp, and after that we'll cache the feck of it.'

Leithen's quarters during these days were in the spare room of the Bay postmaster. Fort Bannerman was a small metropolis, for besides the Bay store it had a Mounted Police post, a hospital run by the Grey Nuns, and an Indian school in charge of the Oblate Brothers. With one of the latter he made friends, finding that he had served in a French battalion which had been on the right of the Guards at Loos. Father Duplessis was from Picardy. Leithen had once been billeted in the shabby flat-chested château near Montreuil where his family had dwelt since the days of Henri Quatre. The Fathers had had a medical training and could at need perform straightforward operations, such as that on an appendix, or the amputation of a maimed limb. Leithen sat in his little room at the hospital, which smelt of ether and carbolic, and they talked like two old soldiers.

Once they walked together to where the Big Hare strained to the Mackenzie through an archipelago of sandy islets.

'I have been here seven years,' Father Duplessis told him. 'Before that I was three years in the eastern Arctic. That, if you like, was isolation, for there was one ship a year, but here we are in a thoroughfare. All through the winter the planes from the northern mines call weekly, and in summer we have many planes as well as the Hudson's Bay boats.'

Leithen looked round the wide circle of landscape – the huge drab Mackenzie two miles broad, to the east and south interminable wastes of scrub spruce, to the west a chain of tawny mountains, stained red in parts with iron, and fantastically sculptured.

'Do you never feel crushed by this vastness?' he asked. 'This country is out-size.'

'No,' was the answer, 'for I live in a little world. I am always busy among little things. I skin a moose, or build a boat, or hammer a house together, or treat a patient, or cobble my boots or patch my coat – all little things. And then I have the offices of the Church, in a blessedly small space, for our chapel is a midget.'

'But outside all that?' said Leithen, 'you have an empty world and an empty sky.'

'Not empty,' said Father Duplessis, smiling, 'for it is filled with God. I cannot say, like Pascal, "le silence éternel de ces espaces infinis m'effraie." There is no silence here, for when I straighten my back and go out of doors the world is full of voices. When I was in my Picardy country there were little fields like a parterre, and crowded roads. There, indeed, I knew loneliness – but not here, where man is nothing and God is all.'

2

THEY left Fort Bannerman on a clear fresh morning when the sky was a pale Arctic blue, so pale as to be almost colourless, and a small cold wind, so tiny as to be little more than a shudder, blew from the north. The boat chugged laboriously up the last feeble rapids of the Big Hare, and then made good progress through long canal-like stretches in a waste of loess and sand. Here the land was almost desert, for the scrub pines had ceased to clothe the banks. These rose in shelves and mantelpieces to the spurs of the mountains, and one chain of low cliffs made a kind of bib round the edge of the range. There was no sound except the gurgle of the water and an occasional sandpiper's whistle. A selvedge of dwarf willow made the only green in the landscape, though in distant hollows there were glimpses of poplar and birch. The river was split into a dozen channels, and the Hares kept the boat adroitly in deep water, for there was never a moment when it grounded. It was an ugly country, dull as a lunar landscape, tilted and eroded ridges which were the approach to the granite of the high mountains.

The three days at Fort Bannerman had done Leithen good, and though he found his breathing troublesome and his limbs weak, the hours passed in comparative comfort, since there was no need for exertion. On the Arctic shore and in the journey thence he had realised only that he was in a bleak infinity of space, a natural place in which to await death. But now he was conscious of the details of his environment. He watched the drifting duck and puzzled over their breed, he noted the art with which the Hares kept the boat in slack and deep water, and as the mountains came nearer he felt a feeble admiration for one peak which had the shape of Milan cathedral. Especially he was aware of his companion. Hitherto there had been little conversation, but now Johnny came into the picture, sitting on the gunwale, one lean finger pressing down the tobacco in his pipe, his far-sighted eyes searching the shelves for game.

Johnny was very ready to talk. He had discovered that Leithen was Scots, and was eager to emphasise the Scottish side of his own ancestry. On the little finger of his left hand he wore a ring set with a small blood stone. He took it off and passed it to Leithen.

'Dad left me that,' he said. 'Lew has a bigger and better one. Dad was mighty proud of the rings and he told us to stick to them, for he said they showed we come of good stock.'

Leithen examined it. The stone bore the three cinquefoils of Fraser. Then he remembered that Frizel had been the name for Fraser in the Border parish where he had spent his youth. He remembered Adam Fraser, the blacksmith, the clang of his smithy on summer mornings, the smell of sizzling hooves and hot iron on summer afternoons. The recollection gave Johnny a new meaning for him; he was no longer a shadowy figure in this fantastic world of weakness; he was linked to the vanished world of real things, and thereby acquired a personality.

As they chugged upstream in the crisp afternoon, hourly drawing nearer to the gate of the mountains, Leithen enjoyed something which was almost ease, while Johnny in his slow drawling voice dug into his memory. That night, too, when they made camp at the bottom of a stone-shoot, and, since the weather was mild, kept the driftwood fire alight more for show than for warmth, Johnny expanded further. Since in his experience all sickness was stomachic, he had included invalid foods among the stores, and was surprised when Leithen told him that he need not fuss about his diet. This made him take a more cheerful view of his companion's health, and he did not trouble to see him early to bed. In his sleeping-bag on a couch of Bay blankets Leithen listened to some chapters of Johnny's autobiography.

He heard of his childhood on Great Slave Lake and on the

Liard, of his father (his mother had died at his birth), of his brother Lew – especially of Lew.

'We was brothers,' said Johnny, 'but also we was buddies, which ain't always according to rule.'

He spoke of his hunting, which had ranged from the Stikine to the Churchill, from the Clearwater to the Liard, and of his trapping, which had been done mostly about the upper waters of the Peace. Johnny as talker had one weak point – he was determined that his auditor should comprehend every detail, and he expounded in minutiae. He seemed resolved that Leithen should grasp the difference in method between the taking of mink and marten, the pen on the river bank and the trap up in the hills. He elaborated also the technique of the spearing of muskrats, and he was copious on the intricate subject of fox . . . In every third sentence there was a mention of Lew, his brother, until the picture that emerged for Leithen from the talk was not that of wild animals but of a man.

It was a picture which kept dislimning, so that he could not see it clearly; but it impressed him strangely. Lew came into every phase of Johnny's recollections. He had said this or that; he had done this or that; he seemed to be taken as the ultimate authority on everything in heaven and earth. But Johnny's attitude was something more than the admiration for an elder brother, or the respect of one expert for a greater. There was uneasiness in it. He seemed to bring in Lew's name in a kind of ritual, as if to convince himself that Lew was secure and happy . . . What was it that he had said on the Arctic shore? He had called Lew mad, meaning that he was possessed by a dream. Now Lew was hot on the trail of that dream, and Johnny was anxious about him. Of that there was no doubt.

Leithen laughed. He looked at Johnny's bat ears and bullet head. Here was he, one who had seen men and cities and had had a hand in great affairs, with his thoughts concentrated on an unknown brother of an Indian half-breed! Galliard had almost gone out of the picture; to Johnny he was only Lew's 'pal,' the latest of a score or two of temporary employers. Even to Leithen himself the errant New Yorker, the husband of Blenkiron's niece, the pillar of Ravelstons, seemed a minor figure compared to the masterful guide who was on the quest for a mysterious river. Had Lew inspired Galliard with his fancies? Or was the inspiration perhaps Galliard's? What crazy obsession would he find if and when he overtook the pair somewhere in that wild world behind which the sun was setting?

That night they made camp at the very doorstep of the mountains, where the river, after a string of box-canyons, emerged from the foothills. It was an eerie place, for the Big Hare, after some miles of rapids, drowsed in a dark lagoon beneath sheer walls of rock. Leithen's mind, having been back all day in the normal world, now reacted to a mood of black depression. What had seemed impressive a few hours before was now merely grotesque and cruel. His errand was ridiculous – almost certainly futile, and trivial even if it succeeded. What had he to do with the aberrations of American financiers and the whims of half-breeds? Somewhere in those bleak hills he would die – a poor ending for a not undignified life! . . . But had his life been much of a thing after all? He had won a certain amount of repute and made a certain amount of money, but neither had meant much to him. He had had no wife, no child. Had his many friends been more, after all, than companions? In the retrospect his career seemed lonely, self-centred, and barren, and what was this last venture? A piece of dull stoicism at the best – or, more likely, a cheap bravado.

3

ALL next morning they smelt their way through the box-canyons, sometimes with the engine shut off and the Hares poling madly. There were two dangerous rapids, but navigation was made simpler by the fact that there were no split channels and no shallows. They were going through the limestone foothills, and the cliffs on either side were at least seven hundred feet high, sheer as a wall where they did not overhang. Johnny had a tale about the place. Once the Hares had been hunted by the Crees – he thought it was the Crees, his own people, but it might have been the Dogribs. At that time the Big Hare River had come out of the mountains underground. The Hare boats were no match for the fleet Cree canoes, and the wretched tribe, fleeing upstream, looked for annihilation when they reached the end of the waterway. But to their amazement they found the mountains open before them and a passage through the canyons to the upper valley where was now the Hares' hunting camp. When they looked back there were no pursuing Crees, for the mountain wall had closed behind them. But some days later, when the disappointed enemy had gone back to their Athabaska swamps, the passage opened again, and the Hares could return when they pleased to the Mackenzie.

'Big magic' said Johnny. 'I reckon them Hares got the story out of the Bible, when the missionaries had worked a bit on them, for it's mighty like the children of Israel and old Pharaoh.'

Suddenly the boat shot into a lake, the containing walls fell back, and they were in a valley something less than a mile wide, with high mountains, whose tops were already powdered with snow, ringing it and blocking it to the north. The shores were green with scrub-willow, and the lower slopes were dark with spruce and pine.

At the upper end of the lake, on a half-moon of sward between the woods and the water, was the Hares' encampment. Big Klaus and Little Klaus set up a howl as they came in sight of it, and they were answered by a furious barking of dogs.

The place was different from Leithen's expectation. He remembered from old days the birch-bark lodges of eastern Canada; but in this country, where the birches were small, he had looked for something like the tall teepees of the Plains, with their smoke-holes and their covering of skins. Instead he found little oblong cabins thatched with rush-mats or brushwood. They had a new look as if they had recently been got ready for the winter, and a few caribou-skin tents showed what had been the summer quarters. On the highest point of ground stood what looked like a chapel, a building of logs surmounted at one end by a rough cross. Penned near it was an assortment of half-starved dogs who filled the heavens with their clamour.

The place stank foully, and when they landed Leithen felt nausea stealing over him. His legs had cramped with the journey and he had to lean on Johnny's shoulder. They passed through a circle of silent Indians, and were greeted by their chief, who wore a medal like a soup plate. Then a little old man hobbled up who introduced himself as Father Wentzel, the Oblate who spent the summer here. He was about to return to Fort Bannerman, he said, when his place would be taken for the winter by Father Duplessis. He had a little presbytery behind the chapel, where he invited Leithen to rest while Johnny did his business with the Hares.

The priest opened the door which communicated with the

chapel, lit two tapers on the altar, and displayed with pride a riot of barbaric colours. The walls were hung with cloths painted in bedlamite scarlets and purples and oranges – not the rude figures of men and animals common on the teepees, but a geometrical nightmare of interwoven cubes and circles. The altar cloth had the same byzantine exuberance.

'That is the work of our poor people,' said the priest. 'Helped by Brother Onesime, who had the artist's soul. To you, monsieur, it may seem too gaudy, but to our Indians it is a foretaste of the New Jerusalem.'

Leithen sat in the presbytery in a black depression. The smells of the encampment – unclean human flesh, half-dressed skins of animals, gobbets of putrefying food – were bad enough in that mild autumn noon. The stuffy little presbytery was not much better. But the real trouble was that suddenly everything seemed to have become little and common. The mountains were shapeless, mere unfinished bits of earth; the forest of pine and spruce had neither form nor colour; the river, choked with logs and jetsam, had none of the beauty of running water. In coming into the wilderness he had found not the majesty of Nature, but the trivial, the infinitely small – an illiterate half-breed, a rabble of degenerate Indians, a priest with the mind of a child. The pettiness culminated in the chapel, which was as garish as a Noah's Ark from a cheap toyshop . . . He felt sick in mind and very sick in body.

Father Wentzel made him a cup of tea, which he could barely swallow. The little priest's eyes rested on him with commiseration in them, but he was too shy to ask questions. Presently Johnny arrived in a bustle. He would leave certain things, if he were permitted, in the presbytery cellar. He had arranged with the chief about dogs when they were wanted, but that was not yet, for it would be a fortnight at least before snow could be looked for, even in the high valleys, and, since they would travel light, they did not need dogs as pack animals. They would take the boat, for a stage or two was still possible by it; after that they would have the canoes, and he had kept the Hares as canoe-men – 'for the portagin' business would be too much for you, mister.'

He had news of Lew. The two men were not more than a week ahead, for a sudden flood in the Big Hare had delayed them. They had canoes, but no Indians, and had gone in the first instance to Lone Tree Lake. 'That's our road,' said

Johnny. 'Maybe they've made a base camp there. Anyhow, we'll hit their trail.'

He had other news. It was the end of the seven years' cycle, and disease had fallen on the snow-shoe rabbit, upon which in the last resort all wild animals depend. Therefore the winter hunting and trapping of the Hares would be poor, and there might be a shortage of food in their camp. 'You tell Father Duplessis that when you get back to Fort Bannerman,' he told the priest. Their own camp, if they were compelled to make one, might run short. 'Lucky we brought what we did,' he told Leithen. 'If we catch up with Lew we'll be all right, for he'd get something to eat off an iceberg.'

They passed one night in the presbytery. While Johnny slept the deep, short sleep of the woodsman, Leithen had a word with Father Wentzel.

'The two men who have gone before?' he asked. 'One is the brother of my guide, and the other is a friend of my friends. How did they impress you?'

The child-like face of the priest took on a sudden gravity.

'The gentleman, he was of the Faith. He heard mass daily and made confession. He was a strange man. He looked unhappy and hungry and he spoke little. But the other, the guide, he was stranger. He had not our religion, but I think he had a kind of madness. He was in a furious haste, as if vengeance followed him, and he did not sleep much. When I rose before dawn he was lying with staring eyes. For his companion, the gentleman, he seemed to have no care – he was pursuing his own private errand. A strong man, but a difficult. When they left me I did not feel happy about the two messieurs.'

4

OUT of the encumbered river by way of easy rapids the boat ran into reaches which were like a Scottish salmon stream on a big scale, long pools each with a riffle at its head. The valley altered its character, becoming narrower and grassier, with the forest only in patches on infrequent promontories. The weather, too, changed. The nights were colder, and a chill crept into even the noontide sunshine. But it was immensely invigorating, so that Johnny sang snatches of Scots songs instead of sucking his pipe, and Leithen had moments of energy which he knew to be deceptive. The air had a quality which he was unable to describe, and the scents were not less baffling. They were tonic and yet oddly sedative, for they moved the blood rather to quiescence than to action. They were aromatic, but there was nothing lush or exotic in them. They had on the senses the effect of a high violin note on the ear, as of something at the extreme edge of mortal apprehension.

But the biggest change was in Leithen's outlook. The gloomy apathy of the Oblate's presbytery disappeared, and its place was taken by a mood which was almost peace. The mountains were no longer untidy rock heaps, but the world which he had loved long ago, that happy upper world of birds and clouds and the last magic of sunset. He picked out ways of ascent by their ridges and gullies, and found himself noting with interest the riot of colour in the woods: the grey splashes of caribou moss, the reds of partridge-berry, cranberry, blueberry, and Saskatoon; the dull green interspaces where an old forest fire had brought forth acres of young spruces; above all the miracle of the hardwood trees. The scrub by the river, red-dog-willow, wolfberry willow, had every shade of yellow, and poplar and birch carried on the pageant of gold and umber far up the mountain sides. Birds were getting infrequent; he saw duck and geese high up in the heavens, but he could not identify them. Sometimes he saw a deer, and on bare places on the hills he thought he detected sheep. Black bears were plentiful, revelling among the berries or wetting their new winter coats in the river's shallows, and he saw a big grizzly lumbering across a stone shoot.

Three long portages took them out of the Big Hare valley to Lone Tree Lake, which, in shape like a scimitar, lay tucked in a mat of forest under the wall of what seemed to be a divide. They reached it in the twilight, and, since the place was a poor camping-ground, they launched the canoes and paddled half-way up till they found a dry spit, which some ancient conflagration had cleared of timber. The lake was lit from end to end with the fires of sunset, and later in the night the aurora borealis cast its spears across the northern end. The mountains had withdrawn, and only one far snow peak was visible, so that the feeling of confinement, inevitable in the high valleys, was gone, and Leithen had a sense of infinite space around him. He seemed to breathe more freely, and the chill of the night air refreshed him, for frost crisped the lake's edges. He fell asleep as soon as he got under his blankets.

He awoke after midnight to see above him a wonderful sky of stars, still shot with the vagrant shafts of the aurora. Suddenly he felt acutely his weakness, but with no regret in his mind, and indeed almost with comfort. He had been right in doing as he had done, coming out to meet death in a world where death and life were colleagues and not foes. He felt that in this strange place he was passing, while still in time, inside the bounds of eternity. He was learning to know himself, and with that might come the knowledge of God. A sentence of St Augustine came into his head as he turned over and went to sleep again: '*Deum et animam scire cupio. Nihil ne plus? Nihil omnino.*'

5

HE woke to find himself sweating under his blankets. The weather had changed to a stuffy mildness, for a warm chinook wind was blowing from the south-west. Johnny was standing beside him with a grave face.

'Lew's been here,' he said. 'He's left his mark all right. Eat your breakfast and I'll show you.'

At the base of the promontory there was a stand of well-grown spruce. A dozen of the trees had been felled, stripped, cut into lengths, and notched at each end. An oblong had been traced on a flat piece of ground, and holes dug for end-posts. A hut had been prospected, begun – and relinquished.

'Lew's been on this job,' said Johnny. 'You can't mistake his axe-work.'

He stood looking with unquiet eyes at the pile of cut logs. 'Him and his pal put in a day's work here. And then they quit. What puzzles me is why Lew quit. It ain't like him.'

'Why shouldn't he change his mind?' Leithen asked. 'He must have decided that this was not the best place for a base camp.'

Johnny shook his head.

'It ain't like him. He never starts on a job until he has thought all round it and made sure that he's doin' right, and then hell fire wouldn't choke him off it. No, mister. There's something queer about this, and I don't like it. Something's happened to Lew.'

The mild blue eyes were cloudy with anxiety.

'They've back-packed their stuff and gone on. They've cached their canoe,' and he nodded to where a bulky object was lashed in the lower branches of a tall poplar. 'We've got to do the same. We'll cache most of our stuff, for when we catch up with Lew we can send back for it. We'll take the Indians, for you ain't fit to carry a load. Their trail won't be hard to follow. I've been over the first bit of it. Lew pushed on ahead, and the other was about fifty yards back of him and limping. Looks like they've quarrelled.'

6

THE trail led away from the lake shore up a tributary stream towards what looked like the main wall of the divide. The berry-clad, ferny hillside made easy walking, and since the timber was small there were few troublesome windfalls. Johnny carried his .44 rifle, his axe, and a bag containing his own personal effects and most of Leithen's; the Hares, Big Klaus and Little Klaus, had the heavy stuff, tent, cooking utensils, portable stove, stores; while Leithen had no more than a light haversack about the weight which he had often carried in the Alps. The pattern of his day was now so familiar that he found it hard to fit into it the astounding novelties in his life – his quest for a man whom he had never seen, in the least-known corner of North America – the fact that presently somewhere in this wilderness he must die.

New also in his experience were the weather and his own weakness. The sun was getting low and the days were shortening; each night frost crisped the edges of the streams, and the first hour of the morning march was through crackling pools and frozen herbage. But by noon the sun was warm and it set daily over their left shoulders in a haze of opal and pearl. The morning and evening chills were keenly felt, but the tonic air seemed to soothe his coughing. It was the very quintessence of air, quickening every sense so that he smelt more keenly, heard more clearly, saw things in sharper outline. He had never used spectacles, and he found that his eyes were fully the equal of Johnny's when he knew what to look for.

He might have had an appetite, too, had it not been for his fatigue. He was so tired when they made camp for the night that he could scarcely eat, and Johnny had to turn his beans and bacon into a kind of soup before he could swallow them. He would lie in a half-stupor drawing his breath painfully for the better part of an hour, while Johnny and the Hares built the fire. Johnny was merciful, and accommodated his pace to his dragging feet, but the easiest gait was too much for him, and soon he had to have hourly rests. The trail went in and out of the glens, rising slowly to the higher benches, and, but for a few patches of swamp and one laborious passage over a rockfall, it was a road a child could have walked. But except for a very few minutes in the day it was for Leithen one long purgatory.

He started out in the morning with wobbling legs. After a mile or so, when his blood moved more briskly, he had a short spell of comfort. Then his breath began to trouble him, and long before midday he was plodding like a conscientious drunkard. He made it a point of honour to continue until Johnny called a halt, and, though Johnny did this often, he found himself always near the limits of his strength, and would drop like a log when the word was given. He returned unconsciously to an old habit of his mountaineering days, when he had had a long dull course to complete, counting his steps up to a thousand and walking to the rhythm of 'Old Soldiers never Die.' . . .

At the head of a little pass Johnny halted, though the march had only been going for twenty minutes. The Hares, when they came up, set down their packs and broke into a dismal howling, which seemed to be meant for a chant. There was a big jack-pine with the lower branches lopped off, and some fifty feet from the ground a long bundle was lashed to the trunk, something wrapped in caribou skin tanned white.

Johnny removed his disreputable hat. 'That's a chief up there. Good old scout he was – name of Billy Whitefish . . . Passed out last fall.'

7

ONE blue day succeeded another, and each was followed by a colder night. The earth was yawning before it turned to its winter sleep. Leithen, though the days tired him to desperation, yet found the nights tolerable, and could let his thoughts stray from his bodily discomfort. He listened to Johnny's talk.

Johnny talked much, for he had lost his shyness of Leithen, and this kind of trip was child's play to him.

'This is a pretty good land,' he said, 'to them that knows their way about. I guess a man could starve in the barrens, but not in the woods. Why, there's forty kinds of berries – and a whole lot of different sorts of mushrooms – and rock-tripe – and bark you can boil to make porridge. And there's all the animals that Noah had in the Ark. And there's nothing to hurt a body provided the body's got sense, and don't tackle a grizzly up-hill.'

He had strong views on food. 'B'ar's right enough in the fall when he's fat. A young un's as good as mutton, but an old un's plain shoe leather.' He did not care for moose meat, preferring caribou or deer, and he liked best partridge or ptarmigan in half-plumage.

'What's here? Grizzly, black b'ar, brown b'ar, moose, caribou, three kinds of sheep – everything except goats. The Almighty left goats out when He stocked them mountains.'

It was clearly his purpose to picture the land as an easy place even for a sick man to travel in. 'Canadians,' he said (he used the word as the equivalent of strangers, embracing everybody except the men of the North-west), 'think we've got hell's own climate up here. They're wrong. We get milder winters than the Prairies. Besides, winter's a fine time to travel if you know the ways of it. You'll be snugger in a hole in the snow at forty below than in an apartment house in Winnipeg, and a darn lot healthier.

'But you've got to watch your step in the Northland,' he would add. He would tell experiences of his own to show the cruelty of the wilds, though he was always careful to explain that his misfortunes were due to his own folly. He was a white-water man, though not of Lew's class, and above all things he hated towing a boat with a long trackline. 'The thing's just waitin' to murder you,' he said, 'trip you over a cliff, or drown you, or get round your neck and saw your head off.' . . .

He had been near starvation. 'I can go three days without food and not feel it, and I've done it pretty often. I reckon Lew could go five. But there's never been no reason for it except my own dam' folly. Once I lost all my kit in a river, including my knife which I had in my teeth, and I had to make shift with flint-flakes to kill and skin. I once lived for a week on berries and one porcupine.'

He had had his accidents, too, as when a pine he was chopping down split with the cold and sent a sliver through his shoulder. He had once walked twenty miles to find a bottle of painkiller which he had cached, his throat choking with laryngitis. But his worst adventure – he seemed shy in telling it – was when he was caught without snow-shoes in an early fall blizzard, and crossed unknowingly a bottomless half-frozen sphagnum swamp which heaved under his tread and made him vomit up his soul.

He would talk, too, about the secret lore of the woods. He could make the crows speak to him, and the squirrels, but not the whisky-jacks, because they were fools with only a cry and no speech. Lew could make anything talk.

It was always Lew, the mentor, the magician. But he never spoke his brother's name, or so it seemed to Leithen, without an accent of disquiet. He followed unerringly Lew's blazing of the trail, and often the blazes were so small that only a skilled woodman could have noticed them. He studied carefully every bivouac. Sometimes in marshy places he found the moccasin tracks still fresh, and then his anxiety seemed to increase.

'Lew's settin' a terrible pace,' he said, 'and the other's laggin'. They're still messin' together at night, but the other must be getting in pretty late, and he can't be having much sleep, for each morning they starts together . . . I don't like it somehow. I wonder what brother Lew's aiming at?'

8

THE trail wound intricately along the slopes of deep parallel glens, now and then crossing from one to another by a low pass. Johnny had been over it before, and was puzzled. 'Them rivers run down to the Yukon,' he told Leithen. 'But Lew swears the Sick Heart don't do that, and we're over the divide from the Mackenzie. I reckon it can't have nothin' to do with the Peel, so it must disappear into the earth. That's my guess. Anyhow, this trail ain't going to get us nowhere except to the Yukon.'

The celestial weather continued, wintry in the small hours of the night, but in the sun as balmy as June. Leithen had fallen into a state which was neither ease nor mal-ease, but something neutral like his bodily condition at the end of a hard term at the Bar, when he was scarcely ill but assuredly not well. He could struggle through the day and have a slender margin for the interests of the road.

There was one new thing – the wild animals were beginning to show themselves, as if they were stretching their legs for the last time before the snows came. One morning he saw the first moose – well up the hillside in a patch of dwarf spruce, showing against the background like elephants.

'Them beasts ain't happy here,' Johnny said. 'They want the

hardwood country, for they ain't like caribou that feed on moss – they likes the juicy underbrush. I guess they'll come down before the snow to the bottoms and stamp out a *ravage* so as to get to the shoots. I'll tell you a queer thing. The moose is pushin' further north. I mind the day when there wasn't one north of the Great Slave Lake, and now Lew has seen them on the Arctic shore east of the Mackenzie. I wonder what's bitin' them?'

The caribou had not yet appeared, being still on the tundras, but there were birds – ptarmigan and willow grouse – and big Arctic hares just getting into their winter coats. Also there were wolves, both the little grey wolves and the great timber wolves. They did not howl, but Johnny – and Leithen also – could hear them padding at night in the forest. Sometimes dim shapes slipped across a glade among the trees. One night, too, when Leithen could not sleep, he got up and watched the northern heavens where the aurora flickered like a curtain of delicate lace wrought in every tint of the rainbow. It lit up the foreground across which stalked a procession of black forms like some frieze on a Greek urn.

He found Johnny at his side. 'That's the North,' he said solemnly. 'The wolves and the Aurory. God send us a kind winter.'

9

ONE day the trail took an odd turn, for it left the parallel ridges and bore away to the east to higher ground. Johnny shook his head. 'This is new country for me,' he said. 'Here's where Lew has taken the big chance.'

Mountains prematurely snow-covered had been visible from the Hares' settlement, and Leithen at Lone Tree Camp had seen one sharp white peak in a gap very far off. Ever since then they had been moving among wooded ridges at the most two thousand feet high. But now they suddenly came out on a stony plateau, the trees fell away, and they looked on a new world.

The sedimentary rocks had given place to some kind of igneous formation. In front were cliffs and towers as fantastic as the Dolomites, black and sinister against a background of great snowfields, sweeping upward to ice arêtes and couloirs which reminded Leithen of Dauphiné. In the foreground the land dropped steeply into gorges which seemed to converge in a deep central trough, but they were very unlike the mild glens through which they had been ascending. These were rifts in the black rock, their edges feathered with dwarf pines, and from their inky darkness in the sunlight they must be deep. The rock towers were not white and shining like the gracious pinnacles above Cortina, but as black as if they had been hewn out of coal by a savage Creator.

But it was not the foreground that held the eye, but the immense airy sweep of the snowfields and ice pinnacles up to a central point, where a tall peak soared into the blue. Leithen had seen many snow mountains in his time, but this was something new to him – new to the world. The icefield was gigantic, the descending glaciers were on the grand scale, the central mountain must compete with the chief summits of the southern Rockies. But unlike the Rockies the scene was composed as if by a great artist – nothing untidy and shapeless, but everything harmonised into an exquisite unity of line and colour.

His eyes dropped from the skyline to the foreground and the middle distance. He shivered. Somewhere down in that labyrinth was Galliard. Somewhere down there he would leave his own bones.

Johnny was staring at the scene without speaking a word, without even an exclamation. At last he drew a long breath.

'God!' he said. 'Them's the biggest mountains in the Northland and only you and me and Lew and his pal has seen 'em, and some Indians that don't count. But it's going to be a blasted country to travel. See that black gash? I reckon that's where the Sick Heart River flows, and it'll be hell's own job to get down to it.'

'D'you think Lew and Galliard are there?' Leithen asked.

'Sure. I got their trail a piece back on the sand of that little pond we passed. We'll pick it up soon on them shale slides.'

'Is the road possible?'

'Lew thinks it is. I told you he'd seen the Sick Heart once but couldn't get down the precipices. It couldn't have been this place or he wouldn't have gone on, for he don't try impossibilities. He sure knows there's a way down.'

Leithen, sitting on the mountain gravel, had a sudden sharp pang of hopelessness, almost of fear. He realised that this spectacle of a new mountain-land would once have sent him wild with excitement, the excitement both of the geographer and the mountaineer. But now he could only look at it with despair. It might have been a Pisgah-sight of a promised land; but now it was only a cruel reminder of his frailty. He had still to find Galliard, but Galliard had gone into this perilous labyrinth. Could he follow? Could he reach him? . . . But did it matter after all? The finding of Galliard was a task he had set himself, thinking less of success than of the task. It was to tide away the time manfully before his end so that he could die standing. A comforting phrase of Walt Whitman's came back to him, 'the delicious near-by assurance of death.'

Sometimes lately he had been surprised at himself. He had not thought that he possessed this one-idea'd stoicism which enabled him to climb the bleak staircase of his duty with scarcely a look behind . . . But perhaps this was the way in which most men faced death. Had his health lasted he would be doing the same thing a dozen or a score of years ahead. Soon his friends would be doing it – Hannay and Lamancha and Clanroyden – if they were fated to end in their beds. It was the lot of everyone sooner or later to reach the bleak bag's-end of life into which they must creep to die.

10

THEY soon picked up the tracks of their forerunners in the long spouts of gravel, and as they slowly zigzagged downhill to the tree line the weather changed. The cold blue sky beyond the mountains dulled to a colder grey and all light went out of the landscape. It was like the coming of the Polar Night of which he had read, the inexorable drawing down of a curtain upon the glory of the world. The snow began to fall in big flakes, not driven by any wind, but like the gentle emptying of a giant celestial bin. Soon there was nothing but white round them, except the tops of the little gnarled firs.

Luckily they had reached the tree line before the snow began, for otherwise they might have lost the trail. As it was, Johnny soon picked it up from the blazes on the diminutive trunks. It led them down a slope so steep that it was marvellous that any roots could cling to it. They had to ford many ice-cold streams, and before they reached flat ground in the evening Leithen was tottering on the very outside edge of his strength. He scarcely heard Johnny's mutter, 'Looks like Lew has lost his pal. Here's where he camped and there's just the one set of tracks.' He was repeating to himself Whitman's words like a prayer.

Johnny saw his weariness and mercifully said no more, contenting himself with making camp and cooking supper. Leithen fell asleep as soon as he had finished his meal, and did not wake until he heard the crackling of the breakfast fire. The air was mild and most of the snow had gone, for the wind had shifted to the south-west. Every limb ached after the long march of yesterday, but his chest was easier and there seemed more pith in his bones.

Johnny wore an anxious face. 'We've made up on 'em,' he said. 'I reckon Lew's not two days ahead.'

Leithen asked how he knew this, but Johnny said he knew but could not explain – it would take too long and a stranger to the wilds would not understand.

'He's gone on alone,' he repeated. 'This was his camping-ground three nights back, and the other wasn't here. They parted company some time that day, for we had the trail of both of 'em on the shale slides. What in God's name has happened? Lew has shook off his pal, and that pal is somewhere around here, and, being new to the job, he'll die. Maybe he's dead already.'

'Has Lew gone on?'

'Lew's gone on. I've been over a bit of his trail. He's not wastin' time.'

'But the other – my friend – won't he have followed Lew's blazes?'

'He wouldn't notice 'em, being raw. Lew's blazed a trail for his use on the way back, not for any pal to follow.'

So this was journey's end for him – to have traced Galliard to the uttermost parts of the earth only to find him dead. Remembrance of his errand and his original purpose awoke exasperation, and exasperation stirred the dying embers of his vitality.

'Our job is to find Mr Galliard,' he said. 'We stay here until we get him dead or alive.'

Johnny nodded. 'I guess that's right, but I'm mighty anxious about brother Lew. Looks like he's gone haywire.'

The snow was the trouble, Johnny said. It was disappearing fast under sun and wind, and its melting would obliterate all tracks on soft ground, almost as completely as if it still covered them. He thought that the Hares were better trackers than himself and they might find what he missed. He proposed that Leithen should lie up in camp while he and the Indians went back on yesterday's trail in the hope of finding the place where the two men had parted.

Johnny packed some food and in half an hour he and the Hares were climbing the steep side of the glen. Leithen carried his blankets out to a patch which the sun had already dried, and basked in the thin winter sunshine. Oddly enough, Johnny's news had not made him restless, though it threatened disaster to his journey. He had wanted that journey to succeed, but the mere finding of Galliard would not spell success, or the loss of him failure. Success lay in his own spirit. A slight increase of bodily comfort had given him also a certain spiritual ease. This sun was good, though soon for him it would not rise again.

The search-party did not return until the brief twilight. Johnny, as he entered the tent, shook his head dolefully.

'No good, mister. We've found where the other feller quit the trail – them Hares are demons at that game. Just what I expected – up on the barrens where there ain't no trees to blaze and brother Lew had got out of sight. But after that we couldn't pick up no trail. He might have gone left or he might have gone right, but anyhow he must have gone down into the woods. So we started to beat out the woods, each of us takin' a line, but we've struck nothin'. Tomorrow we'll have another try. I reckon he can't have gone far, for he's dead lame. He must be lyin' up somewhere and starvin'.'

Johnny counted on his fingers.

'Say, look! He's been three days quit of Lew – he's dead lame, and I reckon he wasn't carryin' more'n his own weight – if he didn't catch up with Lew at night he didn't have no food – maybe he wasn't able to make fire – maybe he didn't carry more'n one blanket – if he's alive he's mighty cold and mighty hungry.'

He was silent until he went to bed, a certain proof of anxiety.

'This sure is one hell of a business,' he said as he turned in. 'Lew kind of mad and streakin' off into space, and his pal aimin' to be a corpse. It's enough to put a man off his feed.'

II

JOHNNY and the Hares were off at dawn next morning. The weather was mild, almost stuffy, and there had been little frost in the night. Leithen sat outside the tent, but there was no sun to warm him, only a grey misty sky which bent low on the hills.

He was feeling his weakness again, and with it came a deep depression of spirit. The wilds were brutal, inhuman, the abode of horrid cruelty. They had driven one man mad and would be the death of another. Not much comfort for Felicity Galliard in his report – 'Discovered where your man had gone. Followed him and found him dead.' That report would be carried by Johnny some time down into the civilised places, and cabled to New York, signed with the name of Leithen. But he would not see Felicity's grief, for long before then he would be out of the world.

In the afternoon the weather changed. The heavens darkened and suddenly burst into a lace-work of lightning. It was almost like the aurora, only it covered the whole expanse of sky. From far away there was a kind of muttering, but there were no loud thunder peals. After an hour it ceased and a little cold wind came out of the west. This was followed by a torrential rain, the heaviest Leithen had ever seen, which fell not in sheets but with the solid three dimensions of a cataract. In five minutes the hillside was running with water and the floor of the tent was a bog. In half an hour the brook below was a raving torrent. The downpour ceased and was followed by a burst of sunshine from a pale lemon sky, and a sudden sharpening of the air. Johnny had spoken of this; he had said that the winter would not properly be on them until they had the father and mother of a thunderstorm and the last rains.

Leithen pulled on his gum-bots and went out for a breath of air. The hill was melting under him, and only by walking in the thicker patches of fern and berries could he find decent foothold. Somehow his depression had lifted with the passing of the storm, and in the sharp air his breath came easier. It was arduous work walking in that tangle. 'I had better not go far,' he told himself, 'or I'll never get home. Not much chance for Johnny and the Indians after such a downpour.'

He turned to look back . . . There seemed to be a lumbering body at the door of the tent trying to crawl inside. A bear, no doubt. If the brute got at the food there would be trouble. Leithen started to slither along the hillside, falling often, and feeling his breath run short.

The thing was inside. He had closed the door-flap before leaving, and now he tore it back to let in the light. The beast was there, crouching on its knees on the muddy floor. It was a sick beast, for it seemed to nuzzle the ground and emit feeble groans and gasps of pain. A bear! It's hinder parts were one clot of mud, but something like a ragged blanket seemed to be round its middle. The head! The head looked like black fur, and then he saw that this was a cap and that beneath it was shaggy human hair.

The thing moaned, and then from it came a sound which, though made by dry lips, was articulate speech.

'Frizelle!' it said. 'Oh, Frizelle! . . . pour l'amour de Dieu!'

12

IT took all Leithen's strength to move Galliard from the floor to his bed. He folded a blanket and put it under his head. Then he undid the muffler at his throat and unbuttoned the shirt. The man's lips were blue and sore, and his cheeks were shrunk with hunger and fatigue. He seemed to be in pain, for as he lay on his back he moaned and screwed up his eyes. His wits were dulled in a stupor, and, apart from his first muttered words, he seemed to be unconscious of his environment.

Leithen mixed a little brandy and tinned milk and forced it between his lips. It was swallowed and immediately vomited. So he lit the stove and put on the kettle to boil, fetching water from the nearby spring. The moaning continued as if the man were in pain, and he remembered that Johnny had guessed at a wounded foot. The sight of another mortal suffering seemed to give Leithen a certain access of strength. He found himself able to undo Galliard's boots, and it was no light task, for they were crusted thick with mud. The left one had been sliced open like a gouty man's shoe, to give ease to a wound in his shin, a raw, ragged gash which looked like an axe cut. Before the boot could be removed the moaning had several times changed to a gasp of pain. Leithen made an attempt to wash the wound, and bound it up with a handkerchief, which was all he had in the way of a bandage. That seemed to give Galliard relief, and the moaning ceased.

The kettle was boiling and he made tea. Galliard tried to take the pannikin, but his hands were shaking so that Leithen had to feed him like a child. He swallowed all that he did not spill and seemed to want more. So Leithen tried him again with brandy and milk, the milk this time thinned and heated. Now two brown eyes were staring at him, eyes in which consciousness was slowly dawning. The milk was drunk and Galliard lay for a little blinking at the tent wall. Then his eyes closed and he slept.

Leithen laid himself down on Johnny's mattress and looked at the shapeless heap which had been the object of his quest. There was the tawny beard which he had come to expect, but for the rest – it was unfamiliar wreckage. Little in common had it with the gracious portrait in the Park Avenue hall, or the Nattier, or the Aubusson carpet, or Felicity's rose-and-silver drawing-room. This man had chosen the wilderness, and now the wilderness had taken him and tossed him up like the jetsam of a flood.

There was no satisfaction for Leithen in the fact that he had been successful in his search. By an amazing piece of luck he had found Galliard and in so doing had achieved his purpose. But now the purpose seemed trivial. Was this derelict of so great importance after all? The unaccustomed bending in his handling of Galliard had given him a pain in his back, and the smell of the retched brandy and milk sickened him. He felt a desperate emptiness in his body, in his soul, and in the world.

It was almost dark when Johnny and the Hares returned. Leithen jerked his thumb towards the sleeping Galliard. Johnny nodded.

'I sort of suspicioned he'd be here. We got his tracks, but lost them in the mud. The whole darned hill is a mud-slide.' He spoke slowly and flatly, as if he were very tired.

But his return set the little camp going, and Leithen realised what a blundering amateur he was compared with Johnny and the Indians. In a few minutes a fire was crackling before the tent door. Galliard, still in a coma, was lifted and partly unclothed, and his damaged leg was washed and rebandaged by Johnny with the neatness of a hospital nurse. The tent was tidied up and supper was set cooking – coffee on the stove and caribou steaks on the fire. Johnny concocted a dish of his own for the sick man, for he made a kind of chicken broth from a brace of willow grouse he had shot.

'You'd better eat,' he said. 'We'll feed the soup to that feller when he wakes. Best let him sleep a little longer. How you feelin' yourself? When I come in you looked mighty bad.'

'I found Galliard more than I could manage; but never mind me. What about him?'

Johnny's bat's ears seemed to prick up as he bent over the sleeping figure. He was like a gnome in a fairy-tale; but he was human enough when he turned to Leithen, and the glow of the fire showed his troubled blue eyes.

'He'll come through a' right,' he said. 'He's been a healthy man and he ain't bottomed his strength yet. But he's plumb weary. He can't have fed proper for three days, and I reckon he can't have slept proper for a week.'

'The wound?'

'Nasty cut he's got, and he'll have to watch his self if he don't want to go lame all his days. He can't move for a good spell.'

'How long?'

'Ten days – a fortnight – maybe more.'

Leithen had the appetite of a bird, but Johnny was ordinarily a good trencherman. Tonight, however, he ate little, though he emptied the coffee-pot. His mind was clearly on his brother, but Leithen asked no questions. At last, after half an hour's sucking at his pipe, he spoke.

'I figure that him' – and he nodded towards Galliard – 'and brother Lew has been agreein' about as well as a carcajou and a sick b'ar. Lew'd gotten into a bad mood and this poor soul didn't know what the matter was, and got no answer when he asked questions. But he was bound to hang on to Lew or get lost and perish. Pretty nasty time he's been havin'. Lew's been actin' mighty mean, I'd say. But you can't just blame Lew, for, as I figure it, he don't know what he's doin'. He ain't seein' his pal, he ain't seein' nothin' except the trail he's blazin' and somethin' at the end of it'.

'What's that?'

'The old Sick Heart River.'

'Then he's gone mad?'

'You might say so. And yet Lew for ordinar' is as sane as you, mister, and a darn lot saner than me. He's gotten a vision and he's bound to go after it.'

'What's to be done?'

'Our first job is to get this feller right. That was the reason you come down North, wasn't it? Every man's got to skin his own skunk. But I don't mind tellin' you I'm worried to death about brother Lew.'

The attention of both was suddenly diverted to Galliard, who had woke up, turned on his side, and was looking at them with wide-awake eyes – pained eyes, too, as if he had awakened to suffering. Johnny took the pannikin of soup which had been heating on the stove, and began to feed the sick man, feeding him far more skilfully than Leithen had done, so that little was spilt. The food seemed to revive him and ease his discomfort. He lay back for a little, staring upward, and then he spoke.

His voice was hoarse, little above a croak. Johnny bent over him to catch his words. He shook his head.

'It's French, but Godamighty knows what he means. It don't sound sense to me.'

Leithen dragged himself nearer. The man was repeating some form of words like a litany, repeating it again and again, so that the same phrase kept recurring. To his amazement he recognised it as a quotation from Chateaubriand, which had impressed him long ago and which had stuck to his fly-paper memory.

'*S'il est parmi les anges*,' the voice said, '*comme parmi des hommes, des campagnes habitées et des lieux déserts*.'

There was a pause. Certain phrases followed, '*Solitudes de la terre*,' '*Solitudes célestes*.' Then the first sentence was repeated. Galliard spoke the words in the slurred patois of Quebec, sounding harshly the final consonants.

'He is quoting a French writer who lived a century ago,' Leithen told Johnny. 'It's nonsense. Something about the solitary places of heaven.'

Galliard was speaking again. It was a torrent of *habitant* French and his voice rose to a pitch which was almost a scream. The man was under a sudden terror, and he held out imploring hands which Johnny grasped. The latter could follow the babble better than Leithen, but there was no need of an interpreter, for the pain and fear in the voice told their own tale. Then the fit passed, the eyes closed, and Galliard seemed to be asleep again.

Johnny shook his head. 'Haywire,' he said. 'Daft – and I reckon I know the kind of daftness. He's mortal scared of them woods. You might say the North's gotten on his mind.'

'But it was a craze for the North that dragged him here.'

'Yep, but having gotten here he's scared of it. His mind's screwed right round. It's a queer thing, the North, and you need to watch your step for fear it does you down. This feller was crazy for it till he poked his head a wee bit inside, and now he's scared out of his life, and would give his soul to quit. I've known it happen before. Folks come down here thinking the North's a pretty lady, and find that she can be a cruel, bloody-minded old bitch, and they scurry away from her like jack-rabbits from a forest fire. I've seen them as had had a taste of her ugly side, and ever after the stink of smoke-dried Indian moccasins, and even the smell of burning logs, would turn out their insides . . . I reckon this feller's had a pretty purifyin' taste of it. Ever been lost?'

'Never.'

'Well, it ain't nice, and it tests a man's guts.'

The air sharpened in the night and the little tent with its three occupants was not too stuffy. Galliard never stirred. Johnny had the short sound slumbers of a woodman, waking and rising before dawn; but Leithen slept badly. He had found his man, but he was a lunatic – for the time being. His task now was to piece together the broken wits. It seemed to him a formidable and unwelcome business. Could a dying man minister to a mind diseased? He would have preferred his old job – to go on spending his bodily strength till he had reached the end of it. That would, at any rate, have given him peace to make his soul.

Johnny set the camp stirring and was everywhere at once, like a good housewife. Galliard was washed and fed and his wound dressed. Leithen found that he had more power in his legs, and was able to make a short promenade of the shelf on which the camp stood, breathing air which was chilly as ice and scented with a thousand miles of pines. Johnny and the Hares were busy with measurements.

Leithen, huddled in the lee of the fire, watched the men at work. They were laying out the ground plan of a hut. It was to be built against the hillside, the gravel of which, when cut away, would make its back wall, and it seemed to be about twenty feet square. The Hares did the levelling of the shelf, and presently came the sound of Johnny's axe from the woods. In a couple of hours the four corner posts were cut, trimmed, and set up, and until the midday meal all three were busy felling well-grown spruce and pine.

Johnny's heavy preoccupation lightened a little as they ate.

'We need a hut whatever happens,' he said. 'The feller' – that was how he referred to Galliard – 'will want something snugger than a tent when the cold sets in, for he ain't goin' to get well fast. Then there's you, a mighty sick man. And, please God, there'll be brother Lew.'

'Is there no way of getting back to the Hares' camp?'

'For Lew and me – not for you and the feller. We got to plan to spend the winter here, or hereabouts. We can send the Indians back for stores and dog teams, and maybe we could get out in February when the good snows come. But we got to plan for the winter. I can fix up a tidy hut, and when we get the joints nicely chinked up with mud, and plenty of moss and sods on the roof, we'll be as snug as an old b'ar in its hole. I'm aimin' to fix a proper fireplace inside, for there's the right kind of clay in the creek for puddlin'.'

'Let me help.'

'You can't do nothin' yet, so long as we're on the heavy jobs, but I'll be glad of you when it comes to the inside fixin'. You get into the tent beside the feller and sleep a bit. I'm all right if I wasn't worried about Lew.'

Johnny was attending to the bodily needs of the sick man like a hospital nurse, feeding him gruel and chicken broth and weak tea. Galliard slept most of the time, and even his waking hours were a sort of coma. He was asleep when Leithen entered the tent, and presently, to the accompaniment of Johnny's axe in the woods, Leithen himself drowsed off, for by this time of the day he was very weary. But sleep was for him the thinnest of films over the waking world and presently he was roused by Galliard's voice. This time it sounded familiar, something he had heard before, and not the animal croak of yesterday.

Two dull brown eyes were staring at him, eyes in which there was only the faintest spark of intelligence. They moved over his person, lingering some time at his boots, and then fastened on his face. There was bewilderment in them, but also curiosity. Their owner seemed to struggle for words, and he passed his tongue over his dry lips several times before he spoke.

'You are – what?'

He spoke in English, but his hold on the language seemed to slip away, for when Leithen replied in the same tongue the opaque eyes showed no comprehension.

'I am a friend of your friends,' he said. 'We have come to help you. I have the brother of Lew Frizel with me.'

After a pause he repeated the last sentence in French. Some word in it caught Galliard's attention. His face suddenly became twisted with anxiety, and he tried to raise himself on his bed. Words poured from him, words tumbling over each other, the French of Quebec. He seemed to be imploring someone to wait for him – to let him rest a little and then he would go on – an appeal couched in queer childish language, much of which Leithen could not understand. And always, like the keynote of a threnody, came the word *Rivière* – and *Rivière* again – and once *Rivière du Coeur Malade*.

The partner of Ravelstons had suffered a strange transformation. Leithen realised that it would be idle to try to link this man's memory with his New York life. He had gone back into a very old world, the world of his childhood and his ancestors, and though it might terrify him, it was for the moment his only world.

The babbling continued. As Leithen listened to it the word that seemed to emerge from the confusion was Lew's name. It was on Lew that Galliard's world was now centred. If he was to be brought back to his normal self Lew must be the chief instrument . . . And Lew was mad himself, raving mad, far away in the mountains on a crazy hunt for a mystic river! A sudden sense of the lunatic inconsequence of the whole business came over Leithen and forced from him a bitter laugh. That laugh had an odd effect upon Galliard for it seemed to frighten him into silence. It was if he had got an answer to his appeals, an answer which slammed the door.

13

NEXT day the cold was again extreme, but the sun was out for six hours, and the shelf in the forest was not uncomfortable. Johnny, after sniffing the air, pronounced on the weather. The first snow had fallen; there would be three days of heavy frost; then for maybe ten days there would be a mild, bright spell; then a few weeks before Christmas would come the big snows and the fierce cold. The fine spell would enable him to finish the hut. A little drove of snow-buntings had passed yesterday; that meant, he said, since the birds were late in migrating, that winter would be late.

'You call it the Indian Summer?'

'The Hares call it the White Goose Summer. It ends when the last white goose has started south.'

That day Leithen made an experiment. Galliard was mending well, the wound in the leg was healing, he could eat better, only his mind was still sick. It was important to find out whether the time had come to link his memory up with his recent past, to get him on the first stage on the road back to the sphere to which he belonged.

He chose the afternoon, when his own fatigue compelled him to rest, and Galliard was likely to be wakeful after the bustle of the midday meal. He had reached certain conclusions. Galliard had lost all touch with his recent life. He had reverted to the traditions of his family, and now worshipped at ancestral shrines, and he had been mortally scared by the sight of the goddess. These fears did not impel him to mere flight, for he did not know where to flee to. It drove him to seek a refuge, and that refuge was Lew. He was as much under the spell of Lew as Lew was under the spell of his crazy river. Could this spell be lifted?

So far Galliard had been a mere automaton. He had spoken like a waxwork managed by a ventriloquist. It was hardly possible to recognise a personality in that vacant face, muffled in a shaggy beard, and unlit by the expressionless eyes. Yet the man was regaining his health, his wound was healing fast, his cheeks had lost their famished leanness. As Leithen looked at him he found it hard to refrain from bitterness. He was giving the poor remnants of his strength to the service of a healthy animal with years of vigour before him.

He crushed the thought down and set himself to draw Galliard out of his cave. But the man's wits seemed to be still wandering. Leithen plied him with discreet questions but got an answer to neither French nor English. He refrained from speaking his wife's name, and the names of his American friends, even of Ravelston's itself, woke no response. He tried to link up with Chateau-Gaillard, and Clairefontaine – with Father Paradis – with Uncle Augustin – with the Gaillards, Aristide and Paul Louis, who had died on the Arctic shores. But he might have been shouting at a cenotaph, for the man never answered, nor did any gleam of recognition show in his face. It was only when Leithen spoke again of Lew that there was a flicker of interest; more than a flicker, indeed, for the name seemed to stir some secret fear; the pupils of the opaque eyes narrowed, the lean cheeks twitched, and Galliard whimpered like a lost dog.

Leithen felt wretchedly ill all that day, but after supper, according to the strange fashion of his disease, he had a sudden access of strength. He found that he could think clearly ahead and take stock of the position. Johnny, who was labouring hard all day, should have tumbled into bed after supper and slept the sleep of the just. But it was plain that there was too much on his mind for easy slumber. He sucked at his pipe, kept his eyes on the fire outside the open door, and spoke scarcely a word.

'How is he getting on?' Leithen asked

'Him? The feller? Fine, I guess. He's a mighty tough body, for he ha'n't taken no scaith, barrin' the loss of weight. He'll be a' right.'

'But his mind is gone. He remembers nothing but what happened in the last weeks. A shutter has come down between him and his past life. He's a child again.'

'Aye. I've known it happen. You see he was scared out of his skin by something – it may have been Lew, or it may have been jest loneliness. He's got no sense in him and it's goin' to take quite a time to get it back. That's why I'm fixin' this hut. He wants nursin' and quiet, and a sort of feel that he's safe, and for that you need four walls, even though they're only raw lumber. If you was to take him out in the woods you'd have him plumb ravin' and maybe he'd never get better. I've seen the like before. It don't do to play tricks with them wild places.'

'I don't understand,' said Leithen. 'Lew goes mad and terrifies Galliard and lets him lag behind so that he nearly perishes. Galliard has the horror of the wilds on him, but no horror of Lew. He seems to be crying for him like a child for his nurse.'

'That's so. That's the way it works. The feller don't know that his troubles was all Lew's doin'. He's gotten scared of loneliness in this darned great wild country, and he claws on to anything human. The only human thing near at hand is brother Lew. But that ain't all. If it was all you and me might take Lew's place, for I guess we're human enough. But, as I figure it, Lew has let him in on his Sick Heart daftness, and kind of enthused him about it, and, the feller bein' sick anyhow, it has got possession of his mind. You told me back in Quebec that he'd a notion, which runs in his family, of pushing north, and we seen the two graves at Ghost River.'

'Still I don't understand,' said Leithen. 'He's frightened of the wilds and yet he hankers to get deeper into them, right to a place where nobody's ever been.'

Johnny shook out his pipe.

'He's not thinkin' of the Sick Heart as part of the woods. He's thinkin' of it the same as Lew, as a sort of Noo Jerusalem – the kind of place where everything'll be a' right. He and Lew ain't thinkin' of it with sane minds, and if Lew's there now he won't be lookin' at it with sane eyes. Sick Heart is a mighty good name for it.'

'What sort of place do you think it is?'

'An ordinary creek, I guess. It's hard to get near, and that's maybe why Lew's crazy about it. My father used to have a sayin' that he got out of Scotland, "Far-away hills is always shiny."'

'Then how is Galliard to be cured of this madness?'

'We've got to get Lew back to him – and Lew in his right mind. At least, that's how I figure it. I mind once I was huntin' with the Caribou-Eaters in the Thelon, east of Great Slave Lake. There was an Indian boy – Two-sticks, his name was – and he come under the spell of my Chipewyan hunter, him they called White Partridge. Well, the trip came to an end and we all went home, but next year I heard that Two-sticks had been queer all winter. He wasn't cured until they fetched old White Partridge to him. And that meant a three-hundred-mile trip from Nelson Forks to the Snowdrift River.'

'How can we get Lew back?'

'Godamighty knows! If I was here on my own I'd be on his trail like a timber wolf. Maybe he's sick in body as well as mind. Anyhow, he's alone, and it ain't good to be alone down North, and he's all that's left to me in the family line. But I can't leave here. I took on a job with you and I've got to go through with it. There's the feller, too, to nurse, and he'll want a tidy bit o' nursin'. And there's you, mister. You're a pretty sick man.'

'Go after Lew and fetch him back and I'll stay here.'

Johnny shook his head.

'Nothin' doin'. You can't finish this hut. The Hares are willin' enough, but they've got to be told what to do. And soon there'll be need of huntin' for fresh supplies, for so far we've been livin' mostly on what we back-packed in. And we've got to send out to the Hares' camp for some things. Besides, you ain't used to the woods, and what's easy for me would be one big trouble for you. But most of all you're sick – god-awful sick – a whole lot sicker than the feller. So I say Nothin' doin', though I'm sure obliged to you. We've got to carry on with our job and trust to God to keep an eye on brother Lew.'

Leithen did not reply. There was a stubborn sagacious

dutifulness in that bullet head, that kindly Scots face, and those steadfast blue eyes which was beyond argument.

14

HE spent a restless night, for he felt that the situation was slipping out of his control. He had come here to expend the last remnants of his bodily strength in a task on which his mind could dwell, and so escape the morbidity of passively awaiting death. He had fulfilled part of that task, but he was as yet a long way from success. Galliard's mind had still to be restored to its normal groove. This could only be done – at least so Johnny said – by fetching and restoring to sanity the man who was the key to its vagaries. Johnny could not be spared, so why should he not go himself on Lew's trial, with one of the Hares to help him? It was misery to hang about this camp, feeling his strength ebbing and getting no further on with his job. That would be dying like a rat in a hole. If it had to be, far better to have found a hole among the comforts of home. If he followed Lew, he would at any rate die in his boots, and whether he succeeded or failed, the end would come while he was fighting.

He told Johnny of his decision and at first was derided. He would not last two days; a Hare might be a good enough tracker, but he wanted a white man to guide him, one who was no novice. The road to the Sick Heart was admittedly difficult and could only be traversed, if at all, by a fit man; there might be storms and mountains made impassable. Moreover, what would he say to Lew, to whom he was a stranger? If Lew was found he would for certain resent any intrusion in his lair. This was the point to which Johnny always returned.

'You've heard of mad trappers and the trouble they give the Mounties. If Lew's mad he'll shoot, and he don't miss.'

'I know all that,' said Leithen, 'and I've made my book for it. You must understand that anyhow I am going to die pretty soon. If I hurry on my death a little in an honest way, I won't be the loser. That's how I look at it. If I never get to Lew, and perish on the road, why, that's that. If I find Lew and his gun finds me, well, that's that. There is just the odd chance that I may persuade him to be reasonable and bring him back here, and that is a chance I'm bound to take. Don't you worry about me, for I tell you I'm taking the easiest way. Since I've got to die, I want to die standing.'

Johnny held out his hand. 'You got me beat, mister. Lew

and myself ain't reckoned timid folk, but for real sand there's not your like on this darned continent.'

15

LEITHEN found the ascent of the first ridge from the valley bottom a stern business, for Lew had not zigzagged for ease, but had cut his blazes in the straight line of a crow's flight. But once at the top the road led westerly along a crest, the trees thinned out, and he had a prospect over an immense shining world.

The taller of the Hares, the one he called Big Klaus, was his companion. He himself travelled light, carrying little except a blanket and extra clothing, but the Indian had a monstrous pack which seemed in no way to incommode him. He had the light tent (the hut being now far enough advanced to move Galliard into it), a rifle and shot-gun, axes, billy-can, kamiks to replace moccasins, and two pairs of snow-shoes. The last were of a type new to Leithen – not the round 'bear-paws' of eastern Canada made for the deep snow of the woods, but long, narrow things, very light, constructed of two separate rods joined by a toe-piece, and raised in front at a sharp angle. The centres were of coarse babiche with a large mesh, so as to pick up the least amount of snow, and since the meshing entered the frame by holes and was not whipped round it, the wooden surface was as smooth as skis. On such shoes, Johnny said, an active man could travel forty miles in a day.

Once the ridge had been gained, Leithen found that his breath came a little more easily. He seemed to have entered a world where the purity of the air was a positive thing, not the mere absence of impure matter, but the quintessence of all that was vital in Nature. The Indian Summer forecast by Johnny had begun. There was a shuddering undercurrent of cold, but the sun shone, and though it gave light rather than warmth, it took much of the bleakness out of the landscape. Also there was no wind. The huge amphitheatre, from the icy summit of the central peak to the gullies deep-cut in the black volcanic rock, was as quiet as a summer millpond. Yet there was nothing kindly in this peace; it seemed unnatural, as if the place were destined for strife. On the scarps the little spruces were bent and ragged with the winds, and the many bald patches were bleached by storms. This cold, raw hill-top world was not made for peace; its temporary gentleness was a trap to lure the unwary into its toils.

It was not difficult to follow Lew's blazes, and in a little swamp they found his tracks. He must be a bigger man than Johnny, Leithen thought, or else heavily laden, for the footprints went deep.

The Hare plodded steadily on with his queer in-toed stride. He could talk some English, and would answer questions, but he never opened a conversation. He was a merciful man, and kept turning in his tracks to look at Leithen, and when he thought he seemed weary, promptly dropped his pack and squatted on the ground. His methods of cooking and camping were not Johnny's, but in their way they were efficient. At the midday and evening meals he had a fire going at miraculous speed with his flint and steel and punk-box, and he could make a good bed even of comfortless spruce boughs. His weapon was a cheap breech-loader obtained from some trader, and with it he managed to shoot an occasional partridge or ptarmigan, so that Leithen had his bowl of soup. The second night out he made a kind of Dutch oven and roasted a porcupine, after parboiling it, and he cooked ash-cakes which were nearly as palatable as the pease-meal bannocks which Leithen had eaten in his youth.

That second night he talked. It had been a melancholy summer, for it had been foretold that many of the Hare people would presently die, and the whole tribe had fasted and prepared for their end. The manner of death had not been predicted – it might be famine, or disaster, or a stupendous storm. They had been scolded for this notion by Father Duplessis at Fort Bannerman and by Father Wentzel at the mountain camp, and before the end of the summer the spirits of the tribe had risen, and most believed that the danger had passed. But not all; some wise men thought that bad trouble was coming in the winter.

'It is not good to wait too long on death,' said Big Klaus. 'Better that it should come suddenly when it is not expected.' He looked reflectively at Leithen as if he knew that here was one who was in the same case as the Hares.

For three days they followed the network of ridges according to Lew's blazing. They seemed rarely to lose elevation, for they passed gullies and glens by the scarps at their head waters. But nevertheless they had been steadily descending, for the great rift where the Sick Heart was believed to flow was no longer in the prospect, and the hanging glaciers, the ice couloirs and arêtes, and the poised avalanches of the central peak now overhung and dominated the landscape.

It was a strange world through which Leithen stumbled, conserving his strength greedily and doling it out like a miser. There was sun, light, no great cold, no wind; but with all these things there was no kindness. Something had gone out of the air and that something was hope. Night was closing down, a long night from which there would be a slow awakening. Scarcely a bird could be seen, and there were no small innocent frightened beasts to scurry into hiding. Everything that could move had gone to sanctuary against the coming wrath. The tattered pines, the bald, blanched pastures, were no more a home for life than the pinnacles of intense ice that glittered in mid-heaven. Dawn came punctually, and noon, and nightfall, and yet the feeling was of a perpetual twilight.

In these last weeks Leithen's memory seemed to have become a closed book. He never thought of his past, and no pictures from it came to cheer or torture him. He might have been like the Hare, knowing no other world than this of laborious days and leaden nights. A new discomfort scarcely added to his misery, and food and fine weather did not lighten it. Every hour he was looking at marvels of natural beauty and magnificence, but they did not affect him. Life now awoke no response in him, and he remembered that some wise man had thus defined death. The thought gave him a queer comfort. He was already dead; there only remained the simple snapping of the physical cord.

16

THEY came on it suddenly in the afternoon of the third day. The scraggy forest of jack-pines, which seemed to stretch to the very edge of the snows, suddenly gave place to empty air, and Leithen found himself staring breathlessly not up, but down – down into a chasm nearly a mile wide and two thousand feet deep. From his feet the ground fell away in screes to a horizontal rib of black rock, below which, in a blue mist very far down, were the links of a river. Beyond it were meadows and woods, and the woods were not of scrub pine, but of tall timber – from one or two trees in scattered clumps he judged them to be a hundred feet high. Beyond them again the opposite wall rose sheer to fantastic aiguilles of dark rock.

He was looking at some mighty volcanic rift which made a moat to the impregnable castle of the snows.

The strength seemed to go from his limbs, and he collapsed among the crowberries and pine cones. He fumbled in a pocket to find his single Zeiss glass, but gave up the search when he realised the weakness of his hands. This sudden vision had drained the power from his body by intense quickening of his senses and mind. It seemed to him that he was looking at the most marvellous spectacle ever vouchsafed to man. The elements were commonplace – stone and wood, water and earth – but so had been the pigments of a Raphael. The celestial Demiurge had combined them into a masterpiece.

He lay full in the pale sun and the air was mild and mellow. As his eyes thirstily drank in the detail he saw that there was little colour in the scene. Nearly all was subfusc, monochrome, and yet so exquisite was the modelling that there was nothing bleak in it; the impression rather was of a chaste, docile luxuriance. The valley bottom, so far as he could see it, seemed to be as orderly as a garden. The Sick Heart was like a Highland salmon river, looping itself among pools and streams with wide beaches of pebbles, beaches not black like the enclosing cliffs, but shining white. Along its course, and between the woods were meadows of wild hay, now a pale russet against the ripple of the stream and the evergreen of the trees . . . Something from his past awoke in Leithen. He was far up in the Arctic north; winter had begun, and even in this false summer the undercurrent of cold was stinging his fingers through his mitts. But it was not loneliness or savagery that was the keynote of this valley. Pastoral breathed from it; it was comforting and habitable. He could picture it in its summer pride, a symphony of mild airs and singing waters. Stripped and blanched as it was, it had a preposterous suggestion of green meadows and Herrick and sheep.

'We'll camp here,' he told Big Klaus. 'There's nothing to show us the road down. It'll take some finding.'

He found the Zeiss glass at last and tried to make out further details. There must be hot springs, he thought, natural in a volcanic country; that would explain the richness of the herbage. The place, too, was cunningly sheltered from the prevailing winds, and probably most of the river that he could see never froze. That would mean wildfowl and fish, even in the depths of winter . . . He pocketed his glass, for he did not want to learn more. He was content with what he saw. No wonder the valley had cast its spell on the old Indian chief and on Lew Frizel. It was one of those sacred places on which Nature had so lavished her art that it had the magic of a shrine.

Big Klaus made camp in a little half-moon of shingle on the verge of the cliffs, with trees to shelter it on north and east. He built an enormous fire on a basis of split wood, piled like a little wigwam, and felled two spruces so that they met in the centre of the heap, and as their ends burned away would slip further down and keep alight without tending until morning.

'It will be very cold,' said the Hare, sniffing towards the north like a pointer dog.

Leithen ate little at supper, for his mind was in a fever. He had won a kind of success as he was nearing the brink of death, for he had found something which other men had longed to find and about which the world knew nothing. Some day there would be books of travel and guide-books, and inevitably it would be written that among the discoverers of the secret valley was one Edward Leithen, who had once been His Majesty's Attorney-General in England, and who had died soon afterwards . . . This unexpected feat obscured the fact that he had also found Galliard, for, setting out on one task he had incidentally accomplished a greater, like Saul the son of Kish who, seeking his father's asses, stumbled upon a kingdom.

The big fire roared and crackled at the mouth of the little tent, and beyond it was a blue immensity, sapphire in the mid-heaven, but of a milky turquoise above the mountains where the moon was rising.

He fell asleep early, and awoke after midnight to a changing world. The fire had sunk, but it was still fierce around the point where the spruce trunks intersected. The moon had set and the sky was hung with stars and planets – not inlaid, but hung, for the globes of sheet light were patently suspended in the heavens, and it seemed as if the eye could see behind them into aboriginal darkness. The air had suddenly become bitterly cold, cold almost beyond bearing. The shudder which had for some days lurked behind the sunlight had sharpened to an icy rigour. Frost like a black concrete was settling over everything, gumming the eyes and lips together. He buried his head under his blankets but could not get warm again . . .

Some time towards dawn he fell into an uneasy sleep. When

he awoke Big Klaus was tending the fire, white as an icicle and bent double against the fury of the north-west wind. Snow was drifting in flakes like pigeons' eggs. With a bound winter had come up on them.

Movement was impossible, and the two men lay all day in the tent, Leithen half in a stupor, for the sudden onrush of cold seemed to have drained the remnants of his strength. With the snow the first rigour abated, and presently the wind sank, and the smoke of the fire no longer choked the tent. The Hare split wood and rose every hour or so to tend the fire; for the rest he dozed, but he had a clock in his brain and he was never behindhand in his stoking. There was no fresh meat, so he cooked bacon and camp biscuit for luncheon, and for supper made a wonderful stew of tinned bully-beef and beans.

At twilight the snow ceased, and with the dark the cold deepened. The silence deepened, too, except for trees cracking in the fierce stricture of the frost. Leithen had regained some vitality during the day, enough to let him plan ahead. It was his business to get down into the valley where, beyond question, Lew had preceded him. It would be hard to find Lew's route, for there were no trees to blaze, and the weather of the past week would have obliterated his trail. To a mountaineer's eye it seemed an ugly place to descend, for the rock did not fissure well into foot-holds and hand-grips. But the snow might solve the problem. The wind from the north-west had plastered it against the eastern side of the valley, the side on which they had made camp. It must have filled the couloirs and made it possible to get down by step-cutting or glissade. He had only two fears – whether his body was not too feeble, and whether the Hare was sufficient of a mountaineer for the attempt.

Morning brought no fresh snow, and the extreme cold seemed to slacken. Leithen thought that it could not be more than ten degrees below zero. Having an immediate practical task before him, he found himself possessed of a certain energy. He ate his meagre breakfast almost with relish, and immediately after was on his feet. There must be no delay in getting down into the valley.

With Big Klaus he explored the rim of the cliffs, following the valley downward, as he was certain Lew had done. Mercifully it was easy going, for with the trees withdrawn from the scarp there was no tangle of undergrowth, and what normally might have been loose screes was now firm snow.

For a little the cliffs overhung or fell sheer. Then came fissures by which, in open weather, a trained mountaineer might have descended, but which now were ice-choked and impossible. Leithen had walked more than a mile and come very near the limit of his strength before he found what he sought. The rocks fell back into a V-shaped bay, and down the bay to the valley floor swept a great wave of snow, narrow at the top and spreading out fanwise beneath. The angle was not more than thirty or thirty-five degrees. This must have been Lew's route, and no doubt he had had to face awkward rock falls and overhangs which now were obliterated in one great smooth white swirl. Leithen got out his glass and searched the lower slopes. No, there seemed to be no snags there; a good skier would tackle the descent without a thought.

'We must shift our stuff here,' he told the Hare. 'But first make a fire or I will freeze.'

He cowered beside the blaze until Big Klaus had brought up the camp baggage. They cooked the midday meal, and then ransacked the stores. There was rope, but not enough of it. First they must pack their kit so that it would be kept together in the descent, for Leithen knew what a sepulchre snowdrifts could be for a man's belongings. Then he would have liked another hundred feet of rope for the Hare and himself. He meant to go down slowly and carefully, feeling his way and humouring his wretched body.

The baggage took up every inch of rope. Leithen had the gun and rifle lashed on his own back, and the rest made up a huge bundle which was attached to Big Klaus and himself by short lengths of cord. It was the best he could do, but it was an unwieldy contraption, and he prayed that there might be no boulders or pockets in the imperfectly seen lower reaches, for it would be impossible to steer a course. The Hare was sent into the wood to cut two long poles. He did not seem to realise the purpose until he returned and Leithen explained what must be done.

'The snow is firm enough,' he said. 'It will give good foot-holds. One step at a time, remember, and we must never move together. I stand still when you move. For God's sake keep your balance. If you slip, turn on your face and dig in your hands and feet. Don't let the kit pull you out of your steps. You understand?'

He repeated the instructions several times, but Big Klaus

stared at him dully. When at last he realised that it was proposed to descend the shoot, he shook his head violently. He patted his stomach and made the motions of one about to be sick. Twice he went to the edge and peered down, and each time there was something like panic in his heavy eyes.

'Come on! There's no time to be lost. Even if we roll all the way it won't kill us.'

Leithen took two steps down, leaning inward as he moved. 'Come on, you fool!'

The Hare put out a foot, like a timid bather in cold water. He was a brave man, for, though he was mortally afraid, he kept his eyes away from the void and imitated Leithen in hugging the slope.

At first all went well. The grade was steeper than had appeared above, but not much, and, though the baggage wobbled and swayed, they managed to keep their balance.

They had emerged from the throat of the couloir, and were out on the fan of the lower and easier slopes when disaster overtook them. The Hare miscalculated a foot-hold at a place where there was glazed ice on the snow, and shot downward on his back. He, and the weight of the baggage, plucked Leithen from his stance, and the next second the whole outfit had started a mad glissade. The rope round Leithen's middle choked the breath out of him. He cannoned into the baggage and ricochetted off; he cannoned into Big Klaus; his mouth and eyes were choked with snow; some rib of rock or ice caught his thigh and hurt him . . . Once, climbing at Courmayeur alone, he had slipped on a snowfield and been whirled to what he believed to be his end in a *bergschrund* (which happened to be nearly full of snow into which he had dropped comfortably). Now once again, before his senses left him, he had the same certainty of death and the same apathy . . .

17

HE recovered consciousness to find the Hare attempting a kind of rough massage of his chest. For a minute or two he lay comatose, breathing heavily, but not suffering pain except for his bruised thigh. Slowly, with immense difficulty, he tested his body for damage. There seemed to be little – no concussion – the bruise – the breath knocked out of him but returning under the Hare's ministrations. It was not until he tried to get to his feet that he realised how much the glissade had taken toll of his strength.

The valley bottom was like a new creation, for the whole flavour of the landscape was changed. It was no longer the roof of the world where the mind and eye were inured to far horizons, but a place enclosed, muffled, defended by great rock bastions from the bleak upper air. Against the eastern wall the snow lay piled in big drifts, but there was no snow on the western side and very little in the intervening meadows. In these same meadows there was what looked like frozen pools, but the rigour of the frost had not touched the whole river, for below one of the patches of forest there was a gleam of running water. There was not a breath of wind, the slanting sunlight gilded the russet grasses and snow patches, the air was unbelievably mild. Here in this fantastic sanctuary was nothing of North America. Apart from the sheer containing walls, the scene might have been a Northumbrian pasture in an English December.

But all the pith had gone out of him. It seemed as if the strain of the descent had damaged some nerve control, for his weakness was worse than pain. He struggled to his feet and clutched at the Hare to keep himself from falling. The latter had got the baggage straightened out and was restrapping the guns. He nodded down the valley—

'He has gone that way,' he said. But how he had guessed Lew's route he did not tell, nor did the other inquire.

For to Leithen it looked as if in this strange place he had got very near his journey's end. He toiled in the wake of the Hare for something less than a mile, counting each step, utterly oblivious of anything but the dun herbage under foot. He tried to step in the Indian's prints, but found them too long for his enfeebled legs. He who had once had the stride of a mountaineer now teetered like an affected woman. He made little bets with himself – how many steps until he fell? – would Big Klaus turn back, see his distress, and stop of his own accord? . . . The latter guess was right. The Indian, turning, saw a face like death, and promptly flung down his pack and announced that he would make camp.

There was a patch of gravel where the stream made a sharp bend, and there, in the lee of a tall coppice, a fire was lit. The Hare had to loosen the light pack from Leithen's shoulders, for he had lost all muscular power. His fingers seemed to bend back on him if he tried to lift a blanket. Also his breath was so troublesome that in that open place he panted like a man suffocating in a hole. The fit passed and by the time the tent was up and the beds laid his main trouble was his desperate weakness. Big Klaus fed him for supper with gruel and strong tea, but he was able to swallow little. His throat was as impotent as his hands and legs.

But his mind was no longer wholly apathetic, for he had stumbled on a queer corner of recollection. He had been conscious of the apathy of his memory, for, had he been able to choose, he would have been glad in those evil days to 'count his mercies,' to remember with a wry satisfaction the many pleasant things in his life. No present misery could kill his gratitude for past joys. But the past had remained a closed book to him, and he had had no thoughts except for the moment.

Now suddenly, with blinding clearness, he saw a picture. Outside his bedroom door in a passage on the upper floor of the old Scots country house of his boyhood, there had hung a print. It was a Munich photogravure called *Die Toten-Insel*, and showed an island of tall cliffs, and within their angle a grove of cypresses, while a barge full of bent and shrouded figures approached this home of the dead. The place was Sick Heart Valley – the same sheer cliffs, the same dark, evergreen trees; the Hare and he, bowed and muffled figures, were approaching the graveyard . . . As a boy he had been puzzled by the thing, but had rather liked it. As he dashed out on a spring morning its sombreness had pleased him by its contrast with his own sunlit world . . . Now, though he saw the picture of those April days, he could not recapture the faintest flavour of that spring rapture. He saw only the dark photogravure on the distempered passage wall, and his interest was faintly touched by its likeness to his present environment . . . Surely he was already dead, for he had ceased to react to life!

Through the open tent door he could see the northern heavens ablaze with the aurora. The frost was closing down again, for the Dancers seemed to give out a crackling sound as if the sky were the back-cloth of a stage with the painted canvas strained to cracking-point. The spectacle did not stir his apathy. This blanched world was rioting in colour, but it was still blanched and bleached, the enemy of all life.

As he lay wakeful, scarcely conscious of the dull pain in his chest or of the spasms in his breathing, but desperately aware of his weakness, he felt the shadow of eternity deepening over him. Like Job, the last calamities had come on him. Thank Heaven he was free from loquacious friends. Like Job he bowed his head and had no impulse to rebel. The majesty of God filled his universe. He was coming face to face with his religion.

He had always been in his own way a religious man. Brought up under the Calvinistic shadow, he had accepted a simple evangel which, as he grew older, had mellowed and broadened. At Oxford he had rationalised it in his philosophical studies, but he had never troubled to make it a self-sufficing logical creed. Certain facts were the buttresses of his faith, and the chief of them was the omnipotence and omnipresence of God. He had always detested the glib little humanism of most of his contemporaries.

But his creed had remained something aloof from his life. He had no communion with the omnipotent God and no craving for it. It rarely impinged on his daily experience. When things went well he felt a dim gratitude to Omnipotence; when badly, it was a comfort to tell himself that it was God's will and to take misfortune cheerfully. In the War it had been different. Then he felt a relation so close as to be almost communion – that he was not only under God's ultimate command, but under His direct care. That was why his nerves had been so steady. It was foolish to worry about what was pre-ordained.

Then had come long years of spiritual sloth. The world had been too much with him. But certain habits had continued. Still in his heart he had praised God for the pleasures of life, and had taken disappointments with meekness, as part of a divine plan. Always, when he reflected, he had been conscious of being a puppet in almighty hands. So he had never been much cast down or much puffed up. He had passed as a modest man – a pose, some said; a congenital habit, said others. His friends had told him that if he had only pushed himself he might have been Prime Minister. Foolish! These things were ordained.

Now his castles had been tumbled down. Pleasant things they had been, even if made of paste-board; in his heart he had always known that they were paste-board. Here was no continuing city. God had seen fit to change the sunlight for a very dark shadow. Well, under the shadow he must not quail but keep his head high, not in revolt or in defiance, but because He, who had made him in His image, expected such courage. 'Though Thou slay me, yet will I trust in Thee.'

There was no shade of grievance in Leithen's mind, still less self-pity. There was almost a grim kind of gratitude. He was now alone with God. In these bleak immensities the world of man had fallen away to an infinite distance, and the chill of eternity was already on him. He had no views about an after-life. That was for God's providence to decree. He was an atom in infinite space, the humblest of slaves waiting on the command of an august master.

He remembered a phrase of Cromwell's about putting his mouth in the dust. That was his mood now, for he felt above everything his abjectness. In his old bustling world there were the works of man's hands all around to give a false impression of man's power. But here the hand of God had blotted out life for millions of miles and made a great tract of the inconsiderable ball which was the earth, like the infinite interstellar spaces which had never heard of man.

18

HE woke to a cold which seemed to sear that part of his face which the blanket left exposed. There was a great rosy light all about the tent which the frost particles turned into a sparkling mist.

The Hare stood above him.

'There is a man,' he said, 'beyond the river under the rocks. I have seen a smoke.'

The news gave Leithen the extra incentive that made it possible for him to rise. He hung on to the Hare's shoulder, and it was in that posture that he drank some strong tea and swallowed a mouthful of biscuit. The smoke, he was told, was perhaps a mile distant in a nook of the cliffs. The long pool of the river was frozen hard, and beyond it was open ground.

Leithen's strength seemed suddenly to wax. A fever had taken him, a fever to be up and doing, to finish off his business once for all. His weakness was almost a physical anguish, and there was a horrid background of nausea . . . But what did it all matter? He was very near his journey's end. One way or another in a few hours he would be quit of his misery.

The Hare guided him – indeed, half carried him – over the frozen hummocks of the pool. Beyond was a slight rise, and from that a thin spire of smoke could be seen in an angle of the cliffs. In the shelter of the rise Leithen halted.

'You must stay here,' he told the Indian, 'and see what happens to me. If I am killed you will go back to where we came from and tell my friend what has happened. He may want to come here, and in that case you will show him the road. If I do not die now you will make camp for yourself a little way off and at dawn tomorrow you will come where the smoke is. If I am alive you may help me. If I am dead you must return to my friend. Do you understand?'

The Hare shook his head. The orders seemed to be unacceptable, and Leithen had to repeat them again before he nodded in acquiescence.

'Good-bye,' he said. 'God bless you for an honest man.'

The turf was frozen hard, but it was as level as a croquet lawn and made easy walking. All Leithen's attention was concentrated on his crazy legs. They wobbled and shambled and sprawled, and each step was a separate movement which had to be artfully engineered. He took to counting them – ten, twenty, thirty, one hundred. He seemed to have made no progress. Two hundred, three hundred – here he had to scramble in and out of a small watercourse – four hundred, five hundred.

A cry made him lift his eyes, and he saw a man perhaps two hundred yards distant.

The man was shouting, but he could not hear what he said. A horrid nausea was beginning to afflict him – the overpowering sickness which comes to men who reach the extreme limits of their strength. Then there was a sound which was not the human voice, and something sang not far from his left shoulder. He had taken perhaps six further steps when the same something passed somewhere on his right.

His dulled brain told him the meaning of it. 'He must be bracketing,' he said to himself. 'The third shot will get me in the heart or the head, and then all will be over.' He found himself longing for it as a sick man longs for the morning. But it did not come. Instead came the nausea and the extremity of weakness. The world swam in a black mist, and strength fled from his limbs, like air from a slit bladder.

19

WHEN Leithen's weakness overpowered him he might lose consciousness, but when he regained it there was no half-way house of dim perception to return to. He alternated between a prospect of acid clarity and no prospect at all . . . Now he took in every detail of the scene, though he was puzzled at first to interpret them.

At first he thought that it was night and that he was lying out of doors, for he seemed to be looking up to a dark sky. Then a splash of light on his left side caught his attention, and he saw that it outlined some kind of ceiling. But it was a ceiling which lacked at least one supporting wall, for there was a great blue vagueness pricked out with points of light, and ruddy in the centre with what looked like flames. It took him some time to piece together the puzzle . . . He was in a cave, and towards the left he was looking to the open where a big fire was burning . . . There was another light, another fire it seemed. This was directly in front of him, but he could not see the flames, only the glow on floor and roof, so that it must be burning beyond a projecting rib of rock. There must be a natural flue there, he thought, an opening in the roof, for there was no smoke to make his eyes smart.

He was lying on a pile of spruce boughs covered with a Hudson's Bay blanket. There was a bitter taste on his lips as he passed his tongue over them – brandy or whisky it seemed; anyhow some kind of spirit. Somebody, too, had been attending to him, for the collar of his dicky had been loosened, and he was wearing an extra sweater which was not his own. Also his moccasins had been removed and his feet rolled snugly in a fold of the blanket . . .

Presently a man came into the light of the inner fire. The sight of him awoke Leithen to memory of the past days. This could only be Lew Frizel, whom he had come to find – a man who had gone mad, according to his brother's view, for he had left Galliard to perish; one who a few hours back had beyond doubt shot at himself. Then he had marched forward without a tremor, expecting a third bullet to find his heart, for it would have been a joyful release. Now, freed from the extreme misery of weakness, he found himself nervous about this brother of Johnny's – why, he did not know, for his own fate was beyond caring about. Lew's madness, whatever it was, could not be wholly malevolent, for he had taken some pains to make comfortable the man he had shot at. Besides, he was the key to Galliard's sanity, and Galliard was the purpose of his quest.

He was a far bigger man than Johnny, not less, it appeared, than six feet two; a lean man, and made leaner by his dress, which was deer skin breeches, a tanned caribou shirt worn above a jersey, and a lumberman's laced boots. His hair, as flaxen as a girl's, had been self-cut into a bunch and left a ridiculous fringe on his forehead. It was only the figure he saw, a figure apparently of immense power and activity, for every movement was like the releasing of a spring.

The man glanced towards him and saw that he was awake. He lit a lantern with a splinter from the fire, and came forward so that Leithen could see his face. Plainly he was Johnny's brother, for there was the same shape of head and the same bat's ears. But his eyes were a world apart. Johnny's were honest, featureless pools of that indistinct colour which is commonly called blue or grey, but Lew's were as brilliant as jewels, pale, but with the pallor of intense delicate colour, the hue of a turquoise, but clear as a sapphire, and with an adamantine brilliance. They were masterful, compelling eyes, wild, but to Leithen not mad – at least it was the madness of a poet and not of a maniac.

He bent his big shoulders and peered into Leithen's face. There was nothing of the Indian in him, except the round head and the bat's ears. The man was more Viking, with his great high-bridged nose, his straight, bushy eyebrows, his long upper lip, and his iron chin. He was clean-shaven, too, unlike his brother, who was as shaggy as a bear. The eyes devoured Leithen, puzzled, in a way contemptuous, but not hostile.

'Who are you? Where do you come from?'

The voice was the next surprise. It was of exceptional beauty, soft, rich, and musical, and the accent was not Johnny's *lingua-franca* of all North America. It was a gentle, soothing Scots, like the speech of a Border shepherd.

'I came with Johnny – your brother. He's in camp three days' journey back. We've found Galliard, the man who was with you. He was pretty sick and wanted nursing.'

'Galliard!' The man rubbed his eyes. 'I lost him – he lost himself. Come to think of it, he wasn't much of a pal. Too darned slow. I had to hurry on.'

He lowered his blazing splinter and scanned Leithen's thin face and hollow eyes and temples. He looked at the almost transparent wrist. He lifted the blanket and put his head close to his chest so that he could hear his breathing.

'What brought you here?' he asked fiercely. 'You haven't got no right here.'

'I came to find you. Galliard needs you. And Johnny.'

'You took a big risk.'

'I'm a dying man, so risk doesn't matter.'

'You're over Jordan now. The Sick Heart is where you come to when you're at the end of your road . . . I had a notion it was the River of the Water of Life, same as in *Revelation*.'

The man's eyes seemed to have lost their glitter and become pools of melancholy.

'Well, it ain't. It's the River of the Water of Death. The Indians know that and they only come here to die. Some, at least; but it isn't many that gets here, it being a damn rough road.'

He took Leithen's hand in his gigantic paw.

'You're sick. Terrible sick. You've got what the Hares call *tfitsiki* and white folk T.B. We don't suffer from it anything to signify, but it's terrible bad among the Indians. It's poor feeding with them; but that's not what's hunting you. Where d'you come from? Edmonton way, or New York like the man Galliard?'

'I come from England. I'm Scots, same as you.'

'That's mighty queer. You've come down north to look for Galliard? He's a sick man, too, sick in his mind, but he'll cure. You're another matter. You've a long hill to climb and I doubt if you'll win to the top of it.'

'I know. I'm dying. I made my book for that before I left England.'

'And you're facing up to it! There's guts left in the old land. What's your name? Leithen! That's south country. We Frizels come from the north.'

'I've seen Johnny's ring with the Fraser arms.'

'What's brother John thinking about me?'

'He's badly scared. He had to stay to attend to Galliard, and it's partly to ease his mind that I pushed on here.'

'I guess his mind wanted some easing. Johnny's thinking about mad trappers. Well, maybe he's right. I was as mad as a loon until this morning . . . I've been looking for the Sick Heart River since I was a halfling, and Galliard come along and gave me my chance at last. God knows what *he* was looking for, but he fell in with me all right, and I treated him mighty selfish. I was mad and I don't mind telling you. That's the way the

Sick Heart takes people. I thought when I found it I'd find a New Jerusalem with all my sins washed away, and the angels waiting for me . . . Then you come along. I shot at you, not to kill, but to halt you – when I shoot to kill I reckon I don't miss. And you came on quite regardless, and that shook me. Here, I says, is someone set on the Sick Heart, and he's going to get there. And then you tumbled down in a heap, and I reckoned you were going to die anyway.'

Lew was speaking more quietly and the light had gone from his eyes.

'Something sort of clicked inside my head,' he went on, 'and I began to look differently at things. The sight of you cleared my mind. One thing I know – this is the River of the Water of Death. You can't live in this valley. There's no life here. Not a bird or beast, not a squirrel in the woods, not a rabbit in the grass, let alone bear or deer.'

'There are warm springs,' Leithen said. 'There must be duck there.'

'Devil a duck! I looked to find the sedges full of them, geese and ducks that the Eskimos and Indians had hurt and that couldn't move south. Devil a feather! And devil a fish in the river! When God made this place He wasn't figuring on humans taking up lots in it . . . I got a little provender, but if you and I don't shift we'll be dead in a week.'

'What have you got?'

'A hindquarter of caribou – lean, stringy meat – a couple of bags of flour – maybe five pounds of tea.'

'There's an Indian with me,' said Leithen. 'He's gone to earth a mile or so back. I told him to wait to see what happened to me. He'll be hanging about tomorrow morning, and he's got some food.'

Lew rapped out a dozen questions, directed to identifying the Hare. Finally he settled who he was and gave him a name.

'What's he got?' he demanded.

'Flour and oatmeal and bacon and tea, and some stuff in tins. Enough for a week or so.'

'That's no good,' said Lew bitterly. 'We've got to winter here or perish. Man, d'you not see we're in a trap? Nothing that hasn't wings could get out of this valley.'

'How did you get in?'

Lew smiled grimly. 'God knows! I was mad, as I told you. I found a kind of crack in the rocks and crawled down it like a squirrel, helping myself with tree roots and creepers. The snow hadn't come yet. I fell the last forty feet, but by God's mercy it was into a clump of scrub cedar. I lost nothing except half my kit and the skin of my face. But now the snow is here and that door is shut.'

'The Hare and I came down by the snow, and it's the snow that's going to help us out again.'

Lew looked at him with unbelief in his eyes.

'You're a sick man – sick in the head, too. Likewise you're tireder than a flightin' woodcock. You've got to sleep. I'm goin' to shift your bed further out. Frost won't be bad tonight, and you want the air round you. See, I'll give you another blanket.'

Leithen saw that Lew was robbing his own bed, but he was too feeble to protest. He dropped straight away into the fathomless depths of exhausted sleep.

When he woke, with rime on his blankets and sunlight in his eyes, he saw that the Hare had been retrieved and was now attending to the breakfast fire. For a little he lay motionless, puzzling over what had happened to him. As always now at the start of a day, he felt wretchedly ill, and this morning had been no exception. But his eyes were seeing things differently . . . Hitherto the world had seemed to him an etching without colour, a flat two-dimensioned thing which stirred no feeling in his mind of either repulsion or liking. He had ceased to respond to life. A landscape was a map to him which his mind grasped, but which left his interest untouched . . .

Now he suddenly saw the valley of the Sick Heart as a marvellous thing. This gash in the earth, full of cold, pure sunlight, was a secret devised by the great Artificer and revealed to him and to him only. There was no place for life in it – there could not be – but neither was there room for death. This peace was beyond living and dying. He had a sudden vision of it under a summer sun – green lawns, green forests, a blue singing stream, and cliffs of serrated darkness. A classic loveliness, Tempe, Phaeacic. But no bird wing or bird song, no ripple of fish, no beast in the thicket – a silence rather of the world as God first created it, before He permitted the coarse welter of life.

Lew boiled water, gave Leithen his breakfast, and helped him to wash and dress.

'You lie there in the sun,' he said. 'It's good for you. And listen to what I've got to say. How you feeling?'

'Pretty bad.'

Lew shook his head. 'But I've seen a sicker man get better.'

'I've had the best advice in the world, so I don't delude myself. I haven't got the shadow of a chance.'

Lew strode up and down before the cave like a sentry.

'You haven't a chance down here, living in a stuffy hole and eating the sweepings of a store. You want strong air, it don't matter how cold, and you want fresh-killed meat cooked rare. I've seen that work miracles with your complaint. But God help you! there's no hope for you here. You're in your grave already – and so are all of us. The Hare knows. He's squatting down by the water and starting on the dirges of his tribe.'

Then he took himself off, apparently on some futile foraging errand, and Leithen, half in the sun, half in the glow of the fire, felt his weakness changing to an apathy which was almost ease. This was the place to die in – to slip quietly away with no last convulsive attempt to live. He had reacted for a moment to life, but only to the afterglow of it. The thought of further effort frightened him, for there could be no misery like the struggle against such weakness as his. It looked as if the fates which had given him so much, and had also robbed him so harshly, had relented and would permit a quiet end. Whitman's phrase was like a sweetmeat on his tongue: 'the delicious nearby assurance of death.'

Lew and the Indian spent a day of furious activity. They cut huge quantities of wood and kept both fires blazing. Fire-tending seemed to give Lew some comfort, as if it spelled life in a dead place. He wandered round the outer fire like a gigantic pixie, then, as the evening drew on, he carried Leithen into the cave, and, having arranged a couch for him, stood over him like an angry schoolmaster.

'D'you believe in God?' he demanded.

'I believe in God.'

'I was brought up that way too. My father was bed-rock Presbyterian, and I took after him – not like brother Johnny, who was always light-minded. There was times when my sins fair bowed me down, and I was like old Christian in *The Pilgrim's Progress* – I'd have gone through fire and water to get quit of 'em. Then I got the notion of this Sick Heart as the kind of place where there was no more trouble, a bit of the Garden of Eden that God had kept private for them as could find it. I'd been thinking about it for years, and suddenly I saw a chance of gettin' to it and findin' peace for ever more. Not dying – I wasn't thinking of dying – but living happily ever after, as the story books say. That was my aim, fool that I was!'

His voice rose to a shout.

'I was mad! It was the temptation of the Devil and not a promise of God. The Sick Heart is not the Land-of-Beulah but the Byroad-to-Hell, same as in Bunyan. It don't rise like a proper river out of little springs – it comes full-born out of the rock and slinks back into it like a ghost. I tell you the place is no' canny. You'd say it had the best grazing in all America, and yet there's nothing can live here. There's a curse on this valley when I thought there was a blessing. So there's just the one thing to do if we're to save our souls, and that's to get out of it though we break our necks in the job.'

The man's voice had become shrill with passion, and even in the shadow Leithen could see the fire in his eyes.

'You're maybe thinking different,' he went on. 'You think you're dying and that this is a nice quiet place to die in. But you'll be damned for it. There's a chance of salvation for you if you pass out up on the cold tops, but there's none if your end comes in this cursed hole.'

Leithen turned wearily on his side to face the speaker.

'You'd better count me out. I'm finished. I'd only be a burden to you. A couple of days here should see me through, and then you can do what you like.'

'By God I won't! I can't leave you – I'd never hold up my head again if I did. And I can't stay here with Hell waitin' to grab me. Me and the Hare will help you along, for our kit will be light. Besides, you could show us the road out. The Hare says you know how to get along on steep snow.'

'Have you any rope?' Leithen asked.

Lew's wild face sobered. 'It's about all I have. I've got two hundred feet of light rope. Brought it along with the notion it might come in handy and I can make some more out of caribou skin.'

Leithen had asked the question involuntarily, for the thing did not interest him. The deep fatigue which commonly ended his day had dropped on him like a mountain of lead. Death was very near, and where could he meet it better than in this gentle place, remote alike from the turmoil of Nature and of man?

But after his meagre supper, as he watched Lew and the Indian repack their kit, the power of thought returned to him.

This was the last lap in the race; was he to fail in it? Why had he come here when at home he might have had a cushioned death-bed among friends? Was it not to die standing, to go out in his boots? And that meant that he must have a purpose to fill his mind, and let that purpose exclude foolish meditations on death. Well, he had half-finished his job – he had found Galliard; but before he could get Galliard back to his old world he must bring to him the strange man who had obsessed his mind and who, having been mad, was now sane. Therefore he must get Lew out of the Sick Heart valley. He did not believe that Lew could find his way out alone. The long spout of snow was ice in parts, and Lew knew nothing of step-cutting. Leithen remembered the terror of the Hare in the descent. Mountaineering to men like Lew was a desperate venture. Could he guide them up the spout? It would have been child's play in the old days, but now! . . . He bent his knees and elbows. Great God! his limbs were as flaccid as india-rubber. What kind of a figure would he cut on an ice slope?

And yet what was the alternative? To lie here dying by inches – by feet and yards, perhaps, but still slowly – with Lew in a panic and restrained from leaving him only by the iron camaraderie of the North. His own utter weakness made him crave for immobility, but something at the back of his mind cried out against it. Why had he left England if he was to cower in a ditch and not stride on to the end? That had always been his philosophy. He remembered that long ago in his youth he had written bad verses on the subject, demanding that he meet death 'with the wind in his teeth and the rain in his face.' It was no false stoicism, but the creed of a lifetime.

By and by he fell asleep, and – a rare thing for one whose slumbers seemed drugged – woke in the small hours. Lew could be heard snoring, but he must have been recently awake, for he had stoked both fires. A queer impulse seized Leithen to get up. With some difficulty he crawled out of his sleeping-bag and stumbled to his feet, wrapping a blanket round him . . .

It was a marvellous night, cold, but not bitterly cold, and the flames of the outer fire were crimson against a sky of burnished gold. Moonshine filled the valley and brimmed over the edge of the cliffs. Those cliffs caught no reflection of light, but were more dark and jagged than by day; except that on the eastern side, where lay the snowdrifts, there was a wave of misty saffron.

Moonlight is a soothing thing, softening the raw corners of the world, but suddenly to Leithen this moonlight seemed monstrous and unearthly. The valley was a great golden mausoleum with ebony walls, a mausoleum, not a kindly grave for a common mortal. Kings might die here and lie here, but not Edward Leithen. There was a tremor in his steady nerves, a fluttering in his sober brain. He knew now what Lew meant . . . With difficulty he got back into his sleeping-bag and covered his head so that he could not see the moon. He must get out of this damned place though he used the last pennyweight of his strength.

20

LEW and the Indian had Leithen between them, steadying himself with a hand on each of their huge back-packs. The Hare's rope had gone to the cording of the dunnage, and Lew's was in a coil on Leithen's shoulder. The journey to the snow shoot was made in many short stages, across a frozen pool of the river, and then in the snow-sprinkled herbage below the eastern crags. The weather was changing, for a yellow film was creeping from the north over the sky.

'There'll be big snow on the tops,' said Lew, 'and maybe a god-awful wind.'

It was midday before they reached the foot of the couloir. The lower slopes, down which Leithen and the Hare had rolled, were set at a gentle angle, and the firm snow made easy going; it was up in the narrows of the cleft that it changed to a ribbon of ice. The problem before him stirred some forgotten chord in Leithen's mind, and he found himself ready to take command. First he sent Lew and the Hare with the kit up to the edge of the ice, and bade them anchor the packs there to poles driven into the last soft snow. That done he made the two men virtually carry him up the easy slopes. He had a meagre remnant of bodily strength, and he would need it all for the task before him.

In an hour's time the three were at the foot of the sunless narrows where the snow was hard ice. There he gave Lew his orders.

'I will cut steps, deep ones with plenty of standing room. Keep looking before you, and not down. I'll rope, so that if I fall you can hold me. If I get to the top I'll try to make the rope fast, and the Hare must follow in the steps. He will haul up the kit after him; then he will drop the rope for you, and you must tie it on. If you slip he will be able to hold you.'

Leithen chose the Hare to go second, for the Indian seemed less likely than Lew to suffer from vertigo. He had come up the lower slopes impassively while Lew had had the face of one in torment.

'Lew's hatchet was a poor substitute for an ice axe. Leithen's old technique of step-cutting had to be abandoned, and the notches he hacked would have disgusted a Swiss guide. He had to make them deep and sloping inward for the sake of Lew's big moccasined feet. Also he had often to cut hand-holds for himself so that he could rest plastered flat against the ice when his knees shook and his wrists ached and his head swam with weariness.

It was a mortal slow business, and one long agony. Presently he was past the throat of the gully and in snow again, soft snow with a hard crust, but easier to work than the ice of the narrows. Here the wind, which Lew had foretold, swirled down from the summit, and he almost fell. The last stage was a black nightmare. Soon it would be all over, he told himself – soon, soon, there would be the blessed sleep of death.

He reached the top with a dozen feet of rope to spare, and straightway tumbled into deep snow. There he might have perished, drifting into a sleep from which there would be no awakening, had not tugs on the rope from Lew beneath forced him back into consciousness. With infinite labour he untied the rope from his middle. With frail, fumbling, chilled hands he made the end fast to a jack-pine which grew conveniently near the brink. He gave the rope the three jerks which was the agreed signal that he was at the summit and anchored. Then a red mist of giddiness overtook him, and he dropped limply into the snow at the tree roots.

21

WHEN Leithen came to his senses he found it hard to link the present with the past. His last strong sensation had been that of extreme cold; now it was as warm as if he were in bed at home, and he found that his outer garments had been removed and that he was wearing only underclothes and a jersey. It was night, and he was looking up at a sky of dark velvet, hung with stars like great coloured lamps. By and by, as his eyes took in the foreground, he found that he was in a kind of pit scooped in deep snow with a high rampart of snow around it. The floor was spread with spruce boughs, but a space had been left in the middle for a fire, which had for its fuel the butt-ends of two trees which met in the middle and slipped down as they smouldered.

He did not stay long awake, but in those minutes he was aware of something new in his condition. The fit of utter apathy had passed. He was conscious of the strangeness of this cache in the snow, this mid-winter refuge in a world inimical to man. The bitter diamond air, like some harsh acid, had stung him back to a kind of life – at any rate to a feeble response to life.

* * *

Next day he started out in a state of abject decrepitude. Lew put snow-shoes on him, but he found that he had lost the trick of them, and kept on tangling up his feet and stumbling. The snow lay deep, and under the stricture of the frost was as dry and powdery as sand, so that his feet sank into it. Lew went first to break the trail, but all his efforts did not make a firm track, so that the stages had to be short, and by the midday meal Leithen was at the end of his tether. The glow of a fire and some ptarmigan broth slightly revived him, but his fatigue was such that Lew made camp an hour before nightfall.

That night, in his hole in the snow, Leithen's thoughts took a new turn. For long his mind had been sluggish, cognisant of walls but of no windows. Now suddenly it began to move and he saw things . . .

Lew was taking shape in his thoughts as a man and not as a portent. At first he had been a mystery figure, an inexplicable Providence which dominated Johnny's mind, and which had loomed big on Leithen's own horizon. Then he had changed to a disturbing force which had mastered Galliard and seemed to be an incarnation of the secret madness of the North. And then in the Sick Heart valley he had become a Saul whose crazy fit was passing, a man who was seeking something that he had lost and had reached his desired goal only to find that it was not there. Lew and Galliard were in the same boat, sufferers from the same spell.

But Lew had returned by way of panic to normal life. For a

moment this strong child of Nature had been pathetic, begging help and drawing courage from Leithen himself, a dying man. The splendid being had been a suppliant to one whose body was in decay. The irony of it induced in Leithen a flicker of affection. He seemed, too, to draw a transitory vigour from a creature so instinct with life. His numb stoicism was shot with a momentary warmth and colour. Lew on the trail, shouting oddments of Scots songs in his rich voice, and verses of the metrical Psalms of his youth, engaged in thunderous discourse with the Hare in his own tongue, seemed to dominate the snowdrifts and the blizzards and the spells of paralysing cold. Leithen found that he had won a faint warmth of spirit from the proximity of Lew's gusto. And the man was as gentle as a woman. His eyes were never off Leithen; he arranged the halts to suit his feebleness, and at each of them tended him like a mother. At night he made his bed and fed him with the care of a hospital nurse.

'This ain't the food for you,' he declared. 'You want fresh meat. It's time we were at Johnny's camp where I can get it for you.'

Half a gale was blowing. He detected the scepticism in Leithen's eye and laughed.

'It don't look good for hunting weather, says you. Maybe not, but I'll get you what you need. We're not in the barrens to depend on wandering caribou. There's beasts in these mountains all the year round, and I reckon I know where to find 'em. There's caribou, the big woods kind, and there's more moose than anyone kens, except the Hares. They'll have stamped out their yards and we've got to look for 'em.'

'What's that?'

'Stamping the snow to get at the shoots. Yards they call 'em down east. But the Hares call 'em *ravages*. Got the name from the French missionaries.'

Next day the stages were short and difficult. There was a cruel north-east wind, and the snow was like kitchen salt and refused to pack. The Hare broke the trail, but Leithen, who followed, often sank to his knees in spite of his snow-shoes. ('We need bear-paws like they use down East,' Lew proclaimed. 'These northern kind are too narrow to spread the weight.') An hour's march brought him to utter exhaustion, and there were moments when he thought that that day would be his last.

At the midday meal he heard what stung his sense of irony into life. Lew had placed him in the lee of a low-growing spruce which broke the wind, and had forgotten his presence, for while he and the Indian collected wood for the fire they talked loudly, shouting against the blast. The Hare chose to speak English, in which he liked to practise himself.

'Him lung sick,' he said. There could be no doubt about his reference.

'Yeah,' Lew grunted.

'Him soon die, like my brother and my uncles.'

The reply was an angry shout.

'No, by God, he won't! You chew on that, you bloody-minded heathen. He's going to cheat old man Death and get well.'

Leithen smiled wryly. It was Uncle Toby's oath, but Uncle Toby's efforts had failed, and so would Lew's.

That night, since the day's journey had been short, his fatigue was a little less than usual, and after supper, instead of falling at once into a heavy sleep, he found himself watching Lew, who, wrapped in his blankets, was smoking his short pipe, and now and then stirring the logs with the spruce pole which he used as a poker. His eyes were half-closed, and he seemed to be in a not unpleasant reverie. Leithen – to his surprise, for he had resolved that his mind was dead to all mundane interests – found his curiosity roused. This was one of the most famous guides in the North. The country fitted him as a bearskin fitted the bear. Never, surely, was man better adapted to his environment. What had shaken him loose from his normal life and sent him on a crazy pilgrimage to a legendary river? It could not have been only a craving to explore, to find out what lay far away over the hills. There had been an almost mystical exaltation in the quest, for it had caused him to forget all his traditions, and desert Galliard, and this exaltation had ended in a panicky rebound. When he had met him he had found a strong man in terror, shrinking from something which he could not name. It must have been a strange dream which resulted in so cruel an awakening.

He asked Lew the question point-blank. The man came out of his absorption and turned his bright eyes on the questioner.

'I've been trying to figure that out myself,' he said. 'All my life since I was a callant I've been looking for things and never findin' 'em.'

He stopped in some embarrassment.

'I don't know that I can rightly explain, for you see I'm not used to talking. When I was about eighteen I got kinda sick of my life, and wanted to get away south, to the cities. Johnny was never that way, nor Dad neither. But I reckon there were Frizels far back that had been restless too. Anyway, I was mighty restless. Then Dad died, and I had to take on some of his jobs, and before I knew I was deep in the business of guiding and feeling good about it. I wanted nothing except to know more about pelts than any trapper, and more about training than any Indian, and to keep my body as hard as whinstone, and my hearing like a timber wolf's, and my eyesight like a fishhawk's.'

'That was before the War?'

Lew nodded. 'Before the War. The War came and Johnny and me went overseas. We made a bit of a name as snipers, Johnny pretty useful and me a wee bit better. I enjoyed it right enough, and barring my feet, for I wasn't used to wearing army boots, I was never sick or sorry. But I was god-awful homesick, and when I smelt a muskeg again and saw the pointed sticks I could have grat with pleasure.'

Lew shook out his pipe.

'But the man that came back wasn't the same as him that crossed the sea. I was daft about the North, and never wanted to leave it, but I got a notion that the North was full of things that I didn't know nothing about – and that it was up to me to find 'em. I took to talking a lot with Indians and listening to their stories. And then I heard about the Sick Heart and couldn't forget it.'

Lew's embarrassment had returned. His words came slowly, and he kept his eyes on the hot ashes.

'It happened that I'd a lot of travelling to do by my lone – one trail took three months when I was looking for some lost gold-diggers. For two years I hadn't much guiding.'

'You were with Mr Walter Derwent, weren't you?'

'Yeah. Mr Derwent's a fine little man and my very good friend. But mostly I was alone and I was thinkin' a lot. Dad brought us up well, for he was mighty religious, and I got to puzzling about my soul. I had always lived decent, but I reckoned decent living wasn't enough. Out in the bush you feel a pretty small thing in the hands of God. There was a book of Dad's I had a fancy for, *The Pilgrim's Progress*, and I got to thinking of myself as the Pilgrim, and looking for the same kind of thing to happen to me. I can see now it wasn't sense, but at the time it seemed to me I was looking at a map of my own road. At the end there was the River for the Pilgrim to cross, and I got to imagining that the River was the Sick Heart. I guess I was a bit loony, but I thought I was the only sensible man, for what did it matter what the other folks were doing, running about and making money, and marrying and breeding, when there was this big business of saving your soul?

'Then Mr Galliard got hold of me. He was likewise a bit loony, but his daftness and mine was different, for he was looking for something in this world and, strictly speaking, I was looking for something outside the world. He didn't know what I wanted, and I didn't worry about him. But as it fell out he gave me the chance I'd been looking for, and we took the trail together. I behaved darned badly, for I wasn't sane, and by the mercy of God you and Johnny found the man I deserted . . . I pushed on like a madman and found the Sick Heart, and then, praise God, my daftness left me.

'I don't know what I'd expected. A land flowing with milk and honey, and angels to pass the time of day! What opened my eyes was when I found there was no living thing in that valley. That was uncanny, and gave me the horrors. And then I considered that that great hole in the earth was a grave, a place to die in but not to live in, and not a place either for an honest man to die in. I'm like you, I'm sworn to die on my feet.'

Lew checked himself with a glance of apology.

'I had to get out,' he said, 'and I had to get you out, for there's no road to Heaven from the Sick Heart. What did I call it? – a by-road to Hell!'

'You are cured?' Leithen asked.

'Sure I am. I'm like a man getting better of a fever. I see things in their proper shape and size now, and not big as mountains and dancing in the air. I've got to save my soul, and that's to be done by a sane man, and not by a loony, and in a man's job. I'm the opposite to King David, for God's goodness to me has been to get me away from yon green pastures and still waters, back among the rocks and the jack-pines.'

22

IN two days, said Lew, they should make Johnny's camp and Galliard. But he would not talk about Galliard. He left that problem to the Omnipotence who had solved his own.

The man was having a curious effect on Leithen, the same effect on his spirit that food had on his body, nourishing it and waking it to a faint semblance of life. The blizzard died away, and there followed days of sun, when a rosy haze fell on the hills, and the air sparkled with frost crystals. That night Leithen was aware that another thought had stabbed his dull mind into wakefulness.

When he left England he had reasoned himself into a grim resignation. Life had been very good to him, and, now that it was ending, he made no complaint. But he could only show his gratitude to life by maintaining a stout front to death. He was content to be a pawn in the hands of the Almighty, but he was also a man, and, as Lew put it, must die standing. So he had assumed a task which interested him not at all, but which would keep him on his feet. That task he must conscientiously pursue, but success in it mattered little, provided always he relaxed no effort.

Looking back over the past months, he realised that his interest in it, which at first had been a question of mere self-coercion, was now a real thing. He wanted to succeed, partly because of his liking for a completed job, and partly because the human element had asserted itself. Galliard was no longer a mathematical symbol, a cipher in a game, but a human being and Felicity's husband, and Lew was something more, a benefactor, a friend.

It was the remembrance of Lew that convinced Leithen that a change had come over his world of thought. He had welcomed the North because it matched his dull stoicism. Here in this iron and icy world man was a pigmy and God was all in all. Like Job, he was abashed by the divine majesty and could put his face in the dust. It was the temper in which he wished to pass out of life. He asked for nothing – 'nut in the husk, nor dawn in the dusk, nor life beyond death.' He had already much more than his deserts! And what Omnipotence proposed to do with him was the business of Omnipotence; he was too sick and weary to dream or hope. He lay passive in all-potent hands.

Now there suddenly broke in on him like a sunrise a sense of God's mercy – deeper than the fore-ordination of things, like a great mercifulness . . . Out of the cruel North most of the birds had flown south from ancient instinct, and would return to keep the wheel of life moving. Merciful! But some remained, snatching safety by cunning ways from the winter of death. Merciful! Under the fetters of ice and snow there were little animals lying snug in holes, and fish under the frozen streams, and bears asleep in their lie-ups, and moose stamping out their yards, and caribou rooting for their grey moss. Merciful! And human beings, men, women, and children, fending off winter and sustaining life by an instinct old as that of the migrating birds. Lew nursing like a child one whom he had known less than a week – the Hares stolidly doing their jobs, as well fitted as Lew for this harsh world – Johnny tormented by anxiety for his brother, but uncomplainingly sticking to the main road of his duty . . . Surely, surely, behind the reign of law and the coercion of power there was a deep purpose of mercy.

The thought induced in Leithen a tenderness to which he had been long a stranger. He had put life away from him, and it had come back to him in a final reconciliation. He had always hoped to die in April weather when the surge of returning life would be a kind of earnest of immortality. Now, when presently death came to him, it would be like dying in the spring.

23

THAT night he spoke of plans. The laborious days had brought his bodily strength very low, but some dregs of energy had been stirring in his mind. His breath troubled him sorely, and his voice had failed, so that Lew had to come close to hear him.

'I cannot live long,' he said.

Lew received the news with a stony poker face.

'Something must be settled about Galliard,' he went on. 'You know I came here to find him. I know his wife and his friends, and I wanted a job to carry me on to the end . . . We must get him back to his own people.'

'And who might they be?' Lew asked.

'His wife . . . His business associates. He has made a big place for himself in New York.'

'He didn't talk like that. I never heard him mention 'em. He hasn't been thinkin' much of anythin' except his old-time French forebears, especially them as went North.'

'You went to Clairefontaine with him?'

'Yeah. I wasn't supposed to tell, but you've been there and you've guessed it. It was like comin' home for him, and yet not comin' home. We went to a nice place up the stream and he sat down and grat. Looked like it had once been his home, but that his home had shifted and he'd still to find it. After that he was in a kind of fever – all the way to the Arctic and then on here. He found that his brother and his uncle had died up there by the Ghost River.'

'I know. I saw the graves.'

Lew's eyes opened. 'You and Johnny went there? You stuck mighty close to our trail . . . Well, up to then Galliard had been the daft one. I could get no sense out of him, and most of the time he'd sit dreaming like an old squaw by the fire. After Fort Bannerman it was my turn. I don't rightly remember anything he said after that, for I wasn't worryin' about him, only about myself and that damned Sick Heart . . . What was he like when you found him?'

'He was an ill man, but his body was mending. His mind – well, he'd been lost for three days and had the horrors on him. But I won't say he was cured. You can have the terror of the North on you and still be under its spell.'

'That's so. It's the worst kind.'

'He kept crying out for you. It looks as though you were the only one that could release him. Your madness mastered his, and now that you are sane again he might catch the infection of your sanity.'

Lew pondered. 'It might be,' he said shortly.

'Well, I'm going out, and it's for you to finish the job. You must get him down country and back to his friends. I've written out the details and left them with Johnny. You must promise, so that I can die with an easy mind.'

For a little Lew did not speak.

'You're not going to die,' he said fiercely.

'The best authorities in the world have told me that I haven't the ghost of a chance.'

'They're wrong, and by God we'll prove them wrong!' The blue eyes had a frosty sternness.

'Promise me, anyhow. Promise that you'll see Galliard back among his friends. You could get him out, even in winter?'

'Yeah. We can get a dog-team from the Hares' camp if he isn't fit for the trail. And once at Fort Bannerman we can send word to Edmonton for a plane . . . If it's to do you any good I promise to plant the feller back where he belongs. But you've got to take count of one thing. He must be cured right here in the bush. If he isn't cured before he goes out he'll never be cured. It's only the North can mend what the North breaks.'

24

NEXT day Leithen collapsed utterly, for the strength went from his legs, and his difficult breathing became almost suffocation. The business of filling the lungs with air, to a healthy man an unconscious function, had become for him a desperate enterprise where every moment brought the terror of failure. He felt every part of his decrepit frame involved, not lungs and larynx only, but every muscle and nerve from his brain to his feet. The combined effort of all that was left of him to feed the dying fires of life. A rough sledge was made and Lew and the Hare dragged him laboriously through the drifts. Fortunately they had reached the windswept ridges, where the going was easier. Twenty-four hours later there was delivered at Johnny's camp a man who looked to be in the very article of death.

Part Three

I had a singular feeling at being in his company. For I could hardly believe that I was present at the death of a friend, and therefore I did not pity him.

PLATO, *Phaedo* 58

I

IN the middle of January there was a pause in the sub-zero weather, and a mild wind from the west made the snow pack like cheese, and cleared the spruce boughs of their burden. In front of the hut some square yards of flat ground had been paved by Johnny with stones from the brook, and, since the melting snow drained fast from it, it was dry enough for Leithen to sit there. There was now a short spell of sun at midday, and though it had no warmth it had light, and that light gave him an access of comfort.

He reminded himself for the thousandth time that a miracle had happened, and that he was not in pain. His breath was short, but not difficult. He was still frail, but the utter overwhelming weakness had gone.

As yet he scarcely dared even to hint to himself that he might get well. His reason had been convinced that that was impossible. There had been no doubts in the minds of Acton Croke and young Ravelston . . . Yet Croke had refused to be too dogmatic. He had said, 'in the present position of our knowledge.' He had admitted that medical science was only beginning to understand the type of tuberculosis induced by gas-poisoning. Technicalities had begun to recur to Leithen's memory: Croke's talk of 'chronic fibrous infection,' and 'broncho-pulmonary lesions.' Sinister-sounding phrases, but he remembered, too, reading or hearing somewhere that fibrous areas in the lungs could be walled off and rendered inert. That meant some sort of cure, at any rate a postponement of death.

Lew and the Hares had no doubt about it. 'You're getting well,' the former repeated several times a day. 'Soon you'll be the huskiest of the lot of us.' And the Indians had ceased to look at him furtively like something stricken. They ignored him, which was a good sign, for they knew better than most the signs of the disease which had decimated their people.

Lew's nursing had been drastic and tireless. Leithen's recollections of his arrival in camp from the Sick Heart River were vague, for he had been in a stupor of weakness. He remembered his first realisation that he was under a roof – the smoke from the fire which nearly choked him – alternate over-doses of heat and cold – food which he could not swallow – horrid hours of nausea. And then his memories were less of pain and weakness than of grim discomfort. Lew's tyrannical hand had been laid on him every hour. He was made to eat food when he was retching, or at any rate to absorb the juices of it. His tongue was like a stick, and he longed for cold water, but he was never allowed it. He was wrapped in blankets like a mummy and kept in the open air when frost gummed his lips like glue, and every breath was like swallowing ice, and the air smote on his exposed face like a buffet.

He bore it dumbly, wretched but submissive. He might have been in a clinic, for he had surrendered his soul – not to a parcel of doctors and nurses, but to one fierce backwoodsman. Lew was life incarnate, and the living triumphed over what was half dead. The conscious effort involved in every hour of his past journey was at an end. He was not called on for decisions; these were made for him, and his mind sank into a stagnation which was almost painless.

Then strange things began to happen. He was stirred out of his apathy by little stabs of feeling which were remotely akin to pleasure. The half-raw meat seemed to acquire a flavour; he discovered the ghost of an appetite; he actually welcomed his morning cup of tea. He turned on his side to sleep without dismal forebodings about his condition when he woke . . . His beard worried him, for in his old expeditions he had always shaved regularly, and one morning, to his immense surprise, he demanded his razor, and with Lew's approval shaved himself clean. He made a messy business of it, and took a long time over it, but the achievement pleased him. Surely the face that he looked at in the mirror was less cadaverous, the eyes less leaden, the lips less pallid, the texture of the skin more wholesome!

There was one memorable morning when, the intense cold having slackened, Lew stripped him to the buff, and he lay on a pile of skins before the fire while one of the Hares massaged his legs and arms. After that he took tottering walks about the hut, and one midday ventured out to the little platform. Presently Lew made him take daily exercise and in all weathers.

He was becoming conscious, too, of his surroundings. First came the hut. Assuredly Johnny was no slouch at hut-making. The earthen floor had been beaten flat and smooth by the Hares, whose quarters were a little annexe at one end. The building was some sixty feet square, but the floor space within was oblong, since four bunks had been built into one side. The walls were untrimmed spruce logs, and the roof was the same, but interwoven and overlaid with green boughs. Every chink in both walls and roof was filled with moss or mud. Johnny had constructed a fireplace of stones, with a bottle-shaped flue made of willow saplings puddled with clay. The fire was the special charge of the smaller Hare, and was kept going night and day to supplement the stove.

Warmth was a simple matter, but, though Leithen did not know it, food soon became a problem. Lew and Galliard had had scanty supplies, for they had set out on their journey with fevered brains. Johnny and the Hares had back-packed a fair amount, but the bulk of what they had brought from Fort Bannerman was cached at the Hares' camp or at Lone Tree Lake. It had been Johnny's intention to send the hares back to bring up the reserves with a dog-team, and in the meantime to supplement the commissariat by hunting. He was a good shot, Lew was a famous shot, and the Indians were skilled trappers. That was well enough for the first weeks after Lew and Leithen joined them. There were ptarmigan and willow grouse to be got in the bush, and the woodland caribou, still plump from his autumn guzzling, whence came beef tea and under-done steaks for Leithen, and full meals of flesh for all.

But in the tail-end of December for ten days a blizzard blew. It came out of the north-east and found some alleyway into the mountains, for these gave no protection, so that it raged as fiercely as in the open barrens. The cold was not great, and it was therefore possible to keep the fire low and prevent the back smoke from choking the hut. But there was little fresh air for Leithen, though in the gaps of the storm Lew carried him out of doors and brought him back plastered like a snow man. There were three days when a heavy weight of snow fell, but for the rest it was rather a carnival of the winds, which blew sometimes out of a clear sky, swirling the fallen snow in a *tourmente*, and sometimes filled every aisle of the woods with thick twisting vapours.

Hunting was all but impossible – whether in the driving snow or in the Scots-mist type of weather the visibility was nil. Leithen was aware that the men were out, for often he was left alone, and in the few light hours there was never more than one at home, but his mind was still dull and he had no curiosity about what they were doing. It was as well, for he did not notice the glum faces and the anxious eyes of the others. But he did notice the change in his food.

He had come to like the fresh, bitter flavour of the half-raw caribou meat. That was his staple fare, that and his carefully measured daily dose of tomato juice; he rarely tasted Johnny's flap-jacks. Now there was little fresh meat, and instead he was given pemmican, which he swallowed with difficulty, or the contents of one of the few remaining tins.

Johnny was getting very grave about supplies. As soon as the weather cleared an attempt must be made to get up the reserves from the Hares' camp. They were out of sugar, almost out of tea and coffee, and their skins would give trouble unless they had fruit juice. But, above all, the hunting must be resumed. That was their main source of supply, and since Christmas the caribou had been harder to get, and February might bring savage weather.

Of these anxieties Leithen knew nothing. He was overwhelmed with the miracle of vigour creeping back into his moribund body. On the road from the Sick Heart River he had found himself responding again to life, and had welcomed the change as the proper mood in which to die. But this was different – it was not the recognition of life, but life itself, which had returned to him.

At night in the pit in the snow with Lew and the Hare he had become suddenly conscious of the mercifulness of things. There was a purpose of pity and tenderness in the iron compulsion of fate. Now this thought was always with him – the mercy as well as the omnipotence of God. His memory could range over the past and dwell lovingly and thankfully on its modest pleasures. A little while ago such memories, if he could have revived them, would have been a torment.

* * *

His mind ran up and down the panorama of his life, selecting capriciously. Oddly enough, it settled on none of the high lights. There had been moments of drama in his career – an adventure in the Aegean island of Plakos, for example, and more than one episode in the War. And there had been hours of special satisfaction – when he won the mile at school and college, his first big success at the Bar, his maiden speech in the House, his capture of the salmon when he and Lamancha and Palliser-Yeates poached in the Highlands. But though his memory passed these things in review, it did not dwell on them. Three scenes seemed to attract it especially, and he found that he could spend hours contentedly in reconstructing them and tasting their flavour.

The first belonged to his childhood. One morning in spring he had left his Border home determined to find what lay beyond the head of a certain glen. He had his rod with him, for he was an ardent fisherman, and lunch in his pocket – two jam sandwiches, a dainty known as a currant scone, two bread-and-butter sandwiches, a hard-boiled egg, and an apple – lovingly he remembered every detail. His short legs had crossed the head of the glen beyond the well-eye of the burn, and had climbed to the tableland of peat haggs and gravel, which was the watershed. Here he encountered an April hailstorm, and had to shelter in a hagg, where he ate his luncheon with intense relish. The hail passed, and a mild blue afternoon succeeded, with the Cheviots clear on the southern sky-line.

He had struggled across the peat bog, into the head of the glen beyond the watershed, where another burn fell in delectable pools among rowans and birches, and in these pools he had caught trout whose bellies were more golden and whose spots were brighter than the familiar fish in his own stream. Late in the evening he had made for home, and had crossed the hills in an April sunset of rose and saffron. He remembered the exultation in his small heart, the sense of being an explorer and an adventurer, which competed with a passionate desire for food.

Everything that day had gone exactly right. No one had upbraided him for being late. The trout had been justly admired. He had sat down to a comfortable supper, and had fallen asleep and rolled off his chair in the middle of it. Assuredly a day to be marked with a white stone. He could recall the sounds that accompanied it – the tinkle of the burn in its tiny pools, the perpetual wail of curlews, the sudden cackle of a nesting grouse. And the scents, too – peat, wood smoke, crushed mountain fern, miles of dry bent, the pure, clean odour of icy water.

This memory came chiefly in the mornings. In the afternoons, when he was not asleep, he was back at Oxford. The scene was always the same – supper in the college hall, a few lights burning, the twilight ebbing in the lancet windows, the old portraits dim as a tapestry. There was no dinner in hall in the summer term, only supper, when you could order what you pleased. The memory of the fare almost made him hungry – fried eggs, cold lamb and mint sauce and salad, stewed gooseberries and cream, cheese and wheaten bread, and great mugs of home-brewed beer . . . He had been in the open air most of the day, riding over Shotover or the Cumnor hills, or canoeing on the upper Thames in the grassy meadows above Godstow, or adventuring on a bicycle to fish the dry-fly in the Cotswold streams. His body had been bathed in the sun and wind and fully exercised, so his appetite was immense. But it was not the mere physical comfort which made him dwell on the picture. It was the mood which he remembered, and could almost recapture, the mood which saw the world as a place of long sunlit avenues leading to marvellous horizons. That was his twentieth year, he told himself, which mankind is always longing to find again.

The third memory was the most freakish. It belonged to his early days at the Bar, when he lived in small ugly rooms in one of the Temple courts, and had very little money to spend. It was the first day of the Easter vacation, and he was going to Devonshire with Palliser-Yeates to fish the Exmoor hill streams. The cheapest way was to drive with his luggage direct to Paddington, after the meagre breakfast which his landlady provided. But it seemed an occasion to celebrate, so he had broken his journey at his club in St James's Street, a cheerful, undistinguished young man's establishment, and had breakfasted there with his friend. It had been a fresh April morning; gulls had been clamorous as he drove along the Embankment, and a west wind had been stirring the dust in Pall Mall . . . He remembered the breakfast in the shabby old coffee room, and Palliser-Yeates' fly-book which he spilt all over the table. Above all he remembered his own boyish anticipations. In twenty-four hours he would be in a farmhouse which smelt of paraffin and beeswax and good cooking, looking out on a green valley with a shallow brown stream tumbling in riffles and drowsing in pools under banks of yellow bent. The larch plantations would be a pale mist on the hillsides, the hazel coverts would be budding, plovers would be everywhere, and water ouzels would be flashing their white breasts among the stones . . . The picture was so dear and home-like that he found himself continually returning to it. It was like a fire at which he could warm his hands.

But there came a time when this pleasant picture-making ceased, and his mind turned back on itself. He had lost the hard stoical mood in which he had left London, but he was not clear as to what had replaced it. What was he doing here in a hut inside the Arctic Circle, among mountains which had never been explored and scarcely visited, in the company of Indians and half-breeds? . . . And then he slowly became conscious of Galliard.

All these weeks he had not noticed Galliard's presence or inquired what had happened to him. This man, the original purpose of his journey, had simply dropped out of his line of vision. He pondered on the queer tricks which the mind can play. The Frizels and the Indians were the human background to his life, but it was a background undifferentiated, for he never troubled to distinguish between the two Hares, and Lew, who was his daily ministrant, seemed to have absorbed the personality of Johnny. Galliard had sunk also into this background. One evening, when he saw what appeared to be three Frizels in the hut, he thought his mind wandering.

Moreover, the broken man, bedridden, half crazy, whom he had left behind when he set out for the Sick Heart River had disappeared. What he saw now was a big fellow, dressed in the same winter kit as Lew and Johnny, and busy apparently on the same jobs. He cut down young spruces and poplars for fuel, he looked after the big fire which burned outside and was used chiefly for melting snow and ice into water, and sometimes he hunted and brought back game. Slowly his figure disentangled itself from its background and was recognised. It had followed Leithen's example and shaved its beard, and the face was very much like that of the picture in the Park Avenue apartment.

Leithen's vitality had sunk so low that he had spoken little during his early recovery, and afterwards had been too much engaged with his own thoughts. This detachment had prevented him listening to the talk in the hut. His attention was only engaged when he was directly addressed, and that was done chiefly by Lew. But now, while he did not attempt to overhear, he was conscious of the drone of conversation after supper in the evening, and began to distinguish the different notes in it. There was no mistaking Lew's beautiful rich tones with their subtle Scots cadences, and Johnny's harsher and more drawling voice. Then he became aware of a third note, soft like Lew's, but more nasal, and one afternoon, at the tailend of a blizzard, when Leithen lay abed in the firelight and the others were getting kindlings from the wind-felled trees, this voice addressed him.

'Can we talk now?' it said. 'I've been waiting for this chance now that you're mending. I think we have much to say to each other.'

Leithen was startled. This was what he had not heard for months, an educated voice, a voice from his own world. A stone had been thrown into the pool of his memory and the ripples stretched to the furthest shore. This was Galliard; he remembered everything about Galliard, reaching back to Blenkiron's first mention of him in his Down Street rooms.

'Tell me who you are,' the voice continued.

Leithen did not answer. He was wondering how to begin an explanation of a purpose which must seem wholly fantastic. He, the shell of a creature, had set out to rescue this smiling frontiersman who seemed to fit perfectly into his environment.

'Johnny says that you know some of my friends. Do you mind telling me your name? I don't trust Johnny's ear, but I think he said "Leven."'

'Not quite. Leithen.'

Galliard repeated the word, boggling, like all his countrymen, at the 'th.' 'Scotch, aren't you?'

'Yes, but I live in England.'

'You've been a pretty sick man, I gather, but you're mending fast. I wonder what brought a sick man to this outlandish place in midwinter? These mountains are not exactly a sanatorium . . . You don't mind my asking questions? You see, we come out of the same world, and we're alone here – the only people of our kind for a thousand miles.'

'I want you to ask questions. It's the easiest way for me to tell you my story . . . I crossed the Atlantic last summer thinking that I was a dying man. The best English authority said so, and the best American authority confirmed his view. I'm unmarried, and I didn't want to die in a nursing-home. I've always been an active man, and I proposed to keep going until I dropped. So I came out here.'

Galliard nodded. His brown eyes had a smiling, comprehending friendliness.

'That I understand – and admire. But why to America? – Why just here? – And on a trip like this?'

'I had to have a job. I must be working under orders, for it was the only way to keep going. And this was the job that offered itself.'

'Yes, but please tell me. How did it happen that a sick Englishman was ordered to the Arctic Circle? What kind of job?'

Leithen smiled. 'You will think it fantastic. The idea came from a kinsman of yours – a kinsman by marriage. His name is Blenkiron.'

Galliard's face passed from an amused inquisitiveness to an extreme gravity.

'Our Uncle John! Tell me, what job did he give you?'

'To find out where you had gone, and join you, and, if possible, bring you back. No, not *bring* you – for I expected to be dead before that – but to persuade you.'

'You were in New York? You saw our Uncle John there?'

'No. In London. I know his other niece, Lady Clanroyden – Clanroyden was at school and college with me – and I had some business once with Blenkiron. He came to my rooms one morning last summer, and told me about you.'

Galliard's eyes were on the ground. He seemed to have been overcome by a sudden shyness, and for a moment he said nothing. Then he asked—

'You took on the job because you liked Blenkiron? Or perhaps Lady Clanroyden?'

'No. I happen to like Lady Clanroyden very much – and old Blenkiron, too. But my motive was purely selfish. I wasn't interested in you – I didn't want to do a kindness to anybody – I wanted something that would keep me on my feet until I died. It wouldn't have mattered if I had never heard the name of any of the people concerned. I was thinking only of myself, and the job suited me.'

'You saved my life. If you and Johnny hadn't followed our trail I would long ago have been a heap of bones under the snow.' Galliard spoke very softly, as if he were talking to himself.

Leithen felt acutely uncomfortable.

'Perhaps,' he said. 'But that was an accident, and there's no gratitude due, any more than to the policeman who calls an ambulance in a street accident.'

Galliard raised his head.

'You were in New York? Whom did you meet there? My wife?'

'Yes. The Ravelstons, of course. And some of your friends like Bronson Jane, and Derwent, and Savory. But principally your wife.'

'Can you' – the man stuttered – 'can you tell me about her?'

'She is a brave woman, but I need not tell you that. Anxious and miserable, of course, but one would never guess it. She keeps a stiff face to the world. She tells people that you are in South America inquiring into a business proposition. She won't have any fuss made, for she thinks it might annoy you when you come back.'

'Come back! She believes I will come back?'

'Implicitly. She thinks you had reached cross-roads in your mind and had to go away and think it out and decide which one to take. When you have decided, she thinks you will come back.'

'Then why did she want you to go to look for me?'

'Because there was always a chance you might be dead – or sick. I sent her a message from Fort Bannerman saying that I had ascertained you were alive and well up to a week before.'

'How did you find me?'

'I guessed that you had gone first to Clairefontaine. I got no news of you there, but some little things convinced me that you had been there. Then I guessed you had gone North where your brother and your uncle had gone. So I followed. I saw their graves, and then Johnny told me about Lew's craze for the Sick Heart River, and I guessed again that he had taken you there. It was simply a series of lucky guesses. If you like, you can call them deductions from scanty evidence. I was lucky, but that was because I had made a guess at what was passing in your mind, and I think I guessed correctly.'

'You didn't know me – never met me. What data had you?'

'Little things picked up in New York and at Clairefontaine. You see I am accustomed to weighing evidence.'

'And what did you make of my psychology?'

'I thought you were a man who had got into a wrong groove and wanted to get out before it was too late . . . No, that isn't the right way to put it. If it had been that way, there was no hope of getting you back. I thought you were a man who thought he had sold his birthright and was tortured by his conscience and wanted to buy it back.'

'You think that a more hopeful state of affairs?'

'Yes. For it is possible to keep your birthright and live in a new world. Many men have done it.'

Galliard got up and pulled on his parka and mitts. 'I'm going out,' he said, 'for I want to think. You're a wizard, Mr Leithen. You've discovered what was wrong with me; but you're not quite right about the cure I was aiming at . . . I was like Lew, looking for a Sick Heart River . . . I was seeking the waters of atonement.'

For a moment Leithen was alarmed. Galliard had seemed the sanest of men, all the saner because he had divested himself of his urban trappings and had yet kept the accent of civilisation. But his last words seemed an echo of Lew – Lew before his cure. But a glance at the steady eyes and grave face reassured him.

'I mean what I say,' Galliard continued. 'I had been faithless to a trust and had to do penance for it. I had forgotten God and had to find Him . . . We have each of us to travel to his own Sick Heart River.'

2

IN the days of short commons Lew was a tower of strength. He ran the camp in an orderly bustle, the Indians jumped to his orders, and Johnny worked with him like an extra right hand. His friendly gusto kept up everyone's spirits, and Leithen was never aware of the scarcity of rations.

It was a moment when he seemed to have reached the turning-point of his disease. Most of his worst discomforts had gone, and only weakness vexed him and an occasional scantiness of breath. The night sweats had ceased, and the nausea, and he could eat his meals with a certain relish. Above all, power was creeping back into his limbs. He could put on his clothes without having to stop and pant, and something of his old striding vigour was returning to his legs. He felt himself fit for longer walks than the weather and the narrow camp platform permitted.

Lew watched him with an approving eye. As he passed he would stop and pat him on his shoulder.

'You're doing fine,' he would say. 'Soon you'll be fit to go huntin'. You much of a shot?'

'Fair.'

Lew laughed. 'If an Old Countryman 'lows he's a fair shot, it means he's darned good.'

One evening just before supper when the others were splitting firewood, Lew sat himself down before Leithen and tapped him on the knee.

'Mr Galliard,' he said – 'I'd like to say something about Mr Galliard. You know I acted mighty bad to him, but then I was out of my senses, and he wasn't too firm in his. Well, I'm all right now, but I'm not so sure that he is. His health's fine, and he can stand a long day in the bush. But he ain't happy – no happier than when he first hired me way back last spring. I mean he's got his wits back, and he's as sensible as you and me, but there's a lot worryin' him.' Lew spoke as if he found it difficult to say what he wanted.

'I feel kind o' responsible for Mr Galliard,' he said, 'seeing that he's my master and is paying me pretty high. And you must feel kind o' responsible for him or you wouldn't have come five thousand miles looking for him . . . I see you've started talking to him. I'd feel easier in my mind if you had a good long pow-wow and got out of him what's biting him. You don't happen to know?'

Leithen shook his head.

'Only that he wasn't happy and thought he might feel better if he went North. But the plan doesn't seem to have come off.'

The conversation, as it fell out, was delayed until early in February, when, in a spell of fine weather, Johnny and the smaller Indian had set off to the Hares' camp to bring back supplies by dog-team. It was about three o'clock in the afternoon, and the sun was beginning to go down in a sea of gold and crimson. Leithen sat at the hut door, facing the big fire on the platform which Galliard had been stoking. The latter pulled out a batch of skins and squatted on them opposite him.

'Can we talk?' he said. 'I've kept away from you, for I've been trying to think out what to say. Maybe you could help me. I'd like to tell you just how I was feeling a year ago.'

Then words seemed to fail him. He was overcome with extreme shyness, his face flushed, and he averted his eyes.

'I have no business to trouble you with my affairs,' he stammered. 'I apologise . . . I am a bore.'

'Get on, man,' said Leithen. 'I have crossed half the world to hear about your affairs. They interest me more than anything on earth.'

But Galliard's tongue still halted, and he seemed to find it impossible to start.

'Very well,' said Leithen . . . 'I will begin by telling you what I know about you. You come from the Clairefontaine valley in Quebec, which Glaubsteins have now made hideous with a dam and a pulp mill. I believe your own firm had a share in that sacrilege. You belong to an ancient family, now impoverished, and your father farmed a little corner of the old seigneury . . . When you were nineteen or so you got sick of your narrow prospects and went down to the States to try your luck. After a roughish time you found your feet, and are now a partner in Ravelstons, and one of the chief figures in American finance . . . Meantime your father died, soon after you left him. Your brother Paul carried on the farm, and then he also got restless, and a year or two ago went off to the North, pretending he was going to look for your uncle Aristide, who disappeared there years before. Paul got to the river which Aristide discovered, and died there – the graves of both are there, and you saw them last summer . . . At the other end something happened to *you*. You started out for Clairefontaine with Lew, and then you were at Ghost River, and then came on here. Is that sketch correct?'

Galliard nodded. His eyes were abstracted, as if he were in the throes of a new idea.

'Well, you must fill out the sketch. But let me tell you two other things. I went to Clairefontaine after you, and after you to the Ghost River, and I saw the crosses in the graveyard. Also, long ago, when I was a young man, I went hunting in Quebec, and I came out by way of Clairefontaine. I found the little meadow at the head of the stream, and I have never forgotten it. When I knew I had to die, my first thought was to go there, for it seemed the place to find peace.'

Galliard's face woke to a sudden animation.

'By God! that's a queer thing. I went to that meadow – the first thing I did after I left New York. There's a fate in this! . . . I think now I can get on with my story . . .'

It was a tale which took long in the telling, and it filled

several of the short winter twilights. There were times when the narrative lagged, and times when it came fast and confusedly. Galliard had curious tricks of speech; sometimes elaborate, the product of wide reading, and sometimes halting, amateurish, almost childlike, as if he were dragging his thoughts from a deep well.

From the village school of Château-Gaillard, he said, he had gone to the University of Laval. He was intended for the law, and his first courses were in classics and philosophy. He enjoyed them, and for a little even toyed with the notion of giving his life to those studies and looking for a university post. What switched his thoughts to another line was a slow revolt against the poverty-stricken life at Clairefontaine. He saw his father and brother bowed down with toil, for no purpose except to win a bare living. In the city he had occasional glimpses of comfort and luxury, and of a wide coloured world, and these put him wholly out of temper with his home. He did a good deal of solid thinking. If he succeeded as a lawyer he would exchange the narrow world of a country farm for the narrow world of a provincial city – more ease, certainly, but something far short of his dreams. He must make money, and money could only be made in big business. In Canada his own French people did little in business, having always left that to the English, and in Canada he might have to fight against prejudice. So he determined to go to the country where he believed there was no prejudice, where business was exalted above all callings, and where the only thing required of a man was to be good at his job.

He left Laval and went to a technical college, where he acquired the rudiments of accounting and a smattering of engineering science. The trouble came when his father discovered the change. The elder Gaillard had something of the seigneur left in him. There was a duty owed to gentle birth. A gentleman might be a farmer who laboured from dawn to dusk in the fields; he could be a priest; he could be a lawyer; but if he touched trade he forfeited his gentility. Moreover, the father hated the very word America. So when the son frankly announced his intention there was a violent family quarrel. Next day he left for Boston and he never saw his father again.

Galliard scarcely mentioned his early struggles. They had to be taken for granted like infantile ailments. He took up the tale when he had come to New York and had met Felicity Dasent.

To Leithen's surprise he spoke of Felicity without emotion. He seemed to be keeping his mind fixed on the need to make his story perfectly clear – an intellectual purpose which must exclude sentiment.

He had fallen deeply in love with her after a few meetings. To him she represented a new world very different from the tough world of buying and selling in which he had found his feet. It was a world which satisfied all the dreams of his boyhood and youth, a happy, gracious place with, as its centre, the most miraculous of beings. It was still more different from Clairefontaine with its poverty and monotony and back-breaking toil. Felicity seemed far further removed from Clairefontaine than from the grubbiest side of Wall Street. The old petty world of Mass and market was infinitely remote from her gracious and civilised life. It was a profanation to think of the two together. Only the meadow at the head of the stream seemed to harmonise with his thoughts about her.

Then came their marriage, and Galliard's entry into society, and his conspicuous social success. After that the trouble began in his soul . . .

He was not very clear about its beginnings. He found things in which he had had an acute interest suddenly go stale for him. He found himself in revolt against what he had once joyfully accepted, and when he probed for the reason he discovered, to his surprise, that it was because it clashed with some memory which he thought he had buried. At first he believed that it was only regret for his departing youth. Boyish recollections came back to him gilded by time and distance. But presently he realised that the trouble was not nostalgia for his dead boyhood, but regret for a world which was still living and which he had forsaken. Not exactly regret, either; rather remorse, a sense that he had behaved badly, had been guilty in some sense of a betrayal.

He fought against the feeling. It was childish, with no basis of reason. He was a rich man, and, if he liked, could have a country house in Quebec, which would offer all the enchantments of his youth without its poverty . . . But he realised miserably that this was no solution. It was not Quebec that he wanted, but a different world of thought, which was hopelessly antagonistic to that in which he now dwelt. To his consternation he discovered that distaste for his environment was growing fast. What had been the pleasures of his life became its boredoms; high matters of business were only a fuss about trifles; men whom he had once reverenced seemed now trivial and wearisome. A lost world kept crowding in on him; he could not recover it, but he felt that without it there was no peace for him in life. There was only one stable thing, Felicity, who moved in a happy sphere of her own, from which he daily felt more estranged.

Ridiculous little things tormented him – a tune which reminded him of a French *chanson*, the smell of a particular tobacco which suggested the coarse stuff grown at Clairefontaine. He dared not go shooting or fishing because of their associations; golf, which belonged wholly to his new world, he came to loathe.

'It was like a cancer,' he said. 'A doctor once told me that cancer was a growth of certain cells at a wild pace – the pace at which a child grows in the womb – a sort of crazy resurgence of youth. It begins by being quite innocent, but soon it starts pressing in on other cells and checking their growth, and the thing becomes pathological. That was what happened to me. The old world came to bulk so big in my life that it choked the rest of me like a cancer in the mind.'

He had another trouble, the worst of all. He had been brought up a strict Catholic, but since he left home he had let his religion fall from him. He had never been to Mass. Felicity was an Episcopalian who took her creed lightly, and they had been married in a fashionable New York church. Now all the fears and repressions of his youth came back to him. He had forgotten something of desperate importance, his eternal welfare. He had never thought much about religion, but had simply taken it for granted till he began to neglect it, so he had no sceptical apparatus to support him. His conduct had not been the result of enlightenment, but flat treason.

'I came to realise that I had forgotten God,' he said simply.

The breaking-point came because of his love for Felicity. The further he moved away from her and her world, the dearer she became. The one thing he was resolved should not happen was a slow decline in their affection. Either he would recover what he had lost and harmonise it with what he had gained, or a clean cut would be made, with no raw edges to fester . . . So on a spring morning, with a breaking heart, he walked out of Felicity's life . . .

'You have guessed most of this?' he asked.

'Most of it,' said Leithen. 'What I want to know is the sequel. You have been nearly a year looking for your youth. What luck?'

'None. But you don't put it quite right, for I was willing enough to grow old decently. What I had to recover was the proper touch with the world which I had grown out of and could no more reject than my own skin. Also I had to make restitution. I had betrayed something ancient and noble, and had to do penance for my sins.'

'Well?' Leithen had to repeat the question, for words seemed to have failed Galliard.

'I did both,' he said slowly. 'To that extent I succeeded. I got into touch with my people's life, and I think I have done penance. But I found that more was needed. I belong to the North, and to go on living I had to master the North . . . But it mastered me.'

Leithen waited for Galliard to expound this saying, but he waited a long time. The other's face had darkened, and he seemed to be wrestling with difficult thoughts. At last he asked a question.

'I cannot explain,' said Galliard, 'for I don't quite know what happened . . . I thought that if I found my brother, or at least found out what had become of him, that I should have done the right thing – done the kind of thing my family have always been doing – defied the North, scored off it. It didn't work out like that. Up there on the Ghost River I was like a haunted man – something kept crushing me down. Yes, by God! I was afraid. Naked fear! – I had never known it before . . . I had to go on or give up altogether. Then Lew started in about his Sick Heart River. He was pretty haywire, but I thought he was on the track of something wonderful. He said it was a kind of Paradise where a man left his sins behind him. It wasn't sense, if I'd stopped to think, but I was beyond thinking. Here was a place where one could be reconciled to the North – where the North ceased to be a master and became a comforter. I can tell you I got as mad about the thing as Lew.

'But Lew was no good to me,' he went on. 'He forgot all about me. Being mad, he was thinking only of himself. I hurt my foot and had a difficult time keeping up with him. Pretty bad days they were – I don't want to go through anything of the sort again. Then I lost him and would have perished if you hadn't found me. You know the rest. Johnny nursed me back to bodily health, and partly to sanity, for he is the sanest thing ever made. But not quite. Lew has come back cured, but not me, though I dare say I look all right.'

He turned his weather-beaten, wholesome face to Leithen, and in his eyes there was an uncertainty which belied the strong lines of mouth and jaw.

'I will tell you the truth,' he said. 'I'm afraid, black afraid of this damned country. But I can't leave it until I've got on terms with it. And God knows how that is to be managed.'

3

LEITHEN found that his slowly mending health was having a marked effect upon his mind. It was like a stream released from the bondage of frost. Before, he had been plodding along in a rut with no inclination to look aside; now he was looking about him and the rut was growing broad and shallow. Before, he had stopped thinking about his body for it was enough to endure what came to it; now he took to watching his sensations closely, eager to find symptoms of returning strength. This must mean, he thought, a breakdown of his stoicism, and he dreaded that, for it might be followed by the timidity which he despised.

But this new mental elasticity enabled him to reflect on the problem of Galliard – on Galliard himself, who was ceasing to be a mere problem and becoming flesh and blood. For months Leithen had been insensitive to human relationships. Even his friends at home, who had warmed and lit his life, had sunk into the background, and the memory of them when it revived was scarcely an extra pang. His mind had assessed the people he met in New York, but they might have been ninepins for all he cared about them, though for Felicity he had felt a certain dim tenderness. But the return journey from Sick Heart River had wrought a change. His sudden realisation of the mercifulness behind the rigour of Nature had made him warm towards common humanity. He saw the quality of Lew and Johnny, and thanked God for it. Now he was discovering Galliard, and was both puzzled and attracted by him.

A man – beyond question. Leithen saw that in him which had won him an enchanting wife and a host of friends. There was warmth, humour, loyalty. Something more, that something which had made Clifford Savory insistent that he must be brought back for the country's sake. There was a compelling charm about him which would always win him followers, and there was intellect in his brow and eyes. Leithen, accustomed all his life to judge men, had no doubt about Galliard.

But he was broken. As broken by fear as Lew had been at Sick Heart River, and, being of a more complex make-up than Lew, the mending would be harder. A man of a stiff fibre had been confronted by fear and had been worsted by it. There could be no settlement for Galliard until he had overcome it.

Leithen brooded over that mysterious thing, the North. A part of the globe which had no care for human life, which was not built to man's scale, a remnant of that Ice Age which long ago had withered the earth. As a young man he had felt its spell when he looked from the Clairefontaine height of land towards the Arctic watershed. The Gaillard family for generations had felt it. Like brave men they had gone out to wrestle with it, and had not returned. Johnny, even the stolid Johnny, had confessed that he had had his bad moments. Lew – Heaven knows what aboriginal wildness was mingled with his Highland blood – had gone hunting for a mystic river and had then got the horrors of the unknown and fled from it. But he was bred to the life of the North and could fall back upon its ritual and defy it by domesticating it. Yet at any moment the fire might kindle again in him. As for Galliard, he was bound to the North by race and creed and family tradition; it was not hard for the gods of the Elder Ice to stretch a long arm and pluck him from among the flesh-pots.

What puzzled him was why he himself had escaped. He had had an hour of revulsion at Sick Heart River, but it had passed like a brief nightmare. His mind had been preoccupied with prosaic things like cold and weariness, and his imagination had been asleep. The reason was plain. He had been facing death, waiting stoically on its coming. There was no space for lesser fears when the most ancient terror was close to him, no room for other mysteries when he was nearing the ultimate one.

What had happened to him? Had he come out of the Valley of the Shadow, or had the Shadow only shifted for a moment to settle later on, darker and deeper? He deliberately refused to decide. A sense of reverence, almost of awe, deterred him. He had committed himself to God's hands and would accept with a like docility mercy and harshness. But one thing he knew – he had found touch with life. He was reacting to the external world. His mind had feelers out again to its environment.

Therefore Galliard had assumed a new meaning. He was not a task to be plodded through with, but a fellow-mortal to be helped, a companion, a friend.

4

JOHNNY and the Hares reached camp when a sudden flurry of snow ended the brief daylight. Lew and the other Indian ran to receive them, and presently Galliard joined the group.

'Queer folk in the North,' Leithen thought. 'They don't make much fuss over a reunion, though it's three weeks since they parted.' Out of the corner of his eye he saw the team of dogs, great beasts, half wolf, half malamute, weighing a hundred pounds each, now sending up clouds of grey steam into the white snowfall. He had a glimpse, too, of Johnny, who looked tired and anxious.

The better part of an hour passed, while Leithen sat alone in the hut mending a pair of moccasins. Then Johnny appeared with a grave face, and handed him a letter.

'Things ain't goin' too well with them Hares,' he said. 'They've got a blight on 'em like Indians get. They're starvin', and they're goin' mad.'

The letter, written on a dirty half-sheet of mission paper, and secured between two pieces of birch-bark, was from the priest, Father Duplessis, who had taken Father Wentzel's place for the winter. It was written with indelible pencil in a foreign pointed script.

'They tell me you are recovering health, my friend, and for your sake I rejoice. Also for my own, for I am enabled to make you an appeal. My poor people here are in great sorrow. They have little food, and they will not try to get more, for a disease has come upon them, a dreadful *accidie* which makes them impotent and without hope. Food must be found for them, and above all they must be roused out of their stupor and made to wish to live. I wrestle with them, and I have the might of the Church behind me, but I am alone and I am but a weak vessel. If you can come to my aid, with God's help we may prevail, but if not I fear this little people will be blotted out of the book of life.'

5

THAT night after supper four men sat in council. Johnny made his report, much interrupted by Lew's questions, and once or twice the two Hares were summoned to give information. Johnny was a very weary man, for his bandy legs had broken the trail for the dogs through the snow-encumbered forest, and he had forced the pace for man and beast. His pale blue eyes, which had none of Lew's brilliance, had become small and troubled. One proof of his discomfort was that when he broke off to speak to his brother it was in the Cree tongue. Never before had Leithen heard him use his mother's speech.

Leithen found himself presiding over the council, for the others seemed to defer to him, after Lew had cross-examined his brother about what supplies he had brought.

'Father Duplessis says there's trouble in the Hares' camp,' he said. 'Let's hear more about it. Father Wentzel in the fall was afraid of something of the sort.'

Johnny scratched the tip of one of his bat's ears.

'Sure there's trouble. Them darned Hares has gone loony and it ain't the first time neither. They think they're Christians, but it's a funny kind of religion, for they're always hankerin' after old bits of magic. Comin' up in the fall I heard they'd been consultin' the caribou bone.'

He explained a little shamefacedly.

'It's a caribou's shoulder-blade, and it's got to be an old buck with a special head of horns. They'd got one and there's a long crack down the middle, and their medicine men say that means famine.'

Lew snorted. 'They needn't have gone to an old bone for that. This year the hares and rabbits has gone sick and that means that every other beast is scarce. The Hares ain't much in the way of hunters – never have been – but they know all about rabbits. That's how they've gotten their name. Maybe you thought they was so-called because they hadn't no more guts than a hare. That ain't right. They're a brave enough tribe, though in old days the Crees and the Chipewyans had the upper hand of them. But the truth is that they haven't much sense and every now and then they go plumb crazy.'

'You say they're starving.' Leithen addressed Johnny. 'Is that because they cannot get food or because they won't try to get it?'

'Both,' was the answer. 'I figured it out this way. As a general thing they fish all summer and dry their catch for the winter. That gives 'em both man's meat and dog's meat. But this year the white fish and pike was short in the lakes and the rivers. I heard that in the fall when we were comin' in. Well then, it was up to them to make an extra good show with the fall huntin'. But, as Lew says, the fall huntin' was a washout anyhow. Moose and caribou and deer were scarce, because the darned rabbits had gone sick. It happens that way every seven years or so. So them pitiful Hares started the winter with mighty poor prospects.'

Johnny spat contemptuously.

'For you and me that would've meant a pretty hard winter's work. There's food to be got up in them mountains even after the freeze-up, if you know where to look for it. You can set bird traps, for there's more partridges here than in Quebec. You can have dead-falls for deer, and you can search out the moose's stamping grounds. I was tellin' you that the moose were shifting further north. The Hares ain't very spry hunters, as Lew says, for they've got rotten guns, but they're dandies at trappin'. Well, as I was sayin', if it'd been you and me we'd have got busy, and, though we'd have had to draw in our belts, somehow or other we'd have won through. But what does them crazy Hares do?'

Johnny spat again, and Lew joined him in the same gesture of scorn.

'They done nothin'! Jest nothin'. The caribou shoulder-blade had 'em scared into fits. It's a blight that comes on 'em every now and then, like the rabbit sickness. If a chief dies they mourn for him, sittin' on their rumps, till they're pretty well dead themselves. In the old fightin' days what they lost in a battle was nothin' to what they lost afterwards lamentin' it. So they're takin' their bad luck lyin' down and it jest ain't sense. It looks as if that tribe was fixed to be cleaned out before spring.'

Johnny's contemptuous eyes became suddenly gentle.

'It's a pitiful business as ever I seen. Their old chief – Zacharias they call him – he must be well on in the eighties, but he's the only one that ain't smit with paralysis. Him and Father Duplessis. But Zacharias is mighty bad with lumbago and can't get about enough, and the Father ain't up to the ways of them savages. He prays for 'em and he argues with 'em, but he might as well argue and pray with a skunk. A dog whip would be the thing if you'd the right man to handle it.'

Johnny's melancholy eyes belied his words. They were not the eyes of a disciplinarian.

'And yet,' he went on, 'I don't know, but I somehow can't keep on bein' angry with the creatures. They sit in their shacks and but for the women they'd freeze, for they don't seem to have the strength to keep themselves warm. The children are bags of bones and crawl about like a lot of little starved owls. It's only the women that keep the place goin', and they won't be able to stick it much longer, for everythin's runnin' short – food for the fire as well as food for the belly. The shacks are fallin' into bits and the tents are gettin' ragged, and the Hares sit like broody hens reflectin' on their sins and calculatin' how soon they'll die. You couldn't stir 'em if you put a charge of dynamite alongside of 'em – you'd blow 'em to bits, but they'd die broody.'

'Father Duplessis has the same story,' Leithen said.

'Yep, and he wants your help. I guess he's asked for it. He says it's a soldier's job and you and him are two old soldiers, but that he's a private and you're the sergeant-major.'

Galliard, who had been listening with bowed head, suddenly looked up.

'You fought in the War?' he asked.

Leithen nodded. His eyes were on Lew's face, for he saw something there for which he was not prepared. Lew had hitherto said little, and he had been as scornful as Johnny about the Hares. The brothers had never shown any pride in their Indian ancestry; their pride was reserved for the Scots side. They had treated the Hares with friendliness, but had been as aloof from them and their like as Leithen and Galliard. It was not any sense of kinship that had woke the compassion in Lew's face and the emotion in his voice.

'You can't be angry with the poor devils,' he said. 'It's an act of God, and as much a disease as T.B. I've seen it happen before, happen to tougher stocks than the Hares. Dad used to talk about the Nahannis that once ranged from the Peace to the Liard. Where are the Nahannis today? Blotted out by sickness of mind. Blotted out like the Snakeheads and the White Pouches and the Big Bellies. And the Hares are going the same way, and then it'll be the turn of the Chipewyans and the Yellow Knives and the Slaves. We white folk can treat the poor devils' bodies, but we don't seem able to do anything for their minds.'

No, it was not race loyalty. Leithen saw in Lew and Johnny at that moment something finer than the duty of kinship. It was the brotherhood of all men, white and red and brown, who have to fight the savagery of the North.

His eyes turned to Galliard, who was looking puzzled. He wondered what thoughts this new situation had stirred in that subtle and distracted brain.

'We'd better sleep over this,' he announced, for Johnny seemed dropping with fatigue . . .

Yet Johnny was the last to go to bed. Leithen was in the habit of waking for a minute or two several times in the night. When his eyes opened shortly after midnight he saw Johnny before the fire, not mending it, but using its light to examine something. It was the shoulder-blade of a caribou, which he had dug out of the rubbish-heap behind the camp. The Hares were not the only dabblers in the old magic.

6

LEITHEN slept ill that night. He seemed to have been driven out of a sanctuary into the turmoil of the common earth. Problems were being thrust on him, and he was no longer left to that narrow world in which he was beginning to feel almost at ease.

Of course he could do nothing about the wretched Hares. Father Duplessis' appeal left him cold. He had more urgent things to think about than the future of a few hundred degenerate Indians who mattered not at all in his scheme of things. His business was with Galliard, who mattered a great deal. But he could not fix his mind on Galliard, and presently he realised something which made him wakeful indeed and a little ashamed. At the back of his head was the thought of his own health. The curtain which had shut down on his life was lifting a corner and revealing a prospect. He was conscious, miserably conscious, that the chief hope in his mind was that he might possibly recover. And that meant a blind panicky fear lest he should do anything to retard recovery.

He woke feeling a tightness in his chest and a difficulty in breathing, from which for some weeks he had been free. He woke, too, to an intense cold. The aurora had been brilliant the night before; and now in the pale sky there were sun-dogs, those mock suns which attend the extreme winter rigours of the North. Happily there was no wind, but the temperature outside the hut struck him like a blow, and he felt that his power of resistance had weakened. This was how he had felt on the road to the Sick Heart River.

He was compelled by his weakness to lie still much of the day and could watch the Frizels and Galliard. Something had happened to change the three – subtly, almost imperceptibly in Galliard's case, markedly in the other two. Johnny had a clouded face; he had seen the Hares' suffering and could not forget it. In Lew's face there were no clouds, but it had sharpened into a mask of intense vitality, in which his wonderful eyes blazed like planets. The sight made Leithen uneasy. Lew had shed the sobriety for which he had been conspicuous in recent weeks. He looked less responsible, less intelligent, almost a little mad. Leithen, intercepting his furtive looks, was unpleasantly reminded of the man who had met him at Sick Heart River. As for Galliard, he was neither dejected nor exalted, but he seemed to have much to think about. He was doing his jobs with a preoccupied face, and he, too, was constantly stealing a glance at Leithen. He seemed to be waiting for a lead.

It was this that Leithen feared. For some strange reason he, a sick man – till the other day, and perhaps still, a dying man – was being forced by a silent assent into the leadership of the little band. It was to him that Father Duplessis had appealed, but that was natural, for they had served together under arms. But why this mute reference to his decision of the personal problems of all the others? These men were following the urge of a very ancient loyalty. Perhaps even Galliard. Who was he to decide on a thing wholly outside his world?

His own case was first in mind. All his life he had been mixed up in great affairs. He had had his share in 'moulding a state's decrees' and 'shaping the whisper of a throne.' He had left England when Europe was a powder magazine and every patriot was bound to put himself at the disposal of his distracted land. Well, he had cast all that behind him – rightly, for he had to fight his own grim battle. In that battle he seemed to have won a truce, perhaps even a victory, and now he was being asked to stake all his winnings on a trivial cause – the *malaise* of human kites and crows roosting at the end of the earth.

It may have been partly due to the return of his malady, but suddenly a great nausea filled his mind. He had been facing death with a certain courage because an effort was demanded of him, something which could stir the imagination and steel the heart. But now he was back among trivialities. It was not a surrender to the celestial will that was required of him, but a decision on small mundane questions – how to return a batch of lunatics to sanity, what risks a convalescent might safely run? He felt a loathing for the world, a loathing for himself, so when Lew sat himself down beside him he found sick eyes and an ungracious face.

'We've got to leave,' Lew said. 'We're too high up here for the winter hunting, and it'll be worse when the big snows come in February. We should be getting down to the bird country and the moose country. I reckon we must take the Hares' camp on our road to see about our stuff. There's a lot of tea and coffee left cached in the priest's cellar.'

Leithen turned a cold eye on him.

'You want to help the Hares?' he said.

'Why, yes. Johnny and me thought we might give the poor devils a hand. We could do a bit of hunting for them. We know the way to more than one moose *ravage*, and a few meals of fresh deer meat may put a little life into them.'

'That sounds a big job. Am I fit to travel?'

'Sure you're fit to travel! We've got the huskies and we'll go canny. It's cold, but you'll be as snug in a hole in the snow as in this camp. When you're in good timber and know the way of it you can be mighty comfortable though its fifty under. Man! it's what's wanted to set you up. By the time the thaw-out comes you'll be the toughest of the bunch.'

'But what can I do? Hunt? I haven't the strength for it, and I would only be an encumbrance.'

'You'll hunt right enough.'

Lew's frosty eyes had a smile in their corners. He had clearly expected argument, perhaps contradiction, but Leithen had no impulse to argue. He was too weary in body and sick in soul.

It was different when Galliard came to him. Here was a man who had nothing to suggest, one who was himself puzzled. Confined for months to a small company, Leithen had become quick to detect changes of temper in his companions. Johnny never varied, but he could read Lew's mutations like a book. Now he saw something novel in Galliard, or rather an intensifying of what he had already observed. This man was afraid, more than afraid; there was something like panic in his face when he allowed it to relax from restraint. This tale of the Hares' madness had moved him strongly – not apparently to pity, but to fear, personal fear. It was another proof of the North's malignity and power.

He was clinging to Leithen through fear, clinging like a drowning man to a log. Leithen could bring the forces of a different world to fight the dominance of that old world which had mastered him. He wanted to be reassured about Leithen, to know that this refuge could be trusted. So he asked him a plain question.

'Who are you? I know your name. You know my friends. But I know nothing more about you . . . except that you came out here to die – and may live.'

The appeal in Galliard's voice was so sincere that his question had no tinge of brusqueness. It switched Leithen's mind back to a forgotten world which had no longer any meaning. To reply was like recalling a dream.

'Yes, you are entitled to ask me that,' he said. 'Perhaps I should have been more candid with you . . . My name is Edward Leithen – Sir Edward Leithen – they knighted me long ago. I was a lawyer – with a great practice. I was also for many years a Member of Parliament. I was for a time the British Attorney-General. I was in the British Cabinet, too – the one before the present.'

Galliard repeated the name with mystified eyes which seemed straining after a recollection.

'Sir Edward Leithen! Of course I have heard of you. Many people have spoken of you. You were for my wife's uncle in the Continental Nickel case. You had a big reputation in the States . . . You are a bachelor?'

'I have no wife or any near relations.'

'Anything else?'

'I don't know. But I was once what I suppose you would call a sportsman. I used to have a kind of reputation as a mountaineer. I was never sick or sorry until this present disease got hold of me – except for a little damage in the War.'

Galliard nodded. 'You told me you were in the War. As what?'

'I was chief staff officer of a rather famous British division.'

Galliard looked at him steadily and in his face there was something like hope.

'You have done a lot. You are a big man. To think of you roosting with us in this desert! – two half-breeds, two Indians, and a broken man like me. By God! Sir Edward, you've got to help me. You've got to get well, for I'm sunk without you.'

He seized the other's right hand and held it in both his own. Leithen felt that if he had been a woman he would have kissed it.

7

GALLIARD'S emotion gave the finishing touch to Leithen's depression. He ate no supper and fell early asleep, only to waken in the small hours when the fire was at its lowest and the cold was like the clutch of a dead hand. He managed to get a little warmth by burying his head in the flap of his sleeping-bag. Drowsiness had fled from him, and his brain was racing like a flywheel.

He had lost all his philosophy. The return of pain and discomfort after an apparent convalescence had played havoc with his stoicism. Miserably, penitently, he recalled the moods he had gone through since he had entered the North. At first there had been sullen, hopeless fortitude, a grim waiting upon death. There had been a sense of his littleness and the omnipotence of God, and a resignation like Job's to the divine purpose. And then there had come a nobler mood, when he had been conscious not only of the greatness but of the mercy of God, and had realised the vein of tenderness in the hard rock of fate. He had responded again to life, and after that response his body seemed to have laboured to reach the sanity of his mind. His health had miraculously improved . . . And now he had lost all the ground he had made, and was down in the dust again.

His obsession was the fear that he would not recover and – at the heart of everything – lay the fear of that fear. He knew that it meant that his whole journey to the North had failed of its true purpose, and that he might as well be dying among the pillows and comforts of home. The thought stung him so sharply that he shut his mind to it and fixed his attention resolutely on the immediate prospect.

Lew and Johnny wanted to go to the Hares' assistance. Lew said that in any case they must be getting down country. Once there they must hunt both for the Hares' sake and for their own. Lew had said that he, Leithen, would be able to hunt – arrant folly, for a few days of it in his present state would kill him.

Had he been a mere subaltern in the party he would have accepted this programme as inevitable. But he knew that whatever Lew might plan it would be for him to approve, and ultimately to carry out. The Frizels were old professionals at the business, and yet it would be he, the novice, who would have to direct it. His weakness made him strongly averse to any exertion of mind and body, especially of mind. He might endure physical torment like a Spartan, but he shrank with horror from any necessity to think and scheme. Let the Frizels carry him with them wherever they liked, inert and passive, until the time came when they could shovel his body into the earth.

But then there was Galliard. He was the real problem. It was to find him and save him that he had started out. He had found him, but he had yet to save him . . . Now there seemed to be a way of salvation. The man was suffering from an ancient fear and there could be no escape except by facing that fear and beating it. This miserable business of the Hares had provided an opportunity. Here was a chance to meet one of the North's most deadly weapons, the madness with which it could affect the human mind, and by checking that madness defeat the North. He had seen this motive confusedly in Galliard's eyes.

He could not desert a man who belonged to his own world, and who mattered much to that world, a man, too, who had flung himself on his mercy. But to succeed in Galliard's business would involve more than hunting docilely in Lew's company with Lew to nurse him.

As he fell asleep to the sound of one of the Hares making up the morning fire he had the queer fancy that the Sick Heart River was dogging them. It had come out of its chasm and was flowing in their tracks, always mastering their course and their thoughts. Waters of Death! – or Waters of Healing?

8

THEY broke camp on a morning which, as Johnny declared in disgust, might have been April. In the night the wind had backed to the south-west and the air was moist and heavy, though piercingly cold. It was the usual thaw which, in early February, precedes the coming of the big snows.

The sledges were loaded with the baggage and the dogs harnessed. Johnny and one of the Hares were in charge of them, while Lew went ahead to break the trail. All of the men except Leithen had back-packs. He carried only a slung rifle, for Lew had vetoed his wish to take a share of the burden. The hut was tidied up, all rubbish was burnt, and, according to the good custom of the North, a frozen haunch of caribou and a pile of cut firewood were left behind for any belated wanderer.

Leithen looked back at the place which for weeks had been his home with a sentimental regret of which he was half-ashamed. There he had had a promise of returning health and some hours of what was almost ease. Now that promise seemed to have faded away. The mental perturbation of the last days had played the devil with his precarious strength. His breath was troubling him again, and his legs had a horrid propensity to buckle under him.

The first part of the road was uphill, out of the woods into the scattered spruces, and then to the knuckle of barrens which was the immediate height of land, and from which he had first had a view of the great mountain country where the Sick Heart flowed. That ascent of perhaps three miles was a heavy task for him. Lew mercifully set a slow pace, but every now and then the dogs would quicken and the rest of the party had to follow suit. Leithen found that after the first half-mile his feet were no longer part of his body, his moccasins clogged with the damp snow, and at each step he seemed to be dragging part of the hillside after him. His thighs, too, numbed, and he had a sickening ache in his back. He managed to struggle beyond the tree line into the barrens and then collapsed in a drift.

Galliard picked him up and set him on the end of one of the sledges. He promptly got off and again fell on his face. A whistle from Galliard brought Lew back and a glance showed the latter where the trouble lay.

'You got to ride,' he told Leithen. 'The dogs ain't too heavy loaded, and the ground's easy. If you don't you'll be a mighty sick man, and there's no camp for a sick man until we get over the divide into the big timber.'

Leithen obeyed, and finished the rest of the ascent in a miserable half-doze, his arms slung through the baggage couplings to keep him from falling off. But at the divide, where a halt was called and tea made, he woke to find his body more comfortable. He was able to swallow some food, and when they started again he insisted on walking with Galliard. They were now descending, and Galliard's arm linked with his steadied his shambling footsteps.

'You're getting well,' Galliard told him.

'I'm feeling like death!'

'All the same you're getting well. A month ago you couldn't have made that first mile. You are feeling worse than you did last week, but you've forgotten how much worse you were a month ago. You remember young Ravelston, the doctor man? I once heard him say that Nature's line of recovery was always wavy and up and down, and that if a man got steadily better without any relapse there was trouble waiting for him.'

Leithen felt himself preposterously cheered by Galliard's words. They were now descending into the nest of shallow parallel glens which ultimately led to Lone Tree Lake. They followed the trail which Johnny had lately taken, and though it required to be broken afresh owing to recent snow, it was sufficiently well marked to make easy travelling. Before the light faded in the afternoon it was possible for Leithen and Galliard to lag well behind the sledges without any risk of losing themselves. The descent was never steep, and the worst Leithen had to face were occasional slopes of mushy snow where the foot-holds were bad. He had a stick to help him, and Galliard's right arm. There was no view, for the clouds hung low on the wooded ridges, and streamers of mist choked the aisles of the trees. Exertion had for Leithen taken the sting out of the cold, and his senses were alive again. There were no smells, only the bleak odour of sodden snow, but the woods had come out of their winter silence. The hillside was noisy with running water and the drip of thawing spruces.

Galliard had the in-toed walk which centuries ago his race learned from the Indians. He moved lightly and surely in difficult places where the other slipped and stumbled, and he could talk with no need to save his breath.

'You left England a month or two after I left New York. What was the situation in Europe in the summer? It was bad enough in the spring.'

'I wasn't thinking about Europe then,' Leithen answered. 'You see, I did not see how it could greatly concern me. I didn't give much attention to the press. But my impression is that things were pretty bad.'

'And in the United States?'

'There I think they took an even graver view. They did not talk about it, for they thought I would not live to see it. But again my impression is that they were looking for the worst. I heard Bronson Jane say something to Lethaby about zero hour being expected in September.'

'Then Europe may have been at war for months. Perhaps the whole world. At this moment Canadian troops may be on the seas. American, too, maybe. And up here, on the same continent, we don't know one thing about it. You and I have dropped pretty completely out of the world, Sir Edward.

'Supposing there is war,' he went on. 'Some time or other Lew and Johnny will get the news. They won't say much, but just make a bee-line for the nearest end of steel, same as they did in '14. They won't worry what the war is about. There's a scrap, and Britain is in it, and, being what they are, they're bound to be in it too. It must be a wonderful thing to have an undivided mind.'

He glanced curiously at his companion.

'You have that mind,' he said. 'You've got a hard patch to hoe, but you've no doubts about it.'

'If I live I shall have doubts in plenty,' was the answer. 'But *you* – you seem to fit into this life pretty well. You go hunting with Lew as if you were bred to it. You're as healthy as a hound. You have a body that can defy the elements. What on earth is there for you to fear? Look at me. I'd be an extra-special crock in a hospital for the sick and aged. You stride like a free man and I totter along like a sick camel. The cold invigorates you and it paralyses me. You face up to the brutishness of Nature, and I shrink and cower and creep under cover. You can defy the North, but my only defiance is that the infernal thing can't prevent my escape by death.'

'You are wrong,' said Galliard solemnly. 'You have already beaten the North – you have never been in danger – because you know in your heart that you do not give a cent for it. I am beaten because it has closed in on me above and below, and I cannot draw breath without its permission. You say I stride like a free man. I tell you that whatever my legs do my heart crawls along on sufferance. I look at those hills and I am terrified at what may lie behind them. I look at the sky and think what horrid cruelty it is planning – freezing out the little weak sprouts of life. You would say that the air here is as pure as mid-ocean, but I tell you that it sickens me as if it came from a charnel house . . . That's the right word. It's a waft of death. I feel death all around me. Not swift, clean annihilation, but death with torture and horror in it. I am in a world full of spectres, and they are worse than the Wendigo ghoul that the Montagnais Indians used to believe in at home. They said that you knew it was coming by the smell of corruption in the air. And I tell you I feel that corruption – here – now.'

Galliard's square, weather-beaten face was puckered like an old woman's. He had given Leithen his arm to support him, and now he pressed the other's elbow to his side as if the contact was his one security.

9

THAT night when Leithen stumbled into camp he found that even in the comfortless thaw Lew had achieved comfort. The camp was made in an open place away from the dripping trees. The big hollow which the men had dug with their snow-shoes was floored with several layers of spruce branches, and on a bare patch in the centre a great fire was blazing. The small tent had been set up for Leithen, but since there was no fall the others were sufficiently dry and warm on the fir boughs.

Movement and change had revived him and though his legs and back ached he was not too much exhausted by the day's journey. Also he found to his surprise that his appetite had come back. Lew had managed to knock down a couple of grouse, and Leithen with relish picked the bones of one of them. All soon went to sleep except Johnny, who was busy mending one of his snow-shoes by the light of the fire.

Leithen watched him through the opening of his tent, a humped, gnome-like figure that cast queer shadows. He marvelled at his energy. All day Johnny had been wrestling with refractory dogs, he had been the chief worker in pitching camp, and now he was doing odd jobs while the others slept. Not only was his industry admirable; more notable still were his skill and resourcefulness. There was no job to which he could not turn his hand. That morning Leithen had admired the knots and hitches with which he bound the baggage to the sledges – each exactly appropriate to its purpose, and of a wonderful simplicity. A few days earlier one of the camp kettles was found to be leaking. Johnny had shaved a bullet, melted the lead, and neatly soldered a patch to cover the hold . . . He remembered, too, what Galliard had said about the summons to war. Lew and Johnny were supremely suited to the life which fate had cast for them. They had conquered the North by making an honourable deal with it.

And yet . . . As Leithen brooded in the flicker of the firelight before he fell asleep he came to have a different picture. He saw the Indians as tenuous growths, fungi which had no hold on the soil. They existed in sufferance; the North had only to tighten its grip and they would disappear. Lew and Johnny, too. They were not mushrooms, for they had roots and they had the power to yield under strain and spring back again, but were they any better than grassy filaments which swayed in the wind but might any day be pinched out of existence? Johnny was steadfast enough, but only because he had a formal and sluggish mind; the quicker, abler Lew could be unsettled by his dreams. They, too, lived on sufferance . . . And Galliard? He had deeper roots, but they were not healthy enough to permit transplanting. Compared to his companions Leithen suddenly saw himself founded solidly like an oak. He was drawing life from deep sources. Death, if it came, was no blind trick of fate, but a thing accepted and therefore mastered. He fell asleep in a new mood of confidence.

10

IN the night the wind changed, and the cold became so severe that it stirred the men out of sleep and set them building up the fire. Leithen awoke to an air which bit like a fever, and a world which seemed to be made of metal and glass.

The cold was more intense than anything he had ever imagined. Under its stress trees cracked with a sound like machine-guns. The big morning fire made only a narrow circle of heat. If for a second he turned his face from it the air stung his eyelids as if with an infinity of harsh particles. To draw breath rasped the throat. The sky was milk-pale, the sun a mere ghostly disc, and it seemed to Leithen as if everything – sun, trees, mountains – were red-rimmed. There was no shadow anywhere, no depth or softness. The world was hard, glassy, metallic; all of it except the fantasmal, cotton-wool skies.

The cold had cowed the dogs, and it was an easy task to load the sledges. Leithen asked Johnny what he thought the temperature might be.

'Sixty below,' was the answer. 'If there was any sort of wind I reckon we couldn't have broke camp. The dogs wouldn't have faced it. We'd have had to bury ourselves all day in a hole. Being as it is, we ought to make good time. Might make Lone Tree Lake by noon tomorrow.'

Leithen asked if the cold spell would last long.

'A couple of days. Maybe three. Not more. A big freeze often comes between the thaw and the snows. The Indians call it the Bear's Dream. The cold pinches the old bear in his den and gives him bad dreams.'

He sniffed the air.

'We're gettin' out of the caribou country, but it's like they'll be round today. They're not so skeery in a freeze. You keep a rifle handy, and you'll maybe get a shot.'

Leithen annexed Johnny's Mannlicher and filled the magazine. To his surprise the violent weather, instead of numbing him, had put life into his veins. He walked stiffly, but he felt as if he could go on for hours, and his breath came with a novel freedom. Galliard, who also carried a rifle, remarked on his looks as they followed the sledges.

'Something has come over you,' he said. 'Your face is pasty with the cold, but you've gotten a clear eye, and you're using your legs different from yesterday. Feeling fine?'

'Fine,' said Leithen. 'I'm thankful for small mercies.'

He was afraid to confess even to himself that his body was less of a burden than it had been for many months. And suddenly there woke in him an instinct to which he had long been strange, the instinct of the chase. Once he had been a keen stalker in Scottish deer forests, but of late he had almost wholly relinquished gun and rifle. He had lost the desire to kill any warm-blooded animal. But that was in the old settled lands, where shooting was a sport and not a necessity of life. Here in the wilds, where men lived by their marksmanship, it was a duty and not a game. He had heard Lew say that they must get all the caribou they could, since it was necessary to take a load of fresh meat into the Hares' camp. Johnny and the Indians were busy at the sledges, and Lew had the engrossing job of breaking the trail, so such hunting as was possible must fall to him and Galliard.

He felt a boyish keenness which amazed and amused him. He was almost nervous. He slung his Zeiss glass loose round his neck and kept his rifle at the carry. His eyes scanned every open space in the woods which might hold a caribou.

Galliard observed him and laughed.

'You take the right side and I'll take the left. It'll be snap shooting. Keep your sights at 200 yards.'

Galliard had the first chance. He swung round and fired

standing at what looked to Leithen to be a grey rock far up on the hillside. The rock sprang forward and disappeared in the thicket.

'Over!' said a disgusted voice. The caravan had halted and even the dogs seemed to hold their breath.

Leithen's chance came half an hour later. The sledges were toiling up a hill where the snow lay thin over a maze of tree-roots, and the pace was consequently slow. His eyes looked down a long slope to a little lake; there had been a bush fire recently, so the ground was open except for one or two skeleton trunks and a mat of second-growth spruce. Something caught his eye in the tangle, something grey against the trees, something which ended in what he took to be withered boughs. He saw that they were antlers.

He tore off his right-hand mitt and dropped on one knee. He heard Galliard mutter '300,' and pushed up his sights. The caribou had its head down and was rooting for moss in the snow. A whistle from Galliard halted the sledges. The animal raised its head and turned slightly round, giving the chance of a rather difficult neck shot.

A single bullet did the job. The caribou sank on the snow with a broken spine, and the Indians left the sledges and raced downhill to the gralloch.

'Good man!' said Galliard, who had taken Leithen's glass and was examining the kill.

'A bull – poorish head, but that doesn't matter – heavy carcase. Every inch of 350 yards, and a very prettily placed shot.'

'At home,' said Leithen, 'I would have guessed 120. What miraculous air!'

He was ashamed of the childish delight which he felt. He had proved that life was not dead in him by bringing off a shot of which he would have been proud in his twenties.

The caribou was cut up and loaded on one of the sledges, maddening the dogs with the smell of fresh meat. For the rest of the afternoon daylight Leithen moved happily in step with Galliard. The road was easy, the extreme cold was abating, he felt a glow of satisfaction which he had not known for many a day. He was primitive man again who had killed his dinner. Also there was a new vigour in his limbs – not merely the absence of discomfort and fatigue, but something positive, a *plus* quantity of well-being.

When they made camp he was given the job of attending to the dogs, whose feet were suffering. The malamutes, since their toes were close together, were all right, but with the huskies the snow had balled and frozen hard, and in biting their paws to release the congested toes they had broken the skin and left raw flesh. Johnny provided an antiseptic ointment which tasted evilly and so would not be licked off. The beasts were wonderfully tractable, as if they knew that the treatment was for their good. Leithen had always been handy with dogs, and he found a great pleasure in looking into their furry, wrinkled faces and sniffing their familiar smell. Here was something which belonged most intimately to the North and yet had been adapted to the homely needs of man.

That night he dined with relish off caribou steaks and turned early to bed. But he did not fall asleep at once. There was a pleasant ferment in his brain, for he was for the first time envisaging what life would be if he were restored to it. He allowed his thoughts to run forward and plan.

It was of his friends that he thought chiefly, of his friends and of one or two places linked with them. Their long absence from his memory had clarified his view of them, and against the large background of acquaintances a few stood out who, he realised, were his innermost and abiding comrades. None of his colleagues at the Bar were among them, and none of his fellow-politicians. With them he had worked happily, but they had remained on the outer rim of his life. The real intimates were few, and the bond had always been something linked with sport and country life. Charles Lamancha and John Palliser-Yeates had been at school and college with him, and they had been together on many hillsides and by many waters. Archie Roylance, much younger, had irrupted into the group by virtue of an identity of tastes and his own compelling charm. Sandy Clanroyden had been the central star, radiating heat and light, a wandering star who for long seasons disappeared from the firmament. And there was Dick Hannay, half Nestor, half Odysseus, deep in Oxfordshire mud, but with a surprising talent for extricating himself and adventuring in the ends of the earth.

As he thought of them he felt a glow of affection warm his being. He pictured the places to which they specially belonged: Lamancha on the long slopes of Cheviot; Archie Roylance on the wind-blown thymy moors of the west; Sandy in his Border fortress; and Dick Hannay by the clear streams and gentle pastures of Cotswold. He pictured his meeting with them – restored from the grave. They had never been told about his illness, but they must have guessed. Sandy at least, after that last dinner in London. They must have been talking about him, lamenting his absence, making futile inquiries . . . He would suddenly appear among them, a little thinner and older perhaps, but the same man, and would be welcomed back to that great companionship.

How would he spend his days? He had finished with his professions, both law and politics. The State must now get on without him. He would be much at Borrowby – thank Heaven he had not sold it! He would go back to his Down Street rooms, for though he had surrendered the lease he would find a way of renewing it. He had done with travel; his last years would be spent at home among his friends. Somebody had once told him that a man who recovered from tuberculosis was pretty well exempt from other maladies. He might live to an old age, a careful, moderate old age filled with mild pleasures and innocent interests . . . On the pillow of such thoughts he fell asleep.

II

THE snow began just as they reached Lone Tree Lake. At first it came gently, making the air a dazzle of flakes, but not obscuring the near view. At the lake they retrieved the rest of their cached supplies, and tramped down its frozen surface until they reached its outlet, a feeder of the Big Hare, now under ten feet of ice and snow. Here the snow's softness made the going difficult, for the northern snow-shoes offered too narrow a surface. The air had become almost mild, and that night, when a rock shelf gave them a comparatively dry bivouac, Leithen deliberately laid his blankets well away from the fire.

Next day they halted to hunt, looking for fresh meat to take to the Hares' camp. Johnny and Lew found a small stamping-ground of moose, and since in the snow the big animals were at a disadvantage, they had no difficulty in getting two young bulls. Leithen helped to drag in the meat and found that the change in the weather had not weakened his new vigour. His mind was in a happy maze, planning aimlessly and making pictures which he did not try to complete.

Lew watched him with satisfaction.

'I've got to learn you things,' he said. 'You haven't got the tricks, and you're wasting your strength, but' – and he repeated his old phrase – 'you're going to be the huskiest of the lot of us. And I seen you shoot!'

They reached the Hares' camp late on an afternoon, when the snow had so thickened that it had the look of a coarse-textured cloth ceaselessly dropped from the skies. Huts, tents, the little church were for the moment buried under the pall. Lew chose a camping site about a quarter of a mile distant, for it was important to avoid too close a contact at first with the stricken settlement.

Johnny and the Indians went off to prospect. Half an hour later Johnny returned with startled eyes.

'I got news,' he stammered. 'The Father told me – seems there was a dog-team got down to the Fort, and come back. There's fightin' in Europe – been goin' on for months. Seems it's them darned Germans again. And Britain's in it. Likewise Canada.'

12

THE taller Indian spoke from behind Johnny.

'My father is dead,' he said, and slipped back into the dusk.

'Yes,' said Johnny, 'there's been a lot of deaths among them Hares. Their camp's like a field hospital. Talkin' of field hospitals, what about this war?'

'We'll sleep on that,' Leithen answered.

Lew did not open his mouth, nor Galliard. Supper was prepared and eaten in silence, and each man by tacit consent went immediately to his blankets. Leithen, before turning in, looked at the skies. The snowfall was thinning, and the air was sharpening again. There was an open patch in the west and a faint irradiation of moonshine. Tomorrow would be very cold.

His bodily well-being continued. The journey down from the mountains had left its mark, for his face was scarred by patches of frost-bite, his lips were inflamed, the snow-shoes had made the calves of his legs ache like a bad tooth, and under his moccasins his feet were blistered. Nevertheless he felt that vigour had come back to him. It reminded him of his mountaineering days, when he would return to London with blistered cheeks and aching shoulder muscles and bleared eyes, and yet know that he was far fitter than the smoothly sunburnt creature that emerged from a holiday at home.

But though his body craved for it his mind would not permit of sleep. He had been living with life, and now suddenly death seemed to have closed down on the world. The tall Indian's cry rang in his ears like a knell.

What had become of the bright pictures he had been painting?

The world was at war again and somewhere in Europe men were grappling with death. The horrors of campaigning had never been much in his mind, for as a soldier he had been too busy to brood over the *macabre*. But now a flood of dimly remembered terrors seemed to flow in upon him – men shot in the stomach and writhing in no-man's-land; scarecrows that once were human crucified on the barbed wire and bleached by wind and sun; the shambles of a casualty clearing station after a battle.

His thoughts had been dwelling on his reunion with friends. Those friends would all be scattered. Sandy Clanroyden would be off on some wild venture. Archie Roylance would be flying, game leg and all. Hannay, Palliser-Yeates, Lamancha, they would all be serving somehow and somewhere. He would be out of it, of course. A guarded flame, a semi-invalid, with nothing to do but to 'make' his soul . . . As he fell asleep he was ashamed of his childishness. He had promised himself a treat which was not going to come off, and he was whining about it.

He woke with a faint far-off tinkle in his ears. He had been dreaming of war and would not have been surprised if he had heard a bugle call. He puzzled over the sound until he hit on the explanation. Father Duplessis in his little church was ringing the morning Angelus.

That tinny bell had an explosive effect on Leithen's mind. This was a place of death, the whole world was full of death – and yet here was one man who stood stubbornly for life. He rang the bell which should have started his flock on their day's work. Sunk in weakness and despair they would remain torpid, but he had sounded the challenge. Here was one man at any rate who was the champion of life against death.

13

IT was a silent little band that broke camp and set out in the late winter dawn. Johnny's face was sullen with some dismal preoccupation, and Lew's eyes had the wildness of the Sick

Heart River, while Galliard's seemed to have once again the fear which had clouded them when he was recovering from his exhaustion.

To his surprise Leithen found that this did not depress him. The bell still tinkled in his ears. The world was at war again. It might be the twilight of the gods, the end of all things. The globe might swim in blood. Death might resume his ancient reign. But, by Heaven, he would strike his blow for life, even a pitiful flicker of it.

The valley opened before them. Frost had stiffened the snow to marble, and they were compelled to take off their snow-shoes, which gave them no foot-hold. The sky was a profound blue, and the amphitheatre of peaks stood out against it in a dazzling purity, matched below by the unbroken white sheet of the lake. The snow was deep, for the near woods were so muffled as to have lost all clean contours, and when they came to the flat where the camp lay the wretched huts had no outlines. They might have been mounds to mark where the dead lay in some hyperborean graveyard. Only the little church on the higher ground looked like the work of men's hands. From the adjoining presbytery rose a thin wisp of smoke, but elsewhere there was no sign of humanity.

Lew spoke at last.

'God! The Hares have gone to earth like chipmunks! Or maybe they're all dead.'

'Not all,' said one of the Indians, 'but they are dying.'

They soon had evidence. They passed a small grove of spruce and poplar, and in nearly every tree there was a thing like a big nest, something lashed to snowy boughs. Lew nodded towards them. 'That's their burying-ground. It's new since we was here before.' Leithen thought freakishly of Villon and 'King Louis's orchard close.' There were funny little humps, too, on the flat, with coverings of birch and spruce branches peeping from under the snow.

'Them's graves,' said Johnny. 'The big ones go up in the trees, the smaller ones are under them humps, and them of no account, like babies and old folk, just get chucked out in the drifts. There's been a power o' dyin' here.'

Lew turned to Leithen for orders.

'Which comes first?' he asked, 'Zacharias or the priest?'

'We will go to the presbytery,' was the answer.

14

THERE was at first no sign of life in the irregular street of huts that made the ascent to the presbytery. The roofs of some of them were sagging with the weight of snow, and one or two had collapsed. But there were people in them, for, now that they were seen at closer quarters, wraiths of smoke came from the vents, which proved that there were fires within, though very meagre ones. Once a door opened and a woman looked out; she at once drew back with a scared look like an animal's; a whimper of a child seemed to come from indoors.

Then suddenly there rose a wild clamour from starving dogs picketed in the snow. Their own dogs answered it and the valley resounded with the din. After the deathly quiet the noise seemed a horrid impiety. There was nothing in it of friendly barking; it was like the howling of a starving wolf pack lost and forgotten at the world's end.

The sound brought Father Duplessis to the presbytery door. He was about Leithen's own age, but now he looked ten years older than at Fort Bannerman. Always lean, he was now emaciated, and his pallor had become almost cadaverous. He peered and blinked at the newcomers, and then his face lit up as he came forward with outstretched hands.

'God be praised!' he cried. 'It is my English comrade-in-arms.'

'Get hold of the chief,' Leithen told Johnny. 'Take the Indians with you and make a plan for distributing the meat. Then bring Zacharias up here.'

He and Galliard and Lew followed the priest into the presbytery. In Father Wentzel's time the place had smelt stuffy, like a furniture store. Now it reeked of ether and carbolic, and in a corner stood a trestle table covered with a coarse linen cloth. He remembered that Father Duplessis was something of a doctor.

He was also most clearly a soldier, a soldier tired out by a long and weary campaign. There was nothing about him to tell of the priest except the chain which showed at his neck and which held a cross tucked under his shirt. He wore kamiks and a dicky of caribou skin and a parka edged with wolverine fur, and he needed all his clothing, for the presbytery was perishing cold. He might have been a trapper or a prospector but for his carriage, his squared shoulders and erect head, which showed the discipline of St Cyr. His silky brown beard was carefully combed and trimmed. A fur skull-cap covered the head where the hair had been cut to the bone. He had the long, high-bridged nose of Picardy gentlefolk, and a fine forehead, round the edges of which the hair was greying. His blue eyes looked washed out and fatigued, but the straight lines of the brows gave an impression of power and reserve. The osseous structure of his face was as sharply defined as the features on a newly minted coin.

'Thank Heaven you have come,' he said. 'This campaign is too hard for one man. And perhaps I am not the man. In this task I am only a subaltern and I need a commanding officer.'

He looked first at Galliard and then at Leithen, and his eyes remained on the latter.

'We are fighting a pestilence,' he went on, 'but a pestilence of the soul.'

'One moment,' Leithen broke in. 'What about this war in Europe?'

'There is war,' said the priest gravely. 'The news came from the Fort when I sent a dog-team for supplies. But I know no more than that the nations are once again at each other's throats. Germany with certain allies against your country and mine. I do not think of it – Europe is very far away from my thoughts.'

'Supplies? What did you get?'

'Not much. Some meal and flour, of which a balance remains. But that is not the diet for the poor folk here. Also a little coffee for myself. See, I will make you a cup.'

He bustled for a minute or two at the stove, and the pleasant odour of coffee cut sharply into the frowst of the room.

'A pestilence of the mind?' Leithen asked. 'You mean—?'

'In myself – and in you – it would be called *accidie*, a deadly sin. But not, I think, with this people. They are removed but a little way from the beasts that perish, and with them it is an animal sickness.'

'They die of it?'

'But assuredly. Some have T.B. and their sickness of the mind speeds up that disease. Some are ageing and it makes them senile, so that they perish from old age. With some it unhinges the wits so that the brain softens. Up to now it is principally the men who suffer, for the women will still fight on, having urgent duties. But soon it will mean the children also, and the women will follow. Before the geese return in spring, I fear, I greatly fear, that my poor people will be no more in the land.'

'What are you doing about it?'

Father Duplessis shrugged his shoulders and spread out his hands.

'There is little I can do. I perform the offices of the Church, and I strive to make them worship with me. I preach to them the way of salvation. But I cannot lift them out of the mire. What is needed is men – a man – who will force their life again into a discipline, so that they will not slip away into death. Someone who will give them hope.'

'Have you no helpers?'

'There is the chief Zacharias, who has a stout heart. But he is old and crippled. One or two young men, perhaps, but I fear they are going the way of the rest.'

15

LEITHEN had asked questions automatically and had scarcely listened to the replies, for in that dim, stuffy, frigid presbytery, where the only light came through the cracks in the door and a dirty window in the roof, he was conscious of something in the nature of a revelation. His mind had a bitter clarity, and his eyes seemed to regard, as from a high place, the kingdoms of the world and men's souls.

His will was rising to the same heights. At last, at long last, his own course was becoming crystal clear.

Memories of the war in which he had fought raced before him like a cinema show, all in order and all pointing the same truth. It had been waste, futile waste, and death, illimitable, futile death. Now the same devilment was unloosed again. He saw Europe as a carnage pit – shattered towns, desecrated homes, devastated cornlands, roads blocked with the instruments of war – the meadows of France and of Germany, and of his own kind England. Once again the free peoples were grappling with the slave peoples. The former would win, but how many free men would die before victory, and how many of the unhappy slaves!

The effluence of death seemed to be wafted to his nostrils over the many thousand miles of land and sea. He smelt the stench of incinerators and muddy trenches and bloody clothing. The odour of the little presbytery was like that of a hospital ward.

But it did not sicken him. Rather it braced him, as when a shore-dweller who has been long inland gets a whiff of the sea. It was the spark which fired within him an explosive train of resolution.

There was a plain task before him, to fight with Death. God for His own purpose had unloosed it in the world, ravening over places which had once been rich in innocent life. Here in the North life had always been on sufferance, its pale slender shoots fighting a hard battle against the Elder Ice. But it had maintained its brave defiance. And now one such pathetic slip was on the verge of extinction. This handful of Hares had for generations been a little enclave of life besieged by mortality. Now it was perishing, hurrying to share in the dissolution which was overtaking the world.

By God's help that should not happen – the God who was the God of the living. Through strange circuits he had come to that simple forthright duty for which he had always longed. In that duty he must make his soul.

There was a ring of happiness in his voice. 'You have me as a helper,' he said. 'And Mr Galliard. And Lew and Johnny. Between us we will save your Hares from themselves.'

Lew's face set, as if he had heard something which he had long feared.

'You mean we've got to feed 'em?'

Leithen nodded. 'Feed them – body and mind.'

Lew's eyebrows fell.

'You coming out in the woods with us? I guess that's the right thing for you.'

'No, that's your job, and Johnny's. I stay here.'

Lew exploded. Even in the dimness his eyes were like points of blue fire.

'Hell!' he cried. 'You can't do it. You jest can't do it. I was afeared you'd have that dam' foolish notion. Say, what d'you think life here would be like for you? You're on the road to be cured, but you ain't cured yet. Come out with me and Johnny and you'll be living healthy. We won't let you do too much. It's a mighty interesting job hunting moose in their *ravages* and you'll get some fine shooting. We'll feed you the kind of food that's good for you, and at night we'll make you as snug as a wintering bear. I'll engage by the spring you'll be a mighty strong man. That's good sense, ain't it?'

'Excellent good sense. Only it's not for me. My job is here.'

'Man, I tell you it's suicide. Fair suicide. I've seen plenty cases like yours, and I've seen 'em get well and I've seen 'em die. There's one sure way to die and that's to live in a shack or among shacks, and breathe stinking air and be rubbing shoulders with sick folks, and wearing your soul out trying to put some pep into a herring-gutted bunch of Indians. You'll be sicker than ever before a week is out, and a corp in a month, and that'll be darned little use to anybody.'

Lew's soft rich voice had become hoarse with passion. He got up from his seat and stood before Leithen like a suppliant, with his hands nervously intertwining.

'You may be right,' Leithen said. 'But all the same I must stay. It doesn't matter what happens to me.'

'It matters like hell,' said Lew, and there was that in his voice which made the presbytery a solemn place, for it was the cry of a deep affection.

'This is a war and I obey orders. I've got my orders. In a world where Death is king we're going to defy him and save life. The North has closed down on us and we're going to beat the North. That is to your address, Galliard.'

Galliard was staring at him with bright comprehending eyes.

'In this fight we have each got his special job. I'm in command, and I hand them out. I've taken the one for myself that I believe I can do best. We're going to win, remember. What does my death matter if we defeat Death?'

Lew sat down again with his head in his hands. He raised it like a frightened animal at Leithen's next words.

'This is my Sick Heart River. Galliard's too, I think. Maybe yours, Lew. Each of us has got to find his river for himself, and it may flow where he least expects it.'

Father Duplessis, back in the deep shadows, quoted from the Vulgate psalm, '*Fluminis impetus laetificat civitatem Dei.*'

Leithen smiled. 'Do you know the English of that, Lew? *There is a river, the streams whereof shall make glad the city of God.* That's what you've always been looking for.'

16

THE place was suddenly bright, for the door had opened. A wave of icy air swept out the frowst, and Leithen found himself looking into a radiant world, rimmed with peaks of bright snow and canopied by a sky so infinitely far away that it had no colour except that of essential light.

It was the old chief, conducted by Johnny. Zacharias was a very mountain of a man, and age had made him shapeless while lumbago had bent him nearly double. He walked with two sticks, and Johnny had to lower him delicately to a seat. The Hares were not treaty Indians, but nevertheless he wore one of the soup-plate Victorian silver medals, which had come to him through a Cree grandmother. His heavy face had a kind of placid good sense, and age and corpulence had not dimmed the vigour of his eye.

He greeted Leithen ceremonially, realising he was the leader of the newcomers. He had a few words of English, but Johnny did most of the interpreting. He sat with his hands on his knees, like a schoolboy interviewed by a headmaster, but though his attitude suggested nervousness his voice was calm.

'We are a ver' sick people,' he repeated several times. It was his chief English phrase.

What he had to tell was much the same story that Johnny had brought to the mountain camp. But since then things had slipped further downhill. There had been more deaths of children and old people, and even of younger men. They did not die of actual starvation, but of low diet and low spirits. Less than half a dozen went hunting, and not many more brought in fuel, so there was little fresh meat and too little firewood. People sat huddled in icy shacks in all the clothes they could find, and dreamed themselves into decay. The heart had gone out of them. The women, too, had ceased to scold and upbraid, and would soon go the way of their men-folk.

'Then our people will be no more,' said Zacharias grimly.

Leithen asked what help he could count on.

'There is myself,' said the chief, 'and this good Father. I have three sons who will do my bidding, and seven grandsons – no, five, for two are sick. There may be a few others. Say at the most a score.'

'What would you advise?'

The old man shook his head.

'In our fathers' day the cure would have been a raid by Chipewyans or Dog-ribs! Then we would have been forced to be up and doing or perish. A flight of arrows is the best cure for brooding. Now – I do not know. Something harsh to get the sullenness out of their bones. You are a soldier?'

'The Father and I served in the same war.'

'Good! Soldiers' ways are needed. But applied with judgment, for my people are weak and they are also children.'

Leithen spoke to the company.

'There are a score of us for this job then. Mr Galliard and I stay here. Lew and Johnny go hunting, and will take with them whom they choose. We shall need all the dog-teams we can get to bring back meat and cordwood. But first there are several jobs to be done. You've got to build a shack for Mr Galliard and myself. You've got to get a mighty big store of logs, for a fire must be kept burning day and night.'

He was addressing Lew, whose eyes questioned him.

'Why? Because these people must be kept in touch with life, and life is warmth and colour. A fire will remind them that there is warmth and colour in the world . . . Tomorrow morning we will have a round-up and discover exactly what is the size of our job . . . You've made camp, Johnny? Mr Galliard and I will be there by supper-time. Now you and Lew go along and get busy. We've got a lot to do in the next few days.'

The door opened again and disclosed the same landscape of primitive forms and colours, its dazzle a little dimmed by the approach of evening.

This second glimpse had a strange effect on Leithen, for it seemed to be a revelation of a world which he had forgotten. His mind swooped back on it and for a little was immersed in memories. Zacharias was hoisted to his feet and escorted down the hill. Father Duplessis prepared a simple meal. There was a little talk about ways and means after Lew left, Galliard questioning Leithen and getting answers. Yet all the time the visualising part of Leithen's mind was many thousands of miles away in space and years back in time.

The stove had become too hot, so the door was allowed to remain half open, for the year had turned, and the afternoon sun was gaining strength. So his eyes were seeing a segment of a bright coloured world. The intense pure light brought a flood of pictures all linked with moments of exultant physical vigour. Also with friendships. He did not probe the cause, but these pictures seemed to imply companionship. In each Archie Roylance, or Clanroyden, or Lamancha was just round the corner waiting . . . There was a July morning, very early, on the Nantillons glacier, on his way to make a traverse of the Charmoz which had once been famous. There was a moonlit night on an Aegean isle when he had been very near old mysteries. There were Highland dawns and twilights – one especially, when he sat on a half-submerged skerry watching for the wild geese – an evening when Tir-nan-og was manifestly re-created. There were spring days and summer days in English meadows, Border bent with the April curlews piping, London afternoons in May with the dear remembered smells fresh in his nostrils . . . In each picture he felt the blood strong in his veins and a young power in his muscles. This was the man he once had been.

Once! He came out of his absorption to realise that these pictures had not come wholly through the Ivory Gate. He was no longer a dying man. He had been reprieved on the eve of execution, and by walking delicately the reprieve might be extended. His bodily strength was like a fragile glass vessel which one had to carry while walking on a rough road; with care it might survive, but a jolt would shatter it . . . No, that was a false comparison. His health was like a small sum of money, all that was left of a big fortune. It might be kept intact by a stern economy, or it might be spent gallantly on a last venture.

Galliard and Father Duplessis were sitting side by side and talking earnestly. He caught a word of the priest's: '*Dieu fait bien ce qu'il fait*' and remembered the quotation. Was it La Fontaine? He laughed, for it fitted in with his own mood.

He had found the right word both for Galliard and himself. They were facing the challenge of the North, which a man must accept and repel or submit to servitude. Lew and Johnny and their kind did not face that challenge; they avoided it by walking humbly; they conciliated it by ingenious subterfuges; its blows were avoided and not squarely met, and they paid the price; for every now and then they fell under its terrors.

He was facing, too, the challenge of Death. Elsewhere in the world the ancient enemy was victorious. If here, against all odds, he could save the tiny germ of life from its maw he would have met that challenge, and done God's work.

Leithen's new-found mission for life gave him a happy retrospect over his own career. At first, when he left England, he had looked back with pain at the bright things now forbidden. In his first days in the North his old world had slipped from him wholly, leaving only a grey void which he must face with clenched teeth and with grim submission. He smiled as he remembered those days, with their dreary stoicism. He had thought of himself like Job, as one whose strength lay only in humbleness. He had been crushed and awed by God.

A barren creed! He saw that now, for its foundation had been pride of defiance, keeping a stiff neck under the blows of fate. He had been abject but without true humility. When had the change begun? At Sick Heart River, when he had a vision of the beauty which might be concealed in the desert? Then, that evening in the snow-pit had come the realisation of the tenderness behind the iron front of Nature, and after that had come thankfulness for plain human affection. The North had not frozen him, but had melted the ice in his heart. God was not only all-mighty but all-loving. His old happinesses seemed to link in with his new mood of thankfulness. The stream of life which had flowed so pleasantly had eternity in its waters. He felt himself safe in the hands of a power that was both God and friend.

Father Duplessis was speaking, and Galliard was listening earnestly. He seemed to be quoting the New Testament – '*Heureux sont les morts qui meurent dans le Seigneur*.'

He had been inhuman, Leithen told himself, with the dreary fortitude of a sick animal. Now whatever befell him he was once again in love with his fellows. The cold infernal North magnified instead of dwarfing humanity. What a marvel was this clot of vivified dust! . . . The universe seemed to spread itself before him in immense distances lit and dominated by a divine spark which was man. An inconsiderable planet, a speck in the infinite stellar spaces; most of it salt water; the bulk of the land rock and desert and austral and boreal ice; interspersed mud, the detritus of aeons, with a thin coverlet of grass and trees – that vegetable world on which every living thing was in the last resort a parasite! Man, precariously perched on this rotating scrap-heap, yet so much master of it that he could mould it to his transient uses and, while struggling to live, could entertain thoughts and dreams beyond the bounds of time and space! Man so weak and yet so great, the chief handiwork of the Power that had hung the stars in the firmament!

He was moved to a strange exaltation. Behind his new access of strength he felt the brittleness of his body. His stock of vigour was slender indeed, but he could spend it bravely in making his soul. Most men had their lives taken from them. It was his privilege to *give* his, to offer it freely and joyfully in one last effort of manhood. The North had been his friend, for it had enabled him, like Jacob, to wrestle with the dark angel and extort a blessing.

The presbytery had warmed up, and Galliard had fallen asleep. He slept with his mouth shut, breathing through his nose, and the sleeping face had dignity and power in it. It would be no small thing to release this man from ancestral fears and gird him for his task in the world. In making his own soul he would also give back Galliard his. He would win the world too, for now the great, shining, mystic universe above him was no longer a foe but a friend, part with himself of an eternal plan.

Father Duplessis' voice broke in on his meditation and seemed to give the benediction words. He was reading his breviary, and broke off now and then to translate a sentence aloud in his own tongue. – '*Car celui qui voudra sauver sa vie la perdra; et celui qui perdra sa vie pour l'amour de moi, la retrouvera.*'

17

From a report by Corporal S——, R.C.M.P., Fort Bannerman, to Inspector N——, R.C.M.P., Fort Macleod.

'PURSUANT to instructions received, I left Fort Bannerman on the 21st day of April, accompanied by Constable F——, and after some trouble with my dog-team arrived at the Hares' winter camp on Big Hare Lake at 6.30 p.m. on the 22nd. The last part of the journey was in the dark, but we were guided by a great blaze coming apparently from the camp which was visible from the outlet of the lake. At first I thought the place was on fire, but on arrival found that this evening bonfire had become a regular custom.

'Rumours of distress among the Hares had reached Fort Bannerman during the winter. Father Wentzel, on his return to the Fort, had predicted a bad time, and Father Duplessis, who replaced him, had sent an urgent message asking not only for supplies of food but for someone to go up and advise. I duly reported this to you, and received your instructions to take an early opportunity of visiting the camp. This opportunity I was unable to find for several months, since the Force was short-handed, owing to the departure of men to the provost company in France, and, as you are aware, I was compelled to make two trips to Great Bear Lake in connection with the dispute at the Goose Bay Mine. So, as stated above, I could not leave Fort Bannerman until the 21st inst.

'Constable F— and I were put up by Father Duplessis, and I received from him a satisfactory account of the condition of the Hare tribe. They are now in good health, and, what is more important, in good heart, for it seems that every now and then they get pessimism, like the measles, and die of it, since it prevents their looking for food. It appeared that they had had a very bad bout in the winter, of the risk of which Father Wentzel had warned us. Up to the beginning of February they were sitting in their huts doing nothing but expecting death, and very soon getting what they expected. A schedule attached to this report gives the number of deaths, and such details as could be ascertained.

'The Hares were saved by an incident which I think is the most remarkable I have ever heard of in my long experience of the Territory. In the early fall a party went into the Mackenzie mountains, travelling up the Big Hare River to a piece of country which has been very imperfectly explored. Or rather, two parties who ultimately joined hands. The party consisted of an American gentleman named Galliard, a New York business man, and an Englishman named Leithen. It had with it two Hare Indians, and as guides the brothers Frizel. The Frizels, Lew and Johnny, are men of high character and great experience. They both served with distinction in the —— Battalion of the Canadian Expeditionary Force in the last war, and have long been favourably known to the Police. The younger, until recently, was a game warden at the National Park at Waskesieu.

'I received further information about the Englishman, Leithen. It appears that he was Sir Edward Leithen, a famous London lawyer and a British Member of Parliament. He was suffering from tuberculosis, and had undertaken the expedition with a view to a cure. The winter in the high mountains, where the weather has been mild for a Mackenzie River winter, had done him good, and he was believed to be on the way to recovery.

'The party, coming out early in February, reached the Hares' camp to find it in a deplorable condition. Sir E. Leithen at once took charge of the situation. He had been a distinguished soldier in the last war – in the Guards, I believe – and he knew how to handle men. With Mr Galliard to help him, who had had large administrative experience in America, and with the assistance of Father Duplessis and the old chief Zacharias, they set to work at once.

'Their first job was to put some sense into the Hares. With the help of the Frizels, who knew the tribe well, a number of conferences were held, and there was a lot of straight talk. Father Duplessis said that it was wonderful how Sir E. Leithen managed to strike the note which most impressed the Indian mind.

'This, of course, was only the beginning. The next step was to organise the survivors into gangs, and assign to each a special duty. Food was the most urgent problem, for the Hares had been for a long time on very short commons, and were badly under-nourished. As you are aware, the moose have been moving north in recent years. The two Frizels, with a selected band of Hares, made up a hunting party, and, knowing how to find the moose stamping-grounds, were able to send in a steady supply of fresh meat. They also organised a regular business of trapping hares and partridges, at which the Hares are very skilful, but which they had been too dispirited to attempt.

'The tribe had also got short of fuel, so wood-cutting parties were organised. Sir E. Leithen insisted on a big fire being kept going by night and day in the centre of the camp, in order to hearten the people.

'Transport was a serious problem. The dogs of the tribe had been allowed to become very weak from starvation, and many had died, for the fishing in the summer had been poor and the store of dried fish, which they use for dog feed, was nearly exhausted. Sir E. Leithen made them start again their winter fishing through the ice in the lake. Here they had a bit of luck, for it turned out very productive, and it was possible to get the dogs back into condition. This was important, since the dog-teams were in constant demand, to haul in firewood from the wood-cutters and fresh meat from the hunters.

'The Frizels did the field work, and Sir E. Leithen and Mr Galliard managed the camp. I am informed by Father Duplessis that Leithen obtained almost at once an extraordinary influence over the Hares' minds. 'Far greater than mine,' the Father said, 'though I have been living for years among them.'

This was partly due to his great ability and the confidence he inspired, but partly to the fact that he had been a very sick man, and was still regarded by the Hares as a sick man. The Indians have a superstitious respect for anyone whom they believe to be facing death.

'Sick man or not, in a month Sir E. Leithen had worked little short of a miracle. He had restored a degenerating tribe to something like health. He made them want to live instead of being resigned to die.

'And now, sir, I come to the event which kills all satisfaction in this achievement. It seems that the elder Frizel had repeatedly warned Sir E. Leithen that the work which he was undertaking would undo all the good of his sojourn in the high mountains, and would lead to certain death; but that Sir E. Leithen had declared that that work was his duty, and that he must take the risk. Frizel's prophecy proved only too true.

'I understand that his strength slowly declined. The trouble with his lungs revived, and, while he continued to be the directing mind, his power of locomotion gradually lessened. Lew Frizel, who came in frequently from the bush to inquire into his health, and implored him in vain to lessen his efforts, told me that by the end of March he had reached the conclusion that nothing could save him. The shack in which he lived was next door to the presbytery, and Father Duplessis, who has some knowledge of medicine, did his best to supply treatment. According to his account, the malady was such that only a careful life could have completed the cure begun in the mountains, and Sir E. Leithen's exertions by night and day were bound to bring it back in a violent form. The sick man, the Father told me, attended the Easter Mass, and after that was too weak to move. Myocarditis set in, and he died without pain during the night of April 19th.

'As I have already informed you, I arrived with Constable F— on the evening of the 22nd. The camp was in mourning, and for a little there seemed danger of the Hares slipping back to their former state of melancholy supineness. From this they were saved by the exhortations of Father Duplessis, and especially by Lew Frizel, who told them they could only show their love for Sir E. Leithen by continuing the course he had mapped out for them. Also, the tribe was now in a better mood, as spring was very near.

'Mr Galliard was anxious that Sir E. Leithen should be

buried at a spot in Quebec Province for which he had a special liking. On April 24th we started by dog-team with the body, the party being myself, Constable F—, Mr Galliard, and the two Frizels. We had considerable difficulty with the ice in the Big Hare River, for the thaw-out promised to be early. We reached Fort Bannerman on the 25th, and were able, by radio, to engage a plane from Edmonton, Mr Galliard being willing to pay any price for it.

'I have since heard by radio that the destination at Quebec was safely reached. The two Frizels were dropped at Ottawa, it being their intention, at all costs, to join the Canadian Forces in Europe . . .'

18

An extract from the journal of Father Jean-Marie Duplessis, O.M.I., translated from the French.

'IN this journal, which I have now kept for more than twenty years, I shall attempt to set down what I remember of my friend. I call him my friend, for though our intercourse was measured in time by a few weeks, it had the intimacy of comradeship in a difficult undertaking. Let me say by way of prologue that during our friendship I saw what is not often vouchsafed to mortal eyes, the rebirth of a soul.

'In the fall I had talked with L. at Fort Bannerman. He was clearly a man in bad health, to whom the details of living were a struggle. I was impressed by his gentleness and his power of self-control, but it was a painful impression, for I realised that it meant a continuous effort. I felt that no circumstances could break the iron armour of his fortitude. But my feeling for him had warmth in it as well as respect. We had been soldiers in the same campaign, and he knew my home in France.

'When things became bad early in the New Year I was in doubt whom to turn to. Father Wentzel at Fort Bannerman was old and feeble; and I could not expect the Police to spare me a man. Besides, I wanted something more than physical assistance. I wanted a man of education who could understand and cope with the Hares' *malaise*. So when one of L.'s guides reached the camp in early February I thought at once of him, and ventured to send him a message.

'It was a shot at a venture, and I was not prepared for his ready response. When he arrived with Monsieur Galliard I was surprised by the look of both. I had learned from Father Wentzel that Galliard was a man sick in the spirit, and I knew that L. was sick in body. Now both seemed to have suffered a transformation. Galliard had a look of robust health, though there was that in his manner which still disquieted me – a lack of confidence, an air of unhappy anticipation, a sense of leaning heavily upon L. As for L., he was very lean and somewhat short of breath, but from my medical experience I judged him to be a convalescent.

'The first day the party spent with me I had light on the situation. L. was all but cured – he might live for years with proper care. But proper care meant life in the open, no heavy duties, and not too much exertion. On this one of the hunters, Louis Frizelle, insisted passionately. Otherwise, he said, and M. Galliard bore him out, that in a little time he would be dead. This L. did not deny, but he was firm in his resolution to take up quarters in the camp and to devote all his powers to saving what was left of the Hare tribe. On this decision plans were made, with the successful result explained in the Police corporal's report, which I here incorporate . . .

'At first I thought that L.'s conduct was that of a man of high humanitarian principles, who could not witness suffering without an attempt at relief. But presently I found that the motives were subtler, and if possible nobler, and that they involved his friend, M. Galliard. L., not being of the Church, made no confession, and he did not readily speak of himself, but in the course of our work together I was able to gather something of his history.

'We talked first, I remember, about the war in Europe. I was deeply apprehensive about the fate of my beloved France, which once again in my lifetime would be bled white by war. L. seemed curiously apathetic about Europe. He had no doubts about the ultimate issue, and he repeated more than once that the world was witnessing again a contest between Death and Life, and that Life would triumph. He saw our trouble with the Hares as part of the same inscrutable purpose of the Almighty, and insisted that we were on one battle-front with the allies beyond the Atlantic. This is said often to M. Frizelle, whom it seemed to comfort.

'I observed that as the days passed he showed an increasing tenderness towards the Hares. At first I think he regarded their succour as a cold, abstract duty. But gradually he began to feel for them a protective and brotherly kindness. I suppose it was the gift of the trained lawyer, but he mastered every detail of their tribal customs and their confused habits of thought with a speed that seemed not less than miraculous. He might have lived most of his life among them. At first, when we sat at the conferences and went in and out of the huts, his lean, pallid face revealed no more than the intellectual interest which might belong to a scientific inquirer. But by degrees a kind of affection showed in his eyes. He smiled oftener, and his smile had an infinite kindliness. From the beginning he dominated them, and the domination became in the end, on their part, almost worship.

'What is the secret, I often ask myself, that gives one human being an almost mystical power over others? In the War I have known a corporal have it, when it was denied to a general of division. I have seen the gift manifest in a parish priest and lacking in an archbishop. It does not require a position of authority, for it makes its own authority. It demands a strong pre-eminence in brain and character, for it is based on understanding, but also, I think, on an effluence of sincere affection.

'I was puzzled at first by the attitude of Monsieur Galliard. He was a Catholic and had resumed – what he had for a time pretermitted – the observances of the Church. He came regularly to Mass and confession. He was ultimately of my own race, though *Les Canadiens* differ widely from *Les Francais de France*. He should have been easy for me to comprehend, but I confess that at first I was at a loss. He was like a man under the spell of a constant fear – not panic or terror, but a vague uneasiness. To L. he was like a faithful dog. He seemed to draw strength from his presence, as the mistletoe draws strength from the oak.

'What was notable was his steady advance in confidence till presently his mind was as healthy as his body. His eye cleared, his mouth no longer twitched when he spoke, and he carried his head like a soldier. The change was due partly to his absorption in his work, for to L. he was a right hand. I have rarely seen a man toil so devotedly. But it was largely due to his growing affection for L. When the party arrived from the mountains he was obviously under L.'s influence, but only in the way in which a strong nature masters a less strong. But as the days passed, I could see that his feeling was becoming a warmer thing than admiration. The sight of L.'s increasing weakness made his face often a tragic mask. He fussed as much as the elder Frizelle over L.'s health. He would come to me and implore my interference. 'He is winning,' he would repeat, 'but it will be at the cost of his life, and the price is too high.'

'Bit by bit I began to learn about Galliard, partly from L. and partly from the man himself. He had been brought up in the stiff tradition of *Les Canadiens*, had revolted against it, and had locked the door on his early life. But it was the old story. His ancestry had its revenge, a revenge bound to be especially harsh, I fancy, in the case of one of his breeding. He had fled from the glittering world in which he had won success and from a devoted wife, to the home of his childhood. And here came a tangle of motives. He had in his blood the pioneer craving to move ever further into the wilds; his family, indeed, had given more than one figure to the story of Arctic exploration. He conceived that he owed a duty to the family tradition which he had forsaken, and that he had to go into the North as an atonement. He also seems to have conceived it as part of the penance which he owed for the neglect of his family religion. He is a man, I think, of sentiment and imagination rather than of a high spirituality.

'But his penance turned out severer than he dreamed. He fell into a *malaise* which, it is my belief, was at bottom the same as the Hares' affliction, and which seems to be endemic in the North. It may be defined as fear of the North, or perhaps more accurately as fear of life. In the North man, to live, has to fight every hour against hostile forces; if his spirit fails and his effort slackens he perishes. But this dread was something more than a rational fear of a potent enemy. There was superstition in it, a horror of a supernatural and desperate malevolence. This set the Hares mooning in their shacks awaiting death, and it held Galliard, a man of education and high ability, in the same blind, unreasoning bondage. His recovered religion gave him no defence, for he read this fear as part of the price to be paid for his treason.

'Then L. came on the scene. He saved Galliard's life. He appeared when Frizelle, in a crazy fit, deserted him, and he had come from England in the last stage of a dire sickness to restore Galliard to his old world. In L.'s grim fortitude Galliard found something that steadied his nerves. More, he learned from L. the only remedy for his *malaise*. He must fight the North and not submit to it; once fought and beaten, he could win from it not a curse but a blessing.

'Therefore he eagerly accepted the task of grappling with the Hares' problem. Here was a test case. They were defying the North; they were resisting a madness akin to his own. If they won, the North had no more terrors for him – or life either. He would have conquered his ancestral fear.

'Then something was added to his armour. He had revered L., and soon he came to love him. He thought more of L.'s bodily well-being than of his own nerves. And in forgetting his own troubles he found they had disappeared. After a fortnight in the camp he was like the man in the Scriptures out of whom the devil spirit was cast – wholly sane and at peace, but walking delicately.

19

'BUT L. was my chief concern. I have said that in him I witnessed the rebirth of a soul, but that is not quite the truth. The soul, a fine soul, was always there. More, though not of the Church, I do not hesitate to say that he was of the Faith. *Alias oves habeo quae non sunt ex hoc ovili*. But he had been frozen by hard stoicism which sprang partly from his upbringing and partly from temperament. He was a strong man with an austere command of himself, and when he had to face death he divested himself of all that could palliate the suffering, and stood up to it with a stark resolution which was more Roman than Christian. What I witnessed was the thawing of the ice.

'He had always bowed himself before the awful majesty of God. Now his experience was that of the Church in the thirteenth century, when they found in the Blessed Virgin a gentle mediatrix between mortal and divine. Or perhaps I should put it thus: that he discovered that tenderness and compassion which Our Lord came into the world to preach, and, in sympathy with others, he lost all care for himself. His noble, frosty egoism was merged in something nobler. He had meant to die in the cold cathedral of the North, ceasing to live in a world which had no care for life. Now he welcomed the humblest human environment, for he had come to love his kind, indeed, to love everything that God had made. He once said (he told me he was quoting an English poet) that he 'carried about his heart an awful warmth like a load of immortality.'

'When I first met him at Fort Bannerman he seemed to me the typical Englishman, courteous, aloof, the type I knew well in the War. But now there seemed to be a loosening of bonds. He talked very little, but he smiled often, and he seemed to radiate a gentle, compelling courtesy. But there was steel under the soft glove. He had always the air of command, and the Hares obeyed his lightest word as I am certain they never obeyed any orders before in their tribal history. As his strength declined he could speak only in a whisper, but his whispers had the authority of trumpets. For he succeeded in diffusing the impression of a man who had put all fear behind him and was already in communion with something beyond our mortality.

'He shared his confidences with no one. Monsieur Galliard, who had come to regard him with devotion, would never have dared to pierce his reserve. I tried and failed. With him I had not the authority of the Church, and, though I recognised that he was nearing death, I could not offer the consolations of religion unless he had asked for them. I should have felt it an impiety, for I recognised that in his own way he was making his soul. As the power of the sun waxed he liked to bask in it with his eyes shut, as if in prayer or a daydream. He borrowed my Latin Bible and read much in it, but the book would often lie on his knees while he watched with abstracted eyes the dazzle of light on the snow of the far mountains.

'It is a strange fact to chronicle, but I think his last days were his happiest. His strength was very low, but he had done his work and the Hares were out of the pit. Monsieur Galliard tended him like a mother or a sister, helped him to dress and undress, keeping the hut warm, cooking for him and feeding him. The hunters, the Frizelles and the Hares, came to visit him on every return journey. Old Zacharias would remain for hours near his door in case he might be summoned. But all respected his privacy, for they felt that he had gone into retreat before death. I saw him oftenest, and the miracle was that, as the spring crept back to the valley, there seemed to be a springtime in his spirit.

'He came often to Mass – the last occasion being the High Mass at Easter, which for the Hares was also a thanksgiving for recovery. The attendance was now exemplary. The little church with its gaudy colouring – the work of old Brother Onesime, and much admired by Father Wentzel – was crowded to the door. The Hares have an instinct for ritual, and my acolytes serve the altar well, but they have none for music, and I had found it impossible to train much of a choir. L. would sit in a corner following my Latin with his lips, and he seemed to draw comfort from it. I think the reason was that he was now sharing something with the Hares, and was not a director, but one of the directed. For he had come to love those poor childish folk. Hitherto a lonely man, he had found a clan and a family.

'After that Easter Sunday his body went fast downhill. I do not think he suffered much, except from weakness. His manner became gentler than ever, and his eyes used often to have the pleased look of a good child. He smiled, too, often, as if he saw the humours of life. The huskies – never a very good-tempered pack, though now they were well fed – became his friends, and one or two of the older beasts would accompany him out of doors with a ridiculous air of being a bodyguard. One cold night, I remember, one of them suddenly ensconced itself in an empty box outside the presbytery door. I can still hear L. talking to it. "I know what you're saying, old fellow. 'I'm a poor dog and my master's a poor man. I've never had a box like this to sleep in. Please don't turn me out.'" So there it remained – the first time I have seen a husky with ambitions to become a house dog.

'He watched eagerly for the signs of spring. The first was the return of the snow buntings, shimmering grey flocks which had wintered in the south. These he would follow with his eyes as they fluttered over the pine woods or spread themselves like a pied shadow on the snow. Then the mountain we call Baldface suddenly shed most of its winter covering, the noise of avalanches punctuated the night, and the upper ribs were disclosed, black as ink in the daytime, but at evening flaming into the most amazing hues of rose and purple. I knew that he had been an alpinist of note, and in these moments I fancy he was recapturing some of the activities of his youth. But there was no regret in his eyes. He was giving thanks for another vision of the Glory of God.

'The last time he was able to go abroad Monsieur Galliard and I assisted him down to the edge of the lake. There was still a broad selvedge of ice – what the Canadian French call *batture* – but in the middle the ice was cracking, and there were lanes of water to reflect the pale blue sky. Also the streams were being loosed from their winter stricture. One could hear them talking under their bonds, and in one or two places the force of water had cleared the boulders and made pools and cascades . . . A wonderful thing happened. A bull moose, very shaggy and lean, came out of the forest and stood in an open shallow at a stream's mouth. It drank its fill and then raised its ugly head, shook it and stared into the sunset. Crystal drops fell from its mouth, and the setting sun transfigured the beast into something magical, a beneficent dragon out of a fairy tale. I shall never forget L.'s delight. It was as if he had his last sight of the beauty of the earth, and found in it a pledge of the beauty of Paradise; though I doubt if there will be anything like a bull-moose in the Heavenly City . . . Three days later he died in his sleep. There was no burial, for Monsieur Galliard wished the interment to be at his old home in Quebec. The arrival of two of the R.C.M.P. made it possible to convey the body to Fort Bannerman, whence it would be easy to complete the journey by air.

'Such is my story of the end of a true man-at-arms whose memory will always abide with me. He was not of the Church, but beyond doubt he died in grace. In his last hours he found not peace only, but beatitude. *Dona aeternam quietem Domine et lux perpetua luceat ei.*'

20

THE chief beauty of the Canadian spring is its air of fragility. The tints are all delicate; the sky is the palest blue, the green is faint and tender, with none of the riot of an English May. The airy distances seem infinite, for the mind compels the eye to build up other lands beyond the thin-pencilled horizons.

A man and a woman were sitting on the greening turf by the well of the Clairefontaine stream. The man wore a tweed suit of a city cut, but he had the colour and build of a countryman. The woman had taken off her hat, and a light wind was ruffling her hair. Beneath them was a flat pad of ground, and on it, commanding the sources of both the north and south-flowing rivulets, was a wooden cross which seemed to mark a grave.

The eyes of both were turned northward where the wooded hills, rising sometimes to rocky scarps, shepherded the streams to the Arctic watershed.

Galliard slowly filled a pipe. His face had filled out, and his jaw was firmer. There were now no little lines of indecision about his mouth. Also his eyes were quiet and content.

For a little the two did not speak. Their eyes followed the

slender north-flowing stream. It dropped almost at once into a narrow ravine, but it was possible to mark where that ravine joined a wider valley, and where that valley clove its way into the dark tangle of forested mountains.

'What happens away up there?' the woman asked. 'I should like to follow the water.'

'It becomes a river which breaks into the lowlands and wanders through muskegs and bush until it reaches the salt. Hudson's Bay, you know. Dull, shallow tides at first, and then the true Arctic, ice-bound for most of the year. Away beyond are the barrens, and rivers of no name, and then the Polar Sea, and the country where only the white bear and the musk ox live. And at the end a great solitude. Some day we will go there together.'

'You don't fear it any more?'

'No. It has become part of me, as close to me as my skin. I love it. It is myself. You see, I have made my peace with the North, faced up to it, defied it, and so won its blessing. Consider, my dear. The most vital forces of the world are in the North, in the men of the North, but only when they have annexed it. It kills those who run away from it.'

'I see,' she said after a long pause. 'I know what you mean. I think I feel it . . . But the Sick Heart River! Wasn't that a queer fancy?'

Galliard laughed.

'It was the old habit of human nature to turn to magic. Lew Frizel wanted a short cut out of his perplexities. So did I, and I came under the spell of his madness. First I came here. Then I went to the Ghost River. Then I heard Lew's story. I was looking for magic, you see. We both had sick hearts. But it was no good. The North will always call your bluff.'

'And Leithen? He went there, didn't he?'

'Yes, and brought Lew away. Leithen didn't have a sick heart. He was facing the North with clear eyes. He would always have won out.'

'But he died!'

'That was victory – absolute victory . . . But Leithen had a *fleuve de rêve* also. I suppose we all have. It was this little stream. That's why we brought his body here. It is mine, too – and yours – the place we'll always come back to when we want comforting.'

'Which stream?' she asked. 'There are two.'

'Both. One is the gate of the North and the other's the gate of the world.'

She faced round and looked down the green cup of the Clairefontaine. It was a pleasant pastoral scene, with none of the wildness of the other – the white group of farm buildings in the middle distance and the patches of ploughland, and far beyond a blue shimmer which was the St Lawrence.

The woman laughed happily.

'That is the way home,' she said.

'Yes, it is the way home – to our home, Felicity, which please God will never again be broken. I've a lot of atoning to do. The rest of my life cannot be long enough to make up to you for what you have suffered.'

She stroked his hair. 'We'll forget all that. We're starting afresh, you know. This is a kind of honeymoon.'

She stopped and gazed for a little at the glen, which suddenly overflowed with a burst of sunlight.

'It is also the way to the wars,' she said gravely.

'Yes, I'm bound for the wars. I don't know where my battlefront will be. In Europe, perhaps, or maybe in New York or Washington. The North hasn't sent me back to malinger.'

'No, of course not. But, anyhow, we're together – we'll always be together.'

The two by a common impulse turned their eyes to the wooden cross on the lawn of turf. Galliard rose.

'We must hurry, my dear. The road back is none too good.'

She seemed unwilling to go.

'I feel rather sad, don't you? You're leaving your captain behind.'

Galliard turned to his wife, and she saw that in his eyes which made her smile.

'I can't feel sad,' he said. 'When I think of Leithen I feel triumphant. He fought a good fight, but he hasn't finished his course. I remember what Father Duplessis said – he knew that he would die; but he knew also that he would live.'